The
Later India
Novels
Part A

The Collected Novels of P. C. Wren
Volume 5A

Fiction Titles by P. C. Wren

Dew and Mildew. 1912
Father Gregory. 1913
The Snake and Sword. 1914.
Driftwood Spars. 1916
The Wages of Virtue. 1916
The Young Stagers. 1917
Stepsons of France. 1917
Cupid in Africa. 1920
Beau Geste. 1924
Beau Sabreur. 1926
Beau Ideal. 1928
Good Gestes. 1929
Soldiers of Misfortune. 1929
The Mammon of Righteousness. 1930 (U.S. title: Mammon)
Mysterious Waye. 1930
Sowing Glory. 1931
Valiant Dust. 1932
Flawed Blades. 1933
Action and Passion. 1933
Port o' Missing Men. 1934
Beggars' Horses. 1934 (U.S. title: The Dark Woman)
Sinbad the Soldier. 1935
Explosion. 1935
Spanish Maine. 1935 (U.S. title: The Desert Heritage)
Bubble Reputation. 1936 (U.S. title: The Cortenay Treasure)
Fort in the Jungle. 1936
The Man of a Ghost. 1937 (U.S. title: The Spur of Pride)
Worth Wile. 1937 (U.S. title: To the Hilt)
Cardboard Castle. 1938
Rough Shooting. 1938
Paper Prison. 1939 (U.S. Title: The Man the Devil Didn't Want)
The Disappearance of General Jason. 1940
Two Feet From Heaven. 1940
The Uniform of Glory. 1941
Odd—But Even So. 1941

The Later India Novels

Part A

by

Percival Christopher Wren

BEGGARS' HORSES
EXPLOSION

Edited

by

John L. Espley

Riner Publishing Company
Culpeper Virginia
2019

ISBN
9780999074947

The text of *Beggars' Horses* will be in the Public
Domain as of 1 January 2030 since it was originally
published in 1934

The text of *Explosion* will be in the Public Domain as of
1 January 2031 since it was originally published in
1935

Contents

PREFACE

The Later India Novels Part A and *The Later India Novels Part B* by Percival Christopher Wren are the fifth of a multi-volume series, *The Collected Novels of P. C. Wren*. The purpose of publishing this series is to make the novels written by P. C. Wren more available to the reading public. His novel, *Beau Geste*, is usually recognized by most of the book dealers I have met over the years, but his other works are not so easily remembered.

I have been collecting P. C. Wren for over fifty years, and have been working on a comprehensive bibliography for almost as long. The text of the twenty-eight novels was easily obtained from copies in my own collection. For that collection, I certainly need to thank the hundreds of used book dealers I have purchased items from, and I need to thank some by name: Steven Temple, David Mason, Walt Barrie and, especially, the late Denis McDonnell for the advice and help they have provided over the years.

Mr. John Venmore and Mr. Philip Fairweather, both descendants of the late Mr. Richard Alan Graham-Smith, Wren's stepson and the executor of Wren's estate, have both been very helpful in providing information about Wren.

As it has been over seventy years since the death of P. C. Wren (November 21, 1941), Wren's works have passed into the public domain in the United Kingdom. In the United States, fourteen of the twenty-eight novels are still under copyright. Thanks to information provided by Messrs. Venmore and Fairweather, the heirs to Wren's literary estate, Mr. Danny Adekoya Campbell and Mr. Christopher Oladipo Graham-Smith, were located and permission has been granted to reprint Wren's works.

I also need to acknowledge the help and guidance of my family members: my daughter and son-in-law,

Dawn and Andrew; my son and daughter-in-law, Jared and Claudia; and my long-suffering wife, Cathy. Thank you.

In conclusion, I need to thank Percival Christopher Wren for the many years of great enjoyment that his stories have provided. I know that Wren is not a literary or critical success, but, for me, he is one of the great storytellers of the early twentieth century.

John L. Espley
Culpeper, Virginia
June 14, 2019

INTRODUCTION

Percival Christopher Wren is best known as a novelist, publishing twenty-eight novels from 1912 to 1941, the most famous being *Beau Geste* (1924). Wren also published seven short story collections; *Stepsons of France* (1917), *The Young Stagers* (1917), *Good Gestes* (1929), *Flawed Blades* (1933), *Port o' Missing Men* (1934), *Rough Shooting* (1938), and *Odd—But Even So* (1941), containing a total of 116 stories. There were also two omnibus collections, *Stories of the Foreign Legion* (1947) and *Dead Men's Boots* (1949), containing stories selected from *Stepsons of France*, *Good Gestes*, *Flawed Blades*, and *Port o' Missing Men*. All 116 short stories can be found in the five volume collection, *The Collected Short Stories of Percival Christopher Wren.*[1]

Wren was a man of mystery in that the majority of biographical statements about him seem to be more fiction than fact. A typical biography places his birth in Devon in 1885, his education at Oxford, and his career as that of world traveler, hunter, journalist, tramp, British cavalry trooper, legionnaire in the French Foreign Legion, assistant director of education in Bombay, and a Justice of the Peace. Most of the above biography, however, is false or has not been verified.

Wren was born Percy Wren on November 1, 1875 in Deptford, a district of South London on the banks of the Thames. He did attend Oxford University, graduating in 1898 with a 3rd class honours in History leading to a Bachelor of Arts degree. He attained his "M.A." in 1901. In those days, a person acquired a "M.A." after a certain number of years (three in Wren's case) and upon payment of a fee.

After leaving Oxford, he married Alice Lucie Shovelier in December 1899 with whom he had a

---

[1] For further information on *The Collected Short Stories of Percival Christopher Wren* see rinerpublishing.wordpress.com

daughter, Estelle Lenore Wren, born in February 1901, and a son, Percival Rupert Christopher Wren, born in February 1904. Percy worked as a teacher at various commercial schools until 1903, when he and his family left England for India.

From 1903 to approximately 1919, Wren was employed as an educator by the Indian Educational Service (I.E.S.). During that time he published a number of educational textbooks, some of which are still in use in Indian schools today. It was during this period that he started using the name Percival C. and Percival Christopher on the textbooks.

From 1905 to 1915, he also served in the Volunteer Corps (Sind and Poona) in India (see the novel *Driftwood Spars*, which contains a description of a Volunteer Corps), and was appointed a Captain in the Indian Army Reserve of Officers, the 101st Grenadiers of the Indian Infantry, in November 1914. He probably saw action in the East African campaign of World War I (see the novel *Cupid in Africa*, which takes place in East Africa during the War), and resigned from the Indian Army Reserve of Officers in November 1915.[2]

Wren's first novel, *Dew and Mildew*, was published by Longmans, Green in 1912. His first novel of the French Foreign Legion, *The Wages of Virtue*, was written in 1913 and published by John Murray in 1916. One of the many questions about Wren is whether he did serve in the French Foreign Legion. Given the chronology of his documented biography it is hard to see where he had time to actually serve in the Legion.[3] Wren himself always maintained that he had served and his stepson, Richard Alan Graham-Smith,

---

[2] Most of the biographical information about Wren has been obtained through certificates, documents, and original research at the British Library, Bodleian Library, and the India Office papers. Further information on Wren and his works was obtained during a three week research visit in September 2018 at the John Murray Archives in the National Library of Scotland. Detailed documentation and sources will be cited in the biographical essay to be included in the forthcoming publication, *An Annotated Bibliography of Percival Christopher Wren*.

[3] After examining just over half of the available files at the John Murray Archives, it is evident that Wren was consistent about serving in the Legion. The only available time though would have been between 1891, when Wren was fifteen and 1894 when he entered Oxford, shortly before he was nineteen.

who died in 2006, "strongly maintained that Wren had indeed served in the French Foreign Legion and was always quick to refute those who said otherwise."[4]

* * * * * * *

The series, *The Collected Novels of P. C. Wren,* is intended to include all twenty-eight novels in seven thematic omnibus volumes. The number of physical volumes will be fourteen, with each thematic volume divided into Part A and Part B. The individual titles will not be in Wren's original publication order, but will instead have a connecting theme such as characters or locale. The seven volumes are:[5]

> v. 1 - The Geste Novels
>> Part A:
>>> Beau Geste
>>> Beau Sabreur
>> Part B:
>>> Beau Ideal
>>> Spanish Maine
> v. 2 - The Sinbad Novels
>> Part A:
>>> Action and Passion
>>> Sinbad the Soldier
>> Part B:
>>> Fort in the Jungle
>>> The Disappearance of General Jason
> v. 3 - The Foreign Legion Novels
>> Part A:
>>> The Wages of Virtue
>>> Sowing Glory
>> Part B:
>>> The Uniform of Glory
>>> Paper Prison
> v. 4 - The Earlier India Novels
>> Part A:

---

[4] wikipedia.org/wiki/P._C._Wren
[5] The order of volumes four through seven has been modified since the publication of volume two.

*　　*　　*　　*　　*　　*　　*

Volume Five of *The Collected Novels of P. C. Wren, The Later India Novels*, contains four novels located primarily in India that Wren published later in his career: *Beggars' Horses, Explosion, The Man of a Ghost,* and *Worth Wile.* All four novels are loosely connected in that characters in *Beggars' Horses* and *Explosion* appear or are mentioned in *The Man of a Ghost* and *Worth Wile.*

*　　*　　*　　*　　*　　*　　*

---

[6] Previous to May 2019 volume seven's title was "The Other Novels".

The Later India Novels Part A

The Later India Novels Part A contains two novels, *Beggars' Horses* and *Explosion*, that were written during 1933 and 1934, the period when Wren, bitterly disappointed in the American sales from the publisher Frederick A. Stokes, was trying to find a new publisher in the United States. *Beggars' Horses* was eventually published as *The Dark Woman* (1943) in America after Wren's death in 1941, and *Explosion* never saw an American publication.

Beggars' Horses is the story of six British army officers who during a hunting trip have an encounter with an Indian fakir or Holy Man. Two of the officers, Harrington-Spens and Hazelrigg, are members of the Secret Service and are on assignment to see if the fakir will become a problem for the British Raj. The other four officers, Wallingford, Wogan, Burlestone, and Easterwood are, unknown to them, cover for the investigation. After the fakir disrupts the hunting trip by having the local villagers boycott the party, the six men visit the fakir. During the visit, Easterwood asks about any psychic powers the fakir has and Wallingford and Wogan become belligerent and mocking, talking about wish fulfillment and the need to beware of a "dark woman". During the discussion and confrontation, the six officers are asked what they would "wish" for. Easterwood asks for great strength. Burlestone asks to be healthy. Wallingford asks to live a long life. Wogan asks for happiness. Harrington-Spens asks for great wealth. And Hazelrigg asks for great courage. The rest of the story is how the six men obtain their wishes and how "a dark woman" interacts with them.

An interesting aspect of *Beggars' Horses* is that several of the themes of psychic powers, boxing and physical fitness, health and doctors, mental illness, and sea voyages echo many issues in Wren's own life. Wren had numerous health problems, extensive ocean cruises, a penchant for boxing, and claimed to have had several "psychic" visions[7].

The original title for *Beggars' Horses* was "The Little Gods Laugh", and Wren also considered changing the title to "Such Sport". William Farquharson, Wren's editor at his publisher John Murray, felt that "Such Sport" was too flippant, and Wren decided to leave the title as *Beggars' Horses*.[8]

In November 1933 Wren sent an incomplete manuscript, about two-thirds of it finished, of *Beggars' Horses* to his publisher to see if serial publication (in a fiction magazine) was possible. Sir John Murray, the owner of the publishing company, read the manuscript and wrote to Wren about liking the story, but was critical of each section ending in a death or suicide, feeling that the public would not be receptive to that type of story. Also, the manuscript seemed to be four or five distinct stories linked together. Wren replied to Murray that the story was incomplete and that he had sent it in early for possible serial publication, which was why it looked like a series of six short stories. Wren's intention for the completed manuscript was for *Beggars' Horses* to be a novel with six heroes and one heroine whose lives are mingled. In the end, three of them would die, one would be in a lunatic asylum, another one would be in permanent captivity in Africa, and the sixth would lose his sight. Wren believed that the novel would be more powerful with these tragedies, but he was willing to change them all, except for the death of Easterwood. Wren rewrote the endings and changed the "story to averted tragedies instead of actual tragedies of fulfilled desire", with "no suggestion whatsoever of separate stories." Wren concluded that *Beggars' Horses* "is another departure and unlike any other book I have written."[9]

Wren had become very discouraged with the American sales of his books by the Frederick A. Stokes

---

[7] See the articles "I Saw a Vision" and "Meaning of Dreams" in volume 5 of *The Collected Short Stories*.

[8] John Murray Archives, National Library of Scotland (hereafter cited as JMA), file Acc. 1297/237 CO3, 23 and 24 November 1933.

[9] JMA, file Acc. 12927/237 CO3, 18 December 1933 through 30 January 1934.

Company, and wanted *Beggars' Horses* to be published by a different company in the United States. The first publisher the manuscript was submitted to was Little, Brown, but they were disappointed in it and rejected it, feeling that the story was very loosely written, too disconnected, and with the plot very mixed and not sustainable.[10] During April, May, and June 1934, the manuscript was considered and rejected by Farrar & Rinehart, Doubleday, Coward & McCann, Dodd Mead, Bobbs-Merrill, and Reynal & Hitchcock.

In July 1934, the manuscript was submitted to the Houghton Mifflin Company in Boston who were very interested in acquiring Wren as one of their authors. Houghton Mifflin's comments about the story were "Wren's new book *Beggars' Horses* presents a pretty tough problem. It's episodic in construction and in places hectic and unconvincing in tone. On the other hand it has that peculiar *je ne sais quoi* of intensity that has marked all of his work, and might have a moderate sale, notwithstanding the steady down curve of his sales and none too good a repute at the moment in the book stores." Houghton Mifflin went on to say that they thought it would be a mistake to publish it as it would damage Wren's reputation and future books, but Houghton Mifflin believed in Wren, and so would publish *Beggars' Horses* with "the understanding that it would have only modest and normal production, and with an option on his next full length novel."[11]

Wren and John Murray accepted the offer, but since they wanted simultaneous publication of Wren's books in England and America, it was decided that Houghton Mifflin would instead publish Wren's next novel, *Sinbad the Soldier*. Wren was negotiating for the publication of *Beggars' Horses* by the American publisher Macrae-Smith in 1940, but it was not published, by Macrae-Smith under the title *The Dark Woman*, until 1943 which was after Wren's death in November 1941.

There are some textual differences between the

---

[10] JMA, file Acc. 12927/237 CO3, 6 March 1934.
[11] JMA, file Acc. 12927/237 CO3, 25 July 1934.

British edition published by John Murray and the American edition published by Macrae-Smith. Besides the usual differences between British and American spelling and punctuation, there are words and phrases that differ between the two versions. The differences are not of the same significance as in the earlier India novels first published by Longmans, Green, and then revised by Wren and published by John Murray after the success of *Beau Geste*, but at least in one place the reader is left uncertain as to whether a character has actually died.

At the end of the train ride by Harrington-Spens and his wife Mary at the end of the chapter, the last paragraph in the American edition has "[. . .] whispered Colonel Harrington-Spens, white-faced and blue-lipped, as the train came to a standstill." The British edition has an additional paragraph: "And incontinently collapsed . . . Bad heart attack."

It is unknown who by or when the changes were made but some possibilities include an editor at Macrae-Smith, or that Wren's wife, Isabel, made the changes after Wren's death, or that the differences are between an older version originally made by Wren before he made the changes requested by John Murray and Macrae-Smith subsequently received the older version of the manuscript. Regardless of the origin of the changes, the significant differences are included in Appendix A herein.

Beggars' Horses was published by John Murray, in the UK, and Longmans, Green, in Canada, on August 27, 1934. Wren had asked that the book be published on this particular date since August 27th was his wife's birthday, and *Beggars' Horses* was dedicated to her. *Beggars' Horses* was published in the fiction magazine, *The Passing Show*, from 16 June through 29 September 1934 which meant that the serial publication was not complete when the book was published, but the magazine was aware of this and did not consider it to be a problem.[12] *Beggars' Horses* was also serialized in *The Australian Women's Weekly* from 17

---

[12] JMA, file Acc. 12927/237 CO3, 26 April 1934.

November 1934 through 16 February 1935.

Explosion is the most political of Wren's novels. The main storyline is about a plot by Indian agitators to use a large bomb to kill British officials and destroy several buildings: a literal explosion. Wren was an ardent Imperialist and *Explosion* is not very complimentary of the Indians who were considered agitators and terrorists before India's and Pakistan's independence.

The two main characters are Anthony Steele, the Superintendent of Police, and Betty Gopaldas, a young English woman married to an Indian who is one of the group of agitators planning the explosion. With Betty being infatuated with Steele, he is able to persuade her to help him uncover the bomb plot.

There are minor plots about British society in an Indian city during the British Raj, and Wren is able to convey the thoughts and feelings of a strong Imperialist in favor of British rule. The dedication provides a very good summary of Wren's feelings about India and British rule. "Dedicated to the Friends of India, the real India of three hundred million unrepresented peasants, whose sole "political aspirations" are that the peace, the security, the justice and the protection provided by the British Raj may for ever remain to them undisturbed, unweakened and unchanged."

Explosion was written in the latter part of 1934, with the contract between Wren and John Murray signed on 28 December 1934, and publication in the UK following on 5 June 1935.[13] *Explosion* has not been published in the United States until this edition by the Riner Publishing Company, although it is entirely possible that some copies of the Longmans, Green edition were carried across the border from Canada for sale in the United States. *Explosion* was not accepted by Houghton Mifflin, possibly due to its strong political stance.

Nevertheless, it is an interesting view on British society in India and how the Indian independence

---

[13] JMA, file Acc. 13328/16 CU22, 28 December 1934 and 5 June 1935.

movement was viewed by an Imperialist.

*   *   *   *   *   *   *

The original spelling, punctuation, and grammar, except for obvious errors, has been preserved as found in the latest editions/printings of the stories during Wren's lifetime (1875-1941). The footnotes, in the novels, are also as found in the original source material.

BEGGARS' HORSES

"The Little Gods laughed to see such sport,
For the Wish ran away with the Boon."
                    Nursery Rhyme
                        (Revised Version).

To

ISABEL

MY TWENTY-FIRST NOVEL

AND

ALL MY LOVE

PART I

CHAPTER I

Colonel Ormesby of the Political Department, secret head of the Secret Service in India, gazed, unseeing, upon the broad beautiful Simla scene that lay spread beyond and beneath the open doors of the wide verandah of his office-room in the Secretariat.

Once again he pondered the problem of the reason for the systematic starvation of the Service upon which the safety of the country and the very existence of the British Raj, at times, depended.

Bricks without straw, and those the very bricks that must underpin and buttress the tottering Wall, so badly eroded by the swirling, rising waters of sedition, disruption, disaffection, disloyalty.

Poor old Wall that he and his fathers had so long defended. . . . Increasingly powerful foes without, increasingly dangerous traitors within. . . .

And at Home, indifference and ignorance among the masses; ignorance, more inexcusable, among the politicians who misinformed and misled them—well-meaning ignorance; windy, platitudinous folly; or self-seeking opportunism. India and her helpless millions, pawns in the mean base game. . . . India, the key-stone of the Empire, endangered for a vote!

And now this new portent; this new cloud on the political horizon, at present no bigger than a man's hand. Would it grow and spread until the whole sky was blackened?

A knock at the door.

And to Colonel Ormesby's cry of, "Come in," entered Major Marcus Harrington-Spens—also of the Political Department and the Secret Service—ushered in by a *chuprassi*, glorious in scarlet and gold.

§2

"That's it, my son," concluded Colonel Ormesby,

half an hour later, as he rolled up a big map. "Then we shall know for certain whether it is pure religion or—impure politics. I trust Mahbub Ali—up to a point. And according to him, the man's an Influence, an absolute Power, in the land. That portion of the land, anyway. I don't know if he could raise the country against an army, whether invading or defending, close the passes, cut communications, stop supplies, start stone avalanches, and that sort of thing; but, according to Mahbub Ali, he could certainly hold up any survey-party, advance-guard, or scouts. Apparently his word is absolute Law in that part—and it's an important part for us.

"What we want to know is whether he is likely to be what the Mahdi was to Egypt, and the Mad Mullah to Somaliland, or—what Christ was to Rome. Quite possibly he has not the very faintest interest in politics. . . . 'Render unto Cæsar the things which are Cæsar's, and to God the things that are God's' sort of fella."

Major Harrington-Spens nodded.

"And, as between us and Russia, says 'A curse on both your houses,'" he mused.

"Exactly. He may be a genuine danger and menace to British rule in India, or he mayn't care a tuppenny damn who rules India, so long as he can sit in peace on the top of a mountain, contemplating the Excellent Law and acquiring merit."

"Shall I take Mahbub Ali with me?" asked Major Harrington-Spens.

"No. No, I think not. He might be recognized locally, and he might—I won't say warp your judgment, but . . . you know. . . ."

Major Harrington-Spens smiled.

"Prejudice, and pre-conceived ideas, eh?" he said. "Sub-conscious bias . . . Nothing like the open mind. M-m-m, I think I'll disguise myself as a shooting-party and muck about in the Holy Man's back-yard."

Colonel Ormesby nodded.

"Splendid! Pack a theodolite and a few funny maps, and drop an occasional word of Russian, accidental-like."

"Might be able to join up with a genuine shooting-party or wangle one," mused Harrington-Spens. "Any-how, I'll get well into the gent's sphere of influence, and see what his game is."

"Yes. Take old Ganesh with you. He knows that country . . . and the difference between Peshawur Pushtu and the real article—if you have to do any disguise and play-acting. You could pick him up on his way back from Gilgit."

"Yes," agreed Major Harrington-Spens. "I'd like to have Ganesh Hazelrigg with me. He's a wise old horse. Very dependable. No-one cooler and braver."

"And I can let you have Shere Khan. He's here in Simla now—just down from Bokhara, Samarkand, Penjdeh, Herat and Kabul," continued Colonel Ormesby.

"Splendid!" smiled Major Harrington-Spens. "None better—and few as good. Pity it wasn't he instead of Mahbub Ali. More level-headed."

"Yes," agreed the Colonel. "But, in any case, I should have got you to go and have a look. It's not a place where we can afford to take chances—or let a holy Bad Man 'sit pretty,' just now. . . . When can you start?"

CHAPTER II

The shooting-camp, pitched on a little plateau, ten thousand feet above sea-level, occupied one of the loveliest sites on earth.

From it, Major Marcus Harrington-Spens and his colleague, Captain Bartholomew Hazelrigg, proposed to make two-day and three-day shooting-trips to the north; Major Anthony Moresby Wallingford and his brother officer, Captain Geoffrey Hennessy Wogan, to the east; and the other two members of the shooting-party, Captain Stacey Burlestone and his great friend Lieutenant Aubrey Easterwood, to the west.

It was generally agreed that Major Harrington-Spens had arranged things splendidly; had been simply indefatigable, and most generous of his time and labour in working everything out, and getting the party to this *shikaris'* paradise of big game, glorious scenery, perfect mountaineering, and all that the heart of a soldier-on-leave could desire.

Wogan and Wallingford agreed that it really had been a wonderful stroke of luck that Harrington-Spens had blown into the Quetawur Club just at the right moment. Burlestone and Easterwood congratulated themselves on having been invited by Hazelrigg to join the party.

The four agreed that it makes all the difference in the world, having a man who knows the ropes, speaks the language, has done it all before, and knows a hairy yak from a woolly Llama.

Splendid!

§2

To Major Marcus Harrington-Spens, seated inside his little green tent, entered, stooping, a burly broad-shouldered native, unkempt, unshaven, wearing an ill-

8

tied *puggari* wound loosely round a *kullah*,[14] a long
dirty shirt outside dirtier baggy trousers, and carrying
in his hand a thick stick of heavy *kan* wood.

Kicking the woven grass sandals from his feet, the
ostensible *shikari* salaamed low. Not even his comrades
would have recognized Havildar Shere Khan of the
Guides.

"Well, any more *khabar*[15]?" asked Major Harrington-Spens.

"No, Sahib," was the whispered reply. "None at all.
The villagers there, too, are all simple men and without
the wit to make a story. Since the hairy-faced white
men and their party had to turn back, no stranger has
been here save one—and that one must have been
Mahbub Ali."

"None others from the north, eh?"

"Not through any of these passes, Sahib; and not to
the knowledge of these people. And they would know.
Not an ibex shifts his stamping-ground but these
people know."

"M-m-m. And the Holy Man?"

"Just that, Sahib. A Holy Man of great power. They
speak of him with the deepest reverence . . . and they
whisper with bated breath of a 'Great One.'"

"Aren't the Great One and the Holy Man the same
person, then?"

"It seems not, Sahib, but it is difficult to tell. They
fear to speak."

"They are a superstitious lot, full of *būt-parasti*,"[16]
added the Havildar, with the True Believer's scorn of all
those of other religions.

"In fact, you learned no more in this village than in
any of the rest?"

"Nothing new, Sahib. They have neither concern
nor interest beyond the task of filling their miserable
bellies—and keeping their wives in order."

"And you discovered there no new trace of the hand
of this Holy Man?"

---

[14] *Conical cap.*
[15] *News.*
[16] *Idolatry.*

"None, Sahib."

"Nor whether he is a friend of the British or an enemy of the British?"

"None, Sahib. Nothing save that he is to them as God."

"And you learned nothing new concerning the party of what the villagers called 'hairy-faced white men'?"

"Nothing of interest or importance, Sahib. Undoubtedly they were Russians."

"Why 'undoubtedly'?"

"They came from the north; they made their tea in the Russian way; their clothes, especially their boots, were Russian; so were their habits, manners, speech. The headman still remembers a Russian word or two that they frequently shouted. And then there was this."

"This" proved to be a scrap of paper, evidently used for a wrapping of some kind, and on it were some printed words.

"I think that is Russian writing, Sahib."

"It is," replied Major Harrington-Spens. "Good work, Shere Khan. Why exactly did they turn back, I wonder?"

"Because they could not go on, Sahib. The Holy Man said they were not to."

"What, simply went down from his cave and told them so? They'd have booted him from there to the top of Mount Everest."

"I don't mean that he told them they were not to go on. His *chela*[17] came and told the headmen of all the villages. So their coolies and servants all ran away, and they had the choice of staying there till they starved, or going back."

"Well, if they could go back, couldn't they go forward?"

"No. Directly they tried to go forward, things began to happen to them. All sorts of strange things, according to this headman also. When at last they decided to go back because they must, their path was made smooth. Their coolies, wood-cutters, grass-cutters, *shikaris* and servants returned, and the white

---

[17] *Disciple, follower and servant.*

men went back."

"Is it known what became of them?"

"Only that they were helped back along their road. It was rumoured that, at length, they got back over the pass just before the snow closed it for the winter. They may thereafter have been caught, and have perished. It is not known."

"Did the Holy Man's *chela* tell the headmen why the white men must be stopped and turned back? Had the Holy Man anything against them?"

"Only that they were *purdeshis*,[18] Sahib. He didn't want them in this country."

"Because they commandeered supplies without paying for them; made the villagers carry for them without payment; beat people, and interfered with the women-folk?"

"The *chela* doesn't seem to have given that for a reason, Sahib. He just brought the message,

"'*Foreigners are approaching and will camp at Kha-bakdir. They must go no farther. They are not to be slain, hurt, or robbed; but no man is to raise a finger to help them—for any pay or bribe whatsoever.*'"

"And this headman and his people obeyed, like those of every other village?"

"Absolutely, Sahib. It is to all the people of this land as it would be if they were Mussulmans and the Holy Man were Allah and his *chela* were Mahomet—the Prophet, Servant and Messenger of Allah."

"H'm. And you feel certain in your own mind that the Holy Man cared nothing concerning the politics, nationality, object, business or doings of these people?"

"Nothing, Sahib. He neither knew nor cared."

"Didn't turn them back *because* they were Russians —if they were?"

"No, Sahib. He'd have done the same had they been Turkomans, Afghans, Persians, Germanis, or any other strangers who came as strong men armed, map-making, exploring, shooting, spying; fore-runners of invasion and war."

"He's not an agitator, a sedition-monger, then?"

---

[18] *Foreigners.*

The Pathan smiled.

"Not he, Sahib. . . . He is no Powindah Mullah. He's not a preacher; a leader. He has no politics whatever. No policy. No mission. No gospel even.

"Save that of *Peace*," he added somewhat contemptuously.

"And all the people believe in him and obey him?"

"Absolutely, Sahib. To them the voice of the Holy Man is the voice of God. His words are their Law."

"And you think that he will do the same thing again now—not caring whether we be British or Russian?"

"The same thing, Sahib."

"Really neither knowing nor caring whether we be British or Russian?"

"I think he will know, Sahib, but he will not care."

"Well, get in touch with this *chela*. Bring him along and I'll have a talk with him, and try to arrange an interview with the Holy Man himself. It ought to be very interesting. Very interesting indeed."

CHAPTER III

"The thing's absurd," expostulated Captain Geoffrey Hennessy Wogan, a red-headed, red-faced, freckled man, thick-set, broad-shouldered, brawny, with powerful-looking hairy arms and large strong hands that were usually clenched into fists.

He puffed angrily at his pipe as he spoke, his red eyebrows drawn together over very pale blue eyes in which seemed to burn an angry light.

"It's simply ridiculous, and we've got to do something about it. We're not going to have our leave spoilt and the shooting-trip ruined because some rascally humbugging old *fakir* can put the fear of God and the Devil into a lot of superstitious natives. . . .

"Holy Man!" he growled. "Probably some *bhang*-sodden brute dressed in wood-ash, dirt, and a handkerchief. A filthy, loathsome parasite who never did a stroke of work in his life. Living on wretched half-starved villagers. . . . Holy! I'd like to make him a little more holey with a peppering of Number Eight shot. Make him run for the first time in his life. Lousy, loafing swine. They are all damned frauds."

"Not all," contradicted Major Marcus Harrington-Spens, a tall, lean, dark man, handsome and austere, his black hair and moustache beginning to turn slightly grey. Pleasant, quiet and almost gentle of address, with a low persuasive voice, sad ascetic face, kindly and courteous manner, he was not only a favourite, but a person of considerable influence among his companions.

"Probably," he continued, "the vast majority of *fakirs* and *sanyasis* are just rogues and vagabonds, humbugs and frauds; but there are genuine Holy Men among them.

"And they are apt to be uncommon genuine," he added, "and possessed of most amazing powers—or at any rate, amazing knowledge. Some of the real *yogis* have what seem to be positively superhuman powers, as well as a complete grasp of sciences that the European has scarcely heard of."

"What? See into the future and tell you what's going on in some distant place—all that sort of thing, eh?" said Captain Bartholomew Hazelrigg, a big, slow, heavy man, rather bald, with a large sagacious face, thick moustache and ponderous manner; a man whose nickname 'Ganesh'—the Elephant God—suited him admirably.

"Yes, I know, for a fact, of a case of one of them who was buried alive for forty days. And was un-buried alive, too. Not only a complete fast—neither food nor water—but no air, either. It's a proven fact, you know, that they can communicate with each other across hundreds or thousands of miles of space. Sort of telephonic—or telepathic—wireless. Chap seated on top of a peak in the Himalayas can let the Abbot of a monastery in Burma or Ceylon know that their old pal So-and-so of the Such-zen Lamassery has popped off, or something of that sort. Projection, too; levitation; suspended animation. . . ."

"Don't believe a word of it," interrupted Major Anthony Moresby Wallingford, a quick, dapper little man; alert, sharp, active. "Simply don't believe it. . . . Like ghosts. We all know somebody who has seen one, but we never see one ourselves. Same with these swindling humbugs. We've all heard of somebody who's beheld their marvels, but somehow you never meet that somebody in the flesh. Absolute bunkum, bilge and bosh."

"Yes?" smiled Captain Hazelrigg pleasantly.

"Yes, he's right. Quite so," agreed Captain Geoffrey Hennessy Wogan. "Tripe, hokum, boloney. . . . Where would they get their wonderful superhuman powers and knowledge? Where would they learn their supernatural science? Lhassa University Extension Lectures? Garn! . . ."

"Ever made any sort of a study of *Yoga*? Taken any interest in it, I mean, or know anything about it?" asked 'Ganesh' Hazelrigg.

"No; and don't want to. Damned mumbo-jumbo," replied Hennessy Wogan angrily, his strong square teeth tightly gripping the stem of his pipe, his strong square chin protruded aggressively. "I should want to know that a thing was worth wasting time on, first. Hearing is listening—but seeing is believing."

"There's that case of the old bird whom the three subalterns turfed off his pitch, you know," drawled Captain Stacey Burlestone, a somewhat delicate-looking man who, perhaps by reason of ill-health, gave the impression of languor, apathy, heaviness of mind.

"That's an established case. Undisputed fact, you know, Major," he added, turning to Moresby Walling-ford.

"Yes; there's no getting away from that," agreed 'Ganesh' Hazelrigg. "Pure gospel truth."

"Coincidence," objected Moresby Wallingford. "Mere coincidence; and a tremendous lot of nonsense talked about it. Gave this *Yoga* tosh a lot of publicity and a lot of undeserved credence, too. . . . Why, damn it all, you might as well believe in African witch-doctors and their rain-making. If, on three separate occasions, I say it will rain to-morrow, and it does, is that a proof that I've got superhuman powers and supernatural scientific knowledge? . . . Gift of prophecy for a start? Of course it was pure coincidence—that the three youngsters pegged out within the year."

"What happened?" asked Lieutenant Aubrey Easterwood, a thoughtful-looking cavalry subaltern, slender and lean, but hard as nails; handsome, whole-some and debonair. "Before my time, I think."

"Curious case," replied Major Harrington-Spens, "and I vouch for the truth of it."

"So do I," chimed in 'Ganesh' Hazelrigg. "I knew the Colonel of one of the youngsters personally, and I knew all about the other two."

"They were on a shooting-trip," continued Major Harrington-Spens. "Just as we are. But, unlike ourselves, they were young and foolish. Went out of their way to make trouble with one of these people. Just went and ragged him, for a lark. Silly thing to do.

He was one of the naked, ash-smeared variety, who sit in the same spot for a hundred years and meditate. . . ."

"'*Om mane padme om*' . . . pom, pom," contributed Captain Stacey Burlestone.

"Contemplate One-ness, Nirvana, Nothingness—and the navel, excuse me," continued Major Harrington-Spens. "Have one grain of rice three times a day, and a goat-milk cocktail when the sun's below the yard-arm.

"Well, these merry lads stepped into the sacred circle in which he squatted, or let their shadows fall on his evening grain of rice, or offered him a beef-steak or a pork-sausage or something. . . . Anyhow, they annoyed him.

"The *fakir* got angry and told them off, good and proper. Called them all sorts of names. And this amused them so much that, finally, they ran him off his pitch and gave him a bath. Dipped him in the river. The whole business very childish, all in the worst of taste, and shocking bad form. Quite inexcusable.

"Then the *fakir* got really mad. And he up and told them not to mind him, but to go on and enjoy themselves—while they could. For they wouldn't enjoy themselves much longer. Neither themselves nor anything else. Because they were all three going to die within the year. And there wasn't so very much left of the year, either. One was going to die on bloody ground; one in bloody water; and the other in a bloody bed. Excuse my language, won't you—but that was the *fakir's* prophecy. . . . That amused them, too; quite a lot; and, next day, they went on their way rejoicing.

"Unfortunately one of them did a silly thing, a few days later. Climbed up-hill after a bear—until the bear came down-hill after him. His right barrel missed fire and his left missed the bear. He certainly died on bloody ground, poor chap. The bear made a nasty mess of him.

"The others went back to Cantonments, and, about a month afterwards, a crocodile took one of them.

"The third chap did his best for him, and damned

pluckily, too; but without avail. The sight of the blood-tinged water rather preyed on his mind, and he got a bit morbid. Used to sit and think about the *fakir* and his prophecies.

"His Colonel—my friend—was a bit worried about him. Especially when it came to his ears that the boy had given up the habit of going to bed. Never went to bed at all. When it got so late at night that everybody else had pushed off, and there was no-one to talk to, he would sleep in a long chair—without undressing.

"When the Colonel tackled him about it, he frankly admitted that he didn't want to 'die in a bloody bed.'

"The Colonel got the M.O. to give him a month's sick leave, and sent him to stay with some people he knew the other side of India, where he would have a good time. Got him to promise that he'd go to bed there, too.

"He did, and got a lot better.

"Unfortunately he woke up, one night, to see a couple of naked dacoits carrying his trunk out of the room, while a third one, with a long knife in his hand, stood over him, watching.

"Half awake, he went to jump up. The dacoit stabbed—and the poor chap died in a bloody bed."

"By Jove!" murmured Aubrey Easterwood. "What an amazing thing."

"Coincidence," growled Captain Hennessy Wogan.

"Queer coincidence," amended Aubrey Easterwood, smiling.

"Bit thick, for coincidence, if you ask me," observed Major Harrington-Spens.

"Well, assuming it's not coincidence—what is one to substitute?" enquired 'Ganesh' Hazelrigg. "Are we to take it that this *fakir* or *sanyasi* was clairvoyant—as most undoubtedly a good many people, even in the West, are clairvoyant—and foresaw that these three poor fellows were going to die? Or are we to suppose that he brought about their deaths? Murdered them, in fact, in revenge for their interfering with him?"

"Pretty stiff vengeance, what?" murmured Captain Stacey Burlestone. "Rather heavy punishment for a bit of a rag!"

"Well, it wouldn't be 'a bit of a rag' for the *fakir*," replied Major Harrington-Spens. "It would probably be a mixture of blasphemy, defilement and sacrilege; his idea of the Sin against the Holy Ghost; the unforgivable sin; in addition to the fact that they'd imperilled his chances in the Future Life, by interfering with his holy doings. . . . Well, if he had the power of punishing them with death, he might very well have considered himself justified in doing so."

"Do you think he had the power, Major?" enquired Aubrey Easterwood.

"Dunno. . . . Shouldn't be surprised. Much more likely that it was a case of clairvoyance. He knew they were going to die, and he paid them out by telling them so."

"In fact he'd just as much marvellous and mysterious superhuman power and supernatural knowledge as any Bond Street palmist, eh?" sneered Captain Hennessy Wogan.

"Anyhow, there it is," asserted Harrington-Spens. "The youngsters ragged the *fakir*, and the *fakir* told them they'd all come to a sticky end within the year. And they did."

"And personally I don't rag *fakirs*," he added. "Good manners apart."

"Do you mean to say that you think one could hurt you, if you upset him?" asked Major Moresby Wallingford.

"Dunno. . . . I don't think that I do. But I do think that he might give me a nasty glimpse of the future."

"Frighten you?" enquired Hennessy Wogan, with a suspicion of a sneer in the tone of his voice.

"Yes. Probably make me quite uncomfortable. Give me something to think about—that is better not thought about. Introspection and all that," was the quiet reply of Major Harrington-Spens.

"Well, this doesn't get us any for'arder," exploded Hennessy Wogan suddenly. "The question is: what are we going to do about this blighter? Are we going to take it lying down? Just turn back, and push off with our tails between our legs, simply because he has made the camp taboo, and told the coolies not to go on, and the villagers not to sell us supplies? I'm damn well going to have a few words with him first, if we are."

"So am I," agreed Anthony Moresby Wallingford.

"What's more," he added, "if he tells me something that's going to happen to me in the future, I'll tell him something that's going to happen to him in the present. It will happen to him, too. . . . Yes, I'm certainly going to have a few words with him."

"We all will," stated Major Harrington-Spens. "I've interviewed his *chela* and learned that His Holiness is At Home from 12 a.m. till 12 a.m., twenty-four hours daily—seven days a week. We'll wait on the gentleman in a body."

"And in a spirit of sweet reasonableness," he added. "Try to see his point of view, and try to show him ours."

"Show him a boot in the seat of his—*dhoti*,"[19] mumbled Hennessy Wogan.

"No, no! In the first place he couldn't see it there. In the second place he probably doesn't wear one. And, in the third, that's not the way to get him to help us," smiled Major Harrington-Spens. "We shall absolutely queer our own pitch if we antagonize him. Let's try and make friends with the old Mammon of Righteousness. From what I hear, I doubt if we can do a thing without his permission. It seems he's just God in these parts."

"Permission?" sneered Captain Hennessy Wogan. "Pretty state of affairs! Naked old image sitting up there in front of his damned cave, like a dog scratching fleas in front of its kennel. And half a dozen British officers have got to go and ask his *permission* to shoot over a few hundred square miles of mountains."

"Anyhow, that alone makes him worth a visit," observed 'Ganesh' Hazelrigg. "I agree with the Major. We'll all go and have a look at him. Something we ought not to miss."

"I won't miss him," grinned Hennessy Wogan, "if I take a rotten egg up there with me."

---

[19] *Loin-cloth.*

§2

The individual to whom the members of the shooting-party had variously and indifferently referred as the *fakir*, the *swami*, the *sanyasi*, the *yogi*, the Holy Man, the filthy loafer, and the old image, provided something of a surprise for all of them. Practically naked, he was. Dirty, ash-smeared, emaciated, bloated, *bhang*-sodden, evil-looking, repulsive, he was not.

As the party debouched, from the steep narrow path up which they had climbed, on to the little terrace eyrie, they saw the *yogi* seated, cross-legged, at the mouth of his cave. Around him, a well-swept circle of flattened earth; beside him, a beggar's bowl: a middle-aged man with an extremely intelligent face, of which the large and lustrous eyes, high forehead and aquiline nose, were, in the opinion of the present beholders, contradicted by lips thicker than those of a European.

On the whole, even to the most prejudiced of his visitors, the Holy Man had a fine face; intellectual, austere; the face of a thinker, of a man of lofty ideals, of self-denial, self-knowledge, self-control.

The language problem settled itself immediately, as, in admirable English, the *yogi* bade his visitors good evening, requested them to be seated, and smilingly apologized for the entire absence of furniture.

"I'm afraid I have nothing here on which you can sit, save the whole world," he said; and, somewhat to their own surprise, the party seated itself about him.

"I trust we do not intrude, *Guru-ji*,"[20] began Major Harrington-Spens. "I mean to say, I hope that our feet do not defile what you consider holy ground, nor our shadows cast a desecrating . . ."

"Of course not. Most certainly not," smiled the Holy Man, with a quick movement of the hand that brushed away the suggestion.

Captain Hennessy Wogan snorted.

"Good!" said Major Harrington-Spens. "What we wanted to talk to you about was the—er—embargo that

---

[20] *Honoured teacher.*

you seem to have laid on our arrangements here. As, of course, you know quite well, you've spoilt our *bando-bast*.[21] The coolies we brought from Drimerg have gone back. They have deserted. Left us stranded; and we can't get others locally. Nor will the villagers help us in any way. Apparently all the hens have ceased to lay eggs, and the cows to give milk; and even the chickens —the skinny *moorghis* by which we live—have all left home. Moreover, even our own servants, our *shikaris*, *syces*, *hamals*, cooks and such like, seem very dis-gruntled—especially those among them who are more or less of the Hindoo persuasion."

"In fact, you are completely held up, eh?" smiled the *yogi.*

"Completely," admitted Major Harrington-Spens quietly. "And there seems every reason to believe that we have you to thank, or to blame, for the fact that our expedition has been brought to a halt."

The *yogi* smiled.

"*Khabar* and *bandobast* are the mainspring of a shooting-trip, as you know, and we can get no *khabar* and make no *bandobast*. What about it? We should . . ."

"And it's no good your denying it," burst in Captain Hennessy Wogan, "and telling us a pack of damned lies. We happen to know that you are at the bottom of it."

"Absolutely," agreed Major Moresby Wallingford. "And we are not going to stand it."

Ignoring the last two speakers, the *yogi* addressed Major Harrington-Spens.

"I am to blame—or to praise," he said. "Without raising a hand, I have stopped your expedition. With-out raising my voice, I have called a halt to your shooting-trip."

"Why?" enquired Captain Bartholomew Hazelrigg. "Why?"

"Why?'" smiled the *yogi*. "What a word is 'why.' Let *me* ask 'why' in turn. Why have you come, at great cost in effort, time and money, to this ineffably lovely lonely

---

[21] *Organization, arrangements.*

spot, this paradise on earth, this haunt of ancient peace—to slaughter its harmless inhabitants?"

"Slaughter *whom*?" snapped Major Anthony Moresby Wallingford. "What the devil . . . ?"

"To pursue and hunt and slay my harmless, peaceful brothers who . . ."

"Your *brothers*?" interrupted Captain Hennessy Wogan angrily. "The man's mad. Who wants anything to do with your beastly brothers? Or you either?"

"My kindly gentle brothers, the ibex, the oorial, the burrhel, the barasingh and the bear."

"Huh!" grunted Captain Hennessy Wogan. "If you met your Brother Bear alive one evening, you'd be glad we'd shot him dead before you met him."

"You are Irish, one perceives," smiled the *yogi*.

Captain Hennessy Wogan glared angrily.

"In point of fact," continued the *yogi*, "a very fine black bear visited me here, last night, and shared my evening meal. He sat just where you are sitting. Incidentally he displayed excellent manners. He had a white horse-shoe mark on his chest."

"Faith! We shall know him again then," sneered Hennessy Wogan.

"Not necessarily. All the bears in this part of the world have it."

"Do the villagers whose crops they destroy, and whom they occasionally kill, also regard them as brothers?" enquired Major Moresby Wallingford.

"Certainly. Brothers expiating, on a lower plane of life, sins committed in a former existence. They realize that bears must eat, as well as men. And a man, dying from the stroke of a bear's paw, knows that this fact was written on his forehead by the finger of God."

"*Bunkum!*" snapped Hennessy Wogan. "What about it being written on the forehead of Brother Bear that I should come from Quetawur to shoot him?"

"Undoubtedly it is so written—in the case of such bears as you will shoot," replied the *yogi* gravely. "But personally I doubt if there are any."

"Well, what of my 'why'?" he continued, turning to Major Harrington-Spens. "Why should you kill my innocent and harmless friends, the ibex, the oorial, the mountain sheep and goat and deer?"

"Sport," was the reply. "Er . . . trophies. The stalking and circumventing, you know, are as much as the actual shooting."

"Would it not be equally fine sport, or finer, to stalk them with a camera? The photographs being your trophies and proofs of your great prowess?"

"*Bah!*" growled Hennessy Wogan.

"No, in point of fact," replied Major Harrington-Spens. "Personally I should get no pleasure whatever from stalking ibex or oorial with a camera. I suppose, in theory, I ought to do so, but in practice it would not be at all the same thing. I don't know why, but . . ."

"Blood lust," said the *yogi*. "Man's primeval passion for destruction. Implanted in the race in the days when he had to hunt and to slay, in order to live. 'Nature red in tooth and claw' . . ."

"Well, it is natural then, isn't it?" drawled Stacey Burlestone, "if it's implanted by Nature in man's nature?"

"Not at all," was the reply. "Man has progressed far along the Excellent Way since then. In those days he married his wife by clubbing her insensible, and dragging her away by her hair. And if another man possessed something that he desired, he awaited his opportunity and simply killed him and took it. Civilized man has abandoned those customs. Isn't it time he abandoned the custom of slaughtering animals for his sport and pleasure, even if he thinks he must slaughter them for food?"

There was a brief silence.

"I'm afraid it wouldn't be much good our trying to give you our idea of sport, *Swami-ji,*"[22] said Captain 'Ganesh' Hazelrigg.

"No, I don't think it would," replied the *yogi*.

"But there it is," continued Hazelrigg. "We've come all this way for a bit of shooting, and we're going to have it."

"You won't have it here," replied the *yogi* quietly.

---

[22] *Respected holy man.*

"I'm not boasting or threatening or trying to annoy you. I am merely stating a fact."

"Who's going to stop us?" asked Hennessy Wogan angrily.

"Well, you yourselves have come to tell me that you have been stopped," was the reply.

"You mean *you're* going to stop us? Doesn't it occur to you that, if you choose to turn nasty and use the local power you seem to have, we might turn nasty, too?" growled Wogan.

The *yogi* smiled again.

"You will shoot nothing here," he repeated quietly.

Captain Hennessy Wogan sprang to his feet, and Major Harrington-Spens seized his wrist.

"Now look here, *Guru-ji*," he said in pleasant conciliatory manner, as Hennessy Wogan tried to snatch his hand away. "Let's make a bargain and settle everything pleasantly. You withdraw your opposition, and we'll march on out of your—er—territory. . . . We'll undertake not to fire a rifle or a gun within a day's march of you. You break the spell and raise the ban, and all that, and we'll—clear out."

And so it was agreed.

The *yogi*, albeit with obvious reluctance, undertook to withdraw his opposition, and Major Harrington-Spens, in the name of the shooting-party, undertook that the Holy Man's ears should not be offended by the sound of a gun; and that the lives of none of his four-footed personal friends and neighbours should be endangered.

For Major Harrington-Spens had learnt all he wanted to know, and was satisfied.

The party was about to break up, friendliness expressed by the faces of *the yogi*, Major Marcus Harrington-Spens, Captain Bartholomew Hazelrigg, Captain Stacey Burlestone and Lieutenant Aubrey Easterwood, who, hitherto, had uttered no word; sulky resentment and annoyance exhibited by the counte-nances of Major Anthony Moresby Wallingford and Captain Geoffrey Hennessy Wogan.

As the visitors were about to rise to their feet,

young Aubrey Easterwood, obviously intrigued and deeply interested, found voice.

"Excuse me, Sir," said he, and no-one seemed surprised that a Cavalry subaltern should have addressed the naked *sanyasi* as 'Sir,' "but do you *yogis* of the highest rank possess what you might call supernatural powers? I mean, can you see into the future; and can you do supernormal things that seem incredible to the ordinary person?"

"Work miracles, in fact?" sneered Major Wallingford.

"Yes, couldn't you show us a few tricks before we go?" jeered Hennessy Wogan. "What about the rope trick? What about the-boy-in-the-basket, and the miraculous mango-plant?"

Again ignoring the last speakers, the *yogi* answered Aubrey Easterwood.

"*Yoga* is the greatest of all sciences," he replied gravely, "and of all religions. The Excellent Law. It is the only True Way. Those who have explored it to the end, or as near the end as mortal man may reach, have powers that the ignorant call miraculous."

"And you, Sir?" enquired the boy. "Have you reached—er—the end of the Way?"

Again the *yogi's* enigmatic smile bared his shining teeth.

"Can you do—er—extraordinary things?" asked the subaltern.

"You want me to 'show you a few tricks,' as your friend here put it? A little conjuring, eh?" asked the *yogi*.

Young Aubrey Easterwood coloured slightly.

"No, I didn't mean that, for a moment. I only wanted to know. I was interested, that's all," and he made to rise.

"Stay a moment," said the *yogi*. "You are interested, eh?"

"Oh, come along," cried Hennessy Wogan, springing to his feet. "We've wasted enough time here already. He's going to grant you three wishes and tell you to '*beware of a dark woman*'."

"I could tell you that much, myself," he added, with a contemptuous laugh.

"Three wishes," jeered Major Moresby Wallingford, "and *'beware of a dark woman'*! That's it. Let's see if His Reverence can grant us some wishes, all to come true within a certain time, eh? Then we shall know whether he's 'the goods' or not.

"Can you grant wishes, Your Holiness?" he asked, turning to the *yogi* with a grin.

The *yogi* looked Wallingford in the eyes for a long moment.

"Haven't you a proverb, or a saying, *'If wishes were horses, beggars would ride'*?" he smiled.

"To Hell with your damned impudence. . . . 'Beggars!' . . . What d'you mean?" answered Wallingford.

Still looking him in the eyes:

"'Can I grant wishes,' you ask?" continued the *yogi*. "Wishes have a way of granting themselves sometimes, haven't they?"

"How d'you mean, *Guru-ji*?" asked Major Harrington-Spens, intervening as one who would cast oil on troubled waters.

"Haven't you also a saying that if you want a thing badly enough, it comes to pass?" was the smiling reply. "Don't misunderstand my use of the word 'badly'!"

"Yes; but I suppose it really means that if you want a thing tremendously, you'll scheme and plot and plan to get it; and if you work for it tremendously you *will* get it," replied Harrington-Spens.

"Ah . . . Yes . . . Perhaps . . . You don't take the view, then, that the High Gods sometimes punish us—by granting our wishes?" asked the *yogi*.

"Punish us for what?" growled Hennessy Wogan.

"For desiring the foolish things that we do desire. For wanting and wishing for ourselves instead of striving to understand *Their* wishes and desires, and to fulfil them; to follow the Excellent Law."

"Oh, to Hell with the Excellent Law," growled Hennessy Wogan.

"Haven't you also a saying that 'a man is known by the company he keeps'?" asked the *yogi*—and it is possible that, as he did so, his eyes flickered from Harrington-Spens in the direction of Hennessy Wogan. "Well, in some of the languages of which I have a poor smattering, one finds the proverb, '*You may know a man by his wishes*' and . . ."

"There you are," interrupted Hennessy Wogan, turning to young Aubrey Easterwood. "What did I tell you? Three wishes—and '*beware of a dark woman*'," and he guffawed loudly.

The *yogi* regarded him thoughtfully, his face expressing no trace of resentment or annoyance.

"'*Beware of a dark woman*,' eh? That's *very* interesting . . . And wishes . . . I wonder what the Sahib's own wish would be," he said, "provided he were offered the desire of his heart."

"What would I wish for?" replied Hennessy Wogan somewhat truculently. "I'll tell ye, and if ye can better it, then ye're cleverer than ye look. . . . And if your Excellent Law or any other Law provides for something better, oblige me by mentioning it. . . . I'd ask for *happiness*."

"Ah!" smiled the *yogi*. "Happiness. . . ."

"Just that. Good enough, what?"

"You'd ask for happiness. . . . Your own?" asked the *yogi*.

"Whose else?"

Once again the *yogi*'s gleaming teeth were bared in a kindly, if enigmatic, smile.

"And you?" he asked, turning to the young man who watched him so intently, and with such obvious interest.

"I?" replied Aubrey Easterwood, his ingenuous face again colouring slightly. "Well, do you know, *Yogi-sahib*, if I were offered my choice, and granted one great wish, I'd . . . well, to be quite honest, I'd ask for great *strength*. I'd . . . I'd like to be the strongest man in the British Army."

He laughed lightly.

"Gosh! I'd like to be the strongest man in the world. Yes, *Guru-ji*, I'd like to be a really strong man."

His friends regarded him with interest and

amusement.

"None so dusty either," smiled Captain 'Ganesh' Hazelrigg, slowly nodding his big head.

"And you, Sir?" asked the *yogi* of Easterwood's neighbour. "What would be your wish?"

"Mine?" replied Major Anthony Moresby Wallingford, pursing his lips, a look of deep consideration displacing the sneer upon his clever face. "Well . . . well . . . do you know, I think I'd ask for very long life. I've often thought life is far too short for all there is to see. The sands run out so quickly. Yes, I'd ask for the gift of long, long life. *'Man that is born of a woman is of few days and full of trouble. He cometh forth like a flower and he is cut down.'*

"Yes, *Swami-ji*," he added, with a contemptuous laugh. "You can give me long life, thank you."

"And you, Major-sahib?" asked the *yogi*, turning to Harrington-Spens.

The Major smiled a little sadly.

"Frankly and without a blush," he said, "I'll make a shocking admission. I'd ask for wealth; and I wouldn't care who heard me do it. Wealth. . . . Wealth unlimited —and, by Jove, I'd make some use of it!

"Wealth isn't happiness, I know," he added, turning to Hennessy Wogan, "but *a rich man who can't be happy is a damned fool.* I haven't the least faith in that 'poor but happy' slogan. No. There's more sense in *'When poverty comes in at the door, Love flies out of the window'*—since we're dealing in proverbs.

"*Love* in a cottage!" he continued. "Splendid—until the roof begins to leak, and the dear little conservatory becomes the day-nursery."

"Yes," agreed Moresby Wallingford, "and you can't get out of the front door, on account of the perambulator; or out of the back one, on account of the butcher with his bill. . . ."

"You'd ask for wealth," said the *yogi*.

"Any amount of it, *Guru-ji*," laughed Harrington-Spens. "Don't be afraid of overdoing it."

"And you, Sir," the *yogi* continued, turning to Captain Stacey Burlestone, who lay gracefully reclining upon his elbow, stolid, silent, tired.

"Health," replied Burlestone. "I'd have perfect health. God! I've envied the raggedest, filthiest, lousiest tramp that ever cadged a crust. *Envied* him—because he was bursting with health. What's the good of wealth or long life or anything else, if you are not fit? How can you be happy if you're not healthy? I tell you, life's a burden, a curse. It's plain Hell, if you are always ill. Especially if you're not ill enough. Just able to carry on. Drag along, in pain and misery. Unable to enjoy anything at all. No pleasure in work or play or anything else. Life no good to you. No hope, faith or charity. Food no good to you, and a night's natural sleep unknown to you. No, give me perfect health—and you can have the rest."

His outburst appeared to have exhausted him, for he lay back upon the ground, his clasped hands beneath his head, his face turned to the sky.

"You must study *Yoga*," said the Holy Man, eyeing him compassionately.

"And what are you going to give this Sahib, eh, Mr. Miracle-monger?" asked Wallingford, an unpleasant edge to his voice, as he indicated 'Ganesh' Hazelrigg.

"I'm afraid I'm going to give nobody anything," smiled the hermit, "except the advice about the dark woman!"

"No, I don't think you are," was the reply.

"Nevertheless, it would interest me to know what you would demand, if I were a—miracle-monger," said the *yogi*, turning to Captain Bartholomew Hazelrigg.

"Well, since you are so kind, could you give me some courage?"

There was a general laugh. 'Ganesh' Hazelrigg asking for more *courage*!

"No, I wouldn't at all mind being the most courageous man alive.

"Better than being the strongest man, even," he added, turning to young Easterwood.

"Faith, ye're right, Ganesh," grinned Hennessy Wogan. "Anybody going home?" he asked, "or are we going to jabber here all night? Who's for a spot?"

And he rose to his feet.

"Yes. Afraid we've wasted a lot of your time, *Guru-ji*," agreed Major Harrington-Spens pleasantly.

"Wasted his time!" objected Wogan, yawning and stretching himself. "And what about our time, Major? And what about his damned impudence in holding us up?"

"Well, we'll say no more about that," replied Harrington-Spens, with a frown and shake of his head at Wogan. "It's all settled now—and no hard feelings. None of us will shoot within a day's march of this spot; and *Yogi-ji* will tell the lads-of-the-village to come into line again."

"Plenty of coolies and plenty of supplies," put in Hennessy Wogan, "and no trickery. And I'd like to add that it's the first time I ever heard of such damned impudence before in my life. Don't know what things are coming to."

"And I don't mind telling you," he added, turning angrily on the *yogi*, "that if I'd had my way, the matter would have been handled differently. You can thank these two Sahibs that . . ."

The *yogi* stared unseeingly at a far-distant snow-capped peak.

"Here, you, I'm talking to you, damn you!" burst out Hennessy Wogan, and prodded the Holy Man sharply with the rough and heavy walking-stick that he always carried when mountaineering.

Without removing his eyes from the distant horizon, the *yogi* stretched forth a thin arm, took the stout stick from Wogan's hand and, without effort, broke it and laid the pieces of wood aside.

Before any of his friends could move to interfere, Hennessy Wogan, with open hand, struck the *yogi* heavily across the face, knocking him backward.

"Damn y'r soul, ye impudent black swine!" he shouted.

The other members of the party stood aghast, shocked, almost horrified.

"May my eyes be not blinded by the red mists of anger," said the *yogi*, quietly resuming his sitting position and recrossing his legs, so that the right foot rested upon the left thigh.

"And may I punish myself justly and as I deserve. I erred grievously in breaking your stick," he added. "I apologize to you, Sahib."

"Begod, you black brute, I . . ." shouted Wogan, as Ganesh Hazelrigg caught at his uplifted hand, and Harrington-Spens seized his other arm.

"I *say*," cried young Aubrey Easterwood, "you . . ."

"*Really*, Wogan!" began Stacey Burlestone. "You can't . . ."

And suddenly silence fell, a stillness, a cessation of all movement, as in the mouth of the cave appeared an amazing apparition—an old man, so aged, so withered, so shrunken, that to some of the beholders he seemed a corpse; to others, a living skeleton; something scarcely of this world. Shrivelled, hairless, dead; dead save for the burning eyes that shone in the livid, lipless, parchment face.

And as they stared, impressed, momentarily astounded beyond speech or movement, this Figure of Age personified, raised an arm of bone, skin-covered; extended a hand, lean as a claw, and a finger semi-transparent, a thin brittle stick; and pointed.

The toothless, lipless mouth opened and incredibly gave birth to sound.

"Go!" said the voice, thin, hollow and distinct. "Go in peace . . . And your wishes will be granted."

"Your wishes . . . *Health!* . . . *Wealth!* . . . *Happiness!* . . . Strength! . . . Courage! . . . Long Life!*"

Slowly, remorselessly, without tremor, the finger pointed at Major Marcus Harrington-Spens, and the burning eyes gazed into his.

"You will have Wealth," said the voice. "Wealth beyond the dreams of avarice. Go in peace."

Slowly, inevitably, the finger turned, and with it the eyes, to where Major Anthony Moresby Wallingford stood staring, all expression but that of utter amazement wiped from his neat clever face.

"You will have Long Life. To the age of a hundred

years you will live. . . . Go in peace."

And like that of the hand of Fate, the skeleton finger passed on to Captain Stacey Burlestone, no longer languid and weary-looking.

"You will have Health. Perfect Health," said the hollow voice. "Health unfailing and unbroken. Go in peace."

To Captain Bartholomew Hazelrigg the dreadful finger turned.

"You will have Courage. You will indeed be courageous. . . . Yea, all your life. . . . The Bravest of the Brave. . . . Go in peace.

"And you, my son, will have Strength. You will be strong. . . . As your days, your strength shall be. . . . Yea—as the strength of ten."

And the glowing eyes seemed to soften as they gazed on the now anxious countenance of Aubrey Easterwood.

And, at last, the eyes rested on the red angry face of Captain Geoffrey Hennessy Wogan; and if their glow had softened as they gazed on Aubrey Easterwood, they now blazed again.

"And *you*," said this living mummy, this resuscitated corpse, this apparent Incarnation of Age itself; "go. Go in peace. For you too will have your wish— Happiness. Perfect happiness. . . . Go. . . ."

CHAPTER IV

Returned after weary months, from a long and arduous pilgrimage, seeking knowledge and acquiring merit, the *chela* again sat at the feet of the Holy One and talked, asking of many things.

For to him, the Holy One—whom he reverenced, worshipped, and adored to a point but little on the sane side of idolatry—was a fountain of knowledge infallible, a tower of spiritual strength unassailable, a well of truth inexhaustible, unplumbable and undefileable.

"Has the new *chela*, my *budli*,[23] done well in my absence, Holy One?" he asked, reverently stroking the feet of his *guru*. "Cooked and swept, waited on thy word, and given thee all his care and obedience and love?"

"He has done well, my son," smiled the Holy One.

"As well as—as well as I did? As well as I shall do—now that I have returned to thee from Benares and Hurdwar, from Leh and Ladakh?"

"Who shall do more than it is in him to do?" was the gentle reply. "He, like you, gave of his best."

A long silence of contemplation; of adoration.

"Is it permitted to ask questions of a small matter that has been often in my mind, Holy One?"

"Ask freely, my son."

"Those six Sahibs, angry men bound to the Wheel of Life, of whom one committed in wrath a sin that shall for ever . . ."

"Judge not, my son. . . . What of the six Sahibs?"

"Will those things, that the Great One promised them, really come to pass? Just as he promised? Or was there hidden meaning in his words; and were the promises . . . ?"

"I heard the Great One promise nothing. Never have

---

[23] *Substitute.*

33

I heard the Great One make a promise," replied the *yogi.*

"Forgive me, Master. I thought . . . it seemed . . . it was as though he promised them Health, Wealth, and Happiness, Strength, Courage, and Long Life."

"Prophecy is not promise. The Great One prophesied."

"Then those things will come to pass?" said the *chela* wonderingly.

"Assuredly. For the Great One is a seer, a holy prophet like unto the Prophets of old, one to whom the future is at times revealed."

"And those angry and violent men will receive blessings? Receive great boons and gifts—in return for . . . what they did?"

"Nothing was said of blessings, boons and gifts, my *chela*. They had laid bare the desires of their own hearts; had made known what things, beyond all others, they desired. And the Great One—prophesied . . ."

"And the Great One, his hour being upon him, spake and prophesied," murmured the youth. "Prophesied those blessings to each of them."

"What is a blessing?" asked the Holy Man.

"Which of us knows what is a stroke of good fortune and what a misfortune? In their own tongue they themselves say, 'Call no man happy until he is dead'," he added.

"One of them asked that he might be happy, the worst man of them all! He who, blinded by impious rage, lifted up his hand . . . I cannot say it. . . .

"He asked that he might be happy," continued the *chela*, "and the Great One granted his wish."

"Once again, oh, foolish and ignorant," smiled the Holy Man, "I tell you that the Great One promised nothing. He prophesied that the Sahib will be happy."

"And will he?"

"Did not the Great One say it? Then assuredly the Sahib will be happy."

"A boon and a blessing, in very truth," marvelled the *chela*.

The Holy Man gave him a kindly tolerant glance; a look of patience blended with amusement.

"And so with the others, surely?" continued the disciple with meek, humble, and respectful stubbornness. "Gifts, rewards, boons and blessings."

"Nay. Prophecies," smiled the Holy Man. "I tell you again, it is prophesied that their wishes will be fulfilled. And assuredly they will be so fulfilled.

"It is written on their foreheads," he added, "and nothing can save them. Fruition of the seeds of the deep desires of their hearts will come to pass."

For long the disciple pondered the sayings of his Teacher, and regarded his face.

"Master," said he at length, "were they not good wishes, worthy desires—Health and Happiness, Courage and Strength, Wealth and Long Life?"

"All those are good things, rightly used, my son."

Another long silence, broken this time by the Holy Man.

"My *chela*, what is thine own wish; the true desire of thy soul?

"The truth," he added, smiling, "for I can read that same soul of thine."

The *chela's* long eyes slid round and gazed to where, far across a valley of stupendous depth, a village nestled against the mountain-side; a village wherein dwelt a comely hill-woman, desirable and lovely in the sight of the young man. Her apple-cheeked fair-skinned face came between him and his contemplation of higher things, and was never for long absent from his thoughts.

He swallowed, drew deep breath, faced the compelling eyes of his Teacher, and spoke the truth.

"Love," he said, and looked again across the valley.

"And if you were propounding a wish, asking a boon that should be granted, would you ask to love—or to be loved?"

"To love," replied the *chela*. "It is even better to give than to receive—love."

"A great truth," was the reply. "It is well spoken.

"And would you limit your love? To one person? To

a woman? Or would you ask that you might be given the power to love all mankind and the Creator of all mankind?"

The disciple laid his forehead upon the feet of the Holy Man.

"The power to love all created things and their Creator with all my heart and soul and mind and strength," he said, tears trickling from his eyes.

Laying his hand upon the youth's head:

"Pray for the gift of the power to love," said the Holy Man. "Pray for Good-will. For the only thing upon this earth of which Man cannot have too much is Good-will. Ponder my saying."

The disciple arose to go and prepare food for his Master, and, as he turned, averted his eyes from the distant village.

"And, perchance," said the Holy Man, "I may live to hear the Great One prophesy that thou too shalt attain thy desire and be given Love, that greatest of all gifts—even as those Sahibs will attain their desires, and be given the great gifts of Health, Wealth, and Happiness, Strength, Courage, and Long Life."

PART II

"*What we call Fate is even, heartless, and impartial. . . . We may fret, fume, and fight; but the thing called Fate everlastingly sustains an armed neutrality . . . and in our own hearts we fashion our own gods. . . .*

In two senses, we are precisely what we worship. Ourselves are Fate."

HERMAN MELVILLE.

CHAPTER I

The Manager of the Imperial Hotel, Mayfair, was on his mettle.

Kings, Princes, Dukes, Presidents, Ambassadors, Field-Marshals and Film Stars had frequently been "guests" of the Imperial Hotel, and the Manager was perhaps a little *blasé*.

But to-day, three men, brothers, reputed to be the three richest men in the world, were to meet, and to sojourn, beneath the roof of the Imperial Hotel.

One was coming from Berlin, another from New York, and the third from Buenos Ayres.

Between them they represented a sum of money so large as to be beyond the average comprehension. Even in plain figures, it was not plain to the ordinary understanding. In fact, it sounded rather silly; but to the man in the street their names were as familiar and revered as those of Rothschild, Morgan, Vanderbilt, and Rockefeller; Carnegie, Ford and Croesus.

It seemed that, like the unfortunate Midas, they were endowed with the gift of turning into gold all that they touched.

And, curiously enough, they were Englishmen, unenriched by one drop of Scottish, American, Greek, Armenian or Jewish blood.

Plain, hard-headed Yorkshiremen, one in Russian minerals and timber; another in American railways, steel and oil; and the third in Argentine cattle, in Brazilian rubber and diamonds, and in Chilean nitrates, the Askroyds had made, each, separately and individually, a truly colossal fortune. They had, of course, helped each other, played into each other's hands; and had at times united to form a financial interest of international weight and importance.

Three most interesting men, John, Richard and Henry Askroyd, hard, benevolent, ruthless, charitable, over-worked; two of them innocent and ignorant of love, leisure, peace, joy and enjoyment; loveless, unloving, unlovable, bachelors all.

Henry was the only one of them who had ever turned aside from the straight and narrow path of money-making; the only one who had ever worshipped false gods—or a goddess.

Henry—regarded by the others as a weaker vessel—had not only made a million less than either of his brothers, he had actually had an "affair" with a woman. But for a friend of Henry's, and but for them and their lawyers, their timely and powerful intervention, the literally saving grace of their stern virtue, the foolish Henry might have been very badly stung indeed, might have been badly damaged, might indeed have been married. This last calamity would have been less intolerable had the woman been of the right sort—daughter of some mighty Magnate, heiress of some Financial Power, link between the Askroyds and some such House as that of the Fuggers, Rothschilds, Coutts, or Vanderbilts.

They would have said nothing against such a woman being a Jewess or a Papist, albeit they were the straitest and sternest puritanical Protestants, brought up in the tenets of the Strict Ebenezer Baptist Faith.

But, alas, and incredible, the girl was a nobody or less. Some singer or dancer or artists' model or painter or—worse. An Italian wench, too, whom Henry had picked up in Naples, having gone there from Rome, whither he had come on business from Berlin. Luckily he was meeting John and Richard at Naples, they having come over together from New York to confer with Henry and the *Herren* Ballin and Krupp in Hamburg and Berlin, after they had done some business in Rome, Vienna and Paris.

Yes, an Italian girl, called, or calling herself, Minna Minelli, who spoke perfect English by reason of having an English mother.

An adventuress. A siren. A gold-digger. And Henry might have married her—for the fool was infatuated.

Well, it had cost him a bit to get rid of her, and it had been a narrow escape.

John and Richard had never thought as much of Henry after that . . . Nobbut a domned fule of a gowk of a brass-wasting Jezebel-chaser.

Their vast wealth had made the brothers suspicious and distrustful of all men; more suspicious and distrustful of all women—especially since Henry's shocking lapse—with the sole exception of their sister Julia. Her it was impossible to suspect and distrust.

John, the oldest brother, regarded her as a half-wit; Richard, the second, thought this an exaggeration, and regarded her as not-nearly-a-half wit; while Henry, the youngest, regarded her not at all, but, like each of the others, made her an annual allowance of three thousand three hundred and thirty-three pounds, six shillings and eight pence.

On this ten thousand pounds a year, Miss Julia Askroyd lived in a small Bayswater flat, with a cat, a Pekinese dog, a canary, and another companion, to whom she paid annually the sum of one hundred pounds.

To anyone eavesdropping at their dinner-table in the dining-room of John Askroyd's blue and silver suite (in which, as John said, every gard-damned thing was either a dad-blamed blue or a dod-gasted silver, if it weren't a gol-darned silvery-blue or a doggoned bluey-silver) the conversation would have been disappointing.

They discussed cigars, and took John's word for it that the only cigar worth smoking was a Havana cigar smoked in Havana. None of them smoked much.

They talked of wines, and Henry spoke of an Imperial Tokay Essence of which he had drunk at a banquet given in his honour in Berlin. The wine had come from the private vineyard and cellars of the Emperor of Austria, a gift to the Emperor of Germany.

"Eh, but 'twas a champion wine, yon," he said.

None of the brothers drank much, save Henry, who was a secret drinker of weak China tea.

They talked of ships and sealing-wax
And cabbages and kings.

41

At least, they certainly talked of Kings, not to mention three Emperors. Nor, curiously enough, of the financial affairs of Kings, but of their "goings on," their tastes, their peculiar habits and customs, their strange way of life, and the amazing, the prominent, part that women played therein.

Yes, they let women moock oop their lives for them proper!

They agreed that, on the whole, and with notable exceptions, Kings were a poorish lot; but that, in extenuation, it was to be borne in mind that theirs was a rotten job.

Cabbage was mentioned, as John demanded some, with roast beef and Yorkshire pudding; an order which the *maître d'hôtel* received without any amazement.

And they talked of ships, deciding finally that they would cross the Atlantic in the *Colossus* on Friday, this giving them time to see the Prime Minister, who was nobbut a fool; the Chancellor of the Exchequer, who was a champion twister; the Governor of the Bank of England, who was a grand man; and Julia—who was a daft owd lass.

And, in due course, on the *Colossus* they sailed, each installed in a magnificent, grand, super-de-luxe, royal, private suite, consisting of a large bedroom, a fairly spacious dining-room, a cosy sitting-room of adequate proportions, and a beautifully-appointed tiled bath-room.

But, as all the world knows, the *Colossus*, tearing at high speed through dense fog, was sunk in collision with a wretched oil-tanker, with the loss of over a thousand lives. Nor could the united wealth of John, Richard and Henry Askroyd, some forty-five million pounds, purchase them a little boat in which to save their lives, nor even a seat each in the little boat in which the few survivors escaped.

§2

So Julia, that daft lass, next-of-kin and, indeed, sole relation, inherited, after the payment of death duties and other iniquitous charges upon the respective estates of her poor brothers, more than twenty million pounds.

She gave the cat, Jasper, a new collar and bell, which he disliked intensely.

She gave Maudie, the Pekinese, a winter garment which was viewed with cold contempt, Maudie's expression saying as plainly as words, that she would fain in the fire of Spring this Winter garment in repugnance fling.

Mildred, the canary, did better out of the twenty millions, for Julia bought her a bigger and a finer cage. To the manifest annoyance and despair of Maudie, Mildred thoroughly approved of her mistress's gift, and was happy.

Natheless, Mildred regarded the two sweet little breeding-boxes, neatly provided with horse-hair nests, thoughtfully and with puzzled eye, speculative, concerned, not to say shocked. Possibly she considered horse-hair furniture a bit Victorian and *vieux jeu*.

The fourth companion, one Mary Hazelrigg, also benefited from the twenty millions—to the extent of a new hat. But as Julia herself chose the hat, Mary Hazelrigg's satisfaction approximated less to Mildred's than to that of Jasper and Maudie.

But on the whole, Julia found her brothers' bequests a great nuisance. Ten thousand a year had been more than ample—indeed about nine thousand a year more than ample—for her needs in the little Bayswater flat, even including what she gave to poor Minna Minelli whom Henry had treated so abominably, leading her on, getting her into trouble, and then jilting her!

Yes, a great nuisance. Mr. Hanstey, of Hanstey and Itchin, her Solicitors, was always coming in, nowadays, with papers for her to sign, and wanting her authority to appoint trustees, agents, secretaries, managers, controllers, all sorts of things. Nor was he satisfied even when she said,

"My good man, do whatever you think best. Do what you like—only don't bother me."

And when he had said that he thought the best thing his firm could do would be to drop all other business and devote themselves wholly and solely to the management of her estate, she had fully agreed and approved. Anything they liked. Besides, she hadn't got an estate. Hadn't one anywhere and didn't want one. All she'd got was a flat—and a terrible lot of money, and it was a great nuisance.

Probably she'd lose it all—and then where would she be—and poor Jasper, Maudie and Mildred?

And she wasn't going to give any more to that Minna Minelli either, for Mr. Hanstey had told her that poor Henry hadn't really jilted her at all—hadn't even proposed to her; and that if Henry had got her into trouble, she had also given Henry a lot of trouble.

She wasn't deserving—and anyhow, she'd leave Julia with nothing at all if Julia gave her the hundred pounds she always asked for at Christmas and on her birthday—and sometimes when it wasn't her birthday either. A million or two wouldn't last long at that rate. Why, one way and another, Minna Minelli must have had hundreds of pounds out of her!

CHAPTER II

"What sort of a man is Colonel Harrington-Spens, Barty?" asked Mary Hazelrigg of her brother, Major Bartholomew Hazelrigg, as they sat at breakfast in the Devonshire cottage which the latter had bought for his use when on furlough.

"Oh, one of the best," he replied.

"Doubtless, naturally, of course, and *cela va sans dire*, my good Barty. . . . What sort of a man is this Colonel Harrington-Spens?"

"I've told you, haven't I? A thundering good sort."

"Splendid description. That gives me the clearest impression of him. I feel that I know him inside out. Along what particular lines does he thunder?"

Major Hazelrigg lowered his newspaper and gazed across the breakfast-table at his young sister.

"Eh?" said he. "What's the girl talking about? What? Who thunders along lines?"

"Trains do and—er—have you never heard trams thunder along the ringing grooves of change? 'Let the great world spin for ever down the ringing grooves of change.'"

"The girl's mad," murmured Major Hazelrigg, taking up the paper. "Don't wonder. I expect Mildred the canary was, too. And Jasper the cat. And the Pekinese."

"Do Chinese girls have Pekin knees?" asked Mary.

Ganesh Hazelrigg again lowered his newspaper and stared at his flighty and flippant sister who, to his secret joy, had bubbled with high spirits since coming to keep house for him, on the day of her release from the companionship of Julia.

"The girl's very mad," he murmured. "Don't you bite anybody. What do I know about Chinese girls' knees?"

"And what do I know about Colonel Harrington-Spens, beyond the fact that he is one of the best and a thundering good sort?"

"What more do you want to know? You'll see him to-morrow."

"Well, there are one or two little details omitted. Is he old, young, fat, thin, handsome, ugly, married, single; is he chatty like you—three remarks per day—or does he sometimes utter? Put that paper down. Your coffee is cold and your bacon congealial."

"What d'you want to know about him? I've told you, haven't I, that he's one of the very best? My oldest friend."

"Is he a woman-hater, like you?"

"W-e-l-l, he's a sensible chap," replied her brother, a serious, considering look upon his strong sagacious face as slowly he nodded his big head.

"I see. He won't mind my being here? He won't object to your having a housekeeper—as she is your sister?"

"No. He won't mind."

"Awfully good of him."

Silence.

"Er—Barty, what sort of a man is Colonel Marcus Harrington-Spens, D.S.O., C.M.G., Indian Army, Political Department?"

Again Major Hazelrigg lowered his paper and looked at his sister Mary.

"Oh, one of the best," he replied. "Thundering good chap."

Mary Hazelrigg rose to her feet, threw her napkin on to the table, and departed to hold her morning interview in the kitchen with the village lady who, in her own parlance, obliged, and came to do for them; and, in Major Hazelrigg's parlance, damn nearly did do for them, too.

At the door, Mary Hazelrigg paused and eyed her annoying, aggravating, maddening, adored brother.

"I'm glad I know all about him before he comes," she said. "He sounds nice. But there's one thing about him I do hope . . ."

"Eh?"

"That he's not dumb—that he's nothing like you, Barty."

"Good Lord, no!" replied Ganesh Hazelrigg. "Nothing like me. Taller than I. Thin, dark chap."

At Wolvercombe station, next morning, Mary Hazelrigg paced the little platform, awaiting the train that should bring her brother's guest; paced the dusty gravel as though she trod on air, her face alight and alive with sheer *joie de vivre*.

How good life was!

Glorious Devon, after years of beautiful Bayswater.

Life in a lovely cottage, after existence in a stuffy flat.

Fresh air, after flat air; fresh life, after flat life; everything joyous, lovely, glorious, after being flat, flat, flat.

Dear old Barty. Wise old Ganesh. What a dear he was.

As good as he was modest and as modest as he was brave. . . . Brave! When the truth of the Gilgit business came to light, all the papers had spoken of his amazing courage. One big London paper had headed a leader about him with the caption, "The Bravest of the Brave." And Ganesh had flushed deep red, growled angrily and been quite upset and annoyed.

Ganesh and his grunts, his pipes, his deep rumbling laughter; his marvellous stories of India when, late at night, a story could be wrung from him; his cleverness, knowledge, wisdom and understanding; his fundamental goodness, charity, kindness.

Ganesh—after years of Julia . . . alone with Julia except when that queer, sophisticated and rather frightening Minna Minelli came and stayed in the flat—rather like a hawk in a hen-coop. How uncomfortable she had made one feel; how ignorant of the world; how dull, stupid, narrow, inexperienced and—virtuous.

Here came the train.

The short train idled into the little station with an air of not really having stopped to pick wild flowers but only to watch some hilarious cows swiftly gobbling their Lucullan repast. One munch per minute; and the same food always; and always eating it. Anyway, here was a station and it would puff and puff and pretend it had been running.

"Colonel Harrington-Spens?"

"Miss Hazelrigg?"

Mary Hazelrigg saw a tall, square-shouldered, lean man with brown leathery face, clipped moustache and cropped hair, now going grey; eyes that (she told herself, whimsical ever) had always been grey; a grim straight mouth that unbent, softened, and relaxed into a charming smile, displaying strong and regular teeth; a firm chin, jutting but not heavy.

As he raised his hat, she noted a deeply-lined forehead, and corner-creased eyes that had been screwed up against the glare of the sun, the wrinkles possibly increased by laughter.

No, she didn't think he would laugh very much, but his smile was charming. One of those smiles that literally light a face up.

Being somewhat romantic as well as whimsical, Mary Hazelrigg thought of a rather grim and forbidding scene that she had beheld from a hotel balcony in Switzerland, a scene whose grimness had been suddenly, almost magically, changed to friendliness, warmth, and beauty, as the sun came from behind a cloud.

No, this man wouldn't smile much, but . . .

What a fool she was!

Nice and warm and brown and hard, his hand was, as it took hers. Strong.

Not one of those silly hand-clasps that crush your knuckles, dislocate your bones and bend your ring if you have one, any more than it was one of those cold, dead-fish-in-your-hand efforts that some rotten people give you.

And such a nice voice. Not a growl and not a squeak. Of course, any life-long friend of Barty's would be "one of the best and a thundering good sort." That she had expected; but this man was handsome into the bargain. Thoroughly attractive in appearance, figure and speech; nice face, nice voice, nice handshake.

A strong man, a gentleman, and . . .

And a nice sort of fool was silly Mary Hazelrigg. What on earth . . . ?

"My brother is so sorry he couldn't come to meet you, Colonel Harrington-Spens. He particularly asked me to apologize for my presence—if not for his absence."

Colonel Harrington-Spens smiled again. Delightful. He smiled at you—and not at what he was thinking about you, as Minna Minelli always did. Nothing contemptuous, superior, or faintly derisive about this smile as there was about Minna's. Warm and friendly and kind.

"I don't think the apology really necessary, Miss Hazelrigg," he said, his eyes smiling into hers. Not that beastly stare-in-the-eyes that she had so often incurred from Minna in Miss Julia Askroyd's flat, and from unpleasant men in London omnibuses, tubes and streets, but the direct look that any honest person likes to receive.

She was going to like this man, and she was going to make him talk. *Make* him talk.

Heaven knew she'd had practice enough in that art, otherwise Barty would never have told her a thing; neither would that rather charming Major Moresby Wallingford, when he spent a week of his leave with them; nor that very attractive young subaltern, Aubrey Easterwood, when he, too, had come to stay with them.

Yes, she'd make this Colonel Harrington-Spens talk; and he'd be worth listening to, if ever a man was. As interesting as any man alive; if he'd talk about India and Afghanistan and Persia and all the wonderful places and people—that she'd never see. He had been to Bokhara, Khiva, Lhassa, Samarkand. . . . The Golden Road to Samarkand. . . .

And they shouldn't send her to bed, either, when they got down to it, late at night, with their pipes alight and the whisky decanter between them. She'd just curl up in an armchair in the corner where they wouldn't notice her—and listen.

The things these aggravating men had seen and heard and done—and would not talk about. . . .

And before he'd released her hand, the foolish young woman, impulsive, warm-hearted, eager, romantic, knew that she was going to like Colonel Harrington-Spens tremendously, and enjoy his visit enormously.

Thus, Mary Hazelrigg.

As he stepped down from the cursed meandering rattle-trap of an alleged train, so different from those to which he had been accustomed in India, the Colonel's irritation evaporated as a girl stepped forward, extended a tiny gauntleted hand, and said,

"Colonel Harrington-Spens?"

"Yes . . . Miss Hazelrigg? You are not a bit like your brother."

"You must tell Barty that," smiled Mary Hazelrigg. "It will please him."

The Colonel's hard and leathery face appeared to crack in numerous places ere it broke—into the smile that Mary Hazelrigg found so charming.

Nice girl this. Extraordinarily pretty. Neat. Good style. Humorous. Ganesh had never told him. What a singularly attractive face.

Thus, Colonel Harrington-Spens.

§2

For a week Mary Hazelrigg listened with silent delight to the talk between her brother and his visitor; and, night after night, blandly and firmly ignored her brother's pointed suggestions that it was time she went to bed.

When the two men went for their day-long tramps across the Moor, she repressed her longing to suggest accompanying them. She had no intention of being an inescapable burden and bore. But when they were in the house they were fair game, her lawful prey.

On one occasion, when her brother was obliged to go into Tavistock, she herself went for a long walk with Colonel Harrington-Spens, an exasperating, delightful, disturbing experience.

Did it hurt the man to speak? What would he think if she said to him,

"You remind me of my Cairn, Mac. Intelligent. He's so intelligent he can do anything but talk."

Not that the Colonel was boorish, lumpish, heavy-in-hand; not that he was monosyllabic, snubbing, disagreeable. He would answer promptly and pleasantly, but oh, so briefly; turning what should have been a feast into a tabloid.

And his face . . . so grim and grey; so shut and guarded. A closed door of a face, banged, barred and bolted.

What a reward and a joy when she could make it soften, open, light up—with the most delightful smile she had ever seen. Why couldn't he wear a smiling face? Would one get tired of a smiling face?

Anyhow, she'd made him smile several times. Could many people make him smile? Was he smiling at her as Minna Minelli always did, or with her as Minna never did? Did he think she was a fool? Was he really interested at times; or was that just his good manners, concealment of boredom? For, with all his grim coldness, reticence and reserve, he had charming manners.

Would he remember her face, or so much as her name, a few days after he had gone?

On the last night of his visit, Colonel Harrington-Spens and Major Hazelrigg sat late; very late.

About midnight, Hazelrigg rose to his feet.

"Good night, my dear," he said to Mary. "Sleep well."

"Going to bed?" replied Mary. "Why, I thought you'd be sitting up ever so late . . . to-night."

"I daresay we shall," replied Hazelrigg. "The Colonel and I still have a lot to talk about. Good night."

And, with more than brotherly politeness, he opened the door.

"Oh, Barty, I . . . thought . . ."

"Never mind, child. That's all right. No need for you to sit up for us."

And there was nothing for it but to go.

She hoped that her face was as non-committal, blank and impassive as that of Colonel Harrington-Spens.

"Good night," she said shortly.

"Er—good night, Miss Hazelrigg. I shall see you at breakfast, I hope," said the Colonel.

"Probably. If you look hard enough," said Mary rudely, and shut the door.

At about two o'clock, Major Hazelrigg ended a silence with a long loud yawn.

"Well, well," said he. "What about a last one, Mark, and then a spot of bed?"

"Wouldn't do us any harm," agreed Colonel Harrington-Spens, yawning also.

"By the way, I suppose you've never thought of getting married, Ganesh?" he asked.

"Good God, no! Marry? Why should I? What should I want to marry anybody for?"

"People do, you know," smiled Colonel Harrington-Spens.

"They do. I've often wondered why."

"Well, there are extenuating circumstances at times, of course," mused the Colonel. "Peers—and people who want an heir to carry on a great name."

"Yes, they have to, of course," nodded Ganesh Hazelrigg. "And there are Viceroys and Lieutenant-Governors and such, who must have a 'hostess' at Government House. They are practically driven to it.

"Though I did know of one," he continued, "who brought a lady out from home—and didn't marry her. . . . Said she was his sister . . . till the General wanted to marry her. Then he said 'she wasn't exactly his sister—but let sisterly love continue, without the General butting in.' . . . Shocking scandal."

He yawned again.

"Then, of course, some of these old businesses that have been handed on, from father to son, for generations. Those people have to marry. . . . And working-men have to have someone to cook and mend and clean for them. They need wives and a home. One wife, anyhow. . . . Otherwise, it seems to me an extraordinarily damn silly thing to do. Look at the youngsters who can't afford to keep themselves, and start trying to keep a wife as well.

"Is there any more pitiable object than a stone-broke subaltern with a wife? Ruled, governed, snubbed and squashed flat by the 'Colonel's lady,'" he added.

"Unless it's the Colonel," he added. "Often, Colonel commands the Regiment, and wife commands the Colonel. Pitiful."

"Absolutely," agreed Colonel Harrington-Spens.

"Y'know, speaking generally and taking it by and large, precious few people ought to marry—and of all the people who ought not, soldiers and sailors come first. What's a wife to sailor, except a living expense whom he occasionally encounters in the flesh? What's a wife to a soldier but a tie and a nuisance and a bother, who blubbers when he's going on active service and who takes his mind off his job?

"Or at any rate," he added, "whom he's got at the back of his mind when he should have nothing in his mind at all, except his business. Why, many a good man has funked a thing, or evaded it, because it wasn't fair to his wife and kiddies that he should take a hundred per cent risk when he needn't."

"True," agreed Colonel Harrington-Spens, and leant back in his chair with closed eyes.

"Yes, 'the curse of a soldier,'" said Major Hazelrigg, and murmured a quotation:

> "'*Make 'im take 'er and keep 'er: that's Hell for them both,*
> *An' you're shut o' the curse of a soldier.*'"

Colonel Harrington-Spens smiled.
"Yes," he said.

> "'*The bachelor 'e fights for one*
> *As joyful as can be;*
> *But the married man don't call it fun,*
> *Because 'e fights for three . . .*'"

as Mr. Kipling also says.

"Of course a man inevitably goes to the front happier in his mind," he continued, "freer, so to speak, if he is not cursed with a wife—and children. Naturally a wife is a tie and a burden, particularly to a man in the Secret Service. . . . How can he push off on a dangerous job that may last for years, and take him a long way past the Back o' Beyond, with his life in his hand, and the hand slippery, through sweating with fear, if he's got a wife whom he—adores?"

Ganesh Hazelrigg yawned again, rose to his feet and emptied his glass.

"Just what I say. Why are we worrying about it?" he smiled.

"Because I want to marry your sister, if you don't mind, Ganesh."

Major Hazelrigg collapsed into his chair.

"*What?*" he asked.

"I want to marry Mary, if she'll have me."

"*What?* . . . Whatever for? . . . What for?"

"Because I'm in love with her."

"You're *what?*"

"In love. In love with your sister Mary."

"Why?"

"Because she's the dearest, sweetest, loveliest, most attractive, charming, wonderful . . ."

"Who? Mary?"

"Yes. D'you think I'm too old? Do you think she'll turn me down?"

"She'd better not! Good Lord! My dear Mark. Well, I'm damned! Have you said anything to her?"

"No."

"Well, I shouldn't, if I were you, old man. You don't want to go about marrying people, at your time of life."

"That's what worries me," said Colonel Harrington-Spens, stroking his greying hair. "'At my time of life.' I must be twenty years older than Mary."

"Well, what of it? That's twenty years wiser. Twenty years more experienced, twenty years more . . . you wouldn't have her marry some dam' boy, would you?"

"No, I wouldn't have her marry some dam' boy," replied the Colonel. "Do you mind, Ganesh?"

Major Hazelrigg extended his hand.

"Mark," he said, "if you must be such a silly old fool, damn it, Mark, there's not a man in this world I'd sooner see married to Mary than you. My God, Marky, old man. . . ."

"Probably won't have me," replied Colonel Harrington-Spens in his sad and quiet voice. "That clock right?"

§3

"And how does one set up housekeeping in India, darling?" asked Mary Hazelrigg, some three months later, as she sat snuggled as close as she could get to her *fiancé* in a heathery nook beneath a great grey granite tor—Fox Tor. "Now suppose we've got off the ship at Bombay . . ." and she pressed his knee with her thumb.

"Got into the train at Bombay . . ." and changed the pressure of the thumb for that of a forefinger.

"Got out of the train at What-is-it? . . ." and changed the pressure of the forefinger for that of the second.

"And driven into the Cantonments . . ." and the second finger was changed for the third.

"Oh, isn't it a lovely ring?" she broke off.

"Like it? I wish I could have afforded a worthier one," said Colonel Harrington-Spens.

"I love it. I *adore* it."

And Mary Hazelrigg kissed it impulsively.

"What happens then? How do we start housekeeping?" she continued.

"Well," smiled Colonel Harrington-Spens, "we go to my friend's bungalow—chap named Burlestone. Captain Stacey Burlestone. He'll put us up until we can get into a bungalow of our own. You'll like him. Very good sort. Bachelor, but he knows how to run a bungalow comfortably."

"What's an Indian bungalow like?"

"Oh, pretty biggish house, all on one floor. Built of bricks and mud; whitewashed and thatched; big wide verandahs enclosed with lattice-work; rooms large and lofty; very thick walls."

"Papered?"

"No, whitewashed. If your Parsee or Hindu landlord is a bit of a nut, he may chuck a blue-bag into the whitewash—and that makes it distemper."

"And the floors?"

"Mud. Beaten mud."

"Help!"

"Oh, you don't notice that. Cover it all up with carpets and rugs."

"What sort of carpets and rugs?"

"Oh, awful rubbish called *dhurries*, made in the nearest gaol; and Persian rugs if you're wealthy, worth a hundred pounds per square yard. Wish to Heaven I *were* wealthy!"

"And the furniture? What sort of furniture does one have, and how does one get it?"

"Well, we take a drive down to a shop-fronted shed in the bazaar, kept by Mr. Coconutwallah, or Mr. Ibrahim Currimbhoy. He bows low, hopes that all the children are well, says that he has heard I shall be gazetted General next week, and leads the way into what looks like a railway goods-shed, stacked from floor to corrugated-iron roof with furniture, varying from egg-cups to vast early-Victorian four-poster beds with canopy complete. Out of that howling wilderness of furniture you, my poor dear, select a drawing-room, a dining-room, a few bedrooms, a sort of morning-room for yourself, a sort of office-room den for me, and a lot of verandah stuff."

"All second-hand?"

"A hundred-and-second-hand. 'Battered and bruised and battle-scarred,' but amenable to treatment. Cover it all up with chintz. When you've made your selection, Mr. Ibrahim Currimbhoy reminds you of all the things you've forgotten, and they will by far out-number the things that you've remembered. Then he'll pretend to do lightning calculations and tell me that that will be one hundred and fifty rupees eight annas, a month; but that he'll take off the eight annas for the sake of the love he bears me and the fact that I'm the Protector of the Poor and his father and his mother. And I shall thank him. Also point out to him that I'm not buying the stuff, but only want to know the price of its monthly hire. He will then inform me that that *is* the monthly hire—a hundred and fifty rupees a month. And I shall laugh hilariously."

"I can hear you doing it," smiled Mary. "It'll be worth going to India for that alone."

". . . and shall offer him a quarter of that amount. And by and by we shall strike a bargain that makes us both happy—he much happier than I—and the home will then be furnished. On the hire-and-no-purchase system."

"Of course, I shall have to go over the house first," mused Mary.

"Oh, I shouldn't do that."

"Why not?"

"Big rats, little mosquitoes, huge spiders, stout cobwebs. Cockroach on his back in every cupboard and on every shelf and ledge. Big nail-holes in the walls, damp-stains, ceiling-cloth hanging down, ragged punkah very filthy, half-an-inch of dust everywhere. One tarantula, two scorpions. Can't guarantee a snake, but I will guarantee you can't see through the glass of the windows, if any. . . . Hadn't you better give up this marriage idea?"

"No, Mark. We've done it now—nearly. What's a ceiling-cloth?"

"A cloth that looks like a ceiling. Canvas. White, once. When other pursuits pall, you can sit and watch rats and things running about on the other side of it. That is to say you can trace their progress—as they progress. If there's a hole they fall through. Before you've been there long you'll be able to tell the movements of a snake from those of a rat at a glance . . . 'The snake's progress.'"

"That'll do for the moment, Mark. Hadn't I better take out a lot of stuff?"

"Yes, I take a lot every time. Saddlery, clothes, quinine, calomel, favourite tobacco."

"'Stuff,' I said. For curtains, hangings, loose covers, cushions, linen."

"Oh, stuff! Stuff, you mean. Yes, any amount. Some people go in for making the interior of the bungalow absolutely English. Not a single Oriental thing in it. Once inside you might be in Devonshire."

"Would you like that, Mark?"

"Love it."

"Oh, Mark, I shall die. I shall positively die of joy and excitement and happiness."

"Don't talk about dying, Mary; even in jest."

"Oh, Mark . . . *you* . . . and India . . . and travel . . . and the glorious, glamorous . . . Mark, I'm *too* happy. The loveliest man and the most wonderful, marvellous country. . . ."

"Well, it's wonderfully hot and marvellously dirty, dusty and disappointing. And I *think* you're the first person who ever called me lovely."

And the happy-eyed, grim face again creased and cracked into a smile that, to Mary Hazelrigg, literally was lovely.

"Oh, Mark, you're a pig. Isn't it a romantic land of glow and of glamour—the shining East?"

"'In fee,'" murmured Harrington-Spens. "Talking of which, my dear, my fees don't amount to much. We shall be poor, you know. It'll run to an annual trip to Simla in the hot weather; but we shall be poor. Enough to eat, y'know. Respectable clothing; a horse or two; fairly adequate house and grounds, dry grounds—dust, in fact; a baker's dozen of servants; a car that will—er —go."

"In fact, all that heart can desire, Mark," interrupted the girl. "Do you think I shall want anything else while I've got you?"

"Do you think anything in the whole wide world matters anything at all, or is worth anything at all, while I've got you, Mary? Only I don't want to get you under false pretences; or let you think you are going out to an India that doesn't exist. It will be Heaven for me. Absolute Heaven on earth, but . . . Gad—if only I weren't so poor."

And the unwonted warmth and fervour of his voice changed to its normal cool quietness.

"To avoid disappointment, Madam, please examine the goods before leaving the shop—and count your change. There won't be much change to count, and the goods include terrifying heat; drought; dust; troublesome servants; malaria; insects; boring monotony, especially with regard to food; catty women, whom you meet daily and nightly and eternally; at times, weariness unutterable; illness; and constant danger—even in the water you drink; and . . ."

"And Colonel Marcus Harrington-Spens," added Mary Hazelrigg, taking his brown hand in hers.

CHAPTER III

Mahommedabad in the Punjab . . .

"Much mail, darling?" cried Colonel Harrington-Spens as he swung himself down from his horse, handed the reins to the *syce*, and stepped into the shady coolness of the broad verandah in which his wife sat by a tea-table, awaiting his arrival.

"Fair average, Sweetheart. I've not got much, but quality makes up for quantity. There's a joke. A really amusing letter from a firm of gentlemen of whom I actually know. They are called Arding . . ."

"Mind your aitches, darling. We're very particular in this Station."

". . . called Arding, Hanstey and . . ."

"Yes, Harding, Anstey . . . I see."

". . . called Arding, Hanstey, Itchin, Itchin and Itchin."

"Itchin' three times. Wonder what's bitten them?"

"Something's bitten them badly. Be quick and I'll tell you. Boy! *Char lao.*"[24]

"Well, and what's the joke, Mary?" asked Colonel Harrington-Spens, as he re-entered the verandah a few minutes later.

"You remember Julia?"

"Er—Julia? No, try again. There's no Julia in my blameless past."

"There is in mine, though. Miss Julia Askroyd."

"Oh, yes, I remember. You took me to see her. The old devil who imprisoned you in a Bayswater flat and gave you two pounds a week—to do everything for her, practically to be her personal maid. I'd like to boil her alive."

"Too late, my dear, she's dead."

"Good."

---

[24] *Bring the tea.*

"And she's left me a legacy."

"Oh, Mary, my *dear*! I *am* glad. God bless the old duck. Enough to give you that little extra margin that makes such an almighty difference?"

"Yes, quite enough. She has left me ten million pounds—approximately."

"Only approximately?"

"Yes, what they call round numbers."

"A figure one and seven round numbers, eh? Funny joke, I call it," mused Colonel Harrington-Spens. "What's behind it?"

The two stared at each other.

"After I left her, on the strength of Barty's invitation to keep house for him for his year's furlough, she inherited about twenty million pounds, being the sole heiress of her three brothers who were drowned in the *Colossus*."

"I remember. The three Askroyd multi-millionaires."

"Yes. Well, she hadn't a soul in the world, so far as she knew, who was in any way related to her; and according to Messrs. Arding, Hanstey, Itchin, Itchin and Itchin, she has left most of it to me; and after death duties and all that sort of thing have been paid, I inherit ten million pounds."

"Approximately," murmured Colonel Harrington-Spens. "Roughly. In round numbers. Whose joke is it?"

"I don't know, darling. Messrs. Arding, Hanstey, Itchin, Itchin and Itchin were her Solicitors, I know. They are mostly a Mr. Septimus Matheson, who used to come and see her on business. Her lawyers. I have met him several times, both at her flat and at the offices of Arding, Hanstey and all the Itchins. I think there is only one Itchin now; Matheson and Itchin. Do Solicitors joke? Read their letter."

Colonel Harrington-Spens studied the document with some care, and could find no fault with the envelope, seal, paper, printed heading, wording or signature.

It certainly appeared to convey the sober and serious statement of a sober and serious firm of Lincoln's Inn Solicitors; and it stated, without very much unnecessary verbiage, that their late esteemed and respected client, Miss Julia Askroyd, had made a Will—which incidentally they themselves had drawn up—by which she left everything, of which she died possessed, to her former companion, Miss Mary Hazelrigg, now Mrs. Marcus Harrington-Spens, "in consideration of her faithful service and unfailing kindness, sweetness and the gentle forbearance she had shewn to a cross and crotchety old woman. . . ."

Mary Harrington-Spens, *née* Hazelrigg, was to receive the entire income from the estate during her life; and, should she survive her husband, was then to become possessed of the whole of the capital in her own right, to use, enjoy, and dispose of, as she thought fit. Should she pre-decease her husband, the entire estate should become his.

Here followed Miss Julia Askroyd's reasons for this provision. Evidently she had highly approved of Colonel Harrington-Spens.

"Neither posted nor received on April the First," remarked Colonel Harrington-Spens. "It's really rather cleverly done. I wonder whose joke it is. Do you know anybody who is blessed with this particular kind of humour, Mary?"

"No, dear, I don't. I can't think of anyone who'd take all that trouble to be funny; or be as funny as all that if they took the trouble. Barty wouldn't do it."

"Ganesh? Of course he wouldn't. Besides, he's here in India."

"And how would anybody get hold of a sheet of the firm's note-paper?" asked Mary. "Besides—the signature! I know it nearly as well as I do yours. Julia sometimes made me write to them. If the butcher sent a tough cutlet she 'placed it in the hands of her solicitors.' The answers were always signed like that. . . . Suppose it were true, Mark?"

"Don't let's suppose anything so awful."

"Why 'awful'?"

"Well, a man who, with difficulty, knocks up fifteen hundred a year, doesn't want to be bothered with a ten-million-pound wife, does he?"

Husband and wife gazed at each other in silence for a few moments.

"Of course it's some funny person's idea of—being funny. Meanwhile, the tea is getting cold. Let's have some fresh. We could afford it on ten millions."

"My God!" suddenly ejaculated Colonel Harrington-Spens, rising to his feet and standing staring before him, unseeing; staring into the future—or the past.

"What is it, dear?"

"Nothing. . . . God grant it isn't true."

"Of course it isn't. *Boy!*"

"*Memsahib?*"

A bare-footed, white-clad figure appeared in the doorway.

"*Dusra char lao. Yih thanda hai. Juldi lakerao.*"[25]

"Marvellous flow of purest Urdu!" smiled Colonel Harrington-Spens, re-seating himself on the sofa beside his wife, and placing his hand over hers. "What does it mean?"

"Anyhow, he understands me," replied Mary. "That's the great thing."

"Yes, he's an intelligent lad. . . . Wonder who's the equally intelligent lad that wrote that letter. Do you know, I wouldn't in the least mind introducing the toe of my heaviest boot to the . . ."

"Mark, what's the interest on ten million pounds?"

"Oh, about . . ."

Colonel Harrington-Spens calculated for a few seconds.

"About a thousand pounds a day, if it's reasonably well invested. That is, after you've paid income-tax and super-tax. Yes, I'm afraid it won't run to more than a thousand a day, my dear. Of course, if those three Askroyd Wise Men of Gotham, or Get-'em, had it all in really good things, as they probably did, you may get as much in a day as I get in a year, ha, ha!

"Any other letters, not so funny?" he asked.

But Mary was again reading the one purporting to come from Messrs. Arding, Hanstey, Itchin, Itchin and Itchin.

---

[25] *"Bring some more tea. This is cold. Bring it quickly."*

"Wouldn't you like to be a rich man, Mark?"

"I should. I should like to be one of the richest men in the world."

"Well . . ."

"But that's not the same thing as being the poor husband of a rich woman, is it?"

"Of course it is."

"Of course it isn't. It would be a hideous situation to be a respectable, hard-working man whose wife's daily income was equal to his hardy annual."

"But, Mark . . ."

"Anyway, it's bosh, darling. And here's the tea; second issue. Of course it's bosh."

But it wasn't.

§2

England, Home and Beauty; all the Beauty of Life— that wealth can purchase.

For Miss Julia Askroyd had indeed bequeathed an income of some three hundred and fifty thousand pounds per annum to her former companion, Mary Harrington-Spens, *née* Hazelrigg: and to the latter's husband, should he survive her, the capital sum which produced this colossal revenue.

What had really been at the back of her muddled mind, Mr. Henry Matheson (who somehow was also the long-deceased Messrs. Arding, Hanstey, and at least two Itchins) could not tell his inordinately-esteemed clients, Colonel and Mrs. Harrington-Spens.

"She was always making Wills," said he, leaning back in his revolving desk-chair and tapping his blotter with a pencil. "She made one in favour of a plausible adventuress, a Minna Minelli, who professed to be her sister-in-law. Henry Askroyd's wife. Yes, she made many Wills, and, fortunately, this one happened to be the last."

"Fortunately indeed," and he bowed gravely, first to Mary and then to her husband, who eyed him stonily.

"I think she had some idea that, so long as we were

Trustees of the property, Mrs. Harrington-Spens would have no bother; would have nothing to do, in fact, but sign quarterly receipts. Miss Askroyd had the greatest horror—as Mrs. Harrington-Spens may remember—of anything in the nature of what she called 'business bother,' though she liked to threaten contumacious tradespeople with the terrors of our wrath.

"I rather gathered, too, that she felt it might be a little uncomfortable and *infra dig* for Colonel Harrington-Spens to be compelled to have his business affairs managed for him. Hence the provision that the total capital should become his, in the event of his surviving his wife."

"So that if my wife becomes a widow," remarked Colonel Harrington-Spens, "she promptly does get all the business worry attached to inheriting the capital! A bit of muddled thinking, I should say."

"Er—yes," agreed Mr. Septimus Matheson, "poor Miss Askroyd was given to muddled thinking; and she was obstinate, too, like most rather weak-minded and weak-willed people. But there it is, in a nut-shell. Mrs. Harrington-Spens receives the income for life; and Colonel Harrington-Spens receives the capital if he survives his wife."

"It's a silly Will," sighed Colonel Harrington-Spens.

"But it isn't. It isn't," smiled Mr. Septimus Matheson. "*Or*, at any rate, there's nothing silly about the income—and Mrs. Harrington-Spens gets that as long as she lives, though she would have to assume charge of the capital upon widowhood. And you, my dear Sir, would have to do so upon—er—widowerhood."

"A damn silly Will," repeated Colonel Harrington-Spens, as he rose to his feet.

Mr. Septimus Matheson (or Messrs. Arding, Hanstey, Itchin, Itchin and Itchin) eyed the Colonel appraisingly and with some curiosity.

In a long, wide, and deep experience of men, and of women, he had not yet discovered a specimen of either sex who considered a Will, under which he or she received a colossal fortune, to be a silly one; much less a damn silly one. What did the man want? He didn't look a hog.

Was he aggrieved that Miss Askroyd hadn't left the money to him out-right?

Surely he was on velvet, whatever happened? He'd got his three hundred and fifty thousand pounds a year for as long as he lived, whether he survived his wife or not. And if he did survive her, he got the capital. What more did he want?

As he rose and bowed them to the door, he again shot one of his long, keen, appraising glances at the face of Colonel Harrington-Spens.

No. It was a good face, if he knew anything of faces —and he fancied he knew a good deal.

What more could he want?

In point of fact, what Colonel Harrington-Spens wanted was less. A great deal less. Ten million pounds less.

For, from the day that conviction had come, and they had realized the incredible truth, a cold fear had settled about his heart, the fear that he should become a rich man—through the death of his wife.

Wealth beyond the dreams of avarice—and misery beyond the conception of anyone but himself.

For, with the bitter gain would come the cruel loss, the loss of all that made life worth living; the loss of the woman whom he so adored that ten thousand times ten million pounds, and all the world beside, was less than a grain of dust weighed in the scales against her.

CHAPTER IV

It has to be admitted that their accession to an income, greater than they could spend, added little or nothing to the actual happiness of Colonel and Mrs. Harrington-Spens.

True, every conceivable form of pleasure could be bought; but pleasure is not happiness. In point of fact the one has small relation to the other.

At first there threatened to be a rift within the lute that made the sweet music of their lives; a dark cloud upon the clear and sunny skies of their perfect happiness.

For Colonel Harrington-Spens began by stoutly refusing to give up his job and be kept by his wife; to resign from the Service he loved and take distasteful service as the assistant-spender of his wife's income.

He said that he would feel humiliated—a parasite, "a jumping gigolo"—and that his wife would soon be keeping a cat, a canary, a Pekinese . . . and himself . . . to look after the canary and the dog.

Frankly he was jealous of the legacy, of its awful power, its power to come between them, to give his wife all those things that he had so longed himself to give her.

But both the Colonel and his wife were too wise, too anxious each to act in the best interests of the other, too much in love—to let money come between them.

So he listened to all that she had to say on the subject of the money really being their joint possession, and she listened to all that he had to say on the subject of a man being kept by his wife; and in the end they found a common denominator, used their common sense, and regarded the money as their common property.

Together they visited every part of the world that Mary wished to see, together enjoyed every form of sport that appealed to them, followed the sun, entertained the charmingest people in the loveliest places, and bought the most beautiful toys—the most satisfying of which was a magnificent yacht that was a floating home, a wonderful house-on-the-water that took them over the said water at a steady twenty knots.

Mary's only fear was that wealth might make her vulgar, lazy, cynical, ostentatious or self-indulgent. Her husband's only fear was that he might become one of the richest men in the world—and in his own right; that in finding vast wealth he would lose the only thing he really valued; that he might become a multi-millionaire widower, Midas-rich and Midas-wretched.

Sub-consciously desiring to propitiate the little gods, he gave lavishly, sending empty away none who appealed to him for money. This, in addition to the enormous sums that he and Mary devoted to hospitals, and similar deserving bournes of benevolence.

But far greater than the satisfaction, the superstitious re-assurance, that he gained from giving to the poor and needy, the sick and the suffering, were the anxiety, apprehension and dread, that he suffered each time that he helped Mary to buy some new dangerous toy.

When they took a house in Leicestershire for the hunting, and filled the stables with the finest hunters that money could buy, each horse that Mary rode was to him a fresh source of anxiety. When he had been poor, one of his greatest pleasures, his keenest joys, his most appreciated luxuries, had been a run with a good pack, even on a screw, a hireling hack, or the dubious mount provided by a host only less penurious than himself.

In India he had been able to afford good horses and membership of the Vale of Peshawar Hunt. In England, on furlough, badly mounted, it had, of course, been different; not a case of "good hunting" at all.

But how different are English turf, horses, foxes, weather, and conditions generally, from their Indian prototypes.

And what pure joy, what exhilaration, thrills incommunicable to the non-hunting person, had not his former second-rate English hunting given him.

Pure delight; pure joy.

And now that he could hunt under the most perfect conditions imaginable, enjoy the very finest hunting in the very finest style that money could procure, he did not enjoy it at all.

The whole time when he, hard-riding thruster, was not following his wife, it was a case of,

Where's Mary? What is Mary doing? Is that horse too strong for her? Suppose it's a bolter. Suppose it's come down with her, and rolled on her. Suppose it's thrown her, and that patent stirrup has not acted, and she's been dragged. Did she get over the brook safely? People had been drowned under their horses in three or four feet of water. Does she know about that chalk-pit?

And instead of enjoying the sights and sounds so enthralling to the heart of the hunting man, he constantly saw, in imagination, his wife thrown, dragged, rolled on, drowned, crushed, meeting with that sooner-or-later inevitable "accident in the hunt-ing-field"; and heard above the music of the hounds and of the Master's horn, the sound of a thud, a crash, a cry for help, a scream of pain.

And, if possible, Mary's wonderful car which she drove with such dash and skill and verve was a greater source of anxiety to him than was her string of hunters. That she drove as well, or better, than he did, he was quite aware; but, as he told himself, it isn't what you do, it's what the damned-fool-whom-you-meet does. The cur, the swine, the criminal homicidal maniac that suddenly whizzes round the bend in front of you on the wrong side of the road, and just has time to miss you by a hair's breadth, with a fatuous grin on his foolish, oafish face.

How many times had he longed to stamp some such face into the mud? To kneel up in the car that his wife was driving and let off a magazine-ful of rapid fire at the disappearing car that had been within an ace of smashing them.

The most perfect driver can be wrecked and

maimed, blinded or burned alive, by the most brainless ape-in-goggles that chooses to make himself a road-hogging menace to pedestrian and fellow-motorist alike. And not the most competent of drivers is immune from dangers due to mechanical defects, tyre-bursts, skids, or self-sacrifice in swerving to avoid the sudden rush of a child, or even a dog, for that matter.

No, when Mary was motoring, life was nearly as wearing and carking an anxiety as when she was hunting.

But neither of these pursuits gave him one tithe of the anxiety he suffered when she talked of going up in one of these flying-machines! Balloons had always attracted her, and now she wanted to own one! Good God! . . .

On board the yacht, things weren't so bad; though his obviously painful interest in meteorological conditions and in the behaviour of the barometer, caused the Captain to mis-judge his employer and write him down as about the most nervous man who had ever put to sea.

Fortunately, Captain Holsen was a man who never discussed his employers and indeed rarely discussed anything at all, so the Captain asked no-one to find the answer to the question that so frequently presented itself to his thoughtful mind,

"Why on earth does the man ever go to sea at all? What does he want a yacht for? She must have cost a big fortune to buy, and must take another big fortune to maintain, and he doesn't enjoy one hour of the time he spends on board her."

This was of course something of a *façon de parler* and a slight exaggeration, for Colonel Harrington-Spens did enjoy many hours on board the *Witch Hazel*. (Hazel was Mary's second name, her facetious father having wished to christen her Hazel Hazelrigg and compounded with her protesting mother on "Mary Hazel".)

In snug harbours on the Riviera, in Norwegian fjords, in land-locked bays such as that of Mytilene or Arosa, with anchors down and the pure clear sea-water still as that of a lake, Colonel Harrington-Spens was happy—as happy as any man can be across whose mind fall the shadows of coming events, dangerous events, such as hunting-runs, motor-runs, balloon flights, stormy passages in a yacht . . . even drinking-water in Continental, African, and Oriental hotels, notoriously unsafe.

§2

Everything seemed unsafe. All life was unsafe. And not only things, but people, were dangerous. One grew suspicious of them—of everybody, almost.

"No," reflected Colonel Harrington-Spens, "we mustn't let this wretched wealth make us cynical or suspicious, make us lose our faith in our fellow-men and women—as Mary says."

There was danger of it, for the notoriously-wealthy are daily invited to view something of the seamy side of human nature, and are early compelled to realize the worthlessness and dishonesty of the average begging-letter writer, of the pseudo-philanthropist, of the false charity-monger, the wholly unattested raiser of funds for noble public schemes—which are private schemes.

And there were worse people than these begging and swindling pests.

Minna Minelli, for example.

That had been a most unpleasant experience.

As privately and quietly as was possible, Colonel Harrington-Spens and his wife had crossed from London to Paris, "on high matters of state—the state of my wardrobe," as Mary observed. Of the fact that the buying of clothes gave her unlimited satisfaction and uncloying pleasure, she made no secret whatever.

In the great over-gilded and all-glorious lounge of the Ritz-Meurice, Colonel Harrington-Spens sat one afternoon, awaiting his wife's return from the *ateliers* of the greatest of Europe's gown-confectioners. She had promised to join him for tea at about four o'clock, and he was engaged in making an imaginary bet of a million pounds that she would not pass through the revolving door-way before five o'clock, when he was aware of a lady of whom he had been aware before.

Once or twice he had caught sight of her, just recently, and had taken note of her because she had a remarkably striking face—whether pretty, handsome or beautiful he did not know—and because she had looked at him in a certain way, and in no uncertain way.

Each time that he had seen her, he had been with Mary, and he had rather gathered the impression that she had turned aside and avoided Mary, and that, had he been alone, the woman would have spoken to him.

Colonel Harrington-Spens was very gifted at gathering correct impressions, savouring mental and social atmospheres, receiving and de-coding telepathic messages—in short, at summing up people and situations with swift observation, intuition and instinct.

It had been part of his business to do this when he was in the Secret Service.

This woman had something to say to him. Something important. Important to her, at any rate. And she wanted to say it privately, and to him alone.

Rather interesting.

Was she a vamp?

The Colonel smiled to himself at the notion of Mary's husband being a suitable subject or object for the attentions and machinations of the female adventuress—though not all his professional experiences of the sisterhood had been wholly amusing.

This woman didn't look like any sort of a harpy, however. Nothing of the common gold-digger or man-trap about her. The more reason to be wary, when she showed her hand—or her claws. For he felt quite sure that he was going to see and hear more of her: her glance at him had been too meaning to mean nothing.

A secret agent? Friend or foe? Might be a spy who knew him by sight, and did not know that he had retired from the Service. Looked a gentlewoman, though. Nothing of the pirate-craft about her, trim, taut and smart as paint though she was.

She must be staying in the hotel. This would be the fourth or fifth time that he had seen her, either in or near the place. She could hardly haunt the Ritz-Meurice like this if . . . By Jove—here she came.

"Colonel Harrington-Spens?"

The Colonel rose and bowed.

What a pleasant, low, sweet voice, and, yes, she was more than pretty or handsome, she was beautiful . . . lovely.

"Could I have a few minutes' private conversation with you? Quite private, I mean."

"Certainly . . . until my wife returns. I am expecting her every minute."

"What I want to say concerns her. Her happiness. I don't want her to come in and interrupt. It is of the utmost importance. I don't want her even to see me. I have been trying to speak to you alone."

Colonel Harrington-Spens smiled kindly.

"I have no secrets from my wife," he said.

"No, Colonel? Well, you're going to have one now."

Colonel Harrington-Spens smiled even more kindly.

"Without being so rude as to contradict—I very much doubt it," he said.

"Well; as you like. I'm trying to do your wife a good turn—save her from infinite trouble, anxiety, publicity . . . from pain and loss. If you don't want me to," and the lady shrugged her shoulders with a pretty and very expressive gesture that the Colonel noted as being definitely foreign, quite at variance with her perfect English.

"Naturally I should want you to do anything that would save my wife from trouble, anxiety and pain," he said. "But why the—mystery and privacy? Why mustn't she see you?"

"Come into the further Louis Quinze drawing-room. Tea isn't served in there, and it will be empty, or nearly so—and I will tell you."

Colonel Harrington-Spens rose to comply. He had his doubts, but this might be something genuine and important. He could soon put an end to the interview if it were not. And she was undeniably a most attractive

73

young woman. Really beautiful.

"Let's sit over there, Colonel. Absolutely private," she said, as they entered the most ornate room, "and Mary will not see us, unless she institutes a search for you."

"You know my wife then?" observed Colonel Harrington-Spens as he seated himself facing the girl, with his back to the light.

"Oh, yes! You may have heard her mention me. My maiden name was Minelli. Minna Minelli. I knew her very well when she was—er—companion to my sister-in-law, Julia Askroyd."

"Your sister-in-law?"

"Yes. Although I was always known as Miss Minna Minelli, I was Henry Askroyd's wife. The marriage was kept a secret, by his wish. I never quite understood why. . . . However, I am his widow, Mrs. Minna Askroyd," and the girl produced from a small vanity-bag a visiting-card bearing that name.

"Ah!" observed Colonel Harrington-Spens non-committally.

He began to see daylight or, rather, darkness.

"Yes. And as Mrs. Henry Askroyd I have, presum-ably, some legal right to a share of his fortune, however iniquitous and inequitable his Will may have been."

"I am afraid I'm no authority on law—or on the vested rights of inheritance, Mrs.—er—Askroyd," replied the Colonel.

"But doubtless my Solicitors are," he added, "and I am sure yours are."

"Quite so," agreed the lady; "but need the matter be left to Solicitors? Need there be an unsavoury law-suit, a public washing of dirty linen?"

"Oh, I think my—er—linen is all right, Mrs.—ah—Askroyd."

"Well, a judge and jury may not," was the prompt and business-like reply.

"Or, rather, your wife's linen," continued the girl. "It was to save her that I came to see you."

"That was nice of you," smiled the Colonel. "But to save her from what?"

"Exposure!"

"*Exposure?*"

Colonel Harrington-Spens rose from his chair.

"I wish you were a man," he said quietly, and, "If you'll excuse me," he added, "I'll see whether my wife has come back yet. Good afternoon—er—Miss Minelli, and believe me, if you go on, you're heading for bad trouble."

"Wait! Listen! If you really care for your wife's welfare and interests. I warn you I shan't give you—or her—this chance again," was the reply. "I'm not vindictive, but I want my rights. Your wife unduly and improperly influenced my sister-in-law and got her to make an infamous Will, leaving everything to her—her paid companion; and not a farthing to me, her own brother's wife!

"Now then. I'm going to contest that Will—and I shall win my case. I hate doing it, but I'm not going to be robbed like this. It has taken me some time to raise the money for the law-suit; and to collect my proofs and witnesses; but now I'm ready. I am going to claim my husband's money and also to contest my sister-in-law's Will. And unless you are wise enough to settle the matter out of Court—into Court it goes, and you lose everything . . . *everything*. I am, of course, entitled to my husband's estate; and I am also the sole heiress of the two Askroyd brothers, as soon as a Court of Justice has quashed the iniquitous Will—made by a wrongfully-influenced and senile half-wit at the dictation of her companion . . . a person who hadn't the faintest shadow of a claim on her, and . . ."

"Excuse my interrupting," said Colonel Harrington-Spens smoothly, "but tell me quickly. End the suspense and put me out of pain. For how much will you consent to settle the matter out of Court?"

"For five million pounds," was the reply.

"Madam, I marvel at your moderation," said the Colonel, and laughed merrily.

The lady who was, or was not, Mrs. Henry Askroyd, possessed what is known as a poker face, but the tip of her tongue moistened dry lips.

"It will be no laughing matter," she said, "as you'll find when . . ."

"No," interrupted Colonel Harrington-Spens without apology. "No laughing matter at all, if I treat this as an impudent attempt at blackmail, and myself set the law in motion. Be advised—and don't be silly, Miss Minelli. Henry Askroyd was never married at all—according to his Solicitors."

"I have my proofs . . . proofs . . . *proofs*, I tell you."

"You'll find them useful then—if I am driven to prosecute. Good afternoon."

"My last word, Colonel—and your last chance to save your wife from exposure as a cheat, a swindler, a *thief*. . . . What will you pay—to save her, and settle out of Court?"

"Ninepence ha'penny—in coppers," replied Colonel Harrington-Spens.

Yes, a most unpleasant business. And such a delightful, charming, beautiful woman, too. Perfect, except for being a liar, a swindler, a rogue and—a real danger to Mary's peace of mind.

§3

Although the syndicate financing the *soi-disant* Mrs. Henry Askroyd lost the case and their money, the trial was an unspeakably painful affair—and public opinion was fairly evenly divided as to whether Mrs. Harrington-Spens had been extremely clever in getting the fortune and extraordinarily lucky in keeping it; or whether the alleged Mrs. Askroyd had been extremely unlucky in losing it and extraordinarily clever in putting up so fine a fight for her rights.

Yes—a most unpleasant experience. Enough to make one wish the beastly money had perished with the unfortunate brothers who had amassed it.

All pleasure in it was spoilt. It was tainted. And its present possessors felt tainted by it.

Mary Hazelrigg, Mary Harrington-Spens, of all people on this earth, held up to the consideration of all readers of newspapers as a possible swindler and schemer; to many as a probable, and to some as a certain, if unconvicted, one.

"Poor Mrs. Harrington-Spens!" sympathized many kindly people.

"Poor Mrs. Askroyd!" sympathized just as many equally kindly people.

§4

Colonel Harrington-Spens need not have worried on the score of bolting hunters; racing, skidding motor-cars and road-hogs; storm-destroyed balloons; sinking yachts; or germ-laden drinking water and ptomaine-poisonous food.

As a wise man has said, we suffer far more from the misfortunes that never happen to us than from those that do.

And no misfortune ever befell Mary when hunting, swimming, ski-ing, big-game shooting, travelling in uncivilized savage lands, motoring, mountaineering, yachting, or even ballooning, though they voyaged, by air, from England to Germany, unhurt.

"Markie," said Mary one day, as they walked across the heather of their Highland moor, from the butts to the road, after their last grouse-shoot of the season, "I've just thought of an extravagance."

Colonel Harrington-Spens stopped.

"No!" he said. "Well, well, what a brain! Splendid. I really didn't think it was possible."

"We aren't really bored, are we, Mark?"

"I'm not, Mary. Nor likely to be while you're alive. No, of course we're not bored. But to have thought up some new way of getting rid of some money! What is it?"

"We've never had a special train, Mark."

"By Jove! Neither have we. Let's have one each."

"Oh, no. Be matey. Let's have a special train and take everything south, all-under-one-like, as you say. We can take the whole party; the cars, the servants, the kit and everything."

"Great idea. We will. After all, having a special train to yourself is nothing. I believe some of the really wealthy people in America not only take a special train, but own one."

"What, live in it?"

"No, only when they feel that a little travelling would broaden their minds, if not narrow the credit column in their pass-books."

"Where do they garage when they are not using them? At the bottom of the garden?"

"No. I imagine the train's broken up, and the private cars—drawing-room, dining-room, bedroom . . ."

"Billiard-room, ball-room, library, music-room bath-room . . ." interrupted Mary.

". . . and so forth, stand in some corner of the nearest big terminus railway-sheds."

"Of course, there's a Royal Train in England, isn't there?" asked Mary.

"Sure to be."

"Shall we have a train of our own, Mark?"

"Be a bit—well—royal, wouldn't it?"

"No, it could be a perfectly ordinary train; only we could fit it up just as we wanted it, and have a special siding for it and all that."

"It would certainly be a way of getting rid of a little money, wouldn't it?" mused Colonel Harrington-Spens. "Rather a joke to give railway-parties, railway-holidays."

This latest idea of his wife's certainly sounded safer than those anent private balloons, fast cars and fast horses. She'd be as safe in a British train on British railways as in her own house.

"Might be amusing," he said. "So long as we kept it quiet, and it didn't look ostentatious. People needn't know we hadn't chartered it for the occasion. Be much more fun in a country like India, though, where you could tootle out to a suitable place and make a shooting-camp of the train. Lots of places in the East where you could shunt a train into a siding by some little jungle station quite close to tiger country, or near a good duck and snipe *jheel*. Come to think of it, you couldn't really do much with a private train in England, except simply go there and back. Couldn't use it as a glorified caravan, like you could in India."

"No," agreed Mary. "It'd be rather like the man's description of life in a country village,

"'Oh yes. Lots to do, in the country. Any amount. Walk up the street; down the street; ask the age of the goat . . .'

"No, silly idea. Anyhow, we'll take a special one, won't we, Mark, just for once. Great fun."

"Yes, rather. I'll ring up the Station-Master at Kildrossie when we get back to the Castle. We can arrange to stop where any of our guests want to get off, if they aren't all going back to London. . . ."

CHAPTER V

The Dream . . . Was this a dream?

It must be a dream, of course.

For a second or so, Colonel Harrington-Spens thought he was on the Frontier again. . . . Chitral Fort? . . . Mahsud watch-tower?

Fort blown up. . . . Buried alive. . . . Pinned down. . . . Badly wounded, too, apparently, but, thank God, not suffocated. No heavy beam crushing his face. No earth covering his mouth and nostrils.

Well, they'd dig him out, sooner or later, no doubt. In the meantime, breathing had better be gentle and shallow, in case there was not much air in the space in which he was imprisoned.

This was probable, as some sort of roof was only a foot or two above his head.

No, the problem of air-supply was all right. There would be no question of suffocation, as he could feel a breeze blowing across his face. Good.

But the sooner they dug him out, the better, for the pain was pretty bad. Dreadful. And he felt as though he might have lost a lot of blood; or perhaps he'd had a smack on the head from a falling beam, a stone, or possibly a great lump of earth. . . .

Colonel Harrington-Spens half awoke, felt acute pain in the heart, and then fainted. The dream faded.

Was this a dream, or was it not?

When he came to, he found he was in the same place and position.

So they hadn't dug him out yet. And yet he could hear voices quite distinctly. And someone else, close by, was badly wounded. He could hear a faint moaning.

Curious. If he could hear them talking, and somebody, badly wounded, was close by, he could hardly be buried alive.

The Fort wall might have fallen in on him, though, and there was an aperture through which he could hear the men; and somebody else might be pinned down close beside him. It was quite feasible—and yet it was curious that they weren't trying to get him out.

Who had been in the watch-tower with him when the crash came? Where was he? It must have been a Royal Engineer petard at the Gate . . . Gone off too soon. No—too late. Caught the attackers themselves. Biggest, smashing, rending crash he'd ever heard. . . . Malakand? Tirah? Chitral?

Pain wasn't so bad now, or was he getting numb?

What was that? . . . Whose voice?

"Are you a doctor, Sir? Thank God you've come. There's a couple of passengers pinned here and nothing on earth'll ever get 'em out, short of a steam-crane—or an amputation."

"And the train on fire!" said another voice.

"Thank God I've got some morphia and a hypodermic," said somebody.

What was this? A train? A crane? A train on fire? . . . Not the Frontier? . . . South Africa? A troop-train derailed by the Boers again?

Blessed oblivion. The dream faded again. . . .

What was this? A troop-train?

No. *A special train!*

Oh, blessed wealth, oh, lovely riches! *'He who has wealth is a fool if he cannot secure happiness.'* . . . A special train, wrecked and burning.

Slowly, painfully, Colonel Harrington-Spens turned his head toward the sound of faint moaning, faint gasping, and an occasional word, appeal, prayer, in a voice he knew, only just audible above and through the crackle and roar of flames, the sounds of burning.

Mary! . . . By the light of some flickering flare he could see her face; white, dreadful. White, even in that awful light, light from the fire of a burning train. Fire driven toward them by the steady wind.

"Mary! . . . Mary!"

A gasping moan.

"Oh, Mark, Mark. . . . *Save me! Save me!*"

But neither Colonel Harrington-Spens nor the surviving uninjured passengers and personnel of the train could save Mary Harrington-Spens, it seemed.

The weight of half a railway-carriage across her legs . . .

The doctor, haled from his bed, and arriving just in time, did what he could to lessen her sufferings.

Colonel Harrington-Spens, almost unconscious through injury, pain and morphia, found himself saved, dragged forth, just in time, by almost superhuman effort and the fact that some of the *debris* of the wrecked carriage that crushed him down was, for a brief second, movable by the power of human hands, applied to a lever.

And so Colonel Marcus Harrington-Spens found himself a rich man, wealthy beyond the dreams of avarice. . . .

But wasn't it *all* a dream?

Being the man he was, he took the blow bravely, showed the mettle of his pastures, the courage of his breed, and the results of his life's training.

Only those who knew him well, realized that his loss was irreparable, his hurt incurable, the blow mortal.

One day he walked down Bond Street from end to end, and then back again up Bond Street on the opposite side of the road. Into the window of every shop he looked, bestowing but a cursory glance upon the windows of some of them, more carefully examining those of others. A dream of course . . . Very real . . .

Himself he believed to be invisible.

Before some shops he spent several minutes, not with vacant stare, but as though looking for something.

Arrived at the end of his journey, he noticed a man selling matches—obviously an old soldier, obviously half-starved, obviously broken, ill, and hopeless. His face seemed familiar, in the dream.

From his note-case Colonel Harrington-Spens took a five-pound note and put it on the man's match-tray.

With apathetic glance, the man looked at the note and then at the Colonel's face.

"No good to me, Sir," he said.

"No? . . . I see . . . Difficulty in changing it, eh?"

"Prison, if I tried to."

"Well . . . I'll give you what silver I've got, and make it up in sovereigns. You can use those, I suppose?"

"More easily than the 'flimsy,' anyhow. What's the game, Sir?"

The man looked half-dazed, half-suspicious, wholly incredulous.

"Well, I came out to buy something. Just to pass the time away," replied the Colonel. "Just to help me through the morning. I've walked from one end of Bond Street to the other, both sides; and there's not one single, solitary thing in the whole street that's any good to me. There's not a thing I'd want the trouble of unpacking if they'd send it home to me, free. No—not if they'd give it to me for nothing, and send it home free of charge."

"Rough luck," said the man. "I've been dodging about in Bond Street, on both sides of the road, for a month, and have taken enough to keep me alive. Coffee-stall and the Embankment. Didn't run to a Rowton House."

"Old soldier?"

The man unbuttoned his ragged coat and displayed a row of medals: South Africa, Egypt, and the North-West Frontier.

"M-m-m. Now look here. Here's my card. Send me your name and address, and I'll do something for you. Something permanent. Don't be a fool and let the chance slip. Don't vanish . . ."

"Thank you, Sir," said the man, still staring, incredulous and stupid. Suddenly he vanished.

"Poor devil's head is about as empty as his stomach, at the moment," thought the Colonel as he turned away.

This little encounter gave him an idea, and he made it his daily practice to sally forth from his Club with pockets laden with half-crowns. These he would slip as surreptitiously as possible into the hands, trays, tin-cans, or hats of such down-and-outs as he could find; his quarry varying from blind beggars, some of whom had excellent sight, to pavement-artists, some of whom couldn't draw a line, although in charge of pictures.

To those who begged of him he gave nothing.

To aged people; to such as were obviously ill; to the halt, lame and deformed, who didn't beg; and to hungry-looking children, he gave double.

But quickly he grew more and more conscious of the terrible bulk of his possessions. It was like emptying a pond with a teaspoon; like removing a mound of sand, grain by grain. It was a nightmare.

It was all a dream—a nightmare—of course!

And his frequent nightmares took this form. Labours of Hercules, toils of Sisyphus, and a terrific, mad, hopeless endeavour to stem a rushing river of gold, to dam a mighty rising tide of gold, to remove a Mount Everest of sovereigns, with a tiny shovel.

To every charity that he felt was worthy, human, and deserving, he contributed lavishly. No hospital but blessed his name.

For years or for centuries, it seemed that he strug-gled on, fighting gamely against temptation. Striving staunchly to defeat the insidious foe, struggling bravely against the almost overwhelming desire to find Release.

Curiously enough it was against the thought of Release—and not of relief—that he had to fight. The idea of mere relief scarcely occurred to him. It was beneath contempt. Not for the man who had been the husband of Mary Hazelrigg, the brief relief of the kindly devilish drug, the friendly fatal alcohol.

But Release! The mere pressure of a trigger—to end it all. That was Temptation Incarnate.

But he had been a soldier all his life—and surely he could fight Temptation.

There was one thing though! Fate had made him

colossally rich—but Fate couldn't keep him rich against his desire. Made rich by Predestination, he could become poor again of his own free will. One had that amount of Free Will anyhow.

And once again Colonel Harrington-Spens visited Mr. Septimus Matheson of Arding, Hanstey Itchin, Itchin and Itchin, and bade that apparently astonished solicitor set to work to divest his client, as quickly as possible, of all his property and money. He would retain nothing but his army-pension.

Mr. Septimus Matheson was to draw up, for the approval of Colonel Harrington-Spens, a schedule of Charities, the most deserving that he could discover.

Incidentally a million pounds was to be allotted to the foundation and up-keep of houses to which any poor woman could go and spend the night. No qualification save need; no inquisition as to religion or morals; no restriction save entry at nightfall and departure after breakfast.

To be called the Mary Hazelrigg Homes.

A mad idea.

But of course the man was mad; must be, sighed Mr. Septimus Matheson, who, it seemed, had come to like him—and had hitherto admired him.

Mad! . . .

Why did people stare at him nowadays? Did he look queer? Behave queerly? Or was it by reason of this wretched habit of talking aloud to himself?

He must try to cure himself of that.

There! He'd said it out loud. Of course people in hotels, trains, the streets, shops, the Club, would stare at a man who said aloud,

"I must cure myself of that."

And there, he'd said all that out loud.

He'd better accept Ganesh's invitation. Ganesh was home on leave again. He'd better go and stay with him a little while—dreadful as it would be to go back to the house where he'd first seen Mary. He would see Mary more plainly there than anywhere else.

Perhaps he would really see her. Perhaps she'd speak to him. He'd only had brief fleeting glimpses of her hitherto: but of course a hotel-bedroom or a club reading-room was hardly the place where one would expect to get *en rapport* with the dead, to receive visits from . . .

What nonsense was he talking now? Really, he must . . .

Yes, he'd go and visit Ganesh. Everyone took his troubles to Ganesh. The cottage would be open for some time before Ganesh went back to India. Things couldn't be worse there than they were everywhere else. And they might be better.

And, anyhow, he was only dreaming, of course.

She might really visit him, and remain when he spoke to her instead of vanishing. Possibly talk to him.

Major Bartholomew Hazelrigg was obviously shocked at the terrible change in his brother-in-law and old friend.

Evidently he wished that the Colonel had persisted in his refusal to meet him "until he felt more equal to it . . . until it was less painful," as he had written.

Something would have to be done about it. He couldn't go back to India and leave Mark alone, he said. Not while he was like this. Poor chap was positively queer. What a tragedy!

How would it be to try and get him to come back East with him? Get him to travel with him when he went up Gilgit way again? Might even get him to come along on a job when he went to Samarkand, Bokhara, Khiva and such places. He knew the ropes. Been that way himself. Give him an interest in life. It would be more than even chances that neither of them ever came back—and that might not be a bad thing for poor Mark, either.

Thank Heaven he'd come down to Devonshire. He ought to have gone and fetched him as soon as the cottage was opened up again. But you can't very well force yourself on a man, even your oldest friend and brother-in-law, when he writes and tells you he simply does not want to see you just at present. Colonel Harrington-Spens felt that he knew exactly what Ganesh was thinking.

He dreamed that Ganesh Hazelrigg turned away from the window as Mrs. Cobley entered the room bearing a tray laden with coffee, eggs-and-bacon and breakfast impedimenta.

Going to the foot of the stairs Ganesh shouted, "Come along, Mark. Don't let breakfast get cold."

"Shan't be a minute, Ganesh. Don't wait," replied Colonel Harrington-Spens.

A minute or two later, the Colonel thought he came into the little dining-room.

"Morning, Ganesh."

"Morning, Markie."

"I say, Ganesh, did Aubrey Easterwood ever sleep in the room I've got?"

"Er . . . yes . . . Er . . . Why?"

"I saw him last night, sitting in the arm-chair by the window, and I could tell you exactly what he wore when he was staying here."

"Seen the paper this morning?" asked Ganesh Hazelrigg as he passed the toast-rack, his face wooden, expressionless.

"He wore a shooting-jacket of that red-lined sun-proof stuff and fawn-coloured jodphurs. Kit he must have brought home from India with him."

"Probably," replied Ganesh Hazelrigg. "Will you do something for me, Mark?"

"Is it likely?" smiled Colonel Harrington-Spens, in his dream.

"Come back East with me, next month. I shall be in Srinagar for a bit, and we could have quite a good time. Then, hey for the Pamirs, what?"

"Did Mary always occupy the room she had when I was here before?"

"Yes. You know I rather funk going alone on this next job, Markie. Come with me, will you? Wouldn't you like another sniff of wood-smoke on a cold-weather morning? Another pop at the ducks at sunrise by the Nawar Lake? Perhaps another gallop after a pig, eh, Markie, before we go north? Wouldn't you like to sleep on a bed of spruce-cuttings again, after a day's march under the deodars? Wouldn't you like to jog up through the Khyber again, playing 'possum, and getting *khabar* again with Havildar Shere Khan and Mahbub Ali?"

"Would you mind if I moved into it to-night, Ganesh?"

"Eh?"

"The room Mary had when I was here before. I think she'd stay a bit longer, perhaps, if she came to see me there. She came last night, but it was only a glimpse again. I awoke at about four. As I opened my eyes, there she was; but as I sprang up and called her name, she disappeared. She didn't vanish as she's done before but—faded out, so to speak. Perhaps I startled her by my sudden movement, and shouting her name like that. Did you hear me?"

"I did," replied Major Bartholomew Hazelrigg. "I thought you were dreaming. Perhaps you were. Perhaps you are now."

Colonel Harrington-Spens laughed in his dream.

"Dreaming! . . . But of course she wouldn't be alarmed by anything I said or did, would she? But I do think she might stay a bit longer if I moved into her room. D'you mind?"

"Do anything you like, my dear chap," replied Ganesh Hazelrigg. "What are you going to do this morning?"

"I'm—er—I'm going for a walk."

"Good. I'll come with you."

"Oh . . . You and I will go for a walk this afternoon, I think. I rather wanted to go alone this morning. I want to go up to Fox Tor."

Colonel Harrington-Spens could see that Ganesh understood. That was where Mark and Mary had been in the habit of going when they were engaged. He had proposed to her up there.

"Poor dear old Mark . . . He must certainly get him into harness again, somehow," he was thinking. His brother-in-law could see him doing it.

The dream was fading again. . . .

Now growing clear and bright. . . .

Colonel Harrington-Spens strode swiftly across the grass and heather, erect and vigorous. He was feeling happier than he had done since . . . Mary's . . . since Mary . . .

There was the Tor. He and she had climbed up this very path, and sat on that very slab of granite. Had squeezed themselves into that very fissure, cave-like between the gigantic boulders of the Tor, that day when it had come on to rain.

Curious. Very curious. He had said to her,

"You know, if a man forced his way sideways in there and got stuck, he might never be found again."

Yes, he had actually made that somewhat foolish remark to her. He was sure he had, because he could remember how they'd talked about the origin of the expression,

"Somebody has just walked over my grave."

He had given a slight shiver or shudder, and had wondered whether he was in for a go of malaria. Doubtless the temperature had dropped considerably, owing to the rain.

She had asked him if he were cold, and, not wishing to allude to malaria, he'd said,

"Oh, no. It's nothing. Somebody's just stepped over my grave."

Over his grave.

Why had he put the little automatic in his hip-pocket?

Oh, of course, he'd wondered whether he could still hit a running rabbit at forty yards. Probably not. A sitting one wasn't too good a target.

Why did he always take the little automatic about with him wherever he went? He'd never been in the habit of keeping a pistol by him. Something sub-conscious, no doubt. Possibly to be accounted for by his sense of defencelessness, nowadays. Not so much a sub-conscious feeling of being unprotected, of course, as being so *alone* in the world. Something of that sort, possibly. Unarmoured . . . unarmed . . . against the blows of Fate.

Curious. Something like those men who, leading the most humdrum lives in circumstances of the utmost safety, always carry a sword-stick.

Blows of Fate . . . Predestination . . . Still—he had exercised Free Will all right, in the matter of getting rid of the damned accursed wealth.

Colonel Harrington-Spens dreamed that he took the pistol from his pocket.

It was foolish actually to carry the thing about on one's person. He couldn't think why he did it.

The cowardly or weak-minded or weak-willed person might find it a temptation. An awful temptation . . . to the sort of man who found that his mind wondered a lot; fancied he saw things; had visions; talked to himself aloud; and so forth. That sort of chap.

Neat little thing. Interesting how neat, efficient and deadly-looking small lethal weapons are. He'd have a pot at something with it.

Yes . . . by-and-bye. Sit awhile here, where he and Mary had sat.

Now step into the fissure place. Yes, this was the exact spot in which he and Mary had stood sheltering from the rain . . . Just see how far one could squeeze in sideways . . .

Quite a long way. And round a corner. Invisible from outside.

He'd wait here awhile, quiet and still, and perhaps she would come. Nice and dark. Surely she'd come . . . He must watch. Watch and pray . . . The dream faded . . . No . . . Look . . . Look . . .

Suppose he looked along the pistol barrel, would he get a glimpse of . . . ?

And for the first, and last, time in his life Colonel Harrington-Spens found himself looking along a pistol barrel—the wrong way.

CHAPTER VI

Colonel Harrington-Spens sat up in bed, switched on the light, and looked across to the other bed in which slept his wife.

For a few seconds he stared blankly; then, gazing round the familiar room, moistened dry lips.

God! What a dream! . . .

Did ever man before dream so detailed, so realistic, so "sensible" a dream—one so free from the ordinary absurdities, incongruities, impossibilities, of the ordinary dream?

God! What a nightmare!

There must be something wrong with a mind that could dream like that.

It had been—life itself. . . . He had lived it. . . . The only dream-like thing about it had been his knowing what other people were thinking. He had read Ganesh's thoughts, and known exactly how Ganesh had felt toward him. . . . Scarcely, even now, could he be sure where reality had ended and the dream had begun.

Special trains! . . . He wouldn't get into a special train for a million pounds.

A million pounds! Pah! What was that to him? He'd give a million pounds to regain his former peace of mind. . . .

Did ever man dream a dream like this before?

Surely he had not merely dreamed it. He had lived it. Who was the fellow—poet or philosopher or something—who was not quite sure whether our waking daily daylight life was the real one; or whether the real one were the dream? What we call our dream-life the reality.

Anyway, that was an idle speculation, for here he was, alive, actual, sitting up and talking to himself aloud. There was Mary, thank God, alive and well. Here they were, Harrington-Spens and his wife, Mary

Harrington-Spens, in the huge bedroom of their castle in Scotland. . . . Not a "castle in Spain."

He tapped his head hard with his knuckles, reached for the little travelling-clock that stood on his bed-side table, and put it to his ear; opened a book and read a few lines; switched off the light, switched it on again.

Yes, of course, it was all real. This was reality and the dream was a dream, a nightmare, a foul damnable devilish vision from Hell. Nothing but a dream.

But one or two more dreams like that would . . . well . . . He'd soon be afraid to go to sleep at all. . . . He wouldn't care to live through that again. Why, he'd sooner be the poorest . . .

Yes, by God, the poorest man alive. That was the word—poorest. Oh, to be poor. Blessed poverty. This torture . . .

Was this reality? Really and truly? He must wake Mary and talk to her.

"*Mary!*"

No answer. No movement.

Good God, was this Hell or Heaven or dream or fact?

"*Mary!*"

Mary Harrington-Spens opened her eyes, looked round, raised her head from the pillow, and, leaning on her elbow, smiled across to her husband.

"What's up, Mark?"

"I say, darling, I've just had the most hellish nightmare. It was the most incredibly realistic dream. I lived it."

"Poor old Mark."

Mary suppressed a yawn.

"Did you do St. Andrews in eighteen and wake up on the nineteenth? Like the time I putted with a putty putter when going in for the Club medal, and the ball was a cannon-ball?"

"Mary, darling . . . Let's get rid of this cursed money! If I had another dream like this I should be afraid ever to sleep again. I should go mad. My dear, I saw and heard you being burnt alive, within a yard of me, under the wreck of that special train we're *not* going to take to-morrow."

"But, Mark, you're not going to begin taking notice of dreams, are you? You'll be going in for omens, like the Hindus—signs, tokens, divinations, propitious days, horoscopes, clairvoyance. . . . Keep a private fortune-teller, witch-doctor, dream-interpreter, diviner and . . ."

Mary yawned long and loud.

"My dear, if I could only give you the very faintest ghost of a notion of what I've just been through you'd . . ."

"I'll scold the *chef*," interrupted Mary. "I must watch over your dinner-doings; absolutely prohibit lobster in every shape or form; soup, savouries, red meat; snatch the port bottle from your trembling hand . . ."

"I say, old girl, I woke up more absolutely terrified than I have ever been before in my life. I didn't know what suffering was until to-night; and when I woke I thought I was in Hell and . . ."

"Called up the other little devil, eh, Markie? I'm so sorry, old chap."

Mary yawned again.

"Tell me all about it," she said apologetically, patting her mouth.

He must be joking. It was perfectly impossible for Mark to be frightened. He didn't know what fear was.

Fancy his making all this fuss about a silly nightmare. Everybody had nightmares. But then, men were like that. They'd suffer Chinese tortures without a groan, and make a frightful moan over a headache or a touch of liver. Pity themselves to death nearly. Poor old Mark. He was as brave as Ganesh himself, and here he was talking about being terrified to death over a dream, like a small boy waking up in a dark room and squawking for his nurse.

"Mary, my dear, for God's sake! . . ."

Heavens, what a fuss about a nightmare. Perhaps she'd better be a little firm. Really, he was taking himself too seriously.

"Same to you, old son. 'For God's sake' let me go to

sleep. Poor Markie had a nasty nightmare. What a shame! Now sleep on your right side and don't get your head under your pillow. Night-night, Markie."

Colonel Harrington-Spens, with a deep sigh, switched off the light and said no more; but he was at some pains to keep himself from sleeping again that night.

At breakfast, next morning, he re-opened the subject. To the utmost of his ability he described the long and detailed dream, the misery of the life he lived in it; the agony of horror he suffered beneath the wrecked train; and his final defeat and suicide.

"Listen, Mary," he continued. "If you had a dream, an incredibly actual, unspeakably hellish nightmare, in which you clearly and really saw me die screaming in agony, crushed and burned alive, with yourself pinned down close by and unable to raise a finger to help me—can you conceive how you'd suffer?"

"Don't, Mark . . . No, I can't. . . . It doesn't bear thinking of. But, dear, it would only *be* a dream."

"Yes, but suppose you felt in your bones that it was *prophetic*, a warning; and that in this dream you were tortured almost to death in order that you might save what was more to you than life—wouldn't you act on it?"

"How d'you mean, 'act on it,' Mark?"

"Well, wouldn't you avoid the chance of such a thing happening? Would you take this special train?"

"*I* wouldn't, Mark. But I'd hate the thought of *your* not doing so. I am only a silly woman—though I don't think I am superstitious—but you, Mark, you are such a tower of strength. You are so brave and cool and strong. Oh, I'd hate to see you do a thing like that—take notice of a dream."

The Colonel sighed again.

"Well, Mary, I have done my best to tell you what I suffered, and what I feel. Do you still want us to take that special train?"

Mary Harrington-Spens studied her husband's face, thought for a moment and replied,

"Yes, Mark. I do."

"You really do. Exactly why?"

"Because I'd feel I'd done you harm, if we didn't. I'd feel I'd—how shall I put it?—weakened you; softened your fibre; been your heel of Achilles, so to speak; been the cause of Marcus Harrington-Spens acting weakly and foolishly for the first time in his life. Been the cause of his giving way to superstition like some sooth-sayer-consulting old woman."

"Mary, I *am* afraid. I'm afraid for you. And for me."

"There you are! Exactly. You're afraid. And I am the cause of it. Oh, Mark, I couldn't bear to think that *I* had made *you* afraid."

"My dear, I have been afraid ever since we had this damned money. I have *lived* in a state of fear. At times, I have hardly been able to sit my horse for fear of what your horse might do with you. I'm afraid the whole time we are on the yacht. I'm afraid every time you drive your car."

"And yet you wouldn't be afraid to go to war, Mark. You've never been afraid when you were tiger-shooting; pig-sticking; on Secret Service in dangerous places and tight corners."

"Well, no. Not actual funk. Not terrified to death for myself . . . for my own life."

"No, it's left for me to make you afraid, Mark. Nice thing. Now you stop it, old son. You can't expect me never to ride a horse again, to go to sea, or to drive a car; be wrapped in cotton wool. It's awfully dear of you —but it's all wrong, Mark. Oh, don't look like that."

Mary Harrington-Spens rose from her chair, came round to her husband's end of the table, perched on the arm of his chair, stroked his hair and kissed him.

"Let's take that special train, Mark; defy that beastly dream-warning. I shall feel so guilty, so wretched, if you let this fear, for me, get you down. Just think of *you*—and fear! Let's have the special, Mark."

"Then for God's sake let's wait a little while. I don't feel . . ."

"No, Mark, we'll go to-day. We'll just carry out all we'd arranged."

"Mary . . . Don't . . ."

"Mark . . . Do."

"Don't, Mary—for my sake. I could not bear it."

"Mark, do, for my sake. I should be miserable for the rest of my life if I felt I'd done you harm. And this would be real harm. Your nerve would go. You know, yourself, that the only way to conquer a fear is to do the thing of which you are afraid. I have heard you speak of men thrown, when learning to ride, or when racing, steeple-chasing, pig-sticking—being thrown and half-killed—and then getting back on to the horse immediately, for fear they should lose their nerve. Let's take the special to-day, Mark."

Again the unhappy man sighed heavily.

"So be it, Mary."

Distressed, Mary Harrington-Spens furtively watched her husband's face throughout the journey, a face strained, anxious and drawn, as she had never seen it. From time to time, surreptitiously, he dried it with his handkerchief.

Suffering almost as much as her husband did, she yet felt that she was doing right, was acting wisely.

And at last, at the end of the longest day that Harrington-Spens had lived, a day that told him his heart was strained and tired, the special drew safely into the London terminus.

"Thank God! . . . Thank God! . . ." whispered Colonel Harrington-Spens, white-faced and blue-lipped, as the train came to a standstill.

And incontinently collapsed . . . Bad heart attack.

CHAPTER VII

Captain Stacey Burlestone and Lieutenant Aubrey Easterwood sat after dinner, cheroots alight, in the verandah of the bungalow that, at the time, they were sharing, neither yet being married.

With feet outstretched and higher than their heads, legs upon the long leg-rests, and eyes idly scanning the moon-lit garden that looked so beautiful by night and so arid and unattractive by day, they took their ease.

Ease of body, at least, for the mind of Lieutenant Aubrey Easterwood of the 1st Bombay Lancers, was not at ease; and his mentor, guide, philosopher and friend, Captain Stacey Burlestone, was a little concerned and uneasy about him.

The incident of the midnight intruder had undoubtedly made a very deep impression on Easterwood's mind. What Captain Stacey Burlestone really began to fear was that it might positively affect it.

In his opinion there was a distinction and a difference between the two things. A mind may be deeply impressed and be quite undamaged; in fact, may be greatly improved. On the other hand, an event which "affects" a person's mind, gives it a bias, a complex, an *idée fixe*, and does it an injury. If you say that a person's mind is "affected," you say something sinister and serious.

So he argued—and argued so with his young friend, for whom he had very great admiration, very strong affection, and considerable respect.

"Yes, I know, I know, my dear chap," he said. "I know it has made a deep impression on your mind. Very deep, that's obvious enough. But you mustn't let it *affect* your mind, you know. Don't let it get on your nerves. India is a queer place, particularly for people blessed or cursed with an imagination. Imagination is a noble horse so long as you can ride it; but when it bolts, God help the rider. Especially, as I say, in India."

"The climate, d'you mean?" began Aubrey Easter-wood. "Or . . . ?"

"Oh, everything. Especially the heat; and what you might call its foreign-ness. We are bubbles on an ocean into which we can't sink, and of the depths of which we know nothing. Yes, climate; way of life; incompatibility of self and circumstance; the earth, the sky and the people; the air and the water; they are all against us; as well as celibacy, mental loneliness, depolarization, monotony of strangeness—not to mention the power of the local gods."

Aubrey Easterwood laughed.

"D'you believe in that?" he asked. "The power of the Little Gods?"

"I don't know. Anyhow, I don't go out of my way to defy it; and I do go out of my way to watch my step. That's a 'bull' worthy of Hennessy Wogan. . . . Watch myself and watch my nerves. I began watching my nerves when I was subject to that cursed malaria and dysentery. Nerves! Many a good man's nerves have got him—court-martialled . . . hanged.

"And when you find you are getting something on your mind—get it off again, quick. Whatever you do, don't brood. Don't get introspective. That sitting alone in a little bungalow, all day, with the doors closed and the windows shuttered, as one has to, through the hot weather—is bad. One of the bad things of India. Worse than whisky."

"Yes," agreed Easterwood. "When one's read all there is to read, the day seems pretty long from break-fast to tea-time, when you're alone, and it's too hot to go out of the house."

"You were getting like a broody hen," said Stacey Burlestone. "I know it's easy to say 'forget it,' but that is what you've got to do. And the best way to get something out, and keep it out, is to put something else in. Get this worry out of your mind and something else into it—a hobby of some sort.

"Now tell me all about it, thrash it all out, and then don't let's refer to it again. Get it in its proper per-spective and see it in the proper light—as other people will. Believe me, nobody else looks at the matter as you do."

"They didn't suffer the . . . the *humiliation*," was the reply.

"Humiliation be damned. Nothing of the sort. No more than taking a toss at hunting, pig-sticking, or steeple-chasing. You wouldn't call that 'humiliation,' would you?"

"No, I wouldn't. But there's no comparison. One can't help one's feelings; and ever since it happened I've felt—humiliated."

"'One can't help one's feelings,'" mused Stacey Burlestone. "Well, there I don't agree with you. I think one can."

"One can disguise them, of course," said Easterwood. "I've tried to."

"I know you have, my dear chap. I'm not talking about disguising one's feelings. That's mere repression, and, however admirable, doesn't do any good at all. I say one can *change* one's feelings. . . . Anyhow, we're going to try to change yours.

"Now, first of all, tell me all about it. Just exactly what happened; what you thought, and felt and did. Get it all up and out, and ventilate it. Let's get your mind swept and garnished."

"And then seven devils worse than the first will enter in?" smiled Easterwood.

"No, they won't. Not if I know you. Let one wholesome god—not goddess, mind you—enter in, instead of this miserable devil of doubt and depression and distrust of self. . . . Well, get on with it."

"I was asleep on the verandah," began Aubrey Easterwood. "I'd had my light camp-bed set up outside the bedroom door. I didn't have it out in the garden because it was full moon, and moon-light wakes me up and keeps me awake.

"I'd turned in at about eleven, and had gone to sleep fairly soon. I was awakened by a noise inside the bungalow. Somebody had either dropped something or knocked it over.

"As the servants sleep in their houses at the bottom

of the compound, there should, of course, have been no-one in the bungalow but myself.

"A beam of moon-light came through the lattice at the corner of the verandah, and I could see by my watch that it was a quarter to three; much too late, and much too early, for any of them to be about the place.

"I pulled up the mosquito-curtain, got out of bed, and looked into the bedroom. That's the end room; and the moon was shining in. . . . Nobody there. . . . I then went into the living-room and struck a match. I always keep a box in the breast-pocket of my pyjamas. Nobody there."

"Did you feel at all nervous?"

"Not in the very slightest degree," replied Aubrey Easterwood. "I then went into the next room, where I keep my kit, boots, guns, and so forth. There's a desk and chair in the room. . . . Nobody there.

"But just as the match was going out, I noticed something wrong with the pattern of my bright-stuff on the wall, and also realized that there was a lamp on the shelf.

"I struck another match and lit the lamp, and held it up to the wall where a large oblong of green baize was nailed up. On this baize hung all my bright-stuff, in a sort of trophy pattern: sword, scabbard, spurs, chain-mail shoulder-straps, bits, badges, belts, buckles, stirrups, revolver—and all that.

"But the revolver was gone.

"And then I noticed that a drawer of the desk was open.

"Well, as I'd heard the noise only half a minute before, I realized that there was somebody in the place and that, if they'd got no other weapon, they had got my revolver."

"Did you feel nervous then?" asked Stacey Burlestone. "I don't mean frightened, mark you, but keyed-up, trembling with excitement, that sort of thing."

"Not in the least," replied Easterwood. "I felt annoyed, and only hoped that I'd catch the blighter. As there was only one other room, he must be in that, or in the back verandah.

"None of these rooms opened into each other, so I had to go out into the front verandah, each time, to get from room to room.

"I at once nipped round into the remaining room. . . ."

"With the lamp in your hand?" interrupted Stacey Burlestone. "Bad tactics, my son—making yourself a perfect target, and also heralding your arrival."

"Anyway, the room was empty. So was the back verandah. That puzzled me, because it meant that the man had escaped by way of the front verandah while I'd been looking for him, and that didn't strike me as probable."

"Couldn't he have got out at the back?"

"No, the doors of the back verandah were shut, and still bolted on the inside.

"I returned to the front verandah, put the lamp down on the table, and went back to the bedroom. I kept my despatch-box in a uniform-case in there, and what cash and small valuables I have were in it. Studs, links, gold watch, a ring, a few things like that; and it occurred to me that one's trunk would be the first thing that a thief would go for.

"As I entered the bedroom, a man was coming out of it. I suppose that, when I first looked in, he'd been hiding in the bath-room or in the shadow of an almirah, having heard me get out of bed.

"I imagine he'd then waited till he thought the coast was clear, before making a dash for it; but he'd left it too late.

"He was a big chap, taller than I, and broad; a heavy burly sort of fellow; a Pathan, I should say."

"Were you at all nervous then?" asked Stacey Burlestone. "Don't misunderstand me. Once again, I don't mean frightened. I mean, were you rattled—the opposite of calm, cool, and collected?"

"No," replied Easterwood. "I wasn't rattled. I wasn't frightened, and I was calm, cool, and collected. Those are absolute simple facts."

"Good. A Pathan, eh? Lucky for you he wasn't one

of the low-caste Hindu professionals—dressed in a suit of oil and a long knife."

"Yes, this chap was clothed, even to a *kullah*[26] and *puggari*. I should say he was wearing baggy trousers, long shirt outside them, and a velvet waistcoat over the shirt. He'd nothing in his hands, as I realized when he rushed at me with them extended, open, for a sort of catch-as-catch-can wrestler's grab. . . . I suppose he had got my empty revolver stuck in the back of his cummerbund, or somewhere.

"Well, I met him more than half-way, and aimed with my right fist, the best punch that I could deliver, at the point of his jaw.

"It didn't get home.

"He caught my right hand with his left, seized my left arm in his right hand, pulled me towards him, then shifted his right-hand grip to my throat and threw his left arm around me, pinioning my right arm to my side.

"With my free hand I got hold of his wrist and tried to tear his hand away from my throat. And in half a second I realized that the fellow was about twice as strong as I was. I hadn't a chance. It was absolutely humiliating; and, as I've told you, I've felt humiliated ever since."

"Just because this fellow was bigger and stronger than you?"

"Not quite that. Not wholly that. It would have been bad enough if it had happened in England, and I'd been up against a regular Bill Sykes of a burglar, who was bigger and stronger than I. That would have been bad enough. But here in India. A native . . ."

"So it's really because he was a little brown brother —but still bigger and stronger than you—that you feel it so badly?"

"To be quite candid, yes. I think if I'm to be honest with myself—and with you—I have to admit that what upsets me is the fact that, in a fair hand-to-hand, man-to-man tussle and trial of physical strength, I was absolutely no-where."

"Well, lots of natives of India are immensely

---

[26] *Skull-cap.*

powerful. The professional wrestler and Rajah's strong-arm man—not to mention the average Jat cultivator, big Sikh, Punjabi Mussulman, Mahratta athlete, and most Pathans. . . . Surely any up-country Regiment, in fact any Regiment at all, has got any number of men in it who are physically stronger than any Officer in it. Besides, in point of fact, the Pathan is not a native of India at all."

"Well, that's a bit of casuistry, isn't it?" smiled Easterwood. "Anyway, I tackled what we are pleased to call a 'native,' and he proved to be a damn-sight better man than I."

The two fell silent.

"Exactly what happened next?" asked Stacey Burlestone.

"Well, I struggled, with all my might—and about as effectively as a small boy would struggle if you'd caught him stealing apples in your orchard. It was really rather like that, except that it was the thief who'd caught me—and it was a bit more serious, for he was choking the life out of me, and, by exerting my utmost strength, I couldn't budge a fraction of an inch."

"Did you try to shout at all?"

"I couldn't have uttered a whisper."

"Did you shout for help before he'd closed with you?"

"No."

"Why not?"

"Well; damn it all. . . . There was only one of him; and a white man, a soldier, ought to be able to deal with a sneak-thief creeping about his bungalow in the night."

"It simply didn't occur to you to call for help?"

"Not for a moment."

"Well?"

"We came down with a crash."

"D'you mean you managed to get him down, and fell with him?"

"Not a bit of it."

"He threw you and fell with you?"

"No, he had no need to. He was simply holding me

and throttling me quite successfully and satisfactorily. What caused our downfall and probably saved my miserable life, was the fact that we were on a rug, one or both of us, and the thing slid and shifted, and we came down together, knocking over the table and its contents, including a mirror—an awful crash. I think that frightened him off, for he knelt on my chest, gave me two awful clouts, left and right, with his closed fists, jumped up, kicked me in the ribs and then ran for it.

"And what was, I think, the most humiliating touch of all, was the fact that he gave a contemptuous laugh as he jumped up and dashed through the doorway."

"Did you follow him?"

"I was bare-footed."

"What did you do?"

"Pulled on a pair of shoes and, without stopping to lace them, ran after him."

"Did you see anything of him?"

"No. He had darted across the compound into the black shadow of the banyan trees; dark as a tunnel. I'd no earthly means of knowing whether he'd turned left or right, or whether he'd merely rushed across the road and was standing still and quiet, behind one of the trees."

"Had you picked up a weapon of any sort?"

"No."

"Well, what would have happened if he'd been concealed behind a tree-trunk, and you'd found him, or he had jumped out on you?"

"Why, I should have taken another hiding, I suppose. That's what worries me."

"Lucky for you that he'd been unable to find any ammunition for the revolver. Well, what did you do?"

"I decided that he'd probably bolt for the city and go to earth in the bazaar, rather than run through Cantonments out into the open country. So I turned left and ran as hard as I could go, in the direction of the town. And when I couldn't run any longer, I turned round and walked back again; and that was that.

"It's a nice thought, isn't it?" added Easterwood,

"that I've taken a licking from an unarmed native, and that, save for the accident of the small light rug and the slippery floor, he would probably have killed me with his bare hands. Just throttled me."

Captain Stacey Burlestone threw his cigar-butt out into the garden.

"Would I, or the Major or the Colonel or Hennessy Wogan of the Gurkhas have put up a better show than you did? Wouldn't the same have happened to any of them?"

"The point is that it didn't happen to them," replied Aubrey Easterwood shortly.

"Can you box?"

"No."

"Wrestle?"

"No."

"Well then, with how many men in your own Troop do you suppose you could deal triumphantly, in what you call a 'fair man-to-man tussle and trial of physical strength'?"

"The point is that I don't happen to need to," snapped Easterwood.

"Nevertheless, the fact remains that in a stand-up, 'all-in,' wrestle-punch-strangle-kick-bite-and-gouge scrap with one of your men, it's probable you'd be defeated. . . . You certainly would be, by at least half of them. They've led the physical life from babyhood and are as strong as their horses. Just accept the plain fact that they are bigger, stronger, hardier men than you. . . . Well, what about it? Doesn't make you any the less valuable as an Officer, does it?

"An Officer is there for his superior brains, knowledge, training, professional skill, character, birth, breeding, education and so forth. According to your idiotic idea, the Colonel should be the strongest man in the regiment, the Major next, the senior Captain third, and so on, downwards. I never heard such bosh. Bless my soul, next time there's a vacancy for Rissaldar-Major, Drill-Major or Woordi-Major, would you propose the strongest man in the Regiment?"

"No," growled Easterwood.

"No," continued Stacey Burlestone, "we don't promote from the ranks by physical strength, nor by ability in a rough-and-tumble. Very useful things, no doubt, but they come a long way after the qualifications for which we do promote: seniority, experience, conduct, discipline, character, education, brains and so on. I should say that, as a broad rule, the strongest man in any regiment, native or British, is the biggest fool. Great brain and great brawn don't generally go together."

"No," replied Aubrey Easterwood, "but of the two I think I'd rather have the brawn."

"Well, my son, since God has been pleased to endow you with the brain, you yourself can gather in the brawn. There you have the advantage over the strong man. The strong man can't get brainy, but the brainy man can get strong. Provided, of course, that he is healthy and of reasonable physique."

Aubrey Easterwood turned and looked at his friend and mentor.

He was a young man of remarkable character, one of the strangest traits of which, was his way of regarding his seniors as being probably his betters—at least in point of learning, wisdom and understanding. He actually cherished the belief that the man who had been about the world thirty or forty years longer than he, might have wider experience than he, and be possessed of those priceless jewels of knowledge that experience, and experience alone, can give. Stacey Burlestone was not thirty or forty years older than Easterwood, but he had been fifteen years longer in the Army and in India.

"Now you, my son," continued Stacey Burlestone, "are as healthy as the devil, and are of perfect physique. Or shall we say, have the makings of a perfect physique, since you are not particularly well-developed. Well then, what about pushing out this morbid idea of 'humiliation,' and putting in the healthy idea of making yourself as strong as any one of your men? Making yourself the strongest man in the Regiment, if you like."

Aubrey Easterwood sat up.

"Do you nothing but good mentally, and won't do you any harm physically, unless you over-do it. Make a hobby of it. Be your salvation. As you are now, you're positively morbid; what they call 'mouldy' in the Navy. And when young men in India go morbid and mouldy, it too often ends in their wanting to clean a pistol—and have an accident with it. Seen lots of cases."

Young Aubrey Easterwood sprang to his feet and gripped his friend's hand.

"God!" he cried, "I'd give my soul to be the strongest man in the Regiment! . . . I'll have a shot at it. I'll start to-morrow."

"Wonder you don't start to-night, before you've finished your cheroot," smiled Captain Stacey Burlestone, former sufferer from ill-health, against which he had put up a heroic struggle.

"Did you ever go in for that sort of thing?" asked Easterwood, as he sat down again in his long chair and put his feet up on the rests.

"Very keen on it, until I had enteric and had to give it up for a time. That left me wrong inside, and I got dysentery. Couldn't shake it off. Then it was malaria. What energy I'd got left, just carried me through the day. None to spare for physical jerks or the milder forms of relaxation, like boxing and rugger. . . . Then I took myself in hand and got down to it. Simply fought for health with all my heart and soul, strength and energy; absolutely lived for it. Well, I fairly earned it— and I got it. Fit as a fiddle now. Enjoy perfect health, but I shall soon turn the forty mark, and go a bit easy on violent exercise. . . . But *you*—never had a day's illness in your life, I should think, have you?"

"Never."

"Well then, you take my tip. . . . Do what I say—and come off this mouldiness."

§2

Aubrey Easterwood came off this mouldiness; and, with whole-hearted and single-minded determination, vigour and energy, settled down to his new body-building and soul-saving hobby of Physical Culture. Not to the exclusion of mental and spiritual exercises, interests, and pursuits, but in addition thereunto.

As a soldier he was ambitious. And strange as it may seem to some people who talk much, while knowing nothing, concerning Public Schools, there had been implanted in him, at his own school, a love of reading, a desire for knowledge, a keen appreciation of books, and the habit of thought.

Now, for a very gradually increasing portion of the long Indian day, when all Europeans and most natives of those parts were confined, perforce, to the protection and relative coolness of their respective abodes, Aubrey Easterwood systematically and scientifically developed his muscles and his strength.

He wrote Home for books on systems of Physical Culture, and steadily worked through each one.

From the system of one country he learned the science and art of muscle-building; from that of another, the gaining of elasticity and general muscular strength; from a third, muscle-control; from a fourth, that of organic health and development, a system that considered nothing of muscles but everything of the heart, the lungs, the stomach, the liver, the nerves, and so forth.

Having worked through all the systems of which he could obtain information—Swedish, English, German, American, Japanese—he perfected a system of his own, which he believed to combine all the virtues of the others. At this he worked as religiously and regularly as does a conscientious and ambitious Scholar working for an Honours Degree.

Particularly he attended to the resurrection and development of what he called "lost muscles," and endeavoured to provide himself with an abdominal front as corrugated as that of the statue of Hercules.

As the months passed, he was surprised to find that his physical culture and muscle-building labours involved and connoted mental and moral culture almost equally marked and valuable. Gone was the morbid self-distrust, the feeling that he had been, and again might be, "humiliated." Self-confidence grew, and with it self-knowledge, and self-respect; and, to Stacey Burlestone's delight, Aubrey Easterwood grew up, grew strong, and, better still, grew ever finer—developed a fineness of mind as well as of body and soul that Burlestone loved to note and enjoyed to see.

When satisfied with his physical condition— satisfied, that is to say, that he could make his magnificent muscles no bigger or stronger, and need only exercise sufficiently to keep them as they were— Aubrey Easterwood turned his thoughts to the application of his strength in boxing.

Now a marvel of development and might, he would make himself an expert boxer, wrestler and swordsman. Then he would study the art of jiu-jitsu—and go to Japan to perfect his skill, if necessary.

Boxing first; the noble art of self-defence. And no more "humiliations" for Aubrey Easterwood.

To this end, he engaged the services of Sergeant Buckley of the Royal South Lancashire Regiment, who was Divisional Heavy-weight Champion and considered likely to become Champion of India at the next year's tournament.

It was Easterwood's good fortune that the South Lancashires were stationed at Quetawur, and that the famous Buckley was available. Moreover, the man was not only a magnificent boxer but an unusually good teacher, very keen, and quite as much interested in his pupils' progress as in the fees which they paid for his services as instructor.

Once he grasped the fact that Lieutenant Aubrey Easterwood of the 1st Bombay Lancers was not merely in need of exercise, recreation, and amusement, but intended to be thoroughly and completely taught and trained as a boxer, Buckley's interest was really awakened and his zeal aroused.

He began at the very beginning, and set his new pupil exercises in foot-work and bag-punching as monotonous, regular, exacting, and necessary, as is scale-practising to a pianist or singer.

Systematically, Buckley widened the scope of Easterwood's training, until the day arrived when he released him from the practice of elementary boxing-exercises and punching-practice, and began to teach him the science and art, the precept and practice, of guarding, ducking, dodging, side-stepping, and the general principles of evasion.

Having tested the length, depth and strength of Easterwood's patience, zeal and determination, and the genuineness of his desire to become a real boxer, Buckley now promoted him to actual sparring—permitting, however, no rough-and-tumble knock-about business for the sake of exercise and pleasure. Every lesson was a lesson in something definite in the way of blow or guard, and the lessons were progressive.

And in the fulness of time, the instructor passed his pupil out from what he called "recruits' course" to "full private" as a boxer, and proceeded to box with him.

Gradually the relative positions of the teacher and the taught changed, and, although the master remained the master, the pupil, with increasing rapidity, approximated to his science, power, knowledge, ability, and skill. Increasingly the instructor, perforce, took more and more care of himself; and, literally perforce, gave his pupil "something to think about," both in the latter's interests and his own.

One day, in the Brigade Gymnasium, Easterwood knocked Buckley down. It was during a set two-minute round, in which Buckley had told him to "go all out" and, incidentally, to "take care of himself."

No-one more delighted than Buckley, though, springing to his feet, he gave Easterwood an undeniably *mauvais quart d'heure*, or rather, *de minute*. For the remaining quarter-minute of the round, Buckley went for his pupil as though fighting a Champion for a Championship. Definitely he did his best to knock Easterwood out, and for two reasons—that he might retain his prestige and easy complete superiority, and also that his pupil might not begin to fancy himself too soon, too quickly, and too much.

Within three months of this episode, Sergeant Buckley told Aubrey Easterwood that he ought to go in for the Officers' Heavy-weight Championship of India.

"I'm going to do so," replied Easterwood. "That has been my intention from the beginning."

"Well, you'll win it, sir," Buckley assured him. "You'll have a walk-over in the Novices, easily win in the Brigade and the Divisional Tournaments, and you'll win the All India Officers' Heavy-weight Championship. I don't say you'll do it the first time, because it's held by a most remarkable good man, but you're younger than he is and—you'll get it. Captain Mackleworth oughter been a professional. He'd 'ave come to the top as a pro—and he won't lose the Championship easy, but . . . I say you'll beat him. For why? You are bigger than he is, and I should say you're stronger; and I reckon that, by the time you meet him, you'll be as good a boxer. He's got the ring-craft, but you've got ten years advantage of him in age. Anyhow, I'll stake my last rupee that you get into the Finals with him—and that it'll be a fight, whoever wins. . . . Now I must get you some sparring-partners and some quiet little matches with some of the useful lads of the Brigade. By and bye I might get Gypsy Jones to come up 'ere if you'd like to have a punch at him. It wouldn't cost you much, and I'd like to try meself out on him, too. He only lost the Heavy-weight Championship of India on points last year, and there was many as thought he should have had the verdic'. It wouldn't cost you much."

"Splendid," agreed Easterwood. "We could get the Gymnasium to ourselves, I suppose."

"Yes sir. I'll fix it with Staff-Sergeant Instructor Gilman and nobody needn't know anything about it except him and you and me, and anybody you like to invite."

And soon a new star appeared and shone brighter and ever brighter in the somewhat empty boxing firmament of Officers in India; and the name of Lieutenant

Easterwood became the subject of conversation among those interested in the sport.

CHAPTER VIII

"My dear old Tony," wrote Captain Geoffrey Hennessy Wogan, to his friend Major Anthony Moresby Wallingford.

"How goes it, old son? I'm awfully happy here at Kirkee and shall be very sorry when the course is over. Poona's a good spot—only a few minutes' drive, across the river. Splendid Gymkana Club and the Club of Western India. Fine Race-course and a jolly good pack of hounds—Poona and Kirkee Hunt—not bad going. No foxes, of course, but the local jackal runs well. What with the Gunners and the Sappers here, the Northumberland L.I. and the Highland Fusiliers, not to mention two Native Infantry Regiments and one Cavalry, there's always a good field . . ." and so forth.

*   *   *   *   *

"And talking of the Northumberland L.I., it's rumoured they're being moved to Quetawur. A jolly good crowd too—you'll like them. Bar Mackleworth, that is. He's a terror. Both in the ring and out. It's a treat to see him in the ring—a real heart-warming treat —but he ought to stay there. Only place for him. I never struck such a bearish boor in my life. Not that I have 'struck' him—or want to, though I love a good scrap, with the gloves or without. He's above my weight altogether, both avoirdupois and style.

"They had the annual Divisional Boxing Tournament here, last week, and a stout lad in the Durhams had a whang at him. A very plucky effort—but it was murder. Mackleworth simply battered him for about ninety seconds and then knocked him cold. Everybody thought he might have given the chap a run for his money and shown us some boxing. He could have knocked him out in the last round (they were only three-round contests) if he must, but there was no need for that, even. He knew he could win each round on points—and get ninety-nine per cent of the points too.

"But no—he just set about him as though he were fighting Jack Johnson for his life. He's a killer, all right. And, my faith, so's his wife, begorra! A real beauty—and a goer. They say he beats her! People tell you so—quite seriously. I daresay he has good cause. I'd give him cause myself if I had the chance. Tim O'Leary of the 84th Battery is the white-headed boy— at the moment—only he's red-headed. It's confidently and hopefully expected that Mackleworth, who's a jealous devil, will put his foot down one fine day, or his fists up one fine night, and then there'll be a hell of a bust-up; for Tim, as you know, is about as wild an Irishman as ever came out of Galway. He has got it badly too. . . . Goes about confiding to people that Mackleworth isn't good enough for her, a proposition which nobody disputes. Not with Tim, anyhow. Just as well they're being transferred, though it'll be a dark day for Tim O'Leary. Been a darker one, though, if they'd stayed on and he'd shot Mackleworth up, or something of that sort.

"I wonder what you'll make of her, and whether she'll disturb the holy calm of Quetawur. She disturbs mine all right, though I never had any. Otherwise I shouldn't be writing about her, I suppose.

"I've been puzzling my mind for a long time, wondering of whom she reminds me. I found out last night, turning over some old magazines. There was a full-page illustration, a reproduction, of that smiling lass, La Gioconda by a Mr. Leonardo da Vinci or words to that effect. It was in colour, and there she was—Mrs. Mackleworth, I mean. At least, there was what I'd had at the back of my mind, ever since I first saw her. It's the smile. I don't mean that she's one of those women who are for ever grinning, but she has what a poetic cove would call 'a haunting smile,' like this Gioconda Tottie. I think the usual adjective with regard to the Mona Lisa smile is 'enigmatic.' Well, she's like that. Mrs. Mackleworth, I mean. You don't know what she's thinking. Sure, 'tis like a Killarney lake; beauty in sunshine or shadow, and you don't know, for the life of you, whether 'tis deep or shallow. What you do know is that it's lovely, and it's all you want to know. There may be currents and weeds and whirlpools, and sharp rocks under the surface. Or not. It may be unfathomably deep and as cold as the Polar sea. Or hot as the ground floor of Hell. You don't know—and you don't care.

"Anyhow, Tony, me bhoy, you'll be beginning to think *I* care.

"And, faith, you won't be far wrong.

"I'll look forward to hearing from you about her, by-and-bye, and what sort of a stir she creates in Quetawur.

"Mackleworth too. He's generally in the news for some outrage or other. Drinks like a fish—and turns morose and nasty when he's full, instead of carrying his liquor like a gentleman.

"By the way, the boxing people down here are wondering whether young Easterwood is going to have a shot at the Heavy-weight Championship. Personally I'd advise him not to, although he's shaping so splendidly. He might get a sort of licking that would spoil him as a boxer, for Mackleworth really is a tough proposition. He stops drinking when he goes into training, and in about a fortnight he's in the perfect pink. And begod, he can both box and fight. I'd back him with my last bean to win the World's Amateur Championship, and if he turned pro it wouldn't surprise me, in the least, to see him World's Heavy-weight Champion. This is talking, I know, but wait till you've seen him at it—going all out. And he goes all out, all the time. I haven't seen Easterwood at work, but unless he's a colossal fighter as well as an almost unique boxer, he'd be just 'a burnt offering and a bloody sacrifice' on the altar of Mr. Moloch Mackleworth. Very bloody.

"Well, I wish you'd stop chattering. When are we going to have another shooting trip together?

"So-long, old son. Best salaams to the Missus.

"Yours ever,
GEOFF."

CHAPTER IX

So, one day, Aubrey Easterwood learned something that interested him deeply.

"Heard the news?" asked Captain Stacey Burlestone as Easterwood came from his bedroom, pyjama-clad, for *chota-hazri*—the early morning tea and toast, with which the notoriously lazy Anglo-Indian begins his day at about five o'clock in the morning.

"No," yawned Aubrey Easterwood. "Are we both promoted in undue course for unexceptional conduct in un . . ."

"The Northumberland L.I. are going to relieve the South Lancs instead of . . ."

"By Jove!" interrupted Easterwood, "that means Mackleworth!"

"It does, my son. It means Goliath of Gath; and David will be able to have a look at him. Before taking a sling at him—with his fist."

"Officers' Heavy-weight Championship of India," breathed Aubrey Easterwood.

"He's a tough nut, old son. I've seen him defend the Championship three times. Some defence too. K.O. in the first round each time. Still, that won't hurt you. Do you all the good in the world to try.

"By Gad, old chap," he added, "you're a different man from what you were when you were brooding over the Pathan episode."

"Yes, a bit," smiled Easterwood. "Thanks to you, Stacey."

"Thanks to yourself and your good guts. I gave you a sound tip and you took it. Absolutely a different man."

"I wish that same Pathan lad would roll up again one night, now," said Easterwood as he lit a cigarette. "It would be rather interesting to try conclusions."

"Be conclusion for the Pathan, I should think," smiled Stacey Burlestone. "You'd either give him as noble a hiding as one man ever gave another, or else put him out for a long count, first poke. Yes, it would be very interesting. However, failing the Pathan, Mackleworth'll do."

"Do for me, probably," said Easterwood. "Stiff proposition, but . . . I'm going to have a stab at it. And I've got another eight months. Tournament isn't till after the Autumn Manœuvres."

§2

Aubrey Easterwood, taking his ease in a club armchair after a day of hard going, glanced up from his newspaper as someone came to the big near-by table on which, in orderly array, lay the latest magazines and newspapers from Home, all three weeks old.

A woman. . . . A stranger.

What an arresting face. A remarkable, unusual face.

For the first time in Aubrey Easterwood's life, a woman's face interested him—as a face. Of what or whom did she remind him? She could scarcely remind him of another person, because he knew of no-one at all like her. He would remember such a person instantly, for it was an extraordinary face. Most unusual. To begin with, the enormous eyes surely were black, or was it a trick of light?

She glanced at him, and his eyes met hers.

Instantly he raised his newspaper, colouring to the roots of his hair as he did so. But he had seen that the eyes were almost black. And not that opaque black of marble, but transparent black. . . . Nonsense, they were darkest velvet-brown. And the pupils very large.

Perhaps that was what made the face so striking, so arresting, their almost-blackness, and their—what was the word?—transparency, translucency? As though the iris was made of black glass, and not of wood, painted black or deep-brown and then varnished.

What rot he was thinking . . . He must have another look . . .

Folding his paper Easterwood glanced again, this

time underneath it.

Yes, it was partly the size and colour of the eyes, but partly the long black lashes and the thin arched black eyebrows.

No, it was probably the fact that she wore a fringe. Most unusual, surely. Lovely silky soft curly hair, and yet a definite little fringe. And what a complexion! She couldn't be long out from Home.

And what a "live" face! Was the mouth a little hard? No, of course not. A lovely mouth, a lovely face. Really, one couldn't help looking at it.

But where on earth . . . ?

Of course! Of course! He had it. A Barribal girl. He'd seen a magazine cover. No, surely not. That was unworthy. A picture, somewhere, of a girl by that artist —and this one might have sat as his model. He had evolved a type—or rather had given his name to a type, and here was a specimen of it. Beautiful. And not only beautiful, lovely.

Who could she be?

The girl selected a magazine and turned from the table. The young man hoped that she wasn't going to take it out on to the verandah. He could hardly go out there and stare at her. Nor could he very well turn his chair round if she remained in the reading-room but sat somewhere behind him.

No. Good. She was going to sit just to his left in the big inviting chair that stood facing him. It really was the most interesting, attractive, piquant, provoking face he'd ever seen.

And how smartly she was dressed; and with what charming taste. She looked, in some indefinable way, quite different from the other ladies of the Station. It must be the fashion and the newness of her clothes, straight out from Home.

Who could she be? Very neat small feet, tiny ankles, small beautifully-gloved hands.

How extremely effective the long jade earrings were against her shining black hair. Her eyes seemed the blacker for the jade, or at any rate, of a clearer brighter black. She was absolutely . . .

Suddenly the eyes again met those of Aubrey Easterwood, and instantly he made a poor pretence of looking over her head at the clock, and back again to his paper.

Clumsy fool that he was. How rude she would think him. He'd like to get up and apologize, and assure her that he wasn't looking at her at all. Perhaps that would hardly be complimentary. In any case, what a fool he'd look if she said,

"Presumably that is why your eyes twice caught mine."

Or, worse still, if she said,

"Not at all. I was not aware that you were in the room."

Good Heavens, what on earth was he thinking about? Had he gone mad?

He had.

The madness of love had descended upon Aubrey Easterwood for the first time in his life, and at first sight.

That night Aubrey Easterwood lay awake trying to conjure up a vision of the face; to reconstruct it, feature by feature; to see it again with his mind's eye as he had seen it that afternoon.

To his surprise he was entirely unsuccessful.

Never mind. He knew what it was like, and he knew that he would see it again to-morrow. Sooner or later he would be introduced to her, and then he gravely feared that, though not in the least socially-awkward, he would stutter and stammer and blush, and appear an even bigger fool than he was.

Who could she be?

That didn't really very greatly matter, so long as she continued to exist in the same world as Aubrey Easterwood.

And suddenly he burst into song.

> "*There is a ladye sweet and kind,*
> *Was never face so pleas'd my mind;*
> *I did but see her passing by,*
> *And yet I love her till I die!*"

A bed at the other end of the verandah creaked.

"Don't think me unappreciative, or less than delighted, but would you kindly shut that bloody row?" said the voice of Stacey Burlestone.

Good Heavens, he'd absolutely forgotten that he was not alone in the verandah.

"Sorry, old man," he said. "I must have been singing in my sleep."

"Well, so long as you don't sing in my verandah . . . G'night."

She proved to be Mrs. Colin Mackleworth and, curiously enough, it didn't in the least disturb Aubrey Easterwood to learn that she was married.

Young love is like that. While, as we all know, subject for amusement and ridicule, it is fleshless and bloodless; of the most crystal purity; ethereal; of the soul, the spirit and the mind; and, while the beauty on which it feeds includes beauty of face and form, it is not of the body. Nor, as a rule, does a youth's first love, gracefully known as calf-love, turn to ordinary love, its pure lambent flame light the fierce red fires of passion.

So Aubrey Easterwood was perfectly happy, gloriously happy in his love, in his adoration, of Daphne Mackleworth.

Life turned suddenly bright and smiling, and his heart sang within him.

Constantly was her face—and in sober truth it was a very unusual face and definitely beautiful—before him; her image in his mind.

Trotting through the dust at the head of his troop; following hounds at break-neck pace across terrible country in pursuit of the enduring jackal; schooling recruits over the jumps in the ride; at polo (and how he played when she was watching!); when attempting, or pretending, to read a book; in the Club bar when having the evening spot; at Mess when apparently listening respectfully to the words of wisdom emitted by his seniors; at his Physical Culture exercises; and especially at night—more especially and particularly at night—when, there being no other distractions, he could lie in the warm darkness and think of her, rehearse again every word of any brief conversation that he had been privileged to hold with her, consider ways and means and hopes and chances of seeing her again soon.

§3

It was not long before Captain Stacey Burlestone discovered the ingenuous youth's secret.

An observant man, delighted with the success of his scheme for rousing the boy from his introspective despondency, he had quickly noticed the sudden access of joyousness, light-hearted vitality, the new high spirits, the gaiety. The boy was *tête-montée*, bubbling with the pure joy of life, a new man. There could be but one cause for this.

There had been a marked improvement in his spirits and attitude to life soon after he had taken up his hobby of Physical Culture; and again when he found himself making unexpected, and indeed rather remarkable, progress in boxing; but this was something quite different.

If the other was good strong ale, this was champagne.

And even had he not developed the distressing habit of bursting into song—invariably love-song—and trolling snatches of ballads about ladies fair; and not only reading, but actually writing, or attempting to write, poetry, Stacey Burlestone would have known that Aubrey Easterwood was in love.

Captain Stacey Burlestone did not approve.

The less that impecunious subalterns had to do with love, the better. It interfered with work. Marriage was fatal. When they married as young as that, it generally meant that they were in debt for the rest of their service. Not only in debt, but on short commons. Always anxious and bothered. Spoilt their polo, too. Couldn't afford proper ponies.

Aubrey had "great expectations," for he was the

only nephew and heir of a very rich man—but it might be many and many a long year before those expectations were realized—and there's many a slip 'twixt the cup and the lip.

However, it was not long before Burlestone, to use his own expression, located the seat of the trouble; for Aubrey Easterwood could not keep Mrs. Mackleworth's name out of the conversation.

This changed the direction of Stacey Burlestone's faint anxiety on behalf of the boy of whom he had grown so very fond. Handsome is as handsome does—and woman is as woman does. There can be no better friend for a young man than a married woman—of the right sort and the right age.

Mrs. Mackleworth might be of the right sort. On that point Stacey Burlestone reserved judgment. But she was not of the right age. She was far too young.

Nor did the impression and opinion that Burlestone had formed concerning her, coincide with those of Aubrey Easterwood. Burlestone had a prejudice against huge dark eyes, for a start; and he didn't like "type" girls—artists' type, that is to say—whether Rubens, Burne-Jones, Dana Gibson, Barribal or Kirschner.

No, he didn't like "type" women; and especially he didn't like the Barribal type, in general—and he was not quite sure that he would like Mrs. Mackleworth, in particular.

Certainly he loathed "the man Mackleworth," as he called him.

Mrs. Mackleworth might be all right. Mackleworth himself was all wrong, and, in the event of any sort of trouble, would do something wrong. Something nasty.

Yes, he felt he was not being uncharitable in deciding that whatever Mackleworth did, in that event, would be nasty. However, it might be only a passing infatuation, the inevitable silly calf-love of a virgin boy.

But what a ghastly thing if so amazingly and extraordinarily nice a boy as Aubrey got involved in something—nasty.

He was so decent, so sensitive, so upright, so

guileless, so ingenuous. It might be shattering, soul-searing; and do him infinite harm. Might do him every kind of harm there was, if he really fell in love with the woman and she led him on until there was—an affair.

He'd make it his business to get to know her, and to know as much as he could about her. Find out, as far as possible, on what sort of terms she was with Mackleworth. One could hardly imagine a nice woman being on any sort of terms with a man like Mackleworth, but you never knew. Women saw, or imagined, virtues, in men, that were certainly hidden from the eyes of their fellow-men. She might be in love with Mackleworth; or, at any rate, love him—and all might be well.

And she might be a thoroughly nice, normal, ordinary, good woman, fond of her husband and likely to be merely amused by Aubrey's devotion, even supposing she ever became aware of it.

But somehow he didn't think so.

His first impression of her was not wholly favourable. She was conscious of her undeniably good looks; pleased with herself; a trifle hard about the mouth and eyes perhaps; and probably as sophisticated as Aubrey was ingenuous.

And according to Moresby Wallingford, she was, on the authority of his pal Hennessy Wogan, a lady of experience. But—Hennessy Wogan! One would prefer to trust Wogan's judgment in the matter of a horse rather than in that of a woman, perhaps.

On the whole, the other would have been better—Aubrey's falling in love with somebody's daughter, and the course of true love running smoothly . . . until it ran into the troubled waters of matrimony.

§4

"Notice Mrs. Mackleworth at the meet this morning?" asked Easterwood, one day, as he and Burlestone sat at tiffin.

"Yes."

"Looking most amazingly pretty, wasn't she?"

"Yes."

"Wonderful seat on a horse."

"Yes."

"Hands, too. And an extraordinarily plucky rider. That's twice she's been the only woman to finish, or at any rate, in at the death."

"Yes."

"Amazing how a woman can finish a run like that, in this heat, and look as cool as a cucumber."

"Yes."

"Wonderfully 'all-round' woman. Very musical, you know."

"Yes."

"And reads Italian. Talks it fluently. She's reading a paper on Dante at the Literary Society show on Saturday, with recitations from the *Paradiso* and *Inferno* in the original Italian. Extraordinarily well-read and well-educated woman."

"Yes."

"Paints too."

"Surely no need!"

"I mean water-colours, of course," said Aubrey Easterwood coldly.

A brief silence and a quick recovery.

"Dances divinely; absolutely."

"Who?"

"Mrs. Mackleworth."

"Yes."

"Plays a jolly good game of tennis, too."

"Yes."

"I say, don't you like her, Stacey?"

"I don't know her as well as you do."

"No. You would if you did, I'm sure."

"Yes?"

"I can't understand what she sees in that fellow Mackleworth, can you?"

"No."

"You don't like him either?"

"No."

"I think he's perfectly detestable. Absolutely mannerless. The Compleat Bounder."

"Yes."

"They can't have a thing in common."

"Don't know about that, I'm sure," growled Stacey Burlestone. "They may have a lot."

"What on earth do you mean?"

"Well, as I've said, I don't know Mrs. Mackleworth as well as you do. And Mackleworth may, in the domestic circle, display virtues and charms which—well, which he keeps for the domestic circle."

"He certainly does that, if he's got 'em," observed Easterwood.

"You haven't boxed with him yet, have you?" asked Burlestone.

"No, and I don't think I shall—until—well, until I've got to."

"Until the Finals, you mean? Mightn't it be a good thing to spar with him a bit, get a few friendly bouts, and take his measure?"

"Well, somehow I don't feel like it," replied Easterwood. . . . "I did speak about it to Sergeant Buckley before the South Lancs went, and he said something that strikes me as sensible. While you're taking another man's measure, he is also taking yours."

"That's so," agreed Burlestone.

"If I don't box with Mackleworth and he doesn't see me boxing, I shall be as much an unknown quantity to him as he is to me. So there isn't much in it, really, is there? No, I don't think I want to spar with him."

"That's interesting. That's very interesting," mused Stacey Burlestone aloud, in his thoughtful way. "I wonder why. I wonder what's the real psychological phenomenon behind that."

"Oh, I don't know."

"No, you probably don't. I fancy that most of us don't know, most of the time, the real motive behind most of our actions. I don't mean ordinary actions, of course, like feeding your face or putting your boots on; but things like this. F'r instance, a case in point. There's a certain person to whom I owe a letter and to whom I ought to write a letter; but for the life of me I can't bring myself to do it; and I simply and honestly don't know why. There's no reason—in my conscious mind at least—why I shouldn't do it; but I can't. . . . I wonder why you feel you can't box Mackleworth, or rather why you feel you don't want to."

"Oh, I don't know," was the reply.

"Well, we admit that; but why don't you know? Dip into it a bit. Come now, think up some reason why you don't want to spar with Mackleworth."

"Perhaps I'm afraid of a hiding," smiled Easterwood.

"Bosh! You know that's nonsense, because you are going for him, anyhow. You do still mean to go for the Championship, don't you?"

"Rather."

"D'you mean you're afraid that you might find him so good that you'll be compelled to abandon the idea?"

"No, I don't. I should hate to say it to anyone but you, Stacey; but I feel pretty confident."

"Of the Officers' Heavy-weight Championship of India?"

"Well, I didn't exactly mean that I feel confident of that, though what I said implied it. What I really meant was that I feel quite confident of my ability to take care of myself in a ring with Mackleworth."

"H'm. It's not that, then."

A brief silence.

"Now then, Aubrey, why don't you want to spar with Mackleworth? Come on. Out with it."

"Don't know."

"Well, dig in and find out. Is it because he's Mrs. Mackleworth's husband?"

"What d'you mean? What has that got to do with it?"

"Well, has it got anything to do with it? D'you mind this Third Degree, old chap? Am I bothering you, or being impertinent?"

"Good Lord, no . . . I dunno—his being her husband may have something to do with it."

"Not the old 'humiliation' idea?" asked Burlestone. "You don't sub-consciously feel that the one man in the world from whom you don't want a hiding is Mrs. Mackleworth's husband—*because* he is Mrs. Mackleworth's husband?"

"Well, if it were sub-conscious I shouldn't know it, should I?"

"No, unless my question had brought it up into your conscious mind. Give it a thought. Do you feel like that?"

Aubrey Easterwood stirred his coffee reflectively.

"Well, it's a difficult question to answer, Stacey. I certainly should loathe to take a good beating from Mackleworth, but I believe that's because he is—Mackleworth."

"And not because he is Mrs. Mackleworth's husband?"

"I really don't think so. No, honestly I don't. I think it's because I dislike him so intensely."

"And why do you dislike Mackleworth so intensely?"

"Oh . . . you know. . . . You detest him yourself. I hate everything about him."

"Including the fact that he is Mrs. Mackleworth's husband?"

Aubrey Easterwood leaned back in his chair, brought forth his cigarette case, tapped a cigarette, lit it, and blew a long cloud of smoke, before answering.

"I don't like him any better for being Mrs. Mackleworth's husband; but honestly I think I should dislike him just as much as I do, if he were a bachelor, or somebody else's husband."

"I wonder," mused Stacey Burlestone.

"Another idea," he added, a moment later. "Do you think the reason why you don't want to spar with him is that you might lose your temper? From what I've seen of you in action, and from what I've heard from Buckley and other people, you are a remarkably imperturbable boxer. . . . Is that it? You think you might see red and go wild?"

"Oh, I don't know. I don't think so," replied Easterwood. "Hope not, anyhow. Fatal thing to do."

"Absolutely," agreed his friend. "Wonder if that's it, and if so, why should you lose your temper with him more than with anybody else?"

"Well, I admit I detest the fellow," was the reply,

"and I should certainly accept a bang on the nose from him with less gratitude than I should from anybody else."

"And then follows the question why, and the vicious circle's complete, eh?" smiled Burlestone as he rose from his chair.

"Anyhow, I don't want to box with Captain Colin Mackleworth—and I'm not going to do so until I must," said Easterwood doggedly.

"Interesting," murmured Stacey Burlestone again as he rose and turned to take up his helmet and riding-whip.

§5

"No, I don't know Mrs. Mackleworth as well as you do, my son, but I'm jolly well going to," murmured Captain Stacey Burlestone to himself, as he rode out of the compound.

"Without being one of those funny fools who imagine that they understand women," he thought to himself, "I think I've enough both of intuition and experience to form a fairly accurate opinion. . . . What about a dance or two, and a sit-out or two, in a *kala jugga*[27] with her, on Thursday night? Sacrifice my rubber of bridge in a good cause. And then what? Suppose I detested her. I can't pass that on to young Aubrey. Or if I found out that she really did have a past—been the Worst Woman in Widdecombe—it would be a dirty job telling him anything about her, apart from the fact that he wouldn't believe a word of it."

At the Thursday evening dance at the Gymkana Club, Captain Stacey Burlestone made himself particularly agreeable to Mrs. Mackleworth; and he was a man who had the power to make himself—particularly agreeable.

Three times he danced with her, and greatly he enjoyed it.

Aubrey Easterwood danced, and sat out with her,

---

[27] (Lit.) *Dark place. A sitting-out place.*

five times; but the remainder of the dances she gave to Mr. Clarence Wellingson, Assistant-Magistrate of Quet-awur.

An honest man, Burlestone frankly admitted—to himself—that he found her delightful, charming. Yet curiously enigmatic. Pleasant, friendly, easy and agreeable, she was anything but flirtatious. Not once in conversation did she strike a note that jarred; nothing cynical, malicious or unkind. Her comments on the Station and its inhabitants, though witty and amusing, were never satirical, unfriendly or cruel.

While reserving judgment, he decided that, so far, he had formed the impression that she was a nice amusing clever woman, probably quite a good sort, and certainly far too good for Mackleworth.

Still, he didn't like huge dark eyes, and wasn't certain that, at times, her mouth was not a little hard, her extremely beautiful eyebrows inclined to draw together, her red lips too thin, the line of her jaw too marked and strong.

But there again, her frowning was probably just a nervous trick . . . headache . . . habit. And anyhow, surely any woman who'd lived, for however brief a space, with Captain Colin Mackleworth, might well suffer a little hardening of the mouth, and a tendency, at times, to frown.

Yes, if young Aubrey hadn't been involved in the matter at all, probably he himself would have liked Mrs. Mackleworth very much.

Very much indeed.

He didn't know when he'd seen so interesting a face.

An interesting talker, too. Knew how to be pleasant to a man.

To a man? . . . To any man? . . . Every man?

What about women? It would be interesting to find out what the women-folk thought of her. It might not be conclusive, but it was indicative, if she were unpopular with them.

On the other hand, is any extremely attractive—nay beautiful—woman, who is also fashionable, smart, *chic*, fascinating, accomplished, likely to be very popular among the women of an Indian station? Do they love the loveliest when they see it? Speaking generally, that is?

Anyhow, she was an extremely interesting subject for study.

Captain Stacey Burlestone found himself pursuing his studies.

Literally pursuing? The devil of it was that it was so extremely difficult to get near her; *tête-a-tête, c'est à dire*. It was easy enough to see her every day, and more than once every day, in the company of other people. But it was almost impossible to see her alone, thanks to young Aubrey, not to mention Clarence Wellingson, Moresby Wallingford and a dozen more.

And what did old Tony Wallingford want to go chasing a married woman for? Especially when he had a wife like Joan Wallingford. A jolly sight too good for him.

Anyhow—there they were—flies round the honey-pot.

And, of course, one cannot study people satisfactorily in public. It is inevitable that, in a crowd, they are not quite their natural selves.

It was almost impossible to get a morning ride alone with Mrs. Mackleworth, thanks to one or other, or a dozen, of her gay cavaliers—who were anything but gay when together in her society. It was equally difficult to ride home alone with her after the bi-weekly hunt. Flies round the honey-pot indeed, then, in numbers.

Why, it was becoming none too easy to get a dance with her; for, at the weekly dances, the flies simply swarmed.

And he didn't wish to copy the tactics of Aubrey, or Moresby Wallingford and young Clarence Wellingson, who obviously booked dances with her, a week ahead. Probably on each Thursday night they booked the same dances for the following week.

And you couldn't really talk to anybody while playing tennis with her; and when the set was over, you simply joined the crowd, sitting in a row and looking on.

Jolly difficult. Ten thousand pities dear Mary Harrington-Spens had gone Home. She'd have helped. She'd have been invaluable.

§6

Captain Stacey Burlestone, a man of ideas, had—an idea.

For things were getting worse. Definitely worse. Gradually, imperceptibly, the situation had developed until, somehow or other, it had come to pass that it was an established, recognized and accepted fact in the bungalow—that Aubrey Easterwood was madly in love with Mrs. Mackleworth.

There had been no sudden declaration, statement, confession.

It had not come to pass that Aubrey Easterwood had seized his friend's hand and, with shame-flushed face and hanging head, had, with halting words and faltering voice, admitted the painful truth.

It had not come to pass that, with squared back-thrust shoulders and up-thrown head, he had definitely trumpeted forth, bravely and proudly, the fact, naked and unashamed, that he loved Daphne Mackleworth.

Nor had it come to pass that, stricken down by malaria or other illness, he had, in his delirium, called upon her name; or in his weakness whispered to his friend that his heart was breaking for love of her.

Nothing of the sort. But in his ingenuous guilelessness he had talked of her so frequently and at such length that—well, there it was, and something really must be done before something really happened. Something—nasty.

Hence the idea.

Mrs. Moresby Wallingford, of course! She'd help. And naturally, she'd hold no brief for Mrs. Mackleworth if she knew that Tony was philandering with her. Be only too glad to put a spoke in her wheel—being a human woman.

Joan Wallingford was one of the very best. A jolly good sort, and one of those married women who really are good for a young man. She'd advise him. And her advice would be worth having, too. She had liked Aubrey ever since he had stayed with her and old Tony, when they were on furlough.

And most women, particularly the best of them, loved rescuing men, especially desirable, presentable, eligible young men, from the "clutches" of another woman—apart from any personal reasons.

On the afternoon of the very day on which the idea occurred to him, Captain Stacey Burlestone sought out Mrs. Moresby Wallingford, where, briefly a grass-widow, her husband away, shooting, she sat alone in the Club, reading a magazine.

"Will you do something for me—and for Aubrey Easterwood—Mrs. Wallingford?" he asked.

"Of course I will. Only too delighted," replied Joan Wallingford, who had a particular liking for both men. "Even if I weren't deep in your debt for your great kindness to me when we arrived here."

"Oh, that! . . . Pleasantest month of my life, when you and Tony stayed with me."

"What can an ignorant new-comer here, like myself, do to help you?"

"Well, it's like this. . . . You know Mrs. Mackleworth."

"Yes. We've exchanged calls and I have talked to her at the Gymkana."

"What do you think of her?"

"Well, in what way? From what point of view?"

"D'you like her?"

"I don't dislike her. She's enigmatic. . . . But I think she's terribly attractive. One of the smartest, cleverest and most amusing women I . . ."

"Yes, as you say, terribly attractive. That's the trouble."

Joan Wallingford opened her eyes. She had rather gathered, from what her husband had said, that Stacey Burlestone was something of a misogynist, or at any rate was a confirmed bachelor. Was he going to ask her to help him to meet Mrs. Mackleworth? Well, why not? Better the bachelor, Captain Burlestone, than her Tony.

"You find her so?"

"I? Er . . . Oh, no! No! It's young Easterwood. Dark secret, of course, strictly between ourselves. He's fallen head over ears in love with her."

Joan Wallingford smiled.

"How dreadful," she said.

"Well, yes, it is—or might be—literally that. He's a splendid boy; absolutely one of the very best. Clean as a whistle and straight as a die; and it might be, well, pretty ghastly. Might end in a tragedy."

"Oh, surely not. I . . ."

"Well, you see, one doesn't know what line Mrs. Mackleworth might take. Still less what the man Mackleworth might do, in the event of—well, trouble. And whatever he did would be something . . . nasty."

"I don't like Captain Mackleworth," admitted Joan Wallingford. "Horrible man."

"Yes, quite so. I think there's no possible doubt that, if it came to trouble, he'd make all the trouble he could. That's quite certain. So what is vital is the question of what sort of person Mrs. Mackleworth really is; what sort of line she'd take if things developed."

"What can I do in a matter like this? What had you in mind?"

"Well, I thought perhaps you'd hold a watching brief, so to speak; and do anything you could."

"Such as . . . ?"

"Well, could you get to know Mrs. Mackleworth better? Make up your mind about her? Form an opinion as to the sort of terms on which she is with her husband?"

"Really, Captain Burlestone, I . . ."

"Don't say you won't help."

"Of course I'll help, if there's anything I can possibly do; but you are sketching out a rather—tall order."

"Yes, I know. It does sound like that; but if you cultivated her, she might tell you things."

"She doesn't strike me as a very on-coming and

communicative sort of person," mused Joan Wallingford. "Where women are concerned, anyhow."

"No?"

"And it isn't as though I were an old friend—or a
new bosom-friend, is it? She's hardly likely to discuss
her husband with me."

"No, but you might get an idea, an inkling. And
being a clever woman . . ."

Joan Wallingford gave a slight ironical bow.

". . . you might be able to find out what her attitude
really is, to Aubrey Easterwood. You might introduce
his name and see how she re-acted."

Mrs. Moresby Wallingford laughed.

"What—a sudden gasp, a guilty flush, the vapours,
smelling-salts, a swoon . . . ?"

"No, don't rag, Mrs. Wallingford. It really is serious;
or rather it might be frightfully serious if Mackleworth
is one of those violent jealous brutes—or a mean
vindictive fellow—or one of those men who are on the
look-out for a chance to get rid of their wives."

Mrs. Moresby Wallingford studied Stacey Burlestone's face and smiled again, this time to herself.

How funny men were . . . the dears.

"What do you think of Mrs. Mackleworth?" she
asked. "Do you agree that she is an outrageous flirt?"

"Good gracious, no! Who says such a thing?

"The old cats of the station, I suppose," he added
bitterly.

"You don't believe any of the stories that have
drifted here, after her, from Poona?"

"Never heard any," replied Burlestone shortly. "Not
about her. Only about him."

"You don't agree with those people who sympathize
with him for having such a 'handful' of a wife?"

"Most certainly not. Handful? People say anything
about a beautiful woman."

"Yes. She dances well, doesn't she?"

"Divinely."

"Tennis, too."

"Oh, championship form."

"Dresses extraordinarily well, doesn't she?"

"Oh, marvellously, marvellously. Always looks as though she'd come straight out of a band-box."

"And so well-read. Italian and German poetry and all that."

"Yes."

"In fact, you yourself have formed a very high opinion of her, Captain Burlestone?" asked Joan Wallingford artlessly, and with no trace of a smile upon her kindly friendly countenance.

"I? Oh, no. Not at all. You see, I really know nothing about her. Young Easterwood knows her far better than I."

"So does Mr. Wellingson, I imagine," observed Joan Wallingford, and pondered as to how well her Tony knew the woman.

"Wellingson! Yes. Confounded pup. Must be a perfect nuisance to her. Simply shadows her about. I gather from Aubrey that he absolutely haunts the Mackleworth bungalow."

"Well, isn't that rather useful—from your point of view?" smiled Joan Wallingford. "Surely. Much better than if Mr. Easterwood were her sole and conspicuous —attendant."

Stacey Burlestone frowned.

"Er—m'm . . . Yes. . . . No, I think it makes Aubrey all the worse. Jealousy and rivalry and all that, you know. Spurs him on, so to speak. Not that he needs any spurring on. But it makes him, if possible, all the keener to cut-in, quick, before Wellingson does him down. Dances and teas and morning rides and all that."

"No, I think it makes Aubrey all the worse," said Burlestone again, after a brief silence.

"Yes, I can understand that. We are apt to value things—and people—more, because others value them," mused Joan Wallingford.

"Yes. I shouldn't be surprised if half the trouble now isn't . . . well . . . the competitive spirit, if you know what I mean. Jealousy of Clarence Wellingson."

Mrs. Moresby Wallingford pinched her lower lip as she sat in thought. Suddenly she looked up at

Burlestone with her frank, charming, and delightful smile.

"I know!" she said. "You cut them both out. Surely she'd prefer the society of a man like you, with your experience of life, to that of callow youths like those boys."

True enough—and it would be one more attractive bachelor between the woman and poor flirtatious inconstant Tony. And Stacey Burlestone was a man who could take care of himself.

Captain Burlestone perpended.

"Well, do you know, Mrs. Wallingford," he said. "I'm ashamed to confess that the idea had occurred to me. I'm not a ladies' man as you know, but . . ."

"Probably makes you all the more interesting to her," smiled Mrs. Wallingford, "quite a feather in her cap. As I've said before, the woman's a living enigma, but she is a woman, and I should think she'd be simply thrilled to find that you, of all people, took an interest in her."

"I'm no good at that sort of game, y'know, Mrs. Wallingford. I've never in my life . . ."

"That'll be the attraction, the charm; and I don't mind telling you, Captain Burlestone—if you won't let it go any further, nor let it spoil you—that I, for one, find you an extremely charming person."

Stacey Burlestone actually blushed.

"And I'll tell you what suddenly does occur to me," continued Mrs. Wallingford. "Do you realize that we're talking about a married woman, and quite probably a thoroughly nice, well-behaved, self-respecting married woman at that?"

"Yes," admitted Stacey Burlestone. "That's the trouble of it. I shouldn't be here bothering you, or rather I shouldn't be bothering you on this particular subject, if she were an eligible spinster. It's the fact that she is a married woman, and married to the man Mackleworth, that makes me so anxious about young Aubrey. . . . And, anyhow, we weren't really talking scandal, were we? We're not proposing that I should elope with her—before Aubrey does. She's an extremely popular woman."

"With men," smiled Joan Wallingford. "And she's got to have friends—naturally."

"Well, it's better that she should have men friends who—well—who know the rules of the game, and are not likely to come a cropper . . . get into a mess and . . . No, I don't mean that exactly. I mean men friends who can keep it . . ."

"Platonic," suggested Mrs. Wallingford.

"Exactly. Men friends who can have a safe pleasant harmless friendship with a married woman; neither of them a penny the worse, and both of them all the better for it."

"Yes. And you'd be a better lightning-conductor—if there were any lightning—than Aubrey Easterwood."

"Yes, I could certainly deal with Mackleworth better than Aubrey could; if he chose to be—nasty," he growled.

"Why can't men let women alone," he added.

Joan Wallingford laughed outright.

"Why, indeed," she smiled. "We women are terrible people."

"It'll all fizzle out," she continued. "Either Aubrey or the Mackleworths will go on leave or be transferred, sooner or later."

"Yes, but there might be the Devil's own explosion before—er—the flame does fizzle out."

"What d'you really fear?"

"Well, trouble in general, and Mackleworth in particular. What I fear is the spoiling of Aubrey Easterwood. Soiling and spoiling—of his nature, I mean; his character. He's such an extraordinarily, amazingly nice boy. And Mrs. Mackleworth is, to say the least of it, just what you called her—an enigma, an unknown quantity; and, as you just mentioned, a married woman. And what I also fear is his professional and social ruin. . . . Smash. . . . And suppose on top of that, there's a divorce case, with Mackleworth doing his uttermost, and perhaps a whole string of co-respondents. . . . Trumped up by Mackleworth, I mean, of course. And young Aubrey with a badly damaged

Mrs. Mackleworth on his hands for the rest of his life. It would be his utter damnation. Destruction.

"Or again," continued Stacey Burlestone, "if it didn't come to that, there might be a frightful row and a horrible scandal. I gather that Mackleworth is that sort of chap. Anyhow, I can't just stand by and see Aubrey riding straight for a precipice, and not do something about it."

"No," agreed Joan Wallingford. "You really came to ask me what I could do about it. . . . Would you like me to ask Mrs. Mackleworth to tea—and you drop in? We'll see what we make of her; and I could leave you alone with her for a while. You could fix up a ride or some dances or something."

"That's awfully good of you, Mrs. Wallingford. Thanks so much."

"It'll be a start, anyway, and we may decide that she's as nice a woman as ever lived, and thoroughly good for our young friend."

"Yes, possibly as good for him as you'd be. Why on earth couldn't he have fallen in love with you?"

"Well, thank Heaven he didn't, anyway," smiled Joan Wallingford. "Oh, this love business! . . . Silly boy."

§7

And so it came to pass.

Her husband still being away on his shooting-trip, Joan Wallingford wrote Daphne Mackleworth a friendly little note, inviting her to tea at four o'clock on Saturday. And at four-thirty Captain Burlestone called —and found that Mrs. Wallingford was At Home.

With Mrs. Mackleworth he got on famously, splendidly, and, incidentally, quite corrected the wrong impression that that lady had formed of him.

Why did people call him a crusty bachelor, a cynic, a surly hermit, a woman-hater, and all that?

Why, he was perfectly delightful. Charming. And it was natural charm, too. One could always tell when a man was laying himself out deliberately to captivate.

He was just as attractive and interesting when he was sitting silent as when he was talking in his slow grave way. A solid, reliable person. A gentleman, and, albeit witty, graceful, delightful, he was no hill-captain, no captivating woman-hunter. No *gigolo* and carpet-knight.

How different from the wretched boys who pestered her; the more experienced almost professional flirts; the furtive married men whose wives did not understand them; the old *roués* who sickened her . . . Oh, men, men, men. . . .

And how different from the boorish bear she'd been fool enough to marry. Dull, drunken beast.

And, somehow, when Joan Wallingford left them alone together as she went to interview her *dirzie* who was working, sitting on the floor in the back verandah (efficiently manipulating the sewing-machine with the toes of his right foot), the name of Aubrey Easterwood was not mentioned.

No, somehow they talked about Captain Stacey Burlestone. And Mrs. Mackleworth, having metaphorically turned him inside-out and upside-down, liked him more and more; liked him enormously; but came regretfully to the conclusion that, like all the nicest men, he'd got no money; nothing much but his pay; and had transferred to the Indian Army for that reason.

Sad.

Nevertheless . . . he was a dear. Just the sort of man she adored—if only by reason of his being in such sharp contrast with the vast majority of the young fools, middle-aged scamps and aged flirts who flocked around her.

A pity that Captain Stacey Burlestone didn't occupy the pretty financial situation enjoyed by young Aubrey Easterwood, or have the pleasing prospects of dear little Clarence Wellingson.

For here was a man who attracted her tremendously, and at first sight. Actually a man whom she could admire and respect. Frankly and plainly, a man with whom she could fall in love. . . . Real love.

CHAPTER X

Flies round the honey-pot.

Captain Stacey Burlestone sat on one side of Mrs. Mackleworth in the Gymkana Club ball-room. On the other side sat Lieutenant Aubrey Easterwood. In front of her, Major Moresby Wallingford and a group of young men and not-so-young men joined in the conversation, asked for dances, and generally displayed their liking for honey.

The conductor of the band of the Northumberland Light Infantry, up in the musicians' gallery, rapped smartly with his bâton, and Mr. Clarence Wellingson, the Assistant Magistrate of Quetawur, pushed a little brusquely and importantly through the group of courtiers and into the immediate Presence.

"Our dance, I think, Mrs. Mackleworth," he said proudly, triumphantly; and, in the opinion of Stacey Burlestone and Aubrey Easterwood, too possessively and very fatuously.

Smiling, Mrs. Mackleworth rose to her feet and, with a "Mind this for me," handed her bag to Stacey Burlestone.

Aubrey Easterwood frowned.

"And you mind this, Aubrey," she said, giving him a small fan.

Easterwood's frown turned to an ecstatic smile and then to a cold glare, as he regarded the retreating form of Mr. Clarence Wellingson, and then the bag entrusted to Stacey Burlestone.

"Damned little squirt," he said.

"Can't stand the bumptious pup," agreed Stacey Burlestone, as from his forefinger he dangled Mrs. Mackleworth's little bag, by its golden chain.

Coldly and doubtfully he eyed the fan which, in Easterwood's powerful fist, looked incongruous, especially when, opening it, he began gently to fan his heated face.

141

Honours divided.

Circling past, in Clarence Wellingson's arms, Mrs. Mackleworth bestowed a brilliant, charming and delightful smile which, beginning with Burlestone, ended with Easterwood.

As she and her partner passed the big open doors that gave on to the large front verandah, a big, burly, thick-set man stepped into the door-way, glanced around, and then, raising a large hand, beckoned urgently, imperiously. Not with the beckoning finger of request, but with the quick-moving hand and arm that command; definitely the ordering-gesture of superior to subordinate, of master to servant.

Mr. Clarence Wellingson, ardently gazing at Mrs. Mackleworth's face, saw that she suddenly flushed, that her eyes flashed as she looked over his shoulder.

Being in the act of turning, he immediately saw the cause of her change of countenance, and found himself the recipient of the urgent call conveyed by the insistently beckoning hand.

"Your husband . . ." he said, as his back turned again to the door-way and Mrs. Mackleworth again faced it.

"My husband," she agreed.

"He—er—seems to want to speak to you—or me . . . or both of us," tittered Wellingson.

"Yes," replied Mrs. Mackleworth.

"I don't think it can be anything as urgent as all that. He might wait until the dance finishes, mightn't he?" asked the young man.

"He's going to, anyway," said Mrs. Mackleworth.

But he wasn't.

As, in their course round the rather crowded floor, the couple again passed the door-way, the big man stepped into the ball-room, confronted them, impeded their progress, and indeed definitely arrested it.

"I'm going home," he growled.

"Well? Good night, then," replied Mrs. Mackleworth.

"I'm going home, I said. Come along," replied the man.

"Really, Captain Mackleworth!" interposed Clarence

Wellingson. "In the middle of a . . ."

The man turned his heavy face and the hard stare of his angry sullen eyes toward the speaker, but made no other reply.

Turning her back upon him, Mrs. Mackleworth replaced her hand upon Wellingson's shoulder, and took a step to continue the dance.

"Come along, I said," growled Captain Mackleworth, and seizing his wife's wrist, jerked her roughly in the direction of the door-way; led, or pulled her through it; and, with a quite unmistakable swing of his powerful arm, slung her in the direction of the steps, at the bottom of which his car was standing.

Recovering her balance, Mrs. Mackleworth drew herself up, turned, and faced her husband.

"We won't have a scene here," she said quietly. "Do you think I might be permitted to get my bag and fan?"

"Oh, to Hell with your bag and fan. . . . Or send your little dog for them."

Clarence Wellingson was forced to accept the evidence of his eyes and ears. It was part of his profession to accept or reject evidence.

Obviously with truth, his eyes and ears had told him that a man, a member of the Club, had stepped into the Club ball-room, interrupted a lady and her partner in the middle of a dance; ordered, and then hustled, the lady out of the ball-room; spoken to her as though she were a dog—and had then actually called her partner one!

But this was incredible, impossible.

Such things did not happen in civilized society.

This man was an "officer and a gentleman." A very notorious one, it was true. Famous for his shocking manners, gross rudeness to all and sundry, and general bearishness and brutality. People said he trained too hard and wore his nerves to a frazzle. Others said that he drank like a fish. . . . Anybody would think he drank, but of course that couldn't be the case with a boxing champion.

On the other hand, though, he might have regular drinking-bouts between periods of training. After all, he only had to go into training and get himself fighting-fit once a year. Yes, perhaps he drank. Probably he'd been drinking now. Spent the whole night in the bar.

Yes, he must be drunk; and he must be carefully handled. Any person with a grain of common sense knows that a drunken man must be humoured and carefully handled.

Mustn't have a scene, especially with such a huge and powerful ruffian as Mackleworth the boxer. Be all the more difficult for Mrs. Mackleworth, if there were a row, and the fellow's foul temper were made worse.

Discretion definitely the better part of valour.

Yes, he must be humoured and . . .

"Fetch my wife's bag and fan."

Clarence Wellingson almost jumped, so threatening was the glare of those savage, sullen eyes, so ugly the growl of that menacing voice.

Drunk—of course. And to be humoured.

"And my wrap—if you'd be so kind, Clarence. I left it on my chair."

"Yes—*Clarence* dear," jeered Mackleworth, and Wellingson obeyed promptly. Obeyed Mrs. Mackleworth of course.

Nimbly and gracefully the young man threaded his way across the crowded ball-room to where sat Stacey Burlestone and Aubrey Easterwood, the one dangling a little *petit point* bag on his finger, and the other somewhat sullenly opening and shutting a fan. Both, looking up, eyed him with surprise and what—to a young man less sure of himself and his welcome—would have seemed distaste.

"Er—Mrs. Mackleworth is—er—just going. I've come for her bag and fan."

"Just going!" exclaimed Aubrey Easterwood. "But I'm having the next dance with her."

"You're not," tittered Wellingson.

"And I was under the impression that I was having the one after next," growled Stacey Burlestone.

"Well, you're not," Wellingson assured him.

The friends rose as one man.

"I'll take her bag to her myself—thank you," said

Burlestone.

"And I'll take her fan—thank you," said Easterwood.

"And I'll take her wrap—thank *you*," scored Wellingson.

And, followed by Wellingson, the other two made their way round the ball-room to the verandah.

Evidently something was "up."

Men had come to the door of the bar at one end of the verandah; others were standing about, by that of the card-room at the opposite end; people who had been lounging in the ball-room door-way, watching the dancers, were now watching Captain and Mrs. Mackleworth who stood at the top of the steps leading down to the drive. Someone had seen something and the news had spread.

Mackleworth again . . .

Mrs. Mackleworth was calm, self-possessed, apparently unperturbed. Captain Mackleworth, fists on hips, arms akimbo, feet astride, stood looking like an angry bull, his back to his wife, glowering toward the ball-room.

Suddenly he guffawed.

"Here's the procession," he said.

And indeed, the three men in single file, each bearing the property of Mrs. Mackleworth, did rather suggest that idea.

"Enter slaves, bearing gifts," jeered Mackleworth.

"Here, give that to me," he added, as Wellingson went gracefully to drape the light shawl about Mrs. Mackleworth's bare shoulders.

Swiftly the wise young man obeyed.

"And that," said Mackleworth, extending a huge hand for the tiny bag that Burlestone carried, still dangling by its gold chain, from his finger.

Eyeing him with all the contempt that he felt, Stacey Burlestone, with an ironical bow, handed the bag to Mackleworth.

As he did so, Aubrey Easterwood gave Mrs. Mackleworth her fan.

And with the tail of his eye, Mackleworth saw him do it.

"Oh, thanks so much," she murmured. "I'm so sorry about our dance, but . . ."

And she smiled the peculiar and intriguing smile that Aubrey Easterwood so loved.

"So sorry, Captain Burlestone," she added, "but . . ."

And again she smiled with an almost imperceptible shrug of the shoulders.

"And no 'buts' for dear Clarence?" rasped Mackleworth.

His wife eyed him coolly.

"So sorry, Clarence," she said quietly. "To be continued in our next."

"Well, that being settled, you can return that fan to dear Aubrey, and he can give it to me."

Aubrey Easterwood was young, impulsive, quick-tempered, and desperately in love. To his credit he turned away with a brief.

"Good night, Mackleworth. Come and have a drink, Stacey; I'm for a strong peg of neat—soda-water."

There should be no scene, so far as he was concerned.

But Mackleworth held other views, if the whims, fancies and impulses of a man under the influence of alcohol can be considered views.

With a stride surprisingly swift and light in so big a man, and an outflung arm, he seized Easterwood by the shoulder, swung him about and thrust his inflamed, scowling face, lowering and menacing, close to that of the younger man.

"Take that fan back from my wife, and then give it to me," he growled.

Easterwood returned the stare of the hard and cruel eyes, in which a fire seemed to smoulder when it did not flare and blaze.

He smiled.

"Why certainly," he said lightly. "All things according to ceremonial as laid down in the book, and so forth."

And with a bow he held out his hand for the fan.

With an equally ironical bow and enigmatic smile,

Mrs. Mackleworth handed the bone—or ivory—of contention to Easterwood, who, taking it, offered it upon his joined open palms, as though upon a cushion, to Mackleworth.

The obvious mockery of the gesture enraged that gentleman.

Seizing it with his left hand, he delivered with his open right a tremendous cuff or clout upon the side of Easterwood's head—almost. But for the swiftest of movements, Easterwood had received a ringing box on the ear, which would probably have knocked him down.

"Playful to-night, Sir," laughed Easterwood, and turning swiftly on his heel, made for the bar.

Mrs. Mackleworth's eyes followed his retreating figure, and there was no smile upon her face.

Stepping up to the glowering Mackleworth, Burlestone took him by the arm.

"I'm an older man than you," he said quietly, "and considerably your senior in the Army List. Listen. People lose their commissions for things like that, reported in the proper quarter—with witnesses' affidavits attached. . . . Pull yourself together, man. There are ladies present—and a brace of perfectly good Generals in the card-room. Now then, come along home."

For a moment it looked as though Mackleworth was going to strike Burlestone.

"I'll drive you," added that wily man, "for I'm quite sure you can't drive."

"*What?*" growled Mackleworth. "You're a damned liar. What d'you mean, can't drive? Drive the car backwards at sixty if I wanted to."

"Bet you can't drive it forwards at ten miles an hour, for a start," replied Burlestone; and Captain Mackleworth promptly descended the steps, threw his wife's things into the car, and got into the driver's seat.

"Come along, Daphne," he said. "We'll show 'em."

"Good night, Captain Burlestone, and thank you so much," smiled Mrs. Mackleworth; and the look she gave him caused Stacey Burlestone's whole being to thrill. A new experience indeed.

He raised eyebrows of enquiry and was answered by a short reassuring nod. Yes, she'd be safe enough in the car with her husband. Drink didn't affect his body.

And a moment later, driven rather fast, but with complete accuracy, the car sped down the drive, through the Club gates and out on to the dusty moonlit road.

If that swine wrecked the car with her in it, Stacey Burlestone would . . . would . . . wreck Mackleworth.

CHAPTER XI

Clad in a heavy dressing-gown, a white singlet, blue shorts and thin kid boots, Aubrey Easterwood climbed into the ring, and, seating himself in his corner, laid his arms along the ropes, leaned back against the padded post, closed his eyes, relaxed all his muscles and endeavoured to make his mind a blank.

In the last-named effort he was not successful. Thoughts would come, of course.

First thoughts:

How fortunate were those boxers whose contests were staged in the open air, the glorious fresh clear air, instead of in halls and such ill-ventilated places where hundreds of selfish and unsporting spectators puffed forth clouds of cigarette, cigar, and pipe-tobacco smoke into the already fetid twice-breathed atmosphere. A pity some of them couldn't be made to take the place of the distressed boxer whose labouring lungs panted for air and for dear life.

Very fortunate indeed. . . . Thank God for the cool gentle breeze and for the sweet sense of space, cleanness and freedom . . . the star-jewelled moon-lit sky for roof . . . No enclosing roof.

Second thoughts:

Those big acetylene lamps were very powerful and gave a strong glare. But that was all to the good, since one would not be looking upward. Couldn't have too much light when dealing with the great Mackleworth. Bright light, pure air, space . . . in which to try conclusions with Mackleworth. Conclusions . . . ?

Third thoughts:

What a crowd! Probably a couple of thousand British soldiers present, not to mention civilians. Hundreds of those—a white sea of dress-shirt fronts surrounded by a sand-coloured shore of khaki uniforms . . . That would make the sea a lake, since it was entirely surrounded by the sand-coloured shore . . . A

149

lake—and in the middle of it was the little island, the raised ring in which he was seated. And the murmur of voices was like that of the waves of the sea—an insistent yet monotonous susurrus of sound—with, here and there, a wave that broke higher than the rest, as some soldier called across to a friend.

Curious to think that that ocean of sound would be stilled the moment that he rose to his feet and confronted Mackleworth. Curious to think that thousands of pairs of eyes were staring at him and that hundreds of tongues were talking about him.

What were they saying, the majority of them? That he hadn't a ghost of a chance against Mackleworth. Well, that remained to be seen. To be seen very soon, too. Perhaps it was just as well that he couldn't hear what they were saying. Not that they'd be able to give him any feeling of defeatism. No, not if every soul in that vast canvas-walled enclosure thought he was going to be beaten.

Fourth thoughts:

Was it a good thing or a bad thing, so far as winning a fight was concerned, to have a personal animus against one's opponent? In fact, to hate him with all one's heart and soul? Would that lend strength to one's blows, cunning to one's defence, determination and doggedness to one's will to endure; or would it mar one's coolness, warp one's judgment, detract from one's scientific detachment, so to speak?

Anyway, however much he loathed Mackleworth, whatever reasons he had for hating him, however much he longed to hammer him, smash him, defeat him, for his treatment of Daphne, as well as for his own sweet sake, one must, before all things, be cool, calm, clear-headed, single-minded.

Yes, of course it was a bad thing to hate your opponent, to see him through the red mists of wrath. Why, it was part of ring-craft to make your opponent angry, wild—literally so—in order that his blows might be equally wild.

Still, when it came to the chance of delivering the blow that he'd practised and delivered ten thousand times at the punching-ball, there might be a little extra in it, a little added weight behind it, that might not have been there had his opponent been anybody but Mackleworth.

This wouldn't do. There he was, getting all taut again, clenching his fists and his teeth, and fighting Mackleworth before he got into the ring. Absolute waste of energy, vitality and force.

Now then, to relax properly and to make his mind a blank.

Aubrey Easterwood opened his eyes as a hush was followed by a ragged cheer. The extremely popular Lieutenant-General commanding the Division had entered, accompanied by the Brigadier-General commanding the Quetawur Brigade; a visiting Inspector-General of Cavalry; and a fourth General, a stray, passing through Quetawur on his way from Simla to Bombay. It was, of course, pure coincidence that the two latter happened to be in Quetawur at the time of the All India Boxing Tournament and the Heavy-weight Championship contest.

"Is it going to be a fight or another Mackleworth murder?" asked the Inspector-General of Cavalry of the Divisional General.

"Well . . . I don't know," was the reply. "The youngster there is a bit of a dark horse, and I've heard interesting things about him. He's most amazingly strong. I'm glad it's only a three-round contest, though. Strength isn't everything."

"No," agreed the other. "I should say it isn't anything against science, and Mackleworth's got that all right. And strength as well. Strong as two people. Ever seen him box?"

"Yes. Saw him at Quetta and at Poona. Boxes much more like a pro than an amateur."

"Hope it goes the three rounds," observed the Brigadier.

"So do I, for Easterwood's sake," agreed the General. . . . "It'll be worth seeing, if it does."

"Yes. Particularly so. There's a little bit of a drama

behind it," he added. "A little personal feeling, apart from rivalry and the championship."

"Oh? What's that?" enquired the Inspector-General of Cavalry.

"Well—there's a certain amount of ill-feeling. At any rate, on Mackleworth's part. He behaved very badly at the Gymkana, one evening. It didn't come to my notice officially, of course, but I rather gather that Mackleworth displayed 'conduct unbecoming an officer and a gentleman' and so forth. Thought Easterwood had been dancing with his wife too much, or something of the sort. According to gossip, Mackleworth wanted to start the Championship contest then and there. With bare fists."

"What, they were scrapping all over the Gymkana, d'you mean?"

"Oh, no. I believe Easterwood's conduct was extremely correct. If it hadn't been, there would have been a bit of a scene. Anyway, it's common knowledge that there's no love lost between them."

"Mackleworth's got rather a murky reputation altogether, hasn't he?" asked Brigadier-General Erskine.

"And his wife rather a brilliant one," smiled General Craddock. "A lovely girl. I was on the boat by which she came out. Danced with her at the Yacht Club at Bombay. Gave me quite a shock when I learned that she had come to marry Mackleworth. . . . Hope this lad wallops him well."

"Shame!" laughed the Quetawur Brigadier. "*I* hope the best man will win," he said virtuously.

"And I hope the best man is Easterwood," he added.

§2

Captain Colin Mackleworth climbed into the ring, cast a glance at his opponent, and looked round the big enclosure.

A thin cheer greeted his appearance, a cheer raised largely by the sporting fraternity whose money he carried. These worthies were not numerous, for few indeed could be found to take a risk on his opponent even at the longest odds.

Ten to one on Mackleworth was freely offered—and freely refused.

Aubrey Easterwood opened his eyes.

There he was then, a picture of the Perfect Pugilist; cropped hair; slightly bent and flattened nose; massive projecting bone where the nose joined the forehead, and above the eyes; heavy jaw; very thick neck; magnificent shoulders, not too square, but sloping to enormous arms; deep chest; flat, corrugated stomach, huge thighs and tremendous calves.

A grand gnarled oak-tree of a man; a bruiser; a fighter. And, in addition—a boxer.

Well, well! Perhaps he wasn't as quick as he was strong. A fight is not lost until it's won by the other party; and there is always the fortune of war, the luck of the game; and the God of Battles has handed out some amazing luck at times, and isn't always on the side of the big battalions.

When, the time being come, Aubrey Easterwood rose to his feet, threw off his dressing-gown and handed it to his second, Sergeant Buckley, present again in Quetawur for his own fight, loud and hearty applause started from the ring-side seats, and spread to those occupied by the soldiers of the Garrison.

"By Jove!" said Lieutenant-General Sir Archibald Helstone, "he peels well."

"Magnificent!" murmured his Brigadier. "Apollo *versus* Hercules."

"Or Hercules *versus* a gorilla," suggested the Inspector-General.

"If only he can box . . ." said General Craddock, and left his sentence unfinished.

Aubrey Easterwood looked round in amazement.

Could they be cheering him?

Apparently they were, for everyone was looking at him, and Mackleworth was still seated in his corner.

Well, that was very nice of them. Very heartening. He'd like to bow or wave his acknowledgments, but that would be an absurd thing to do. He only hoped he'd be able to put up a show and give them a run for their money. Not one of those miserable exhibitions of ten seconds' "weaving," one smack, and the count; all over in the first minute.

No, he'd keep his temper, be absolutely cool, scientific and detached—and play for safety. Or, at any rate, for time. Long enough to make it a contest and not an execution.

The brief preliminaries. Fitting of gloves, announcement of names and weights.

"Seconds out of the ring."

"Time."

And with a look of quiet calm confidence on his exceedingly handsome face, Aubrey Easterwood strode to the middle of the ring, extended both hands, and, with a smile and sufficient cordiality, shook those of his opponent.

Both men stepped back and assumed each his fighting stance.

A complete, unbroken silence, in which two thousand pairs of eyes watched critically what should befall.

§3

Round one.

Well, here was the man who, on several occasions, had insulted him, and on one of them had attempted to punch his head, smack his face, or box his ears. Here was the man who made Daphne's life a burden to her, sneered at her, and humiliated her in public. Here he was, for Aubrey Easterwood to do to him what he could.

Well, he had his plan of campaign well thought out, his strategy and tactics, based on the fact that Mackleworth was older than he, and probably was not in such good training and condition. He felt that he himself was in absolutely perfect condition, that he was the strongest man in his Regiment, probably in his Brigade, possibly in the Division, conceivably the strongest man in the British Army.

Why, for all he knew, or anybody else knew, he

might be the strongest man in the world.

He felt like it; though, at the moment, it was not so much a matter of strength as of boxing, and by the lighting up of Mackleworth's sullen eyes, he was about to do something.

Mackleworth took a sudden swift step forward, feinted with his right, ducked below Easterwood's excellent straight left, changed the same feint into an actual blow, and, cross-countering also, struck Easterwood a tremendous blow, full on the mouth, splitting both lips and sending him heavily to the boards.

Mackleworth the Killer was in good form.

"Over in five seconds!" growled the Divisional-General, Sir Archibald Helstone.

The referee rose to his feet to count, and, with him, rose Aubrey Easterwood, earning a cheer as he did so. Evidently there was some fight, some pluck, and some guts in the lad who was not down for a second from a blow like that, a full-strength long-arm blow from the shoulder, and Mackleworth's shoulder at that.

As Easterwood's hands left the canvas, Mackleworth rushed, swinging a tremendous upper-cut at the face of his half-risen opponent. This Easterwood dodged, as he drove at Mackleworth's mark.

Mackleworth blocked the blow with his left, and right-hooked viciously at Easterwood's jaw. The heavy blow sent him reeling sideways against the ropes, Mackleworth instantly springing after him like a tiger, and aiming left and right again at Easterwood's jaw.

Ducking swiftly, the latter side-stepped under Mackleworth's left arm, and sprang clear.

Whirling left, Mackleworth again rushed, to be met by Easterwood's long and strong straight drives, harmless defensive blows which Mackleworth guarded or blocked, but treated with the respect they deserved. Three times his attack was thus repulsed, and the fourth time, side-stepping and cross-countering, Mackleworth repeated the blow that had knocked Easterwood down.

A little higher this time, on the nose and mouth, came the blow, like the kick of a mule, and Easterwood, almost knocked from his feet, was sent reeling back to the ropes, the upper one catching the back of his neck, the lower taking him behind the knees.

Through the ropes he went, and to the ground five feet below.

Knocked clean out of the ring.

"I'll spoil his beauty for him," growled Mackleworth.

To the accompaniment of loud cheers, Aubrey Easterwood climbed back into the ring, evaded Mackleworth's immediate rush by a swift side-step and a dancing, dodging, ducking retreat—a running-away, a flight, which stopped suddenly as, flinging his left arm across his down-turned bleeding face, he bent low, and, with legs and body in the position of a lunging fencer, drove with his right at the charging Mackleworth, just above the belt.

The terrific blow stopped Mackleworth's rush. It was as though a man, running swiftly in darkness, had dashed suddenly against the end of a horizontal scaffold-pole.

The gasp with which the breath was driven from his body was audible throughout the arena. Instinctively he dropped his right to the spot where the blow had fallen, as his opponent straightened to his full height.

And then Easterwood really struck.

With all his strength, with all his heart and soul and might, with all his anger and hatred, he struck the blow that he had practised ten thousand times, as, day after day, he had striven to increase its force, striven so to strike his punching-bag ever harder and more heavily.

Rising to his full height and proper stance, he struck with perfect timing, with every ounce of his fourteen stone of weight behind the blow, and with the absolute utter whole of all his mighty strength.

Unguarded, unblocked, undodged, the blow fell straight and true and full on Mackleworth's jaw, and, like a statue flung from its pedestal, Mackleworth went down.

He twitched, quivered and lay still.

In dead silence the referee counted the fatal

seconds. Not at the seventh, the eighth, nor the ninth, did Mackleworth stir.

Not at the tenth, not at the cry of "*Out!*", not at the tremendous salvo of ringing cheers, did Mackleworth move.

Neither then—nor ever again.

For he was dead.

In fair fight, under strictest supervision, rules, regulations and conditions, Aubrey Easterwood had, by sheer strength, killed Colin Mackleworth.

CHAPTER XII

More trouble for Captain Stacey Burlestone.

The boy was going morbid again.

Of course it was a shocking tragedy. A terrible thing to happen to any youngster. But it had happened many a time before, and it would happen many a time again.

Fellows had killed other fellows at polo, too. Driven a ball smack against a man's temple, or knocked him and his pony flying, ack over tock. But nobody blamed them.

"Bless me," growled Burlestone, "how many men have accidentally killed others at Rugger; at wrestling; at cricket, even. What about that case of the man whose foil broke as he thrust, and he shoved it clean through his opponent's eye into his brain? What about that chap who missed the lion, in Kathiawar, and shot his friend who'd moved from his post and got into the line of fire? What about the chap who accidentally fouled, at a jump, the man against whom he was riding a match—and broke his neck?

"Accidents will happen.

"Poor old Aubrey. First he gets the fantods because he's not strong enough and a native nearly kills him; and then he gets them because he's too strong and quite kills the Heavy-weight Champion.

"Cruel rough luck, of course, but, damn it all, accidents will happen—in the best-regulated boxing-contests."

Well, he wanted to win the Officers' Heavy-weight Championship of India, and by Jove, he'd done it! And then said he'd never put a boxing-glove on his hand again.

Talk about wanting to be strong!

Strong! The Civil Surgeon, the Surgeon-General, and the R.A.M.C. doctor officially present in case of need, had all agreed that Mackleworth's death was due to pure shock. Nothing whatsoever wrong with heart, blood-vessels, or anything else. He was simply killed by the force of the blow, as though he'd been sand-bagged or struck with a padded hammer.

Poor old Aubrey!

And what made it ten times worse was his feeling about Mrs. Mackleworth. It would have been bad enough if the fellow had been a bachelor. Worse if he'd been a married man whose wife was a complete stranger. But as things were, worst of all.

It was not as though he was one of those fellows who could shrug their shoulders and take the sensible view that it was pure accident, and pursue to its logical conclusion the thought that the woman whom he loved was now a widow.

Poor old Aubrey!

Now, if somebody else had killed Mackleworth, the position would be mightily different; and the fact of her being a widow wouldn't be one to grieve over.

Anyhow, she was a widow, begad. Yes, she was a widow now, all right.

And, rising to his feet, Stacey Burlestone paced up and down the verandah.

Yes, lovely Daphne Mackleworth . . . intriguing, provocative, enigmatic, Mona Lisa was a widow. And doubtless La Gioconda was none the less a *gioconda*—none the less jocund—for her deliverance from the late Captain Mackleworth.

A widow . . .

H'm!

§2

"I feel I must do it," said Aubrey Easterwood to his friend, after dinner that evening.

"I shouldn't," replied Stacey Burlestone. "You can't do any good and you might do harm . . . to yourself."

"I must. I simply must. I don't think I shall sleep again until I have."

"But, my dear chap, what can you say? Come down to brass tacks. You can't send in your card as soon as her Not-at-Home box is down, and when you are shown into the drawing-room say,

"'I've just called—er—to—er—say I'm so sorry I killed your husband.'"

"I can. And I will," replied Easterwood. "Not exactly in those words, of course. But I must see her and try to tell her how I feel about it."

"Well, how do you feel about it? So far as she is concerned, I mean? Don't you realize that you've done her just about the best turn one person ever did another?"

"Please don't talk like that."

"Why not? I'm talking sense. She hated Mackleworth. She must have hated him. And you've been the means of setting her free from an intolerable bondage. It's not as though you deliberately murdered him, either. You've nothing on earth to be ashamed of, and if she were to be perfectly honest, perfectly frank, perfectly truthful, she'd tell you that your—er—unfortunate accident had brought her happiness, freedom, relief from . . ."

"When you say honest, frank and truthful, don't you mean cynical?" interrupted Easterwood.

"Well, I should think she is a bit cynical. I imagine anybody who'd lived with Mackleworth would be. I don't know that I'd call her a cynical woman—but there's a definite tang about her observations and remarks. She sees life pretty clear-eyed, you know, and has a fairly just estimate of values. Nothing sloppy or sentimental about Mrs. Mackleworth. And if you ask me . . ."

"Look here, Stacey," broke in Aubrey Easterwood. "Supposing you had a motoring accident, and, absolutely through no fault of your own, killed a child. Wouldn't you want to go and see its parents—however painful the interview? Even though you were completely exonerated, and nobody had a word of blame for you? Wouldn't you want to go and tell the kid's mother how sorry you were?"

"Yes, I would," agreed Burlestone, "but this is different."

"Anyhow, that's how I feel about it," continued Easterwood. "I feel I must go and see her—in just that spirit . . . and tell her how terribly sorry I am."

"And are you terribly sorry—really deep down in your mind? Really right away at the back of your mind, are you absolutely sincerely sorry that Mackleworth is dead?"

Angrily Aubrey Easterwood rose to his feet and turned to go.

Halting he turned back.

"Whether I'm sorry that he's dead or not, I'm sorry —more sorry than words can tell—that I killed him. I'd give anything to wake up from this nightmare and find that I'd not done it.

"I'd a thousand times rather that he'd killed me than that I had killed him, I tell you," he added.

"And that's that," murmured Stacey Burlestone as his friend strode out of the bungalow.

§3

The minutes during which Aubrey Easterwood sat in Mrs. Mackleworth's drawing-room, awaiting her, were among the most distressing of his life.

Now that he was there, and about to face her, he began to wonder if his friend had not, as usual, been right.

What could he say?

What earthly good could his visit do? Was not his action purely selfish, incredibly selfish? Calculated to inflict pain in order that he himself might obtain a little relief from pain? Was he there merely to tell her that he was sorry—as though that information would be either surprising or interesting to the woman whose husband he had killed, the widow of the man who was "scarcely cold in his grave"? Or was he really there simply and solely because he craved for the sight of her face and the sound of her voice?

Was he there hoping that she'd speak words of comfort and kindness, telling him not to blame himself, because neither she nor anyone else did so?

Of course many women, most women indeed, would never, never forgive the man who had done such a thing—by accident or not. Women weren't logical. They were swayed by emotion and not by reason.

How difficult it was for a somewhat introspective and reasonably conscientious person to be absolutely certain of his real motive for any action.

Why had he come? What was it that had led him, impelled him, forced him, to seek this meeting with her, this interview that could not possibly be anything but most painful to them both?

Should he creep out of the bungalow and sneak away before she came?

No, the mental turmoil would start afresh at once, his mind again become the hapless home of doubts and warring impulses.

He rose to his feet.

No, it would be all to do again.

He must see her.

The door opened, and Daphne Mackleworth entered the room.

Easterwood sprang to his feet.

"Mrs. Mackleworth, I can't tell you how . . . What can I say? . . . It's good of you to see me. . . . Have I done wrong by intruding when . . . It's shamefully selfish of me. . . . But I felt I must try to . . ."

Daphne Mackleworth made no reply.

Ignoring Easterwood's outstretched hand, she placed hers upon his shoulders and looked him in the eyes; and, still unspeaking, unsmiling, took his head between her hands, drew it down, and kissed him on the lips.

Her arms went about his neck.

Again and again she kissed him, stroking his hair as she did so.

And in that moment Aubrey Easterwood's love for Daphne Mackleworth died.

He knew it; and hotly he denied it.

Drawing him down beside her upon the deep and

soft divan, again she took his face between her hands.

"Never speak of it any more, Aubrey," she whispered. "Let's never, for the rest of our lives, think of him or speak of him again."

For the rest of their lives?

Oh, joy, unspeakable, incredible! "The rest of their lives!"

Oh, dust and ashes! Oh, bitter, bitter, lovely fruit. . . .

What was dying in his heart?

Nothing, nothing. . . . "*Such love as ours can never die.*" Such love as his . . .

What had happened to him?

Of course, he wasn't himself. It was reaction from the sub-conscious dreadful fear that Daphne Mackleworth would hate him, accuse him, regard him as her husband's murderer, shrink from him in horror.

"The rest of our lives."

But to take her in his arms *now*; to kiss her lovely face—that had so haunted him by night and by day, sleeping and waking—*now*.

No, no. Not now.

Humbly, gratefully, reverently, Aubrey Easterwood kissed the woman's hands.

"Oh. . . . Thank you, thank you . . . from the bottom of my heart," he said, and rose to his feet. "You are kindness itself. . . . But I'm . . . I am dazed. . . . I . . ."

And turning, he hurried from the room.

For minutes, Daphne Mackleworth sat staring at the closed door; a long, long look, considering; her face devoid of expression until, as she rose to her feet, the enigmatic smile lightened her eyes, lit up her face, and softened the lines of her mouth.

§4

So, in due course, Aubrey Easterwood married Daphne Mackleworth and lived "happy" ever after.

Or, at any rate, "happy" until, literally, his dying day.

CHAPTER XIII

There were, of course, flies in the precious ointment. Occasionally elephants in it.

One of them would bob up quite frequently and stick its ugly head above the surface of the said ointment; and, whether of fly or of elephant, the head somehow bore a strong resemblance to that of the late Colin Mackleworth.

By his mighty strength Easterwood had killed Mackleworth. And, in so doing, had killed that beautiful, delicate thing, his selfless, sexless, boyish love for Daphne.

For the woman who had thrown herself into the arms of her husband's slayer, within a few days of his death, was not the goddess he had worshipped.

Oh, to Hell with such thoughts. . . .

She was the woman he did love, anyway. The warm, living, loving, passionate woman whom he worshipped —with his body.

Boys grow up into men, cease to worship goddesses, and love women instead. Women, with all their faults and frailties.

And what about men's faults and frailties?

What of the faults and frailties of Aubrey Easterwood—the Strongest Man in the World, who was so weak that he now lifted his elbow a little; now did things—and enjoyed doing things—that once he would not have done.

The World, the Flesh, and the Devil.

La Belle Dame sans merci.

Oh, to Hell with such thoughts. . . .

She was the most enchanting, intriguing woman in the world, ever fresh and ever new—who kept him ever guessing.

Another fly or snake or crocodile or elephant in the ointment of his happiness was his utter, ever-present dissatisfaction with himself, his life, his lack of object and purpose.

His two boyish ambitions had been fulfilled, achieved. He would once have given almost his immortal soul to be the strongest man in the world. And probably to-day he was.

He would once have given almost his immortal soul for the love of Daphne Mackleworth.

He *had* given his immortal soul. . . . Given it. . . . Lost it. . . .

To Hell with such thoughts. . . .

Oh, bitter gain—of strength that had killed love.

Oh, bitter gain—of love that had killed strength.

Killed love?

To Hell with such thoughts. . . .

Didn't he love her with all his heart? Soul?

No. Body.

The fact was that Stacey had been right when he had called him introspective, morbidly inclined, an introvert. Fact was, he was too cursedly self-centred, selfish. For ever digging over the garden of his soul—to see how his garden grew.

> "*Aubrey, Aubrey, face like a strawberry,*
> *How does your Garden grow?*
> *With Merry Hell's bells and drunken spells*
> *And concubines all in a row.*"

He had degenerated. Degenerated into a pleasure-seeker, a self-indulgent wallower, a woman's well-rewarded lap-haunting lap-dog.

And that brought to the surface another fly in the ointment of his lovely fleshly "happiness."

A fly in the ointment, or a mammoth—a damned great dinosaur?

Stacey!

Could it be possible that this dreadful creature that from time to time raised its head above the surface of the precious ointment, and leered at him, bore a look of his once dear friend, Stacey Burlestone, the man who had saved him and made him?

God, *how* he had deteriorated in the past year or

two, if he were really jealous of Stacey Burlestone; yes —even if it were possible that the faintest breath of suggestion of jealousy could for one moment float like a foul exhalation above the precious ointment of his happiness. How he had deteriorated if he were jealous of Stacey!

Jealous of Stacey Burlestone? Good Lord, what next?

Of course, the scores of little flies in the ointment were nothing but—well—little flies. One couldn't be seriously jealous of a pansy like Clarence Wellingson; couldn't be jealous of a queer wild ruffian like Tim O'Leary; couldn't be jealous of a burly red bear like Hennessy Wogan; couldn't be jealous of a nice chap like Moresby Wallingford.

Why, Wallingford was married to one of the dearest women in India.

They weren't really flies in the ointment at all.

Rotten thoughts of a putrid mind. Why couldn't he keep his mind like his body, that still fairly-glorious piece of almost perfect mechanism, perfectly controlled.

But then, one can't control one's thoughts.

Oh, to Hell with one's thoughts. . . .

Let him be thankful to God for the still incomparable strength in which he still revelled; and for the incomparable woman whom he loved and with whom he was so happy.

Of course he loved her.

Of course he was happy.

Did Stacey Burlestone love her, and was he, therefore, unhappy?

Did she love Stacey Burlestone?

Oh, God, what was he thinking now? He deserved to lose her, to lose her love, to lose his friend.

Shame on him for a hulking mass of . . . deterioration, mental and moral. Not really serious physical deterioration yet, thank God, in spite of a few bad habits that he absolutely must give up. He must smoke far less and stop drinking between meals.

Why had he ever started smoking and drinking?

Daphne had wanted him to smoke because she did; and to join her in a cocktail or sherry-and-bitters before lunch and dinner, and in a bottle of wine at meals. She had said it seemed so un-companionable if he never had a cigarette when she did, and if he never joined her in an *aperitif* or a liqueur. She said it made him seem more human if he smoked and drank. Heaven knew he was human enough; but, of course, it did look priggish and disapproving, to remain a rigid total abstainer and non-smoker when one's wife smoked and enjoyed her drinks.

Anyhow, he'd be a low cad to blame Daphne for the fact that he now certainly smoked too much and probably drank more than was good for him. He must put the brake on, if he wanted to remain what they called him, "The Strongest Man in the Army."

Yes, that was one thing he could do, and would do; must do. It had been easy enough to resign his Heavy-weight Championship and refuse ever to box again: but there was no earthly reason why he shouldn't continue to beat, in private, and for his own satisfaction and amusement, all weight-lifting records and similar feats of strength, as they were achieved and published by the professionals.

No-one knew it, but he could still do anything that any music-hall Strong Man could do—and a little more. Sometimes a good deal more. Anyway, thank Heaven that he was due for furlough next year.

They'd go straight to Switzerland, as they both loved that country—summer or winter. Say June and July. Then they'd have some yachting; glorious sun and air. Then Scotland; long tramps over the moors, a bit of grouse-shooting, and he'd take her stalking and see her shoot her first stag.

After that? Keep away from London. Might do some sun-bathing on the Riviera and then up to Switzerland again for the Winter Sports. He'd teach her to ski.

They'd have a glorious leave, and he'd pull himself together, and come back at the end of it as hard and fit as he'd been—well—before his marriage.

They'd be coming back to a different station, too,

Yusufabad—and he'd be rid of all these little flies in the ointment. Clarence the Pansy, Hennessy Wogan, Moresby Wallingford, and all the rest of them. And it would be beyond even the skill and nerve and brass of Tim O'Leary to get himself transferred from Quetawur to Yusufabad, as he had done from Poona to Quetawur.

And rid of Stacey Burlestone, too.

Heaven help him and forgive him—*what was he saying?* What on earth would he say next? Was he actually rejoicing that he'd be parting from his best friend? Really his only friend—or at any rate, the only man he really loved, or ever had loved.

Rid of Stacey?

What had he come to—that he could harbour such a thought as that?

CHAPTER XIV

Switzerland!

To think that Switzerland and India could exist in the same world! All this glorious air, this ineffable sense of well-being, freedom, health. He'd felt a different man from the day when he had first set foot upon the mountains.

No flies in the precious ointment of his "happiness" here.

For of course it was by the purest chance and coincidence that Stacey had turned up at their Hotel. Purest chance and coincidence, of course. It wouldn't be for very long, either.

What a mean jealous swine he was becoming, to feel anything but pleasure at seeing dear old Stacey again. And if it had given Daphne pleasure, as obviously it had, what else mattered?

Besides, it gave him pleasure to see Stacey again. Of course it did.

Anyhow, he'd walk the old beggar off his feet while he was staying in the same Hotel. Since he was for ever bucking about his wonderful health nowadays, he should put it to the proof. He'd make him do a climb like this every morning while he was with them.

Well, it was splendid to see him in such fine fettle and so hale and hearty again, sound in wind and limb.

Nevertheless, he'd try his wind and limb for *him* before he pushed off somewhere else: by Jove he would.

*   *   *   *   *

"There's the Hotel," said Stacey Burlestone, suddenly halting and pointing down into the valley which, as they rounded a great rock, came into view some three thousand feet below them.

"Wonder if that white speck on the verandah is

Daphne?

"Got your glasses?" he added, looking over his shoulder to Aubrey Easterwood, following a pace or two behind him.

"Yes, here you are," replied Easterwood, taking his field-glasses from their case and handing them to his friend.

"Yes, that's she," said Burlestone, "having a squint up through the telescope. She'll see us better still round the next corner. If I remember rightly, the path runs nearer to the edge."

"Yes," agreed Easterwood. "That nasty bit. She'll enjoy an uninterrupted view of us from head to foot just there."

"Yes," said Burlestone, "from our bowler 'ats to our 'obnail boots."

And he strode on.

The "nasty bit" was rather nasty. The narrow path between high rock and cliff edge sloped slightly downward and was of uncovered stone. Also damp. And, as Burlestone, whistling merrily, and with quickened pace, strode across it, his iron-shod boots slipped, his feet shot out from under him, he fell heavily, and, as Easterwood sprang to his rescue, rolled downwards, slid, slithered, in spite of the presence of mind with which he flung out arms and legs as widely as he could, and did his best with digging heels and clutching hands, to hinder his swift sliding descent toward the edge.

Easterwood's stooping grab caused him also to lose his footing and his balance, and, within a couple of seconds of Burlestone's slip, the pair of them slid down the short slope and over the edge of the precipice. Over the edge of the precipice—and on to a narrow outward sloping ledge, six feet below.

Striking this with his back, and vainly snatching for support, Burlestone went over the edge.

Following on to it in the same second, but on his face, Aubrey Easterwood with his right hand seized Burlestone's wrist and, with his left, grasped the top of a small jagged upstanding ridge of stone, out-cropping, or firmly embedded between the ledge and the precipice.

For one long lasting terrible fraction of a second, the issue was in doubt, their equilibrium was unstable, there was a soul-sickening sense of arm-stretching, of shoulder-breaking, of slipping, giving, and then— equipoise and a brief stability.

The mighty muscles, the iron grip of the Strongest Man in the World triumphed, held firm, made good; and Stacey Burlestone dangled over a three thousand foot drop, held at the wrist by Aubrey Easterwood, himself partly overlapping the edge of the sloping shelf, his left hand and fore-arm hooked about the jagged tooth of upward-jutting rock.

Which would give first, he wondered, as he drew a deep breath? The hand that gripped his friend's wrist, the arm and hand that grasped the stone, or the stone itself?

How long could he hold on?

Was the stone a detached fragment, or part of the living rock? How long would it stand fast?

How long, O Lord, how long?

For a few seconds Aubrey Easterwood lay still, his face against the stone, breathing deeply. The wrench had been tremendous; the shock and uncertainty, as to whether even momentary safety had been achieved, of the kind that might well cause one to tremble.

Slowly he raised his face from the stone and looked over the edge.

Stacey's bare head was bent back, his face turned upward, his eyes tightly closed.

Sensible chap. One glance into those awful depths inclined one to turn faint. He must not look down again.

Easterwood rested his head upon the ledge.

What next?

How long could this last? The tooth of rock was hurting the inner side of his left arm, his right arm felt as though it were being pulled from the shoulder-bone.

Good God! Was Daphne watching through the telescope? Would she watch until Burlestone . . . ?

She'd faint before that happened.

No, she must already be shouting for help, for guides to rush out and climb as they'd never climbed before.

Could he hold on while the swiftest of mountaineers climbed three thousand feet?

Well, was he not the strongest man in the world?

And if they arrived in time, could they get Burlestone up?

Yes, if they had the sense to bring a rope. They could swing a slip-knot under him, bring it up beneath his arms, and haul him up to the path above.

Could he hold him till they came?

Lord, what a feat of strength that would be! There'd be some point in having strength that could do that.

Was it for this that he'd worked and laboured and trained for all those years—to this end, that he might save the life of his friend?

How strong he felt, now he'd settled down to it, got both his grips firm, and realized that he had a chance, that his position was secure, that it was simply a matter of sheer strength.

Thank God that he was "The Strongest Man in the World," now that Stacey's life depended on the might of his good right arm.

"Aubrey. . . . Let go. . . . I can't stand this any longer."

Easterwood looked over the edge. Stacey had one foot poised precariously on a jutting stone. Such a poor little stone.

"You can stand it as long as I can, Stacey. Keep up your heart, old chap. I can hang on for a week."

And Aubrey Easterwood achieved a sound that resembled a laugh.

"Aubrey! Let go! . . . It's only prolonging the agony. . . . It can only be a matter of minutes. . . . Let go. I shall only pull you over."

"I shan't let go . . . until I must."

"Don't torture me, Aubrey. . . . Let go. . . . Your left hand'll give, and we shall both fall. . . . Let me go."

"I shan't. . . . I won't. . . . I can't. . . ."

Easterwood again rested his head upon the ledge.

"Aubrey! Quick!"

Easterwood raised his head and looked over the ledge, into the upturned face of his friend. . . . No, he mustn't look downwards. Those dreadful depths. Again he closed his eyes.

"Aubrey! Quick! I'm about to die, and I've got to say something. I can't die with this on my mind."

"Oh, shut up. Keep still—and keep quiet."

"Listen, Aubrey; and then let go."

"Shut *up*, will you!"

"Daphne and I . . ."

Involuntarily tightening his grip, Easterwood opened his eyes and looked into those of Burlestone.

"*What?*" he whispered hoarsely.

"It's true. . . . *I've been her lover*. . . . For years. . . . Before you married her. In Mackleworth's time. It began just after she came to Quetawur. *Now* will you let go?"

"*What?* No! No! Stacey, *no*! Not—you and Daphne. . . . *You*, Stacey?"

"Yes, let go. Don't torture me any longer. Let go."

Again Easterwood closed his eyes and laid his face against the rock.

Had he been struck a paralysing blow that numbed his body from head to foot?

No, it was only the intolerable ache of arms and shoulders.

Had his mind, his soul, his brain, received a blow that paralysed them so that he could neither think nor feel nor understand . . . nor realize . . . ?

No. For a fearful flood of raging wrath was rising up within his soul; a murderous hatred of this false friend, this thief for whom he himself was suffering that he might be saved, this cur for whom he was risking his life.

"Let go! Let go! I've confessed. Let me die. Quickly.

Now," cried Stacey Burlestone.

The cur was whining . . . crying . . . yelping. . . .

And a convulsive jerking added to the strain of the dead weight upon his arm.

And, by God, he'd let him go. He'd drop him. He'd watch his body turning and turning and turning until it was smashed upon the rocks, three thousand feet below.

The *Judas!*

Smashed and burst asunder, as did the body of Judas Iscariot.

He had but to open his hand. Open his hand—*so.*

And there he went. Look! Look! Turning, turning in mid-air.

Was he suffering as he fell? Was he conscious? Did he feel? Had he some taste of the agony that . . . ?

Crash! . . . Audible for miles . . . surely.

She would hear it, there in the Hotel. Would she ever forget the sound? And the sight? For she was watching, watching, seeing his body turning and turning. She was seeing it all—and serve her right.

Easterwood opened his eyes.

No. He was still holding him. He was not a murderer yet. Not just yet.

Murderer!

If, deliberately, he now opened his hand, he would be a murderer. For the remainder of his days he would walk the earth with the brand of Cain upon his brow.

But none would ever know that he had let go before he must.

None would ever know. Nobody could possibly know.

But he would know. Know and remember and think, think of it always.

Murderer!

But that was nonsense. It was an accident. It was pure accident that had brought Burlestone where he was. He had done his best to avert it; to save him. He had imperilled his own life.

Suppose his left hand, gripping the rock, should fail before his right. He'd be pulled over to his death as Burlestone said, unless he let go in time.

Well then, he must leave go in time. Why should he die because this man was the falsest friend, the most treacherous cur, the meanest, basest, dirtiest scoundrel on God's earth? His *friend*! Why should he die for him?

No. When he found that his left hand was losing its hold upon the rock, he'd relax his right-hand grip, and let this dog drop to his dreadful death.

No-one could ask more of a man than that; ask more than that he should risk his life to save his friend. And here he was, most dangerously risking his life to save his enemy, the man who had done him the most grievous wrong that one man could do another. His friend!

"Let go! Let go, Easterwood," cried Stacey Burlestone.

Again Aubrey Easterwood moved his head an inch or two, opened his eyes and looked into those of Stacey Burlestone.

"*I'm going to!*" he said. "I'm going to hold you here a little longer. Perhaps a good deal longer. You're going to suffer before you die. You're going to suffer nearly as badly as I am suffering now. You . . . you . . . There's nothing I *can* call you, you false-faced, treacherous cheat . . . thief, liar, hypocrite. You sneaking Judas. Oh, I'm going to drop you all-right."

"Leave go then! Leave go, Aubrey. Quick."

"Oh, I'll leave go all-right; but not yet awhile. I'm going to perform a feat of strength, Stacey Burlestone. I'm going to do what only the strongest man in the world could do. . . . It must have been to this end that I made myself so strong."

And Aubrey Easterwood laughed. A dreadful sound.

"I'm going to perform an astounding feat of strength. I'm going to hold you here until help does come. Until they come with a rope. Until they've lowered the bight of it. Until it touches you. Until it is almost in position. Until you are *almost* saved. And then, then—just in time, just in time to be too late, Stacey Burlestone, *I'm going to drop you.*"

And he would be a murderer. For the rest of his days, he would see his friend's face—every night of his life. Every time he laid him down to sleep he would live this intolerable nightmare through again.

No, he could not commit murder. He simply could not do it. The only hope was that his cursed strength would fail. He must hold on to the uttermost end of the last possible second; and Stacey Burlestone must not fall because Aubrey Easterwood intentionally let go of him. Burlestone must fall because Aubrey Easterwood's strength had failed at last. He must have nothing with which to reproach himself, or he could not face life thereafter.

But how could he face life, whether he committed this murder or not? How could he face life, knowing that Daphne was—what she was?

Well, he must face it.

After all, he was man and a soldier. He must tell her that he knew of their conduct—through Burlestone's dying confession and . . .

Good God! Suppose it *were* love. Suppose Burlestone loved her as he himself had loved her. Suppose she loved Stacey Burlestone even as he himself once loved her.

"Burlestone," he cried with parched tongue and cracking lips, "do you love Daphne?"

"With all my heart and soul," replied Burlestone, "and let those be my last words. I'll say it again, and I'll never speak again. For God's sake, let me fall when I've spoken for the last time. . . . *I love and adore and worship Daphne.*"

Aubrey Easterwood again sought relief for the aching muscles of his neck by resting his face upon the rock.

He really loved her, did he? Loved her so that he could declare it at a moment like that. Declare it with his dying breath.

Well, let it be his dying breath, curse him and damn him.

Let it *be* his last breath.

Were his muscles too stiff for him to be able to open his hand? And was it not just Fate's own dirty trick that, in grabbing the wrist of his dear faithful friend, he had seized him round the coat-cuff? Had he got him by the bare wrist, his hand and that wrist would, by now, have been so slippery with sweat, that strength would have been of no avail. But with that wrapping of rough tweed between hand and wrist there was no fear of slipping.

No, there would be no slipping and, unless deliberately he let go, his cursed strength, his damnable fatal strength would hold the dog for minutes yet.

For minutes? For hours.

No hope of any slipping. . . . He must leave go deliberately.

Murder. . . .

Perhaps his hand and arm were too stiff for him to relax the muscles and leave go. . . .

Ah . . . not so. Not too stiff. He had complete control of them. Splendid!

"*Go.* . . ."

"There, you dog! There! How do you like the pain and agony of falling? Horror like jagged spears of ice thrust through your heart? How d'you like torture? . . . Are you conscious; are you thinking while you fall; are you waiting for the dreadful crash? Do you see the whole of your life passing before your eyes? Do you realize that your sin has found you out . . . because you weren't stout enough criminal to conceal it, although you were cur enough to commit it?

"And do you realize, as you fall, that you've told about the woman; eased your own dirty soul by confession; included her in it; accused her? Do you, you dog, as you fall and fall?

"You are not turning and turning and turning in the air as I thought before, when I didn't drop you. You're falling like a plummet, like a stone.

"Straight, straight, straight as a die, to the death that is too good for you.

"And now I'll see you crash; smashed . . . dashed to pieces and . . .

"Oh God, I am a murderer!"

Aubrey Easterwood looked over the edge—into Stacey Burlestone's eyes.

"Drop me, Aubrey. Make an end," said Stacey Burlestone. "Forget the wrong I've done you, and think of any . . . any . . . decent thing I may have done, the good times we've had together, our friendship."

"*Friendship!*" shouted Aubrey Easterwood in a whisper, and again laughed—horribly.

"Aubrey, let go. Why should we both die? If your other arm goes before this one, nothing can save you."

"Aren't you thoughtful for my safety? Aren't you the dear true friend?" was the reply. "Practically saving my life, aren't you? Splendid fellow."

"Aubrey, let go. You wouldn't torture a dog like this."

"No, I wouldn't. Dogs don't commit ad . . . Oh, Christ! I can't say . . ."

And his face fell forward on to the stone.

"Drop me, Aubrey, if you've one spark of humanity."

"Why don't you struggle, you dog, so that I can't hold you? Why don't you twist and turn?"

"Because I don't want to pull you over."

Another bitter, ugly, cruel laugh.

"The ever faithful friend! The love passing the love of woman. 'Greater love hath no man than this, that he lay down his life for his friend.' Wouldn't shorten your own torture by a second, would you, *for fear you pulled me over*? You rotten, hypocritical swine. Kick and struggle, you dog, so that I can't hold you. Don't make your dear friend a murderer. Struggle out of his grip yourself. Go on—struggle. . . . Struggle so that I *can't* hold you. . . ."

Beggars' Horses

"Aubrey, Aubrey, have mercy. Leave go. Leave go before your other arm gives."

"Ha . . . ha . . . ha . . . ha . . . !

"Think of something else," said Easterwood, the spasm of semi-hysterical laughter conquered.

"Listen then," croaked the voice from below. "Daphne loves me as much as I love Daphne. We've fooled you. Fooled you before your wedding and after your wedding. You are our fool, Aubrey Easterwood. You are Daphne's fool. If she's watching now, she is praying that I'm saved and you are killed. She's mine. She has been mine a hundred times."

Then Aubrey Easterwood endeavoured to moisten dry lips.

"She has, eh? Well, she won't be yours again, dear friend. Good-bye. God damn you!"

*   *   *   *   *

And so he was a murderer, was he? A murderer who never could be brought to justice.

Unless he gave himself up.

People did do that.

Some great French detective had written that the murderer's most dangerous pursuer was himself—his own conscience. And if he had no conscience, something drove him to "haunt the scene of his crime," drove him constantly to fear that his fine security was false security. Drove him constantly to fear that his Paradise of safety was a fool's paradise. Perhaps somebody knew. Probably there was a God who knew. Certainly he himself knew. Sooner or later he must confess or go mad. Go mad or confess. Leap up in the night shouting,

"I didn't do it! . . ." to hear a voice reply,

"Huh? Who said you did? Didn't do what?"

"Didn't commit a murder."

"Didn't murder whom?"

And out would slip the name.

That could not happen to him, though. It could not, possibly, because, even if he walked into the nearest

Police Station, gave himself up, and swore an affidavit that he'd murdered Captain Stacey Burlestone, he couldn't prove that he had.

On the contrary. She was watching through the telescope and would testify that he'd risked his life to save him; that he'd held on to him, supported him by sheer strength, for minutes, hours, days, weeks, months, years, centuries. . . .

God, he was going mad now, now, now—and no wonder.

But would she come forward to testify in his favour? Was it not more probable that she would rise up and testify against him; swear that she'd seen him thrust his friend from the path above? That, walking behind him, he had suddenly pushed him violently sideways, and sent him hurtling to his death?

A woman who would do what she had done, would be capable of anything.

She had murdered his soul; and, beside that, the murder of his body would be nothing.

Well, he was a murderer. Let her say she'd seen him commit the murder; for, deliberately releasing his hold, while yet he had the strength to maintain it, was plain—murder.

Murder most foul.

Well, he must get to his feet somehow, or rather to his hands and knees, and painfully crawl back to the path.

In a safe place he would lie and relax and rest, recover his strength.

And then take up the business of life again, some-how, if he could.

Yes, it was time he moved, while he yet had the strength to do so.

Why wouldn't his right arm come up to the ledge? Too numbed? Dead?

What was holding it so stiff and straight?

"Aubrey! Leave go! . . . Aren't you a man at all? Haven't you the self-respect, the decency, the guts, to avenge yourself; to pay me out, to punish me, to even the score? . . . Come, Aubrey. I've smashed your life. Now smash me. Be a man, you weakling, you coward. Be a man and—clean the slate. . . . Go on."

So he had not done it?

Thank God he was not a murderer! Thank God!

That had been a terrible minute.

What an incredible, ineffable relief.

His strong hands were clean. His strong soul was unburdened, untainted.

Strong! The strongest man on earth. Well, he had made Strength his god, and his god had brought him to this, for, without it, he would have been unable to hold Stacey Burlestone for more than a few seconds.

Without it, Daphne would still be Mrs. Mackleworth, for he would not have caused the death of her husband.

Well, in training his body to this strength, he had inevitably trained his mind, his soul, his character, his spirit, his essential inward self, to strength, as well.

Oh, to Hell with his "inward soul!"

Damned cant. This creeping reptile had stolen Daphne's love. Had fouled his home . . . wrecked and ruined his life. How could he carry on, now? How could he face life, after this? How could he ever again trust man or woman, have the slightest faith in any fellow creature?

This filthy, bestial, cheating thief deserved to die. Then let him die—for Fate had placed him where he could be killed without the shadow of suspicion attaching to his slayer. It was the hand of Fate. Fate had willed it so. Fate alone had brought about this situation, and given him his chance of revenge. No, not mere revenge, but just punishment. Punishment for Burlestone the adulterer and for Daphne the harlot. For Daphne who was watching . . . watching. . . . Let her suffer through her lover—while her lover suffered for his sin. It was punishment, not vengeance. It was Justice. Yes, righteous, fair, poetic Justice—that he should die and the woman, his fellow-sinner and lover, watch him die.

Justice!

Also it was—murder.

Having retained the habit from early childhood, Aubrey Easterwood prayed.

"Let my strength fail, O Lord," he implored, "and save me from the sin of murder. I have made Strength my god and now I am punished for this idolatry. Help me to strive while I have the power, oh, God—but let my strength fail soon. Help me to weaken. Help me not to commit this sin. Help me to hold on, while hold I can—but, O Merciful Father, *take away my strength*, quickly. Let me be as a little child again, in all things, especially in strength. . . . Forgive me, oh, God, and weaken me . . . so that this man's death is not through sin of mine. Almighty Father, I will do my utmost to be strong—but do You make me to be weak; to tire and weaken. . . ."

What was he doing? Praying that God might slay Burlestone—encompass his death by weakening Aubrey Easterwood—so that no sin should burden that noble creature's precious soul?

Easterwood raised his head and laughed aloud.

Asking God to be so kind as to do Easterwood's little murders for him, because he wasn't man enough to do them for himself.

Wasn't that what his prayer amounted to? Hadn't he, in effect, said,

"Make this job easy for me, oh Lord. I don't like to kill my enemy deliberately—but I'd be greatly obliged if You'd just weaken my arm for me. Thank You—that's done the trick nicely, and nobody a penny the worse, except my enemy and his paramour."

Was he going mad?

This wouldn't do.

He must pull himself together.

He must be himself.

He must make an end.

§2

Once again he looked over the edge.

Burlestone was hanging limp, his chin upon his chest.

"Stacey, old chap," he said.

And with an effort Stacey Burlestone raised his face, white, terrible, his lips blue, his eyes protruding.

"Leave go, Aubrey," he whispered.

"Stacey, old chap. . . . One can't help loving."

"I know that!"

"Love is stronger than we are, Stacey. Now listen. I'm going to save you, Stacey . . . for her . . . and because you are my friend and I owe everything to you. . . . I've been selfish. . . . Now, old chap, watch the Strongest Man on Earth do a little feat of strength."

But Stacey Burlestone was unable to accept the invitation, for he was near the end of his tether, barely conscious. His eyes closed and his head fell sideways on his shoulder like that of a man who has been hanged. Suddenly the little stone under his foot loosened, and fell . . . down . . . down . . . down to the depths.

And Aubrey Easterwood began the performance of his last great feat of strength, a feat worthy of the Strongest Man in the World.

To and fro, like a pendulum, he began slowly to swing the dangling body of his friend.

Higher and higher it swung. Higher and higher, with a steady but slowly increasing swing, until, at each end of the arc, the body was horizontal.

And at last, with a shout of triumph and an inward jerk of his mighty right arm, Aubrey Easterwood swung his friend on to the sloping ledge, so that, rolling across him, Stacey Burlestone came to rest against the cliff face, and in so doing, thrust Aubrey Easterwood from his precarious place.

And as his numbed left arm, deeply marked by the stone's raised edge, failed him at last, and was forced from its hold, Aubrey Easterwood slowly slipped, slid

. . . lost his grip . . . lost all holds . . . lost everything—
and saved his soul.

CHAPTER XV

In her wide balcony sitting-room at the Hotel at Zermich, Stacey Burlestone faced Daphne Easterwood. "I marvel that you have not been ill," she said. "Nine people out of ten would have suffered from shock, nervous breakdown. I wonder it didn't kill you. An unspeakable, terrible experience. And you haven't seen a doctor or had so much as an extra hour in bed."

For so well-balanced a woman, always so quiet, restrained, poised and self-controlled, she was talking rather fast, was almost loquacious.

"You must have an iron constitution, Stacey."

"I enjoy perfect health. Absolutely perfect," said Stacey Burlestone. "But for the fact that I am so fit nowadays, I shouldn't have been trying to climb with Aubrey. . . . Health! . . . Nothing affects it. Nothing whatsoever."

"Well, if anything could have done so, surely this would. It nearly killed me, merely to watch. I was a nervous wreck by the time Conrad Weiler and his sons reached you."

"Did you watch the whole time?"

"Every second—after I had seen the guides start off. How those men ran! They went up that path like chamois."

"I wonder you could bear to look, Daphne; to watch and wait. Did you actually see Aubrey . . . go to his death?"

"Yes."

"And you didn't faint?"

"No. I had to . . . to . . . to hold on, to cling to consciousness with all my strength. I *had* to fight off faintness—to see what happened to you, Stacey."

"Happened to *me*?" cried Burlestone in utter amazement.

"To *you*, Stacey. Don't you understand?"

"No, I don't," replied Stacey Burlestone, and rose to

his feet. About his black-bruised wrist he could still feel the grip of Aubrey Easterwood's hand.

He had loved this woman, fallen in love with her at Quetawur when pretending to himself that he sought her out but for the purpose of saving Aubrey Easterwood from her.

He had never loved a woman before.

He would never love a woman again.

He loved her now, but if he had rightly interpreted the meaning of her words, the look in her eyes, the smile on her lips, the expression on her face—his love would die, here and now.

Daphne Easterwood got up from her chair, and confronted him.

Ignoring the hand that Burlestone raised, she placed hers upon his shoulders and looked him in the eyes, and unspeaking, unsmiling, took his head between her hands, drew it down and raised her lips to his.

Burlestone threw up his head, and before her arms could go about his neck, stepped back.

"*Daphne!*" he gasped.

"Stacey!"

The man and woman stood silent, gazing each into the eyes of the other; the woman beseeching, beguiling; her look, her pose, her attitude, her whole expression, her whole self—an offering; the man cold, withdrawn, repellent; his face hard, bitter, contemptuous; his look, the expression of his face and figure, his whole self—a refusal.

"Stacey, you love me. You know you love me. I know that you love me. Why pretend? We both know it. And now I'll tell you something that you don't know. I, too, love you. I love you—and I found it out too late. You are the only man whom I have ever loved, the only man I ever shall love. The words are banal but they are utter truth. You are the one love of my life. We love each other. Don't let's pretend . . . be conventional . . . be silly. We aren't children. You are not a boy, such as poor Aubrey was. You are a man of the world—and I am a woman of the world . . . Stacey . . ."

Burlestone withdrew further from this lovely pleading woman whom he had so deeply loved.

"Daphne, you have told me something. Will you listen while I tell you something?"

"Surely, Stacey."

"Sit down again in your chair, and let me tell you everything; for I believe, I hope, it will be the last time that I shall tell you anything at all.

"Aubrey Easterwood was the noblest soul I ever knew. One of the noblest on this earth. The sort of man who never thought of 'doing good'—but did it all the time. Made the world better for his being in it. Made everyone the better for knowing him . . . except you, Daphne. He fell in love with you, as scores of other men have done, and his love was very beautiful, a fine and noble and glorious thing. It was utterly selfless and pure. His love was—lovely. And you knew it, Daphne; you traded on it; and you trapped him. He didn't marry you—you married him. It was his chivalrous wrath against Mackleworth that put such strength into the blow with which he killed him."

Daphne Easterwood wiped her lips, lips which grew thinner and more compressed as she watched the speaker with eyes that narrowed and hardened as the brows above them contracted.

"Do you know," went on Burlestone, "that when he came back from your bungalow to tell me that he was engaged, engaged to marry you, within days of your husband's death, he was filled with—*horror*. I told him so, and he denied it, angrily, hotly. We almost quarrelled. I did my very utmost to prevent his marrying you; and to this day I don't know how much there was of jealousy in my motive, how much there was of disinterested love for Aubrey. You said just now that I loved you. You were right. I did. I fought against it. I hated it. I hated you, Daphne, nearly as much as I loved you. Oh yes, I loved you all right, you *belle dame sans merci*; but I loved Aubrey Easterwood far better."

Daphne Easterwood shrugged shoulders and curled lips of contempt, her livid face a sneer.

"One of 'those,' eh? How very beastly," she observed

coolly.

Stacey Burlestone's stern face hardened.

"Beastly? It's you who are beastly. You're a beastly woman, Daphne. I loved Aubrey Easterwood as a brother, as a son. Literally with a love passing the love of woman. Passing your poor comprehension of love. My love for him was as 'beastly' as was David's for Jonathan. You can't defile his memory, though you defiled him."

"Thank you, Captain Burlestone. Always the complete gentleman in the grand manner, what? . . . Nearly finished?"

"No; not nearly. And you are going to hear all that I have got to say.

"Aubrey was filled with horror, though he did not realize it, and would never admit it, even to himself. You killed his love by offering yourself to him, by throwing yourself at his head, within days of Mackleworth's death—and Aubrey the man who had killed him and who was all but broken-hearted because he had done so. Of his courtesy and chivalry he married you—the fool. The noble fool. But you had killed his love—as you have killed mine. You . . ."

"Nothing of the chivalrous noble fool about you, Stacey Burlestone, eh?"

"No; nothing. I am a fool—but not that sort of fool. Aubrey was a romantic, and a throw-back to the 'knightly years.' He was sheerly purely good and fine and noble. . . . I'm not. But on the other hand, I'm not an utter swine and I'm not going to be turned into one, Circe."

"Always the little gentleman."

"I wonder if I'm wasting my time."

"You are wasting mine."

"I wonder if I am wasting breath in trying to do something for Aubrey's memory? In trying to make you see yourself as I see you, and as he refused to see you."

Daphne Easterwood yawned, tapping her mouth.

"Listen. Try to rise to the occasion. Try to show yourself—just for a few minutes—as worthy to be his widow. *Aubrey Easterwood gave his life to save mine*

because he thought I loved you and you loved me.
Because he thought we were—lovers."

"And why should he think that, pray?"

"Because I told him so."

The Mona Lisa smile which had reappeared on Mrs. Easterwood's face faded.

"You did *what?*"

"I told him that you and I were—lovers. That we had been lovers for years. Lovers when Mackleworth was your husband. Lovers before and after your marriage to Aubrey Easterwood. Lovers ever since."

Daphne Easterwood stared, uncomprehending, her pale face a frozen mask.

"Had you gone mad?" she asked.

"No. Only to the extent of thinking that I could anger a man like Aubrey Easterwood to the point of murderous wrath, to vengeance, to just punishment for a cur, a snake."

"What *was* your game?"

"My game! My 'game' was to make Aubrey let go of me before his strength failed and I pulled him over. Do you know, can you grasp, can you realize, that Aubrey Easterwood would never have let me fall, would never have released the grip of his right hand; and that the end would have come only when the strength of his left hand failed, and he could cling to that sharp piece of rock no longer? Aubrey never in his life left a man in the lurch. Aubrey would never have said, 'It's your death or mine—so naturally it's yours. . . . Good-bye.'

"I knew that, although he was one of the strongest men alive, he could not hold on until help came. No human being could do it. And I knew that Aubrey would go with me if I went, would die if I died, would never, never let go. Not while he was Aubrey Easterwood.

"So, in my folly, I tried to change him. I tried to turn him into a righteously indignant mass of jealousy and rage. Tried, as I have said, to rouse murderous wrath in Aubrey Easterwood—and failed. As I might have known I should fail. I killed him. I killed him as surely as he killed Colin Mackleworth. And you offer yourself to *me*—as you offered yourself to him."

Daphne Easterwood's white face was almost plain. "You killed him?"

"Yes. Instead of so enraging him that he let me fall —as any other man would have done in the circumstances—he used the last of his colossal strength to swing me up on to the ledge—as you saw—knowing that my falling against the rock above him and beside him would surely dislodge him from the sloping ledge. . . . He went to his death because he no longer wished to live, after what he'd learned about you and about me. And I believe, I feel, I *know*, in the inmost depths of my soul, that he wished you and me to be happy. Happy, Circe! Do you hear?"

"But . . . you liar! You foul poisonous liar! You abominable liar!"

"Yes, I was a liar, an abominable liar, in telling him that you and I were lovers. But I told him those lies believing—or at least hoping—that they would cause my death and save his life."

"You filthy liar, to say that you and I had . . . Oh, you upright honourable gentleman! You'd use a woman's name, her reputation, in order to . . ."

"Her *reputation*, Circe! . . . I lied in connecting my name with yours, but . . . *your name*! Your reputation! Your honour and honesty! Why—what of Moresby Wallingford? Wasn't he your lover, and didn't every decent person in Quetawur hope that Mrs. Moresby Wallingford would never find out?

"What of Tim O'Leary? Wasn't he your lover? And wasn't there an awful scandal when Mackleworth thrashed him?

"What of Hennessy Wogan? Wasn't he your lover? Didn't you run the risk of wrecking and ruining Aubrey's life by carrying on with Hennessy Wogan after you'd married Aubrey?

"What of Clarence Wellingson? Wasn't he your lover? And weren't there a dozen others? Only *you* know how many.

"Yes, I lied about you, Circe—but only by substituting my own name for that of a score of men."

"And to save your own precious life," sneered Mrs. Easterwood, through scarce-opened lips.

"Am I wasting my time? Wasting my breath? Beating the air? I told you, and I tell you again, it was to save Aubrey's life—truly precious to me."

"So it *was* pure selfishness on your part. You wanted to save his life because it was so precious to you, eh?"

"Oh, purely selfish," replied Stacey Burlestone coldly, "so selfish that I was trying to make him drop me."

"And did you realize, noble hero, what you were doing to Aubrey Easterwood—not to mention the little matter of a mere woman? Suppose you'd been right, and Aubrey had deliberately let you fall—as I wish to God he had—what would his life have been, afterwards? What about his happiness, knowing that his wife was your lover—your leavings? Did you think of that?"

"I did. I did think of it. I did realize what I was doing, and I hoped and prayed that he'd believe me and, believing me, would save himself and kill me—and cast you off. Cast you off, and escape from your evil influence, the influence that was beginning to make even Aubrey Easterwood deteriorate. And when I say cast you off, I don't mean that I supposed he'd come down here and accuse you and make a scene—as another man would have done. I hoped and believed he would simply have refused to live with you any more. I hoped he'd just have left you."

"And lived happy ever afterwards, do you think?"

"No, lived unhappy for a long time afterwards. But he would have recovered. It would have gone far to kill his faith in human nature—but it would have gone further still to bring him back to what he was before you—took him over."

"Yes, there you are! There it is! 'Took him from you,' you mean. Pure selfishness."

"Call it what you like. I tried to make Aubrey kill me. No, I don't put it like that. Aubrey would never kill anybody. I tried to make him slacken his incredible effort to save me, and I told him lies about you. But those lies were not one-tenth of the truth. Very well. Now perhaps you understand why I don't love you. Why, not being Aubrey Easterwood, I cannot accept your love."

Daphne Easterwood sprang from her chair.

"Oh, *stop* it! Stop it, Stacey! Kiss me! Kiss me! . . . What does it matter? What does anything matter, when we love each other so? I love you, Stacey. I love you, love you, *love* you. . . . And you love me. You do love me. . . . Kiss me, Stacey."

"I'd sooner kiss a poisonous serpent," replied Stacey Burlestone, rising to his feet.

As he strode from the room he turned, his hand upon the door-knob.

"I love you? I did love you, Daphne—and I'm ashamed of it. I thank God I have never told you that I loved you, until to-day. And I hope I shall never see you nor hear of you again."

As the door closed behind him, Daphne Easterwood rose to her feet and stared at it.

"You'll see me again," she whispered. "You'll see me again, all right. You shall. I'll get even with you. You shall hear from me again, Stacey Burlestone. You shall love me again. Make love to me—and then I'll show you what hate can be, since you wouldn't have love. . . . How I could have loved you, Stacey.

"How I do love you, and, God, how I hate you!"

CHAPTER XVI

War . . .

Brigadier-General Sir Hubert Howe was a sick man, and commanded a brigade of sick men. His troops, both British and Native, were already tainted with malaria when they left India. Nor were they strangers to dysentery after an abnormally bad hot-weather season in a notoriously unhealthy Station.

And now, for weeks on end, they had been sitting tight in what must be one of the worst places in the whole world, a low-lying, jungle-enclosed, fever-haunted mangrove-swamp; a place in which the very rain was hot, and the stagnant atmosphere was more steam than air.

Men died like flies or lived like beasts—less fortunate than the other denizens of the swamp, in that it was not their natural habitat.

The doctors were at their wits' end and at their resources' end, having long ago exhausted their slender store of surgical and medical necessities. Medical comforts there had never been.

Across a table, of which the legs were tree-branches and the top was packing-case wood, the General faced his Brigade-Major, whose yellow face, sunken eyes and shaking hands showed how near he was to the end of his tether.

"Well, if it's really certain that the river can be forded there, and has been forded there, we must get busy at once. Stop that earth—or water—before the old fox uses it."

"Yes, Sir," agreed the Brigade-Major. "The K.A.R. people say he could march an army straight across. It's the only ford for a hundred miles—and there's no bridge anywhere, of course. Finding it was a good piece of Intelligence work."

"Quite. Well then, we must establish a strong post there immediately, this side of the river, and run out the field telephone. We must spare a couple of machine-guns."

"Yes, Sir. We shall have to. And some good men."

"And they'll probably be scuppered," said the General.

"What we want is a Company of the best mud-larks we can find, and a brace of the best British officers. Best from the health point of view, I mean," he added.

"Yes, Sir. I think the Gurkhas stand swamp conditions better than most."

"Well, the medical returns will show that, in statistics," replied the General.

"Yes, Sir. I suppose these conditions do approximate more to those of Nepal and the Terai than to those to which the Baluchis and Punjabis are accustomed. And certainly they strike me as being the most cheerful crowd. Among the Indian troops, anyway. The Northumberlands keep their tails up, of course, but there are thirty-seven per cent of the Battalion—er—horizontal."

"And sixty-three per cent more who ought to be," observed the General. "The whole lot ought to be in hospital. Well, let's say a hundred picked men from the Gurkhas. . . . And what about Officers. . . ? It's the devil, the way nobody's with their own men nowadays —what with casualties and transfers and special jobs. There isn't a double-company in the Brigade that's got a single Officer it had in India."

"No, Sir. As to health—there's one man who hasn't been off duty for a day, or had any truck with the R.A.M.C. ever since we left Bombay. Captain Burlestone."

"He's a good man, isn't he?" mused the General.

"Oh, a first-class officer, and with the special qualification for this job, that he's never sick or sorry. I was talking to him yesterday, and he told me that he enjoys absolutely perfect health. Hasn't had an hour's illness of any sort or kind for years."

"Born that way, I suppose," said the General, opening heavy-lidded eyes.

"No, Sir. He's had enteric and was a martyr to

malaria and dysentery once upon a time, he tells me."

"Salted, eh? Had it and done with it. Immune."

"Must be so. He's about the only man in this Brigade who hasn't got either malaria or dysentery or both."

"Well—stroke of luck he's with this Brigade. That's one. Who'd better go with him?"

"I suggest Captain Hennessy Wogan, Sir."

"Is he another bug-proof wonder?"

"No, I don't say that, but he's—cheerful. He's too damned cheerful for words. Known as Happy Geoff in his Mess."

"Bit of a Mark Tapley, eh?"

"That's it, Sir. Fellow's always laughing at something or nothing. Just the man to keep the Gurkhas merry and bright. They love him."

"Good officer?"

"Yes, Sir. Always been a bit wild and all that; but peace-time vices are apt to be war-time virtues."

"A wild Irishman, eh?"

"Yes, Sir. Tough, and a born scrapper."

"Right. That ought to make a good team, then."

"Those two, and a hundred men with the best health-record to date, and my old friend Subedar-Major Ghantu Rawat. . . . Yes, and Jemadar Pahalsing Gurung, and Jemadar Manjit Thapa. They couldn't have better Native Officers than those."

"No, Sir," agreed the Brigade-Major, hiding a smile. The General was himself an old Gurkha and had known these men from their recruit days as young riflemen.

§2

Fighting. . . .

For thirty-six hours the stockaded post, defended on one side by a swift, deep tributary of the main river and, on another, by unpassable, impenetrable jungle, had withstood the German fire, the fire of ten times the number of rifles that the full strength of the post could number, as well as that of two small field-guns.

There could be but one end to the affair, unless help soon came from the Brigade—wading its weary way through swamps and by narrow jungle-paths.

That must come quickly; for, like Caesar, the Gurkhas had already done enough for honour. Possibly more than enough, for of the hundred men, but thirty-two remained alive, and of the three Native Officers, but one.

Captain Stacey Burlestone and Captain Hennessy Wogan met beneath the improvised flag-staff in the middle of the post, during a lull in the almost constant rifle-fire.

"Well, old bird, still in the pink of condition! Faith, I wish I knew how the devil you do it," croaked Hennessy Wogan, a happy grin lighting his drawn, thin, yellow face. "You look like an advertisement for somebody's patent food, or a high explosive tonic. Begad, your face on a label would sell the worst Devonshire cider, for it's more like a rosy-cheeked apple than . . . faith, I dunno what."

Stacey Burlestone smiled.

"Yes, I enjoy perfect health," he said.

"It's a fact that ye do, Stacey, and keep up your weight, too. One'd think you got up in the night and ate double rations—half mine and the men's, too . . . Health, begob! I dunno how you do it."

"And I don't know how *you* do it, Geoff."

"Do what?"

"Keep smiling. You're a walking laugh, and your grin's worth a double-company. Anyone'd think you were happy."

"Faith, and so I am," laughed Hennessy Wogan. "Happy as the day is long."

"Well, you've a damn funny taste in amusement."

"*Chacun à son* guts, as the French say," grinned Hennessy Wogan. . . . "We're both blessed beyond the luck of ordinary men, Stacey, but, begob, 'tis a doubtful blessing we've each got. But for your health ye wouldn't be here to be killed in this stinking swamp. And but for my cheerfulness, I shouldn't be. We should live to fight another day—and get lots more fun out of this fine War. . . . Well, well—*morituri te salute ye*, as the Greeks or . . ."

The noise of a sudden terrific fusillade drowned his words. As it ceased, and was followed by orders bawled in German, and a mixture of cheers, shouts and howls, the two officers rushed to their respective posts on the southern and western walls of the stockade to meet the charge, the hand-to-hand assault that had come at last.

This was the end; for thirty-two men, Gurkhas though they be, cannot repulse the onslaught of hundreds, especially when, of those hundreds, a half are stalwart Europeans, seasoned, trained and fighting-fit; and the remainder are six-foot savages, strong, fierce and brave as lions, fighting in their own country in their own way and for their own object—loot.

Laying about him lustily with *sjambok* and boot, *Herr Ober-Leutenant* von Groener prevented the two wounded and helpless white officers from being butchered by the *askaris*, as every other living soul in the outpost was butchered.

What happened to such scum as the cannon-fodder was of no consequence, of no interest, to the *Herr Ober-Leutenant*, but English officers were *junkers*, and not to be slaughtered like the said cannon-fodder, the *canaille, der Pöbel*.

Besides, General von Lettow Vorbeck would be exceedingly angry if it came to his ears that wounded officers had been—well, murdered—by the Herr Ober-Leutenant's men.

§3

Captain Stacey Burlestone made a marvellous recovery. Never had the *Herr Doktor* known a gun-shot wound heal so amazingly quickly. He took great credit to himself for the fact that he had his patient up and about, and hobbling around on crutches, in what must have been positively record time. A feather in the good

Herr Doktor's cap; though, to himself, he admitted that the Englander must be endowed with a remarkable constitution, wonderful health, and extraordinarily pure blood. Why, he was a walking-case long before others, no worse wounded, could get off their beds, and, indeed, were scarcely out of the wood.

An astounding case of vitality, recuperative power, health, and iron constitution.

And the other Englander who was not an Englander at all, really, but an Irisher, was another interesting specimen. A prisoner of war, badly wounded—and happy as the day was long.

Nor was he of the type that is happy to be out of the fighting; happy because the war was over, so far as he was concerned. Unless the *Herr Doktor* was a far poorer psychologist than he thought, this was a fighting type, one of those who love fighting for its own sake, and are happiest when fighting. And yet here he was—absolutely happy.

A tough fellow that, and not afraid to speak his mind, even when in enemy hands and in the power of a man who could put him to death if he thought fit— which, of course, he never would do—with the prick of a needle or a "mistake" in the medicine. Why, the mad fellow had called him, the *Herr Doktor*, a dirty dog; and the *Herr Doktor* knew English far too well to be mistaken. He knew English—and he knew the Irish. He had practised in Dublin for years, following assiduously both his professions, that of Medicine and that of Secret Intelligence—until warmly invited by the authorities at Dublin Castle to go and practise in his own country.

It had been an interesting and instructive conversation that he had had with the happy officer:

"What I can't understand is why you, an Irishman, should be here, fighting for your hereditary enemies, oppressors, butchers of your compatriots from the days of Cromwell."

A laugh, happy if contemptuous.

"Sure now, *Doktor*, the wicked divils. Sassenachs. Wicked Saxons. You don't happen to be a Saxon yourself, *Doktor?* For I'm all for foightin' 'em."

"And wasn't this your chance of a lifetime; the chance of a Country's lifetime, to throw off the yoke of the invader?"

"Why, of course it was. And have a German one instead. A nice kind German invader—like the Belgians got, eh?"

"*Ach, der liebe Gott,* why talk nonsense? Didn't the Belgians choose to have us as enemies when we offered to be friends? We should have been Ireland's friend."

"Said the wolf to the lamb," laughed Hennessy Wogan.

"And if you were fools enough to think we should be bad friends to you, couldn't you at least have remained neutral? Why fight for the English? *Ach, du liebe Zeit,* that's what I can't understand. I know your folk-lore songs. Hark."

And in a beautiful tenor voice, the *Herr Doktor* actually sang,

> "'And what colour will be seen?'
> Says the Shan Van Voght.
> 'And what colour will be seen?'
> Says the Shan Van Voght.
> 'What colour should be seen
> Where our fathers' homes have been,
> But our own immortal Green!'
> Says the Shan Van Voght.
> 'Our own immortal Green,'
> Says the Shan Van Voght."

Hennessy Wogan solemnly beat time, as solemnly the *Herr Doktor* sang.

"And what of this:

> "'Then since the colour we must wear
> Is England's cruel red,
> 'Twill serve but to remind us of the blood that
>   has been shed;
> You may take the shamrock from your hat
> And cast it on the sod,

But never fear, 'twill take root there,
Tho' under foot 'tis trod.'

"And when war comes you forget your history, your traditions, your murdered patriots—and you fight for the English, fight against us who would have liberated you from them."

"Faith, man, what does it matter who ye foight, so long as you get some foightin'?" laughed Hennessy Wogan.

"Very well then, putting the argument even on that low ground and setting patriotism aside; if it doesn't matter whom you fight, why not fight the English oppressor? Why not fight against the English oppressor and for the German liberator?"

Hennessy Wogan laughed again.

"How you Germans love the little nations, *Doktor*, and how they love you! Belgium, Luxembourg, Schleswig, Holstein, Alsace, Lorraine, Serbia—all those little chaps. I don't know very much History, but I'm sure they love ye."

"And does Ireland love England, *Kapitan*? Does she hate Germany? Has Germany ever harmed Ireland? Or England done anything but harm Ireland from the days of Longbow, Earl of Pembroken?"

"Faith, 'tis you that knows the History, *Doktor*," laughed Wogan. "Now, in me ignorance, I'd have called him Strong-Arrow, Earl of Brokepen."

And once more Wogan guffawed.

"What matter how you call him? The thing is this. Your country has groaned under the iron heel of the jack-boot of John Bull."

"Or the john-boot of Jack Bull," murmured Hennessy Wogan. ". . . And now the hour has come when Ireland shall be free from the mountains to the sea, says the Shan Von Voghtheimer, eh?"

"Every man of honour . . ." began the doctor.

"Faith, I can't stand these 'men of honour,' . . ." interrupted Wogan.

". . . must strike a blow for his Vaterland. Now listen, *Kapitan*."

"I wouldn't miss a word, *Doktor*, for I find your conversation highly divertin'."

"Now listen. When you are feeling a bit stronger—and I will make it my business quickly to make you stronger, specially to feed you up . . ."

"Faith, I'm fed up already."

". . . and get you on your feet again, I will take you to see Major Kraut."

"'Twill be nice for him," smiled Hennessy Wogan.

"Yes, and for you. And you will tell the Major and his Intelligence Officer all the things they want to know about the—defences of Mombasa; the British Navy ships operating from there to Zanzibar; the steps taken for the protection of the Uganda railway; the strength of the Brigade based on Mombasa, and the British troops at Nairobi; the spirit of the Indian troops; the likelihood of reinforcements from South Africa; the strength and disposition of the Colonial forces, the Rhodesians and such; the number of guns; and all such things, including the real political situation in India, and why the second Indian Mutiny failed; and the truth about what happened at Singapore when the 5th Indian Light Infantry shot their Officers. All those things. If you can tell him all that and much more, you'll get very different treatment from what you will otherwise get as a prisoner of war. Why, the General might even set you free, give you an honourable and well-paid appointment, treat you as an ally and a friend, and as what you are by birth—an enemy of England. If you tell us . . ."

"I'll tell you one thing now, *Doktor* dear."

"Yes, yes? And what's that?"

"That you are a dirty dog; and that, savin' me good manners, I'd spit in y'r eye."

Yes, that was how the disappointing fool and *schweinhund* had come to call the *Herr Doktor* a dirty dog.

Well, perhaps the foully pestilential climate of Bulundi, the ever-increasing shortage of all necessary drugs and medicines—including the absolutely essential quinine—all such invalid food as milk, eggs, fresh vegetables, fresh meat, and everything that sick men should have, would make him change his tune.

The *Herr Gott in Himmel* knew that it was bad enough for the good German wounded, not to mention the other poor incapacitated wrecks that malaria and dysentery had made of strong men; and if the German Hospital itself was on short commons, and terribly ill-supplied with necessities, not to mention comforts, what could the English expect?

Yes, let him wait until he found he was surely dying for want of the antiseptics, dressings, drugs, medicines, brandy, broth, milk and such things that he could get by turning from an England-assisting renegade Irelander to an honourable Germany-assisting Irish patriot.

But this other man, this *Kapitan* Burlestone, was indeed a marvel and a credit to the *Herr Doktor*.

If he had failed with the Irelander as a diplomat, he had wonderfully succeeded with the Englander as a *Doktor*.

And the good *Herr Doktor* Kruller made something of a show of his star patient.

§4

An exchange—or an abandonment—of prisoners. . . .

Only those who have been prisoners have any conception of the horrors of being a prisoner, or of the ineffable joy of release; of the terrible rise and fall of the spirit, the fluctuations between the delirium of happiness and madness of despair, attendant upon the fluctuating hopes and fears as the possibility of release advances and retreats.

Bulundi was to be evacuated, and, unless negotiations for an exchange of wounded prisoners were successful, these would be left behind by the retreating German forces. The advancing British would enter Bulundi within a few hours or, at most, a few days, after the German evacuation.

Beggars' Horses

Meanwhile, the wounded would receive attention at the hands of German women, wives of planters on active service, and temporarily working as nurses attached to the German army.

These women would certainly receive good treatment from the English, and the German sick and wounded suffer no hardship. No additional hardship, *c'est à dire.*

The German General approved this arrangement, and had no intention of being hampered with unnecessary transport for wounded prisoners, or by the necessity of feeding useless German mouths.

Scarcely could there have been a happier band of men than the English prisoners-of-war in Bulundi, in spite of grievous sickness or incapacitating wounds.

Release; friends; English nurses, hospitals and doctors.

Not but what the Germans had treated them as well as could be expected, considering their own shortage of most of the necessities of life.

Release; transport to the railway; a hospital train; proper nursing; the peace, quiet and comfort of a real hospital in Nairobi or Mombasa.

A hospital ship; the sea; sea breezes after the hot stagnant air of this poisonous climate, like that of a combination of a sewer and a Turkish bath; sick leave to an Indian hill-station for convalescence and recuperation. Think of Simla, Darjeeling, Mussouri, Naini Tal, Mount Abu, Mahableshwar—after Bulundi. One's own people, the friendly little Clubs and Gymkanas.

Oh, the peace and rest and quiet. And afterwards, a good time, a real good time. A bust. And then—"Back to the Army again, Sergeant."

Release!

Why, most of them were as happy as Happy Geoff himself. Happy Geoff Wogan, whose high spirits nothing could damp.

Those who could hobble, hobbled the faster. Those who'd been unable to face bully-beef, army biscuit, maize and mealies, began to develop an appetite. Those who were dying began to take a hold upon life. They were all to be exchanged for German prisoners of war or, what was much more probable, left behind to fall into the hands of their friends.

That's what would happen, they decided; for why should the British General buy what he could get for nothing? He knew that the Germans must evacuate Bulundi, and he knew they couldn't take the wounded with them, whether German or British.

"Faith, 'twill be a good stroke of business," pointed out Hennessy Wogan, "for the old bhoy to leave all his own sick and wounded to be cared for by the British. He can't take the poor divils with him and he knows right well that they'll get the same treatment from our people as we'll get ourselves."

"Yes," agreed Stacey Burlestone, "the only difference being that it's they who'll be prisoners now. As you say—'poor devils.' . . . Well, on the whole I think I'd sooner be a German prisoner in English hands than an English prisoner in German hands."

"Sure, Stacey, me bhoy, and the German thinks the same thing, t'other way round."

And so it came about that the English sick and wounded in the Bulundi hospital, which consisted of native huts and ragged tents, ceased to be prisoners of war, and, in due course, found themselves in real hospitals.

All save one, and the heart and spirit of that one were almost broken as he said good-bye to his friends and to the man whom circumstances had made his more especial friend—Captain Hennessy Wogan.

For the good *Herr Doktor* Kruller could not bear to part with his prize patient, the man whom he had restored to health so swiftly and so completely.

"I'm sorry, *Herr Kapitan*," said he to Stacey Burlestone, "but you remain with us. I can't conscientiously regard you as coming into the category of sick or incapacitated wounded prisoners of war. Wounded you have been; but sick, never. And you are now as strong and fit and healthy as any man in your army or ours. You will come with me and, if you are wise, will make yourself useful. You will be able to help me in many ways. By the time the war is over you will be almost a qualified hospital-assistant. Yes, you shall stay with me and I shall show you to other doctors who will be greatly interested in my wonderful feat of surgery. Also your food, quarters, treatment, conditions of life generally, will be better if you choose to make yourself useful."

Though, presumably, sorry to say good-bye to Burlestone, there was no perceptible diminution in Hennessy Wogan's happiness.

"Well, well," he said philosophically. "Ye can't have it both ways, Stacey. You've got the perfect health you boasted about—and I hope you'll keep it. You'll need it."

That night Burlestone, having refused his parole, marched out of Bulundi, carefully guarded.

As with heavy feet and heavier heart, he turned his back upon all hopes of distinction, success, promotion, and upon all those lesser lovely things that had seemed to be within his reach, all the things of which he had dreamed, he fought with the devil of Despair.

Suddenly, to the surprise of the worthy *feld-webel* who marched beside him, he laughed aloud.

"What a priceless gift is perfect health, my friend," he observed to the astonished non-commissioned officer.

"But for that I shouldn't now be enjoying your society.

"Perfect health!"

And Stacey Burlestone laughed again.

CHAPTER XVII

As Hennessy Wogan watched his friend Stacey Burlestone march off into the blue, into German East Africa, a prisoner of war "for the duration," the happy smile faded not from his lean, sickly-looking, but ever-cheerful countenance.

Poor old Stacey—he *was* down in the dumps. But Happy Geoff Wogan—not he! He was happy. And if he were marching off with the Huns as Stacey was, he'd still be happy. Happy, happy, happy. . . .

From his youth up; from boyhood; from babyhood, in fact, Geoffrey Hennessy Wogan had, like so many of his Southern Irish compatriots, been a rebel.

A born rebel, he had always been against the government of his nurse, his governess, his mother, his father, his masters and pastors, and all those set in authority over him. And the way of the rebel, like the way of the transgressor, is hard. In consequence of his chronic state of revolt against the authority of whatever powers might be, Wogan's childhood had been an unhappy one, his boyhood more unhappy, his youth and young manhood unhappier still.

His father, Colonel Patrick Hennessy Wogan, having been killed by Dervish spearmen in a broken British square on the banks of the Nile, his mother promptly married again; and married a hard-drinking, hard-riding, fox-hunting squire who detested his stepson, lashed him perpetually with his biting tongue, and frequently with his less biting whip. Colonel Wogan's widow, who had detested her first husband, frankly disliked his son who so resembled him, cast oil on the troubled fires of her second husband's, and young Geoffrey's, temper, and made them blaze the more fiercely.

It is a moot point whether the boy was unhappier at home or at school, where, although he had an admiring loyal following of fellow rebels, rogues, and ruffians, he was popular neither with masters, prefects, nor his seniors generally.

At Sandhurst he was in constant hot water and, more than once, in danger of expulsion, his crimes being insubordination, defiance of authority, and the exercise of an undoubted skill, ingenuity and tenacity in law-breaking—for the sake of breaking a law because it was one.

Both in his British Regiment and the Indian Regiment to which he was transferred, his career was a series of "crimes"; and he lived dangerously in a chronic condition of trouble and distressfulness, due again, and entirely, to his wayward spirit of rebellion and revolt against authority; his ineradicable taste for being agin' the government of whatever powers might be, and his consistent attitude to life, of "Here's a law— let's break it." Naturally and consequently his lot was not a happy one; and, since it was his habit, plan and principle to seek sorrow and ensue it, he found it abundantly and dwelt in its dark shadow.

Only the realization by his superiors that he was fundamentally a real fighting soldier, endued with all the military virtues save obedience, averted disaster.

It was his good fortune that his British Regiment was Irish, and that the Colonel of his Indian Regiment was a Galway Irishman. Behind Wogan's recklessness, quarrelsomeness, wildness, troublesome lack of discipline, violent temper and insubordination, they both saw the contemptuous honesty, high courage, real warmth of heart, fine ability, and dare-devil disregard of dangerous consequence, that formed the solid rock upon which grew the fungus of his folly.

"A bad man and a good divvle; an insubordinate young blackguard and a foine soldier," said Colonel Michael O'Teague, somewhat contradictorily. But if his praise and blame were apt to sound inconsistent, Colonel O'Teague understood his Irishmen, and, in time of war, asked for nothing better than the worst of them. Nevertheless he ground the face of Geoffrey Hennessy Wogan, and scarified his soul to the utmost of his very great ability. He contributed all he could to the young man's unhappiness, and the Colonel's contributions were unfailing, large, and heavy.

Little cause was there, then, to wonder that Geoffrey Hennessy Wogan was unhappy; unhappy as only those can be whose hands are against every man's; who live a life devoid of harmony; who are self-made whipping-posts and chopping-blocks; and who desire to recognize no law but their own; and presume to be laws unto themselves.

Definitely and chronically, for the first thirty years of his life, Geoffrey Hennessy Wogan was, through fault and temperament of his own, unhappy; and unhappily craved for the happiness that he denied himself.

Geoffrey Hennessy Wogan craved for Happiness.

And then, two events changed the course of his life, by changing his outlook upon life. He fell in love with a woman, and he got his Double-Company.

As a Captain and Double-Company Commander, the rebel turned ruler; the law-breaker turned law-maker; the poacher became game-keeper; the maverick outlaw became policeman and guardian of the peace.

As a lover—and for the first time in his life, a lover —the lonely, quarrelsome misanthropist mellowed, thawed and softened, found self-expression, suffered a sea-change, found himself happy at last, and turned his back upon unhappiness.

His great new folly swallowed up his old follies; he loved a woman—but otherwise grew wise.

Having escaped the measles of calf-love, and having had no sisters and only an absentee mother—who transferred to him her dislike of his father—Wogan had no exalted ideals of womanhood, and was capable of the unusual and difficult feat of loving, or of being infatuated with, a woman whom he did not greatly respect.

As a man loves so is he; and, as Wogan was, so he loved Daphne Easterwood.

Alas, for Geoffrey Wogan.

§2

The outbreak of the Great War had set the final seal upon his complete and perfect happiness.

"Power, Love, and War! And the greatest of these is War! What more could any man desire?"

Thus Geoffrey Hennessy Wogan.

His battalion under orders for East Africa, he was happy as the day is long, radiantly and invariably happy, so remarkably happy that his happiness was remarked.

On active service in one of the unhealthiest and deadliest campaigns ever waged by foolish man (*homo sapiens!*), Wogan's unquenchable high spirits and genuine joyousness brought him to the favourable notice of the General, and were rewarded by his selection for a post of honour and of extra danger.

Here, under most appalling conditions of extremest hardship, of suffering, privation, sickness and disease, enduring the worst and unhealthiest climate in the world, Wogan's spirits—and spirit—seemed to rise. To his brother officer in this little stockaded out-post of misery, it was matter for a wondering incredulity that the man should not merely endure uncomplainingly, but be merry; rejoice; be, in fact, genuinely and un-feignedly—happy.

Severely wounded, a prisoner of war in the World War's worst area; in pain; in danger of his life; his professional prospects apparently ruined; he was, even still, perfectly happy. Obviously so, and to a degree that attracted the wondering notice of his captors.

When the Germans evacuated Bulundi, taking with them his comrade-in-arms and in misfortune, Captain Stacey Burlestone, Wogan, as has been said, took a happy farewell of the latter, when he was marched away. Could he have rescued his friend he would have done so, but he felt no sorrow at the parting, and made no pretence of any. He was already so happy that, when the British marched into Bulundi, he could feel no happier. He could only remain himself—Happy

Geoff Wogan, soon to be cause for wonder and admiration on the part of the diseased and weary men who came to the succour of these wounded comrades, late prisoners of war, now mercifully restored to their friends.

Possibly his unbounded and unflagging joyousness was less noticeable in the comparatively luxurious conditions of hospital at Nairobi, at Mombasa, on the Hospital Ship *Madras* that bore him from Kilindini to Bombay, but only by reason of its less contrasting background.

Nevertheless, it was sufficiently noticeable to be approved, admired and emulated. If a man, as badly knocked about as this, could be wildly happy, why should anybody grouse and be glum, groan over the prospect of being lame for life, or of being out of the War, out of the Army, out of—everything?

From the Bombay hospital, Captain Wogan, almost recovered, was sent to the Officers' Convalescent Home at Lanapur, near Quetawur, and there encountered Mrs. Easterwood, that lovely young widow, daintily and romantically nursing, on the staff of Lady Wrattesbury's hospital.

"Faith! 'Journeys end in lovers' meetings,'" quoth he, and fell in love with her afresh.

§3

Captain Geoffrey Hennessy Wogan was very happy in Lanapur with Daphne Easterwood.

He had always admired her tremendously, despite the fact that, concerning her, he had few illusions. To say that he had no illusions whatsoever would be to make a foolish statement. There is no man but has some illusions about the woman who attracts him.

At Poona, where he had been for a space, when she was Mrs. Colin Mackleworth, he had, at first, admired her from afar—one of the many moths that fluttered round the bright light of her beauty, her wit, her grace and her charm.

Into that innermost circle he had not endeavoured

to thrust, albeit an essential thruster, for he realized
that others had an earlier and greater claim to a place
in the delectable ring. He respected the prior claim of
his faithful friend, Tim O'Leary, who, with generous
and noble trust, had introduced him to the lady of his
heart.

Some sticklers for convention did undoubtedly assume that Geoffrey Wogan might rather have respected
the presumably prior claim of Captain Colin Mackleworth to his wife's society and affections; others, more
cynical, that Wogan's respect might have been for the
noted temper and prowess of Colin Mackleworth, a
man whose hand was literally heavy.

Later, in Quetawur, the ingenuous Geoffrey, redis-
covering the incarnate Mona Lisa of his admiration in
the form of Mrs. Easterwood, had decided, with that
accuracy of clear-cut thought for which he was well
known, that Tim O'Leary, left behind in Poona, might
honestly and honourably be considered as left behind
in the race, also.

No, definitely Tim had now no prior claim, begob.
And, with all the power of his artless artfulness, all the
ingenuity of his patent ingenuousness, all the persuasive eloquence and blarney of his gifted Irish tongue,
he had sought to make headway in the good graces of
Daphne Easterwood.

And with no small measure of success. For he was
of a type approved by Daphne Easterwood. Thoroughly
she enjoyed his wit and his wickedness, his high good
humour and his extremely high good stories. A man
after her own heart, she yet admired him, though,
again, without illusions. To say that Daphne Easterwood had few illusions concerning Geoffrey Hennessy
Wogan would be to make a foolish statement, for such
women as she have no illusions whatsoever concerning
their lovers. None whatever.

Accurately and completely such women read the
souls of the ridiculous Good Men whose honour they
admire, detest and despise; of the two-anna Tomlin-
son-soul Men who would make love to them if they
dared, men whose goodness is but lack of courage to

be bad, men who let I dare not wait upon I would (by Jove, I would); the souls of the frankly Bad Men whose honour rooted in dishonour stands, a dung-hill flower, the scent of which offends not the sensitive nostrils of these delicate creatures—the wicked men with whom they feel at home and to whom they are At Home.

So in Quetawur, Daphne Easterwood and Happy Geoff Wogan, of common clay, had met on common ground, each to the other's virtues kind and to their vices wisely blind. Only to some vices, *c'est à dire*, for Daphne strongly objected to Geoff's infidelity and untruthfulness—in relation to his Infidelities.

Nor to one of his virtues was she kind, to wit his generosity—in relation again to his Infidelities. And when she strongly suspected that one of his Infidelities was an Infidel, an *ayah*, in fact, she was shocked, hurt and angry.

No, no illusions concerning dear Geoff. He was brave as a lion and would fight for his—er—mate, like a lion. He was the most amazing man she'd ever met; a real wit, eloquent as Demosthenes, and speaking with the tongues of angels—the Devil's own pet ones. Though anything but handsome, he was gay and debonair, and could carry off a situation or a woman, with an air indeed. He was generous to a fault (a very grave fault occasionally—sometimes quite a miscarriage of generosity) and, finally and chiefly, what an amazingly *happy* soul he was! Really, it made one happy to be with him; to see his exceedingly cheerful smiling face, to hear his happy laugh, even before he spoke and made love to one.

And what a lover he was!

As Daphne Easterwood regarded, estimated and esteemed Geoffrey Wogan, so, to a very great extent, did Geoffrey Wogan, allowing for certain illusions, regard, estimate and esteem Daphne Easterwood.

A foine woman! Lovely as the top of the morning, clever as paint, artful as a bag of monkeys, and able to keep you guessing. Faith, she was the one that could give ye some surprises. And it's when people leave off surprising ye that ye lose interest in them. A woman of the world who knew her world, knew to a fraction how many beans make five, and knew a lot of other things, too. Brought up on cocktails, and caviare with lots of red pepper on it.

Well, no-one could say that Happy Geoff Wogan had much taste for bread-and-butter. Those who wanted that sort of diet could have it, for him. Fancy her having married young Aubrey Easterwood! Bit of a change from Colin Mackleworth, begod. Swing of the pendulum. And Daffy was a lass whose pendulum would swing high in the direction of gold. Very magnetic metal, gold—although the scientists didn't realize it. Aubrey's great-uncle, old General Easterwood, must have been a very warm man. One of the richest men in the Army, in his day.

Well, well, you can't get something for nothing in this wicked world, and if Daffy had wanted the Easterwood money-bags she'd had to earn 'em, though it must have been hard-earned money and badly wanted, for a lass like Daffy to earn it by marrying young Easterwood!

And then for the old boy to have married again, and lived so long that he had brought his grey heirs in sorrow to the grave before him! Rough luck on Daffy. A widow, and not a penny the richer for her Easterwood venture. . . .

Yes, a foine woman. He'd never known a lovelier or a cleverer—or a kinder.

> "*She was a little less than kin*
> *And rather more than kind,*"

hummed Happy Geoff. A real stroke of luck, her having gone to Quetawur, and Aubrey Easterwood keeping her in the family, so to speak. Very nice of him, and he had borne Aubrey no grudge for doing it. Divil a bit. And he hadn't envied him. Not a bit of it. No. With all her virtues, accomplishments and attractions, Daffy wasn't the sort of lass to marry, even if one were given to that foolish pastime. No, not for Geoff! He'd have been happy, married to her, of course, but not as happy as he was unmarried to her. . . .

And here she was again, here in Lanapur, lovely as ever—and as loving.

§4

"Got my marching-orders, Daffy," said Wogan to Mrs. Easterwood one morning, meeting her as she left the Lady Wrattesbury hospital for tiffin (with him) at her nice discreet little bungalow.

"What! Oh, Geoff! Back to Africa?"

"I am not. It's Home I'm going and then to France. I am going to fly."

"What, with me, Geoff?"

"No, without ye, mavourneen. Old Tony Moresby Wallingford has been pulling strings and I'm going to join him in the Royal Flying Corps. Train in England, get my 'wings,' and then to France. Tony has done so well, already, that he's what they call an ace; and, what's more, he's back in England in charge of a flying-school. . . . Faith! 'Twill be better than clod-hopping and mud-larking in the P.B.I."

"You're glad to go, Geoff? Quite—happy—about it?"

"Begob, I am then, Daffy."

"Happy to leave me?"

"As happy as I was to meet ye again—and that's saying something."

"Always happy, eh? In any circumstances."

"Always."

"Then you can be happy to know that I'm coming, too."

"Good for you, Daffy. Can you wangle it?"

"Watch me."

And Geoffrey Hennessy Wogan watched, with much interest and considerable amusement.

CHAPTER XVIII

Major Moresby Wallingford of the Royal Flying Corps, as the Royal Air Force was then called, was quickly justified of his belief that his old friend Hennessy Wogan would prove to be an ideal airman, the right man in the right place. Not only was he devoid of nerves, absolutely fearless, and as cool in the air as he was hot-tempered and rash on the ground, but he had the gift: hands, quickness and air-sense. Moreover, he was invaluable in Mess when nerves were taut, tempers frayed and uncertain, flying-field casualties high, and a fair amount of gloomy depression resultant.

Then it was that Happy Geoff Wogan was worth a squadron, priceless and invaluable, a heart-warming tonic. No "mouldiness" could survive in the same atmosphere as his unfailing infectious laugh, his irrepressible bubbling *joie-de-vivre*, his joyous grin, his incurable optimism and unfailing cheerfulness, his jests and jokes, his genuine, unforced, unaffected, sheer happiness. Never was man more popular with all ranks.

And, for the first time in his life, he was popular with all those set in authority over him. Superiors, suffering from war-strain and from the threat of depression and morbidity due to the repeated sight of the deaths of promising pupils, sought him out, insisted on his company for a trip to Town, and declared that an evening with Happy Geoff Wogan was the finest change, rest, tonic, bracer, cure, that an over-worked, over-anxious, nerve-threatened man could have.

Not that it was always easy to get hold of Happy Geoff Wogan for an evening's binge or a week-end bend, for he had a girl tucked away somewhere. He had been seen with her, once or twice, in Town, and she was reported to be . . . well . . . worthy! A lovely lass—the sort of girl that Wogan *would* get . . . and thoroughly deserved.

At the other extreme of popularity, in fact most definitely and markedly unpopular, was a wretched fellow, a Lieutenant Brettel, who had transferred from the Infantry to the Royal Flying Corps because he knew he simply could not stand a second winter in the trenches. The cold, the sodden misery, the mud, the stench, the hellish racket, had all but broken him. A short life and a merry in the Flying Corps, where men slept in beds; ate real food; did not sit, stand, or lie, in oozy mud; did not have to march, march, march, in rain and snow and sleet till they wished they were dead; and did not live in the midst of a perpetual hell of slaughter and suffering—that would be the place for him.

But the poor chap found that life in the Royal Flying Corps was much more likely to be short than merry—for his nerve had gone. Shell-fire, influenza, deaths of his men and his brother officers, and horrible, unbearable sights in the trenches, had afflicted him more seriously than he knew—until he had to fly an aeroplane solo.

And then, promptly he wished with all his soul that he was back in the trenches. He had no head for heights, he was not "air-minded," he was not interested in machinery, and, alone in an aeroplane, his nerves took charge of him. He was in a state of abject fear, almost paralysed with terror.

Oh, for the blessed solid earth, *terra firma*, firm beneath his cold, cold feet; the good earth, solid, steady, reliable . . . no height from which to fall. He'd love to lie flat on it for the rest of his life. Lying flat on the ground, one could not even fall down, let alone fall from giddy heights. . . . "Giddy" indeed.

And this creature professed to be sick, sorry and tired of what he had the impudence to term "Wogan's eternal braying"; declared that his ceaseless, senseless laughter got on his nerves; and that if he had to stand much more of it, he wouldn't be able to stand it at all— he'd go mad, and either shoot Wogan or run away.

Geoff told Daphne all about him, and she was quite interested. So much so that she made Geoff introduce him to her, the kind-hearted woman. . . .

Possibly there were one or two who agreed with Brettel just to the extent of feeling that, at four o'clock in the morning—routed from their warm beds and cosy tents by a raucous-voiced Sergeant-Major, to fly solo, with empty, sinking stomachs, dry tongues, and shrinking nerves—they did not particularly desire to hear loud bellowing laughter from someone who apparently enjoyed learning to fly at four in the morning, in spite of seven deaths in eleven days.

For laugh, at that terrible hour of the morning, Wogan did.

He laughed when he pan-caked; he laughed when his engine began to splutter and conk; when his plane rose so slowly from its taxi-ing run that it only cleared buildings by inches; when he came down with a galloping-goose run and crashed his under-carriage; when he had to make a forced landing and the machine turned turtle on top of him, caught fire, and he scrambled clear with his clothes smouldering; when, in a fog, he came down straight into a tree and fell out of it, cut about the face, bruised, shaken, and unhurt; when, learning bombing and machine-gunning, he dived at the target and found he had a "dead stick." (He hit the ground and was unconscious for forty-nine hours.)

Always he laughed—and admittedly it was unfortunate that, at a funeral, the ninth that month, in the little Flying Corps cemetery near the training-ground, he should have burst into a loud and hearty peal of laughter when the Chaplain, slipping on the wet clay, fell and—as Wogan said—dirtied his clean pinafore.

Whether Happy Geoff's constant laughter really had anything to do with it, is not known, but Brettel's nerve suddenly failed. Called as usual at four in the morning, for another solo flight, he found that he could not do it. Simply he could not climb into the plane, call "*Contact*," and take off. Flatly he refused to obey orders, and, before he could be reported and put under arrest, he disappeared. He did not go mad, or shoot Wogan, but ran away.

And, curiously enough, in frantic headlong flight, he went to see kind Mrs. Easterwood.

And she showed him how to get out of the country, helped him to do so, enabled him, in fact, to get to Holland.

§2

In due course, or, rather, in record time, Wogan was sent out to France, whither his reputation had preceded him; a reputation for skill, coolness and courage that he proceeded to justify; a reputation for unquenchable joyous high spirits and happiness that he more than justified. If he were a real accession to the fighting-strength and hitting-power of the Squadron, what a priceless accession was he to its *morale*; its cheerfulness; its social amenities; its ability to forget the War, battle, slaughter and sudden death, for a few hours. Indeed when the Squadron Mess entertained French and Belgian squadrons, and the American airmen of the Lafayette *Escadrille*, he notably added to the gaiety of nations.

No man more popular with all who knew him than Happy Geoff Wogan. And quickly he gathered in a "confirmation" and a *marraine*. A confirmation is an officially-admitted victory over an enemy aeroplane, and a *marraine* is an unofficially-admitted and temporary wife.

Of fighting enemy planes, Happy Geoff never tired, and whenever he tired of his *marraine*, who owned and ran an *estaminet* near the Squadron's base, he could wangle leave to Paris, where Daphne could always meet him.

She was now a kind of private secretary to a kind of philanthropic and ubiquitous American millionairess deeply interested in Red Cross work in general, and the care and cure of wounded officers in particular— apparently a good kindly woman who had the highest regard, affection and admiration for Daphne.

And the interest that Daphne took in Geoff's doings, in those of his Squadron and of the Royal Flying Corps, naval and military, British, French and Belgian, was wonderful and delightful.

§3

Before long, Geoffrey Hennessy Wogan was a recognized "ace," and had ten confirmations and three decorations. He grew, if possible, happier and happier, for he loved this form of fighting; the sense of independence and freedom when away on his own, the world before him and beneath him; the sky his, wherein to go almost where he pleased and to do almost as he liked, master of his own ship, if not captain of his own soul.

Successful, praised, courted, decorated, in his element, he had all the fighting that he could want, and unlimited scope, power and permission for destruction. The joy of taking out a B.E.2 bomber and smashing things; of wiping out whole railway-stations; wrecking crowded troop-trains; scattering great banging, popping, burning, exploding, dumps; bombing batteries of artillery, jogging along a road; battalions of marching infantry; observation balloons; camps of weary Huns; villages which were crowded enemy billets; huge factories and munition plants; aerodromes with hangars full of *Fokkers*, *Aviatiks*, *Pfalzes*, or *Albatroses*; cross-road tangles of transport and troops; and best of all, raining ruin and destruction upon great industrial towns.

What he really wanted a go at, was a Zeppelin.

But best sport of all was a dog-fight, an all-on-to-all scrap between a flight of British Bristol Scouts and a bigger flight of *Fokkers*, everybody shooting-up everybody, a wild and whirling *mêlée* from which every now and then, someone went hurtling down to death in a blaze of smoke and fire, and Happy Geoff would yell "Another 'flamer' begob!" and roar with laughter while bullets riddled his nacelle and wings, tore his clothes, and cut his struts, but somehow always spared his engine, his petrol tank and his body.

Once, with his last pint of petrol, he landed at his aerodrome after such a dog-fight, sole survivor of the aerial battle; and, gentle and perfect as was his landing, the faint jolt caused the plane literally to fall to pieces, so riddled with bullet-holes was it. Both wings fell off, and, what had touched the ground an aeroplane, lay on it a useless heap of junk, not worth reassembling and tinkering for one more flight.

As he stepped out of the ruins, after as narrow an escape as ever a man had, Wogan laughed consumedly, literally roared with laughter, at the cosmic jest of Death's defeated attempt to get Happy Geoff Wogan.

So noisily merry was he, that his devoted Scots mechanic, Sandy McAlister, painfully broke his habitual silence and almost broke his record for long-winded speech.

"He's fey," growled dour Sandy McAlister.

Next day was a memorable one.

Starting at dawn with a roving commission to fly along the Front in his new single-seater Bristol tractor bi-plane "fighter," and drive away, or down in flames, any scouting intruders or visiting bombers, he quickly spotted an enemy patrol of three planes, each equipped with balloon-destroying rockets, a dozen to the patrol— whose good deed for the day would be a little balloon-jumping, should they discover any tethered observation-balloons spying upon the behind-the-lines activities of German reinforcements, concentrations, dump-building, battery-placing and artillery movements in general.

Having the height of the patrol, Wogan tilted his machine over to take a good look, and then dived straight down at the nearest. Demonstrating both his experience and his coolness, he held his fire until his victim presented a perfect target, raked the *Pfalz* from end to end, and with a yell of laughter, saw it burst into flames, crumple up, and fall, like a plummet, blazing to the earth.

Looping a big loop he came under the tail of the second *Pfalz* and from its "blind spot" repeated his tactics, this time missing the vitals of the ship but, a moment later, seeing, with another shout of laughter, the pilot slump forward and collapse over his joy-stick. Out of control but uninjured, the plane flew on, to crash behind the British lines.

Tilting his machine to watch this decline and fall, Wogan unconsciously saved his life as a burst of fire from the third *Pfalz* missed his head by inches.

"Now, me bhoy," roared Wogan, unheard in the greater roar of his machine; showed the German leader some acrobatic flying, and gave him the, not wholly erroneous, impression that he was dealing with a wild man of the air who, for two pins, would deliberately collide with him . . . would rather kill the pair of them than let him live.

On his tail, beneath him, alongside, at few yards' range, the English plane darted, dived, looped and manœuvred, and at every opportunity—that is, when-ever he had a retreating or broad-side target—let off a burst of fire.

To the German it was a marvel that his plane held together, that he and his engine were yet whole. Also that, apparently, his opponent was invulnerable. He decided to pull out and break off, and, with that intention, dived down, down, down, as though driven down out of control, inevitably to crash.

Suddenly, and having reached the utmost margin of safety, he flattened out, put the nose of his machine up, and, in the same moment, from below and behind him, heard his enemy's machine-gun again and for the last time.

A few seconds later, the *Pfalz* was a crumpled mass, a mess—from which no pilot stepped.

With a shout of joy and a roar of laughter, Wogan zoomed aloft, looped three loops and flew for home, to replenish petrol and ammunition.

Three more "confirmations."

Would he live to hold the world's record? Could he make a century?

Of course he could—and would.

Coffee, a sandwich, a cigarette in the Mess, and

Wogan returned to his plane, to find his mechanic patching bullet-holes.

"Faith," laughed Hennessy Wogan, "'tis 'The Spotted Dog' I'll call her. . . . Looks as though she's had small-pox."

"Aye," creaked Sandy McAlister.

"Took three of them to make those little holes," laughed Wogan.

"Aye?" said Sandy McAlister.

"But those three have gone where the good Huns go," said Wogan, laughing long and loud.

"Aye?" replied Sandy McAlister.

"Everything all right?"

"Aye."

"Well then, stop jabberin', bejabbers, and swing the prop. . . ."

About half an hour south of the scene of the morning's fight, Wogan spied a three-seater *Aviatik*, flying in the same direction, climbed to a satisfactory height and dived.

The first that the crew of the *Aviatik* knew of him was a burst of fire.

What damage he had done, he didn't know, but obviously it was not fatal, for, instantly, the enemy plane swerved and began a steep climbing turn.

As he came about, manœuvred for the position where the German rear-seat gunner could not see him, by reason of his own tail-plane, Wogan fired, discovered that his gun had jammed, and knew the horrible sensation of a dead gun, than which only that communicated by a "dead stick" is worse.

Well . . . He who fights and runs away lives to fight another day. But there were two words to that. One was that Geoffrey Hennessy Wogan had never run away from man or beast—or aeroplane—yet; and was not going to begin now. The other was that it might be a good deal easier to talk about running away than to do it. If these three birds didn't mean him to pull out and break off, he could not do it.

No, and he was not going to do it, either. Damn them, he'd get above them and throw a spanner at 'em first. Pity he hadn't got a bag of brick-bats.

No, damned if he'd run away.

What a fool he'd been not to carry a rifle or an automatic or a few hand-grenades, as they used to do before machine-guns were mounted in air-craft.

And meantime they were making pretty good shooting. Wires were snapping, struts splintering, holes suddenly materializing before his eyes.

Could holes materialize? Well, anyhow, there they were, suddenly appearing out of nothing.

Yes, a hole is a space with nothing in it. Damn it, they'd spoil his ship in a minute. Two machine-gunners. Shooting away like Hell. Do some damage if they weren't careful.

What they would do, would be to use up all their ammunition. That'd be sport, to dodge all round 'em like a fly round a bald head, till they'd emptied their belts.

One of them might have an accident, though, and put a bullet into his head, or his engine, or his tank.

Hell! A burning, searing pain in his thigh. Got him that time. Well, now he'd get them, damn them. All go roaring down to the Devil together. Now, Mr. Hun, see if you can dodge this.

And with a loud laugh Wogan swung his plane and charged the *Aviatik*, with the hope and intention of striking its tail with his propeller.

But the German pilot was also an ace, one of the best aviators in the German Air Force, and, just in time, pulled his plane out of danger, his manœuvre being aided by the fact that his "wash," the terrific draught from his propeller, affected the flight of the smaller lighter plane, causing it to deviate by yards and sending it momentarily out of control.

Again and again Wogan repeated the manœuvre, each time unsuccessfully, thanks to the German pilot's skill and to the hard facts of aerial draught and current.

Right. Since he couldn't knock the blighter's tail off, he'd knock his wing off. And that'd be the last of two planes and four good men.

Diving, climbing, turning, looping, the while new holes appeared in every part of the fabric of his machine, Wogan gained position for the dive that should end the fight; and, suddenly, like a hawk on a mallard, he dived.

As though instinctively realizing his intention, the German pilot put his rudder hard over, swerved with the utmost suddenness of which he was capable and, to Wogan's utter amazement, shook the right wing from his machine.

Wogan's dead gun had done its work before it jammed.

Missing the falling plane by feet, and saving his own life by a second, Wogan banked and dived to see the end. In No Man's Land, between the French and German trenches, the three-place *Aviatik* crashed, and a great cheer rose from the French trenches.

Another "confirmation."

And so to lunch.

Nor, at lunch, was anyone as merry and bright, as noisy and gay, as Geoffrey Hennessy Wogan, who, for all other signs of weariness, strain or nerves that he exhibited, might have spent the morning playing a leisurely round of golf.

It was certainly Geoffrey Wogan's lucky day. Going for what he termed a flip, that afternoon, and flying at a height of three miles above the ground, he sighted an *Albatros* observation-plane evidently doing a little photography.

Diving, he discovered it to be a two-seater, and that the observer in the rear cock-pit was prompt to change camera for machine-gun.

Not that the *Albatros* was looking for trouble; merely for useful pictures.

But trouble came. Engine trouble. And all that the pilot could do was to head for his own lines in the hope of making a successful landing behind them.

This he might have done had not a tracer bullet struck him between the shoulders. The *Albatros* crashed, an utter wreck, and, ere it did so, the observer jumped from a height of some hundred feet. Wogan wondered why.

He found the incident infinitely amusing.

Apparently, on his return to the aerodrome, he found the fact that he had a slight flesh-wound in the thigh equally amusing; and when the R.A.M.C. surgeon asked him what the devil he was laughing at, he replied that he was laughing because he was so happy.

Always happy. In season and out of season.

There were those who considered that his happiness was occasionally very much out of season.

As, for example, when receiving a French decoration from a very highly-placed and important official at a very ceremonial parade, he applauded that gentleman's serious, solemn and oratorically-intense commendation with a peal of laughter; and, being kissed by the Frenchman upon either cheek, insisted upon warmly returning the kisses ere being rendered almost helpless by his hair-trigger sense of humour, and collapsing from laughter-induced weakness.

As, for example, again, when the Squadron-leader, making a perfect landing in what was left of his torn, riddled and shattered plane from which his blood dripped steadily, climbed out of it, staggered drunkenly and fell on his face unconscious, Wogan roared with laughter. Being asked for the point of the joke that amused him so, he replied that the dour, ascetic Major Permaine had looked so funny, reeling about like an old drunk; that it was very amusing if you came to think of it, that a man who could fly couldn't walk; and anyhow he, Geoff Wogan, felt so happy that he *had* to laugh.

And when he wanted to laugh he was dam'-well going to laugh.

And as, for example, again, when, at a drum-head open-air Church Parade, he suddenly noticed, or remembered, something so amusing that, after chuckling to himself for a minute, he burst into hearty guffaws, so long and loud, that the service was seriously interrupted.

The new Squadron-leader, an observant and experienced man, suggested that Flight-leader Wogan should have a spot of leave, go to Paris for a week, have a thorough change and a rest—and see what his nerves were like when he returned.

Laughing merrily, Wogan assured his Squadron-leader that nothing would suit him better than a binge in Paris; that he'd get through a lot of change and would not have a lot of rest—but that anyone who thought it would affect his nerves to go to Paris, was a fool. His nerves were perfect now, and they'd be perfect when he returned. Yes—whatever sort of a hell-bender of a binge he had. Perfect; and that was why he was so happy. Or else conversely, they were perfect because he was so happy.

"Quite so; quite so; both, probably; and the higher in summer the fewer," agreed the Squadron-leader, eyeing his magnificent ace anxiously, and causing Flight-leader Wogan almost to choke with merriment. "Anyway, I'm going to get you sent to Paris on a little job that'll take a week or so, or else I'll get the M.O. to order you a week-or-two of leave. . . ."

Arrived in Paris, Geoffrey Wogan, having secured a suitable *appartement*, went in search of Daphne Easterwood, and displayed no other emotion than tremendous amusement on discovering that his unannounced visit was inopportune, inasmuch as she was entertaining Major Moresby Wallingford, an old friend of her Quetawur days.

With laughter long and loud, Wogan gave them his blessing; waggishly threatened to tell Joan Wallingford, unless Tony got him promotion, and went on his way rejoicing, to the unofficial headquarters of flying-men in Paris, "*chez Elaine*," where, as usual, his terrific high spirits, unquenchable joyousness and care-free happiness, quickly rendered him noticeable, prominent, and most popular.

With one lady—to whom he was presented by an admiring *cher collégue* of the French flying-service, as a mark of high esteem and great favour—he was an instant success, and made a great hit; a most attractive woman with the curious name of Mata Hari.

Some jealousy was aroused by Mademoiselle Mata Hari's obvious preference for the wild Irishman; but of that Wogan recked nothing. It would have taken a great deal more than the black looks of extremely senior French officers to cast the slightest shadow upon his perfect happiness; and with his new friend—who, although she spoke French, Spanish and English, was either Dutch or Javanese, or perhaps Eskimo or Siamese or something else neutral or allied—he had a glorious time. For not only was she fascinating and *chic* beyond belief, but amazingly intelligent, for a girl whose only job in life was to be ornamental. Wonderful what she knew and wanted to know, about all that the brave soldiers were doing.

And, curiously enough, it turned out that she knew Daffy. Had first met her at a dinner, she said, given by a well-known Belgian General; and then quite frequently at amusing places where one danced or went for supper.

Tony Wallingford, Daffy, Wogan and Mata made a truly merry quartette and had some great evenings—all friends together, no jealousy, and no hard feelings.

And if Tony did once or twice pull Geoff up—for pointing at some grave and reverend Senior at a neighbouring table, calling attention to the old Frog's silly beard, and roaring with laughter—Geoff forgave him, because poor Tony wasn't as happy as Geoff was. No, not nearly.

In fact poor Tony Wallingford wasn't really happy at all, so far as Geoff could make out. Got something on his mind—about Daffy and Mata—and instead of enjoying life, a short life and a merry, or better still, a long life and a merry, he was bothering his head and trying to bother Geoff's head—about what Mata's real business in Paris was, and why she went to Belgium, Holland, Spain and England, if that was where she did go when she disappeared from France.

So far as Geoff could gather, some stuffy old geezers at the *Sureté* were casting their dhirty suspicions at her, probably because she wouldn't play with them in their mouldy back-yards—or grave-yards, the hoary corpses—when they tried to bribe her to do so. . . . And, though he'd been too happy to pay much attention to what Tony said, it seemed that the people at the War Ministry had got their eye on the poor girl, and wanted to know what Daffy had to do with her. Was Daffy trailing her according to British instructions, or were Mata and Daffy birds of a feather?

Ah, to Hell with the ould spalpeens! Why couldn't they be happy, like Geoff, and let the girls be happy, too? And why couldn't Tony make hay while the sun shone, and enjoy life instead of pumping Geoff about the poor colleens and moaning that he'd be in the nastiest position conceivable if Daffy were up to tricks and Tony had to—give her away?

Happy Geoff Wogan had guffawed mightily at the mouldy-minded Tony, and bidden him take note that he wasn't going to give Daffy away at the altar, anyhow —not to Geoffrey Hennessy Wogan, begod. He'd swop Mata for Daffy, with Tony, if he liked, and re-appoint her his Number One girl, but—there's no discharge in the war, and there was no marrying in the game. Not in Geoff's game, anyhow.

And Tony had bidden Geoff shut up and pull himself together, eyeing him anxiously the while, as though he were very perturbed and worried about him.

Ah, to Hell with it; why couldn't Tony be happy and enjoy life? Let him look at Geoff, happy as the day is long, and take pattern by him.

And ten days passed with incredible speed.

So happy indeed was Wogan that when his leave expired, and it was time for him to take train for the Front again, he decided that, on the whole perhaps, he was even happier with Mata and Daffy in Paris than he had been with his Squadron.

And when his old friend Moresby Wallingford tried to hurry him off, Geoff bade him be aisy, for there was no hurry at all, at all. He was much too happy at Elaine's to go back yet awhile; and he wasn't going back till he felt he'd be happier, or at least, just as happy, with the Squadron bhoys.

He loved flying; he loved shooting down Huns; he loved bombing; he loved taking spies over into Germany at night, landing them there and fetching them back later, on another dark night; he loved the bhoys, and his mechanic; he loved it all—and particularly he loved his Squadron-leader—but, just at present, he loved Mata and Daffy even better, and was so happy with them that he wasn't going to leave them, begob.

To an urgent irate telegram, he replied,

Don't worry about me absolutely happy leaving this address having glorious time change and rest I have the change and Daffy has the rest my nerves all right her nerve all right laugh you mouldy blackguard Geoff.

§4

Major Moresby Wallingford did his best, made his friend's business his own, worked swiftly and pulled strings competently, and changed the case from one for the Provost Marshal and a Court-Martial to one for a Medical Board.

The Medical Board was sympathetic with this fine-looking, laughing soldier, wearing the ribbons of the D.S.O., M.C., D.F.C., *Croix de Guerre, Médaille Militaire* and Legion of Honour, this distinguished ace who laughed incessantly and repeatedly assured the members of the Board that he was absolutely happy, so happy, indeed, that he didn't know what to do with himself.

The Board knew what to do with him, however; and Major Moresby Wallingford, who was returning to England, undertook to accompany him thither, see him safely into the proper hands, and produce him before the India Office Medical Board when notified.

Mrs. Daphne Easterwood also did her best, insisted on accompanying him, looking after him, and generally taking charge of him until he recovered from the mental strain . . . nervous break-down . . . or whatever it was that ailed him.

As was most desirable, too, she took charge of his monetary affairs, becoming his financial adviser and guardian—his banker, in fact.

And her dear Geoff was entirely happy to leave all bothersome business in her hands, happy to go to England with her, happy to do whatever she suggested —in fact, completely happy, whatever happened.

And Major Moresby Wallingford was relieved beyond measure that Geoff should leave France before worse befell, and particularly glad that Daphne was going, too; leaving Paris and Mata Hari—and going where she'd be out of mischief.

Or would she be out of "mischief"?

Anyhow, he was returning to France, and if Daphne got into trouble in England, it would be the business of somebody else to deal with her—thank Heaven. A nice thought, a fine thing, for a man to have to arrest, and give evidence against, a woman whom he had known for years; with whom he had been in love; of whom he was still very fond; a woman, in fact, whose lover he had been!

And, in England, Geoffrey Wogan was extremely, extraordinarily, indescribably happy with Daffy. Life was one long laugh.

But the War must be getting on people's nerves; for, occasionally, in hotels, trains, theatres, night-clubs and such places, men—and sometimes even women, women supposed to be daughters of *joy*, forsooth— would ask him for God's sake to shut up, to stop laughing like a cursed hyena and braying like a damned costermonger's donkey.

One chap, on sick leave from India, told him in the Imperial Grill that he reminded him of a blasted jackal —and that made Wogan laugh till he cried. For, as he explained to the nerve-shattered, head-wounded fellow, for all *he* knew, Wogan's name might be Hall, and his Christian name might be John—then, of course, he'd *be* Jack 'All, just as the poor fellow said—Jackal. See?

And the quality of his laughter, the awful noise that Happy Geoff Wogan made, finally decided Daphne that the time had come to take the steps that she had considered and contemplated.

The help of two doctors and a solicitor would be necessary, she believed, before he could be "certified."

§5

Major Moresby Wallingford's hurried visit to the scene of his old friend's incarceration was ineffably painful, almost the most painful occasion of his life.

He didn't want to go and see him in that place, and in that condition. He could hardly bear the thought of seeing him; but he felt it an ineluctable duty, however harrowing, for he was not quite satisfied and easy in his mind, about the "certifying."

Geoff Wogan couldn't be really *mad*!

He had known Geoff for many a long year; soldiered and hunted with him; played cricket and polo; gone on glorious shooting-trips; known him really intimately, and seen him under all sorts of conditions, in fair weather and foul—and had never detected the slightest sign of madness; never even dreamt of suspecting the possibility of such a thing.

Geoff Wogan! True he had been a bit wild; more or less always in hot water; been a bit "mad" in the sense that his type always is a bit "mad," harum-scarum, unexpected and unaccountable. But as for lunacy! Madness in the sense of real lunacy; the sort of madness that means being imprisoned for life . . . perhaps in a padded cell. . . . *No!*

CHAPTER XIX

Yes. Undoubtedly one of the unhappiest hours that, up to that day, Colonel Anthony Moresby Wallingford had ever known, was the hour he spent at the Brackenmoor Private Lunatic Asylum, visiting his poor friend, Geoff Wogan.

To him, it was the most heart-rending experience of the War—for Captain Geoffrey Hennessy Wogan, D.S.O.; M.C.; D.F.C.; *Croix de Guerre*; *Médaille Militaire*; Officer of the Legion of Honour, etc., was happier that afternoon than he had ever been, having discovered that he had exactly the same number of fingers as he had toes; and that, moreover, his thumbs corresponded with his big toes, so to speak, and his little fingers with his little toes.

It was splendid; so interesting, remarkable and convenient.

It gave him an idea, too. He could wear foot-gloves and hand-boots. Make them inter-changeable. And, in spite of the manifest annoyance of his "nurse," a large, strong, unattractive man, he insisted on removing his boots repeatedly, in order to verify his discovery; he also insisted on wearing his boots as gloves; and on demanding that his nurse go and buy him some gloves for his feet. . . .

There was one grain of comfort, one ray of light in that hideous blackness—his friend was quite happy.

Yes, Geoffrey Wogan was perfectly happy—as happy as the day was long.

And, to the utmost of his power, Colonel Wallingford dwelt upon that aspect of the tragedy, and the reflection that, although the mad do not know that they are mad, some of them are obviously suffering, are steeped in misery, and should, in mercy, be put to painless death; but Geoff was genuinely, and perfectly, happy.

Good God! It was well for Geoff Wogan that he did

not carry, written upon his forehead, the fate, the lot, the *kismet* that he, Anthony Moresby Wallingford, did. For Wallingford knew—he did not merely believe—he knew, with absolute certainty, that he himself would live to be a centenarian; would live for at least a hundred years, and possibly for more.

Time after time, in different parts of the world, fortune-tellers, sand-diviners, palmists, clairvoyants, astrologers and soothsayers had told him that he would reach a very ripe old age; would exceed the allotted span of man's life by some decades; would live to be the oldest man in his country; would live to be over a hundred years old, and so forth.

Curiously enough, his father, his grandfather, his great-grandfather and that gentleman's father, grandfather and great-grandfather had, to his certain knowledge, died young, remarkably young; not one of them reaching the age of fifty years.

One had been killed at Badajoz, aged twenty-eight; two had met their deaths before they were thirty; and the rest had died or been killed in their forties.

To these facts, their tomb-stones, as well as family records, testified.

And, from boyhood, it had been the passionate desire of Anthony Wallingford to break the tragic record; to live a long, as well as a full, life; to learn for himself that *chaque âge a ses plaisirs*; to avoid sinking down into the cold and silent tomb until such time as he was so old, so tired, so feeble and disillusioned, that death would be a welcome visitor.

To have to die, as at least six of his immediate ancestors had done, in the hey-dey of life, was terrible. It disturbed one's faith in an omnipotent, omniscient, all-wise and beneficent Deity. . . .

A sensitive, introspective boy, he had brooded upon thoughts of early death; conceived himself to be one of a doomed race; and, steeped in Byronic gloom, walked apart.

Being in point of fact perfectly healthy, endowed with courage, energy, initiative and an unusually enquiring and receptive mind, young Wallingford grew out of this phase, and, by the time he left Sandhurst, was free of this obsessive fear of death, or rather of revolt against unjust sentence of early death; and only occasionally entertained the weakening belief that he had less expectation of life than that enjoyed by his fellows.

By the time he reached India, all that remained of his boyish and youthful trouble was an occasional sense of hopeless *laisser faire*, and an occasional urge to seize, and enjoy to the full, what pleasure might be wrung from the fleeting moment.

Now and again he would surprise his friends with some such half-fatalistic, half-cynical remark as,

"What's the good? I shall be dead before I reap the reward of this virtue."

"Why strive and strain, when Time itself is against one?"

"Why climb, when one knows one will fall by the wayside?"

Now and again he would surprise his friends by a strange unwonted burst of hectic gaiety and dissipation; a curious lapse from his normal quiet, well-ordered way of life. For, apart from these brief occasional aberrations, Wallingford was, and was known as, a studious, ambitious soldier; a man cleverer and more thoughtful than his fellows; the type of officer to whom sport and games are but necessary recreation, and whose objective is the Staff.

Not popular—for he was reserved, abstemious and exclusive; critical, clever and sharp-tongued—he was admired by many and loved by not a few. And those who loved him best were those who knew him best.

Joan Wallingford, knowing her husband through and through, understanding the sense of doom that militated at once against his determination to achieve his ambition and against his natural asceticism, had understood all sufficiently to forgive all: understood his occasional immersion in something near despair; had understood his attraction to merry men and laughing ladies; to Geoffrey Wogan; to Daphne Mackleworth.

Only too well she knew why, at times, her husband would shut himself up and brood; morose, rebellious against Fate; resentful of ineluctable Doom; despairing.

Nothing for it but to be gentle, kind and unobtrusively sympathetic until the dark fit should pass; the black certainty that, in the very flower of his manhood, he would be cut off, mown down, his labours wasted, his ambition unfulfilled . . . wronged, cheated, cursed from the cradle.

And with loving-kindness she would strive to comfort him, to reassure him, to contradict him when half-angrily, half-sadly, he would declaim,

"*Man that is born of a woman is of few days and full of trouble. He cometh forth like a flower and he is cut down.*"

Equally well she understood his brief rare fits of dissipation, his pursuit of Pleasure as she ran, his unhappy snatchings at false happiness, the doubting cry of his tortured soul—

"If a brief life—a merry."

And thus she explained to herself her husband's enduring friendship for so different a man as Geoffrey Wogan, his infatuation for so different a woman as Daphne Mackleworth . . . Daphne Easterwood.

If they could give him ease—then let them.

If Daphne could, intentionally or unintentionally, do anything for Tony that his wife could not do, then, in Heaven's name, let her. And God bless her.

§2

And then his amazing change, his completely new attitude to life.

To Joan Wallingford's ineffable joy and unutterable thankfulness, her husband not only lost his belief in the family fate, his certainty that he was doomed to an early death, but actually began to believe the opposite.

To her unbounded surprise, a surprise as great only as her relief and joy, she discovered that Tony had a new belief—no, a certainty—that he would not only survive his thirties and forties; not only reach the

Biblical three score years and ten of man's allotted span; not only attain a ripe old age, but a remarkable one.

One day, Tony, a changed man, a happy, light-hearted man, had told her that he knew, he *knew*, that he would "make a century, not out"; live to be a hundred years old—and more.

Well, if this were the outcome of his long rides with Daphne, his long and late sessions with her at her bungalow, she couldn't be sufficiently grateful to Daphne.

Jealous? Yes, of course; naturally and healthily jealous—and thankful. It was a poor love that loved itself best.

One day, Joan Wallingford, sitting reading in her deep and shady verandah, had heard the rhythmic, soothing, somewhat musical cry of,

"*Borah, Memsahib; Borah. Borah, Memsahib; Borah.* Silver, turquoise, silk, Kashmir work, Sind work; all things. Silk Borah, Memsahib; silk Borah. Benares, Bokhara, silk, sausage, silver, lace, sardine, salmon, chutney, potted meat, tinned peas, soup, silk, silver, pudding, Persian rugs. All things Borah, Memsahib."

And the leader of a small caravan of laden coolies stood salaaming at the verandah door; a large fat man, clad in snowy white, with a gold-embroidered velvet waistcoat or Zouave jacket, and a velvet pill-box cap to match.

"*Kuch nahin mangta, Borah*," said Joan Wallingford, "I don't want anything to-day."

"But, Memsahib," replied the large fat man, with a beaming smile which exposed snowy and regular teeth, and lighted up big lustrous kohl-encircled eyes. "Memsahib not knowing what Borah got."

"Oh yes, I do," replied Joan. "You've got silver, silk, sausage, soup, salmon, sardines and . . . It sounds like a game."

"No, Memsahib, no game got. Got all other things. I showing Memsahib."

And, at a wave of his hand, the unreluctant coolies dumped each his big bale upon the ground, loosed its bonds, and, turning its *dhurrie* covering into a shop-counter, set forth the contents to best advantage.

Making a choice selection from the large and incredibly varied collection, the Borah set them out upon the rug at Joan's feet.

Chased silver-ware; chaste garments of silk; beautiful embroideries; hideous turquoise-encrusted articles as useless as un-ornamental; specious jewellery; spacious brazen bowls; spurious antique weapons and genuine antique tins of comestibles.

"No, there's nothing there I want," said Joan.

"These very good oysters, Memsahib, and very good gold chain."

"No. I don't think I care about tinned oysters, Borah. And I don't use gold chains—much."

"For Sahib?" suggested the Borah. "For wearing on watch and chain."

"No, the Sahib wears a wrist-watch. How much do you want for that ivory?"

"That very good ivory, Memsahib. Tip ivory."

"What do you mean—tip ivory?"

"Tip of tusk, Memsahib. Very good, very solid, very heavy. Other ivory bad man bring you is tooth ivory or hollow end of tusk ivory. Me good Borah. That good ivory."

"Well, how much do you want for it?"

"More than Memsahib wanting to give."

"I'm sure of that."

"Colonel Sahib offering me one hundred rupees, but I can't do. I let Memsahib have it for one hundred and fifty because Memsahib liking it."

Joan put the ivory statuette, an ordinarily good Japanese Buddha, down on the rug.

"Good joke, Borah."

"How much Memsahib wanting to give?"

"I'm not really wanting to give anything."

"How much Memsahib would give if Memsahib were wanting?"

"Ten rupees."

"Good joke, Memsahib," smiled the Borah, salaaming respectfully and chuckling.

"No, don't want anything, Borah. Sorry you wasted your time."

"No, no, Memsahib, time not wasted. Memsahib will buy something."

"No. Nothing I want."

"Tell Memsahib's fortune."

"I know it, Borah."

"Good joke, Memsahib. Memsahib knowing past and present but not future. I knowing Memsahib's past and future, too. Memsahib lived in very big town. Perhaps London? But often going to *mofussil*[28] and riding horses on green grass after many dogs. Memsahib's father and mother both dead, alas. Memsahib got one sister. No brother. Memsahib been in India five years. Been married three years. No children got. Never mind, Memsahib. Sahib is an Officer-Sahib. Very clever. Sahib away shooting."

Joan was impressed—deeply. How could this man possibly have learnt anything about her?

"I tell Memsahib's fortune?"

Joan shook her head.

"No.

"Look here, Borah," she continued. "Can you tell the Sahib's fortune?"

"When Sahib comes back, yes, Memsahib. Tell it true."

"Oh, you can't tell it while he's away?"

"I try, Memsahib. Memsahib give me something the Sahib worn much; also portrait."

No. What a fool she was. Suppose it was something dreadful! But then he wouldn't tell her anything dreadful. She'd ask him just one question. Just as a matter of curiosity; interest.

"Wait a minute, Borah," she said.

And going into Tony's den, she collected a riding-switch, a boot and a polo-glove.

From her own room she picked up a framed photograph of her husband.

"There you are. Now listen. I don't want you to tell my husband's fortune—unless you can tell me some-

---

[28] *Country districts.*

thing very good—but I want you to answer a question."

The Borah stared long at Anthony Wallingford's photograph, held the riding-switch and glove in one hand, the boot in the other, and closed his eyes.

"Think about the Sahib much, Memsahib. Yes, yes, I am seeing. Yes," continued the man, "Memsahib ask question."

"Will my husband live to be an old man, Borah?"

And immediately came the reply,

"He will, Memsahib."

"Live to be older than his father?"

"He will live to be as old as the years of his father, his grandfather, and his grandfather's father all added together, Memsahib. He will live to be a very, very old man."

And beneath his breath he whispered in tones of amazement, something that sounded to Joan like,

"*Ek sau sal aur dus aur. . . . Wah, wah!*"

"Memsahib, the Sahib will live to be as the father of all Sahibs living."

Curious. Curious . . . and very interesting.

"Thank you, Borah. I shall give you five rupees. And that is fifty times as much as . . ."

"No, no, Memsahib. For I have told you the truth; and I tell you, Memsahib, that the Sahib will be a leader in war. He will be a Gineraal-Sahib. Memsahib, he will go high. High up in the air."

Joan laughed at what she took to be a curious description of success.

"And," added the Borah, rising and salaaming low, "Memsahib will go back to Inglistan soon. Sooner than she thinks. She will be very unhappy . . ."

"That's enough, Borah."

". . . for a little while," hastily added the man, "And then she will be very happy."

"Happy ever afterwards, eh?" smiled Joan.

"Yes, Memsahib. How much Memsahib offering for the ivory?"

"Ten rupees."

"For a hundred-and-fifty-rupee ivory, Memsahib?"

"No, for a five-rupee ivory," replied Joan.

"Very good, Memsahib."

And with a sigh of grief and a grimace of pain, the Borah handed over the Buddha.

"Don't sell me the hundred-and-fifty-rupee ivory for ten rupees, unless you want to, Borah," smiled Joan.

"Take it, Memsahib, take it," replied the Borah hastily, for he was a reasonable man, content as a rule with a hundred per cent profit.

And before long, Joan Wallingford came to accept her husband's belief. Became imbued with it, and genuinely, without self-deception, held it.

Tony was going to break the family tradition, survive middle age, and live to be an old man.

He would, thank God, survive her.

Yes, if Daphne had done for him what this wandering Borah had undoubtedly done for her, then, whatever befell, she would try to feel nothing but gratitude for Daphne.

But nothing would befall—between him and Daphne. Tony would grow out of that sort of thing, now that he had grown out of his belief in the imminence of death, the certainty of a short life, the knowledge that he came of doomed and fated stock.

*   *   *   *   *

Then came the War; and to Joan Wallingford, the Borah's prophecy had, at first, been a slight comfort, for, at times, she believed in it. Soon she believed in it completely.

§3

Holding, as he now did, the unshakeable belief that he would inevitably attain great age, Anthony Wallingford, a logical-minded man, realized and accepted its corollary, its obvious sequel, the fact that he would survive the War.

To him and to his wife, Joan, the belief, the certainty, that he would do so, brought joy unbounded—to her, because Tony would be spared; to him, because there could be no risk he would not take, no danger he could not face.

Thus it was that, having accompanied the Indian Expeditionary Corps to France, and greatly distinguished himself for initiative, coolness, and courage in the trenches, he sought new worlds to conquer, a new sphere of activity, and a greater scope for usefulness, distinction and success—in the air.

Always, from the day that a heavier-than-air machine had left the ground, he had been absorbingly interested in aviation.

To his clever, original and enquiring mind the problem of flight had been the most interesting problem of life. In the doings of Wilbur and Orville Wright, Maurice Farman, Bleriot, Rolls and the other pioneers, he took the deepest interest; with the relative merits of the Gnome, Anzani, Renault motors, the Deperdussin, Breguet, Voisin, Caudron, Nieuport, Morane-Saulnier and other patterns of aeroplanes, he was familiar; and during his last furlough before the War, he seriously "took up" the science of flying and learned to fly in England, and flew in France at Buc. Returning to India, he wrote articles in Service magazines, on the probable future of the heavier-than-air flying-machine as a means of reconnaissance in time of war—articles that attracted considerable attention, and not only in India.

So when, on the return of the Indian Expeditionary Corps to the East and other spheres of glory and invaluable success, Major Anthony Moresby Wallingford applied for transfer to the Royal Flying Corps, now a swiftly-expanding, indispensable part of the British Army, his request was not only granted but welcomed.

His success was immediate and his rise to fame, both as an aviator and instructor, meteoric. Apparently bearing a charmed life; being ignorant of the meaning of danger; crashing fewer machines than any other pilot in the Service; taking greater risks of weather, enemy action, unknown and untried brands of new machine; piling up a bigger record of flying hours, recorded destructions of enemy machines, successful missions, decorations and deeds of desperate daring, Wallingford quickly became Squadron-leader and then, recalled to England, Commandant of the principal School of Instruction in flying, aerial fighting, bombing, reconnaissance, artillery "spotting," and the constantly-developing branches of aerial education and training.

Thus the Great War was Anthony Wallingford's Great Opportunity, and he grasped it, made the very utmost of it, made it his stepping-stone to fame and fortune—secure in the absolute certainty that he would survive it, that he would live to reap his harvest and garner his sheaves; certain, like Napoleon, that upon no bullet was his name inscribed; and, better still, certain that in no aeroplane, however crank, ill-used, ill-engined, however riddled and shattered and torn, would he meet his death.

No, Anthony Wallingford, favourite of the fickle Gods, was marked for long, long life.

And that knowledge gave him the colossal self-confidence at which men marvelled; that knowledge strengthened the ambition that devoured him.

So immersed was he in his work, so absorbed, so literally enthralled, that he forgot Joan, nursing in India—and soon forgot Geoff Wogan, laughing in a mad-house.

Flight. . . . Flight. . . . Flight. . . . The Conquest of the Air . . . the Annihilation of Space and Time. . . .

Yes—when the War was o'er, he'd be as distinguished, successful and recklessly daring in civil aviation as he had been in military flying. He would blaze trails across the world—be the first man to fly to . . . oh, to any country or place to which man had never flown before.

For he was almost immortal; he bore a charmed life, he could not die—for more than half a century at least. That, he *knew*.

CHAPTER XX

"When the war is o'er we'll part no more," hummed Mr. Jack Wellacombe as he sat drinking, out on the lawn of the Bombay Yacht Club.

He was always Mr. Jack Wellacombe, never John, for he was fat and well-favoured, hail-fellow-well-met, and very popular. He was also local agent of the Anglo-China Royal Mail Steam Packet Company, and a very useful man to know. He could do you a very good turn when you were fixing up your passage home, especially in times when there were "three simultaneous Generals to a seat at table, four to a cabin, five to a bath and six to Another Place," as he had said. In need, a very useful friend indeed, ready, willing and able to perform miracles of wangle, when he chose.

When Mr. Jack Wellacombe did use his powers in this way, it was for love, of course, and not for money. Naturally he was entirely unbribeable, but he was neither unlovable nor unloving; and on the occasions on which he had conferred a favour, it had not infrequently been upon a lady.

Well, the damned war was o'er, as he sang, and perhaps things would now settle back to normal, and a man get a chance to call his soul his own, and to work without quite so much outside interference.

Yes, over at last, and about time, too.

He turned his gaze, from the island-studded waters of the beautiful harbour, to the guest-thronged lawn that stretches between the club building and the sea.

By Jove, this was a smart woman. Hadn't he seen her before somewhere? Seemed to think so, yet one would hardly forget a beauty like that.

No, he didn't know her, but he was jolly well going to, if she was a Member and staying in Bombay.

Might only be passing through, of course. What a beautiful . . . And, by Jove, it was toward him that she was coming.

Mr. Jack Wellacombe rose from his seat at the little table beside the low wall that divides the Yacht Club lawn from the lapping waters.

"Mr. Wellacombe?"

"Yes. I'm afraid . . ."

"No, you don't know me, Mr. Wellacombe, but I know you—by sight. So please excuse . . ."

"Won't you sit down. Do have some tea?"

"Oh, thanks so much, I will—if it means you've a few minutes to spare. I wanted to ask you a favour."

Mr. Jack Wellacombe was well accustomed to this gambit. An enormous number of people wanted to "ask him a favour", and he had his stereotyped favourite reply to the gambit. But not to a lovely woman like this. No, no. It was one of the few perquisites of his position, the power to do a favour for a lady of this type.

"You want a passage home, Mrs. . . . . er . . . ?"

"Well, I do and I don't," replied the lady, with a slow smile, charming—enigmatic as her answer.

Mr. Jack Wellacombe also smiled, and made his smile as charming as he could.

"Well," he said quizzically, a twinkle lighting his roguish eye, "shall we act on the do or the don't?"

"Depends."

"On what, Mrs. . . . . er . . . ? If it depends on me, you can . . . er . . . count on me."

"Depends on the passenger list."

"Oh, I see," nodded Mr. Jack Wellacombe. "You want to travel home in the same ship with some friends."

"Or to travel home on some other ship than that chosen by a friend," smiled the lady.

"Quite, quite. H'm. What you really want to know is who's going home on the *King Emperor* on Monday?" guessed Mr. Jack Wellacombe, making a very good shot.

"Or who is *not* doing so," was the untruthful reply. "I'll be quite frank with you, Mr. Wellacombe. There is someone I want to avoid—a horrible man who's been pestering me ever since I had the misfortune to nurse him in the Lanapur Hospital. I am almost certain he's going home on the *King Emperor*, and if he is, I'm going to ask you to book me a passage by the next boat, if you possibly can. But if he's not, can you get me a passage on this boat?"

"Or ship," laughed Wellacombe. "She's a ship—of sorts. Or was before the War, poor old girl. But for that she'd have been broken up five years ago. Passenger list. Well, highly irregular, but if you like to come down to my office to-morrow morning, at—what time shall we say?—at twelve?—I'll let you have a peep at the passenger list, so far as it is made up. There won't be many changes between now and next Monday, and if this fellow's name is on the list, you can take it he's going on the *King Emperor*, and you can also take it that I'll do my very best for you with the next ship—if she doesn't arrive full from Hong Kong. That'll be the *Peshawur*—if that'll suit you."

"Oh, splendidly! Thank you so much. I'm so grateful to you. Then I'll come to the Anglo-China offices to-morrow at twelve, and ask for you."

"And perhaps you'll lunch with me here afterwards, Mrs. . . . er . . ."

"I shall be delighted. Thanks so much."

And scanning the list of passengers proposing to join the *King Emperor*, Daphne Easterwood found, as she had expected, the name of Captain Stacey Burle-stone.

"No, his name is not on the list yet," she informed Wellacombe, "so if you can find me a corner on the *King Emperor*, I'll go by her."

And Mr. Jack Wellacombe, being Mr. Jack Wella-combe, found Daphne Easterwood an extremely comfortable corner on the *King Emperor*.

§2

"*Stacey!*"

"Mrs. Easterwood! Well, this is a surprise."

"It is indeed."

And undoubtedly it was a surprise for Captain Stacey Burlestone, to come suddenly face to face with the last person in the world whom he desired to meet. And not only to meet, but to have as an inescapable, unavoidable fellow-traveller for a fortnight.

How beautiful she still was. . . . How infinitely desirable. . . . How hateful.

If the exception proves the rule, the rule that a beautiful face is the index of a beautiful mind, that a sweet expression is an expression of sweet thoughts, was proven here. This was a lovely mask, a mask that never slipped. Almost never; only "almost"—for, once, he had seen the face behind the mask.

"I didn't know you were in India again," he said.

Heavens above, what rotten luck!

"Yes. I've been nursing. Came out with Mrs. Moresby Wallingford. Lady Wrattesbury, when she rejoined His Excellency, wrote and asked her to hurry back and bring anyone else who'd come and help with her Hospital. Especially anyone who knew India. And you, Stacey? Geoff Wogan told me he left you in Africa."

"Been a prisoner of war in East Africa the whole time."

What infernal luck this was. If the ship hadn't started, he'd have walked straight off and waited for the next ship on which he could get a berth.

"Liked you so much they wouldn't part with you, eh?"

"Exactly. I owe the loss of four years of my beautiful youth to my even more beautiful health."

"Wounded?"

"Badly. But made a record recovery. And never had a day's illness—apart from the wound, of course. Sometimes I was the only man in the force who hadn't malaria or dysentery. I was a joke. Couldn't see the joke myself."

Daphne Easterwood laughed.

"Not even in a mirror, Stacey?"

"No joke to the German surgeon who operated on me. He took me very seriously. Prize exhibit. 'Alone he did it.'"

Why was he talking like this, hurriedly, and for the sake of talking?

What ghastly luck. Daphne Easterwood, of all people.

"Simply couldn't catch anything, and I could hardly blame them for turning me to account when there was a cholera epidemic in one appalling jungle-camp."

"Yes, you look a different man from what you did when I first came to Quetawur."

"Oh, I was pretty fit, even then, though I'd been having quite a bad year or two, previous to that. Rotten health, really."

"And you went all through the campaign on the wrong side, so to speak?"

"I certainly went all through the campaign. Marched every yard that the Germans did, when General Smuts got them on the run. And finished as fit as a fiddle.

"But for that I shouldn't be here now. I should have got across from Africa on a hospital ship, and sailed for home on an earlier ship than this," he added.

Had she detected a note of bitterness in his voice?

If so, it didn't affect the Mona Lisa smile.

"Poor Stacey. What cruel luck."

Was she referring to his meeting her on this ship?

If so, she was right.

"Four years of that awful life! Four years of misery and tantalization, while other people were covering themselves with glory and winning the 'tinkling symbols' thereof."

"Well, I had all the hardships of a campaign with 'that prisoner feeling' added, and none of the . . . er . . . fun of the fair—as you say."

"And they treated you pretty decently?"

"Oh, yes. Yes. Quite a good crowd really. I'd the greatest admiration for the General and for his Brigade-Major, a chap named Kraut. They were all right, except one swine—who said I owed my obvious health and fitness to pinching the medical comforts and the food of the wounded men I was supposed to be looking after."

"You certainly had wonderful luck, to keep so well, hadn't you?"

"Wonderful. Poor Captain Spangenberg, a great friend of mine, had the cruellest luck I ever heard of. He was as tough and fit as I. Went right through the war on his own feet, every day of it—and died of 'flu down at Dar-es-salaam after the Armistice was signed. Can you beat it?"

"Oh, poor man!"

"Yes. Cruel. When mine enemy died I felt I had lost my friend—a real friend. . . . Well, I must go and unpack."

Daphne Easterwood smiled and raised her hand, partly to hide an artificial yawn.

Yes, he must go and unpack. Well, it wouldn't take him a fortnight to unpack.

The same old Stacey Burlestone. What a fool she'd been—for once in her life, anyhow. What a fool to mis-read him as she'd done, and to play her cards so badly that dreadful day in the Hotel at Zermich.

Yes, of all the men she'd ever known, right from the days of Fritz von Voehniger, Stacey Burlestone was the best—or at any rate the one who attracted her most. So solid, so reliable, so sound, so honourable . . . so damned honourable, so everything that she herself was not.

Poor Aubrey had been that, too, but, oh dear, oh dear, what a boy, what a child, what an excellent, virtuous bread-and-butter-hound. And what a whole-some, excellent, nutritious and disgusting diet is bread-and-butter.

Bread and Aubrey Easterwood!

Well, it had been a case of "any port in a storm," for Colin Mackleworth had left her nothing but debts, and Aubrey had been there to hand; madly in love with her; and, though not well off, had great expectations . . . which incidentally hadn't materialized in time to do her any good.

Why couldn't Stacey have shown his hand, or rather his heart, sooner? Before she "took up with"

Aubrey Easterwood. Everybody said Stacey was an absolute what-is-it. A woman-hater; a confirmed bachelor. And when he did begin to hang around, she'd jumped to the conclusion that he was riding her off, as the polo-players say—deliberately coming between them, protecting and preserving his precious Aubrey from contamination.

Well, she'd discovered the truth too late, and misjudged her man, too.

Was it too late now?

She'd be more than willing to forgive him, if he was willing to be forgiven. Or, at least, to make a good pretence of it.

All that was ancient history. Might as well forgive and forget—or, at any rate, put it aside, for the present. And Time had healed the wound, to some extent. Let bygones be bygones. . . . She was growing no younger; she must find another "port" and safe peaceful anchorage; and she had always loved Stacey really. He could have been her *amant de cœur* whenever he liked.

And she was tolerant; a woman who could make allowances. Also she had always possessed, and enjoyed, the power of loving and hating simultaneously. A great gift.

A fortnight with him all to herself. A fortnight of deck-chairs in the light of the moon and the stars. A woman of experience (and God knew she was that) ought to be able to retrieve a mistake and put things right.

So while the good Stacey went and unpacked, she'd go and see the Head Waiter or Chief Steward, and Stacey would find that there'd been another coincidence, and that he was beside her at table.

He'd never suspect; and he wasn't the sort of man to go to the Chief Steward and ask if she'd arranged it.

Well, if she didn't succeed he'd be the first man with whom she'd ever failed. He'd hurt her cruelly, given her pride an almost mortal wound—but life was a battle-field . . . her life had been one long battle . . . and in battle one must expect an occasional wound.

It would be marriage or nothing, with Stacey Burlestone, and it was time she settled down.

She'd settle up, too, with Stacey, if he married her; and she'd pay off that Zermich score.

Yes, if she married Stacey, she'd . . . er . . . retire . . . be good, settle down, feel safe. And still have lots of fun, of course.

He was well-off now, according to Hennessy Wogan; had a place, and knew lots of people. They'd have a flat in town and a good time. Plenty of racing. Hunting. Salmon and grouse. An occasional flutter at Monte. Yes, it would do very nicely. And she'd stay put.

But she'd teach Stacey Burlestone something. Plague the life out of him: teach him a lesson and lead him a dance—within limits, of course. Forgive and forget? She'd never forgive him—and he should never forget what he'd said to her at Zermich. But she'd keep him, once she'd got him. No more free-lancing. She'd been married once and . . . er . . . not married—was it five or six times since Fritz von Voehniger had been such a disappointment?

Time she settled down, and of all the men she'd ever known, Stacey Burlestone was the one with whom she'd be most likely really to settle down—for good. Her good, anyway.

§3

Stacey Burlestone was by nature essentially and fundamentally a kindly man; but long residence in the East and a wide experience of Orientals had led him to the conclusion, right or wrong, that, to the Eastern mind, kindness and weakness are synonymous terms.

While totally disagreeing from those who say that the native of India is devoid of gratitude, he knew enough of him, whether incarnated as Gurkha, Sikh, Pathan or Punjabi Mussulman, to realize how little he knew of him, how little he could grasp his point of view, put himself in his place and think as he thought.

But he did believe that it must be with extreme care that the European exhibits gratuitous kindliness, leniency and "easiness" toward him.

Understanding his language perfectly, he knew that the Indian's mental attitude toward the kindly and easy European is inevitably tinged with contempt; and that his translation of "kind" is a word indistinguishable from "soft."

It had thus been his endeavour, while a regimental officer, to temper his mercy with very strict justice; to be known rather as a hard than a soft man; and, where he wished to act with kindness, to give some reason other than his real one, a reason immediately comprehensible to the beneficiary.

In some ways Daphne Easterwood reminded him of a native, and, though he was perfectly certain that she had nothing of what is delicately termed a touch of the tar-brush, he found it difficult to believe that she was of purely Nordic origin.

As she sat with her deck-chair by his, but facing in the opposite direction, so that, although side by side, they were turned face to face, he once again studied her as so often he had done before—this woman whom he had so loved; so hated; so admired; so despised.

Yes, there was definitely something Oriental about her, especially about her great black eyes. . . . Incidentally he had, of course, seen both Pathans and Berbers with blue-green and grey-green eyes. Yes, and he recalled a case of eyes that were definitely green in a swarthy bearded face beneath a heavy *puggari*. . . . But hers were real Eastern eyes—Indian, Turkish, Moorish; not European at all.

Burlestone studied her.

An Oriental face and certainly an Oriental grace and poise and sinuosity, reminding one of the stately women who, with perfect carriage, walked to and from the well, bearing pitchers of water upon their heads, and of the lithe dancing-girls of perfect figure and beautiful proportion.

No, of course she had no Eastern blood, but it wouldn't surprise him to learn that she was of Latin extraction—Provençal, Andalusian, Sicilian.

By Jove, yes! Had either, or indeed both, of her

parents been Southern French, Southern Spanish, Southern Italian, she might well have Moorish blood; for quite a large proportion of the people of that part of Europe are descended from the Moorish invaders—just as a great many of the natives of Morocco are of Gothic Viking origin.

Yes, Daphne might very well have a strong strain of African blood.

What a rotten thing to think.

Well, one couldn't help one's thoughts, and, anyhow, he'd bet his life she wasn't plain English, or rather, pure British. Definitely something "native" about her; and therefore not to be treated too kindly, although, alas, he was beginning to feel almost kindly toward her—once again.

No, Daphne was one of those people who would mistake kindness for weakness; and with Daphne he would be strong. Against Daphne he would be strong.

"A penny for them, Stacey."

"Worth more than that to me, and worth nothing to you."

"Oh? Thinking of something unpleasant about me, were you?"

"I wasn't thinking about you at all," lied Stacey Burlestone.

"No? Well, you are going to, Stacey, my dear. You are going to think about me a whole lot."

"Well, that might not be to your advantage," fenced Burlestone.

"It might be to yours, dear," whispered Daphne Easterwood, smiling her Mona Lisa smile and giving him a long, long look.

A disturbing look. Definitely a disturbing look. Damn the woman.

Stacey Burlestone rose to his feet.

"Excuse me, Mrs. Easterwood," he said. "I . . ."

"All right, Stacey. I'll see that no-one takes your chair," mocked Daphne Easterwood, smiling still, smiling undaunted.

But as he turned away, her mouth straightened and hardened, her eyes narrowed and she looked less beautiful.

§4

Partly from force of habit, the habit of a life-time, partly as a side line, a little sport without danger, a little reassuring exercise of unfading and unfailing charms and charm, Daphne Easterwood vamped the Third Officer, Mr. Hallington, a very susceptible, romantic and pleasing young man, honest and honourable, clean without and within.

For him Stacey Burlestone felt a little pity, inasmuch as the poor chap was obviously losing his head as well as his heart.

"Sailors are a chivalrous tribe," observed Daphne Easterwood, as Mr. Hallington, rising from the foot-rest of her chair, saluted, and said that he feared he must push off. "Always so nice to women."

"Very," agreed Stacey Burlestone, beside whom she had, as usual, seated herself.

"They don't see much of them, of course," he added, a little bitterly, eyeing the beautiful, hateful woman with whom he was again falling in love—or with whom he had never been really out of love.

"Oh! Cynical. . . . Sailors are more chivalrous than others because they see less of women, eh?"

"I imagine that's the reason, Daphne. They see them as enchanting creatures because distance lends enchantment to the view."

"Are none of them really enchanting—at close range?"

"Oh, yes. I have known—at least one."

"Thank you, Stacey. But whoever would have thought it."

Silence.

"I *do* like Mr. Hallington, Stacey."

"I'm sure you do, Daphne."

"D'you think he likes me?"

"I'm sure he does."

Daphne Easterwood appeared to consider deeply.

"But—I don't know," she said. "Isn't it notorious

that sailors have a 'wife' in every port?"

"It is."

"Very well, then, clever! How can they be chivalrous simply because they know so little about women?"

"*Touché*," smiled Burlestone.

And his smile was so pleasant, so kindly, that Daphne Easterwood slipped her tiny hand into his, giving it a warmly affectionate and meaning squeeze.

A terribly clever woman; determined, shameless, devoid of scruple; a huntress equipped; a goddess revealed, he thought.

A goddess! At times, as she eyed, and narrowly watched, Stacey Burlestone, she was a fury from the hell of women scorned.

It may be safely stated that no man of the type of Stacey Burlestone is a match for a woman of the type of Daphne Easterwood, for her faults are her allies, her armour and her arms: his virtues are his foes, his weaknesses. The greater his chivalry, kindliness, for-bearance, gentlehood, the less his chance of defeating his unscrupulous enemy.

And on the night of the great sea-tragedy of the *King Emperor*, Stacey Burlestone was tempted of the devil—and Daphne Easterwood: Stacey Burlestone, chivalrous and kindly, a greater admirer of robustious King David than of the gentle Joseph; Stacey Burlestone, a man who had loved this woman beyond telling and in all his life had loved none other.

CHAPTER XXI

Few adult people need reminding of the published details of the tragic loss of the *King Emperor*, oldest ship of the Anglo-China Royal Mail Steam Packet Company: of the fact that she filled and sank in a few minutes; that, thanks to the skill and heroism of the Captain, Officers and crew, five of the boats got away; that, owing to the cyclonic storm and roughness of the south-west monsoon sea, four of these were dismasted, swamped and never seen again; and that one of them, handled and commanded with consummate ability and courage, survived to be picked up, a fortnight later, by the *Perseus* of the British Australia Line, proceeding on her lawful occasions and unusual homeward journey from Sydney by way of Singapore, Calcutta and Colombo, the Persian Gulf, Basra, Muscat, Aden, Port Said, Naples, Marseilles and Southampton.

§2

Mr. Hallington, Third Officer of the ill-fated *King Emperor*, was determined to save his life, his boat, and Mrs. Easterwood. To be more exact, Mrs. Easterwood, his other passengers, his crew, his boat and his own life. In spite of his sufferings—from thirst, hunger, sleeplessness, soaked clothing, soreness and anxiety— he was not unhappy. He was saving Mrs. Easterwood and she was watching him do it. A brave woman that. Really brave. Plucky as she was beautiful. Never a groan, a tear, a complaint, nor a snivel out of her.

An example to one or two of the men passengers who didn't come out as strong as some of the others in these tragic and terrible circumstances.

Wasn't it as bad for Mrs. Easterwood as it was for fat Mr. Prollick, for example, who moaned and groaned all day, and wanted the water-ration increased, if not the meagre biscuit issue. Fact was, the plump bird had never missed a meal in his life, and had never slept out of a comfortable soft bed. Do him good to starve for a bit, and to sit upright on a thwart until he fell over from sheer weariness, and slept in an inch or two of water.

Let him and two or three more take example from her.

They weren't cowardly gutless hounds—like that little Cypriote, Maltese, Scorpion or Levantine swine Karouian who begged, blubbering, on his knees, for more water, and who'd started the boat-voyage with a hip-flask that he'd kept to himself—but they didn't show up any too well under hardship and adversity. No, it wasn't so much the danger that daunted them, as the misery and pain. Pity there weren't more like Captain Burlestone.

Now, that was a man.

Might have been at sea all his days—and in a ship's lifeboat too—by the calm way he took things.

Never turned a hair. It had been a stroke of luck, having him in the boat. Just the man to put in charge of the food and water. An officer and a gentleman— whose word and orders no-one would presume to dispute or doubt. And he was accustomed to managing and issuing rations, of course. Not the poorest, meanest creature on board could question his fairness, honesty, or ability for a task like that—and it relieved one of a big responsibility, as well as of an ugly job. Especially when women, children, and one or two things calling themselves men, begged and prayed and wept for more . . . more . . . more. . . .

"More than your share, you mean, eh?" Captain Burlestone would growl. "I'll give you less if you don't shut up; and divide it among the kids."

He was splendid and, what was more, never seemed a penny the worse for wear. He wasn't sea-sick; he didn't appear to be hungry; he scarcely ever slept; and he seemed as fit as a fiddle. Yes; with everybody else looking gaunt, starved, haggard, and just about all-in, sick unto death, Captain Burlestone looked a picture of health. Absolutely a picture of perfect health.

Queer, that.

Mr. Hallington considered himself to be as tough as most people, for he had never had a day's illness in his life—until now; but he knew that he looked and felt as sick and skinny a scare-crow as any of them, almost. And yet Captain Burlestone might have been enjoying four meals a day and an eight-hour night in bed, so far as appearances went. And spirits, too. He was a marvel. And, most remarkable thing of all, one would think he was getting all the water he needed, too, judging by the way he spoke and looked. No cracked lips, leather tongue, glue-coated mouth and closing throat, there. Quite different from the rest—including the stout A.B.'s, the tough stokers, and that fine fellow O'Rourke, the Quarter-master, an old Navy man.

And so it remained, days later, when old Mr. Markess and two children had died; the mother of one of the latter had gone mad—and gone overboard, too, in the night; three of the men passengers were obviously dying, and everybody was in a very bad way indeed. So it remained; Captain Burlestone enjoying perfect health—and Mrs. Easterwood displaying perfect courage. Well, Captain Burlestone could take a double trick at steering to-night, since he was so hale and hearty, for Mr. Hallington was getting pretty near the end of his tether—what with slipping Mrs. Easterwood a share of his biscuit-ration and half his water, on the quiet. That and the responsibility. . . . No, probably the responsibility was a blessing in disguise—kept one up to the mark, and left one less time to pay attention to one's aches and pains and the fact that one was dying of thirst, hunger and weariness.

"Steer as long as you can, Sir," said Mr. Hallington, "and then wake me. For God's sake don't fall asleep and let her broach to—or we shall be swamped. . . . Thank the Lord you can handle a boat as well as I can. If we still split the steering and keep the poor old Quarter-master and Jackson responsible for seeing that their watches don't stop bailing . . . that's . . . the . . . best . . . plan . . . I . . ."

Mr. Hallington fell asleep as he spoke, and slumped

down at Burlestone's feet, all in, done up, for he had had less sleep than anybody except Burlestone (who did not appear to need any), and Hallington had had less food and water too, thanks to his sudden, swift and incandescent love for Mrs. Easterwood.

That lady, seated as usual in the stern-sheets beside Burlestone, also lowered herself to the wet boards, leant her head upon Burlestone's thigh and put her arms about his knees.

A long silence.

Daphne Easterwood awoke, looked up into his face and smiled.

"Well . . . Charon," she whispered. "We're crossing the Styx, eh? A boat-load of the dead."

And indeed, save for themselves, this company might have been a boat-load of dead people. The wind and sea having moderated and the boat been bailed dry by the Quarter-master's "watch" of deck-hands, he and his men had fallen asleep.

"Bosh!" replied Stacey Burlestone. "We're joy-riding. Sky-larking. 'Who's for a sail in the Skylark? Nice morning, Sir. Like a trip round the Bay 'smorning? Thank you, Sir.' Styx? Over the sticks, if you like—steeple-chasing the waves. Aren't you enjoying the sail, Daphne?"

"Kiss me, Stacey. I think I am enjoying it—in a way —so long as you are here. I should enjoy it more if I weren't dying of thirst. Kiss me, Stacey."

"Eyes in the boat," was the reply. "I can't steer you and kiss the boat—I mean I can't . . ."

"Can't steer me? Would you like to try, Stacey, if we get ashore alive. . . . Kiss me, Stacey. . . .

"Stacey, I think you are absolutely noble; and the god-awfullest prig that ever—strutted."

"Pigs don't strut, my dear."

"I said 'prig.'"

"Oh—prig? Perhaps so. I certainly feel I'm one whenever I'm being—er—virtuous."

"Well, then; why be virtuous?"

"A bad habit, I suppose. You're a brave lass, Daphne."

"Oh, Stacey . . . I'm dying. I'm dying of thirst. Don't let me die, Stacey," and Daphne Easterwood buried her face in her hands, while her body shook and trembled.

"'Shaken by dry sobs' is the expression," murmured Stacey Burlestone, forbearing to remark that she had had more water than anybody—a truth of which he was aware by reason of the fact that, while apparently asleep, he had watched Hallington giving her a share of his meagre ration.

What had been his real feeling as he watched and unavoidably listened? Was it *possible* that he was jealous of Hallington? And was that why he had ceased to give her any of his own ration—after he had seen her sharing Hallington's as well? . . . Jealous?

"I'd like to kill you," whispered Daphne Easterwood. "I would if I could."

Stacey Burlestone laughed.

"The world's champion prig," she said. "Did you ever hear of the Jew who was eating a ham-sandwich when a terrific thunderstorm arose, and he said, 'Lord! Lord! What a lot of fuss about a little bit of pork!'?"

"Oh, yes! Was he another prig?"

"No—but I verily believe you think that the *King Emperor* was sunk to save your virtue. Just when you'd decided you weren't weak enough or strong enough to play good Little Joseph to my naughty Mrs. Potiphar . . . 'Lord! Lord! What a lot of fuss about a little bit of virtue!' said you to yourself, Prig Stacey, as you fell—or rather, prepared to fall—and the ship sank, to save you from sin!"

Stacey Burlestone laughed.

"But then, of course, it wasn't ordinary virtue. It was the noble Stacey Burlestone's Virtue," sneered Daphne Easterwood. "That must be saved at the cost of all our lives, naturally. As you couldn't save yourself from me, Heaven must. And sank the ship."

Stacey Burlestone laughed again.

"We must remember that—and tell them, at the Board of Trade Inquiry into the sinking of the *King Emperor*. It will interest the Court—and the public.

"Well, I'm glad you can talk, Daphne," he added.

"Shows you're bearing up and going strong.

"And getting enough to eat and drink," he added.

"Don't be a brute. Enough to eat and drink! I'd give *anything*—all I've got in the world—for a cup of water. . . . Give me some water, Stacey."

"What?"

"Give me some water. I'm dying."

"Aren't the others? Aren't those two poor children and that woman, as well as the injured Quarter-master and all the men? Do you really want me to rob them for you? Of course you don't, Daphne. . . . *Noblesse oblige*, and all that. . . . You consider yourself 'better' than those steerage people and the 'common' sailors and stokers. You wouldn't 'look down' on them—and drink their ration of water, too, would you?"

"Thanks for the sermon. Preach a little more, you . . . you . . . you prig and snob and fool. Yes, *fool*—as you'll find out, if we're saved," and she burst into a flood of tears of rage and misery.

"Cheer up, Daphne. Be yourself. I've been admiring your pluck all the time. Thinking how brave you were. I know it's an awful temptation. Awful. But you wouldn't take any of their fair share, would you, now? Of course not."

"Oh, Stacey, I'm dying of thirst. Don't let me die. I'm not strong like you. . . . And I'm not in charge of the food and water all night—when everybody is asleep— like you are."

This missed Stacey Burlestone, fine-minded man of honour.

"Oh, for pity's sake, give me a little, Stacey. These people aren't old friends of yours. I am, Stacey. Surely something's due to friendship. To one's friends. They come before strangers, don't they? What's friendship for, otherwise? Stacey! I shall go overboard like that other woman. I shall drink sea-water and go mad. Stacey. . . . Help me. Save me, Stacey, and I'll never forget it. There's nothing I won't do for you."

"*Noblesse oblige*, Daphne. If we think we're these people's 'superiors,' we should give them part of our rations, not take theirs."

Beggars' Horses

"Well—you think you're superior to everybody, including me. Especially me. Why don't you *'oblige'* then, out of your great *'noblesse'*?"

"All right, Daphne. You can have half my to-morrow's ration—if you care to drink it. I ought not to do it, because Hallington has an idea that I'm—useful; and that he or I should always be at the tiller. Thinks we have, or ought to have, as officers, the best-developed sense of responsibility, and all that. Leave the oars, the bailing, and the sail to the men, while we keep the bridge and the look-out."

"What's that got to do with it?"

"Those who are responsible for the lives of these people should have their fair share of the food and water. Or more. Especially Hallington—as he is the most important and valuable person in the boat, the one who is going to save the others, save us all, including you. Nobody should accept a share of his water rations. And I come next, Daphne. I can steer and handle a boat in a sea-way; and I can be trusted not to fall asleep and let anything happen to the boat for want of a competent helmsman—nor let the lights of a ship go by unseen, because my eyes were shut. Nobody ought to accept a share of my ration, Daphne."

"Oh, *no!* It would be an awful calamity if anything happened to you, wouldn't it?"

"Shocking."

"You don't look as though it is likely to. Everybody's saying how amazingly fit you look. They can't under-stand it."

"No. I . . . er . . . *enjoy* perfect health."

"You look as though you enjoy it."

"No-one knows how I 'enjoy' it."

"Then you could afford to give a little water to a dying woman, I should think."

"I'm going to."

"Oh, Stacey! I knew you'd . . ."

"My own ration, mind, Daphne. I'll give you half my to-morrow's allowance."

"Oh, *Stacey!* How can I ever . . ."

The Quarter-master sat up, stared, passed his hand

across his roughly-bandaged head, rubbed his eyes, and fell back again.

Daphne Easterwood drank.

Drank and felt better. Felt so much better and, for the moment, so grateful to Stacey Burlestone, that she talked to him of love.

The wind had dropped, and with its falling, the sea had grown calm. From behind a passing bank of clouds the moon shone forth.

"I feel light-headed, Stacey; almost light-hearted. Kiss me . . . ! Stacey, we're going to be saved, I know we are."

"I am a bit light-headed, too, Daphne. It's the short commons makes us feel so."

"Keep like it, Stacey darling. . . . Kiss me, again . . . again . . . *again*. . . .

"Stacey—we must never part, after this, must we? We couldn't."

"Daphne—my dear. God! You do make it hard for a man! Daphne—I . . . I don't love you. I don't really. I can't . . ."

"You *do* love me. You've loved me ever since you first met me. You do. You know you do. You love me, Stacey."

"There's no real solid lasting love—the only sort of love that people ought to marry on—without res . . ."

"Say it. Go on. I know what you were going to say. '*Without respect.*' . . . That's what you were going to say —so don't tell me lies. Yes. '*Without respect—and as I don't respect you, my poor fallen woman, I cannot marry you.*' I understand, Stacey. Thank you."

Silence.

"Is that your last word, Stacey?"

"It was yours, Daphne."

"Oh, be a man, as well as God's Own Perfect Prig and the Devil's Own Silly Snob. Is that your last word, Stacey Burlestone?"

"Yes, Daphne *Easterwood*."

And at dawn that morning, the Fourth Officer of the *Perseus*, walking the bridge, suddenly stopped, raised to his eyes the binoculars that hung upon his broad chest, studied the *King Emperor*'s lifeboat, and shouted an order to the helmsman.

CHAPTER XXII

How it got about, on the *Perseus*, nobody knew—unless it were Mrs. Easterwood.

Everybody somehow had the tale, at second hand, but everybody was uncertain as to how and when and where the rumour had arisen, whence the scandal had spread, and who was responsible for it.

Most people declined to believe it, or said they did; for most people are fundamentally decent—and he seemed such a nice man, this Captain Burlestone.

Still—it couldn't be denied that he looked entirely different from the other poor creatures, the survivors of that terrible experience in an open boat, the sole survivors indeed of the great crowded liner the *King Emperor*.

Entirely different. So healthy. The colour of his cheeks undoubtedly added colour to the story; the fact that obviously he had not lost weight added weight to the accusation.

But who had made the accusation? No-one could say. Even Mr. Hallington, who ought to have known, was only half aware. Much less than half, really.

And certainly the injured Quarter-master had held no converse with the passengers of the *Perseus*.

*   *   *   *   *

"Yes—he's a marvel. As you say, a picture of perfect health." Mrs. Easterwood had agreed, when the Fourth Officer of the *Perseus*—her easy, early slave and jealous rival of Mr. Hallington—had remarked on Captain Burlestone's appearance.

"Looks as though he'd been on a pleasure-cruise in a private yacht," observed the Fourth Officer.

"He does. He was in charge of the food and water, you know, in the boat."

"Yes?" said the Fourth.

264

"Yes."

*   *   *   *   *

One of the children, saved from the boat, was saved, only to die a few hours later.

Mrs. Easterwood, a ministering angel, helped nurse it devotedly, condoled with the distracted mother, and did her utmost to comfort the poor half-demented soul.

"The little darling's happy now," she said. "No more suffering and pain. Perfect peace and purest joy, for ever more. . . . Oh, but only to think that a little more food and water would have saved it, the poor starved mite. Wasted to a skeleton. And some people in that boat came out of it as fit and well—yes, and well fed, too—as they went into it!"

*   *   *   *   *

Mrs. Easterwood, leaning on the forward rail of the promenade deck, caught sight of the Quarter-master of the *King Emperor*, a rough diamond, sunning himself on the hatch of the well-deck, down below. Kindly and graciously she went down and talked to him, enquired about his broken head, now properly dressed by the surgeon of the *Perseus*.

"Well . . . all's well that ends well, they say, Mum," he growled, "but 'twasn't so well for some of them women-passengers and children. Wot time's the poor little nipper's funeral? 'Ope they don't let the poor mother attend it. Bad enough—without seein' 'er there, too. We made a bit of a wreath, we 'ave. Artificial o' course, but the best we c'd do. Shows respect; an' she's a very nice woman. Plucky, too. An' I know she give the kid more'n 'arf 'er own share as well."

And the Quarter-master blew his nose hard, and crudely.

"Yes. It's a pity one or two others couldn't have done the same. One or two who were getting *more* than their share."

"Eh? . . . What's that, lady?" And the Quarter-master stared, passed his hand across his face and rubbed his eyes.

What had the lady said? That last night when he awoke, didn't know where he was, remembered, and fell back again. Hadn't he seen Cap'n Burlestone whacking out a ration of water? Queer, at that time o' night, and everybody else asleep.

But a gent, an officer, wouldn't go for to do a thing like that. . . . Would he?

*   *   *   *   *

At the child's funeral, Captain Stacey Burlestone could not help being aware that people eyed him. Looked at him more than they did at others. Eyed him queerly. Some with quick-shifting glance, as he caught their eye. Others with long appraising stare—rather cold and hard.

Very curious.

What were they staring at *him* for? Why eye him like that? And he returned a hard look, gazing with raised eyebrows at anybody whose stare he caught.

Very curious indeed.

And it grew more and more remarkable, for, by the time the *Perseus* reached Southampton, Captain Stacey Burlestone found himself ostracized—definitely "sent to Coventry."

Far too proud, sensitive and reticent to take any steps in the matter, tax anybody with shunning him, go about asking people why they didn't cultivate his charming society, Burlestone retired into his shell, seemed to notice nothing unusual, sought no-one's society, spoke only when addressed, and generally gave the impression that this was the state of affairs that suited him exactly.

But, for all his apparent calm and indifference, he suffered bitterly, eating his heart out in resentment and anger, oppressed by a sense of the cruellest injustice.

What on earth had he done to be treated as a pariah—a leper? So far as he knew, he had only been guilty of the folly of giving away a good deal of his food-and-water ration, and of taking more than his share of duty at the tiller.

Surely he had behaved as a man should, in that boat; as an officer and gentleman should? True he had been a little rough with some of the men passengers, one or two miserable creatures who had begged him to increase their due allowance. But he had only done his duty in telling them off, as he had; trying to shame them into a sense of decency, self-respect and unselfishness. Things like those fellows Karouian, Kyprion and Skutani. Perhaps they were getting some of their own back now, by spreading lies about him?

Well, well; if people liked to listen to scum like that, believe what they said, and condemn him unheard for something or other that he hadn't done—why, let them. . . . No loss.

Whenever he came face to face with Daphne Easterwood, she smiled her famous smile—now more enigmatic than ever.

She by no means cut him, avoided him, or was unpleasant at all; but she certainly did not seek his society as she had done on the *King Emperor*.

A good job, too—and most certainly he wasn't going to ask her why. Nor ask anybody else. It would be a novelty for Captain Stacey Burlestone to go up to some passenger, late of the *King Emperor*, or to one of the *Perseus* passengers, or to the Captain, or any officer of the ship, and say,

"Look here! You don't seem to love and admire and cultivate me as much as my great charm and merit deserve. Why is it?"

No. But it was no good being foolish about it—and there really was no reason why he shouldn't gently sound Hallington on the subject. Hallington had been not only friendly, but grateful, in the boat, and had gone out of his way to express—well—admiration. And now he was as bad as any of them. Totally different in manner. Avoided him when he could, and was abrupt, unfriendly and anything but grateful and admiring, when he couldn't avoid him. Damn him.

*   *   *   *   *

Mr. Hallington was sitting in a deck-chair on the promenade deck, reading a book.

"Good morning, Hallington," said Stacey Burlestone in pleasant friendly manner.

"Morning."

"Feeling better, now? Putting on flesh a bit?"

"Yes."

"What's the matter, Hallington?"

"Nothing. I am—putting on flesh a bit."

"Yes. I mean—er—what's the matter—as between you and me?"

"There's nothing between you and me. And I don't want there to be. Good morning."

And Mr. Hallington returned to his book with deep exclusive absorption.

"Oh, no, Hallington. That won't do," replied Burlestone. "Kindly favour me with your attention for a moment. In that boat, you and I were the best of friends, and we pulled together. I did all I could to support you—and, so far as a land-lubber can help a sailor, I helped you."

"Helped yourself, too, didn't you?" snarled Hallington. "Literally helped yourself."

"What *do* you mean, my lad? Your sufferings turned your brain?" replied Burlestone, in his best unpleasant manner.

"You know what I mean. You know perfectly well. You helped yourself."

"Well—surely in doing so I helped us all?"

Mr. Hallington made a sound indicative of angry contempt.

"'*Helped us all!*'" he growled.

"Look here, Hallington. Let's have some plain speaking, shall we? I thought sailors were supposed to be blunt, outspoken, fair-dealing people. Now then—out with it."

Mr. Hallington flung down his book and rose to his feet, angry-eyed, with closed fists and clenched teeth.

For a moment he stared Burlestone in the face.

"Fair-dealing!" he growled. "*You* should talk about it!"

"I am," replied Burlestone quietly. "Tell me; did I or didn't I do my best at sailing that boat during your 'watch below,' and in managing and issuing the rations?"

"You certainly did," said Hallington. "You managed the rations, all right. Managed them so cleverly that you climbed aboard this ship as fat and well as you were when you went over the side of the *King Emperor*. Why, look at you, man! You're in perfect health. And look at me—as strong a man as you! Why, I'm a skeleton beside you. A sick skeleton, and you're—in perfect health."

"We were 'in the same boat,' Hallington—literally."

"Yes! We were in the same boat—*but I wasn't in charge of the provisions.* I thought I would put them in charge of a British Officer, a Captain in the Regular Army, and then there'd be fair play and no grumbling. No-one could say I'd unduly favoured the women and children, or my own men—*or* myself."

"Finished, Hallington?"

"Yes. Isn't it enough?"

"No. It's a cowardly mean lying insinuation. Of course it isn't enough! Make a plain accusation in plain English. Go on. Be a man."

"Oh? It's '*be a man*,' is it? Make a plain accusation, eh? Very well. I accuse you, Captain Burlestone, of stealing the food and water committed to your charge for the benefit of all. Committed to your charge because you were above suspicion! Yes—and that's why you were so willing to relieve the helm at night. Always ready, willing and able. When I and everybody else was dead asleep—whacked to the wide. And that's why you could do it when I couldn't. That's why you finished fat and fresh—in perfect health when all the rest . . ."

"Thank you, Hallington. That's much more worthy of you than insinuation and innuendo. That's a plain accusation. Now we know."

"Yes. Now you know."

"Good! Well—the next thing is—the accuser and the evidence. Who brings the charge?"

"I do."

"You do? Did you see me—er—stealing the food and water 'committed to my charge for the benefit of all—because I was above suspicion'? Did you see me doing it, with your own eyes?"

"No."

"Who did then?"

"One of the men."

"A passenger?"

"I'm not going to name him—at present."

"Was it he who told you? Did he come to you with the yarn?"

"No. He didn't tell me. I mean he didn't come to me and bring the charge against you."

"Who did, then?"

"I shall not tell you—at present."

"Why not?"

"I've promised not to do so."

"Why?"

"I gave the promise before I knew what was coming."

"I think that promise ought to be broken."

"I daresay you do. I'm—well—shall we say 'straight'? I solemnly gave my word, and repeated it. And I shall keep it."

"Was it a passenger?"

"I shall not tell you. No doubt you'll know, all in good time."

"I hope so. And somebody, Mr. Hallington, is going to know that there's a pretty stiff and stringent Law of Slander, in England."

"That's your business."

"And it may be yours, Mr. Hallington—among other people's. A damnable, abominable lie, like this, is going to be scotched—and the liar is going to be punished. Also the malicious fools who repeat it."

"Perhaps. . . . A Court of Law may decide first of all whether it is a lie. Evidence given before a Board of

Trade Court of Inquiry isn't 'slander,' I suppose?"

"No. But the spreading of malicious falsehoods on this ship is."

"Malicious falsehoods! I say you drank the water secretly. I tell you a man saw you doing it. I say I . . ."

"Well—for your own sake—don't say it to anybody else."

"Anybody else! Everybody knows it. And all England's going to know it. All the British Isles and the British Empire—and America. Everywhere that the English language is read and spoken. And serve you damn-well right—you thieving swine. I'd sooner pinch pennies out of a blind beggar's tin!"

Stacey Burlestone kept a tight rein upon his temper, and his hands in his pockets. This youngster believed what he was saying. He was in deadly earnest. And he was filled with a burning, righteous indignation. As Stacey Burlestone himself would have been, in like circumstances.

"Listen, Hallington," he said. "Do I strike you as the sort of man to do such a thing as that? Is it likely? Ask yourself. Is it likely now? Would I have believed such a tale about you, Hallington?"

"Or I about you, Captain Burlestone—if your own health hadn't proved it! Go and look at yourself in a glass, man. Go and weigh yourself. You yourself are the strongest evidence against yourself. Why should some of us be dead and all the rest of us be more than half dead—and you in perfect health? Ask yourself. Of course you'd have believed the accusation, if it had been made against me—and I had been in the pink of condition, like you.

"No, it won't do," Hallington added. "Slander be damned."

"We'll see about that when we reach England," replied Burlestone.

"You bet we will," replied Mr. Hallington, resuming his chair, his book, and his air of aloof absorption therein.

CHAPTER XXIII

The Board of Trade Court of Inquiry, of which Mr. Malden Brabazon, K.C., was Commissioner, and Admiral John Fleming, R.N., Engineer-Lieutenant Commander J. B. Moorson, R.N., Colonel Horace Denwood, R.E., Captain H. R. Banning, R.N.R., and Captain P. D. Barr, R.N.R., were Assessors, found, after forty-seven days' "proceedings," that, owing to the loss, by drowning, of the Captain and all deck officers, save one, and the loss of all engineer officers, it was impossible to find the actual origin of the incursion of water which caused the sinking of the *King Emperor*, but that main contributory causes to this shipping casualty, the ship's total loss and the great loss of life of passengers and personnel, were:

"Overloading of the vessel beyond her load-line; the age and tender condition of the ship; the insufficient margin of stability and reserve of buoyancy; heavy weather, high wind and sea causing the vessel to list to port; leaks from port ash-ejector, the booby hatch on the shelter deck and half-doors on the upper deck; upper-deck hatches in port shelter-deck bunker and cross alley-ways not being battened down soon enough in some cases, and not being battened down at all in other cases; water finding its way into lower bunkers, saturating the coal and causing the list to port and probably preventing pumps from working efficiently; the scuppers becoming, after a certain angle of list was reached, a means of incursion of water into the upper deck which, in the *King Emperor*—this being a shelter-deck vessel—was also the weather deck, and these scuppers not being stopped or plugged when the vessel listed, gave ready access of water to the upper deck and so further reduced the margin of stability; wing suctions not fitted in all ballast tanks," and so forth.
. . .

In the Judgment of the Court, on the completion of

the enquiry, great credit, high compliment and warm recommendation were extended to Mr. Hallington, Third Officer, for the part he had played, not only on board the ship before it sank, but on life-boat Number 9, this life-boat, capacity sixty-three persons, being one of the four successfully launched, and the only one to survive.

Mr. Hallington, the most important witness before the Court—all other witnesses being deck or engine-room hands, or else passengers—spent a strenuous forty-seven days, and was more than thankful when the case was brought to its tardy conclusion.

He had done his utmost for his dead ship-mates; and he had strained every nerve, if not the truth itself, to avert blame from the absent, the forever absent.

With regard to the living, he had felt it less incumbent upon himself to put their conduct in the most absolutely favourable light. For them, the truth, the whole truth, and nothing but the truth. They were there to answer any charges. His Captain, the Chief Officer, and the Chief Engineer, all men whom he had liked and greatly admired, were not.

§2

Each member of the Court had received anonymous letters, all referring to the same subject, that of the provisioning of the boat and of the issuing of such provisions as it contained. These anonymous letters each member of the Court read, and, having read them, destroyed—and, having destroyed them, endeavoured to dismiss the contents from his mind.

It is notoriously true that the more one endeavours to dismiss something from one's mind, the more persistently it remains, the more tenaciously it retains its hold. You cannot direct your attention toward the removal of anything without directing your attention to the thing itself.

It was inevitable that the Court took particular interest in the matter of the ship's boats and the questions:

"Were the appliances for the lowering of the boats on board the *King Emperor* in good working order?

"Was the order for boat stations definitely given at any time?

"Was the order to abandon ship definitely given at any time?

"If so, when and by whom were such orders given?

"Did the passengers and crew go to pre-arranged places on such order being given, if it were given? If not, why not, and to what extent, if any, was this the cause of the terrible loss of life which ensued?

"Were the boats, or any of them, promptly got out, passengers placed in them, lowered, put safely into the water, and got away under proper superintendence?

"What boats, in point of fact, were lowered and got away?

"Were the boats, which were got away, properly manned and equipped, and did each boat carry her proper complement of passengers and crew? Could more boats have been got away, and what was the reason for the failure to get them away?

"Were such boats as got away 'properly found' in provisions, according to Board of Trade schedule?

"Was there any lack of order and discipline amongst

(*a*) The crew, or

(*b*) Any particular section of the crew, or

(*c*) Among the passengers?

"To what extent, if any, did such lack of order and discipline contribute to the loss of life which occurred?"

And the Court pursued its enquiries into the subject of the fate of boat Number 9 in particular, and the questions as to whether it was properly launched, properly equipped, properly provisioned and properly handled. Also into the cause of death of those of its passengers who died between the time the boat was launched from the *King Emperor* and that when it was picked up by the *Perseus*.

On this subject, as on all others, Mr. Hallington promptly, clearly, and succinctly answered all questions put to him by the Court. And it is undeniable that certain of the questions put to him would not have been asked but for the anonymous letters which each member of the Court had received. An idea is an idea, however it comes into the mind; thoughts are beyond the control of the thinker; and though the highly-trained, specialized legal mind of Mr. Malden Brabazon, K.C., the Commissioner, may have rejected ideas and thoughts suggested to it by the anonymous letters, those of the other Members of the Court did not. Hence the questions put to witnesses which otherwise would not have been asked.

In the result, although nothing of the sort was so much as glanced at, in the Court of Inquiry's Report, the impression was undoubtedly given that boat Number 9, though skilfully and promptly lowered and got away, properly manned and equipped, carrying due complement of passengers and crew, ably handled and satisfactorily provisioned, did suffer from lack of proper, efficient and fair issue of said provisions.

In this matter Mr. Hallington was only to blame, if he were to blame at all, for an error of judgment, inasmuch as he had done what he considered best in arranging for the issue of rations.

No. No Board of Trade Inquiry, however anxious to find a scape-goat and blame somebody, could allot any portion of blame to Mr. Hallington, the only officer who had kept his boat afloat. He had shown not only courage, coolness and skill, but organizing ability; and, having regard to the fact that he was in charge and command of a boat containing upwards of fifty people, he had done more than well in dividing his crew into watches for the purpose of bailing, and of rowing when necessary; and in appointing certain responsible persons under his command to certain duties (including those of care, apportionment, and issue of rations) while he himself attended to the primary and essential duty of the steering and navigation of the boat. In fact, of keeping it afloat, in the heavy seas and high winds that were, at first, encountered.

Neither the Commissioner nor any one of his five assisting Assessors could fail to know that at least one of the crew and more than one of the passengers were anxious—or if not anxious, definitely inclined—to give more information than was asked for, on the subject of the issue of provisions. Nor could they fail to notice that such supplementary and uninvited information bore out the substance of that contained in the anonymous letters that they had received.

To each Member of the Court it was unspeakably unpleasant and distasteful, and to none more so than to Admiral John Fleming and Colonel Denwood, the latter of whom knew Captain Stacey Burlestone by sight, the former by name.

To them at least the thing was unthinkable.

Absolutely incredible. And whatever innuendo, insinuation, or indeed, accusation, might be made, the fact remained that the provisions out-lasted the voyage, and that there were still both food and water in boat Number 9 when it was picked up.

There was no question whatsoever of going into the matter of the cause of the deaths of the old man and the children who had died. Clearly they had died of exposure; and might, indeed, have died on board the *King Emperor*, had she never been wrecked at all.

It was impossible to say that these people had died of starvation or thirst, while there were still food and water in the boat, and these provisions were being issued twice a day.

They had received the same quantity of food and water as the other passengers.

There were sure to be a certain amount of discontent, dispute, disapproval and jealousy, if not actual wrangling and accusation in such circumstances.

Messrs. Karouian, Kyprion and Skutani didn't make a particularly favourable impression upon the Court; and it was generally felt that any arrangements, whatever, would have failed to meet with the approval of these gentlemen.

As for the lady-passenger, well, many lady-passengers are notoriously—difficult.

Captains Banning and Barr, who had spent the greater part of their lives on liners, were particularly well aware of this fact; and she might have been light-headed. There was a certain type of woman—and Mr. Commissioner Brabazon, K.C., knew the type well— who in honeyed tones, gentle accents, and flattering words would ask you a favour, and, failing to get it, would turn and rend you like a wild-cat. Her uninvited condemnation of Captain Burlestone's stewardship might be based not so much upon his unduly favour- ing himself, as upon his refusal unduly to favour her.

But Mr. Commissioner Brabazon, K.C., was a hard- bitten cynic and something of a misogynist, whereas Admiral John Fleming and Engineer-Lieutenant Com- mander Moorson were, on the contrary, typically kind- hearted and chivalrous sailormen. Upon their soft and susceptible hearts Mrs. Easterwood made a deep impression. Still, she couldn't be allowed to introduce irrelevant matter, in no way germane to the questions asked.

As for the Quarter-master, O'Rourke, he admitted that what with continuous rowing and bailing, bailing and rowing, loss of sleep and a dunt on the 'ead which he'd received from a swinging block, huge and heavy, of the davit-tackle, when the boat was launched—he was muzzy-'eaded and queer.

His story of suddenly awaking, all of a doo-dah, sitting up, looking round, and seeing the gentleman in charge of the water 'avin' a drink all to 'imself was, besides being irrelevant, open to the very gravest doubt.

So, at the end of that part of the proceedings deal- ing with the manning and conduct of boats, Captain Stacey Burlestone, who had given valuable evidence throughout the proceedings, was congratulated by Mr. Commissioner Brabazon, K.C. He was complimented upon his evident coolness, and upon the exercise of considerable powers of observation at the time of the loss of the *King Emperor,* and thanked for his great helpfulness in the absence of all-important official witnesses.

And left the Court with a dark stain on his character.

§3

Well, there was one thing to thank God for, that none of the uninvited comments, innuendoes, insinuations or accusations of the Levantine gentlemen; or of the skull-cracked Quarter-master, O'Rourke; or of the lady-passenger, Mrs. Easterwood, were reported in the Press.

No, not even in the *Journal of Commerce and Shipping Telegraph.*

Thanks to the time-saving promptitude, mental clarity, and impatience of verbosity and irrelevance, for which Mr. Commissioner Brabazon was noted, all extraneous matter, unacceptable as evidence useful to the Court, was rejected and quashed—and, in consequence, ignored by the reporters present at the enquiry.

Thus, although the stain was there—the stain on his character that grew ever deeper and darker, that spread and spread unceasingly, in and through and over and around his own mind—it was not visible to the public eye.

Not yet.

Naturally it would gradually grow and spread, by word of mouth; for every person present at the Inquiry would talk. It would be known, of course, in the Clubs and throughout the Services and to all his friends.

Being a sane, well-balanced and sensible man, Stacey Burlestone quite realized that it was probably only in his own warped imagination, his own foolish fancy, that friends and acquaintances seemed different in their manner. That people in the Club did not seem to see him when he entered the hall, the smoking-room, the reading-room, the lounge, the bar, the dining-room; that acquaintances, approaching him in Bond Street, crossed the road just in time to avoid the choice of greeting him or cutting him dead; that the number of his daily letters dwindled; that he received fewer invitations; that the manner of those men and women who did not avoid him was subtly different; that, while some people were colder, less pleasant, more aloof, others were—what was far worse—extra hearty, jovial and reassuring, as who should say,

"We've heard that nasty story, of course, but, Lord bless you!, it doesn't make any difference to us."

It is a truism that people who look for slights find them.

Those who expect to notice differences in the manner of their friends and acquaintances, do notice them. Those who think that people's attitude toward them is changing, find it changed.

What could he do? It was no use seizing upon any particular man or woman and saying,

"Look here, your manner to me is different from what I should like it to be, and from what it used to be."

He couldn't order people to be as cordial as they were of yore; demand that they invite him to lunch, to dinner, to their dances, their shoots, their house-parties. Of course he couldn't. And no self-respecting man, endowed with any pride at all, could say to any acquaintances, or indeed to any friends,

"I suppose, from your manner, that you've heard the yarn about my conduct when in charge of the food and water in that boat? Well, it isn't true."

And, if one did offend one's self-respect and humble one's pride to the extent of saying such a thing, it would not be pleasant to receive the reply,

"No, I haven't heard any such yarn," or worse still,

"Why should such a charge have been brought?" or worst of all,

"Who's accused you?"

In spite of Stacey Burlestone's determination to face this horrible situation calmly, squarely, and sanely, it was not long before he found himself walking up and down his library at home, his Hotel bedroom or sitting-room, or his Club bedroom, delivering speeches aloud, addressing Mr. Commissioner Brabazon, a General Meeting at his Club, the crowd in Hyde Park, and telling them that the thing was incredible, absurd; that, far from appropriating to his own use the provisions for which he was responsible, he had given part of his own proper ration to other people, to a woman, to a crying child. On one occasion, to the very woman who had accused him of stealing water in the night.

In bed he would find that he lay awake composing letters to the Press; and, when he fell asleep, would awake to find himself dictating such letters aloud.

Now and again, he imagined himself reading answers to his letters, some of which answers were signed by at least five people, and declared that the writers had actually seen him stealing food and water from the common stock.

Sometimes the gist of the imaginary letters would be,

"Why does Captain Stacey Burlestone write to the Press stating that he did not steal food and water from people dying of starvation and thirst? He says he did not. Who says he did? *Qui s'excuse s'accuse.*"

Anyhow, nobody did die of actual starvation and thirst, obviously, inasmuch as there was still a small reserve of food and water when the boat was picked up. On the other hand, the allowance both of food and water was necessarily so small that it must have had a deleterious effect upon the health of young children and old persons.

And supposing their rescue had been postponed for another week?

Well, what could one do about it?

Nothing. Grin and bear it. Bear it, anyhow.

But this obsession; this eternal chewing-over of the indigestible mass of mingled thought, fear, resentment, sense of injustice, anticipation of ostracism; this un-shakeable inescapable *idée fixe*—meant insomnia, a nervous breakdown.

"'This way madness lies,'" quoted Stacey Burle-stone. "I scarcely eat. I scarcely sleep. I worry about this from morning till night, and think of nothing else; and yet, so far, I still enjoy perfect health—oh, *perfect* health. And what a blessing is perfect health!"

Good God, what could he do?

An idea. A bright idea. Brilliant. He'd go and have a talk with Ganesh Hazelrigg before Ganesh went to Turkestan. No wiser, braver man alive. Of his wisdom he would give advice. Of his great courage he would set an example. And God knew Stacey Burlestone needed both. He needed wisdom and courage before all things.

§4

"That's my advice, old chap," said Ganesh Hazelrigg, as he and Stacey Burlestone sat smoking their pipes, after dinner, in the sitting-room of Hazelrigg's *pied à terre*, his Dartmoor cottage. "The thing to do is— nothing. And the thing to aim at is to feel—nothing. *Magna est Veritas et prævalebit.* Not many people know; memories are very short; and anything that strangers may say or think doesn't affect you—and shouldn't really interest you."

"Strangers," murmured Stacey Burlestone. "And what about friends?"

"No friend of yours would believe it, for one moment."

"And acquaintances who are neither strangers nor friends?"

"Do they matter much?"

"Not very much, of course."

"Well, let it be the acid test of acquaintances, deciding whether they shall become strangers or become friends. Let those who eye you askance, or change in their manner, go to Hell. Let those who show that they don't believe it, rank as friends.

"It's easy to talk, I know, Stacey," went on Ganesh Hazelrigg. "Very easy. But there's something in what I say. Take me, for example. When I first heard it, my blood boiled with anger. And then I laughed. And then I did as one does with anonymous letters. I threw the whole thing in the mental waste-paper basket."

Stacey Burlestone turned his sad gaze from the fire to his friend's face.

"Oh? You had heard the story before I came to see you about it, Ganesh?" he said.

Ganesh Hazelrigg looked uncomfortable.

"Yes," he said. "Er . . . yes. I had heard it."

"Exactly. There you are, you see! Good news travels fast, doesn't it? How did you hear it?"

"No, never mind about that, Stacey. That's of no interest or importance whatsoever. What is interesting and important is the effect it had upon—let's say a typical friend. You can safely take me, I suppose, as a specimen of your friends, in and out of the Service. Well, it made me furiously angry; then it made me laugh; then its own intrinsic absurdity and impossibility made me, as I say, chuck it into the waste-paper basket and forget it."

"How did you hear it, Ganesh?"

"I had a letter."

This was something of an under-statement, for in point of fact, Major Bartholomew Hazelrigg had received several letters on the subject. One or two indignant, one or two incredulous, one or two with a note of "Whoever would have thought it?" and one accusatory, a plain definite statement of fact—or fiction.

"May one ask from whom?"

"Er . . . my brother-in-law, Harrington-Spens. Boiling with indignation, of course. Said he'd wring the damned and dirty neck of anybody he heard repeating the foul and filthy libel."

"Wonder who told him?"

"He'd had an anonymous letter," replied Ganesh Hazelrigg, forbearing to add that he himself had received a similar one.

"Ah," exclaimed Stacey Burlestone, "and one can imagine who wrote it, eh?"

"What you can better, and far more profitably, imagine, my dear chap, is the effect of the letter. Made my sister Mary, and Harrington-Spens, see red. And that is the only effect that the story, written or oral, will have on any friend of yours—or on any decent acquaintance."

A long silence, while both men smoked, the one slowly, thoughtfully, the other fast, with quick angry exhalations.

"Slander or libel action? Rubbish. My dear chap," said Ganesh Hazelrigg, "you don't want to broadcast the story through the Press till it's known to twenty million people instead of twenty hundred, as at present. Twenty hundred? One hundred, more likely; or less. Talk about stirring up mud! That would be stirring it up with a vengeance."

"Well, an innocent man has a sort of instinctive desire to defend himself, hasn't he?" remarked Stacey Burlestone. "Why should one sit down under it? Why let them get away with a foul lie like that?"

"Why should one sit down under it? Because one's got to. No help for it. As for getting away with a lie, how far do they get and who believes it?"

"Well, it seems to me that everybody I meet knows it—and believes it," objected Stacey Burlestone.

"Bosh! You know better than that, old chap. One per cent of the people you meet have heard it; and of those few, not one per cent believes it. And, as I say, what is the good of telling twenty million more, through bringing an action against anybody? And, moreover, an action which you would inevitably lose. Your plight would be ten thousand times worse then. Twenty million times worse. . . . And against whom would you bring the action? If it were against this Daphne Easterwood, the three Levantines, and the Quarter-master, would it not be your word against theirs, one against five?

"And what Judge or Jury is going to accept your unsupported word against a sworn statement sup-ported by the testimony of at least four eye-witnesses? And, in any case, I suppose that what they blurted out, uninvited, at that Inquiry, was privileged; although the President rejected it as irrelevant to the terms of his Inquest. All he'd got to find out was if anyone was to blame for the loss of the ship, and whether the boats were properly found and provisioned. Also whether anyone lost his life in that boat owing to negligence on the part of the Company.

"Any wrangling about the whacking-out of water

and provisions was nothing to do with the Court, provided the provisions were there in the boat in suffi-cient quantity, according to the law and requirements of the Board of Trade. The rest is a passengers' squabble, and who—even if they ever heard of it—cares what a gang of fat Levantines and hysterical women said about getting their fair share of it?

"No, of course you can't bring a slander or libel action. As I say, you'd inevitably lose it, and then you *would* have branded yourself! You'd have no-one but yourself to thank if everybody was talking of you as the man who pinched the water belonging to women and children who were dying of thirst."

Stacey Burlestone's pale face set more grimly.

"I suppose you're right, as usual, Ganesh," he said. "I must accept it and sit down under it. Well, well! *Tout passe, tout lasse, tout casse.*"

"*Passe* is right, my boy. The whole thing will be forgotten in nine days by the very few people who have heard of it. . . . What about a spot?"

"D'you know, I think it might be a good thing if I left 'spots' severely alone now, Ganesh."

"Perhaps you're right," smiled his friend. "I'll join you in a leave-it-alone. Have a cheroot instead."

Undoubtedly Stacey Burlestone left the house of Ganesh Hazelrigg comforted, refreshed and strength-ened—for a time.

However, it could not be said that those who narrowly observed him, on his return to his usual haunts, were able to detect any important change in his appearance.

That would be impossible, for, as always, he enjoyed the most perfect health.

CHAPTER XXIV

Of course, magnificent health is a magnificent thing, but—white nights are very long nights.

He found himself yawning a lot, and feeling most infernally tired and sleepy, in the day-time, just when he didn't want to feel tired and sleepy. He'd rather feel ill—within reason or within limits—and get a seven-hour sleep every night. Going to bed became such a farce when one lay thinking painful thoughts, horrible thoughts, and almost physically writhing under a sense of injustice; then turning on the light and reading for a bit; finding that one couldn't concentrate, and was reading the same page time after time; then turning out the light again until one was simply driven to switch it on once more; then getting up and seeing what a biscuit and a whisky-and-soda would do for one; and finding that it did nothing at all except provide an increasing desire to take another and another, and perhaps a few more.

And, after that, to repeat the lying-awake-in-the-dark business, before a little more of the abortive reading effort.

Then getting up and dressing and going out for a walk at three in the morning, and returning to a cold and empty house, feeling remarkably cold and empty, with hours to wait before one could reasonably hope to expect to get any breakfast.

Rotten.

Perfect health! Why, the most terrible wrecks in a Home for Incurables got some sleep at night. The doctors saw to that.

The doctors.

That was an idea. He hadn't spoken to a doctor—as a doctor—since . . . why, not since he was wounded in East Africa.

The good old *Herr Doktor* Kruller, ha, ha. . . .

And that had only been by reason of the wound,

and not ill-health. Yes, it was years and donkeys' years since he'd consulted a doctor; long, long before the War.

Well, he'd consult one now—in spite of his perfect health. Perfect physical health, that is to say.

§2

Sir Andrew McIlraith eyed his new patient with increasing interest.

"And you have absolutely no other symptom than this insomnia," he repeated, as he laid aside his stethoscope.

"Absolutely none, Sir," replied Stacey Burlestone.

"No. I can find nothing wrong. You seem to me to be in perfect health."

(Oh God, that phrase again! Perfect health! Perfect health! Perfect health!)

"I haven't an ache or a pain. I enjoy my food, and . . . no, I can't rake up one solitary symptom—except that."

"You can concentrate all right?"

"Until I go to bed. When I go there, I can do anything but sleep—and concentrate. I can't read a book, with any enjoyment; can't read one at all, in fact. I find I read the same paragraph, or even line, over and over again, without its conveying anything to my mind."

"Interesting," mused Sir Andrew, tapping the case-sheet with the handle of his pen. "Curious. No somatic disturbance whatever, and no apparent ill-effects from the insomnia.

"You simply don't feel ill at all, ever?" he said again, looking up and shooting a sharp glance at his patient.

"Never. The only thing is, I—I dread the night so. I've simply come to hate and fear the night. All right during the day, and I feel all right; but as night comes on, and everybody else goes to bed and I am left alone, well, I simply dread turning in. Very often I don't. Just potter about till the morning. Then have a bath and change and . . . carry on."

"And don't feel too bad?" said the famous doctor, puzzled and interested. "Don't go all to pieces, don't have a shocking headache and feel—as one does feel when one's been up all night? I have to be, on rare occasions, but I'm no good next day, and shouldn't care to do it two nights running. As for three!

"Well, look here now, we'll give you something that'll put you to sleep all right; though, honestly, I'm loth to give drugs . . . medicine . . . to so obviously hale and hearty a specimen as yourself, Captain Burlestone. Seems a sin and a shame to give a narcotic to anybody who is in perfect health."

(Oh God, that phrase again! Perfect health! Perfect health! Perfect health! He'd go mad if he heard it much longer.)

A brief silence, while the doctor—distinguished neurologist as well as physician—studied the strong pleasant face, lined and sad, albeit healthy-looking, of the reserved and quiet man before him.

"I suppose you sleep sometimes?"

"Yes, I suppose I must do, sometimes, Doctor. I fancy one occasionally dozes without realizing it; but, to my absolute certain knowledge, I've been awake for ten consecutive nights at a time, without shutting my eyes, and without taking my clothes off during the night."

"Dream much, when you do sleep?"

"Yes. Nightmare generally."

"Oh, that's interesting. Nightmare. Do you mean always the same one?"

"Yes," lied Stacey Burlestone. He could not bring himself to speak of the boat nightmare—reveal himself as the man who did—*not*—steal the water.

"Ah! Yes. Interesting again. What is it?"

"Dangling over a precipice, waiting to fall and be dashed to pieces. And the extraordinary thing is that I want to fall. I want to be dashed to pieces. And what constitutes the horror of the nightmare is that I cannot."

"Cannot?"

"Cannot fall."

"That's a queer nightmare. Quite a new one in my experience. And that really constitutes the terror, horror—the fact that you cannot fall?"

"Yes, both terror and horror. And a sort of hideous, aching misery in addition. Unbearable."

"And sub-consciously, or otherwise, you do your best to stay awake, to escape having a nightmare, eh?"

"No, Doctor, I think not. If it is so, it's certainly unconscious. I want to sleep, from sheer weariness. Not in the absolute sense, so much as weariness-of-myself, boredom, loneliness. Twenty-four hours is an awful long time when it's an unbroken twenty-four hours; but when it gets to two hundred and forty hours, it is insupportable. I suppose ten days is not a record for complete insomnia?"

Sir Andrew laughed.

"No, nor ten weeks, nor ten months, nor ten years."

"Good Lord above us! Are there really poor devils who . . . ?"

"There's an established case of an old woman living in a place near Buda-Pesth, a place called Ceglad, who has not slept for nineteen years. She's been under observation by Viennese specialists, and there's no possible doubt of the facts of the case."

Stacey Burlestone smiled ruefully.

"I think I'd better go, Doctor," he said.

"No; wait a minute," smiled Sir Andrew. "There is also the case of an officer, also a Hungarian, curiously enough, who was wounded in the head during the War, and who has not so much as closed his eyes ever since. It's not merely a matter of cessation of function by the muscles of the eyelids, either. He just doesn't sleep. It's another definitely and officially established case. . . .

"There's an instance in England, too, at Huddersfield, of a man who has not slept at all since he had a very serious operation, over five years ago. He takes morphia every night; and it's pretty well established that he simply doesn't sleep. His doctor has taken quite satisfactory and stringent measures to assure himself of this.

"And there's also a case at Newcastle-on-Tyne of a man who crashed badly when cycling, in nineteen hundred and ten, and was unconscious for about eight hours. The poor chap's had a permanent headache ever since, and nobody has ever found him asleep. This example is not so fully documented as the others; but what I have just said is true, and it is a good deal. Nobody, since nineteen hundred and ten, has ever seen this man asleep; and the local doctors have done their best to—well, to catch him at it. So you see . . ."

"Yes, I see," smiled Stacey Burlestone. "Compared with those four unfortunates, I'm one of the Seven Sleepers. Dam-me, I'm a dormouse!"

Sir Andrew laughed.

"Yes, but their plight being worse than yours, doesn't make your plight any better, does it?"

"No, Sir, it doesn't. And 'plight' is the word. It's a perfect curse. I've often thought I'd sooner be ill, and get some sleep, than be perfectly well—and be awake for a week. It makes life simply unbearable, insupportable. I feel at times that I shall go mad if it goes on much longer."

"Oh, come, don't talk like that."

"I suppose some mad people are perfectly healthy?" asked Stacey Burlestone.

"Physically so; physically so; certainly. Of course, the word 'insane' itself means unhealthy. Often physically healthy enough, poor souls. I've known madmen who looked, and were, as healthy as you."

"H'm," coughed Stacey Burlestone.

"And amazingly strong, and who lived to a ripe—or unripe—old age. But that's neither here nor there. I'm going to give you something that will put you right. Give you relief whenever you feel you need it."

"Thank you, Sir."

"But mind you. Note this, and don't forget it. The less frequently you take it, the more efficacious it will be—because you must not increase the dose. That's the danger with narcotics . . . the misuse . . . the abuse of them. Too frequent resort to them; and then the increasing dose, to get any result at all."

"No, I won't take it too often, Doctor. Keep it as a stand-by, for when I've come to the end of my tether again."

"Yes. That's the thing to do. Good servant, but a bad master. Now, I'm not going to give you a prescription. I'm going to give you a bottle of the stuff myself; and I want you to bring the bottle back, to let me see how much you've used—and not used."

"Suppose the bottle's empty, Sir?" smiled Stacey Burlestone.

"Well, then, you'll get no more until the end of the month, see? So spin it out. Excuse me a minute."

"There you are. One teaspoonful at night, as required (I've written 'tea' in red ink on the label), in water; a wineglassful. Now, you take my advice. Go to bed to-night, put it on your bedside-table, and say,

"'There it is if I want it; but I'm not going to want it.' Probably the very fact that you know you've got it there, and that you can take it and sleep well, will prevent your needing it."

"I suppose it's sure to act, Doctor?"

"Oh, absolutely," smiled Sir Andrew. "I guarantee *that*, all right. And don't forget, a *tea*-spoonful, in water. Be *very* careful. Exactly a *tea*-spoonful, neither more nor less."

"No, I shan't forget, Sir, thank you. . . . It reminds me of the time I took a prescription to be made up at a chemist's in a little up-country town in India. The Eurasian sportsman behind the counter wrote on the bottle,

'A spoonful three times a day after meals.'

I said to him, 'What do you mean by "spoonful"? A teaspoonful or a table-spoonful?' And promptly he spoke up, smart and bright, 'Yessah; a tea-table spoonful.'"

Sir Andrew laughed.

"Well, you take a *tea*-table spoonful of this when you feel you must, and not before. Exactly a *tea*-spoon, mind. Not a *drop* more. . . . And come and see me one month from to-day and tell me all about it."

§3

A fortnight later, as the clock struck three, Stacey Burlestone sat up in his bed.

"Oh God! I can't stand this any longer," he said. "*Now* Sir Andrew McIlraith!"

And, uncorking the medicine-bottle which, with measured medicine-glass and a carafe of water, stood within reach,

"This has got to be done very carefully," he murmured with a smile. "Exactly a *tea*-spoonful, neither more nor less."

And with hands of iron steadiness, and clear eye of perfect vision, he poured out, with meticulous accuracy, a table-spoonful of the drug.

"And now a little water."

"And a little sleep. . . ."

Stacey Burlestone filled up the medicine-glass with water, and drank. . . .

And composed himself to sleep his last sleep.

CHAPTER XXV

Some hours later, Stacey Burlestone, lying flat upon his back, his hands crossed upon his chest . . . found that he could see.

What was the white expanse above him? The vault of Heaven, literal physical Heaven?

If so, it was adorned with mouldings, and, from its centre, depended an electric chandelier.

No, this was not the vault of Heaven. It was the ceiling of his bedroom.

Was he still alive, then, in spite of having taken four times the dose of sleeping-draught, four times the quantity that the doctor had prescribed with such meticulous and emphatic care; or was he dead, and did the soul, for a period, hover above the body that it had vacated?

Would he now, with the eyes of his astral form, or with strange and new perceptive powers, watch the rites and ceremonies attendant upon the disposal of his body?

And then what would happen?

Once his body was in the grave, would he, in the familiar phrase, "go to Heaven"—or, perchance, elsewhere?

He heard a sound.

Then evidently the ghost, the spirit, the soul, the astral shape, the ectoplasm, or whatever you liked to call it, could hear as well as see.

Could it feel, taste, and smell also?

He tried to move.

No; he could not do that.

Then perhaps the liberated soul lacked the sense of feeling? He was not conscious of any odour of any kind, so perhaps the sense of smell was lacking also?

If only he could have moved, he would have reached out and taken some more of the sleeping-draught that had killed him, just to see whether he could taste it.

Beggars' Horses

How long had he been dead? . . .

If this were the state of "being dead," it appeared, on the whole, to compare unfavourably with the state of being alive. It would be rather dreadful to have to remain like this, conscious of sights and sounds, able to think, but otherwise completely impotent.

What a fool he had been!

How he had let things get on his nerves.

What utterly false values he had come to accept.

To what a pitch his accursed "perfect health" had brought him. The miserable, wretched death of a despicable suicide; and all because he thought people were talking about him.

Which, probably, they were not doing at all.

And if they were, what did it matter? What on earth did it matter, to any sane person, whether a herd of chatterboxes were believing ill—or believing well—of him?

Who was the sensible chap who coined the family motto,

"They say? What say they? Let them say!"?

That was the right spirit. The man whose philosophy that had been, was not only a sound philosopher but a stout lad.

Oh, if he, Stacey Burlestone, were only alive again, how differently he would view things!

How differently he would act.

What a poor fool had Stacey Burlestone been. God's glorious great world around him; perfect health in which to enjoy every hour of his life upon it; and he had moaned and groaned and whined and wept and committed suicide—because he thought a few people were thinking ill of him.

What on earth did it matter?

Suppose he were up in a balloon and looking down upon an assembly of a million people, a half-million of whom were telling the other half-million something about him; something that he couldn't hear, and of which he did not know and never would know—what on earth would it matter to him whether they were all speaking ill or well of him? If one half were telling the other half that he was the noblest fellow that ever lived, would he be any the better for that? And if they were saying he was the most despicable thing in human form, would he be any the worse?

"They say? What say they? Let them say!"

Did every suicide, in the act of death, regret his foolish and wicked act, and then go on regretting it through all eternity? Probably. He believed it was a fact that all suicides who leaped into water, for example, instantly began to swim, and did their utmost to save their lives. Many, realizing that this would be the case, tied their hands together, or heavily weighted themselves, before doing it.

Ah, if only he could put back the clock! That wish as old as the world. . . .

Suppose he were, by a miracle, given back the life that he had lost through his own mad act, how differently he would behave; how immeasurably beneath his contempt would be the back-biting tittle-tattle of enemies and scandal-mongering gossips. It would matter as little to him as does the buzzing of mosquitoes to the swamp-buffalo. He'd get into harness again. He'd start afresh in some foreign land quite new to him. Africa, say.

Yes, get transferred, on promotion, to the W.A.F.F.'s. He was young, strong, and, God knew, had perfect health.

Yes, the West African Frontier Force; or the King's African Rifles. A new life, a new career. He had learnt his lesson, and he would profit by it. He'd go to the War Office to-morrow and see old . . .

But he was dead. What he'd see to-morrow would be the undertakers.

Suddenly he sneezed.

Good Lord!

Stacey Burlestone raised his head from the pillow and looked round his room; sat up; yawned; stretched himself—and laughed. The first laugh for months.

Well, well . . . !

He roared with laughter.

§2

"Er . . . no. In the strict scientific sense of the word, it was not a sleeping-draught, Captain Burlestone," said Sir Andrew McIlraith, "and yet, undeniably, it made you sleep, didn't it?"

"It did. It made me sleep for some hours, and I expected it to make me sleep for ever, for I took just four times the quantity prescribed."

"Why didn't you drink the lot, while you were about it?" asked Sir Andrew McIlraith.

"Well, I thought that, since it had to be one tea-spoonful, measured to the exact drop, surely four tea-spoonfuls would do my business; and it would then look as though I'd taken exactly a table-spoonful in mistake for a tea-spoonful. Wouldn't look so much like suicide; and I should get the benefit of the doubt, or my corpse would. What was it, Doctor?"

"*Aqua pura,*" smiled the physician. "Plain water, slightly coloured and flavoured."

"Then why did it make me sleep, for the first time in —God knows how long?"

"Because you thought it would. Auto-suggestion. Because you *knew* it was a sleeping-draught and *knew* that it would make you sleep—it made you sleep."

"But it wouldn't work again, I suppose, Sir?"

"No, but if I gave you a bread pill, and told you it was an opiate stronger than opium, a sedative as powerful as morphia, and convinced you that I was speaking the truth, that would make you sleep all right."

"What is the moral?"

"Why, go to bed believing that you are going to sleep —and you will sleep. Go to bed firmly convinced that you are going to lie awake all night—and you will lie awake all night."

"You're quite right, Doctor. I've been doing it. As I told you, I went on until I was really at the end of my tether, and then I committed suicide.

295

"I woke up thinking I was dead, and was very sorry for myself. Being 'dead,' I got quite a new angle on life; and, having come back to life, I have retained that angle. And that's an interesting point again, Doctor. I woke up so certain that the quadruple dose had done the trick, and so sure I was dead, that I could not move! I'd got my hands crossed on my chest, all ready for someone to stick a bunch of snow-drops in them— and I couldn't move. Then, of course, I knew I really was dead, in spite of the fact that I could see and hear."

"Auto-suggestion again," smiled Sir Andrew McIlraith.

"And then I sneezed, and decided once and for all that corpses don't."

"Well, a table-spoonful of cold water gave you a peaceful sleep, my friend."

"Yes, and it gave me something more than that, Doctor, and I've come to thank you. It gave me, literally and finally, a new adjustment to life. It was more than a sleeping-draught, it was a cure. It cured me of what was killing me."

"And you'll stay cured," smiled Sir Andrew McIlraith.

"I shall, Sir."

"And what are you going to do now?"

"Going to West Africa. Seconded to the West African Frontier Force."

"West Coast of Africa sounds a good place for a man who enjoys—perfect health."

"Yes, Doctor; with good luck and the help of God I may yet get rid of it."

"Of what?"

"My perfect health."

CHAPTER XXVI

It is relevant to this veracious chronicle to state that Chuku M'Pangano, High Priest of the Great White Ju-ju of Okala, was an exceedingly nasty man; an unsocial person, peculiarly unsocial to white men in general and to the British in particular.

He had little affection for the Portuguese of Angola; he disliked the men of Bula Matadi (the Stone-Breaker), as the negro calls the Belgian Congo Government; he hated the Germanis of Togoland, the Cameroons and elsewhere; he loathed the Frankis of Dahomey and French Equatorial Africa; and peculiarly he abhorred the British of the Gold Coast, Nigeria, and the Oil River Country.

For Chuku M'Pangano was a travelled man, and had encountered specimens of all these white devils. In his opinion, the Portuguese had cheated him over a land and trading deal; the Bula Matadi folk had swindled him with gas-pipe guns that burst, with gunpowder that wouldn't explode, with synthetic gin that was sometimes sheer fatal poison and sometimes merely bottled water; the Germanis had evilly entreated him with strokes of the *kiboko* that cut his back to ribbons; the Frankis had raided his Holy Grove and kicked him out of their territory with grievous loss; and the utterly beastly British had called him a Secret Society promoter, a killing-palaver maker, and a slaver; had seized his stock of the dedicated and sacrificial elect, and clapped him incontinently in gaol at Calabar —where he had to labour among common men, like a common man.

They had, moreover, promised to hang him—him, the High Priest of the Great White Ju-ju of Okala—if they caught him Secret-Society organizing, witch-doctoring, slave-dealing and human-sacrifice trading again.

But all that was in the bad old days before Chuku had discovered the land of Okala, and before the White Men all went mad and fought each other, from one end of Africa to the other—indeed, as some said, from one end of the world to the other.

Travelling very light and in some haste, on his old manœuvre of crossing borders and eluding the persecutions of the wicked white men of the province he was leaving, Chuku had discovered Okala, and, before long, the thrilling fact that apparently it was neither Germani nor Franki country, neither Portuguese nor British, but a place where no writ ran, a no-man's land where there was no law, save that of the strongest, and where a man could be a law unto himself.

The vast tract of swamp and jungle, some fifty miles wide and five hundred miles long, was indeed an enclave, a buffer strip of useless country, claimed by no Great Power and avoided by all as possibly belonging to another.

A boundary line drawn on a map of Africa is a line —length without breadth; but on the surface of the actual country it may be a belt rather than a line, a belt fifty miles wide and five hundred miles long, for example, when the country consists of unpassable swamp and impenetrable jungle. When the country is auriferous or otherwise valuable for its mineral or vegetable products, the case is different of course, and the line definitely without breadth. . . .

In the ill-defined, unadministered enclave, known to its savage and frequently cannibal inhabitants as Okala, the ill-used Chuku M'Pangano settled down, announced himself as a great witch-doctor, did business, and flourished exceedingly, by trading on the superstition of the natives and with the agents of the Arab slave-dealers.

His most profitable concern was the Great White Ju-ju of Okala, his next the Agency which he established for the Supply of Next-World-Retinues to Deceased Chiefs. The retinues were, of course, supplied to the relatives, heirs, and next-of-kin of the dead Chief; but their souls accompanied that of the

Chief into the reputedly Better Land to which it departed. The bigger the Chief, the greater was the number of the retinue suitable for attendance upon him in his new sphere of happiness; and upon Chuku M'Pangano the heirs could always rely to do the thing properly, no order being too large or too small to receive his personal attention. Promptitude, courtesy and despatch were his watch-words and achievement— particularly "despatch."

Naturally a good deal of organization was required to keep the stock of Attendants-to-the-Better-Land equal to the demands upon it; for the expectation-of-life of Chiefs is not as great as they themselves expect, and scarcely a month passed without a fine funeral.

At the best kind, done in the first-class style, as many as a hundred "accompaniers" would—accompany. Their heads would form a noble cairn for the Chief's grave, and their bodies a noble feast for his mourners' stomachs.

So, in death, these worthless bushmen were useful at last; doubly useful, for their bodies did good service here below, and their souls went marching on—in attendance upon that of the departed Chief.

The focus and centre of this organization for supply of the raw material (later to be cooked) was the Great White Ju-ju; the means of making its awful presence, and more awful power, known throughout the twenty-five thousand square miles of Okala, was the Secret Society of the White Ghosts, its priests and missioners.

The Great White Ju-ju, of which Chuku M'Pangano was the High Priest and Chief Witch-Doctor—as well as creator, founder, proprietor and sole patentee—was a Ju-ju of the greatest potency and force; a god, a religion, an oracle, a supernatural Thing, the dread power of which no European can understand.

In comparison with it, the awe-inspiring influence and power of the Holy Inquisition in Spain, in mediæval times, was feeble in the extreme; that of the priests of Israel, weak.

Probably there is no power on earth, there never was a power on earth, to equal that of a well-established Ju-ju; probably there never have been people with more power over their fellow-men than the priests of such a Ju-ju—power entirely unlimited, over mind and body and soul, here and hereafter.

To the people of Okala, the word of the Great White Ju-ju was Law, absolute, unquestioned, infallible; and the members of the Secret Society of White Ghosts carried the word of the Great White Ju-ju, the word spoken by Chuku M'Pangano.

Being the High Priest of the Ju-ju and the Head of the Society, Chuku was the ruler of Okala—and no ruler in the history of mankind ever had more power, more utterly untrammelled arbitrary freedom to do what was good in his sight, or what was bad.

The Thing itself was white and amorphous; terrible and not to be looked upon; roughly of human shape, with a truly dreadful face; seated upon a plinth of human skulls. It dwelt in a great hut, sacred and utterly taboo, built in a Sacred Grove, and was seen but rarely, save by Chuku M'Pangano, and that in darkness relieved only by the dim flickering light of a sacred fire.

On these occasions it spoke, and the least of the words of the oracle were the greatest of laws to the bushmen of Okala.

Nor, when its priests came by night to a village, did any man, woman or child dream of disobeying the summons, the Great White Ju-ju's summons to attend upon the pleasure of Its servant and Great High Priest, the omnipotent witch-doctor, Chuku M'Pangano.

And this, though they knew that the order was the death-warrant of those who were called. Many were called and all were chosen.

These "priests" were naked save for white paint, wherewith their faces were smeared, and the rough representation of a skeleton delineated on their bodies. In imitation of the great and glorious Secret Society of the Leopards, suppressed in neighbouring administered provinces, they wore gloves of skin in which great steel claws were fastened. In the use of these they were very skilful, when playfully pretending to be night-prowling leopards, and could disembowel a man quite neatly. This they did in the case of recalcitrant fools and of aged and useless village headmen, to keep high and fragrant the prestige of the Society, and to ensure that no out-of-the-way jungle hamlet should be so ignorant, benighted and buried-alive as to be unaware of the dread powers, deeds, and omniscience of the White Ghosts.

A good side-line was the great annual stock-taking sale, attended by Arab slave-dealers, who bought freely of Chuku's surplus stock, paying for it with guns, gin, beautiful ornaments for Chuku's innumerable wives, and with trade goods generally.

By the time of the outbreak of the Great War, the (also Great) White Ju-ju of Okala was unshakeably established in Okala, and its High Priest held a position of importance and autocratic power un-equalled by that of any king, chief, or other tribal ruler in Africa.

And during the years of the War, Chuku M'Pangano extended the scope of his operations, going far beyond the admittedly ill-defined boundaries of the Okala enclave, into certain adjacent territories, always loosely administered, whose rulers now had other things to attend to, matters much more important than the doings of Chuku M'Pangano.

During those years and many subsequent, there were vast tracts of country, particularly in what had been German territory, that this enterprising scoundrel annexed to Okala, by the very practical token of levying taxation therein.

For the Great White Ju-ju of Okala was far from content with prestige, power, and religious authority. Brass rods[29] by the thousand, bags of salt by the hundred, goats by the score, as well as basket-loads of yams, dried fish, and other comestibles, and appropri-ate weights and measures of rubber and palm oil were payable, on demand, by every village that desired to remain a village.

But when the times began to grow normal once

---

[29] *Value 2½ d. each.*

again, the shouting and the tumult died, the captains and the kings departed and left civil administrators to proceed with administration, one king, uncrowned, remained—and began to attract the unfavourable notice and attention of two or three of his neighbours.

One of these, an official whose native name was Ear-to-the-Ground, something of a new broom who wished to know exactly the area that he had to sweep, came to the conclusion that quite a few of the villages giving reluctant allegiance to Chuku M'Pangano of Okala were really well within the vast district that he had been appointed to administer.

Making enquiries, as he toured, he learned quite a lot about the Great White Ju-ju of Okala.

Into Okala he sent his spies, picked Houssa men, as brave and trustworthy as they were clever, that he might learn more about that country and its ruler; discover the truth of the rumours that reached him concerning the doings of the Great High Priest of the Great White Ju-ju of Okala; rumours of human sacrifice at its shrine; of slave-dealing; of a murderous Secret Society of White Ghosts; and, particularly, concerning slave-raiding into what was indisputably Mandated Territory.

Was it true, as averred by his chief spy, Sergeant Ali of the West African Frontier Force, that that appalling murder-club, the Society of Leopards, was practically resuscitated and re-established, inasmuch as the majority of the White Ghosts were ex-members of that terrible scourge?

If it could be proved that the Great White Ju-ju of Okala was extending its sphere of influence further and further into Mr. Commissioner Herriott's own little sphere of influence, and that whoever ran the foul thing was raiding into the territory for whose peace and protection he was responsible—so much the worse for the Ju-ju and its High Priest.

He'd root the damn thing out—and its proprietor, too—letting that fiend discover that, if the Great War had been his chance, the Great Peace would now be his mischance, inasmuch as there was no further need for buffer strips and conveniently ill-defined borders; no further need for care lest mighty susceptibilities be offended in Europe.

No—there'd be no more *Panthers* sent to Agadir—and there should be no more Leopards sent into Mr. Commissioner Herriott's district, to rob, slaughter and enslave.

§2

Almost Chuku M'Pangano began, himself, to believe in the Great White Ju-ju; really to wonder whether it were not the great and powerful Ju-ju that all other men knew it to be. How else account for his amazing luck?

It couldn't be luck. No mere happy chance could have brought so amazing a tribute to the Ju-ju's might, as a White Sacrifice—out of the sky.

Actually out of the sky itself—borne on the wings of a great bird—for the greater glory of the Great White Ju-ju of Okala.

Chuku M'Pangano had never heard the words *ad majorem Dei gloriam*, but he uttered their exact trans-lation when the news reached him by *lokali*[30] that a White Man had fallen from the sky into the Okala jungle, and was, of course, being forwarded, forthwith, to Okala Town, to the earth-shaking omnipotent Witch-Doctor High Priest Chuku M'Pangano, and the Great White Ju-ju of Okala.

Chuku licked his lips, rubbed his hands, smiled widely, and, in the joy of his heart, rose from his Stool of State, picked up his razor-edged machete and neatly smote the head from the shoulders of the dancing-girl who was posturing before him.

A White Man!

O! ko! He would know how to deal with a White Man! He should be a red man ere he died, red from his scalp to his toe-nails, and his skin should be stretched on the sacred drum of the Great White Ju-ju of Okala. At the feet of the Ju-ju he should be publicly sacrificed,

---

[30] *Huge drum.*

a White Sacrifice to the White Ju-ju—and *then* what would be the fame and prestige of the Ju-ju that had brought a White Sacrifice to its feet, out of the blue, out of the air, to be a sign and a token to all men of its power and strength, and of the virtue of its High Priest?

Yes. A worthy sacrifice. A truly great occasion and a noble feast. White "beef."

Or—no—a bright idea! Better still.

Far better. No? . . . Yes? . . .

Well, King Chuku M'Pangano would think the great idea over.

CHAPTER XXVII

In the corner of the foul and stinking slaughter-house and human cattle-pen that stood appropriately and conveniently close behind the Ju-ju House of Okala, four men sat.

From time to time, two of them spoke to each other.

One of these was indubitably and completely white, the other of a yellowish brown.

The third and fourth were huge negroes, brutish and dull.

The white man, his chin resting on his knees, his right wrist bound to his right ankle, his left wrist to his left ankle, was chained to the tree-trunk that formed the corner-post of the hut. He was quite naked, bruised, blood-stained, and marked with the welts and cuts of a rhinoceros-hide whip.

In a curious mixture of Coast pigeon-English of the "him fit for die one time, you lib for chop" variety; and of Coast French of the "Bo' jou' M'soo" sort; interspersed with many Arabic and Portuguese words, the yellow man, who was not bound, but merely chained up, chattered freely, and willingly answered the occasional questions of the white man; questions put in careful easy English twisted to imitate the Coast dialect, and repeated in simple French.

The yellow man's French was better than his English, and he professed to be fluent in the Okala tongue—both the northern and the southern languages, which differ widely, Arabic, Portuguese, Swahili, Houssa, Bomongo, Ibo, Munshi, Dama, Yahe and a few other dialects, and to be able to make himself intelligible in German and Spanish.

As this gifted person appeared to be a fellow-prisoner and of quite friendly disposition, the white man asked him who and what he was.

He was Chuku M'Pangano's valued interpreter—that was why he was chained up.

Eh?

Chuku didn't want to lose him. So he kept him chained up. Also because he was a Christian.

A *Christian?*

Oh, yes! A proper God-man. Baptised and every-thing. The good White Fathers had brought him up at the mission at Eyebi. Taught him to pray in French like a gentleman. His father had been a Belgian trader and his mother an Aro woman; so he had good blood, both sides. Oh, yes! Belgian, French, Arab and, well, cheap Cross River stuff; Ibo, or what-not. No, he had never known his father; but his mother had told him all about it . . . French blood? Oh, the Aros have French blood, everybody knows that; and his grandmother had been a Mahommedan woman. Almost certainly Arab. Haussa anyway. That was why he was so white. His good blood.

He had been on the sea, too. Oh, yes! Been quite a trader, like his father. He had made a mistake in coming to Okala though. Chuku M'Pangano had found him too useful—because he could talk Arabic, Haussa, and the bush dialects as well as White Man's talk; and because he was an honest man who would never lie nor cheat. Also Chuku was angry with him because he would not admit, privately or publicly, that the Great White Ju-ju of Okala was more powerful than Jésu Christ, the Ju-ju of the Frankis and Germanis and British.

Chuku was going to blind him on the ninth day of the ninth month, if he did not publicly admit it—on the occasion of the great palaver and feast. It was the Big Day of the Ju-ju, the ninth day of the ninth month. Everything went in nines in the Ju-ju worship.

Oh, no. He wasn't going to rat, and go back on the White Fathers, or admit to black trash like Chuku that his *sale cochon* of a Ju-ju was as great as the Christian God. No. Chuku should have his eyes first.

He'd never bow down to the Ju-ju. If he did—why, he'd be no better than a negro, a black heathen, a cannibal Pagan. . . . *Nom de Dieu*, he was a white man and a Christian—and Chuku shouldn't make him an idolater. Not if he tortured him to death.

But Chuku wouldn't do that—he was too useful to him. Nor would he cut his tongue out. He'd got Chuku there! You can't cut an interpreter's tongue out.

But blind him he certainly would. Do it himself, too.

How?

Oh, gouge with his thumbs and then use his hands.

The white man shuddered.

Would Chuku be likely to do that to him, too?

Oh, yes. Unless the White Man publicly worshipped the Ju-ju. But of course he'd never do that, would he?

The white man licked dry lips.

Besides, Chuku would do it, anyhow; to prevent the White Man from escaping. Cut his tongue out, too, for a certainty. He was very fond of doing that. Besides, dumb men tell no tales.

But, what was more probable, was that Chuku would just sacrifice him to the Great White Ju-ju of Okala.

How?

Oh, torture him to death.

Not burn him alive?

Oh, no! The priests and witch-doctors would grumble at such a waste as that!

Waste of what?

Bœuf blanc. Good white beef—a rare commodity. Might perhaps roast him alive, so that he would *be* a roast, so to speak; *bœuf blanc rôti*; but not burnt. . . .

But, there, you never knew with Chuku: he might get up to all sorts of tricks. If ever he caught his interpreter lying to him, for example, he was going to sew his lips together tightly—after putting a tiny *bicheki* snake in his mouth. Little chap only about four inches long, *mais très méchant*. Very poisonous indeed.

Yes, Chuku was full of ideas. These two big negroes here in the hut, for example, Oko and B'sulo. Special private guards. If the White Man or the Interpreter escaped, Oko was to be pegged out and have a charcoal fire lighted on his belly to keep him *wakeful*.

If the White Man or the Interpreter committed

suicide, B'sulo was to be made to commit suicide himself—by taking a morning swim in the walled pool of the *timsah mugga*, the Sacred White Crocodile of the Great White Ju-ju of Okala on the day he was fed. He had a meal every ninth day. Always human flesh—generally only girl-children though. The idea must make B'sulo disapprove of suicide.

Anyway, Chuku M'Pangano was a dirty black dog, and his Ju-ju a dirty white fraud. Nor should he have the satisfaction of making either the White Man or the Interpreter worship it or bow down to it—much less admit that its power was greater than that of the greatest of all Gods, the Saviour, Jésu Christ, the only true God and the only Son of God.

And at the Great Ninth Month Palaver, the White Man would have a fine chance to testify to the Christian Faith as propounded by the White Fathers, and to die for it. And the Interpreter would have a fine chance to testify, too, and to be blinded for it.

Yes, and unless Chuku cut his interpreter's tongue out, which he wouldn't be such a fool as to do, he'd keep on shouting in the Okala tongue,

"Greatest of all Ju-jus is the power of Jésu Christ! Filthiest of all foul idols and graven images is the stinking, powerless Ju-ju of Okala. Dirtiest of all dogs is the fish-eating mud-worm Chuku M'Pangano. . . ."

Keep on till they choked him, he would. Eyes or no eyes—while he'd got a tongue.

And he'd translate all the White Man said, for Jésu Christ and against the Great White Ju-ju, into the most pungent Okala—adding all the worst insults against the Ju-ju that the Okala language contained. And they were pretty good.

The White Man tried to moisten dry lips.

Was he of the stuff of which martyrs are made?

Had he any particular need to be tortured for his Faith?

Had he any particular Faith to be tortured for, if it came to that?

He had not prayed for years. He had attended no place of worship. He had given no thought whatsoever to religious matters.

What, in point of fact, did he really believe?

If, by prostrating himself before this Ju-ju, he could save himself from hideous tortures, agonies unthinkable, horrible disfigurement, maiming, blindness . . . save himself from having his tongue cut out.

Deny his Faith—if he had any?

Lower the White Man's prestige before this Chuku devil and these brutes, bushmen, cannibals?

Kow-tow—to a painted African idol? At the behest of a savage; a jungle Cetewayo or Lobengula, a blood-bathed, bestial witch-doctor?

In spite of the example of this heroic creature here? This mongrel negroid half-caste, who had loyalty to his religion, pathetic pride in his "superior birth," self-respect?

How could he fall below the standards of this yellow, ignorant nondescript?

But—he was different, this jungle-born son of a slave-woman and a . . .

Different? Yes—alas!

But he *was* different, of course; he hadn't so much to lose; he lived on a so much lower plane of life; he had a far lower nervous organization, infinitely lesser sensitiveness to pain, degradation, deprivation of . . .

No. It wouldn't do. White man, yellow man, brown man, or black man—guts were . . . *guts*. Though, of course, the white man would suffer far more, from the same amount of injury, than a coloured man would.

"What would you do if I said I was not a Christian, and that the Great White Ju-ju of Okala was greater than the God of the White Man?"

"Then I *would* lie," was the reply. "I would be a bad Interpreter and translate all wrong. I would shout that you did not curse the Ju-ju but only laughed at it; and that you did not even spit on it, for it was not worth the trouble. . . . But, of course, no White Man would deny his Faith and worship a ju-ju! Not even the wickedest, lowest gin-trader would do that. Not even a Mussulman slave-dealer would do that. And, if he did, Chuku and the people would never know! I am the only

Interpreter."

The yellow man laughed, and began to chant what sounded to the white man like,

> *Au Père, au Fils, au Saint Esprit*
> *Soit toute la gloire à Jésu Christ. . . .*

§2

The White Man was again brought before Chuku M'Pangano, Witch-doctor and High Priest, who sat on his Stool of State before the great hut that he had caused to be built for his House, at the entrance to the Sacred Grove.

About him stood grouped his priests and deacons, guards and executioners, dancing-girls and plump courtiers, chiefs and headmen, witch-doctors, messengers, poisoners, *lokali* men, *kurli* lion-hunters, and assorted retinue. Also some Arab visitors; a deputation from a slave-selling king across the River; and the invaluable interpreter.

Chuku had made up his mind; and all men were to be informed of his decision.

And all the congregation should say Amen. Any man who didn't say it wouldn't have the opportunity to say much else.

And the decision was,

That the Great White Ju-ju of Okala did not desire that the White Man should be sacrificed to It.

The Ju-ju desired that he should be Its servant, living in Its presence, in the Great Ju-ju House, for ever, chained to a post.

The Ju-ju desired that on the ninth night after the next new moon but one, the Holy Day of the Ju-ju, he should gaze upon Its face and then be blinded, so that he should see nothing thereafter.

The Ju-ju desired that he should praise and worship It, acknowledge Its superiority to the White Man's Ju-ju, and then be rendered dumb, so that he should say nothing thereafter.

The Ju-ju desired that he should hear all the people

acclaim It in a great shout, and then be rendered deaf so that he should hear nothing thereafter.

The Ju-ju desired that, should the White Man ever die, his skull should be hung about Its neck and his flesh eaten by the priests of the temple of the Ju-ju.

Thus would it be known for all time, and unto all men, that the power of the Great White Ju-ju of Okala was greater than the ju-ju of the White Man.

And the interpreter was bidden to announce this oracle of the Great White Ju-ju, in all the languages that he knew.

In the human cattle-pen and slaughter-house, that night, the interpreter made it abundantly clear to the White Man that he was not to be sacrificed to the Ju-ju; but imprisoned for life in the Ju-ju house, and that he would be deaf, dumb and blind for the rest of his life.

"*Alors, M'soo,*" the interpreter consoled him, "*n'importe! N'ayez pas peur. . . . Restez tranquil. . . . M'soo sera mort bientôt!* M'soo will not live very long after the—ceremony. They are very rough, these executioners, with the tongue-cutting, and the ear-drum bursting, and the blinding. Very rough. M'soo will not live very long after the Ninth Day of the Ninth Month, seven weeks hence. No European would be likely to survive the suffering of all three tortures on one day."

"*Man!*" screamed the White Man, "*I shall live another fifty years! . . . I shall live to a great old age! . . . I shall live to be over a hundred years old . . .*" and he laughed noisily, uncontrollably; and was seized with a violent rigor.

CHAPTER XXVIII

Like Chuku M'Pangano, Mr. Commissioner Herriott also had a great idea; and thought it over.

A month later, he sat at chop with the officer commanding the half-battalion of the West Africa Frontier Force that had arrived at his head-quarters a few hours previously.

"We'll do the thing properly, Burlestone," he said. "I've long wanted to make a beginning, and now I'll make an end. This Okala country is simply an Alsatia for all the slave-raiders, slave-dealers, gun-runners, gin-peddlers, ivory-poachers, escaped criminals, and Bad Men of Central West Africa.

"The City of Okala is a robbers'-nest and the head-quarters of this damned White Ju-ju, and of the White Ghost Society, too. That wouldn't have been my official business, but they've been raiding well into my district —putting the fear of Ju-ju into my simple villagers and robbing them right and left—not merely of their women and children but of their precious goats, as well as young men. Human sacrifice, of course. Slavery, any-how.

"And now they've got this white man there—or had. Probably chopped the poor devil by now . . . and eaten him."

"How did you hear about him?" asked Major Stacey Burlestone of the W.A.F.F.

"*Lokali* and spy. I have got a chap who must be about the best *lokali* reader in Africa. Drummer, too. I sent him nosing into the Okala country, as far as he dared go. He's no hero. But he went far enough to hear the 'talk' of the Sacred Drum of the Great White Ju-ju of Okala relayed. Probably relayed several times. Fifty to a hundred miles.

"And he swears that he heard a message or *pronunciamento* which, after the usual rigmarole, said that the Great Ju-ju had shown, once and for all, its infinite superiority to the White Man's ju-ju by bringing a White Man to Its feet, as a sacrifice. Brought him down out of the sky, too, where he was flying about on the back of a bird. . . . One might have disregarded that as the usual Great Ju-ju bunk; but Sergeant Ali, my chief spy, has reported that personally, he's certain they've got a white man. It's all the talk in Okala town."

"How long ago is this?" asked Burlestone.

"The *lokali* man heard it on the 'jungle wireless' a month ago to-morrow, and Sergeant Ali reached Okala town three weeks back."

"Not much hope for the European then—if they did get one," observed Stacey Burlestone.

"No. Probably sacrificed to the Ju-ju, and eaten, by now," agreed Mr. Commissioner Herriott. "We shall be too late to do him any good—but he'll have done us and the Province some good, poor chap. . . . I think he was the last straw—or my tale about him was—that broke the Governor's heart, and got him to agree to my request for you and a quiet little half-battalion expedition. Just to demarcate the boundary between British and Mandated territory, once and for all, and to wipe out this damned Okala enclave, as such.

"Anyhow," he concluded, "we'll push along as quickly as possible."

"Wipe out the Okala Ju-ju, too, eh?" said Burlestone.

"Yes. *And* the slaughter-merchant as well. He's for the right end of a rope if we catch him. You should have seen some of my villages that his 'White Ghosts' had been through. Twenty miles this side of the Okala country, even putting the border-line at its vaguest. I'll make ghosts of them all right," the Commissioner growled.

"We'll be a Boundary Commission as well as a punitive expedition," he added. "Burn Okala town and the Ju-ju grove and temple, and run the line straight through the centre of it. Then it's clear Mandated Territory up to it, on one side; and British on the other. And that'll be the end of the Okala enclave and a blot on civilization."

"And if you hang this black Nero on the exact spot where he murdered the white man, there'll be no more chopping of stray Europeans in this part of the world," said Stacey Burlestone.

"I'll hang him . . . as high as Haman."

A carrier-pigeon flew into the loft at the Commissioner's head-quarters that evening, bearing, attached to its leg, a message pencilled on cigarette papers, from Sergeant Ali, to the effect that there was to be a tremendous *tamasha* at Okala town on the ninth of the month, a great Ju-ju palaver, a feast and a beer-drinking.

"The population from miles round will be flocking in to that," said Herriott. "We'll be there. . . . Drop in after dinner—to coffee and liqueurs, when everybody's merry. Not to say blind drunk. A stroke of luck. We can just do it in the time."

"What about village *lokalis* announcing our gate-crashing—hours before we get there?" asked Burlestone.

"We'll discourage that. Send a good man well ahead, with instructions to see there is no drumming. And leave a sentry over the drum of each village we pass through. With any luck there'll be no fighting to speak of. . . . Though I wouldn't mind an excuse for one or two accidents to a few of the slavers and gin-peddlers. Devils like Marbrouk ben Hassan the Raider, for example. Does a regular trade in slaves with the Touareg. Those Arab slavers are worse than the black catch-'em-alive-ohs who collect the human-sacrifice fodder for Chuku M'Pangano. Yes—we'll attend that party, Burlestone, raid the Club and nab the gang with cards and money on the table.

"In other words, with human flesh in the cooking-pots," he added.

"Is cannibalism really practised, nowadays?" asked Burlestone.

"In the Okala country it certainly is," replied the Commissioner. "But it isn't going to be much longer."

§2

The Ninth day of the Ninth Month, the propitious and sacred Holy Day of the Great White Ju-ju of Okala, and of Chuku M'Pangano, its High Priest and Chief Witch-doctor.

The scene, lighted by the moon and the flames of fires, sacrificial, cooking, ritual, and purely illuminatory, was impressive, with its setting of great trees, the Ju-ju temple, stockade and buildings, archiepiscopal palace and harem huts, the massed soldiery, priests, and people.

Swollen and proud with wine and feasting—*tumbo*, mealie beer, trade gin and human "beef"—Chuku M'Pangano sat upon the Sacred Stool before the Ju-ju House and gave judgment; each sentence being promptly carried out by the stabbing-spears of his young men.

Before him, naked and bound, stood the white man, sick with rage, humiliation, fear and hunger—for in the bowl of mealie mash given him yesterday, he had found a tiny human hand, and had eaten nothing since. Another of Chuku's little jokes.

Beside him, unbound, but carefully watched by Oko the Wakeful, stood the yellowish brown man, the interpreter, whose business it was to make clear the words of Chuku to all men, be they natives of north or of south Okala; men from across the River; traders from Liberia, Dahomey, Timbuktu, or Jericho; Arabs, Haussas, Aros, Touareg, Europeans, Pagans, Turks, or Infidels.

"And now, dog," spake Chuku M'Pangano, "announce that the Great White Ju-ju accepts the offering of the eyes and the tongue and the ears of the White Man, this night. And that from this day he dwells in the Ju-ju House, to be Its servant for ever. Speak this in the two Okala tongues, in Bomongo, in Haussa and Ibo. First tell the White Man that he will fall on his face before the Ju-ju and cast dirt upon his head in token of respect; and that he will then lift up his voice and tell the people that his own ju-ju is powerless, here, as elsewhere. And thrice he will cry aloud,

"Great is the Ju-ju of Okala whose servant I am."

To the White Man the interpreter spoke.

"*Excusez-mo', M'soo.* This black dog says you worship Ju-ju. He is a fool, M'soo. Whatever you say, he will blind you and cut out your tongue; and that *salau'* B'sulo will hit you on the ears with rubber club like paddle, and burst ear-drums. Whatever you say, Chuku will not kill you, because he think it more fame and honour to Ju-ju to have white man chained in Ju-ju House as slave. So, M'soo, I tell Chuku he is god-damned idolater and dirty black dog and M'soo spits in his eye. Myself also, please, M'soo, join you in insulting this heathen."

The European moistened dry lips, and spoke.

"Tell him that if he does this, many White Men will come, soldiers with machine-guns, and will destroy this place and hang him on a tree. Tell him the White Men never forget or forgive the murder of a White Man. Try to frighten him. Tell him my people will avenge you, too, if . . . Oh, for God's sake tell him *something* that . . ."

The interpreter turned to the Ruler of Upper and Lower Okala and shouted as loudly as he could,

"Black jungle-village dog! The White Man spits on you and on your dirty image of a grinning idol. He says the shadow of his God and Jésu Christ His Son are more powerful than all the heathen ju-ju's in Africa put together. They will save him from you. He will not worship your pig of a ju-ju. And the White Men will come and burn it and you and your swines' sty of a village."

Chuku M'Pangano, with a hiccup and a lurch, reached for his stabbing-spear and rose to his feet.

"*I, also, say it,*" shouted the interpreter, "*for I too am a White Man and a Christian. Your ju-ju is a child's toy, a lump of painted wood, without power. . . . It is nothing! . . . I spit on it. And on you. You are a black idolater, a low bush cannibal . . . a dog . . . a thief . . . a liar . . . a coward. . . .*"

And Chuku M'Pangano flung back his arm . . . and

struck.

Chuku was not himself. Had he been sober he would have inflicted quite different punishment, enjoying the sight and sounds thereof, and yet not destroying a perfectly good interpreter.

As the murdered interpreter sank to the ground he rolled his eyes toward the White Man.

"*Adieu, M'soo,*" he said. "*À bas le sale ju-ju. . . . Vive le bo' Dieu et so' Fils Saint Jésu Christ. . . .*"

From the body quivering on the ground, Chuku looked at the White Man, again lost control of his temper, flung back his stabbing-arm . . . and struck.

As he did so, there was a cry, a turning of heads, a swaying of the multitude. . . . Up the sacred grove came a long huge serpent; swift, undulating; silent, brown, with a white head. The White Man's soldiers— with a man, dressed all in white, leading them. . . . *O, ko! . . . O, Ju-ju, n'dewo! . . . O, ko! . . . Ho! . . . Ho! . . .*

Mr. Commissioner Herriott fired from the hip, and Stacey Burlestone, walking, as requested, behind him, fired over the civilian official's shoulder. At the signal, every Haussi soldier fired his rifle in the air and howled a war-cry. Most of them fired, as they had been instructed, over the heads of the people, who with one accord turned and fled, as fast and as far as the extent of the night's feasting and *tumbo*-drinking permitted.

Glancing round the blood-soaked stage of the ceremonies, at the still-bleeding bodies of the executed, at the bound white man, Mr. Commissioner Herriott discovered a vein of hardness.

"Hang that dog, Chuku! Quick," he shouted to Sergeant Ali, "before he dies. There's a good branch. . . . Up with him before he bleeds to death."

For both the heavy soft-nosed bullets had pierced Chuku's broad chest.

"Good God! . . . Look here. . . . I say. . . . Why—*it's Wallingford . . .*" cried Burlestone incredulously, as he turned the white man over on his back. "Wallingford, the aviator . . . !

"Alive, too," he added. "The spear struck the ropes

and only gashed him. . . ."

"Let your men scatter, and drive the devils into the cordon," shouted Herriott. "They must catch every mother's son who's got any white paint on him, or leopard-claw gloves. Sergeant Durundo, take the police-section and set fire to everything here that'll burn. Quick. Start with the Ju-ju House. . . . Herd the White Ghost prisoners into the communal palaver-house, tied in pairs. . . . What's that about an aviator? . . ."

The once notorious Okala enclave no longer exists.

CHAPTER XXIX

On the *Bodiam Castle*, Major Stacey Burlestone and Colonel Moresby Wallingford sailed for Home, the one on furlough, the other to make another attempt to fly round Africa by an all-red route.

"Nearly became red enough for you, last time," smiled Burlestone as the two men sat in their deck-chairs, gazing out across the glorious sparkling blue water, and breathing in new life, health and energy.

"Yes. I thought I was an honoured guest of Mr. Chuku M'Pangano for life," replied Wallingford, "and a long life at that. Fancy being chained up in that ghastly Ju-ju House for—half a century perhaps."

"You wouldn't have lived. Apart from the . . . mutilations."

"That's what the interpreter said. But—I don't know. . . . By gad, he was a brave chap. I never knew his name. . . . A modern martyr. '*The blood of martyrs is the seed of the Church.*' Burlestone, I'd like to build a mission-church on the spot where he died."

"An Unknown Warrior for Christ, eh? . . . Might get Harrington-Spens to endow a complete Mission there— if he's got any money left."

"He can't have got through that little lot yet surely?"

"Got through it? He and his wife have been giving it away as fast as they could find worthy objects. I get a long letter from dear old Ganesh Hazelrigg every now and then. His sister, Mrs. Harrington-Spens, writes them for him when they're staying at his cottage. He's blind, you know."

Anthony Wallingford shuddered.

"Good God! . . . Poor old Ganesh. . . . I've been out of touch since nineteen hundred and eighteen. What happened?"

"Oh, it's a long story. . . . Tell you some time. The reward of courage and the end of the career of the bravest man who ever lived. End of his active life, anyway. He's crippled as well as blind. Some Christian gentlemen left him bound down on a table, and set the house on fire. Bound with thick wire. Not bush cannibals like Chuku M'Pangano. White men. Europeans. He was on the most dangerous job of all he ever did, and was caught. In Tashkhara, I think. He'd have been burnt alive but for two Secret Service agents, Mahbub Ali and Shere Khan, who got him out, just in time, at the risk of their lives. Shere Khan was burnt badly, too. . . . Nobody but Ganesh would have had the nerve and courage to hold on to life at all, in those conditions. Nearly burnt to death, and then hidden in a stable. No medical necessities whatever, and no proper food; and two Pathans for nurses. And in imminent danger of capture and torture, the whole time he lay on the foul earth of that stable. He hung on though—and he pulled through. And crippled and blind as he was—Mahbub Ali and Shere Khan brought him from Tashkhara to the Khyber!"

"It doesn't bear thinking of," said Wallingford, and shivered. "What he must have suffered! And the cold iron courage—to hang on, and fight for life, like that."

"Yes. He'd got the information he went for. And the courage that took him there and carried him through, enabled him to get back with it. Kept him alive . . . and he'd be better dead.

"One knew his pluck and nerve and courage would be his undoing, sooner or later," continued Burlestone, "from that time he went into a cave after a wounded tiger—with a hog-spear."

"Yes," agreed Wallingford. "And when he grabbed the cobra with his bare hands at Barki, as it was crawling over his sleeping syce."

"Yes. And when he joined up with Ibrahim Afzul Khan's robber-gang, disguised as a Mahsud, to learn what the Amir was doing about it. They'd have jointed him alive, if he'd made a slip."

"And that cholera business among the deserted carriers. Another man's coolies, too."

"And his journey into Thibet."

"Talk about living dangerously! Bravest of the

brave—and now he's a blind cripple."

"Yes. And makes light of it, his sister says," observed Burlestone. "Perfectly cheerful; and insists on learning to do everything for himself. Won't leave that cottage, or have anyone to live there and look after him. . . . Marvellous chap. . . . Pushes himself along the Moor roads, in a wheeled chair, and goes for walks, on crutches, blind though he is. There's one blessing— Mary Harrington-Spens settled ten thousand on him, whether he liked it or not, so he can have everything he wants."

"Except his eyes and the use of his legs," said Wallingford sadly. "The price of—courage."

A long silence.

"You know, Burlestone," remarked Wallingford suddenly, "I never understood Ganesh Hazelrigg, though I saw a good deal of him at one time—up in Simla; and on two or three shooting-trips; and in Devonshire. You saw much more of him than I did. What was behind that look of . . . of . . . a sort of gentle bland benevolence and heavy stolid sagacity—besides his real cleverness and incredible courage?"

"A great kindliness," replied Burlestone, "amazingly allied to utter ruthlessness. Nothing squeamish about Ganesh when he was on the job; and not a scruple about doing anything he thought to be in the interests of that job. . . . I've listened to him and Harrington-Spens—and got some eye-openers about Ganesh. He looks soft—and there never lived a harder man. Or, rather, one who could be harder when occasion arose. I'll tell you how I'd put it: Ganesh Hazelrigg has not only the courage to do right, whatever the temptation to shirk—but he has the courage to do wrong."

"To do wrong?"

"Yes. What is usually termed wrong. . . . He has his own views on the subject of right and wrong; and he has the courage of his convictions. The sort of thing I mean . . . well, he would consider that the end justified the means, when the end was his country's welfare, and he'd value the life of the individual, who was a danger to his country, at about the same price as he values his own—nothing.

"Oh, yes," continued Stacey Burlestone, "he's a kind, gentle friend, helpful and generous and altruistic —but I don't know anyone I'd like less as an enemy, especially a professional enemy, so to speak. Ganesh is hard and ruthless all right."

"I'm not surprised," smiled Wallingford. "One somehow felt that Ganesh didn't get to the top of that particular tree on—bland benevolence, brotherly love, and a slow, if sure, sagacity and wisdom. In short, on being what he looked."

"No . . . a very deceptive lad, old Ganesh, in the matter of appearances," said Burlestone. "But what a ghastly tragedy! Ganesh Hazelrigg a blinded cripple— on crutches.

"Through being—the bravest of the brave," he added.

CHAPTER XXX

Stacey Burlestone and Anthony Wallingford came to know, and to like, each other better than they had ever done, as the voyage progressed and they spent more and more of each lovely day and glorious night in each other's company. They talked with greater freedom and with greater intimacy, discussing mutual friends and experiences, old shooting-trips, Indian days, and Eastern nights.

"And poor Geoff Wogan?" asked Burlestone one perfect night as they patrolled the wide deck. "Still in that asylum?"

"Not he, thank God," was the reply. "He came into a comfortable little sum of money."

"Didn't that make him 'happier' than ever?"

"Only at first," replied Wallingford. "But it was his salvation."

"Oh? How?"

"Who do you think got him out? And cured him?" asked Wallingford.

Burlestone thought of the names of distinguished neurologists, alienists and psycho-therapists.

"Not my man, Sir Andrew McIlraith?" he asked.

"No. Nor any other man. . . . It was Daphne Easterwood. She's Daphne Wogan now. And I should say Geoff is about cured of happiness—as long as Daphne's alive, anyhow. Married him and his money and took him to—where do you think? Switzerland, of all places."

"Good God! What a woman." Burlestone's face set like stone.

"One would have thought Switzerland was the last place in the world she'd have gone to, after poor Aubrey Easterwood's tragedy there," he said. "She's not . . . not . . ."

"She's not decent, you mean," agreed Wallingford. "She's not a normal woman. She's a . . . a . . . Well, you've heard of the man who sent ten pounds to the Chancellor of the Exchequer with a letter saying it was conscience-money, for, though he had never kept a dog, his wife was such a bitch that . . . !"

Burlestone frowned angrily, his teeth clenched.

"That's about what Geoff Wogan would have been doing soon, if she hadn't left him and gone off with a Russian, I should think," continued Wallingford. "Unless he puts her in a lethal-chamber instead."

"Best place for her," growled Burlestone. "She wrecked and ruined Aubrey Easterwood's life, and tried to spoil him. She brought me to an attempt at suicide —over that boat-voyage business. And . . ."

"And she plied Wogan with drink and debauchery and devilment when he should have been doing a rest-cure," interrupted Wallingford. "She made him 'happy' all right, collected his cash, and got him put away. And, though I am a cad to say it and was a weakling to let her do it, she 'ran' me, for a time. Lost my head completely—if not my heart. . . . And Joan who's worth a thousand of her—and whom I really love—slaving in a hospital in India. Damn Daphne Easterwood, the fascinating devil. I was hog and ape to her Circe all right in Paris—and in London, too."

"Yes. I called her just that . . . once! Circe," said Burlestone. "She is fascinating all right. I was in love with her, once."

"And she got you?"

"Well—no. She didn't."

"'You're a whiter man than I am,' then, or . . ."

"Not a bit of it. No virtue of mine," interrupted Burlestone. "It was Aubrey Easterwood. If he hadn't been in love with her, hadn't got engaged to her and married her, I should have—er—fallen, all right. I was definitely and deliberately making a dead set at her, when young Aubrey walked into the bungalow, one day, and said he was going to marry her. Another week or so and I could have said,

"'You're not, my lad. She's my mistress,' or pleasant words to that defect."

"To save him, eh?"

"I tell you she fascinated me. I was in love with her," replied Burlestone.

"But how did she get Wogan out of that Home?" he continued. "And how did she know he was worth saving?"

"He'd given her a power of attorney, before he was certified insane. Or rather she'd given him one—to sign. A most comprehensive document, although he'd already put his banking-account in their joint names. Apparently, though, she couldn't get hold of this legacy, as Geoff wasn't competent to sign some necessary papers. So darling Daphne set to work. Moved heaven and earth, especially earth; pulled strings, used her famous charm-of-manner on the right men, did the trick—as usual—and got his case reviewed and revised. Geoff, after a long spell in that asylum, was considerably subdued, and they let him out. She married him at once, and no doubt has been spending his money hard, ever since. I'll bet that married life with her cured him of happiness, especially when the money was gone."

"Queer how she has come into the lives of four of us. All of us—except Ganesh Hazelrigg's and Harrington-Spens'," mused Burlestone. "She first spoiled, and then killed, poor Easterwood; it wasn't her fault she didn't separate you and Mrs. Wallingford; she wrecked Hennessy Wogan; and she pretty nearly finished me. I wonder what she'd have done with Ganesh if they'd ever met."

"Nothing. But I thought at one time she'd finished me, too, I don't mind telling you," replied Wallingford. "I got the fright of my life. I was seeing a lot of her in Paris—and was suddenly requested, politely but very firmly, to come on the carpet at the Ministry of War, Special Department—*contre espionage*! They wanted to know, and very badly, just what I knew about the lady calling herself Mrs. Daphne Easterwood and professing to be the English widow of two English officers, late of the British and Indian Army respectively, Captain Colin Mackleworth and Lieutenant Aubrey Easterwood —a lady who spoke perfect German, incidentally.

"Naturally I told them all I knew—that concerned them—and was just going to give my personal assurance and guarantee, when the old bird in the chair said,

"'Doubtless *Monsieur le Commandant* knows what he knows, and hopes to know a little more, eh? Ah, *oui, oui,* yes, exactly. . . . And about Madame's friend, Mademoiselle Marguerite Zell, calling herself Mademoiselle Mata Hari, also? . . . Now, does Madame know all about Mademoiselle Zell, or are they just acquaintances . . . ?', and so forth.

"Apparently they were on to Margy Zell—Mata Hari —even then, giving her plenty of rope—and considering roping in Daphne Easterwood, too! To this day, I don't know whether she was up to mischief, or whether she was merely making her sort of hay while the sun shone. Certainly she was very thick with 'Mata Hari,' but that may merely have been because they were birds of a feather. And certainly she pursued every soldier, sailor, airman and diplomat, French, Belgian or English, who might know what was doing—or going to be done—and she undoubtedly took an uncannily intelligent interest in military matters, and was always asking questions. But then she *is* intelligent and interested. She was like that in India, you remember, before the War. Could never learn enough. Knew as much about the Army in India as the G.O.C."

"Yes," agreed Burlestone, "and she spoke Italian and German—and took Mackleworth to Russia on language-leave."

"Well, I was frightened, I can tell you, for I was known as her particular *amant de cœur* and current 'proprietor.' Nice thing for me if the French arrested her as a spy!

"Luckily for me, I was returning to England in a day or two. Daphne did a bolt—if it were a bolt—at the same time. She led a hectic life in Town for a while, and then, after Geoff was put away, went to Holland, Switzerland, and Spain, and thence back to India."

"And I had the luck to come home with her," observed Burlestone.

"Then she went to Russia, I know, with a Russian Secret Service Agent, whom she'd known in Switzerland. And she got poor old Geoff," continued Wallingford. "Wonder what the end of that'll be? I'd go over and see him if it weren't for meeting Daphne, who may have returned to him. I funk it, though my conscience rather pricks me about Wogan."

"What do you funk?" asked Burlestone.

"Falling in love with Daphne again. To call it 'love.' She could twist me round her finger, even now. . . . I'm afraid of her. Isn't it despicable?"

"Yes, very. . . . And I'm as bad," replied Burlestone.

CHAPTER XXXI

The first newspaper purchased by Colonel Anthony Wallingford and Major Stacey Burlestone on Southampton platform, contained news of the Dartmoor Woman's Death Mystery. They read it in the boat-train with some interest.

THE GREAT DARTMOOR MURDER MYSTERY

The discovery was made bright and early, one lovely morning, by Mr. George Collins, a farmer and grazier, riding in wide circles about a lonely unfrequented corner of the Moor, on business of strayed or stolen sheep.

Arrived at the dominating granite-bouldered hillock known as Fox Tor, he reined in his sturdy cob, glanced cursorily around in all directions, saw no signs of sheep; and, producing from a capacious side-pocket his pipe and pouch, proceeded to prepare for a leisurely and peaceful smoke, ere making a more careful examination of the surrounding terrain, and continuing his ride.

Having filled his pipe, he returned it to his pocket, shook up his somnolent horse and trotted quickly off across the heather to make quite sure that his eyes were deceiving him.

For, in a little heather-carpeted depression, a natural saucer of but a few yards' diameter, a woman lay sleeping. Or rather, it seemed to Mr. Collins that a girl lay sleeping on a bed of heather in the little hollow —but that could hardly be. Anyone lying asleep there, so early in the morning, must have slept there all night, which was hardly likely.

It must be one of those optical what-you-may-call-'ems, a trick of light and shade. Mr. Collins had been "had" like that before, especially with boulders trying to

look like sheep—and succeeding very well, at a distance. This would be a matter of a shadow and a log
and . . .

No! It was a woman; a lady!

Something wrong?

She wouldn't be the first who'd lost their way. Aye,
lost their lives, too; ignorant in-coming foreigners from
the towns trapesing up-along across Moor as though
'twere Exeter High Street and all. Sound asleep, too . . .
and . . .

Good God Almighty! There were ants running in
and out of her mouth and nostrils. . . . She was dead!

Mr. Collins erroneously believed himself to be turning pale, and knew himself to be turning queasy-like.
. . .

This was terr'ble . . . gashly.

But he must do his duty, make sure the poor
creature was beyond help, and then ride straight to
Sergeant Trevethen over to Hillacombe and tell him the
terr'ble news.

Yes—a police job this.

And it proved to be a job that puzzled, exercised,
and finally defeated, not only Sergeant Trevethen and
his comrades of the Devon Constabulary, but Scotland
Yard itself, in the person of the biggest of the Big Five.

For, at the inquest, evidence was given by Sir
Bertram Selwyn, the great pathologist and uncannily
brilliant criminal-investigation scientist, to the effect
that the dead woman had not lost her way, sprained
her ankle, or for any other reason lain down to rest
and remained to die—of exposure and starvation.

Nor had she committed suicide.

She had met her death by violence. She had been
murdered—or, at least, killed.

Of this, Sir Bertram was absolutely certain, and
upon the truth of this he staked his reputation.

Sensation in Court.

How did Sir Bertram know that she had been
murdered, enquired the Coroner with raised eyebrows

Because her neck was broken.

Further sensation in Court.

But, as the Coroner asked, might not this tragic business be the result of pure accident? Might not the woman have fallen, and broken her neck in doing so?

No, she might not.

And pray why not?

Because, as should be obvious to the meanest intelligence, no-one can break his neck by falling down on a soft bed of heather; and no-one can fall on a rock or other rough hard surface, with sufficient force to break his neck, without there being some external signs of injury. Surely!

And how, pray, could Sir Bertram Selwyn know that the woman was not murdered miles away from the spot where she had been found—if indeed she had been murdered?

Was it not entirely feasible, and a perfectly warrantable assumption, or, at any rate, theory, that the body had been placed there, where it was found by the witness Collins? Placed there by the murderer—or murderers—if any?

No. It was not.

And pray, why not?

Because the woman had walked there, as the evidence of her foot-prints showed. And there she had been murdered—or killed.

He used the expression "murdered or killed" because he was not certain that the woman had been killed by a human being, at all. If she had been killed by a human being—then he would say she had been deliberately killed: in short, murdered. If killed by other agency, then merely—killed.

"And, pray, what other agency could be concerned in the death of this woman?" enquired Mr. Coroner with something like a sneer.

Well, people have been killed by beasts.

The Coroner smiled.

Really, really! This omniscient and infallible Sir Bertram Selwyn was excelling himself. Killed by a beast!

On Dartmoor?

"You are very positive, Sir Bertram Selwyn," said the Coroner, in a tone that was rather accusatory than congratulatory, and as though he deprecated such positive—indeed rash—statements.

"I am," replied the witness.

And then, as one who plays a trump card,

"Very well," said the Coroner. "That being so, perhaps you will tell us how the human being—or the strange wild beast—contrived to commit the murder, contrived to break the woman's neck, without leaving any marks of violence, and without leaving the slightest external trace of injury!

"And, I take it, that you, a physician, surgeon, anatomist, scientist, indeed a man of common sense, do not suggest that a murderer could make so violent, powerful, and brutal an attack upon another person as to break his neck and leave not a finger-mark, not a bruise, not a sign of that tremendous force that must be used before the human neck can be—wrung—dislocated—broken?"

Sir Bertram Selwyn intimated that doubtless the Coroner was right in everything he said; repeated that he had no explanation to suggest; reminded the Coroner that, when all was said and done, the woman's neck *had* been broken by violence, and finally reaffirmed his certainty that she had been murdered by a man—or killed by a beast.

Detective-Inspector Brace of Scotland Yard, a very different type of person, using different methods, did, in his vast, wide and deep knowledge and experience of Magistrates, Judges, Coroners, juries and witnesses, handle the Coroner—differently. And was handled by the Coroner differently—as a man not only of knowledge, wisdom and understanding, but of sweet reasonableness, common sense, and a becoming modesty and diffidence.

Nevertheless, his evidence entirely supported that of Sir Bertram Selwyn and completely confirmed his opinion!

This was a case of murder—wilful murder. Or of

wilful killing.

Deceased had walked to the place where her body was found, and she had walked there alone and un-accompanied.

There were no accompanying foot-prints?

No. No *accompanying* ones. But there were other foot-prints . . . and very curious prints they were.

Very curious indeed—neither human nor animal, so far as Detective-Inspector Brace could make out.

They were not the prints of a man's foot at all—whether shod, bare, or stockinged; for they were not long enough.

Those of a child or a woman shod, bare-footed or in stockings?

No, much too wide to be the foot-marks of a child or a woman.

On the marl, as on the grassy clay, the footmarks, although perfectly plain to be seen, were not sharp-edged, clean-cut, definitely outlined.

Then it was quite obvious and certain that they had not been made by a person wearing any sort of boot, shoe, slipper, moccasin, sandal or other form of foot-wear?

Absolutely. And Detective-Inspector Brace reminded the Coroner that he had already testified that they were not made by the feet of a human being.

It really began to appear that Detective-Inspector Brace had arrived, by different methods and a different route, at the same conclusion that Sir Bertram Selwyn had reached.

That the woman had been killed. Killed by an animal or murdered by a man.

"Well, well," enquired the Coroner, perhaps some-what testily, "if you formed the opinion that these foot-marks were made by an animal—what sort of a beast do you suppose it to have been? Was it an animal with claws, such as a lion, tiger, or bear?"

"No. I should say that there were no claws on the feet of the creature that made the prints. Had there been clear and definite claw-marks in the clay or marl, I should have thought they had been made by a bear."

"A bear! A bear on Dartmoor?"

"They were not made by a bear. Nor by a lion, tiger, panther or any such animal with claws," declared the great detective.

"Well—by what sort of an animal then? . . . A camel? . . . An elephant?"

"No," replied Detective-Inspector Brace gravely. "They were not sufficiently deep. Nor of the shape and size to be made by a camel or an elephant."

"Do you know of any animal that could have made such foot-prints?"

"I think so. I give it merely as an opinion—but I am inclined to believe that they could have been made by one of the larger apes—a chimpanzee, orang-outang, or gorilla."

Renewed Sensation in Court.

"But how on earth could such an animal have got there?"

"I don't know."

"Even if one had escaped from some circus or menagerie, how could it have crossed Dartmoor unseen, killed the woman, and made off again, still unseen? You have ascertained that there is no circus, menagerie, or private zoo in the county. Whence then could an ape have come, and where can it have gone?"

"I do not know. I merely say that the foot-prints are not human, and that they can have been made by no animal that I have ever seen, except an ape."

"There were return foot-prints—going the other way, and showing clearly in which direction the—er—creature left the place?"

"Yes. Equally clear to be seen and equally difficult to be read. Equally puzzling. They were not close to, nor parallel with, the in-going foot-prints, and they yield no clue. Nor can the men whom I have got out, searching the Moor, find anything similar to them. They do not re-appear on the nearest paths or roads. Nothing remotely resembling them."

And, after all evidence had been given, all witnesses heard, all probabilities and possibilities marshalled and estimated by the Coroner, the Jury returned an open verdict.

But for days, weeks, and months thereafter, there were Beasts, and rumours of Beasts, upon the Moor.

Young men dreamed dreams and old men saw visions, when returning late at night full of fear, beer and cider, from the public-houses within a ten-mile radius of the fatal spot.

There being no further manifestations, however, excitement subsided, the nine days' wonder faded slowly out, the affair was gradually forgotten, and the mystery relegated to the limbo of problems unsolved and unsolveable.

CHAPTER XXXII

Ganesh Hazelrigg could still laugh.

"Mrs. Cobley," said he, one morning, "there's a visitor coming to see me, this afternoon. All the way from Exeter, a *masseur.* Don't go defending me from him by saying I'm not at home. The gentleman will tell you he is the *masseur.* We're going to see if he can do something for my legs."

"Very good, Sir."

And when, that afternoon, Mrs. Cobley, knocking and entering, declared,

"The Messiah has come, Sir," Hazelrigg laughed aloud.

"Show Him in," quoth he.

§2

On the very day before Mr. Collins's discovery of the body of the poor lady, upon Dartmoor, Ganesh Hazelrigg rose slowly from his breakfast-table and moved clumsily and carefully to where he could drop into his big arm-chair. No need to use his crutches for so brief a journey, and with the table, a chair-back, and the mantel-piece for support. . . .

And what should he do this merry morn, when he'd had a digestive rest and a pipe? Have a tootle round in the old bath-chair, or make his way over the heather on his crutches?

The former was getting less agreeable as the char-a-banc season waxed—and the latter was very tiring.

Tiring be damned. It was jolly good exercise, and the more exercise he got, the better. For it was still possible that his shrivelled and shrunken legs might improve with use—just as it was still possible that his sight might do so. Lord Morgan-Thomas, the leading oculist, had said it was *possible* he might some day recover, in however small measure, the power to see very, very dimly. Not enough to read, of course, but to tell a white road from moorland grass and heather. Or, at any rate, to tell night from day.

So there was hope.

And if there were no hope, there was always courage. While a man kept up his courage, why—he had courage—and could face anything. Including blindness, horrible facial disfigurement, the maiming of his hands, the loss of the use of his legs—and of the work that had made life worth living.

"So what the hell, Bill; what the hell?" . . . as the soldiers used to recite.

Blind. . . . Blind. . . . Blind. . . . Pity the Blind.

Wonderful how your hearing develops when you're blind, he mused. Almost see with your ears, in time. Wonderful how your arms develop when you're crippled, if you use them properly. Almost as good as legs. . . . Well, well! Jolly old Life—so long as you can feel the sun on your face, snuff the heather-scented breeze, enjoy eggs-and-bacon, coffee, your pipe and a glass of whisky. . . . Curious fact, though, that blindness, while enormously increasing the power and delicacy of the senses of hearing, touch and smell, rather diminishes, if anything, the sensitiveness of the palate. Anyway, he could taste his food and drink, well enough; and his pipe or cheroot, too.

And he was going to enjoy everything he could, and make the best of it. Bad job, not being able to read. . . . But he had his memories!

Memories, begad!

Some memories!

They'd be better when he could push further into the background that memory of the last thing he had ever seen.

Flames! Flames! Flames!

Creeping nearer and nearer.

Smoke. . . . Thick swirling smoke.

That was the very last thing he'd seen—smoke and flames.

Memories. . . .

A semi-Europeanized house in the Carpet Bazaar, and the upper room in which the plotters met and made their little arrangements.

Commissar Yaraslov, the ex-butcher (why "*ex*," by the way!), with the brain of a calf and the strength of a bull, the cunning of a weasel and the ferocity of a panther; ruffian, brute, and callous murderer: Comrade Belinsky, the agitator, with the mind of a scientist, the body of a diseased starveling, the cold inhumanity of a machine, the tongue of a Demosthenes, and the relentless cruelty of a snake; the real brain of the gang, and the power behind the butcher: Comrade Krassin, the specious, wily sea-lawyer from the fo'c'sle of the battle-ship *Borodino*, whose crew had stoked her boilers with the living bodies of their officers; a dangerous, ambitious demagogue, wholly devoid of scruple, who had feathered and fouled his own foul nest in the name of the People whom he exploited: Comrade Wologoff, sincere and terrible fanatic, whose pure and dreadful soul burned up his neglected body; patriot and political theorist, who worked twenty hours a day, slept when he must, and ate when he remembered to do so: Comrade Moskowski, ex-Sergeant-Major, forceful, powerful and violent; full of half-baked theories and windy platitudes; his simple creed—death to the aristocrats, the officers, the *bourgeoisie*, the white-collared, the black-coated, the educated; death, death, death—to all, in short, who were not ignorant, rough, poor, and fit only for manual labour; and the salvation of Holy Russia by the slaughter of all but the workman and the peasant—always excepting, of course, "comrades," agitators and Commissars: Comrade Rodzianova, renegade gentleman and ex-officer, proving the genuineness of his whipped zeal and the purity of his false faith by ever-increasing brutality, savagery, and treachery toward the class to which he belonged by birth; drowning in blood his fear and the shame that gnawed his soul; bathing in blood, to dye himself the requisite Red; most murderously dangerous of them all by reason of his "comrades" suspicion—which he had to allay, avert and lull: Comrade Zilukoff, political theorist and professional agitator, quiet, watchful, deadly enigma, who struck swiftly and silently as the cobra that he somehow resembled: and Comrade Breshko, private soldier, lout, lump, obedient brute, and callous killer.

And the woman! The female of the species!

He had either seen her, or heard her voice, somewhere or other, before. . . . Long ago. . . .

And now she eyed him hard.

The Commissar's wife and Comrade Zilukoff's mistress as well. All things in common and no private property, as Zilukoff had pointed out to Commissar Yaraslov. And when Comrade Breshko had, in turn, pointed out to Comrade Zilukoff that this applied to him also, Zilukoff had replied,

"But, of course, my good *tovarisch*. Take anything you fancy, from the common stock and jointly-owned property—if you think it wise and safe and a—er—wholesome and healthy thing to do," and his smile had been as significant as the gesture with which he idly laid his hand upon the butt of the automatic dangling at his belt.

Yes, the woman! . . . But for *her* . . . It didn't bear thinking of.

As clever as the devil, and as devilish as she was clever.

But he still maintained that it was guess-work on her part; and that she had not really caught him out, not penetrated his disguise, not unmasked him and defeated him. It was pure suspicion—and suspicion was the breath of their nostrils, the air they breathed. It had been luck, chance, guess-work. Ganesh Hazelrigg had not been beaten, at last—by a woman.

She had not shaken his nerve, not made him change countenance and give himself away. Either she remembered him—or else it was a shot in the dark. Just luck. His and hers.

But it had been clever. Clever. Really well done.

Suddenly—in the middle of that eternal chatter of Russian, she had leant across to him and, with a friendly smile, said—so casually, so quietly, so naturally—in faultless easy *English*,

"Got a match?"

And he could swear, could stake his soul on it, that he had not moved his hand by a hair's-breadth towards his pocket, to get the matches he had in his poshteen; he could swear that he hadn't blinked an eyelash, let a gleam of understanding come into his face, given the slightest sign that he had understood what she said.

For he was supposed to be an Afghan. An Afghan sirdar from Cabul, who, because he knew Russian, had been sent by the Amir to see whether Afghanistan and the new Russia could do some mutually profitable business; whether the Bolsheviks were coming much further south; whether they were going to keep their promise to the Asmas Ghazis, to the Hadji of Turgan-zai, the Bulbul-i-Sehwan, Obeidullah's Army of God, the Ghaleb-nameh, the Border Mullahs and the Indian seditionists, and attack India if a simultaneous rising and mutiny were guaranteed there.

And he had played his part to perfection, with nerves of iron. And with a truly wonderful set of cre-dentials, sufficient to convince even such suspicious, distrustful, shoot-him-and-then-enquire people as these. How should they fail to convince these plotters, this half-established "soviet" of fire-brands, agitators, spies and emissaries, since the credentials were actually genuine.

The letter he brought them was the Amir's letter; the clothes he wore were the actual clothes worn by the Amir's envoy; the followers, who had ridden into the town with him, were dressed in the clothes of the envoy's followers.

For Ganesh Hazelrigg, with Shere Khan, Mahbub Ali and his handful of men of the Guides, had followed the Afghan envoy's party from Cabul half across Asia, had overtaken him at a suitable spot—and fought it out. Casualties on both sides—and he had taken care that the Afghan envoy was a casualty.

No—there could not be a shadow of doubt in the

minds of the Comrades that he was what he professed to be. And any faults in his Russian speech would be quite natural in an Afghan—particularly as, now and then, he pretended to be at a loss for a Russian expression, word, phrase or idiom, and would use Afghan words instead.

There had been awkward moments; he was rather fair for an Afghan, in spite of his bushy black beard; and, at any moment, a genuine Afghan might have been brought into the house—into the meetings even. That was the danger. There must have been plenty of Afghans in the town. But his pulse had never quickened; he had never turned a hair; never let an eye-lid quiver.

No—nor when the woman turned to him and said, so conversationally,

"*Got a match?*"

But in spite of his blank look of incomprehension, she had sprung to her feet, thrust a pistol almost against his face and cried,

"Spy! . . . Quick, Krassin, Yaraslov! . . . Grab him. Choke him if he shouts. . . . The door, Moskowski. . . . The window, Rodzianova! . . ." And the powerful butcher, the burly sailor, and the heavy soldier had sprung upon him, while the rest secured door and window, and drew their revolvers.

"He's not an Afghan," said the woman. "I have suspected him all along. I've seen him before. In Europe, too. Or India perhaps. I've never been in Afghanistan in my life. . . . Do you know what this 'Afghan envoy' is, Comrades? He's an Englishman— and if he gets away, we're done for. He knows as much as we do. And he knows us all by sight. . . . And can you guess what the Englishman is? He's advance-agent and spy—of a British army. He . . ."

"How d'you know he's English, Comrade Minelli . . . I mean Comrade Madame Yaraslov?" asked Zilukoff, as the rest closed in, their faces wolfish.

"Because I spoke to him in English—and he understood. . . . I stared into his eyes and read his thoughts. I saw him understand, and then I saw him refuse to understand. He may have controlled his nerves and body, so that he did not start—but his mind, his thoughts, his soul, started. Yes, *jumped*. . . . He's English—and if we let him escape, he'll go straight to the Emir here and tell him everything—and we shall be arrested and shot. . . . Shot if we're lucky. . . ."

Suddenly she turned to Hazelrigg.

"You did understand me when I said '*Got a match?*' didn't you?" she cried, in English.

And almost he replied, in Russian,

"No, I didn't."

Yes, he had very nearly answered, in Russian, the English that she was talking to him!

But he hadn't turned a hair or blinked an eyelash. He had merely looked about from one to another, from her to Zilukoff, Yaraslov, Belinsky, Wologoff, and asked in utter surprise,

"What's the matter? What's Comrade Madame Yaraslov saying about me?"

"Here—torture him till he talks English," said the woman. "There's a coil of barbed wire in the compound, Yaraslov—bind a yard or two of it round his head as tight as you can pull it."

"Shoot him, and be done with it," growled Moskowski, as Yaraslov left the room.

"Noisy. I'll cut his throat," volunteered Rodzianova.

"But what's all this? . . . Why? Why? . . . My master the Amir will . . ." protested the 'Afghan.'

"'Your master the Amir'—won't," sneered the woman, in English.

"Shut up!" Krassin struck him on the mouth. "We'll teach you to come spying here."

"Let's serve him as we did the officers of the *Borodino*," he said, grinning.

Yaraslov entered, carrying a coil of barbed wire.

"Look here," said the woman, "we've got to get out of this. Choose another meeting-place. This beauty has got a gang of tribesmen with him. Pathans from India, I should think. Soldiers of the Indian Army. God knows how much mischief he's done already. May have sent off messengers. . . . Look—this house is going to catch fire; but fortunately we shall not be using it at the time. He will, though. Unless he likes to talk. In English.

"Yaraslov! Wire doesn't burn. You and Krassin and Moskowski bind his arms to his sides and his legs together, then wind the wire round and round him and the table. . . . The fire will then start underneath it. Unless he likes to talk. In English."

"And if he does, Minna?" purred Belinsky.

So she was Minna, was she? And Minelli? *Now* he remembered where he had seen her.

"Well . . . depends on how much he confesses," replied the woman. "What information he gives us. The more helpful he is, the more helpful we'll be—in getting him quickly into Hell. . . . Fetch some lamp-oil and paper, fire-wood—anything that'll burn."

And fight like a lion though he did, six of them overpowered him—a strong man to each arm and each leg, another at his throat, another with a cord, before using the wire.

Gagged and bound, and fastened to the table, they left him, after having tried many and ingenious ways of inducing him to speak English.

And, having replaced the gag, passing a wire across that also, and round the table, they departed one by one, leaving the renegade officer, Rodzianova, to set the place on fire.

They could trust him to do it—because of his fear that they should not trust him.

Memories!

That had been a *mauvais quart d'heure*—but even during that unforgettable time, as he lay there roasting to death, he had had the satisfaction of knowing that they'd been unable to make him speak English—even when Yaraslov the Butcher began cutting his fingers off—one by one; a joint after every unanswered question.

Not many men have been burnt alive—to the point of unconsciousness; to the point of being crippled and blinded; of being a charred, hairless, blackened body on which the clothing has been reduced to brittle charcoal, ash and soot—and have recovered. Without medical aid or skilled nursing. . . . Thank God for brave and devoted followers.

Trust Shere Khan to have been watching the house, and—after seeing the conspirators leave it, one by one, and smoke begin to appear—to have dashed off for Mahbub Ali, waiting close by in the Silk Bazaar, and to have burst into the room, smashing the locked door.

The wire had been red hot in places, he said afterwards.

And those men, their lives not worth an hour's purchase, had hidden him for weeks, in the stable they had rented for the horses; and when he could sit on one, they had brought him safely back, by the way they had come.

Did the ghost of the Afghan envoy jibber and laugh, as his slayer, a blind cripple, rode past the scene of the fight in which the envoy—with five Afghans and three Pathans—had died?

By the end of that blind ride, Ganesh Hazelrigg had known what suffering was.

Ah, well . . . he was alive—and there were other memories than those.

He'd get out in the sun, take some exercise, get up on the moor and hear the larks, smell the heather, count his many blessings and—rejoice.

He still had his courage, all right, thank God.

Rising from his chair, he made his way round the room and out into the little hall. Taking his crutches, he swung off down the garden path, through the gate that opened on to the well-worn track that so few people ever trod, save he and Mrs. Cobley, and, counting every swing of his body, from foot-hold to foot-hold, made his way to the rough road rarely used by motor-cars.

Along this road he swung, still counting, until, accurately as in the days when he could see, he stopped by a gateless stone gate-post, tapped it to verify his position, and turned off on to the heather.

One hundred paces, or measures, from where his feet touched the ground to where they touched it again; another hundred; a third; a fourth; twenty-seven more swings—and he must be at the spot where the ground was always soft, where crutches would sink in, where he might stick like a fly on gummed paper.

Leaning on one crutch he took the other by the middle, and threw it a few yards ahead. Balancing himself for a moment he threw the other after it. Then, sinking forward on his face, he raised his body perpendicularly from the ground and "walked" forward on his hands. At this, he had always been extremely expert; and, like this, he could go quite a long way.

Feeling the heather again beneath his hands, he allowed his body to fall back, and came lightly to his feet. After a few seconds' groping, he found his crutches, rose and resumed his way.

Ah! Here he was! In the hollow wherein he'd loved to sit, upon occasion, almost from boyhood. High and alone and hidden, for the place was a natural saucer, and anyone sitting in it was invisible to passing pedestrians—should there ever be any.

Here, with his lingering agoraphobia, his dread of company, he could be as private as in his own house.

No-one to see him—and to Pity the Poor Blind.

Now for a pipe, and—pleasanter memories; out here in the sunshine and glorious air.

Memories. . . .

Perhaps he'd drop asleep—and not dream that he was burning in Hell.

CHAPTER XXXIII

"Major Bartholomew Hazelrigg?" said a voice. "Excuse me if I intrude."

Instinctively he "looked" up.

"Good God!" whispered the voice. "I didn't know that . . ."

A close and careful observer, had one been present, would have noticed a startled look on the woman's face, a look of incredulity, almost of fear, almost of horror.

The observer might also have noticed that the man held his breath, froze into utter immobility, and listened—appeared to listen with all his soul, as well as with his ears. But his face was expressionless.

"Yes?" he said, after a long silence.

"May I sit down?" asked the woman, her voice now under control again, her eyes examining his blind, disfigured face, his almost fingerless hands, and noting his untidy blind-man's dress, his feeble legs.

"Do," said Hazelrigg.

"I want to talk to you. I saw you come out of your house, and followed you here. What I have to tell you is private. Very private. And I thought this would be a better place in which to say—what I have to say."

"Yes?"

"I am Mrs. Hennessy Wogan. You know my husband, though you don't know me. But . . ."

Ganesh Hazelrigg smiled.

". . . but I know you—or rather, who you are," she continued. "You are Mary Harrington-Spens' brother. It is on her behalf that I have come to see you."

"Yes? You have come from my sister?"

"When I say 'on her behalf,' I do not mean that I have come from her. I have come to do her a kindness, really. To give her a chance of saving herself from—well —from more trouble . . . from another law-suit."

"That is very kind of you."

"As you know, she succeeded in winning the case brought against her by the rightful heiress of Henry Askroyd—his wife. The poor woman whom he secretly married and then disowned."

"Yes?"

"I am she."

"Ah! . . . *Ah!* . . . You are she. Yes?"

"And now—although I then failed to prove the fact that I am Henry Askroyd's wife, and lost my case, lost it because my evidence was stolen and my witnesses bribed—*now* I have another, a perfect, proof that I am the heiress."

"Yes?"

"Yes. I have Julia Askroyd's last Will and Testament. Her *last* Will, you understand. Made after your sister left her service; made months later than the one Julia made in favour of your sister; and which was made under your sister's influence."

"Yes?"

"Yes. And I am going to recover whatever remains of my legal and rightful legacy. I am going to get every penny—unless . . ."

"Yes?"

"Unless you at once pay me back the ten thousand pounds that she made over to you by deed of gift."

"Why trouble about a trifle like that, since you have a later Will?"

"I am not greedy—and litigation costs money. Pay me that ten thousand and I will undertake to waive all claims under the Will—provided your sister pays me another ten thousand also."

"How is your—'husband'?"

"Hennessy Wogan? What has that to do with it?"

"Has he *anything* to do with it?"

"I have not seen him for years."

"Where is he?"

"In Ireland. In the Free State Army or the Irish Republican Army; or both, perhaps."

"No. He is not in both. And he is not your husband."

"What do you mean? Let me tell you something, my

friend. I . . ."

"No, let me tell *you* something, my dear. You have joined two *dossiers* into one—and such a one! You have let a blind man see daylight! I'll tell you. Quite a tale. You have supplied the key that turns the picture-puzzle into a plain pattern. Listen!" and Hazelrigg took the woman's hand in his.

She smiled into his blind face.

Was the fool going to turn amorous—like all the other fools?

Well—the easier her task. . . . Let him get on with it.

The maimed hand slipped to her wrist, and, though it had but a thumb and two fingers, its grip was amazingly strong.

"I've only seen you twice in my life, my dear Mrs.—er—Wogan; and yet your path and mine have often run parallel and quite near to each other—and they have crossed, occasionally. They have crossed again. They won't do so any more.

"No. Sit still, and listen. I have something to say, and you have something to hear. I shan't be very long.

"The first time I saw you was at Miss Julia Askroyd's flat. I had called to see my sister Mary. You were just coming out of the drawing-room as I was shown in. I only had a glimpse of your face. I just heard your voice, too, as you spoke to the maid, before the door was shut. But when I saw you the second time, many years later, I knew that I had seen you before, and had heard your voice before.

"We'll come to that in a minute. . . .

"A Miss Minna Minelli you were, my sister said; and she told me certain things about you.

"Then, not long after my sister married, you brought an action against her, accusing her of getting Miss Julia Askroyd's money by improperly influencing her to make a will in her favour. It was extraordinarily unpleasant for Mary, who had never even heard the word 'will' mentioned by Miss Julia Askroyd. A very nasty case, and horrible front-page publicity. It caused her and her husband a lot of suffering.

"I wasn't in England at the time—and it was the cruellest hard luck for my sister—because, by then, I knew quite a lot about Miss Minna Minelli.

"Sit still! . . . No, I am not going to leave go of your wrist. . . .

"Quite a lot. It was my business to know, as it happened. I knew she was the daughter of an Austrian officer and an Irishwoman. She was born in Rome, and grew up speaking German, Italian and English, and learned Russian as well, later on. She married Captain Fritz von Voehniger, a German Secret-Service agent—a very good agent, too, who did fine work for his country in the War . . . and who is still alive, my dear Frau von Voehniger. She was, for a time, her husband's colleague, the agent's agent—but she required a wider stage for her very marked abilities, as well as a bigger income for her very marked extravagance. So she went off, on her own, and did quite well at her job—soon having a name and number of her own, too, in the German Secret Service.

"She did quite well for herself also, combining pleasure with business, and became quite a noted charmer—generally of Russian, French, and British officers.

"And so to Henry Askroyd. And to a quaint parallelism of our paths, my dear Frau von Voehniger. For it was I who got my sister Mary her job with Miss Julia Askroyd, because I had need and reason to keep in touch with the doings and movements of the Askroyd brothers, particularly the one whose sphere of influence was Germany. It gave me an excuse for calling—and chatting with dear Miss Julia. She loved to talk about her brothers.

"No, Mary knew nothing whatever about the game I was playing. She was absolutely loyal to her employer.

"And, 'to oblige Miss Julia' I called on Henry! . . . *Your* Henry. . . . We had quite a time together—for, although he lived abroad, he was a real patriot, and the less he saw of England, the more he loved her. And he was in a position to be very helpful. Very helpful indeed.

"In time, I helped him, too. The mouse and the lion, you know. I told him that an agent of mine had told me that a certain Miss Minna Minelli—in whom he had been interested and with whom he was now painfully involved—was already married, was a German agent, was Frau von Voehniger in private life, and need not be taken very seriously. In fact, if he liked, we could at once free him from the net.

"He did like—and it was I who put the spoke in your wheel and ended your chance of a career as 'Mrs.' Millionaire Henry Askroyd.

"Eh? . . . Oh, yes, my dear, you got your own back, as you say. But I can still laugh—and he laughs best who laughs last.

"And so, although I had never seen you then, our paths crossed—and again I put quite a kink in yours. . . . Then you turned your attention to Henry's sister in London. And, paid companion to Henry's sister, was my sister; although you didn't know it. And there, as I have said, I got a glimpse of you, though neither of us knew the other.

"Then you disappeared. I lost track of you, and, having gone up north of Afghanistan to the Back of Beyond, only learnt, too late, that you had persecuted and prosecuted Mary. Lost you altogether, my dear—until we met for the second time. . . .

"And now you have come and told me all about yourself—by saying you are Mrs. Hennessy Wogan—so that I can fill in the gap; complete the picture-puzzle.

"Since you are the woman who 'married' poor Hennessy Wogan, you are the woman who spoilt Stacey Burlestone's life with your lying tongue; the woman who very nearly wrecked Moresby Wallingford's career; the woman who 'married' and ruined young Easterwood; the woman who 'married' Colin Mackleworth, in order to take up the agency in India for supplying the German Secret Service with all the latest information about the Indian Army, the political situation in India, and all the news. Here our paths crossed again, although we never met, for your letters to your 'aunt' never reached Germany. They came to me, eventually; for I was in charge of that branch, just then.

"And to think that it was our Minna all the time! Our Frau von Voehniger, in fact!

"When the War came, you were in Germany, and they sent you to Switzerland and thence to Paris, where you worked with Mata Hari. And it was your evidence, later, more than anything else, that sent her to face the firing-squad. You saved yourself at her expense—proving your *bona fides* as a good English ally and genuine *contre-espionage* agent!

"You came to England with Wogan and then went to Holland, Sweden and Italy. Then back to India to carry on the good work. To England again, on the same ship as Stacey Burlestone, and then to Germany, and so to Russia—double-crossing again.

"An extraordinarily clever woman. Amazingly cool and brave. I respect courage beyond all virtues—and had you been a loyal agent of your own country, or an honest agent of any one country, I could almost have respected you. Almost. Not quite. Too personally base and evil, apart from professional dishonesty, taking pay from both sides and betraying both—like your unfortunate friend Marguerite Zell, bird of your feather but lacking your nerve and ability. From both sides? From half-a-dozen—including the foul Bolshevist crew. You served—and cheated—Germany, France, England, Belgium, Austria and Russia. An international spy—and swindler.

"No. I couldn't quite respect you, for you are just a mean, hireling, double-crossing spy—liar, cheat, swindler and evil parasite . . . a conscienceless peril to men and to nations.

"And so to Russia, I say. And there I saw you for the second time, my dear; and though I knew I'd seen you before, I couldn't place you. Had I done so in time, I should now have my two eyes, my ten fingers, the use of my legs—and my fascinating, dangerous work.

"Yes. You won that time. And had me burnt alive.

"And now, feeling safe and secure, you have visited England again . . . to do a little blackmailing, make a little money from Mary and her husband and her silly brother—never dreaming that her silly brother, Bartholomew Hazelrigg, was the man you burnt alive! Hand of Fate, eh, my dear Frau von Voehniger? Paths crossed again—for the last time. . . .

"Have I nearly done? Yes, I have. I apologize for boring you. You could always make men talk, couldn't you?

"Yes. Nearly finished. Don't worry. I am not going to tell you any more. I am going to show you something. Chiefly for England's sake; and partly for the sake of my friends, Harrington-Spens, Aubrey Easterwood, Stacey Burlestone, Moresby Wallingford and Hennessy Wogan. . . . *And*, I fully admit, partly on my own account. . . . Amazing, how you have been concerned in the fates of all six of us. The pure golden thread on which the pearls of our six young lives were strung. . . . '*Beware of a dark woman*,' eh!

"*Keep still!* Don't be impatient. I'm going to show you now. It's a trick I learnt in a country where men take the bull by the horns literally—and turn it into beef, with one twist. I perfected the trick in Japan. Great anatomists, those little men, and wonderful at the application of the powers of leverage. No . . . It is quite useless for you to struggle. I shan't hurt you— and you won't hurt anybody else, ever again.

"Practically painless. Not like being burnt alive. . . . The side of the left hand below the right ear; the right hand on the left side of the head, and a sharp jerk—*so*. . . . Just a click . . . and it's all over. . . . Thank you."

The "click" was audible.

Ganesh Hazelrigg, to the best of his ability, arranged the body of Minna von Voehniger (*née* Minna Minelli), *alias* Daphne Mackleworth, *alias* Daphne Easterwood, *alias* Madame Yaraslov, *alias* Daphne Wogan, in the posture of natural sleep, reached for his crutches, and rose to his feet.

"Vain regrets for the rest of my life, my dear? Yes. Bitter regrets—that I didn't wring your damned neck years ago. . . . And if I hang—well—it'll be a pleasure to hang for you, Minna."

Crossing the clay again, by the same method as before, he retrieved his crutches once more, and returned to his cottage, feeling much better.

CHAPTER XXXIV

A year later, on the anniversary of the day of the murder, Ganesh Hazelrigg threw a party at the Imperial Hotel, Mayfair; a party to celebrate the fact that he could read the headings in a newspaper and was likely to be able to read the rest of it, in course of time; that he could walk a mile without crutches; that his artificial hands were nearly as good as the real ones had been; and that the doctors had built him a new face of sub-cutaneously-injected paraffin wax.

Lord Morgan-Thomas, Sir Andrew McIlraith, and the other physicians and surgeons who had taken pride and interest in his recovery, called it a triumph of courage, and spoke of him as the stoutest and bravest sufferer they had ever known.

There were present at the party his brother-in-law, Colonel Marcus Harrington-Spens, Major Stacey Burlestone, Colonel Moresby Wallingford, and General Hennessy Wogan of the Free State Army.

Never was a jollier or more successful party, although, at one stage, there was a brief unrehearsed silence after the host had proposed the toast of Absent Friends, and added,

"Above ground and below—and especially that fine gentleman, our friend Aubrey Easterwood."

Major Stacey Burlestone's "God rest his gallant soul," came evidently from the heart, and was obviously in the nature of a prayer.

After dinner, in a brief lull of the general happy conversation, the host turned to the General on his left hand, and mentioned that the port was at his elbow.

"Begob it is. I beg its pardon, then. I was thinking, Ganesh, me bhoy . . ." replied Wogan, unsmiling.

"Thinking, Geoff?"

"Yes. Of that damned absentee wife of mine. . . . There's a girl in Ireland, with a heart of gold, eyes of sapphire, teeth of pearl, hair of ebony, complexion of sunset glow on snow-clad peaks. Faith, I . . ."

"Why don't you marry her?"

"They still only allow ye one wife in Ireland."

"I'll tell you something, Geoff. You can rely on its being true—but I want you to say nothing about the matter to anyone, and especially not to give me as your authority, if ever you do. Understand?"

"Absolutely. I'll never repeat what ye say, Ganesh, and when I do, I'll say 'twas not you that told me, for 'twas yourself said it wasn't."

Ganesh Hazelrigg laughed.

"That's it, Geoff. Anyway, whether you quote me as your authority or not, I can't prove what I say—to you or anyone else."

"I'll take your word on it, Ganesh. For you're the best and whitest man God ever made."

"She's dead. You'll never be troubled by her—or by anybody concerning her—if you marry again to-morrow, and put a wedding-notice in every paper in the world."

"Fact, Ganesh?"

"Fact."

"How d'ye know? Secret Service?"

"Very secret."

"Good enough, Ganesh. God bless ye. And thank ye, m'bhoy."

"*What for?*"

"Telling me."

"Oh . . . yes. . . .

"And now I'll tell you something else, Geoff. She never was your wife. Yes, I know you went through a form of marriage with her—but she wasn't a widow. So, if ever she came back, which she won't, you needn't be frightened."

"*What?* Aubrey Easterwood is . . ."

"He never was her husband either. Nor was Colin Mackleworth."

"Sure now, Ganesh. I always said she was a disrespectable woman."

"A bit careless. She never was a widow or a

divorcee. Her husband, Fritz von Voehniger, is alive to this day. And if she were alive she'd be Frau von Voehniger."

"Fancy . . . poor Daphne a 'Frau'! And a corpse, too! She was a great lass."

Ganesh Hazelrigg beamed round at his four friends.

Marky Harrington-Spens—reasonably poor now, and without a care.

Stacey Burlestone—looking less healthy and far happier.

Geoff Wogan—looking less happy and far healthier.

Tony Wallingford—chastened, but on top of the world, now that Joan had decided he shouldn't fly any more.

Poor young Aubrey Easterwood . . . ! Poor? . . . Wasn't his fate perhaps the best of all—because the Gods loved him?

And he himself?

He wished he hadn't been so fool-hardy—rash.

Well, if he had worshipped and painfully cultivated Courage, made it his god, until it had brought him to a fate worse than death, Courage had brought him back again, and saved him.

Yes, whatever he had lost, he had his courage—and no regrets . . . and anyhow, what's the good of wishing? If wishes were horses beggars would ride. . . .

EXPLOSION

DEDICATED TO

THE FRIENDS OF INDIA, THE REAL INDIA OF THREE
HUNDRED MILLION UNREPRESENTED PEASANTS,
WHOSE SOLE "POLITICAL ASPIRATIONS" ARE THAT
THE PEACE, THE SECURITY, THE JUSTICE AND THE
PROTECTION PROVIDED BY THE BRITISH RAJ MAY
FOR EVER REMAIN TO THEM UNDISTURBED,
UNWEAKENED AND UNCHANGED

I

In the huge drawing-room of the vast old bungalow that was the official residence of the Commissioner of the Division, the Bhawalgarh Literary, Dramatic and Philosophical Society was in session.

The Society—which consisted of the Honourable Edward Cornwallis, C.S.I., C.I.E., I.C.S., Commissioner of the Western Division; Mr. Lawrence Herdie, C.S.I., I.C.S., Collector and Resident Magistrate of Bhawalgarh; Mr. Justice Sherdley, I.C.S., Judicial Commissioner; Colonel Brownlow, I.M.S., Civil Surgeon of Bhawalgarh; Colonel Angus Campbell, commanding the Infantry Battalion (Nicholson's Sikhs); Major Murdoch, I.M.S., Governor of Bhawalgarh Gaol; Mr. Anthony Steele, Superintendent of Police; Major Hector Grant, R.F.A., commanding the Bhawalgarh Fort and the half-battery of Field Artillery; the Reverend Byam J. Torrens, Principal of the American Mission College; Mr. Ramrao Narayen Gopaldas, Barrister-at-Law; and others, together with their respective wives, relatives and guests—was the Commissioner's creation, relaxation, pride and hobby.

Every Thursday evening it met at his bungalow, save when he was on tour; and, by means of it, he endeavoured, not without success, to keep the European community of Bhawalgarh a united, if not happy, family, and himself more or less in touch with each of its members.

During the half-hour of informal social intercourse that followed each solemn session, the Commissioner contrived to chat with his civil and military colleagues, subordinates and friends, on matters of interest and importance to them and to himself. When, as usually happened, members of the Society brought friends, a meeting of the Society might include anything from fifty to seventy people.

When the Society was manifesting in its Literary

incarnation, someone could be found to read a more or less interesting paper upon the life and works of some author, more or less well known to his audience; and Mr. Justice Sherdley could always be relied upon to deliver a witty speech of criticism that would keep his audience interested and amused.

Not a few members attended meetings of the Society simply to hear Mr. Justice Sherdley on the subject, whatever that might be.

To him, the Commissioner was wont to allude as a star turn; a tower of strength; a prop and mainstay; his right-hand man; and a damned funny old bird.

To-night, the Bhawalgarh Literary, Dramatic and Philosophical Society was to be Philosophical, by reason of the fact that the Commissioner's wife, the intense, emotional, enthusiastic Rowena Loelia Corn-wallis, *née* Burtwhistle—daughter of that famous Cambridge scholar, philosopher and don—was, as the Commissioner put it, "running" the noted Christian convert from Brahminism, Sant Arjun Rama.

Rowena's enthusiasms were apt, upon occasion, to cause the Commissioner a little embarrassment by reason of their suddenness, unexpectedness, peculiarity and violence, though, happily, the violent enthusiasms, like violent fires, did soon burn out themselves.

When her deep pre-occupation was Indian Widows, he was apt to reply to Mr. Justice Sherdley's sympathetic kind enquiry as to what was troubling him,

"I have an attack of Indian Widows."

At another time,

"I am suffering from Child-Marriage."

Anon,

"I have a bad go of *Yoga*."

Or, perchance,

"I am afflicted with *fakirs*."

In his time the Commissioner had suffered, not gladly but very patiently, many grievous plagues, brought upon him by Rowena as plagues were brought upon the Egyptians by Moses.

And the current one was the Convert, the first, last,

and only genuine Brahmin convert to Christianity, Sant Arjun Rama—to whom Rowena would persistently, and perhaps inaccurately, refer as Saint Arjun—now paying his first visit to Bhawalgarh.

Rowena's own Saint Arjun!

In fact, the man was coming to be known in Bhawalgarh, and indeed throughout the whole of the Western Division, as Saint Arjun.

That he should testify to the members of the Bhawalgarh Philosophical Society and let their critical ears hear his marvellous, nay miraculous, story from his own lips, Rowena insisted. And when Rowena insisted, the Commissioner, for the sake of peace, as well as for that of the love he bore her, gave way whenever possible, Rowena almost invariably contriving to convince him of the possibility.

In vain, in this case, had he pointed out to her that Religion is one of the subjects excluded from the agenda of Debating Societies. For, promptly and conclusively, his wife had pointed out to him that Religion was not in debate at all; that Saint Arjun was merely going to tell the Society the story of his Conversion and the wondrous things that followed upon it; that he was going to explain to the Society, materializing in its philosophical incarnation, his own Philosophy of Life; was going to invite and freely welcome, question, comment and discussion. What more could a Philosophical Society desire? Was not Man the proper study of Mankind; human experience its keenest concern? And when, the coffee-pot in one hand, a marmaladed piece of toast in the other, Rowena, in her fine deep voice had said,

"*Nihil humanum me alienum puto,*" her husband had given way. Hastily.

"Quite so, my dear, quite so. Philosophy of life. Personal experience. No religious—er—controversial—er—wranglings. Quite so. We'll send round the usual invitations for Thursday night, with the notice that Mr. Sant Arjun Rama will address the Society on the subject of his—er—philosophical conclusions; his change of heart—I mean to say, his extraordinary . . ."

"His conversion from Brahminism to Christianity," said Mrs. Cornwallis firmly.

And so, at nine o'clock on that epochal evening, the guests arrived in twos and threes, until most of the European residents of Bhawalgarh had assembled in the Commissioner's drawing-room.

In deep arm-chairs, on comfortable sofas and divans, they seated themselves about the vast room, as their official predecessors had done a hundred years before, and awaited, some with pleasurable anticipation, some with keen interest, some with slight resentment, some with hopes of revelation, and some with deep scepticism, that which should befall.

Having welcomed his friends, the Commissioner took the Chair by seating himself at a table from which, at one end of the huge pillared room, he could see all the assembled guests. Beside, and somewhat behind him, and somehow apparently, but not actually, above him, sat Rowena, holding a watching brief for her Saint and the Minutes Book of the Literary, Dramatic and Philosophical Society of Bhawalgarh, of which she was, of course, the Honorary Secretary.

Ere rising to his feet to ask the Secretary to read the minutes of the last meeting, the Commissioner looked round upon the members, ordinary and honorary, and their guests who accompanied them.

Dear old Sherdley. Thank Heaven he was present, for he could be relied upon to cast the sweetest oil upon the most troubled waters, should there be any: still and deep waters ruffled by anything said by this Sant Arjun Rama that might give offence; or, what was more probable, should any member, in comment, question and discussion, give utterance to expressions unacceptable to the lecturer and his patroness. Lecturer? No, he couldn't call him that exactly. The fellow wasn't there to lecture them. He was merely going to tell his tale. Testify. Anyway, it was a pity that Rowena had conceived this brilliant idea of introducing him to the Society and that he himself had given way. He ought to have put his foot down firmly, like a man. Like a man putting his bare foot down firmly on a tintack.

Still, the announcement had evidently been a great draw. He had rarely seen so many present at a meeting, and he loved to see the room full to capacity. It showed that the Society was healthy and flourishing. It would be a terrible thing if it dwindled and failed; if people lost interest and enthusiasm; and the Society, growing smaller numerically, gradually faded and died.

For it did him real solid good, and every man there, real solid good, to get out of India for an hour or two; to get away from the work, the worry, the heat, the irritation, the anxiety, the carking care of the trivial round, and the painful strain of the heavy responsibility that made the exile's life the somewhat-less-than-joyous thing it was. It did real and solid good to every woman there, to get out of India for a while, to get away from the ever-present worries and troubles of Indian servants; of Indian domestic life; of making ends meet; and of the anxious yearning thought of children at home in England.

Yes, for a time they could forget India, all of them, and remember Books, Plays, Music, Art, Philosophy and the Drama, all the things that adorn and beautify life and make it more worth living.

No, it wasn't for the greater glorification of the Commissioner that the Society existed, though certainly it contributed to his greater happiness, relaxation, comfort and peace of mind.

It actually did comfort him and give him greater peace of mind, to see all these people gathered together in his house; rallying round him, as it were. It gave him—what should he say? An increased sense of safety? No, not exactly that, for he had no sense of safety. Damn it, it did give him something approaching a sense of safety, though. It gave him a little reassurance—a little comfort, as he had said.

For he was afraid.

Definitely he was oppressed by a sense of danger.

He was not afraid for himself, not oppressed by sense of danger to himself, but afraid for Rowena; for the women and children, if not for the men, of

Bhawalgarh; for the women and the children and his fellow-countrymen throughout India; for India herself. He was, he realized and admitted, apprehensive; afflicted with an ever-growing sense of anxiety, fear, that most terrible, devitalizing and deadly of all fatal microbes.

He feared the future—the future to be created by the ignorant or vote-catching British politician, and the Indian agitator.

Waking and sleeping he was troubled with a vague premonition of something about to happen. Something sudden, terrific, and terrible.

Was it possible that those extremely well-worded, well-written, restrained, convincing, matter-of-fact letters, those amazing anonymous letters, had really affected his mind, really found foothold and an abiding-place in his consciousness? Was it? Surely he, the Commissioner of the Western Division, did not dwell in fear of being blown to pieces, annihilated in a second. Surely he was not living in hourly dread, in perpetual fear and constant terror of—explosion.

But he was. He was suffering from fright. Had he been hypnotized in some way?

Yes, waking and sleeping—sometimes very strongly when sleeping—he suffered thus. At times, he was not only afraid of some sudden explosion, material or other, but terribly frightened at the thought of his fear, his ever-increasing fear. Would it continue to grow and increase until it became noticeable, patent? Would Rowena, first of all, suspect, and then discover, that he was afraid; that her husband, the Commissioner of the Western Division, was a frightened man? Would his colleagues be the next to notice it? Would it soon get about that the Commissioner was anxious, worried, and apprehensive, to the point of fear? Would it become common talk that he was—nervous?

He might sound Sherdley on the subject.

No, he couldn't very well do that. It would be silly. . . . How severe, austere, ascetic, Sherdley looked, with his strong calm face, his unruffled imperturbable demeanour. Did ever harder, more unsympathetic, face hide warmer, more kindly, nature? How incredibly must the man whom Elizabeth Sherdley saw in him differ from the Judge whom the Bench and Bar of Bhawalgarh saw, respected and feared—not to mention the criminals who came up for trial before him. It was quite obvious that she adored him.

And there was the excellent Herdie. It must undoubtedly do him a world of good to get away from his files, for no man ever took life more seriously than Lawrence Herdie. He was reputed to work from four till eight every morning, and, having spent the day in Court or *kutcherry*,[31] to go home, dine, and then work from ten until two in the morning. That must be an exaggeration, of course, particularly when it was further stated that the only occasions upon which he failed to rise at four were those upon which he failed to go to bed at all.

When Rowena had tried to interest Jane Herdie in Indian Widows, she had replied,

"Pity Indian Widows? I do. I am one myself."

Poor Jane Herdie! Life must be dull for her, married to an old file—who was wedded to his files.

Well—meetings of the Society gave them both a little change and relaxation from their troubles.

And Jane Herdie, at least, certainly needed it. Now there was a case of genuine and terrible cause for anxiety and apprehension. Every time her husband left the bungalow, she must wonder whether she would ever see him alive again, after those two all-but-successful attempts upon his life, before he was transferred to Bhawalgarh; a bullet through his topi, and his coat torn by a piece of the bomb that killed the man seated beside him; not to mention quite a number of curious inexplicable "accidents" that had happened to him during the past year or two. What must it be like to receive letters by every post, threatening death, and worse, to your husband? What fiend had written in excellent handwriting and perfect English on the white distemper of her bedroom wall,

You think your husband an angel. We are going to

---

[31] *The Collector's secretariat; office-building; treasury and record-room.*

make him one before long.

Just because he was a fearless magistrate, and did his duty.

Talk about a sense of insecurity, a feeling that one dwelt on the edge of a smouldering volcano. And things were now going that way in Bhawalgarh too, it seemed.

Well, no doubt Herdie and his wife could get out of India for an hour or two, when they came to a meeting of the Society.

And there was Anthony Steele. What was he thinking, behind that smooth inscrutable face of his? No-one would ever imagine that he was thinking at all: but anyone who knew him, was very well aware that he thought a great deal and to some purpose. He'd go far. Inspector-General of Indian Police some day. Ought to have been in the Army, for he was a typical soldier and would have had a great career.

On the other hand, it would have been a splendid policeman and detective lost, and Heaven knew they wanted fine policemen here.

Did he go in fear of his life? He certainly went in danger of it. Anyhow, he couldn't possibly go in fear commensurate with the danger, or he'd never be able to carry on. How very interesting it would be to know whether Steele were really frightened, apprehensive, nervous; ever really afraid. Almost certainly not. He didn't look as though he had a nerve in his body; or as though any danger, however sudden and terrible, would make his eyelid quiver, cause him to turn a hair; or as though any danger, however prolonged, uncertain, suspended, would bring a wrinkle to his smooth forehead, a look of anxiety to his clear grey eye.

By Jove, if Anthony Steele were not afraid, he must be a brave man. Only a man with the very highest courage could possibly carry on in Steele's job, if he were capable of fear. Twice they had almost got him. Two hair-breadth, really miraculous, escapes. Did he have any superstition about a third? Did he feel anything at all? Anxiety, worry, fear, or for that matter, anger, hate or love? Well, if he knew even the meaning of the word anxiety, he hid it most remarkably. A

statue of imperturbability. Well might they call him
Cold Steele!

And there was Ramrao Narayen Gopaldas, the
rising young barrister. What went on inside his sleek
head, and to which camp did he really belong? Or had
he a foot in each? What a curious hybrid product of his
day, his environment and his heredity. Bred and born
in an Indian household, of orthodox Hindu parents;
educated at the Bhawalgarh High School, speaking
Urdu in the home and English outside it; sent over the
Black Water, at the age of eighteen, to be further
educated at Oxford, and to qualify as a barrister at one
of the Inns of Court—and then to have married an
English girl.

Why did she do it? How could she? On the other
hand, why not, since she was in utter ignorance of
conditions of life in India?

There should be a law, and if he were a Member of
Parliament he would do his utmost to introduce a Bill,
that no British girl should be allowed to marry an
Indian in England; nor in India, until she had resided
there for a year. Then she would know what she was
doing; would not be taking a leap in the dark; would
know what it really meant, and do it with her eyes
open.

Probably there would be no mixed marriages at all
if such a law were passed; and if there were, the girl
would have no-one but herself to blame if she were
unhappy, as inevitably she would be.

But this position of affairs, allowing a young girl to
marry an Indian without the very vaguest ghost of an
idea of what her life in India was bound to be, should
be ended at once. It was perfectly monstrous.

Of course, Mrs. Gopaldas, Betty Ramrao Gopaldas
—good heavens, what a name, as hybrid and fantastic
as the position she was in, and as the man she had
married—was better off than most English-women who
marry Indians, for he seemed a good fellow, a very good
chap indeed, very anglicized, and in some ways more
English than the English.

But what of his family? His mother, who could not

speak a word of English; his orthodox father; his very *purdah* sisters; his brothers, one of whom was a rather notorious young gentleman, an Indian man-about-town, with his oiled and scented locks, perfumed handkerchiefs, marvellous shirts, ties, and socks; his general flamboyant exuberance. She must find him peculiarly poisonous.

And how the girl must suffer for, and through, her husband when ill-natured people—and some people could be amazingly ill-natured—did not return her call; or invited her to tea without her husband; or observed at the Gymkhana and in her hearing that they simply did not know how a white woman could do such a thing. What a shock it must have been to her to learn that he was not eligible for membership of the Club; to realize that quite a number of people definitely objected to meeting Indians socially; that some hostesses never asked an Indian to dinner; that some women objected to being taken in to dinner by an Indian; and that there were men who objected to it on behalf of their wives.

It was all wrong, of course.

On the other hand, it was the Indians themselves who had set up the great barrier, by their *purdah* system; their utter and absolute refusal to offer hospitality to Europeans, to the extent of inviting them to their houses to meet their wives and daughters.

Well, well, East is East and West is West, and when the twain do meet in such a marriage as this, it can be, under the most favourable circumstances, nothing less than stark tragedy. It would be that, if there were nothing worse to it than the fact that the English-woman came to India to live and die in exile, to grow old in this cruel country, and be buried in its dreadful soil; to go to India to be taken wholly and finally, once and for all, to the terrible embrace of the "grim step-mother of our kind."

Well, whatever it might do for Ramrao Narayen Gopaldas, it must do a world of good to poor Betty Gopaldas to get away from everything for a while, sit in an English drawing-room, talk her own language to her compatriots and the few friends she had, and find a way of brief escape. And to think that there had been people who had actually said, one to another, that they would resign from the Society if she and her husband were invited to become members! If they'd had the courage to say it openly to him, Edward Cornwallis, they'd have heard something to their disadvantage.

Thus reflected the Commissioner during the few moments that elapsed while people settled themselves comfortably, concluded conversations, and rustled softly into silence.

The Commissioner rose to his feet.

"I call upon the Honorary Secretary to read the minutes of the last meeting."

This Rowena Cornwallis did most adequately; and, having concluded her task as Honorary Secretary, became human, and from her warm heart addressed the Society on behalf of the speaker of the evening, appealing not for a fair hearing, which he would naturally get, but for an unprejudiced one; for the open mind, the unbiased attitude and spirit. She begged her hearers to remember that Saint Arjun was a highly educated, highly intelligent man, with a mentality equal to their own, and a breadth of knowledge, a depth of wisdom, a scope of understanding, and a general philosophical equipment that she for one was fain to envy.

Having concluded her little impromptu speech, the while her husband stared at the blotter on the table before him and tapped it, perhaps a little impatiently, with his pencil, Rowena disappeared through the curtains behind her, to return, a minute later, shepherding, and introducing, her latest *protégé*, Saint Arjun, more widely known as Mr. Sant Arjun Rama, Fellow of Jahore University.

The intrigued, interested, and critical members of the Society beheld a smiling, bearded, olive-faced gentleman whose long black hair, parted in the middle, hung down to his shoulders; whose large lustrous eyes seemed to each one of them to look at him or her direct and with a personal message, whether of appeal and allure or challenge and defiance, according to sex; whose forehead was high though narrow; whose teeth shone with white brilliance between moustache and beard; and whose clothing appeared to be modelled upon that of Biblical pictures of the Apostles. Robed rather than dressed, bare-headed, and wearing neat sandals, he looked, in spite of the blue blackness of his hair and little beard, wholly un-Indian, as little like the Hindus and Mussulmans with whose appearance they were familiar, as he was little like a European.

"Now what is he supposed to represent?" asked Anthony Steele of himself. "If I went to a fancy-dress ball got up like that, what should I say I had come as? An Arab? A Syrian? One of the three Wise Men of the East? . . . Something Biblical, anyway. . . . By Jove, if an artist were painting scenes from the Life of Christ, what a model! That's the idea, I think. Our Sant Arjun has simply endeavoured to make himself look as Christ-like as possible. Sant Arjun! What a seraphic face! What a winning smile! No wonder it has won the Lady Rowena. . . . 'Fraid I'm not pure enough to be won. Not by the smile alone. What's his game, I wonder? Just notoriety? Loaves and fishes? Or something else? Nasty suspicious mind I've got. He may be as genuine as Rowena herself. Also he may not. I think we'll keep track of Sant Arjun."

Thus thought Anthony Steele; but to Betty Gopaldas, watching Steele, it seemed that he thought not at all, but with incurious, uninterested, impassive face, merely gazed with cold listlessness at the strange figure that stood beside Mrs. Rowena Cornwallis.

The Commissioner rose to his feet. After all, he was Chairman of the Society, and it was his business to introduce the speaker of the evening.

"Ladies and gentlemen," said he. "Mr. Sant Arjun Rama has kindly consented to address the Bhawalgarh Literary, Dramatic and Philosophical Society on the subject of his—er—metaphysical and philosophical—er—conclusions; his change of outlook and mental attitude; and his experiences, posterior to that—er—change."

Explosion

"*Posterior!*" grunted Mr. Justice Sherdley to himself. "I'd like to kick . . . h'm!"

"In short, why he ratted," thought Major Hector Grant, keen student of psychology and mankind, "and why he professes to have turned Christian. No Brahmin in this world ever did so, genuinely, from pure conviction."

"Saint Peter at the Gate, welcoming . . . me," observed Colonel Angus Campbell to himself. "My God, I wish I were as good as he looks. Almost too good to be true."

Smiling, Rowena seated herself; and Mr. Sant Arjun Rama, nothing loth and in no wise shy, stepped in front of the Chairman's table and, with complete composure, gazed round upon his audience.

"My friends," said he, "I thank Mrs. Cornwallis for affording me this privilege, the honour and the pleasure of addressing this learned and distinguished Society.

"In case it is possible that there are any among you who do not know much about this country of India in which you live and move and have your being—and your appointments and positions, your White Man's burdens—save that it is a hot and dusty land infested by innumerable black men, I should like to say a few words about Brahmins and Brahminism. I do not, of course, propose to inflict a boring disquisition upon this learned Society, but to give some of you some idea of what it means to be born a Brahmin, and then to cease to be a Brahmin. It means, in fact, the achievement of the practically impossible. I don't know how to give you a suitable and satisfactory parallel, unless I were to say that it is as rare and difficult a thing to accomplish as it would be for a full-blooded negro to become the President of the United States of America; or for the Pope of Rome to go upon the music-hall stage as a comedian; or for an Indian *purdah* lady to lead an exploring expedition to the summit of Mount Everest.

"The Brahmin is born a Brahmin . . . twice born. *Nascitur non fit.* He is born privileged, with a privilege beside which that of the Divine Right of Kings pales into insignificance. For he is born with Divine Rights here and hereafter; with spiritual rights as much greater than corporeal rights as the spirit is greater than the body. He is born sacred, sacrosanct, the object of reverence and worship to all other Hindus— and that is to say to hundreds of millions of men and women.

"Any Brahmin can actually do for any Hindu what the Pope of Rome in his palmiest days was supposed to be able to do for any Christian. He is so sacred, exalted, privileged; so different from men of common clay, that any offence committed against him is seven times as great as the same offence committed against an ordinary man. The Brahmins are the spiritual, and will be the temporal, rulers of India, the unfettered, oppressive, and merciless tyrants of India—when the present 'Satanic government' is overthrown."

Here Sant Arjun Rama smiled very sweetly, at his humorous deprecating quotation from the utterances of wicked men in seditious vernacular newspapers.

"I was a Brahmin, brought up in the strictest tenets and observations of the Brahminical faith; brought up to be as spiritually arrogant, spiritually domineering, exclusive and haughty as any Brahmin of them all. To me, countless millions of my fellow-men were as animals. Countless millions of them Untouchables, creatures whose touch, whose very presence, nay, whose mere shadow, was pollution, defilement, dese- cration. I was a Brahmin who received the education and training given to all Brahmins.

"And one day, a day that dawned like any other, I ceased for ever to be a Brahmin. On the morning of that day, after the usual long and intricate ceremony of prayer and purification, I walked forth from my father's house to take the air. Before I had gone far, I suddenly saw a bright light. Although it was a brilliant morning in May, I saw a bright light. So bright was it that, looking upon it, I was blinded. It was as though I had been struck by lightning, for I fell to the ground unconscious. And yet, in the act of falling, in the moment of losing consciousness, I heard a Voice. And the words uttered by that Voice penetrated the ears of my body and reached those of my soul.

"The Voice cried,

"'Arjun, Arjun, why art thou blind in spirit? Now have I blinded thee in body that thou mayest see.'

"And in that moment I saw.

"I saw the error of my ways, the folly of my thought, the presumption of my ignorance, the narrowness of my cruel creed outworn. I knew that, for all my prayers and purifications, for all my hereditary sanctity, privileged selection, eclecticism, I was a sinner, I was less than the dust.

"I knew, in that great moment of Revelation, that there is but one Sin, Selfishness.

"All other offences and misdeeds are ancillary to that one Sin. Be selfless and you will be pure. You will be without sin. All my life, I had regarded Self, seen everything in terms of Self, seen Brahm, God, through Self. And now I knew it, realized it, confessed it. Blind —I saw it. For when I recovered consciousness, I was totally blind.

"All my life I had seen blindly, as through a glass, darkly, and seen nothing but Self. Now, blind, I saw clearly. And I knew that the Voice that had spoken to me was the Voice of the Teacher of Love and Selflessness; of Him who said that all morality, all truth, all ethics, all law, lay in 'Love the Lord thy God with all thy heart and all thy soul, and thy neighbour as thyself.'

"I fell to the ground a Brahmin. I rose from it a Christian. I have said I was unconscious. By that I mean that I was in a state of physical unconsciousness. Unconscious of the material world. My body was as dead. But my mind was never more alive.

"When I returned to physical consciousness I arose, went back to my father's house—and declared the Truth.

"When my unfortunate unhappy parents, my brothers and my sisters, all the members of our family living in that great house, understood what I was saying, and

realized that I was blaspheming their Faith, renounc-
ing my Brahminhood, they passed through a phase of
incredulous horror to one of immeasurable wrath. But
I was blessed in that they did revile me and persecute
me and say all manner of evil against me for righteousness' sake; and in that for Christ's sake I was cast
forth from my father's house to become a homeless,
friendless wanderer upon the face of the earth.

"For when I was cast forth from my father's house, I
was received into my Father's house, in which there
are many mansions."

Mr. Sant Arjun Rama, practised orator, paused and
gazed round upon the faces of his audience. All save
one showed attentive interest.

The face of Anthony Steele, as usual, showed
nothing at all; but he kept his unwavering gaze upon
the face of the speaker. Watching him, Betty Gopaldas
wondered whether he had heard anything whatever; or
whether his mind was engaged with problems of his
work.

Suddenly Steele glanced at her, and though she
forbore to smile, a little colour came into her pale face,
as, for a second, his eyes held hers.

Poor Betty Gopaldas, he thought. Gad, she must be
feeling the heat, especially in that ancient bazaar
bungalow, stuffy and insanitary. The heat and the
strain of life with the good Ramrao Gopaldas and his
mother. Talk of the power-wielding Indian mother-in-
law and her rod of iron. Old "Maharani" Subhadra, as
they called her, must be a terror, even among Indian
mothers-in-law. What a tragedy! What could Betty's
people have been thinking about? Didn't think at all,
probably.

Betty Gopaldas . . . She must hear a lot of
interesting things, and see some, too. What did she
really think of her husband? How much did she really
know about him and his doings? What a very useful
friend she could be—if she'd talk. Just answer simple
questions about a few little interesting odds and ends
concerning the doings at the Gopaldas house; the
comings and goings; a few facts about some of the less

public activities of the brothers; about Ramrao and that fine-feather bird his brother, Motiram; and the curious Jaganath, the brother who did nothing so busily. Was Mr. Ramrao Gopaldas one of the simplest and nicest fellows you could wish to meet, or was he one of the most dangerous Indians in the country—and in the Game? And was brother Motiram just a pure, priceless bounder and anointed flamboyant *boulevardier*, or a very cunning and dangerous criminal? And was brother Jaganath as idle and *fainéant* as he appeared? And the fourth, Tulsiram, the college-student, did he pursue his sociological studies in pure theory only?

Did Betty Gopaldas know anything, and if she knew, would she tell? And if she wouldn't tell, could she be trapped into giving away anything unintentionally, unconsciously? Probably nothing on earth would induce her to split, if she knew: to say a word against her husband, hated she him never so fiercely. Doubtless she had been brought up all fair-play, clean-sport, word-better-than-bond, public-school, and man-to-man; and she might love her Ramrao dearly.

No. Impossible. How could a typical English country-house, county-family, or perhaps Vicarage-and-High-School, type of girl love an Indian; love a man whose attitude, outlook, standards, whether lower or higher, whether better or worse, than hers, were so utterly different; in some cases so diametrically opposed?

What would be the end of it; the end of her? It was bad enough when the young Indian student brought back the lodging-house keeper's daughter, half slavey, half perfect-lady; bad for both; and it invariably and inevitably ended tragically for the girl, and sometimes for the pair of them.

But how many times worse when the girl was of this type, and, at home, had been in as good a social position as any of these women who looked down their noses at her for having lowered the prestige of the white woman. One of the nicest girls he had ever met; proud and, unfortunately, sensitive; thoroughly well-bred; quite well-read and quite accomplished, and with an open, eager, enquiring mind.

Yes, probably that had been her trouble and bane. Eager, impulsive, warm-hearted, with an alert acquisitive intelligence, she most probably owed her present ghastly plight to her mental activity, her eager desire to see life and the world; her refusal to lead the ordinary life of the average small town or village; the routine country-house life—do the flowers, exercise the dog, play the piano a little, read a little, some golf and tennis; perhaps a little hunting; same dull dinner-parties, same cats'-home tea-parties; same flat minds, same flat subjects of conversation. But to exchange life in that green and pleasant land for existence in a native bungalow in the Sudder Bazaar, or at any rate close to it! Life with Ramrao Gopaldas and his family!

Well, if she had suffered from cramped circumstance then, what about now, poor girl? What did she think of it all?

What did she know, and how much of it would she tell?

Betty Gopaldas looked quickly away. Had Anthony Steele smiled at her, or was it just the flickering shadow of the moving punkah?

No, of course he hadn't smiled at her. Why should he? Still, there was no harm in imagining that he had. Perhaps he'd speak to her after the meeting. Possibly he'd remember that he had said,

"We must go for a ride one morning," when she had danced with him at the Gymkhana and she had told him that she rode.

But undoubtedly the "Maharani" Subhadra was watching. More and more frequently the syce declared the horse to be lame and unfit for use to-day. More and more frequently something occurred to prevent Ramrao from taking her to the Gymkhana dances, nor could she really enjoy it, with him sitting pathetically watching her, himself unable to screw up his courage to risk the snub that he might get if he asked anyone but herself for a dance. As he could only dance with her, she couldn't very well dance often with other men.

And when she did, their wives didn't approve. Certainly Ramrao liked to see her dancing with a Sahib. It seemed to give him real pleasure, as though he were vicariously honoured by the compliment and attention paid to his wife. Pathetic.

Yes, why shouldn't she dance, since Ramrao had no objection? What concern was it of the Maharani's? Ramrao had lived in England. He completely understood the spirit and significance—or rather lack of significance—of ball-room dancing. He had loved dancing when he was in England. It had been at a dance that she had first met him and pitied his rather forlorn and appealing foreignness and loneliness.

And why shouldn't she ride? Surely that did no one any harm, and did her a world of good. It was the only time when she felt happy, those hours when she could give herself the illusion of riding away out of it all, riding away from the Hell of that house in the bazaar, into the Heaven of the open country, the jungle, the hills.

What should she do if, or rather when, old Subhadra got her way—as invariably and inevitably she got her way—and she was allowed neither to ride nor to dance? Should she do as she had always done at home and at school and everywhere else—make a stand for what she considered right, and for what were undoubtedly her rights?

What would be the good? Subhadra would win in the end, of course, and her last state would be worse than her first. It was a horrible thought, a hideous feeling, that the only person who had ever really frightened her was this old Indian woman. And she did frighten her. It was useless to deny it.

Partly by sheer personality, will-power, a ruthless forceful determination; and partly by a sinisterly hypnotic power of suggestion, she terrified her. The Maharani had never threatened her, of course, but she was nevertheless horrified at the mere thought of the things Subhadra did not threaten.

She had never heard the word "poison"; didn't even know the Indian name for it; but, without speech or gesture, Subhadra had told her that she would poison her if, and when, she thought fit. Once or twice, after dispute, disagreement and disobedience, she had been taken suddenly ill, had suffered horrible pain such as she had never felt before; and Subhadra had expressed her sympathy with a smile—a smile that held a meaning which she clearly understood.

The one gleam of comfort that she could see in the darkness of her misery was the fact that Subhadra was old, as age goes in India, and the day must come when that dynamic spirit would cease to rule the household.

Perhaps, then, she would be able to induce Ramrao to move away from the terrible, old, airless, smelly warren of a place, insanitary, filthy, crowded, into a bungalow of his own, in the Civil Lines. Surely there could be no objection on the part of her kind white brethren? It would be no real pollution of the sweet air of Cantonments, so long as she was content with a modest little house, unobtrusive and at the end nearest to the bazaar; the house just a sort of link between the European quarter and the native city, as she herself was a link between West and East, between Europe and India? Betty Frobisher, the Missing Link. Elizabeth Ramrao Narayen Gopaldas.

Good God! If only she *were* missing, and had always been missing.

And suppose Anthony Steele left the station, as probably he would. Or suppose they killed him next time. What should she do then? Not that it could make any difference, really. She could hardly see much less of him. She had never once been alone with him for a minute. He had never once said a word to her, or she to him, that the Maharani herself could twist into anything remotely suggestive of evil. But while he was in Bhawalgarh and she could from time to time speak to him, or just see him as she was seeing him now, she could carry on.

Of course, it was only because he stood to her for England. Because he was *the* Englishman, "and all that ever went with evening dress"—or, rather, that went with shady lawns, Devon lanes, cricket fields, joyous house-parties, autumn cubbing mornings, lovely English life. All that went with truth and truthfulness, honour and honesty, trust and trustworthiness; with reality, solidity, loyalty, faith, cleanness, home.

While sinking in this morass of deceit, lies, treachery, enmity, cruelty, ugliness, strangeness, alien incomprehensibility, she could contrive to keep her head above the surface and to breathe, so long as Anthony Steele was there; so long as she could, unknown to him, support herself by his strength, firmness and solidity.

Mrs. Herdie, following the direction of Anthony Steele's glance, saw Betty Gopaldas watching him, saw her colour and look away.

Yes, exactly as she had thought; and entirely useless for Anthony to deny it. Not that he did, or ever would, deny it; for he denied nothing of which she accused him. But it was perfectly plain to her, and doubtless to everybody else; or soon would be. The hussy! Still, what could you expect of the type of woman who'd marry a native? Just think of it!

Mr. Sant Arjun Rama, his oratorical pause concluded, spread his arms abroad, raised his face to Heaven, or at least to the ceiling-cloth, across the other side of which a rat was gaily galloping, and resumed his address.

"And I suffered. Should I be self-pitying, eccentric and ego-centric if I imagined that I suffered as no man ever suffered before, inasmuch as no man before me had ever renounced Brahminism and embraced Christianity?

"I suffered most at the hands of those who had loved me; and then at the hands of those who had known me; and then at the hands of those of my caste-fellows who came to know of me; and, finally, at the hands of those of all other castes and creeds who knew of my conversion and looked upon me as a traitor, renegade from the gods of the East to those of the West; one who had denied not only his faith, his caste, his fellows, but his civilization, his country.

"At length I shook from my feet the dust of my native land.

"Why? Who shall fathom the true main-spring of his actions, accurately judge his own subconscious motives?

"Did I flee, unable longer to bear my martyrdom? Did I yearn to sojourn and be tempted in the wilderness for forty days and nights, forty weeks, forty months? Or did I feel undeniably the impulse to go forth and preach the Word that had come to me, to turn, from those who rejected me, to those in darkness who might receive, through me, the Light?

"I took to the road. I became a fakir, perhaps the first genuine Christian fakir in India, as well as the first converted Brahmin.

"And after a time of testing and trial, I came to a land beyond India, a far-distant country and a heathen town; a town whose inhabitants were worshippers of graven images, men sunk in ignorance, idolatry, and paganism.

"And here I preached and taught, propounded the Gospel of Christ, until the people knew and heard me, their priests knew and hated me.

"And here again I was persecuted for righteousness' sake. First the petty persecution of obstruction and interference, jeers, the breaking-up of my meetings, the throwing of mud and stones; and then more serious persecution. For, one day, I was seized and cast into gaol at the instance of a shop-keeper of the bazaar, a base tool of the priests, from whom I had bought warm clothing against the cold of that place—a coat and other articles for which I had, of course, paid at the time of purchase, paid with money earned by the labour of my hands.

"According to this man and his hireling witnesses, his son, his shop-assistant, his servants and his coolies, I had ordered goods to the value of forty-eight rupees, promising to pay fifty rupees on the first of the following month.

"According to them, the clothing had been carried to my poor lodging by a coolie, to whom I had given a few *pice* in reward.

"According to them, I had worn the clothing daily, had been noticed in the bazaar wearing the new garments; and the shop-keeper seeing me passing, one day, a month later, had gone out and demanded payment.

"According to them, I had asked him what he was talking about, had denied ever having purchased the goods from him, had become threatening and abusive.

"I was a swindler, a thief, a stranger; not to mention the matter of being a disturber of the peace, a gatherer of crowds, a disseminator of new, and therefore wrong, ideas and doctrines; a public nuisance and a danger.

"'One thing at a time,' said the learned Judge. Such matters could be dealt with on another occasion (when there might be a separate opportunity for further graft); the present issue was one of getting goods under false pretences, of having neither the intention, nor presumably the means, of payment.

"'Had the prisoner the money wherewith to discharge this debt?'

"'No,' I told him. 'I had no money and I owed no debt.'

"Then I must go to prison forthwith and remain there until I had got the money.

"This was applauded as an excellent judgment because, if I had got the money, it would now be forthcoming. If I had not got the money, I should be put where I could swindle no more honest tradesmen in the bazaars of that town.

"To me it seemed a peculiarly foolish judgment inasmuch as, if I were a swindler who had no money, prison was hardly the place in which I could earn it; and if I had got the money, all I had to do was to pay up, and I should receive no punishment for the attempted swindle.

"However, to gaol I was taken, there to lie and suffer hunger and cold and the miseries of bondage until such time as I should die, whether of disease or old age.

"However, 'stone walls do not a prison make nor

iron bars a cage,' and I was as near to God in prison as on a Himalayan hill-top, and far nearer to Him than I had been in the house of my father, a stiff-necked, self-centred, arrogant Brahmin.

"All that night I prayed, not for release but for humility and increased power to love my enemies.

"Some days later, the turn-key, a low-browed ignorant man of cruel heart and unenlightened mind, threw open the door of my damp, cold and filthy cell.

"'Come out of that,' he said.

"And as I arose and followed him out of the cell, I wondered if this were the end; if I were to be privileged so soon to suffer, or rather to enjoy, martyrdom for my Faith. Had the priests bribed the Judge, as undoubtedly the shop-keeper had done; and was I to be put to death as a blasphemer, a breaker of the law, a seditionist and a menace to the peace of the State?

"'Where do I go now?' I asked the turn-key.

"'Where you like,' he growled.

"'Has the shop-keeper confessed the truth, then?' I asked, for I had no friend in all that town, who could have interceded for me.

"'What do you mean, confessed the truth?' he asked. 'It's you who've done that, isn't it?'

"'I?'

"'Yes. You sent the money this morning, didn't you?'

"'No.'

"'Well, somebody paid it for you, then. Come on, I can't listen to you all day.'

"And, unlocking the gaol doors, he led me across the courtyard, opened the outer gates and, with a curt and sinister,

"'See you again soon,' he thrust me forth.

"The gates clanged behind me.

"What was this? I could not honestly say I had yet made any real convert to Christianity; that had any group of deeply interested seekers after Truth; much less any church, band of followers, or organized party. I had no Disciple, no Nicodemus, no Timothy. There had been no young man of great possessions among those who had listened to my teaching; no-one who would have paid the sum of fifty rupees to rescue me from gaol and free me from what might prove to be life-long imprisonment.

"I was puzzled.

"The Judge, the men of the Law, the officials, and the public in the alleged Court of Justice had all seemed as inimical to me as was the rascally prosecutor himself.

"How could I discover who had been my benefactor, that I might thank him and redouble my efforts to bring him to the Truth?

"An idea. I could go to the shop-keeper himself, and ask who it was who had paid him the fifty rupees.

"Straight from the prison gates I walked to the bazaar in which was his cotton, cloth and silk shop.

"There was the knave seated among his piled piece-goods.

"But he was changed. He was a different man. I don't quite know how to describe the difference, save by saying that he seemed somewhat nervous, afraid, almost propitiatory.

"'And so the money has been paid?' I asked him.

"'Yes,' he said.

"'And who paid it?' I asked.

"'A stranger,' said he.

"'What kind of a stranger?' I asked.

"'A man of wonderful power, shining presence and great beauty. One speaking with illimitable authority. He was like . . . like . . . an angel.'

"'And what said he?' I asked.

"'"Take thy money,"' he said. '"Withdraw thy false charge, and turn from thine evil ways."'

"'I could not bear to look upon his face, and when I raised my eyes again, he was gone. And the money was here beside me. Straightway I went to the Judge, told him that the money had been paid, and asked for an order that you might be set free.'

"And suddenly I knew, I understood. It was an Angel from Heaven—or else it was Christ Himself who had come to set me free!"

Again the speaker paused and gazed around upon the faces of his audience, all save one of which were turned toward him, and expressive of deep interest.

For a few moments there was silence in the room, broken only by the faint susurrus of the moving punkah, a stillness in which nothing but the punkah moved.

"The age of miracles is not past," continued Mr. Sant Arjun Rama, "as I, unworthy as I am, can testify. For I, in my own person, have been the subject, and the witness, of two great miracles; and those phenomena deserve no less a name. By the first, I was stricken blind that I might see, and my wilfully deafened ears were penetrated by a voice; and by the second, an Angel was sent from Heaven—if it were but an Angel and not Our Lord Himself—to save me from gaol, that I might continue my Master's work."

The speaker smiled sweetly, bowed, and retired to his place behind the table and beside the chair occupied by Mrs. Cornwallis.

The spell was broken and there was a movement and rustling throughout the drawing-room.

The Commissioner rose to his feet.

"On behalf of the Society, I wish to thank Mr. Sant Arjun Rama for his extremely interesting address. As I have already told him, we usually have a discussion, an informal debate, after we have listened to papers, readings, or addresses; and I understand that he will be delighted to remain to hear anything that may be said, and to answer any question that may be put to him."

It was the Commissioner's custom, at this point, to gaze round the room as though expecting immediate response; but it was also the custom of members of the Society to wait until someone had been personally invited to open the debate, and another asked to reply to him thereafter.

The Commissioner's glance travelled round the room and his eye failed to catch that of him who invariably opened the debate.

Mr. Justice Sherdley was staring at the rug before

him, his brows drawn together in a deep frown.

"Mr. Sherdley? . . ." suggested the Commissioner.

"Eh? What? I? . . . I don't believe a word ol it," snapped Mr. Sherdley distinctly.

There was a gasp of amazement.

Mrs. Cornwallis rose to her feet.

The Commissioner stared incredulous. He could hardly believe his ears.

What had happened to his old friend, the most courteous of men, the member upon whom, of all others, he relied for the pouring of oil on troubled waters; for the adroit turning aside of anything approaching acrimony? The man whose motto might well have been *suaviter in modo, fortiter in re.*

What had happened to him? It must be this dreadful heat. But still . . .

Recovering himself before Rowena could usurp the chairmanly functions and intervene, he glanced at the Superintendent of Police.

"Mr. Steele? Would you like to make any comment, or ask any question of the speaker?"

Anthony Steele rose to his feet.

"I thought it a remarkably interesting—er—story," he said slowly, thoughtfully. "I don't think it is one that calls for much comment beyond that. One or two details left my sadly departmentalized mind unsatisfied. While it was lost in admiration of the—er—miracles, and the wonderfully dramatic way in which they were described, it wasn't quite happy about the logical aspect of one or two details.

"For example, to me it didn't seem quite sound and ethical that our friend the wicked shop-keeper should have cleared fifty rupees by his dishonesty."

There were a few smiles at this, a few frowns, one or two impatient movements. The Reverend Dr. Torrens suddenly opened his eyes, stared at Steele, closed them again and murmured something to himself. His nearest neighbour gathered that he was strongly in agreement with Anthony Steele.

"Nor," continued Steele, "does it seem to the finite mind that, the Creator of the Universe of Universes—

being sufficiently interested in Mr. Sant Arjun Rama miraculously to convert him and then miraculously to rescue him from prison—should not have been sufficiently interested in him to intervene in time to prevent his going to prison at all. . . . Anyway, it's a very remarkable and interesting story, and I greatly enjoyed listening to it."

Since everybody was looking at him, it was natural that as, on sitting down, he glanced at Betty Gopaldas, his eyes should again encounter hers. This time, she did smile at him as well as change colour slightly, for she had been smiling at what he was saying and at the way in which he was saying it—without displaying such rudeness as that of Mr. Justice Sherdley, and yet conveying just as much incredulity, as well as indicating the weak points of the story. How cool, assured and easy he was; and how cleverly he had shown his real opinion without saying anything to which Mrs. Cornwallis, or indeed Mr. Sant Arjun Rama, could well object.

And as he glanced at her flushed, eager, smiling face, and caught her eye, he too smiled, in friendly fashion.

Yes, there could be no doubt about it this time. It was not the flickering shadow of the punkah. Definitely he had looked for her as he sat down, and he had smiled at her . . . He had smiled at her.

And so thought Mrs. Herdie. It was abominable. When, in course of time, her husband succeeded Mr. Cornwallis as Commissioner of the Division, and she herself reigned in Rowena's stead, it would be extremely few invitations to meetings of the Society that Mr. and Mrs. Gopaldas would receive. They'd get just exactly none at all. She had no objection to Gopaldas himself, beyond the fact that he was a native; but she had every objection to his wife.

How dare she marry a native and make it plain and clear to every Indian in Bhawalgarh, and indeed throughout the whole Division, that a native was good enough for a white woman to marry; a fit and proper person to be the husband of an English girl? In marrying a native, she had lowered the prestige and caste of every white woman in Bhawalgarh, in India, in the Empire; and if that weren't enough, here she was, making eyes at Anthony Steele.

And Anthony was returning the compliment.

At herself he had not once looked, much less smiled, the whole evening. She'd get hold of him when the meeting ended. And if the girl spoke to him while she was with him, she'd look straight through her. Rowena ought to know better than to countenance her by asking her to Commissioner's House. A line should be drawn somewhere; and it would have been far better policy to have shown Bhawalgarh and the whole Division, that a woman who marries a native either never belonged to the ruling-classes or had forfeited her membership thereof by doing so and going and living in the bazaar with him.

The Commissioner's eye roved round the assembly.

To whom could he appeal? For that was what it had come to. He had drawn two very bad blanks, or rather worse than blanks. His old friend had failed him badly and behaved abominably; and Steele had been much more enigmatic, critical, and evasive than was at all necessary. He rarely called upon a third or fourth speaker by name, save when such an arrangement had been previously made and he had wanted pros and cons, and a proper discussion of some literary or philosophical subject.

What about the Reverend Dr. Torrens? He was a dear chap but very absent-minded, and quite likely to get to his feet if called on, close his eyes, and deliver a scourging harangue if he felt that way, regardless of time and place, and without respect of persons. That would be worse than Sherdley's unpardonable snarl.

Dr. Torrens opened his eyes and stared at the Commissioner. Was the old boy asking to be asked to question and make comment?

"Principal Torrens?" said the Commissioner, rising.

"No, Sir. I have nothing to say, thank you. Less than nothing," replied Dr. Torrens, and closed his eyes, almost with a snap.

H'm. That was that. He might have contented himself with stating that he had nothing to say. The "less than nothing" was definitely unnecessary.

Perhaps one of the ladies? What about Mrs. Herdie? No, unfortunately she was a most prejudiced and biased person. If she said anything at all, it would quite probably be even less pleasant than what had already been said.

The fact was that Rowena had made a mistake, and that he ought to have put his foot down.

Hullo, there was Gopaldas getting to his feet. Good.

"Impudence," thought Mrs. Herdie. "Why couldn't he wait until he was asked? He might have rested quite assured that he would have been asked—by Rowena, if not by the Commissioner."

"Mr. Chairman, Ladies and Gentlemen," began Ramrao Gopaldas, in a high treble voice, as he fingered his black bow tie, adjusted the lapels of his dinner-jacket and smiled nervously. "I should like to express my personal thanks and appreciation to my friend Mr. Sant Arjun Rama and say how I greatly enjoyed his speech. It was most awfully interesting, and I am sure that one and all will agree with me that he is an extremely brave chap. Possibly I know, better than anyone else present, how brave he must be to have renounced Brahminism and ceased to be a Brahmin so far as that is possible; to bear the terrible reproaches of his father and his mother, his brothers and his sisters, his uncles and aunts, his cousins and his nephews, all his family-members, his caste-fellows and club-fellows and all his friends and relations. I don't know that any Christian, be he of the official Church of England, Roman Catholic, Church of Scotland, Presbyterian, Methodist, Baptist, Wesleyan, Congregational, American Mission or other European religion, if any, can quite fathom the depths of his so-called disgrace, or measure the heights of his great courage and faith eternal. I think he would have to be a Brahmin to understand all that; but meanwhile I think an Indian, like myself, can understand better than a European. And I venture to say, without fear of contradiction, that my friend, Mr. Sant Arjun Rama, has had experience unparalleled since the days of Saint Paul, a remarkable similarity . . ."

"*Very* remarkable," murmured Dr. Torrens drily.

". . . to the experience of that great disciple of Jesus Christ. Also the miracle by which he was delivered from gaol. That is, I think, a unique . . ."

"Not quite," whispered Dr. Torrens.

". . . experience, and must go far to bolster up the unshakable faith of the speaker who addressed us so charmingly this evening. Thank you, Ladies and Gentlemen."

"Thank you, Mr. Gopaldas," said the Commissioner, rising to his feet with an air of winding up the proceedings, ere they ran down altogether.

"Would anyone else like to make any further . . . ? No? . . . Then I . . ."

Rowena rose to her feet.

"Yes. I should like to add my voice to that of Mr. Gopaldas, whom I wish to thank personally for his admirably expressed tribute to Saint Arjun's discourse. It did credit to his heart and head, and showed him to be broad-minded, generous and understanding."

Here Mrs. Cornwallis looked hard at Mr. Justice Sherdley, who returned glare for glare; at Anthony Steele, who looked precisely as he always looked; and at Dr. Torrens.

As her glance fell upon the face of the elderly Principal, it hardened rebukingly, almost angrily. It was wasted, for the Doctor's eyes were tightly closed.

"I should like to say that I have never in the whole of my life heard a more moving discourse, a more dramatic statement of facts, nor indeed of facts more absorbingly interesting. The day of miracles is not past, though that of simple faith may indeed be passing. I don't know how anyone could have listened unmoved to Saint Arjun's account of his conversion and of his delivery from bondage. I don't know how ignorance, un-faith, scepticism, cynicism, could prevail in the mind of any intelligent person who listened to him to-night. I thank him from the bottom of my heart. I

firmly believe every word that he said. I venture to congratulate him, not only upon the amazing marvellous
matter of his discourse, but upon the manner of its
delivery; and unhesitatingly I congratulate the Bhawalgarh Literary, Dramatic and Philosophical Society on
the privilege and honour that has been its to-night."

Mr. Sant Arjun rose, smiled with ineffable sweetness upon his patroness, upon the Commissioner,
upon the whole assembly, and, with hands joined as in
prayer, head bowed as in humility and meekness,
turned and disappeared through the curtains.

"That concludes the business of the evening," said
the Commissioner, and seemed with difficulty to
forbear to add,

"And a damned good job too."

The members of the Society rose to their feet, some
even achieving an air or suggestion of stretching and
yawning; the meeting dissolved into a social occasion,
and bare-footed servants clad in snowy garments and
lofty white turbans adorned with the Commissioner's
crest, entered bearing large trays laden, some with
liquid refreshment, some with more solid fare, and
others with cheroots, cigars and cigarettes.

Mrs. Sherdley made her way to her life-long friend
Rowena Cornwallis.

"I'm so sorry, my dear. I don't know what's come to
John. It was extremely naughty of him, and I felt most
ashamed. But he's been strange—queer—for a day or
two. It's this ghastly heat, I think, and he is terribly
worried about something or other. He seems anxious
and—almost apprehensive. So unlike him."

"Quite unlike him," agreed Mrs. Cornwallis a little
coldly. "I don't know when I was more shocked, pained,
and annoyed. He might at least have declined to say
anything at all. Insulting my guest like that!"

"You couldn't be more upset about it than I am, my
dear," placated Mrs. Sherdley. "I can only say again, he
is not himself. He has got something on his mind.
Always now. He's ill."

"He looks well enough."

"Mentally, I mean."

"*Mentally?*"

"Oh, you know what I mean, Rowena. Thoroughly upset, worried, anxious. He seems to go—well, almost in *fear* of something or other. The other day I looked up and found that he was staring at me—without seeing me. Suddenly he said, '*Blown to atoms! It's absurd, impossible, rubbish.*' And when I asked him what on earth he was talking about, he said, 'Eh? What? I didn't say anything,' and he seemed most queer and strange. I'm quite frightened, myself."

"Oh, my dear, I am so sorry." Rowena grasped her friend's wrist. "What is it?"

"I don't know, Rowena. I don't know. I'm worried to death."

"It's only the heat, I expect," she added on a lighter note. "It's dreadful, isn't it?"

"The worst I've ever known," agreed Rowena.

"So electrical, too. One feels all strung up, nervy."

"As you say—dreadful. A sort of brooding, menacing . . . oh, *threatening* kind of weather, generally."

"Yes, dear. That's it, *threatening*. It sounds absurd, but really it seems that one is both prostrated and over-stimulated—nervously prostrated by the heat and yet nervously worked up at the same time—exasperated, exacerbated, frightened."

"We want a thunder-storm to clear the air," observed Rowena.

"We certainly want *something* to clear the air," agreed Mrs. Sherdley. "I must go and make my apologies, or rather John's apologies, to the Commissioner. I am *so* sorry—but I'm sure he'll understand."

"Well, Tony?" smiled Mrs. Herdie. "Haven't seen you since Monday. How are you? God, isn't it hot? I wish I felt as cool as you look. Why were you such a coward to-night?"

"Usual," murmured Steele.

"Why couldn't you have got up and said you thought the man a liar and an impostor and a charlatan?"

"Rude," replied Steele, taking a glass from a passing

tray.

"Would you let that deter you?"

"No."

"Then why didn't you up and say that the man's a humbug?"

"Because I think he's something very much more than that."

"Why, what do you think he is, then?"

"A very clever fellow."

"D'you believe in miracles, Tony?"

"Yes."

"You do? Really?"

"Quite."

"Why?"

"See them every day."

"Oh, tell me one."

"The sons of our fathers losing India, deserting and abandoning the Indian peasant, allowing this country to be turned into another Ireland."

"Oh, don't let's talk politics . . . Can you dine with us to-morrow?"

"Afraid not, Mrs. Herdie. Thanks very much."

"Saturday?"

"Er, no. Busy, Saturday night."

"Bachelor party, Tony?"

"You might call it that."

Anthony Steele did not smile as he visualized the bachelor party which would consist of himself, his Assistant District-Superintendent of Police, a dozen armed policemen and, he hoped, a band of dacoits, lately departed from Almera State and the District adjoining his, and now said to be firmly established in an ancient overgrown hill-fort, in dense jungle, a few miles from the railway.

"When can you dine, then? Sunday?"

"If I'm in the Station. Thanks very much."

"And if you are not? Monday?"

"Thank you, Mrs. Herdie."

Why must he call her that, when she called him Tony and, time after time, had invited him to call her Jenny?

"Sunday then, or Monday," said Steele. "I'll send you a chit over, as soon as I know. Thanks very much."

And turning away, he crossed the drawing-room to where, by one of the great pillars, Betty Gopaldas stood alone, watching her husband in gay and animated converse with the wife of the Commissioner.

"Good-evening, Mrs. Gopaldas. Enjoy the show? Almost he persuadeth thee to be a better Christian?"

She felt her face flushing again. Why couldn't one conquer the wretched habit? She didn't colour in that idiotic way when anybody else spoke to her or looked at her—going all girlish and blushful like a wretched boarding-school flapper.

"Yes, thank you, I did enjoy it."

Would he hear her heart shouting,

"Because you were in the room. Because I could see you. Because Anthony Steele . . ."

Steele suddenly had a very bright idea.

"Very decent of your husband to speak up like that for—er—his friend," he said. "He *is* a friend of your husband's, isn't he?" he added.

"An acquaintance, certainly. He has been to the house, I know," replied the girl.

"Ah; yes?"

"I don't know whether you'd call him a friend."

"No? You don't know whether your husband knew him before he came to Bhawalgarh?"

"No, I don't."

"Come to the house often?"

"Oh, I . . ."

Why on earth must he talk about the wretched man? Why couldn't they talk about England, Home—or, better still, about Anthony Steele?

"I think so. Fairly frequently. I've seen him several times."

"Trying to convert your husband to Christianity?" smiled Steele.

"Not that I know of. He certainly won't succeed while my mother-in-law is alive."

"Does what the 'Maharani' tells him, eh?"

"Oh, all Indian sons have the greatest respect for

their mothers, of course," replied the girl.

Small snub. Anyway, he had learned something very interesting. The worthy Saint was in the habit of visiting Gopaldas. Very interesting indeed.

"And is Sant Arjun *persona grata* to the lady Subhadra?"

"I really couldn't say," replied the girl.

Couldn't, or wouldn't, say? How much did she know? And of what she knew, how much would she tell? Probably nothing—voluntarily.

"Very interesting person," he said. "I wonder if he has made many friends in Bhawalgarh among the nat . . . among the Indians, I mean."

"I don't know."

"I suppose he'd get on best with the Brahma-Samaj people. Does he bring anybody with him to visit your husband?"

"Sometimes. One or two."

That was interesting.

"Oh, really? I suppose he has hopes of making converts among the Europeanized Indians; the non-orthodox who are really only nominal believers in Hinduism."

"He wouldn't have much hope of making any converts among the strict Hindus, I suppose?" replied the girl.

"No . . . There's one chap, I know, he might get hold of. I wonder if you've heard of him? Babu Purshotamdass."

"No . . . No, I don't remember the name."

"A huge great jelly of a man; always wears a frock-coat; *dhoti*; socks, generally pink, held up by coloured garters; and patent-leather shoes."

"Oh, yes," Betty smiled. "I know him. Goes bare-headed. Hair cropped quite short like an English-man's."

"That's the chap. And I shouldn't be at all surprised if Sant Arjun Rama made a convert of him. Very keen enquiring mind. Broke away from orthodox Hinduism long ago. Brahma-Samaj, Arya-Samaj, Theosophy, Agnosticism; and I shouldn't be at all surprised if he doesn't end up a Christian—or rather go through a Christian phase. . . . Does he come to see your husband?"

"Yes, he does. It's at our house that I've seen him."

Very interesting indeed.

"Comes with Sant Arjun, I suppose? Or meets him at the house?"

"Yes, I've seen him come in with him, once or twice."

This marched. The excellent Babu Purshotamdass visited the worthy Ramrao, and with the good Sant Arjun, did he?

"Yes, I thought so. How interesting! Just the man of whom this Arjun might have high hopes. There's another chap, too, a clever little fellow, a 'pleader'—native-trained Indian barrister, you know—used to be a leading light among the local Theosophists, a great hair-splitter and religious argufier. I shouldn't be surprised if Arjun got hold of him, too. A little chap with a pointed beard and big gold-rimmed spectacles; wears complete European kit, tussore silk suit, starched collar and a tie; never wears a turban, but a little brown pill-box cap."

"Yes, I know him," said Betty. "Rather a charming man."

"I'm sure he is. Let's see, what is his name, now?"

"Bhojraj."

"Of course. So it is. Bhojraj Shahani. That's it. Mr. Bhojraj Shahani, M.A., LL.B. Nice little chap."

And so the admirable Bhojraj went with the excellent Babu Purshotamdass and the good Sant Arjun Rama to see the worthy Ramrao.

What an evening's work! Out of the mouths of babes and little English girls . . . How much did she know? Almost certainly nothing at all, or he wouldn't have been able to take her in so easily, and with as simple a line of talk as that.

"That's interesting. We shall be having a native-Christian Church here yet. I wonder who else Arjun hopes to rope in. I suppose they are all Hindus who come and talk 'about it and about'? By birth, I mean, if not by religion? No Mussulmans, I imagine? It would be a feather in his cap if he could really convert a *pukka* Mahommedan. But that's hardly likely."

"Well, I don't know about converting, or whether religion is mentioned at all—because I'm not present, of course—but there's a Moulvie Abdul Haq comes with him sometimes, or rather comes occasionally when he's there. I haven't seen them actually arrive together."

And so the interesting Moulvie Abdul Haq forgathered with the admirable Bhojraj, the excellent Babu Purshotamdass and the good Sant Arjun Rama at the house of the worthy Ramrao!

The girl frowned.

Oh, why must he talk about these people, wasting the few precious minutes? They couldn't be in any way precious to him, of course, or he'd talk about a morning ride, or a dance with her at the Gymkhana.

Anthony Steele smiled.

If he could do such a useful job of work here, in public, so to speak, what could he do if he got her alone and led her on to chatter? He'd have to go carefully, though. She'd shy-off like a restive thoroughbred if he were clumsy. It would have to be a case of light hands and the snaffle, and no hint of curb or spur. Well, he knew something about horses, and that always helped in dealing with women.

How could he find, or make, an opportunity for a quiet talk with her? A dance and a *tête-à-tête* in a *kala jugga*?[32] That would be all right, except that Ramrao would probably notice that he and she had sat-out a dance together, might question her afterwards, enquire as to their subjects of conversation, and discover that he had been pumping her. That would be a pity, for Ramrao must know that the meetings at the Gopaldas bungalow had not been observed.

What a nice little discovery. And what a curious and interesting fact that Abdul Haq, Babu Purshotamdass and Bhojraj should forgather with Ramrao Gopaldas and his brothers Motiram, Jaganath and

---

[32] *lit. Dark place. (A sitting-out place.)*

Tulsiram; and that Sant Arjun should join them.

Just a tiny feather in Steele's cap, that he had shadowed each one of them severally and separately, and now found them in a team. For all the talk of the wonderful detective skill of people who found-out things, there was still a big element of luck in it. Neither he nor his Assistant, neither any of the police nor the C.I.D. people, had spotted it; and here, by pure chance, he had stumbled on a priceless clue, an invaluable piece of information.

Anybody else? Could he risk another direct question without seeming too interested, and spoiling the casualness of the conversation? The religious line had been a good one.

"Really," he said. "Moulvie Abdul Haq. I should hardly think Arjun could have any hopes of him, a moulvie and all! More likely the moulvie thinks he can do something with the depolarized ex-Brahmin."

"What—thinks that if he could change from Brahminism to Christianity, he'd be just as likely to change to Mohammedanism—when he'd got through what you called his Christian phase?"

"Exactly. Anyhow, it must be from mere disputatiousness and the joy of argument that the moulvie goes and listens to Arjun. He's just sufficiently Europeanized and broad-minded to argue on the subject of comparative religion. Of course, the *moulvies* and *mullahs* and *imams* and learned doctors of Mohammedanism will discuss and wrangle and argue all night long among themselves on points of their own religion, but the strictly orthodox don't think other religions are worth arguing about, or their own a suitable subject for discussion with Infidels."

"Nor do I," thought the girl. "Why must he talk about religion? Why can't he talk about himself?"

"I've heard or read that the ten holiest mullahs of Mecca once argued all night long as to how many angels could stand on the point of a needle," she said with a smile.

"And I've no doubt they settled it satisfactorily and placed it on record. . . . It must be awfully interesting to hear them all debating with Arjun."

"Very."

"You've never had the pleasure of listening to them, of course?"

"No. I only hear what they call chit-chat, for a few minutes, when we have callers; but my husband has a room of his own in another part of the house."

"I suppose you get lots of callers besides these four?"

"My husband does. Very few people pay calls on me. Indian gentlemen, both Hindu and Mussulman, seem, somehow, uncomfortable."

"Yes, of course they are not accustomed to meeting the wives of their friends, except the few who've become Europeanized to the extent of abandoning *purdah* and all the 'good old' Indian customs and way of life."

Oh dear, oh dear, why must they talk in this stupid way? Should she summon up courage and be brazen— in other words, behave naturally and sensibly—and remind him of his suggestion that they should go for a ride one morning? Ramrao was bowing and backing away from Mrs. Cornwallis and would probably come straight over; and then, doubtless, Anthony Steele would say good-night.

"Yes, I should love to be present at one of their—er —little debates," he said. "Most interesting subject, Comparative Religion. By the way, when are we going to have that ride? I saw you ride past the Police parade-ground the other morning when I was doing an inspection."

So he had noticed her, and known it was she. Had he wondered why she rode in that direction?

"A ride one morning?" she said. "Yes, riding alone isn't really very much fun. So much better for one's horse, too."

What an incredibly stupid remark. Better for one's horse!

"Oh, yes, rather," agreed Steele promptly. "Horse gets very sluggish and bored. What about Saturday morning?"

"Yes. What time?"

"Let's see. Could you ride past the Police parade-ground about seven?"

"Yes. I will—if my horse isn't lame."

"Lame? What's wrong? Been galloping him too hard? Kicked himself? Over-reach?"

"No. He develops lameness, occasionally, out of his inner consciousness, I think. He's temperamental that way. Or the syce is."

Like that, was it? The dear old "Maharani," no doubt.

"Splendid," he said. "I'll look out for you, and we'll ride to the Ratnapur temple, shall we?"

"Yes, that's my favourite ride."

Did that sound as though she were hinting; telling him where she was to be found sometimes?

"Mine too, I think," agreed Steele. "Good going."

"Ah, there you are, Steele," cried Ramrao Gopaldas, bearing down upon them, beaming joyously and patting Steele on the shoulder. "Won't you have a drink?"

"Having one," replied Steele, raising his glass. "Won't you?"

"Had one," giggled Ramrao, patting his waistcoat.

"Good-night," said Steele, and turned away.

A good evening's work.

§2

After a few words with Mr. Herdie, Collector and Magistrate of Bhawalgarh, on the subject of the dacoits, and of some letters that the Collector had received—promising to blow him to pieces quite soon—Steele left the Commissioner's House. As his own small bungalow, in which he lived alone, was only a few hundred yards from the gate of the grounds of the Residency, he walked, in spite of the heat.

God, how hot it was! One would feel no hotter walking than one would sitting down. The very moon seemed to send forth heat as well as light, and undoubtedly the earth did. One could feel it beating up from the ground. Presumably the thermometer would tell one that the temperature was lower than it had been at midday, but nothing else would.

Well, a cold drink and a cold bath and the comfort of pyjamas. Thank heaven he had not given way to the temptation to have a quiet evening thus, in a long chair.

Babu Purshotamdass . . . Bhojraj Shahani . . . Sant Arjun Rama . . . Ramrao Gopaldas and his brothers Motiram, Jaganath and Tulsiram . . . *and* . . . the Moulvie Abdul Haq!

Very interesting. Very significant. Also definitely ominous. If, and when, the Hindu and Mussulman agitators really joined hands and worked together with the British politician, it would be "Good-bye India." Good-bye to the British Raj and the peace and security that the Indian peasant had enjoyed for the first time in a thousand years and more. When the Hindu and Mohammedan joined in a great conspiracy to overthrow and oust the British, as a preliminary to cutting each other's throats in a struggle for supremacy, the country would be a cock-pit, a welter of slaughter such as it had not known for a couple of centuries. One would have supposed that even the most hare-brained and malignant terrorists would have seen the utter impossibility of an alliance between Hindu and Mussulman that would last beyond the proposed first step, the end of British rule. Not one of them could really imagine that such an un-natural union could last for long.

And how could they contemplate the aftermath?

The Hindus might out-number the Mussulmans by a couple of hundred millions, but which of the two contained the fighting races?

Was there a solitary Hindu who could contemplate with equanimity an India governed by Mussulmans; or a single Mussulman who could bear the thought of an India governed by Hindus?

Could any sane person see anything better for India than the present system of government? The government of India for the Indians by—the British: impartial, just and, whatever its faults, the best government that could be devised by the wit of man?

But these people weren't sane. They were mad with hate, and with lust for power, place and pickings.

What did the Indian peasant want? In other words, what did about three hundred and fifty million Indians want? They wanted peace, justice and light taxation. If there were an honest man among these terrorists, seditionists, agitators, doctrinaire politicians, could he pretend that India would get peace if the British went? Justice under Indian rule? Or lighter taxes—whatever these might, of necessity, now be?

What the devil was this?

As he turned from the road to the gate of his compound, Steele was aware of a man who suddenly stepped out from the shadow of the trees and confronted him with right hand raised to his own face and pointed at Steele's breast.

A pistol.

He saw the gleam of the barrel. . . .

An awkward distance—rather well-chosen. The movement well-timed. A little nearer, and he would have had a chance to spring at the fellow, rush him, knock the pistol up—perhaps—in spite of the fact that he was holding it close to his own face, in that curious manner.

A little further, and he might have had a chance to jump sideways, duck and dodge into the dark shadow, himself.

In the same second that the pistol was levelled, there was a sharp click, a few bright sparks—and nothing more.

Steele leapt forward, struck the weapon sideways with his left hand, knocked his assailant down with his right, and grabbed the pistol—a huge, old-fashioned flint-lock dating from pre-Mutiny days.

He laughed. Nevertheless, had it gone off, he'd have had a ball the size of a big marble in his chest.

The man scrambled to his feet. Holding the pistol by the muzzle, Steele prepared to show him a more effective use for the ancient and unreliable weapon.

"*No! No!*" cried the desperado, shielding face and head with his arms. "No, Sir! Do not strike. Excuse me. I am very sorry."

What sort of an assassin was this?

A lanky lad of the student class, distraught and trembling—but this might be from excitement and agitation rather than fear.

"Sir! Excuse me! Excuse me. I am very sorry."

"Excuse you? Oh, certainly. What are you sorry about? Sorry it didn't go off? I expect you hadn't cleaned out the hole between the priming-pan and the barrel."

"But, Sir, I did that meteeculously."

"Oh. It wasn't that, then. The flint was all-right. It sparked nicely. Perhaps the priming was damp. Or possibly it wasn't good powder?"

"Sir, they told me it was *verree* good powder."

"Who told you?"

Silence.

"Well? Who guaranteed the powder?"

"Sir, I can't say."

"Oh, yes, you can, and what is more, you are going to."

"Sir, I cannot. They would . . ."

"Would what?

No reply.

"Well, whatever they could do to you is nothing to what I can. Walk in front of me. Through the gateway . . . go on. Along the drive . . . go on. Up those steps . . . into the verandah . . . go on. Sit down on the floor there and don't move—while I have a look at this gun."

A Service horse-pistol, Tower brand, 1825 model; and a very good gun, of its time, too. Probably came to India in an officer's holster. Sort of pattern Napier's men had carried. Might even have been used in the Sikh wars, and killed its man at Aliwal, Sobraon, Moodki or Ferozshar. Been well kept and taken care of, too. Very interesting to know its history and where it had been for the last century. How did it come into these fellows' hands? Of course, a good many such weapons were picked up on the battlefields by marauders, or found by peasants; concealed, kept, and sold later. A great many of them were given up at the disarmament, when the Arms Act came into force, were collected and kept in the nearest *kutcherry*. Any European could buy them, nowadays, as well as old native swords, knives, shields, guns and pistols, at two rupees each.

This might have been stolen from such a *kutcherry*, or perhaps have been kept in an Indian family since its British owner lost it. Properly primed, and loaded with good black powder, wads and a well-fitting ball, it would still be a pretty deadly weapon at short range. Make a much more dangerous wound than any modern revolver or automatic, with its tremendous bore and soft leaden ball. But only at short range. And of course it could only be fired once without a long, slow, and clumsy re-loading and re-priming.

Something queer about this! About both the would-be murderer and the weapon. The terrorists had advanced a very long way beyond this sort of thing. There was no shortage of money; no lack of the latest and best eight-shot automatics; no dearth of skilled instruction in the use of them; and certainly no scarcity of cool, courageous and efficient killers.

Why this poor specimen of humanity and this antique blunderbuss? Was it to divert suspicion from the real criminals, the extremely efficient and up-to-date gang of terrorists, the Brethren of India, who were behind this lad and responsible for his actions? Was it to give the impression that there was nothing in Bhawalgarh more dangerous than a few half-baked, hare-brained students?

Steele glanced at the *assassin manqué* and saw that he was trembling violently. Was this rigor due to fear, excitement, fever, or overwrought nerves?

"Where did you get this?" he asked.

"Sir, I cannot tell."

"I think I can, though. Did you load it yourself?"

"No, Sir. I was not loading."

"What's the charge?"

"Attempted murder, Sir, I much fear. Pray excuse

me, Sir." Steele laughed.

"I fear so, too. What I referred to was the charge in the pistol. What's the thing loaded with? Shot, buck-shot, ball, or just rusty nails and brick-bats?"

"Sir, I am knowing nothing."

"Well, we can soon find out. I thought you said you cleaned out the touch-hole in the priming-pan yourself —'meteeculously'."

"Yes, Sir. Very."

"And yet you did not load it?"

"No, Sir. I had to clean the cannon and oil it, and I had to practise pulling up hammer, pushing down priming-cover, pulling trigger, and seeing that sparks arose when flint was striking it up again. Meantime also pointing gun forwards and holding it to eyes and keeping it still while doing same."

"Well, you did it very nicely, and the flint sparked very well."

"Thank you, Sir. I did my best."

"But what I don't understand is, why there was no flash in the pan, and why the pistol did not go off. I suppose you did prime it?"

"Sir, what is that?"

"Put some powder in the pan here, look, and shut the priming-cover down over it . . . so."

"Sir, I am knowing nothing of that. I learnt how to hold cannon and pull trigger without closing eye and thus taking wrong aim."

"And he gave it to you all ready, did he? All ready to be fired?"

"Yes, Sir."

"What, with the hammer up like this?"

"Yes, Sir."

"But didn't Purshotamdass tell you it was very dangerous to you—to carry it under your coat with the hammer up?"

"He warned me, Sir, to be very careful of pulling trigger prematurely."

"'Prematurely' is good . . . Suppose you'd pulled the trigger by accident. You might have shot yourself."

"Sir, he showed me how to keep hand completely

over this part."

"Over the trigger-guard. I see. I shouldn't have thought Purshotamdass would have known very much about guns, but I daresay Ramrao could tell him. He may have learned all about them when he was in England."

"Yes, Sir, perhaps. I followed instructions very carefully, Sir, and don't know how I came to *mis*conduct."

"You didn't drop the bullet and powder out of the gun as you came along, I suppose? Did Bhojraj ram it in with this thing, here, under the barrel—the ramrod? If it was he who loaded it so badly, he ought to have come and tried to fire it, and then he'd have been caught instead of you."

"Sir, his hand is much too small for holding cannon of that size. I, Sir, have much bigger fist."

And the young man held out what was undoubtedly quite a large hand for an Indian.

Steele withdrew the ramrod and inserted it into the barrel of the pistol.

"No, it's wadded all-right. I wonder what went wrong? We'll see what the powder is like, in a minute."

"Sir, possibly it was due to oversight through accident of my pulling back this thing as I am taking it from under coat. It caught in cord of pantaloons, the string holding up my pantaloons."

"What, this?" And Steele raised the priming-cover clamp.

"Yes, Sir. That pulled back, having caught in trouser-string. But seeing this, I pushed it down into its place again, knowing that flint must strike it to cause sparks."

"Well, your belt or 'cord of pantaloons' saved my life. For the priming powder of course fell out when the cover was raised, through the cord catching in it."

"Sir, it was written on your forehead."

"Or on your trousers. I'll write something on . . . I suppose you are at a College here?"

"Oh, no, Sir."

"Where, then?"

"Sir, I'm from Dayaram Jaganath College, Kashigunge."

"Then what the devil are you doing here?"

"Sir, I was brought."

"Brought? What for?"

"Sir, to redeem character."

"What, by committing a murder?"

"Yes, Sir. Formerly also I failed."

"Failed murderer, eh?"

"Yes, Sir."

"Failed B.A., also?"

"Yes, Sir."

"Whom didn't you murder last time?"

"Sir, the Collector of Kashigunge."

"By what method didn't you murder him?"

"Sir, by throwing a bomb through window of his bedroom."

"And didn't the bomb go off, either?"

"Sir, I didn't throw it. I became uncomfortable and dropped it down a well. Then I went back and said I had thrown it but nothing had happened. Then they became suspicious as Collector Saheb seemed in ignorance, and they threatened my death. I mean, Sir, my life."

"And they gave you another chance, eh?"

"Yes, Sir."

"Who brought you here?"

"Sir, I cannot tell."

"Look here, my good idiot. I know all about it, so you might just as well make a full confession. You were brought here and introduced to Babu Purshotamdass; Bhojraj Shahani, M.A., LL.B.; Mr. Ramrao Narayen Gopaldas, M.A., Barrister-at-Law; his brothers Motiram Gopaldas, Jaganath Gopaldas and Tulsiram Gopaldas; Mr. Sant Arjun Rama; Moulvie Abdul Haq and—the Swami Dayanand."

The youth stared wide-eyed and open-mouthed.

"Sir, you are knowing their names?"

"Of course I know. What do you suppose?"

"And you are not arresting?"

"Oh, they'll be arrested all-right, when the time comes. . . . Who brought you?"

"Sir, you must be knowing it was the Swami. He came and fetched me himself."

"Of course I know. Who were the others?"

"But, Sir, you know."

"Of course I do. I'm giving you a chance, don't you see? A chance to make full confession. Why, it may take seven years off your sentence if you make a clean breast of it."

"Sir, I will go silent to scaffold."

"Oh, no, you won't. You'll go noisy. . . . Why did they choose me?"

"Sir, because you are the Collector Saheb."

Steele stared and then laughed.

"Wrong address! So you were to redeem your character by murdering the Collector Sahib, eh? Well, of all the miserable, bungling, rotten plots . . ."

Yes, obviously that was it. Whether the murder came off or not, whether the right man was murdered or not, it was a red-herring. When and where would they really strike? It was like . . . like . . . a king-cobra sending out a harmless grass-snake to tap the leg of a man who knew there was a snake about—that the man might kill the grass-snake and go on his careless and care-free way rejoicing, through his fool's paradise . . . until the king-cobra struck.

Whistling softly to himself, Steele worked away with the screw-pointed end of the ram-rod until he drew out a well-pounded wad of cotton-wool. Into his hand he then tipped out a leaden ball that almost exactly fitted the pistol-barrel. It was a spherical modern sporting bullet, hollow, of the type known as Lethal, for use in twelve-bore shot-guns. It would expand and mushroom on impact, making a hideous wound.

"Good enough," he murmured, and set to work on the second wad.

Having extricated this, he tapped the muzzle of the pistol on the blackwood table that stood beside his chair, and dislodged a charge of gunpowder which poured forth into a little heap.

Taking some of it on the blade of his pocket-knife, he put it on the floor, struck and applied a match, and decided, from the blaze, absence of smoke, the smell, and the residuary products of combustion, that the stuff was modern smokeless powder.

"H'm! I rather fancy that would have burst the barrel," he said.

His thoughts ran on.

"I wonder if it was meant to. I wonder whether that 'red-herring' was to explode, giving the impression that a rather feeble attempt on the Collector's life had failed, owing to the clumsy inexperience of local amateur terrorists. . . . I wonder. But would they have trusted this object not to squeal if the explosion hadn't killed him, trusted him not to give the show away by sheer stupidity when he was put through it?

"I wonder if that charge would inevitably have burst the pistol and blown his head off, if he had fired it. Did the accident, of his letting the priming-powder fall out, save his life—or mine?

"Why did—er, Ramrao Gopaldas, you said?—tell you to hold the pistol close to your face?" he asked.

"Sir, so that I could steady my hand against my chin, if trembling; also look straight along the tub. I mean the barrel."

H'm. . . . A red-herring. And good fun, either way—whether the Collector were killed, or the assassin killed himself in the attempt. In either event, a good scare for the "Satanic" authorities; and the police hood-winked into supposing that all they'd got to cope with in Bhawalgarh was a two-anna[33] seditious conspiracy, on the part of politically-minded students.

Without turning his head, he glanced sideways at the trembling desperado.

It looked as though he were going to sleep! Quite likely. Probably hadn't slept for days.

Yes, nodding; closing his eyes.

Steele watched him in silence for a few minutes. Poor wretch! Probably he began as a burning patriot, with his head filled with lies about "our bleeding Mother India" and the sacrilegious violator; blown up with windy platitudes and nauseous gas about striking

---

[33] Anna = penny.

a blow for the Motherland; a martyr's crown; national hero; world-wide fame; three months' trial and glorious apotheosis—for the noble deed of chucking a bomb under the bed of a sleeping man whose life was devoted to the welfare of India.

Suddenly he shot a question at the lad.

"What were you to do to-night when you'd shot the Collector Sahib?"

"Sir, I was to throw the pistol down beside him and run away. I was to go to the station at three-thirty p.m. and catch mail-train to Mahommedabad Junction for Bombay."

"He gave you the money for your fare?"

"Yes, Sir."

"The Swami did? Are you sure he said three-thirty p.m.?"

"Yes, Sir. Three-thirty in the morning. Or rather in the night, before sunrise."

H'm. So that if the pistol went off without bursting, and poor old Herdie "got the works," the murderer was to bolt. Bolt *via* Mahommedabad to Bombay. And they'd settle his hash when he got there, unless some-one shadowed him and shoved him out of the train *en route*.

And if the pistol burst and killed the wretched youth, that would be very nice, too. Make the *feringhis* uncomfortable; advertise India's "wrongs" to the world; further frighten the weak-kneed, vacillating Secretary of State; and show the police of Bhawalgarh that the terror in their midst was really rather a comic one, some fumbling killers who killed—themselves. And that would do nicely, until the real plot was ripe; the deadly dangerous terrorists of the Brethren of India Secret Society ready to strike the real blow.

Yes, that was how he read it; but it didn't do to theorize too much, build too lofty an edifice upon an insecure foundation; or twist facts to fit a theory.

Perhaps he could get some more information out of this funny murderer.

"What's your name?"

"Lalchand Vasu, Sir."

"Yes? What's your real name?"

"Sir, that is my real name. I would not tell you a lie."

"No? You'd murder me, but wouldn't tell me a lie, eh?"

"Sir, I didn't know that it was you I slew."

"Well, the Collector, then. You'd commit a murder but not tell a lie."

"Sir, we do not call it murder."

"I see. And if I were to get a horse-whip and take your hide off with it, it wouldn't be a flogging if I called it tickling, eh?"

"Sir, European Police Sahebs never inflict torture upon prisoners and captives."

"Oh? We'll come to that in a minute. What good did you suppose you were going to do by murdering the Collector of Kashigunge or the Collector of Bhawalgarh?"

"Sir, to strike a blow for Mother India."

"You mean 'bleeding Mother India', don't you?"

"Yes, Sir. To strike blow that is Death to Tyrants."

"Did you know the Collector of Kashigunge?"

"Yes, Sir. He gave me book and shake hands, at prize-distribution. Also I was, for brief period, in *kutcherry* office under his kind control."

"And did you find him a tyrant—cruel, harsh, brutal, unjust, corrupt?"

"Oh, *no*, Sir. He was very kind officer."

"If a rich man brought a case before him, could he bribe the Collector Sahib?"

"Oh, *no*, Sir. It is well known that such a thing is impossible," was the reply given in a shocked, if not actually reproving, tone.

"Oh? He was always fair and just, kind and pleasant and considerate, accessible and incorruptible?"

"Yes, Sir. He was our father and our mother."

"And spent the whole of his time, from morning till night, doing his best to administer justice and to further the welfare of the people of his District."

"Oh, yes, Sir. All were liking him very much and speaking highly of him."

"I'm quite sure they were—all decent people. I knew him well. A kinder and more conscientious man never lived; nor a better friend to Indians of all castes and creeds."

"Yes, Sir."

"And yet you'd have murdered him, if your nerve hadn't failed."

"Sir, it was Death to Tyrants."

"Oh, don't talk like a damned parrot! You've just said he was precisely the opposite of a tyrant. And suppose you had murdered him, wouldn't another Sahib have come in his place?"

"Yes, Sir."

"Well, what then? Was he to be murdered too?"

"Yes, Sir."

"Until there were no more, I suppose?"

"Yes, Sir."

"Long job for somebody. And suppose, in course of time, your grey-haired great-great-grandchild killed the last British Collector of Kashigunge, do you suppose you'd be better off under a Mussulman Collector?"

"Oh, no, Sir."

"A Hindu Collector?"

"Sir, Hindus would like that better than a Mussulman Collector. If he were of their own caste, that is."

"Would the Mahommedans?"

"No, Sir."

"Then the Mahommedans would kill all the Hindu Collectors and the Hindus kill all the Mussulman Collectors?"

With up-turned palms Lalchand Vasu made a gesture of helplessness.

"Do you know Herdie Sahib, Collector of Bhawalgarh here?"

"No, Sir."

"Do you know anything whatsoever against him?"

"No, Sir."

"Have you heard anything said against him?"

"No, Sir."

"And yet you are prepared to murder him."

"Sir, it is Death to Tyrants."

"It'll be death to half-wits, idiots and cross-eyed parrots in a minute, if you tell me that again. And in any case, suppose he were a tyrant, are you the Law? Who asked you to decide whether people are tyrants or not?"

"Sir, Mr. Ranjit Singh told me."

Another grain of wheat among the chaff at last! Ranjit Singh in it, eh? That was a valuable piece of news. While they were scouring the Punjab for him, he was here in Bhawalgarh, was he? Hence the milk in the coconut. Hence the rise in political temperature—as high as the atmospheric; hence the mutterings and rumblings and sheet-lightning before the storm; and hence this little murder joke, too.

Yes, he'd been right. It was a red-herring, a typical Ranjit Singh trick. While Ranjit Singh and the Swami were up to something really big, they published this evidence of something really small. Very clever! Much cleverer than pretending that Bhawalgarh was a Sleepy Hollow, an Auburn loveliest village of the Plains, where nothing ever could or would happen, in spite of there being a somewhat notoriously politically-minded College, and a tradition of unrest and disloyalty since pre-Mutiny days. This would require careful handling.

He'd handle it himself—and take a leaf from their book.

Yes, by Jove, and use their own tool against them, mystify them with their own trick; and try a little of the lulling-into-security method on his own account.

Ranjit Singh the Agitator!

The seditionist, the terrorist; the boldest, best-equipped, most widely-travelled, most murderous, most cunning plotter of them all; coached, trained, taught and provided, in the Moscow School; with a degree from Vancouver and a post-graduate course in the Irish-American Underground University.

Since blows were advocated, what a blow to the terrorists' gang if he could put his hand on Ranjit Singh, lay him and the Swami by the heels, with a case that even slow-moving, ritualistic, law-worshipping British Justice would find water-tight, and offering no reason or excuse for the discharge of the accused.

Could this lad be used, if he could win him over?

Not a hope. If he read him aright (and he was a fairly experienced reader of such types), he would be worse than useless. Between a perverted, debased, and exploited patriotism on the one hand, and a combination of fear, nervousness, and stupidity on the other, he'd go to pieces as soon as the Brethren got hold of him again.

Nor, to do him justice, was he the type that turns King's evidence to save his skin. He'd much rather "go silent to scaffold," seeing himself a hero-martyr with whose name the Press of the world was ringing, than save his life—only to lose it at the hands of the terrorists soon after; save himself from legal punishment, to lead a hunted brief existence, his name a by-word, as that of a cowardly traitor to the Motherland and to the patriots who had trusted him.

No: worse than useless. His only value would be along the mystification and false-security line; waft him away; puzzle the gang; and keep them guessing.

If he arrested him, ran him in, and prosecuted in the usual way, he'd merely be playing the terrorist gang's game for them. It was just what the Brethren wanted, a small scare, the arresting of a student half-wit for a burlesque "murderous attempt."

"Will Ranjit Singh meet you at the railway-station and see you off by the three-thirty to Mahommed-abad?"

"Sir, I do not know. Nothing was said of that. After committing murder I was to run swiftly away, efface myself, and depart hence by that train."

"Because it connects with the mail-train at Mahom-medabad Junction?"

"Yes, Sir."

H'm. What about sending him off in the opposite direction, by an earlier one? There was an up-train to Jhalni at one-forty-eight. That would take him a hundred miles away from Bhawalgarh and Kashi-gunge. He could lose himself completely in a big city like Jhalni. Or one might send him out of India altogether. What about Srinagar? If he gave him a note to Tweedale-Roscoe, he'd find him a job and keep him safe there; make something like a man of him; and give him a sane outlook on life; convert him, in fact—morally and politically speaking, anyhow.

Meanwhile, was anything more to be got out of him? What a leaky vessel for Ranjit Singh and the Swami to use!

But no doubt they knew their own business best, and either carefully selected him for this job or else invented this job when they had taken stock of him.

"Hi! Wake up."

He stirred the desperado with his foot.

"Sir, excuse me."

"You observed just now that European Police Sahibs don't take bribes. Do the Indian policemen take bribes?"

"Oh, Sir, it is notorious. It is well known to everybody. Your Honour must have heard. When they are quartered on a village it is like plague of locusts. Always no man is safe from them, unless he gives bribe. Any wicked man they will let go, if he pays them. Any good man they will arrest and accuse, if he doesn't pay them. When they go to detect a murder, dacoity, or other crime, always they make a *banao*.[34] If they cannot get true evidence against the man they arrest, they make some up, and hire witnesses."

"*Bosh!* And supposing they were entirely officered by Indians—Indian Inspectors, Indian Assistant-Superintendents, Indian Superintendents, Indian Inspector-Generals, would things be better then?"

"Oh, no, Sir. Far, far worse. Because much heavier bribes would be needed for those officers."

"I see. Then there is at least one respect in which the British are quite useful, eh? Not wholly 'Satanic'?"

"Yes, Sir."

"Well, doesn't the same apply to other Government Officials—Commissioners, Magistrates, Judges, Collectors?"

"Yes, Sir."

---

[34] *Frame-up; false charge.*

"Public Works Department Officers and those in charge of Railways, Roads, Canals? Does the Sahib in charge of Irrigation allow more water to the man who bribes him and less to the man who does not?"

"Oh, *no*, Sir."

"What would Ranjit Singh say if you asked him those questions?"

"Sir, he would say that it is better to govern yourself badly than to be governed well by somebody else."

"Ah! Ask the *ryot*[35] that. Ask him whether he'd rather be taxed to starvation by an Indian government or taxed as lightly as possible by a British one. Ask him whether, when the Hindu and Mussulman mobs have finished slaughtering each other, the peasants will get a more just, fair, impartial and light-handed government from Russians, Japanese or Afghans than they had from the British."

"Oh, Sir. That would be calamity beyond . . ."

"Well, you ask him to-morrow and tell me what he says, will you?"

"Yes, Sir."

"He'll still be in Bhawalgarh to-morrow, will he?"

"Sir, he did not say he was going away."

"Ah! . . . But I am forgetting. You won't be seeing him to-morrow—him or anybody else, except the wicked policemen and the gaoler. You are going to prison."

"Oh, Sir! Excuse me. I am very sorry."

"Yes, going to prison; and from there you will go to the Andaman Islands for the rest of your life—a convict, a criminal, a murderer; and you will live with criminal scum until you die. Never see India again."

"Oh, Sir, I . . ."

The youth broke down and wept.

"Have you ever been in the hands of the police before?"

"Oh, no, Sir, never. We are a most respected family in Kashigunge. My father . . ."

"Yes. Bit rough on your father and your mother, isn't it, to know that their son is a gaol-bird, a convict,

---

[35] *Peasant cultivator.*

herding with the criminal sweepings of the bazaar."

"Sir, I am not a criminal. I am respectable, too. I only wished to be patriot and strike blow for Motherland."

"Respectable! *You?* Why, you're a cowardly slinking murderer who would, if he had the nerve, throw a bomb at a sleeping man who never harmed him or anybody else; a skulking murderer who'd hide in the shadows and shoot an unarmed man whose very name he didn't know. You are a hardened criminal."

"Oh, Sir, I . . ."

The hardened criminal broke down and wept afresh. "So you don't want to be transported for life and die in a gaol?"

"Sir, I'd rather go dumb to scaffold."

"You wish to be hanged—like a filthy dacoit?"

A piteous groan.

"Suppose I were to let you go?"

The youth looked up, a gleam of hope in his eyes.

"Sir, I would ever pray for your long life and prosperity. I would never again murder. But it would be useless. Mr. Ranjit Singh and the Swami would assuredly put me to edge of sword."

"Yes, they'd do you in, all-right, if you went back to them or they caught you. Suppose I were to let you go, and enabled you to get right away beyond their reach, out of India?"

"Sir, someone might be watching at the railway-station and I should be followed and brought back."

"Oh, you think they may come and see you off by the three-thirty to Mahommedabad Junction, eh?"

"I do not know, Sir, but it is both probable and likely. They kept watch on me at Kashigunge, too."

"Well, suppose you went by an earlier train and from the other platform, in the opposite direction. There's a train at one-forty-eight."

"Sir, the station might not be watched as early as that."

"On the other hand it might, eh? Probably would be. Look here, now. The up-train stops at Chinchgad, which is only three miles away. If you went there now, without going back into the native city, you'd be all-right."

"Yes, Sir."

"Well, that's what you've got to do, then. You'll get to Chinchgad easily in an hour. Don't go into the station until the train is signalled. You will be safe enough that way."

"Yes, Sir."

"Now, make no mistake. If you play me a trick and don't go, I will have you arrested before midday to-morrow, and you will get a life sentence for attempted murder. And unless you are lucky, Ranjit Singh and the Swami will catch you before I do, and you will die a very nasty death. They'll say you have failed them here as you failed at Kashigunge. They will say you double-crossed them and that, in any case, you know too much. Anyhow, your one chance of life and freedom is to get away from here. Get away at once, and go as far as possible. I'm going to send you to Srinagar."

"Sir, how can I thank you?"

"Don't, or I might change my mind. But if you want to show gratitude and not be sent to prison for the rest of your life, you can tell me everything you know, just in case there should be any small point on which I have been misinformed."

"Oh, Sir, I cannot betray fellow-conspirators. I cannot be traitor to Motherland."

"Well, I think the better of you for that. But do you really think that Ranjit Singh, the Swami, Babu Purshotamdass, Ramrao Narayen Gopaldas and his brothers, Bhojraj Shahani, Sant Arjun Rama and the Moulvie Abdul Haq are honest fellow-conspirators of yourself? Aren't you just a tool in their hands?"

"Sir, if so, I will be faithful tool and not turn in all their hands, like worm."

"As a matter of fact you are more like a fly in their web. Anyhow, they will treat you as a spider does a fly, if they get hold of you again, for they'll never believe you haven't double-crossed 'em."

"No, Sir, I fear they will never believe it. They are very hard-hearted men."

"Well, they'll certainly bump you off if they catch you, and then you will be the wrong sort of martyr, won't you? They will not only kill you, but they'll blacken your face and your name as a traitor—a traitor to the cause of Mother India, eh?"

"Yes, Sir, that would be *terreeble*."

"Well, why not join the people who are the real friends of India? People from whom she will get nothing but good, or at any rate get more good, more peace, prosperity and justice than she would from any other rulers. Why not help them?

"What was to be the next thing after the murder of the Collector?" Steele added, without change of voice. "Quick now! What was to be the next thing after the murder of the Collector? Quick now! Out with it. What was to be the next thing after the murder of the Collector?"

"Sir, I do not . . ."

"Oh, yes, you do."

"Sir, bombs are to be . . ."

The youth hung his head and stared sullenly at the ground.

Bombs! That was what poor old Herdie had been talking about. Some extraordinarily literary and convincing anonymous letters, promising that he would shortly be blown to pieces, blown into dust. They seemed to have made quite an impression on him. Bombs, eh?

"Yes? At whom are they to be thrown?"

"Sir, bombs are not to be thrown."

"Then what were you going to say about bombs? Quick now! What about the bombs? Come along! You've got to catch that train if you are going to save your life. What about bombs? Not going to be thrown? What then? They aren't going to be eaten, are they? What about the bombs? They are not to be thrown but they are to be . . . ? What? I am waiting. What about the bombs? Bombs. . . . Bombs. . . . Bombs. They are to be . . . ?"

"Sir, they are to be placed."

"Yes, they are to be placed, of course. We all know

they are not to be thrown; and when they are not thrown, they are placed. Yes, you're quite right—they are to be placed. But although you are their fellow-conspirator, you don't know where they are to be placed, do you? They did not tell you that much. Or did they? The time-bombs—where are they to be placed?"

"Sir, I cannot tell."

"No, and I'll tell you why you can't tell. Because you don't know. They didn't trust you enough to tell you. Call yourself a fellow-conspirator! You're not even a tool. Just a spider in their web. You don't know where the time-bombs were to be placed, do you?"

"Sir, nothing will induce me to betray plot."

"I know it won't. Simply because you don't know, do you . . . do you . . . do you?"

"No, Sir."

"All you know is that Ranjit Singh is bringing them here and the Swami is hiding them until Babu Purshotamdass has made arrangements for placing them. Or don't you know that much, even?"

"Oh, yes, Sir. I am knowing that much."

"But they weren't going to let you place one, were they?"

"Well, Sir, it was not actually promised. If I had done well to-night, perhaps I was to be given part in next step."

"I don't suppose they even told you when it was to be, did they?"

"No, Sir. But it is not that they do not trust. It is because they had not yet fixed date."

"No, I know they had not fixed the date, but they didn't even tell you whether it was to be quite soon, or put off until the Governor comes here."

"Sir, it is not known."

"Not known to *you*. You know practically nothing about it, I can see. You don't even know where the Swami is hiding them—out in the jungle, in a cave, in a ruined temple, or whether it is in a house in the native city."

"Sir, I will never betray plot."

Steele laughed.

419

"Won't tell what you don't know, eh! I don't believe you even know where they meet—except at the house of Ramrao Gopaldas."

"Oh, yes, Sir, I am really knowing that."

"Not you. You only know what they tell you. You've never been to the meeting-place at all."

"There, Sir, excusing me, you are wrong. I have been."

Steele drew bow at a venture; took a shot in the dark.

"What, you mean the place behind the *To-day and To-morrow* publishing offices?"

"You are knowing, Sir?"

"Of course I know. And I know you've never been there."

"Excusing me again, Sir, but there you are wrong. I have been. I am trusted fellow-conspirator."

"What, been up to the room right at the top of the house?"

"Yes, Sir."

"You haven't been down into the cellar, though."

"No, Sir. Down there I have not been."

"No, I thought not. I was quite sure they hadn't told you where they were storing the time-bombs, hand-grenades, revolvers and ammunition."

"No, Sir, because first I had to prove worthy, since I had failed at Kashigunge. I am quite sure they would have admitted me to inner circles if I had shot you to-night."

"Even though I am not the Collector?"

"Yes, Sir. I think I should have gained equal number of marks for killing you, because you are Blood-stained Tyrant Hireling of Satanic Government."

"Thanks. Whose blood stains me?"

"Sir, it is metaphorical simile."

"It is silly bilge and bunkum and bosh; and you know it. But I'll tell you what you don't know. You don't know which buildings are to be blown up, besides the *kutcherry*, Commissioner's House and the Collector's bungalow."

"Sir, but I do. Also Railway-station, National Bank

of India, and Commercial Bank, Police Headquarters and Bhawalgarh Fort. Also Post and Telegraph Office. Also gates of Bhawalgarh Gaol and house of Governor of the Prison."

Steele's inscrutable face remained sphinx-like.

"Yes, it's quite an ambitious programme, isn't it? But I don't quite see how they are going to get the bombs into the Banks and the Fort, do you?"

"Sir, they will bribe underlings in some cases, and suborn sepoys and policemen in others."

"Will they, now? And you really think they'd have let you place a time-bomb if you had done your job to-night—and got full marks?"

"Yes, Sir."

"And if you could have got into the Fort or a Bank or Police Headquarters or Commissioner's House in the day-time, and hidden there so that you could place your bomb in just the right spot, when you got the place to yourself at night, would you have been willing to take the risk of not being able to get out?"

"Sir, I would give life for Motherland."

"You'd have risked being shut in with the bomb and blown to pieces?"

"Yes, Sir."

"Even though nobody would ever know that it was you who had given his life?"

"Fellow-conspirators would know, Sir."

"Yes, but they wouldn't tell anybody. You mean to say that you would stay in the building, in the middle of the night, waiting for the bomb to go off?

"It was to be in the middle of the night, of course," he added conversationally, without change of voice.

"Yes, Sir."

"Of course. A conspirator might not be able to put the bomb just where it would do most good, if it had to be done in the day-time."

"No, Sir. Also number of explosions, all occurring at once, in different parts of Bhawalgarh, in the middle of the night, causing great confusion and fear."

Yes, of course. Disorganization. Consternation and alarm. Commissioner gone, Collector gone, Police

Headquarters gone; officers and European soldiers in the Fort gone; Banks blown to pieces; neighbouring houses on fire; Railway-station wrecked; telegraph wires broken; Post Office blown up; telephone wires gone and . . .

"What about the Native Regiment?" Steele suddenly asked. "Quick!"

"Sir, it is of course hoped that they will take advantage of opportunity."

"To join the conspirators, you mean?"

"Yes, Sir."

"And murder their officers?"

"Execute Blood-stained Tyrant Hirelings of Satanic Government."

"Quite so. Much better chance if it is done at night, of course. I should think about four in the morning. Did they fix that definitely?"

"Sir, I am not knowing."

"No, of course they wouldn't fix the hour, I suppose, until they'd fixed the date."

"No, Sir. It is at present awaiting decision until leading gentleman comes from Brethren in Calcutta."

"Yes. Let's see. I've forgotten his name for the moment. It is . . . wait a minute . . . wait a minute. . . . His name is . . . er . . ."

"Sir, I am not knowing his name."

"What! Didn't they even tell you that much?"

"Sir, his name is not spoken."

"Not in front of you, you mean."

"No, Sir; not at all spoken. I am not sure that even all know it—except, of course, Mr. Ranjit Singh and the Swami."

"Just refer to him as The Messenger, I suppose: or is it The Avenger?"

"No, Sir. I have never heard him referred to by those names. Only by number."

"Well, I'll tell you his name when I remember it. He's Number Ten, I think."

"No, Sir. Excusing me, he is Number Seven."

"Ah, yes. Number Seven, of course. It is Bhose . . . or Ghose . . . or Dutt . . . or . . ."

"Sir, I am not knowing. I have never heard."

"And they won't fix the date till he comes. No, I suppose they wouldn't. . . ."

And he had been patting himself on the back and calling it a good night's work on the strength of his chat with Betty Gopaldas. A good night's work before he had encountered this creature!

Thank Heaven it had been himself and not Herdie. If Herdie had handed him over to the Police officially in the ordinary way, they'd never have got a word out of him. Not a hint of this bomb plot; not the name of a single conspirator. He'd have played the game according to his miserable lights and struck the "go silent to scaffold" attitude.

And thank God the pistol hadn't gone off and killed either of them. If the lad had been silenced, this bomb plot would probably have succeeded. And equally so if he himself had been killed.

And who the devil was Number Seven?

When was he coming? How could he be identified and caught? Incidentally, how far had this young fool been hoodwinked? How much of what he knew was false information that he was intended to divulge?

Anyway, there could be no shadow of doubt that the list of names he had unintentionally and unconsciously provided was genuine; or that there was a really big bomb-conspiracy, and that some of the best brains and worst characters in India were behind it.

Was it possible that the Native Infantry battalion was tainted?

How many of the sepoys had been corrupted, and how far; and had the terrorists got hold of any of his police? Probably not, but it would be a wonder if they hadn't, seeing how under-paid and badly treated the police were, all round. Abused or derided, reprimanded or punished, if they took action, because they took too much; the same if they took no action, because they took too little; tried like felons if they defended themselves from assault and used their rifles after sustaining bombardments of stones and savage *lathi* charges. And occasionally burnt alive in their police-

thana.

None but themselves could know what they suffered at the hands of their friends, relations and caste-fellows, for being what this lad called Blood-stained Tyrant Hirelings of a Satanic Government.

And who yelled quicker for the police than their detractors did, as soon as the word dacoits was breathed? Dacoits!

"How's the Swami getting on with Bagu the Robber and his band of dacoits? Are they going to join in the *tamasha* when Bhawalgarh is blown up?" he asked, suddenly.

"Sir, I am knowing nothing of it. I have only heard talk."

"I don't think Bagu quite trusts the Swami, do you?"

"Oh, yes, Sir. He trusts him, doubtless; but he fears, I think, a trap."

"Well, he can't trust him, then."

"Sir, I mean he fears lest he and his band be trapped in the streets of the town, by the police. They are not accustomed to dacoity in cities."

"Not very enterprising, are they? I should have thought that if the Swami gave them good weapons and pay, they'd be only too pleased to have some fighting and looting."

"Sir, I don't think it is considered that the dacoits will be necessary. There are many *budmashes* of the bazaars, and the butchers of the city will join in, also. And of course, the prisoners and captives—the convicts released from the Bhawalgarh Gaol—will be *verree* active and useful."

"Then of course there will be the Sepoys, eh?"

"Yes, Sir. They will be best of all."

"How many of them does the Swami expect to get?"

"Sir, it is not known."

"You mean you don't know."

"Sir, it is not known, for even Ranjit Singh the Sikh cannot be sure of getting his brothers of the Sikh Company to mutiny when the time comes."

"All very difficult, eh?"

"Yes, Sir. *Verree* difficult. But even if Sepoys do not seize opportunity, there will be glorious blow struck for Motherland, and the whole world will ring with sound of bombs."

"Will that do it much good?"

"Sir, it will draw attention to wrongs of bleeding India."

"And what would that do—supposing there were any 'wrongs'?"

"Sir, public opinion is strongest force on earth."

"Yes. And don't they know, by this time, that public opinion is getting more and more horrified at the idea of political assassination, bomb-throwing, cowardly cold-blooded murder?"

"Sir, the blood of martyrs is the seed of . . ."

"Yes?"

"Sir, I have forgotten what it is the seed of; but public opinion is aroused."

"You think the blood of martyrs cannot possibly be shed in vain?"

"*Certainlee*, Sir."

"And don't you think that men like the Collector Sahibs, who have died at the post of duty, who have died *for* their duty, murdered, are martyrs? . . . Are you sure Number Seven's name isn't Dutt? Isn't that it? Quick now. Rabindranath Dutt? Or is it Arabindo Dutt? *Quick!*"

"Sir, I really am not knowing. I have never heard."

And no doubt that was the truth.

Well, there was probably nothing more to be got from this source, and the sooner the fellow was away the better. He'd give him a non-committal note to Tweedale-Roscoe, and write fully by post. Tweedale-Roscoe would keep him safe in the Mission compound, and quite possibly get some more information from him. A great man Tweedale-Roscoe. And he would keep him safe enough; and produce him if, and when, wanted.

Just possibly he might turn King's evidence later; or at any rate give evidence, if Tweedale-Roscoe brought him to see the error of his ways. A thing he could do, if any man alive could do it.

Half an hour later Lalchand Vasu, "failed B.A." and failed murderer, was on his devious way through sleeping cantonment and silent suburb out to the Chinchgad railway-station three miles distant, to take his ticket at the up, instead of the down, platform and to proceed to Srinagar in the extreme North instead of Bombay, far to the South.

§3

Meanwhile, in a curious ancient two-horse cee-spring barouche, magnificent with silver lamps and fittings and silken upholstery that would have been even more magnificent had not the silver been tarnished and blackened, and had the curtains and hangings been less moth-eaten, frayed and filthy, faded and discoloured; the cushions less greasy and torn and inclined to disgorge their stuffing; drawn by a pair of aged horses which, though fine of frame, were pictures of misery; and on the box of which were driver and footman whose bare feet and dirty *dhotis* were unworthy of their magnificent turbans and scarlet coats, Mr. and Mrs. Ramrao Narayen Gopaldas were borne from Commissioner's House to their home at the end of the Sudder Bazaar.

Mr. Ramrao Narayen Gopaldas, M.A., Barrister-at-Law, was in high feather.

"At last I have made speech to the Bhawalgarh Literary, Dramatic and Philosophical Society," he said. "I think I shall add a new degree to my name. Instead of taking LL.B. of Indian University, I will be F.B.L.D.P.S.—Fellow of said Society. Also the Commissioner nodded to me very pleasantly, and I had a long conversation with Mrs. Commissioner. All very pleasant and agreeable. Several noticed us with bows and smiles. What was that fellow Steele saying to you, Betty?"

"Well, we spoke about the address—and the weather—and then the conversation turned on Comparative

Religion."

"Private philosophical debate on your own, you two, eh?" laughed Ramrao.

"Yes."

"And what did he think of Sant Arjun?"

"Just what he said when the Commissioner called on him, I suppose."

"Oah, yes? I thought he seemed a little bit sceptical."

"It did sound rather like that, didn't it?"

"I was glad to see him talking to you."

"Yes, it is nice to . . ."

"To what?"

"Well, I was going to say, to talk to somebody English, sometimes."

"Yes, of course. I quite understand. I like you to talk to Steele. Nice chap. Very intelligent, too. You talk to him just as much as you like. Just whenever you get the chance. And tell me what you talk about, eh?"

"Of course, if it interests you."

"If it interests me? Naturalee anything you say and do interests me, my dear girl. Did he say anything about me?"

"Yes. He said he thought it was very nice of you to stick up for your friend."

"My friend?"

"Sant Arjun Rama."

"Did he call him my friend? How did he know he was my friend?"

"I suppose he used the word as a figure of speech. I believe the Commissioner referred to him as 'My friend Mr. Sant Arjun Rama.' He generally does refer to the speaker of the evening like that."

"But do you think Steele supposes Arjun is a friend of mine? Specially a friend, I mean?"

"No. I remember saying, when he used the word, 'Oh, I don't know that you'd call him a friend.'"

"That's right. Good. Did he ask whether I knew him before he came to Bhawalgarh?"

"I told him you didn't. Or at least I told him I . . ."

"What?"

"Oh, that I didn't know anything about it. Why? Why do you ask?"

"Oh, nothing, nothing, my dear."

If her husband thought he was going to make her report and repeat every word that Steele said to her he was mistaken. She had been perfectly loyal to him, and she always would be; but she was going to draw the line somewhere. He was always advocating emancipation (emancipation, good Heavens!) for women, and professing to believe that a woman, even though married, might have a soul of her own, and she was certainly going to have one.

When he had begged her to marry him, he had promised her—quite untruthfully—that their married life should be in every way European, in circumstance and setting; in kind and conduct; and that she would never realize that she was not married to a Briton, save when she noticed the comparative darkness of his skin.

And here he had pathetically quoted The Prince of Morocco's speech to Portia—

> "*Mislike me not for my complexion,*
> *The shadow'd livery of the burnished sun,*
> *To whom I am a neighbour and near bred*"

—whereupon she had hastened to assure him that she would love him the better by reason of that handicap.

And indeed this might well have been so, had they remained in England where, among people who had never been in the East, his colour might have been merely "interesting"; where there would have been no terrible mother-in-law, no Subhadra; where they would have lived in the kind of house with which she was familiar; where they would have, had the sort of servants to whom she was accustomed; and where she would have had English friends, both men and women.

When he had begged her to marry him, he had promised her that not only in these details, but in her position with regard to him, she should be the normal English wife, her husband's partner and equal, living her own life in her own way; with unfettered freedom to come and go, to have her own interests and follow her own pursuits; that she would have books, music, theatres, games and sport; dancing; entertaining and being entertained by the friends of her own choice.

Making every allowance for the difference between his estimate and hers, every allowance for his seeing everything golden through the sweetening, softening, if distorting, haze of infatuation, the glow and the glamour of love, he must have known perfectly well that she would have no facilities whatever for getting new books; that she would hear no music at all save that of native instruments, the hideous noise of tom-toms, the squealing of gourd flutes, and the minor-key wailing of strange stringed instruments; that there wasn't a theatre for hundreds of miles; that she would be entirely out of it so far as games were concerned, since, as the wife of an Indian, she would not be *persona grata* at the Gymkhana, and only allowed to join on sufferance; that of sport she would see none, there being no hunting, no fishing, no shooting, no point-to-point racing, in which she could take part; and that the "Maharani" would be certain, sooner or later, to veto her riding and dancing; and that as for entertaining and being entertained, practically no-one would call on her; and that few, if any, of the ladies of the Station would take any notice of her at all.

Yes, while making every allowance for his optimism, his very marked inclination to make the wish the father to the thought, his habitual inaccuracy of statement, his habit of seeing the future all *couleur de rose*, it could not be denied that he had deceived her, had married her and brought her to India under false pretences.

Still, she must not judge him as she would an Englishman, and must bear in mind not only the fact that a great deal of what hurt her did not hurt him in the least, but that much of her suffering was really incomprehensible to him.

Even while realizing that he was giving her a quite wrong impression, he could not understand and estimate the extent of her inevitable disillusionment.

Her home life, for example.

True, he had told her that "for a time" they would be living with his people, because the joint-family system was invariable and inevitable in India in certain circumstances; but that they would have their own quarters of course, and be just as private, really, as people who lived in flats.

And, fool that she was, she had promptly visualized a flat in a kind of modest palace; an interior with vast tiled or marble floors, pillars, arches, balconies, Moorish windows, Persian rugs, divans, piled cushions; quite possibly a sunk marble pool and fountain in the middle of the great sunlit, but cool, room—a schoolgirl's dream of the gorgeous East, based on films and on painted pictures by artists who had never been far from Chelsea—*Light of the Harem* sort of thing.

And the reality! Two rooms in a huge ugly house that had no Oriental note save dirt and decrepitude, iron bars instead of windows, semi-cylindrical tiles instead of slates, and a neglected compound instead of a garden.

Two rooms furnished with bazaar stuff; the walls blue-washed to the hideous colour of a butcher's smock; the mud floors covered with ragged matting of plaited palm-leaf; the bedroom bare, save for a vast four-poster iron bed enclosed by a dingy canopy of mosquito-netting; the bathroom a cellar of four dirty walls and a greasy floor on which stood a small zinc wash-tub and an earthenware water-jar.

And every single effort that she had made at improvement, tolerated by her husband, had been opposed tooth and nail, and generally thwarted, by her mother-in-law.

And the food, the dreadful eternal curry and rice, the loathsome Indian vegetables—brinjals, sweet potatoes, ladies'-fingers; the sodden heavy chupatties; the terrible tea, either tasteless or highly flavoured with some appalling scented stuff; the thin milk; the tinned butter; the tough meat, stringy and flavourless when it did not taste far too strongly—of goat. She had never been greedy or particularly interested in food, but oh, for an English meal; afternoon tea on a shady lawn; dinner with snowy napery, bright crystal, steel, and silver; or a British breakfast with delicious coffee and rolls, bacon and eggs.

Well, so long as one could bother over little matters like that, things weren't too bad! And there were better times to look forward to, when she'd have a house of her own, like any other married woman, and she could have something resembling a real drawing-room and dining-room; something remotely resembling an English home. She might even perhaps be able to get decent servants, if Ramrao would get a house in Cantonments or Civil Lines—but it was hardly likely. All the good ones went into Sahibs' service, where they got better pay and perquisites and better *izzat*—prestige and importance.

Nice to have something to look forward to.

But she must not look forward too far. She simply must not think of the time when she would be a lonely old woman in India; isolated; perforce making the worst of two worlds, European and Indian. Never to see Home again, her own people, her friends, the dear faces and places she loved.

No, mustn't look forward too far, not even as far as the inevitable day when Anthony Steele left Bhawalgarh. She must try to put away that ever-recurring thought. It would be bad enough when he went to some other part of India as, sooner or later, he would. Very bad. But when he retired and left India for good, and she knew that she would never see him again . . .

It did not bear thinking about. Nothing did. Except Anthony Steele.

Come, this wouldn't do, for there never was anything so damnable as self-pity. The beginning of self-pity is the end of self-respect, self-help, self-control. She had made her bed and she must lie on it, blinking her eyes to the fact that it wasn't quite the bed that had been promised her.

And meanwhile . . . she was to go riding with Anthony Steele.

Yes, and to that extent at any rate, her soul should be her own. She would have an English friend while she could; and what they chose to say to each other was their own affair. Private. Yes, sacred: and she'd repeat it for nobody. She'd say nothing to Anthony Steele that her husband was not quite welcome to hear; but nevertheless she was not going to repeat it. Nor would Anthony Steele say anything to her that her husband might not hear. But, simply because Anthony had said it, she would not repeat it.

§4

Meanwhile, Mr. Justice Sherdley and his wife went home in their roomy and comfortable car, driven by their uniformed Indian chauffeur, to whom His Honour was wont to refer as the best driver, the cleverest mechanic, and the damnedest rascal in India, averring that the man obviously drank petrol, shod and housed his family with tyres, and had set up his father in a garage—all at the expense of his unfortunate employer.

"John," said Mrs. Sherdley, as soon as she was seated beside him in the car, "I am thoroughly, heartily, and completely ashamed of you."

"Glad you know how to be ashamed of anything," snapped His Honour.

"You are a rude, discourteous, snappy, ill-tempered, abominable old man."

"And you are an old woman. Simply that. Just an ordinary old woman. No adjectives needed. The woman God gave me. No! Why blame God? I did it myself."

Mrs. Sherdley put her arm through her husband's and squeezed it.

"Rude, discourteous . . ."

"What's the difference?" enquired her husband.

"None."

"Tautology," he snapped.

"Well, I won't go so far as to accuse you of that, but it was very bad. Why did you do it?"

"Felt like it."

"What made you feel like it, John?"

"Everything. This damned heat, worry, bother, anxiety."

"Oh, John . . ."

"I'm worried to death. Feel apoplectic."

"Why, *John!* Anything special? Anything particular, or just things in general—and me?"

"Nothing in particular. You—and things in general. I feel . . . Good God, I feel nervous, frightened, apprehensive. Something-going-to-happen sort of feeling."

On the whole, it would be better, wiser, kinder, not to say anything to her about the anonymous letters, of which the style, tone and diction had been so remarkable as deeply to impress him—in spite of himself, in spite of his better judgment, in spite of his contempt for anonymous letters. An explosion that would shortly . . . To the devil with their damned letters. But how curiously and strongly they reminded him of the letter sent to Lord Mounteagle, informing him about the Gunpowder Plot.

"Oh, *John!* Presentiment?"

"Yes. Loathsome feeling. Like I used to feel when I was a small boy and my nurse put the light out and left me in the dark, with the door shut."

What an extraordinary thing for John to say. Doubly extraordinary—because such a man as John should say it and because it was just how she herself had been feeling lately.

Should she tell him that it was just exactly as she herself had been suffering since she had had those letters? A horrible mixture of anxiety, apprehension, nervousness, *fear.* No.

"I apologized to Cornwallis and told him the truth. I said I simply couldn't stand the feller. Like a snake. Do you know, I sat and listened to him in a sort of trance, a sort of nightmare, exactly as though a damned great cobra with a human head sat up on end and talked with its forked tongue. Do you know, Elizabeth, he positively *hypnotized* me; kept on fixing me with those beastly eyes of his. Made me feel queerish; all of a doodah. Don't wonder I was a little brief."

"A little brief! You boorish old man."

"What I'd have liked to do would have been to get up and kick him out of the room. Damned liar."

"What did the Commissioner say when you apologized?"

"It was more what he didn't say. I told him I was sorry, but I thought the feller was a charlatan, a rogue and a liar—and probably worse. And Cornwallis fully agreed by saying nothing. Just glanced at Rowena and back at me. And I nodded. 'Nuff said. Between men of sense."

"You didn't apologize to Rowena, did you?"

"No. Why should I? She's not the Commissioner, and she's not the Chairman of the Society."

"No, but it's her house."

"'Tisn't. Don't talk like a fool. I beg your pardon. I meant don't talk more like a silly old fool than you are. It's the Commissioner's house. Isn't it known as Commissioner's House?"

"It's not her drawing-room, I suppose?"

"When the Society meets there it's the meeting-place of the Bhawalgarh Literary, Dramatic and Philosophical Society—of which she is the Secretary. Of course I didn't apologize to her. It was she who introduced the brute. And not only to the Society, but to Bhawalgarh. Invited him here. . . . Got him living there in the house like a Christian."

"Well, he is a Christian."

"*Bah!*"

"I like it when you bleat, John."

"What?"

"Change from braying."

"What's the woman talking about?"

"Apologies. I'm so glad you had the decency to apologize to the Commissioner. I wish you'd done so to Rowena."

"Well, I didn't."

"Well, I did."

"You apologized for my rudeness?"

"I did."

"Then it was like your confounded impudence, you foolish, ignorant, worthless woman."

"Well, it wasn't like yourself, John, to answer the Commissioner so, when he asked you to make a nice little speech. And you are not to do it again."

"*Bah!*"

"However, I'll forgive you this once."

"You won't do anything of the sort."

"I will."

"You won't."

"Don't shove with your elbow like that, John."

Mr. Justice Sherdley kissed his wife.

"Darling Elizabeth . . ." he murmured.

Quite a different Mr. Justice Sherdley from him whom the Bench and Bar of Bhawalgarh revered and feared.

He was himself now a prey to fear; a prey to an indefinite but terrible Fear. And yet, as whimsically he told his wife that night, when they retired to bed, he could honestly say he was afraid of nothing.

He was afraid of Nothing, a dreadful, indescribable Nothing, vague, without form and void.

For long they lay awake in the insufferably hot darkness, each afraid for the other.

"Did you notice Jenny Herdie gaping at Anthony Steele all the evening, John?"

"No, I didn't. And it's a pity you haven't something better to do than . . ."

"Well, she was. I have half a mind to tell her not to be such a fool in public."

"All right in private, I suppose? You are an immoral and . . ."

"Poor little Betty Gopaldas, too. Watching him like a mouse watching a big cat."

"And you?"

"I?"

"Yes. You must have been staring at him yourself, too."

"He's a most attractive young man. Fascinating."

"*Bah!*"

"He-haw! . . . Feeling better, John darling?"

§5

Meanwhile Mr. Lawrence Herdie, C.I.E., I.C.S., Collector and Magistrate of Bhawalgarh, drove himself and his wife home, in his long, powerful car. He had not cared to employ a driver since his excellent Goanese chauffeur, Felice Pereira, had been killed by his side. The blood of Felice Pereira had been literally upon his head, and he had an uncomfortable feeling that it was so, metaphorically, as well. When his wife insisted on accompanying him, she sat at the back of the car and on the other side of it, a position slightly less dangerous.

As it was not a saloon car, this also rendered conversation impossible, a desirable arrangement.

When the car turned in at the compound gates, a policeman, squatting on his heels in the dark shadow of the porch, rose to his feet, while another man, dark-skinned and naked save for a small loin-cloth, slipped away through the bushes, silently as a snake.

As the car rounded the curve of the long drive, and the light of its lamps illuminated the police sepoy, he was standing stiffly to attention. The car stopped, and he saluted briskly as the doors of the lattice-work verandah were opened by a uniformed *pattiwallah*,[36] and the Collector's English-speaking butler, Paul Jesus Miguel Xavier Manoel Braganza Mascarenhas da Silva, a gentleman who professed to know no Indian tongue and to be of the purest Portuguese descent—in spite of the fact that he had been bred and born in Goa, of low-caste Indian parents who knew not a word of any language save Hindustani—came from the drawing-room through the big open doorway on to the huge lamp-lit verandah.

"Good evening, Sah and Memsahib," he said.

"Evening, Paul. Everything all right?"

"Yes, Sah. All proper," he salaamed.

"Will you have a cup of coffee or anything, my dear?" asked Herdie, turning to his wife.

"Yes, whisky-and-soda. Take them upstairs, Paul."

---

[36] *Uniformed civilian retainer; official messenger and doorkeeper.*

"Very good, Memsahib."

"Bring some coffee along to my office-room," said Herdie. "If you'll excuse me, my dear, I've got a little work I must finish to-night."

"Won't it keep till the morning? You always disturb me when you come up late."

"No, I'm afraid it won't. I must do it to-night."

"I don't suppose the wheels would quite cease to go round if you didn't, would they?"

"Perhaps not."

"Or the Government of India come to a sudden end."

"No, Jenny. Good night, my dear. Sleep well."

"*Sleep!* I?"

Herdie went along the wide verandah and opened the end door, that of the big bare room in which he worked in the early morning before going to Court or *kutcherry*, and again at night, after his day's work was supposed to be done.

In spite of the heat, he closed the shutter of the windowless "window" in the outer wall. No need to make a target of himself.

Removing his patent-leather shoes, dinner-jacket and waistcoat, he put on a silk coat that hung over the back of a chair, ready for his use.

Scarcely had the coat touched his shoulders than his heart seemed to stand still, his blood to freeze, his hair to rise on end. Something alive was wriggling and struggling across his back, between his shoulder-blades. . . . He had a well-developed horror of snakes.

Got him the third time, had they? Was this the Bhawalgarh method, instead of bullet and bomb? What was it, a *krait*, deadliest of snakes? Something small, anyhow. Must be a *krait*. Its tail had flicked his neck. Or had it bitten him? How had it been put inside his coat in such a way that it would stay there until he went to put the coat on? Probably it had been in a sleeve and, as his hand and arm passed down it, the snake had wriggled swiftly up. He had felt something; and, yes, the sleeve of the coat had been bent upward, the cuff resting on the seat of the chair.

437

How could they make the snake remain in the coat-sleeve? . . . They couldn't, of course. They had just taken a chance; and, anyhow, a *krait* anywhere in the room would be a deadly danger.

In the fraction of a second the thoughts passed through his mind. What should he do? To pull the coat off would be almost certain death. He was bound to be bitten, probably on the hand, as it was drawn back through the coat-sleeve.

There was one thing. If he hadn't already been bitten, the snake could not bite while it was held against his body by the coat. But, of course, in a few seconds it would either wriggle upwards and emerge against his bare neck, coil round, and strike; or squirming downwards, fall to the ground, coil, and strike his foot. If only he had kept his shoes on!

Could he hold the reptile there? Could he prevent it from moving, by clutching his coat by the lapels and at the waist? Prevent it from going either up or down? But then it would writhe round sideways and . . . Oh, God —he'd go mad and scream.

An idea!

Suddenly Herdie ran backwards and dashed himself with all his might against the wall. Again. Again. And then against the edge of a heavy cupboard he ground his back as hard as he could. Then, leaning backward, flung himself down as heavily as he could, flat upon his back on the ground.

Here, for a few seconds, he lay still, breathing heavily; then rising quickly to his feet, tore his coat off.

As he did so, a lizard fell to the ground.

Herdie's laugh was not one indicative of good fun and pure enjoyment.

"One up to the terrorists," he said aloud. "Although they don't know it. I suppose Steele would have dealt with that without turning a hair or showing a sign of fear on his frozen face."

"*Boy!*" he called, opening the door of the room.

"Sah?"

The butler came hurrying down the verandah.

"I've trodden on a *gecko*. Take it away and bring me

another coat."

Rather a silly thing to say. Paul would know perfectly well that a house-lizard would not be on the floor, and that it wouldn't stand still to be trodden on if it were. It would have flashed across the floor and up the wall and taken refuge behind a picture in half the time it took to open the door.

How far was Paul trustworthy? Probably quite all-right, and anyhow it was a very sound idea to have a butler who was neither Hindu nor Mussulman. Paul was a devout Christian. Not but what a Goanese Christian was able to divorce Works from Faith as widely as most people, and to keep high noble piety walking hand in hand with low base villainy. Probably quite a good fellow, and anyway, Jenny preferred having a Goanese because, with their bare heads and European clothes, they looked more like what she called human butlers.

Yes, probably one was safer with a Goanese butler and cook than with Hindus and Mahommedans upon whose racial and religious feeling, Hindu or Mussulman terrorists might work. On the other hand, both Hindu and Mussulman servants had shown the noblest loyalty, the most faithful devotion, to their masters during the Mutiny—saving, at the risk of their own lives, a large number of European women and children.

Paul Jesus Miguel Xavier Manoel Braganza Mascarenhas da Silva returned with a fresh coat, thin, loose and cool, though only paradoxically "cool," inasmuch as, in point of fact, like everything else, it was very warm to the touch.

Well, this was not work!

Lawrence Herdie settled down to his desk, drew files toward him, took paper and pen, and endeavoured to concentrate upon the document before him.

Quarter of an hour passed.

What was that?

A stealthy footstep? Had someone tried the shutter?

Good Lord, what *was* it?

Only the punkah that had suddenly started to

swing.

What a state his nerves were in!

Curious that, in spite of the terrible heat, he had not thought of the punkah directly he came into the room, and shouted to the punkah-coolie, who knew quite well that the Sahib would be working here in his office. Probably he'd been asleep on the side verandah, and hadn't even awakened when the shutter had been closed. Were punkah-coolies liable to corruption and use as tools, by the terrorists? No. Too hopelessly stupid for one thing. A man who was content to spend his life pulling a cord up and down, to and fro, through a hole in the wall, wouldn't be of much use for conspiratorial purposes.

What about the *pattiwallahs*?

Probably all quite reliable, quite loyal to him personally, if not to such an abstraction as the British Raj.

That was the thing in India, of course. Personal Government. And more harm had been done to India and the Indian peasant by turning the Collector from a personal, paternal and visible ruler into a glorified clerk, than had any foolish politicians at Home or the seditionists themselves. The Personal Ruler. The rule of the man whom they could see, whom they could approach and speak to, was what the Indian wanted and needed; not rule by paper and print; by section and code; by proclamation, promulgation, and Orders in Council—administered by the Babu.

It was a just and accurate statement that the Indian peasant—and India is ninety-nine per cent peasant—loathes, fears, and despises the Babu, the petty official of his own colour; and respects, admires and likes the British administrator, his official "father and mother" and Protector of the Poor. And the more the peasant sees of the British official, the better he likes him.

Personal contact; personal administration; personal interest; personal justice; and especially personal appeal—as it ever was in the East, from the days when the King sat in judgment in the city gate.

What was that?

Someone on the roof? . . . A monkey, of course. . . .

Really, he must keep better control of his nerves.

Those two hair-breadth escapes in Midnabad had shaken him up. That and having poor Felice's brains spattered over him.

That and Jenny's lapses. . . . Was she getting worse —and jealous as well?

It had been an accusing glare that she had given him that evening when, after looking at Betty Gopaldas he had glanced at her, and she had caught his eye. Could she have known what he was thinking? Rather an absurd thing to imagine. But then, women were undoubtedly marvellously intuitive. No, of course she couldn't have known what he was thinking, but although he had been most careful never to betray himself, she might instinctively and intuitively know what he thought of Betty. And how much, how often, he thought of her.

That was quite possible. She might very well have guessed—to call it guessing, which it could not be, but sheer intuition—that he had fallen in love with the child, that the greatest pleasure he had in life was to get a glimpse of her, a word with her, a rare occasional dance or a ride with her, and that it was almost as great a pleasure merely to close his eyes and think about her.

Yes, he had suddenly realized, with a kind of guilty shock, that she knew; that she had found him out.

In that one glance she had told him; accused him.

On the other hand, of what could she accuse him? Whatever Jenny might know, Betty knew nothing; and it would probably come as the greatest possible surprise to her, if she were informed that Lawrence Herdie, Collector of Bhawalgarh, had ever given a second thought to her.

Of what could Jenny accuse him? It wasn't as though he'd philandered; played the amorous fool; sought the girl in any way. It wasn't as though he'd been ass enough to ask his wife to invite her to the house; or praised her; or talked about her. He had never mentioned her name.

But what a mountain Jenny would make out of a mole-hill or, rather, make on a bare arid spot where there was not so much as a grain of dust.

There was nothing.

And there was everything; for he was hopelessly, desperately, incurably in love with Betty Gopaldas. His wife knew it.

And of course she'd express it in her own terms of love. She would accuse him. And in no measured language.

It was amazing. How infinitely greater are the things of the spirit than the things that are concrete. He had never been alone with Betty Gopaldas, save once, when he had overtaken her on the way home from a morning ride, and their brief conversation, on that occasion, had been solely confined to the subject of horses. He had danced with her five times; never sat out with her once. He had seen her thirteen times at Commissioner's House, at meetings of the Literary Society, and he had seen her in church seventeen times. And he was in love with her.

This evening he had watched her sweet, sad, pensive, beautiful flower-like face, and had forgotten himself. Forgotten where he was; forgotten what his life was; had lost himself in her and in thoughts of her; had then unconsciously, mechanically, as it were, glanced at Jenny whom he was subconsciously contrasting with her—and, in a flash, he had known that Jenny knew.

Without a word spoken, he had, as it were, made love to Betty, admitted to himself that he was in love with her, that the greatest thing in all the world had happened to him; had been angrily accused by his wife of making love to another woman; of being in love with another woman; and had miserably confessed it. All without a spoken word.

And when words were spoken, should he confess it?

No, most certainly not. There was nothing to confess. Surely he could look at the child and take an interest in her? Not only had he never said a word to her that all the world was not welcome to hear, but he had scarcely spoken to her at all. He had never, never once, great as the temptation had been, made any effort to see her; never gone out of his way, or put himself in her way, in order to meet her. So what was there to confess?

Everything.

After all, a man has a right to some reticences, some reservations, some decent privacy of thought, some individual inner life of his own.

Besides, "confession" really implies wrong-doing, and he had done nothing wrong. He had not had the slightest wish to fall in love with Betty Gopaldas. He had not *risked* doing so, as it were. He had not deliberately singed his wings, so to speak, by emulating the foolish moth that flutters around the light. Nothing of the sort. He had seen her at Commissioner's House; Ramrao had proudly introduced him to her; and while her hand was in his, his eyes on hers, it had happened. As suddenly as that.

For the rest of the evening he had kept on glancing in her direction, wondering how on earth so terrible a thing could have come to pass as the inveiglement of that lovely English girl into that native household, presided over by the notorious and sinister "Maharani," as they called old Subhadra Gopaldas. It had seemed a wicked thing to him, and the more he had thought of it, the wickeder it had seemed.

He had spoken to her again after the meeting, and had gone home aware that something had happened to him; that he was a different man; Bhawalgarh a different place; life a different thing. He had lain awake most of the night, thinking of this girl, wondering, scarcely realizing, amazed at himself, almost happy—he who seemed to have forgotten what happiness was and that there was any such thing as happiness. And there was not a soul on earth nor a Recording Angel in Heaven who could accuse him, blame him, for any thought, idea, or intention that was in his mind.

Good God, what was *that*?

Definitely a "click" just outside the window in the

443

side wall.

Herdie sprang to his feet, whirling round as he did so.

The shutters he had closed were slowly opening. What fool had made them to fasten by a small bolt on the outside? When he had shut them the perpendicular bolt must have fallen down into the hole, and the "click" that he had just heard had been made by someone lifting the bolt.

Now what?

Yes, the shutters were opening slowly. Not merely opening, but being opened. If a sudden breeze, or rather blast of hot air, had sprung up and they had been blown open, they would not have moved as slowly, gradually and steadily as this. Nor could a breeze raise the bolt.

Had he been wise in his decision against keeping a revolver handy?

Yes. If they were going to get him, they'd get him, sooner or later; and it was not for the Chief Magistrate of the District to set the example of taking the Law into one's own hands.

Ordinary self-defence?

Yes, but the Law was the proper defence. The sure shield of the Law. Besides, the villager wasn't allowed to keep arms for his own defence against dacoits. When he pleaded to be permitted to do so, he was told that the Law would defend him. Well, the Law must defend the Collector too—after the event.

Another second passed.

Good God, he'd shout in a moment, if the shutters didn't open more quickly.

Thrusting his chair aside and striding to the window, Herdie seized the shutters and flung them back, to be confronted by the vacuous grinning face of the *punkah-wallah*.

"What are you doing?" he growled in Hindustani.

Stepping back and salaaming humbly, the *punkah-wallah* abased himself, body and soul. He was only looking to see whether the *Huzoor* had gone away.

"I'll tell you when I go away," said Herdie.

Confound the fool—frightening him like that!

Frightening him? Was he frightened? Yes, he was. Thoroughly frightened.

He only hoped he'd meet it calmly when it came: behave coolly and decently. . . .

He returned to his desk.

One mustn't carry weapons.

No self-defence. He must do his job and take what came. And he must get his nerves in better order; keep a tighter hold on them.

What was it they had scrawled above Jenny's bed, on the whitewashed bedroom-wall?

"*You think your husband an angel. We are going to make him one.*"

She thought him an angel, eh?

Herdie laughed again; and again the laugh did not sound mirthful. And he had supposed that there had not been a terrorist organization here—until those wretched letters had come. Why on earth was he, after all his experience of India, taking any notice of anonymous letters? . . . "Terrific explosion . . . somewhere, someday—that will blow you to atoms." Probably the brilliant "joke" of some young devil of a student. No. It wasn't a student who had composed those remarkable documents. Anyhow, they had been posted from Midnabad, and there were no signs of any genuine terrorists here in Bhawalgarh, no branch of the Brethren of India. Silly of him to take any notice—and a remarkable thing that he had given them a second thought. He had, though—a good many second thoughts.

Really rather rough luck, in a way. For he had all the trouble he needed, inside the house. Quite as much as was good for him. Trouble at home is bad enough, turning the fruits of life to dust and ashes in the mouth, even when a man could escape to his work and do that in peace and quiet; but when trouble lay thick and heavy on both sides of his front door . . . Well, well, this wasn't work.

A quarter of an hour passed.

Anon, Herdie laid down his pen, straightened himself in his chair and listened.

What was that?

There *was* someone moving about. Someone in the next room.

The butler must have cleared off long ago to his house at the bottom of the compound. He had heard him bolting the verandah doors, and then locking the french windows that opened on to the verandah. Yes, he distinctly remembered hearing him shut and lock the door of the dispense-*khana* behind the dining-room, the only door that led out on to the back verandah.

Quietly going to the door in the long side of the room, the door that led into the drawing-room, he threw it open, and drew back, a look of patent anxiety and alarm upon his face, a smothered exclamation of anger on his lips, as he beheld his wife in nightdress and dressing-gown swaying toward him, a lighted candle shaking in her trembling hand. An odour of whisky assailed him as, angrily thrusting her face close to his, she said,

"Will you come to bed at once! How much longer'm I going to lie awake up there?"

"I'm sorry, my dear. I thought you were asleep."

"Thought nothing about it. You didn't think anything about me at all. You never do. I say you never do. I say you never do think about me, at all. But I know who you *do* think about! Yes—I know. And I won't stand it. I won't have it. I'll leave you. I'll leave you to-night."

"Not to-night, my dear. It's so frightfully late."

"And whose fault is that? I say, whose fault is that?"

"Well, I'm coming now, dear. Now, at once."

"Well, I'm not. I've come down. Now I'll stay down. I'll stay down here all night. You can go upstairs if you want to."

He ought to have gone straight up to bed when they came in; but the papers in the *Very Urgent* dispatch-box simply had to be done, had to be posted to-morrow, without fail.

"You are spilling the candle-grease on your dressing-gown."

"Good job, too. Are you coming up to bed, I said."

"At once, my dear."

And turning out the reading-lamp that stood on his desk, he turned to extinguish the bracket-lamp that hung on the wall. If she refused to go upstairs he'd blow the candle out. She wouldn't stay there in the dark.

Good. She was going. She'd set fire to the bungalow or to herself, one of these days.

Arrived in the big bare bedroom in which were the two widely separated beds, Mrs. Herdie blew out the candle, threw off her dressing-gown, and got into bed. No sooner had her husband tucked in the mosquito-curtain all round, than she raised it and got out again, went over to a table and, with shaking hand, poured out a stiff peg of whisky, added a little soda, drank the mixture, and returned to bed.

Just as well, perhaps. She'd go to sleep soon, or at any rate, after another one. There might be a *mauvais quart d'heure* for him before the next, though. Would a strong man, a man like Steele, have managed her better?

Would he not only have prohibited, but prevented her from drinking?

How could he? If a woman intended to drink she would do so; and no-one could stop her, save by some such drastic step as incarceration. Not even Steele.

Was he, Lawrence Herdie, a weak man? Was he doing, deliberately and intentionally, a diabolically wicked thing in leaving the whisky decanter there now, not only in the knowledge but in the hope that she would soon take another strong peg, fall into a drunken sleep, and leave him at peace; give him a chance to get some sleep himself?

He was very, very tired. Work was endless and overwhelming, and his nerves were in bad shape.

What would happen if he did take the decanter away; hide it, or lock it up; and refuse to let her have any more?

She'd get violent, scream the roof off, scream the place down, as she expressed it.

A nice thing, prolonged and hideous screams coming from the Collector's house in the middle of the night. She had him there—and she knew it. She'd got him beaten. She knew that he couldn't stand it; that he could bear neither the terrible screams themselves nor the hideous fear of scandal; of people coming to see what was happening; to see who was being murdered; to rescue the Collector's wife whom obviously the Collector was beating to death.

Supposing the servants or someone—Steele, for example—came, in response to those dreadful screams, and found Mrs. Herdie raving drunk.

She'd turn maudlin drunk if it were Steele who came.

No, he simply had not the courage to take the whisky away from her now. And how could he do it regularly—or, rather, permanently? How could he give orders at the Gymkhana that Mrs. Herdie was not to be served with whisky and soda when she ordered it? A dreadful thing. Unthinkable.

How could he tell the butler not to bring whisky and soda when his mistress ordered it?

When he had first noticed a tendency toward a slight over-indulgence, he had remonstrated laughingly, playfully, jokingly, and she had immediately taken the greatest offence; immediately increased the amount that she drank. She had asked him whether he imagined that he kept a harem wherein his lightest whim was absolute law. Most certainly she would drink what she liked, when she liked, and where she liked.

He had done far more harm than good by his well-intentioned interference and remonstrance. No, it had hardly been that. It had been nothing more than jesting comment.

And after that, he had done nothing in the matter except become rigidly teetotal himself. And this again had seemed to add fuel to the flames. She had accused him of insulting her by pointedly demanding barley-water at tiffin and dinner and at bedtime, instead of the whisky to which he had been accustomed; had called him pompous prig, fool and cad.

All he had intended had been to minimize the number of occasions, opportunities, and excuses for the appearance of the whisky decanter. And she had been quite wrong when she had remarked,

"Setting the poor fallen woman an example, I suppose?"

Thank God that, so far, no-one knew anything about it but himself; though the butler must think that one of them was a pretty good performer on the bottle, at bedtime.

Thank God that, so far, there had been no sign of excess at the Gymkhana, at their own dinner-table, or when dining out. But it was bound to come. It was inevitable. Her *ayah* was bound to find her intoxicated one night, sooner or later. Suppose the woman came now, for example. Something might cause her to come back one night—something she had forgotten to do in the bedroom. And there is no gossip like an *ayah*. Yes, one of the servants, the *ayah* or the butler or the *hamal* would get to know sooner or later, inevitably.

And then what?

The head of the District, with a drunken wife. He'd have to resign when it became a public scandal. But how could he resign and start life afresh at his age?

Before long there would be not only this worry, anxiety and misery, there would be whispers, public scenes, exposure, scandal and then—just ruin. He'd have to go. Farewell to dreams of becoming Commissioner, Member of Council, and a K.C.I.E.

Well, he mustn't sit in judgment on her, poor soul. The new psychology said that that sort of thing was— psychological; that the drunkard was not an offender, but a victim, in the grip of the unconscious; that it was a mental illness, and not a vice.

What had caused the—illness—in her case? It wasn't just a matter of thirst induced by the appalling heat. The other women felt the heat just as much, and quenched their thirst with lemon squash, barley-water, that sort of thing.

Was it a form of outlet, anti-repression, self-expression or, rather, a craving for self-expression induced by lack of any other means? Doubtless it would have been different if there had been children. Different if she'd had some interest in life, some mental occupation, some hobby, something to do. Occupation is salvation.

Of course, some women busied themselves about all sorts of outside things.

Rowena Cornwallis did, for example. Made her life quite busy with good works, useful causes, philanthropic schemes, various branches of study. Dear old Rowena, with her Indian Widows, Child Marriage, Improvement of the lot of the Untouchables, Slum Dispensaries, Motherhood Teaching, Vaccination, Inoculation, Baby-lore, Snakebite Cures, Quinine for Malaria, Eurasian Girls' Sewing-class, Literary Society —all sorts of things.

So did Elizabeth Sherdley. Always busying herself about something—getting up affairs at the Gymkhana; committees for concerts, fancy-dress balls, moonlight picnics, special dances, mounted paper-chases, pony gymkhanas, *pāgŏl* races, all sorts of things—quite a full and active life.

But nothing seemed to appeal to poor Jenny. She never read anything at all; was not musical; did not play cards; found it too hot for tennis and golf; in fact, seemed to find nothing whatsoever in the way of work or play that interested her in the slightest degree. Nothing, except dancing, and then only if Steele were present. Heavens above, if only there were a dance every night and Steele were present at each one and danced every dance with her! He himself could get on with his work in quiet then.

Was she in love with Steele? Most certainly she was not in love with her husband. Probably never had been. And had only married him to get away from a narrow home and stuffy family, and go to wonderful India and a spacious life.

In the hot weather. What was that about it?

"Oh who will trust the temper of friends or the

new piano's tune;
Oh who will trust the love of his wife at the end
of an Indian June?"

Was that it? Wonderful Bhawalgarh! A hell upon earth. Spacious life! Sitting in a hermetically-sealed bungalow all day long.

Well, thank Heaven for Steele. A pity he couldn't come to dinner every day in the week, and tiffin too. Pity he couldn't come and live in the house.

Yes, Lawrence Herdie, Collector of Bhawalgarh, was a weak-fibred creature, unable to keep his wife from drinking; a creature without the pluck to make a fight of it, win the battle once and for all, and put an end to it. Weak and tottering. Actually glad the decanter was over there, and wishing his wife would go and take the final drink that would send her into drunken slumber.

And what was worse, wishing that another man would fall in love with her and take her off her husband's hands. Perhaps not exactly a wish, but a base and beastly thought, anyhow.

Was she in love with Steele? She was for ever talking about him, quoting him, and comparing him with her husband, to the latter's detriment; always inviting him to the house, making plans to meet him, reserving dances for him, meeting him when out riding.

And Steele? He certainly didn't seem very oncoming. Generally had some excuse for not doing what she proposed. At least, it seemed so to him, but that might be eye-wash. Steele might be as much in love with her as she with Steele. Undeniably she was an extremely pretty woman and could be most charming when she wished; delightful; fascinating.

But Anthony Steele had neither time nor inclination for that sort of thing. Quite right, too. Nevertheless, the more he saw of her the better; both for her and for Lawrence Herdie. No harm, surely, in his wishing her to have the conversation and companionship that she most enjoyed?

Perhaps if she were really in love with Steele, and Steele used the immeasurably powerful influence of

451

love, in the right direction, he might do what her husband had so miserably failed to do, might persuade her to forswear whisky. But before that could happen, it would have to be patent to Steele. It would mean that she was drinking so much that it had become noticeable.

Or could he approach Steele on the subject?

Another foul idea. Disgusting. Of course he couldn't. How could he go up to any man—least of all Steele—and say,

"Look here, my wife's a drunkard. I can't cure her. Perhaps you can."

If Steele were in love with her, he'd feel like knocking down the man who had called her a drunkard. Probably do so, too. And if Steele were not in love with her, what had Steele to do with the matter?

Either way, it would be humiliating beyond expression. It had been a beastly thought, and he ought to be ashamed of himself.

But he was at the end of his tether. He . . .

"Yes, you can lie there sleeping like a log while I lie awake, can't you? Wake up, will you?"

Herdie started, almost like a frightened child that hears suddenly an angry hated voice, or a slave that hears the crack of the whip.

"Why should you sleep when I can't? Why should you bring me to this filthy country and then go to sleep while I lie awake? Answer when you are spoken to, will you? I know perfectly well that you are only shamming sleep. Answer me, will you?"

The thick, monotonous voice rose almost to a shout.

"Answer me, you sulky brute. I'll scream the roof off, I'll scream the house down, if you don't answer me."

"What is it, Jenny? Anything the matter?"

"Yes, anything is the matter. Everything's the matter. Leaving me alone the whole day long and best part of the night, too. Leaving me lying frightened here, and you sitting reading down in that office; reading and drinking and smoking, while I lie here frightened.

Afraid to turn the lamp higher, for fear of what I shall see. Afraid to turn the lamp out, for fear of what I . . . what I . . . shan' see. D'you hear? And I won't be neglected, I tell you. And another thi'g. Why did you tell Tony Steele not to come to dinner to-morrow? Answer me, d'you hear? Answer me, before I scream the roof off. I'll scream, I tell you."

Lawrence Herdie bit back the words that came to his lips,

"Scream, then! Scream your head off. Scream and be damned to you."

He had never used words of that sort to a woman in his life, and was not going to begin with his wife; partly because it was wholly foreign to his nature, and partly because he was afraid. On one occasion when he had made no reply whatever, had given way to a dumb devil of angry indignation and injured pride, she had screamed; screamed with all the strength of her lungs and the violence of her drunken temper; had rushed out on to the verandah, flung open a lattice window, and screamed out into the night.

Tortured, horrified, agonized, terrified by fear of the result, the scandal and disgrace, he had rushed after her, clapped his hand across her mouth, dragged her back to the bed, and fought to prevent her from publishing her shame and his disgrace. A hideous struggle had resulted, a struggle ending with her sudden collapse, and only then had he, with bleeding bitten hands and torn clothing, staggered back to his own bed and flung himself down, with thoughts of murder and of suicide seething in his outraged heart.

He couldn't go through that again. The beaten dog must wag its tail.

"What is it, my dear? I didn't tell Steele not to come to dinner. I didn't even speak to him."

"No, you didn't even speak to him. You did your utmost to show him tha' you don' like him, don' want him to come to the house; and tha' you are jealous of him. You are jealous of him, and you know it. You are jealous of a better man than yourself. A ten times better man. Tha's why you're jealous, isn't it? Ans' me.

Ans' me, will you?"

"I'm not jealous of Steele, my dear."

An ugly laugh.

"Oh, you aren't, aren't you? Well, you've every reason to be. Le' me tell you that. And I love Tony's little finger better than your whole body, mind and soul. Do you hear me? I love Tony and I am going to him. I'm going to him—do you hear me?"

Again Herdie refrained from shouting,

"For God's sake go! And never come back."

This was whisky talking, not his wife, the woman whom he had loved. It was the whisky talking, not Jenny; and the fault was his. If he'd been a stronger man, of finer character, he could have prevented it, if only by keeping her love, a love to which he could have appealed successfully.

No, if he had kept her love, there never would have been the slightest need for such appeal. The fault was his and he must pay for it.

"I tell you he is coming to dinner to-morrow. Or the next day. Or the day after. He's coming to dinner jus' as often as I like. And I will ask him whether you told him not to come."

"I assure you I didn't, my dear."

"You assure me! Who are you to assure anybody? I don't believe a word you say. You are a liar. And I'll tell you another thing. You're in love with that Gopaldas girl, and it's no good your denying it. I saw you, to-night, leering at her, eyeing her and licking your lips like a cat at a saucer of cream. Don't you think you can deceive me. Thought you could carry on behind my back, didn't you? But le' me tell you, I know all about it. I know, and other people are going to know, too. Tony for one. I'll tell him how you treat me, humiliating me like that. As if there weren't a decent woman in the Station, if you *must* go tom-catting about the place at your age. But a woman like that! Why didn't you take up with an *ayah* while you were about it? A beastly woman like that! A woman who could marry a native and go and live in the bazaar with him! What *could* such a creature be like? Would any decent woman do it? And would any decent white man have anything to do with her? No. I'll speak to Mrs. Cornwallis about it to-morrow; and there's one of the places you won't find her any more. Not at Commissioner's House. I'll have you watched, too. I'll have her house watched. I'll see where you go. I'll find out where you meet her when you go riding in the early morning. And I'll tell that wretched Ramrao man to keep . . . to keep . . ."

The voice trailed off into silence.

Soon stertorous breathing took its place.

Thank God she was asleep. No longer any need to watch.

Gently, slowly, as quietly as possible, he turned over on to his right side, his back to the room and to her. Now for peace, quiet, and blessed sleep.

A gurgling snore and a sharp movement in the bed at the other side of the room.

"And if ever you say a word to Tony against me— you will regret it," began the thick, heavy, horrible voice again. "You'll regret it all the rest of your life. Here. Look here. Have you ever told him anything about me? Answer me, will you?"

"No, Jenny. I have never told Steele anything about you."

"Nothing in my favour, eh?" An unpleasant laugh. "Answer me, will you?"

"I have never discussed you with Steele."

"You've never told him that I drank too much?"

"No, I have not."

"Do I drink too much? Answer me, will you? Do I drink too much?"

What should he say? To accuse her might raise the devil himself in her, start a tornado of shrieking that . . . No, he couldn't bear it.

"Answer me, I say."

"No, of course not."

"Well, you're a liar, then. I do, and I'm going to have some more—now."

And, tearing at the mosquito-curtain, Mrs. Herdie arose from her bed. Lurching and stumbling, she crossed the room, fumblingly took the stopper from the whisky decanter, dropped it on the floor, poured out some whisky, drank it neat, staggered back to her bed and fell asleep.

As soon as the heavy breathing was regular and steady, Lawrence Herdie crept across to his wife's bed, saw that her head was on the pillow, tucked the mosquito-net in, turned down the lamp, and retired to rest.

§6

Meanwhile, the Reverend Dr. Byam J. Torrens, Principal of the Bhawalgarh American Mission College, accompanied by his nephew, Mr. Sewell E. Lee, drove home from Commissioner's House to his bungalow, adjacent to the College buildings on the outskirts of the city, in Dr. Torrens' famous *ghari* drawn by Dr. Torrens' famous roan horse, Petra.

> *A rose-red*
> *Quadru-ped*
> *Half as old as Time,*

according to the wags of the Bhawalgarh Gymkhana, who had impudently taken it upon them to christen the enduring animal.

Further, according to these wags, Petra was never unharnessed, living his days and nights entirely in the *ghari*, or, rather, between the shafts thereof, as his unharnessing would be, in a double sense, his undoing.

Doctor Torrens was wont stoutly to deny this allegation, though, on being asked as to whether he had ever seen Petra out of the shafts, he had, with some confusion, perforce to confess that he had not.

The claim of the *ghari* to fame was similar to that of Petra in the matter of shape, antiquity, and colour; but greater, in that to these it added outstanding perform-ance. It did things. It shed its wheels at odd times. It rose and fell, with the motion of a small and storm-tossed boat upon the angry waters, owing to the fact of a certain ovalness, an ellipticality, of its two hind wheels. It was an unmusical-box whose approach was heralded by curious chords, a deep diapason of groans, above which played elfin squeaks and shrieks. It dropped a lamp upon occasion and, much more disconcerting, it dropped its floor boards.

Once, the entire floor gave way as the doctor rose to tap the syce with the handle of his umbrella, his invariable method of communicating with him. Fortunately Dr. Torrens landed upon his feet. Seizing the rail of the driver's seat with his left hand, he smote him heavily between the shoulders. The man, being deaf and accustomed to this form of notification that the doctor desired an acceleration of his speed, promptly passed the blow on to Petra. And the harder and faster Dr. Torrens beat the syce, the harder and faster did the syce beat Petra. Indeed, Petra broke from a trot into a canter, and from a canter into a gallop, and, even as the doctor conveyed intimations of speed through the syce to Petra, so did Petra convey actualities of speed through Petra to the doctor. A very vicious circle. Fortunate it was that the doctor, unlike Petra, was not quite half as old as Time, and that his endurance outlasted the staying powers of his faithful horse. Having given of his best, Petra came at length to a stand-still, and Dr. Torrens got out, or, perhaps, further out, of the *ghari*. Since that occasion the doctor had refrained from standing upon the floor of the carriage and had advised fellow-travellers therein to imitate his example. . . .

"Say; you didn't fall for that lad, Uncle?" observed Mr. Sewell E. Lee as, with care and caution, he removed his feet from the floor of the *ghari* and placed them on the opposite seat.

"Which one, Son?" enquired the doctor.

"Why, the convert."

"Not heavily," replied the missionary.

"I'll say I'd like to have the handling of a lecture-tour by him, through the States. Wouldn't the intellectual dames crowd around and sit at his feet! Dolled-up like that and saying his stuff in the drawing-rooms! Wonder if I could fix . . ."

"Fix nothing, Sewell. If he's genuine, there's no need for him to go to America and preach to the converted. Let him spread the light among his own people. A Mission to the Untouchables, right here, for example. There'd be a better job for him than a Mission to the Too-touchables in New York and Chicago. And if he's not genuine, let him alone. You'd soil your hands foisting a fraud on to a lot of foolish folk ever seeking a new sign, pursuing a new thing, and erecting altars to any old Unknown God."

"I'll do an article on him, anyhow. A rouser. It would read well. The only Brahmin convert to Christianity. Could I get a formal interview with him there at the White House if I sent in a card to her ladyship?"

"No doubt you could, Son. But he's not India. Whether he is a faker or a *faquir*, he's not real India. If he's a humbug you can get that sort in fortune-telling parlours in New York, Paris, and London. And if he's real and honest, he still isn't India. He's an Eastern-Western hybrid."

"Well, he's a Product anyway. Produced right here in India. . . . How did you re-act to that gaol-delivery yarn; and the crib on Saint Paul in the Street called Strait of Damascus?"

"I suspend judgment, Son."

"Yes, but how did you re-act, Uncle?"

"Well, I'll say my skin went goosey, my blood ran cold, and my hair tried to stand on end. Just for a second. Seemed to."

"Sure. So did mine. But I certainly would like a talk with Mr. Sant Arjun Rama. And I think I'll do an interview. Put him in my gallery."

"Not going to be a Rogue's Gallery, is it, Son?"

Mr. Sewell E. Lee laughed.

"Well, the Swami Dayanand is going to be there, I hope. Is he a rogue?"

It was the doctor's turn to laugh.

"By Eastern standards or Western?" he asked. "You've got to bear in mind that there are things done here in India, with the best of intentions, under the compulsion of the highest promptings, with the noblest motives and the most unselfish objects, which, according to Western ideas, are pure sheer crime, police-court business, gaol jobs, hanging matters."

"'*The crimes of Clapham chaste in Martaban*,' eh?" said Lee.

Mr. Sewell E. Lee of Boston, Massachusetts, was a tourist with a difference; a visitor with an object; a bird of passage with the power and inclination to settle and look around with bright observant eye.

A born journalist and a trained reporter, clear-eyed, hard-headed, ambitious, he had conceived the idea of combining good business with great pleasure; of really seeing India, a country that had fascinated him from childhood, and of letting India pay him for his pleasure. A man of personal and professional conscience with which he would not palter, he intended to see India as actually it is, to see it both extensively and intensively, to travel its length and breadth from Simla to Ceylon, from Calcutta to Peshawar. And having seen everything that India has to show the cold-weather visitor, the second part of his programme was to exchange the field-glasses for the microscope. Having seen India in large, to see her in little; to live, move, and have his being in one place, as an inhabitant thereof; to study the microcosm with all his senses— and then to tell the truth, the whole truth, and nothing but the truth.

Innumerable visitors, he realized, had told their truth about India. His aim, object and ambition was to tell *the* truth. The outcome of his visit should be, in the first place, a series of articles to his great newspaper; articles which should be statements of fact unvarnished, unadorned, and uninterpreted; should be, in the second place, a book in which he would endeavour to interpret India to America and to the English-speaking world—a blunt, outspoken, truthful book, in which he would give data and conclusions without fear or favour. He would hold no brief for the white man or the brown; for the British Government or the Indian Congress; for Western civilization or Eastern; for

Christianity, Hinduism or Mahommedanism.

And not only would he see the whole of India by train, by car and by aeroplane, on foot, on horse and on camel; not only would he live, for at least six months, in one place, but he would do what so lamentably few visitors to India do, he would stay through the hot weather and spend that hot weather in the Plains.

And if he could not learn in a year all that he needed to learn, he would take two years. Nor would he imagine, at the end of a year or even two years, that he knew India—for probably no white man knew India; no, not after thirty years of serving her. But the opinions of a man, trained, equipped and devoted; unbiased, unprejudiced and receptive, who had spent his days and his nights in study and investigation of the real India, should be worth hearing, should carry some weight, and deserve some attention.

And he had chosen Bhawalgarh as the scene of his intensive course of study, by reason of the fact that his uncle, the Reverend Dr. Byam J. Torrens, resided there, and had given him warm invitation so to do.

"Any answer from the Swami, Uncle?" he enquired.

"Yes. We are to drive out on Saturday morning to a village called Belgad and walk a piece into the jungle there, to an old temple. He'll be around and will give you an interview."

"What is he, exactly?" asked Lee.

"I don't know," replied the Reverend Dr. Torrens. "I know what he was. Some of the things, anyhow. He was Dewan of Almera State."

"What is a dee-wan really?"

"Wazir. Grand Vizier. Prime Minister. The power behind the throne. The big noise. He has also been a Professor of Philosophy and of Mental and Moral Science; a lecturer, listened to with respect by learned Societies in Europe; he has written books on Metaphysics and Philosophy which are a bit over my head; and he has some of the best degrees that Europe and India can confer on a scholar."

"And now he's a *faquir*, eh?"

"A *sannyasi*, a *swami*, an itinerant mendicant Holy

Man. No home, no clothes, no property, no visible means of support."

"What does he live on?"

"Bananas, rice; any old food that anybody gives him."

"Supposing nobody gives him any?"

"No need to suppose that. Somebody will always feed a Holy Man."

"How does he get on for the other things that he wants?"

"By not wanting them. By reducing his requirements literally to just sufficient food to keep him in health. And I'll say that is mighty little."

"And he has been Prime Minister of a great State; with a fine house and a large salary?"

"Yes. And could be again if he wanted to."

"It's a thing that baffles the Western mind, isn't it?" mused Lee. "Try to imagine a big politician at home, the Governor of a State, walking out on his job and his family, and turning hobo, hitting the main-stem, bumming his way, living on hand-outs, and sleeping beside the track."

"Yes. I can't imagine a Bank President, a Bishop, or a Tammany Boss doing it, can you, Son?"

"I suppose that when a man like this Swami goes from Prime Minister to hobo, voluntarily, and without a thing against him, he's just naturally through with pomps and vanities—because he's had a bellyful. He has just gone clean through and come out the other side. Finds it's all dust and ashes."

"Yes," agreed Dr. Torrens. "Perhaps that is why he goes and sits in the dust, and rubs ashes on his body."

"I'll certainly be glad to interview him. He must be a regular fellow."

"He'll interest you all-right, Son."

"Does he pull this *yoga* bunk?"

"He's got a wonderful reputation. And some of the queerest stories about him seem to be authentic. I am in pretty close touch with all manner of men, from big-wig Officials to my College students; from Indian High Court Judges, Indian District Officers, Indian doctors, solicitors, barristers, and such enlightened people, to the villagers, absolutely illiterate peasants, sunk full fathom deep in blackest superstition and crassest ignorance. And in all ranks and classes, castes and creeds, I find people who firmly believe in the Swami Dayanand and his amazing powers."

"Do you believe in him yourself, Uncle?"

"In his knowledge and ability, yes. He's a far more learned, far more able man, than I am. I take off my hat to him. But as to 'powers,' I don't know. I reserve judgment. Also as to his morality and character."

"Is he vain?"

"All Indians are vain.

"Like Europeans," he added, smiling. "Yes, the Swami is certainly susceptible to flattery."

"Would he swallow it whole if I told him I had come all the way from America to see what he could do, and therefore expected him to do something worthy of the occasion?"

"He would not. Don't try any tricks with the Swami Dayanand. I don't think the man has yet been born who will get the better of him along those lines. If you want a really useful interview, go in a spirit of respectful humility.

"Not that you will deceive him, even then," added the doctor, "but it will be the best line of approach, believe me."

"Will it have any effect if I tell him that the interview is going to appear in one of the most widely circulated papers in the States, and be syndicated too, and read by anything up to ten million people in America alone?"

"Yes. I certainly think it would. Better way to touch his vanity than telling him a lie about having come here on purpose to interview him, anyhow."

"Honesty the best policy, as usual," smiled Lee.

"I'll certainly look forward to Saturday morning," he continued. "It ought to be some interview. And I think I will get one with Mrs. Commissioner's near-Saint, too. He's very interesting; and I don't know whether he'd be more interesting as a fraud or as the goods. Wonderful hokum and boloney the one way—and truly wonderful courage, faith and endurance the other."

"Truly wonderful," agreed Dr. Torrens.

"That cop didn't seem to fall for him," observed Lee.

"Steele, the District Superintendent of Police? No. I don't think he suspended judgment at all. Sat in judgment, rather. He's a young man who makes up his mind quickly."

"Good policeman?"

"Wonderful. Excellent. I've the greatest admiration for Steele. Most efficient at his job; and a charming man to know."

"Good poker face."

"Fine. They call him Cold Steele here. Always the same; and just the same to everybody, high and low. Never hot or bothered. Cool as a cucumber."

"Who's the dame he was talking to? The one who drove off with that native?"

"Mrs. Gopaldas. Betty Gopaldas. Married to Ramrao Gopaldas, poor girl."

"Regular peach. You'd have thought a beautiful girl like that could have done better for herself than to marry an Indian and come and live in the bazaar out here. About twenty million men in England, aren't there?"

"Dreadful tragedy. I did hear from somebody—Mrs. Cornwallis, I think—that her father is a cranky parson with great ideas on the brotherhood of man; black brothers, brown brothers, yellow brothers; all equal in the sight of God.

"Which of course they are," added Dr. Torrens.

"Pity the old man couldn't have demonstrated by marrying an Australian aborigine *gin* instead of letting his daughter show forth his faith and works for him," growled Lee.

"Yes. Whatever the theory may be, the practice must surely be terrible. India is no garden of Eden for the ordinary white woman married to a good fellow of her own class and kind. But in a case like that! It doesn't bear thinking of."

"No, it doesn't," agreed Lee warmly.

"I like the look of that big bug you introduced me

to. What's his name—the Collector, don't you call him?" he continued.

"Herdie? Yes. Collector is the old name, that has come down from the days of John Company, for the Head of the District, the ruler and Chief Magistrate. He governs and administers a District that may be hundreds of square miles in extent; and he's plain Providence to the people."

"Good men, aren't they, these Indian Civil Service officials?"

"None better. As a class they stand for justice, fairness, and devotion. And Lawrence Herdie is one of the best of a magnificent Service. He's a *pukka sahib*."

"That term is getting a bit fly-blown, isn't it?"

"I'm sure I hope not. I should hardly like to think it was. It will be rather a bad day for the world when the appellation and what it stands for are—'fly-blown.'"

"Why? What does it mean exactly?"

"Literally, '*pukka sahib*' means 'true aristocrat'; real ruler; a complete man of honour; solid, thorough and honourable gentleman—in the highest and truest meaning of that abused word. Yes, Son. When *pukka sahib* is a term of contempt, then truth, justice, fineness, honour, faith, loyalty, reliability, self-respect, morality, courage, trustworthiness, kindliness, and all such things as those, will be—contemptible.

"That'll be a bad day, won't it?" he added.

"I'll say it will," agreed Lee. "But I rather thought the *pukka sahib* now ranked among peppery comic Colonels and pompous prancing pro-Consuls."

"May-be, Son, may-be. And yet, do you know, I've never come across one of these 'comic' Colonels. The Colonels I have known in India, and I have met a hatful, weren't a bit comic. Nor peppery. I'd say a composite photograph of a gross of them would show you a quiet, self-possessed man; a very keen, competent, hard-working, professional soldier. . . . No, I wouldn't use the word 'comic' in that connection. I'd sooner say —dangerous. And the best of them become Generals, and have still harder work and more responsibility. I have known quite a few Generals and liked them as much as I've admired them. I honestly don't know where the funny idea comes from. . . . And the pro-Consuls don't prance, either. Much too tired after a heavier day's work than ever was done by the sort of man that laughs at 'em. No, I wouldn't call the job of Viceroy of India, or Governor of one of the Provinces, a job that left much time for prancing; or one likely to be held by the sort of man who'd wish to prance."

"Well, well, Uncle, we live and we learn," yawned Lee.

"We ought to, Son."

"And so Herdie is a *pukka sahib*, is he?"

"He's exactly that. He could not do a mean thing if he wanted to. He wouldn't know how. He's all that the word 'gentleman' stands for, and the best that the word 'man' stands for; and I'll say that there is nobody alive doing better work in a better way than Herdie is doing for the thousands of people whose welfare is the main concern of his life."

"Say, Uncle, you are somewhat in favour of the British Official, aren't you?"

"I? No, Son! No. I have only been watching him for half a century, and am speaking of him as I find him. . . . Here's the College."

"Will the syce be able to stop Petra?"

"He'll stop of himself, Son."

"And we shall certainly know it," opined Mr. Sewell E. Lee.

"By the cessation of sound and violence, if not of progress," he added, as he removed his feet straight from the seat to the step of the *ghari*.

II

Late the following evening, Anthony Steele, District Superintendent of Police, Bhawalgarh, sat, or rather lay, in a long chair in his verandah, his feet, on the upward-sloping leg-rests, a little higher than his head, taking his ease after an extremely tiring and, on the whole, unsatisfactory day.

Disguised as a wandering Pathan *budmash*,[37] with loose ill-wound *puggri*, dirty long shirt worn outside dirty baggy ankle-fitting breeches, the dangling end of his turban drawn across his face and hiding all but his eyes, he had loafed about the bazaars; sat, apparently drugged and sleepy, in the market-place outside toddy-sellers' shops; at the Railway-station; near the entrance to the Post and Telegraph Office; opposite the Gopaldas bungalow; and had squatted on his heels against the actual threshold of the *To-day and To-morrow* offices. He had also travelled in a crowded third-class carriage to Kotgur station, the nearest point on the line to the ancient fortress now used as head-quarters by the dacoit gang whom he intended to raid and catch red-handed or, at any rate, in possession of identifiable stolen property.

Leaving the station and swaggering through the village, the picture of a truculent ruffianly Pathan thief, horse-coper, contractor's railway-and-road labourer, sturdy beggar, gangster, tramp, burglar, and general jack-of-all trades, and those preferably criminal—with his great staff in his dyed and dirty hand, well-worn sandals on his dyed and dirty feet; disguise, kit and make-up perfect (the dress indeed inherited from just such a gentleman, hanged last month in Bhawalgarh), Steele had set off along the dusty faintly-marked bullock-track into the jungle.

And, just as he was thinking how entirely wrong

---

[37] *Ruffian; bad character.*

were the know-alls who said that no European could disguise, and pass himself off, as a native, he heard a pleasant voice greet him casually, lightly, pleasantly, with the words,

"Salaam, Steele Sahib! Whither away?"

And brought up, all standing, he had looked in the direction whence the voice had come, and seen the Swami Dayanand seated cross-legged on a black-buck skin beneath a tree.

He had growled a surly reply in Pushtu.

"Not bad, Steele Sahib, but rather 'bazaar.' I don't mean bizarre. The bazaar Pushtu of Peshawar. . . . Yes, definitely bazaar."

"What do you say, oh man? Peshawar? Yes, I come from Peshawar."

"Quite good, Steele Sahib; but you ought to go back there again and learn just a little more. You want to get the *agh* a little lower in the throat and the *ei* a trifle higher in the nose. And you want just a bit more practice with the sandals. You come down heel-first, you know. And I think, on the whole, I'd suggest a love-lock. You could easily make one and gum it on, under the *puggri*, and bring it down in front of the ear and on to the cheek. Then learn the *Dilkusha*, and sing it very, very nasally as you swagger through the bazaar. . . . Still, it's not a bad performance, on the whole."

Grunting, "Mad, mad. Afflicted of Allah," the pseudo-Pathan had spat upon the ground and swaggered on his way, followed by the mocking voice crying,

"If you are going to call on Bagu the Dacoit, I'm afraid he is out. Definitely Not at Home. I am afraid you will find the place shut up. *For Sale*, or at any rate *To Let*."

Half laughing, half cursing, Steele had given it up. It was no good.

Turning about, he had retraced his steps, seated himself opposite the Swami, and observed in English,

"Now how do you happen to know *that*, Swami-ji?"

"Well, I happen to know *that* in precisely the same way that I happen to know that Steele Sahib passed this way recently in fancy dress, probably intending to impersonate a Pathan. Bagu and Co. passed this way, too. Also in fancy dress."

"Ah! And what was their fancy dress probably intended to represent? What were they impersonating?"

"Wicked men . . ."

"Well, that wouldn't give them much trouble, would it?"

"Wicked men, I was going to say, in charge of about an equal number of police. A very good effort indeed. Highly Commended, if not First Prize."

"Police?"

"Yes. They'd gone to the trouble of procuring the real kit, you know. I fear, Steele Sahib, that they must have raided a police *thana* and denuded some of your sepoys of their honourable liveries. They had red *puggris*, neat blue uniforms with brass buttons, blue putties, everything, including Martini rifles and triangular bayonets. And the roysterers who were impersonating captive wicked men were not more convincing than the others, even though they had provided themselves with gyves and fetters and had linked themselves together in the bonds of bad fellowship with a serviceable-looking cord, even as do the Alpine mountaineers."

"And where do you suppose they were going, Swami-ji?"

"I leapt to the conclusion that they were going on a journey, Steele Sahib."

"A far journey?"

"A train journey, anyway."

"They told you that, did they?"

"Trapped, Steele Sahib!" mocked the Swami. "I am as a child in your hands. Almost you have made me betray myself as a friend and a confederate of evildoers! No, in point of fact they did not tell me anything at all."

"Then how do you know they were going by train?"

"Subtle deduction, Steele Sahib. They were going in the direction of Kotgur Railway-station. And, at the pace at which they were travelling, they would reach the station at a time some ten minutes before I heard the whistle of a train."

"Up or down?"

"As you say, Sahib. Either up or down. Not both, I feel sure."

Returning to the station as quickly as possible, he had learned—by questioning the professional loafers, the station coolies, the ticket-office babu and others who would know—that no party of police and captives had taken train from Kotgur that day, or had indeed been seen in the vicinity of the station.

He had then returned by the next train to Bhawalgarh, assured of the uselessness and futility of reconnoitring the dacoit hiding-place after being recognized by the Swami.

Nevertheless the day had not been wholly wasted. It had been worth the journey to learn that Kotgur was one of the places where the ubiquitous, itinerant, and elusive Swami was, upon occasion, to be found; and that, at any rate, he knew Bagu the Dacoit and his gang when he saw them.

Had the Swami been perhaps a little too clever, a little too pleased at spotting the Police Superintendent in disguise? Had not his vanity perhaps out-run his discretion?

Perhaps not. Vain as the Swami might be, he was far too clever a man for that. The mere fact of his squatting in the jungle between Kotgur Railway-station and the abandoned fortress, and the fact that he admitted to knowing the dacoit gang by sight, inculpated him in no way, established nothing against him.

Were he accused of knowing them, doubtless he would reply,

"Of course I know them—by sight. I know everything. I know Steele Sahib by sight, even when he is amusingly dressed up to resemble a Pathan."

And how the devil had the fellow known him?

Not only was his skin dyed to the colour of that of a Pathan; not only was he dressed in the actual clothes just as they had been taken from the body of an actual

Pathan *budmash*, but his face, all but his eyes, had been completely covered. He had been swaggering along in exactly the manner and style of a Pathan, and, moreover, in a manner and style that had deceived Pathans themselves in the bazaars, drinking-shops and bawdy-houses of Peshawar. How on earth could the fellow, sitting fifty feet away, have known it was he? . . . With his face covered, too. . . . It was uncanny. And really rather disturbing.

Was it possible that the Swami had, as he claimed, supernatural powers and occult knowledge? Occult, that is to say, so far as the European is concerned. Supernatural powers and occult knowledge? . . . Perhaps it would be more accurate to describe them as normal powers unknown to the West; and knowledge of sciences of which the West was ignorant.

Admittedly, of course, the Swami was an extremely clever man, of most exceptional knowledge; highly educated; and widely read far beyond the scope of the ordinarily well-informed person.

To think that the native who had hailed him this morning, the Indian mendicant sitting, practically naked, in the dust, equipped with only a begging bowl and a black-buck skin, was a Fellow of the Royal Society, a Double-First Balliol Prizeman, a Doctor of Philosophy of Heidelberg; and a Sanscrit, Persian and Arabic scholar, who could converse with you in English, French, German, Hindi, Pushtu, Gujerati, Marathi, Bengali and Tamil.

Little wonder if, having assimilated Western learning and philosophy to the extent that he had, he was also learned in Eastern lore, a student, and indeed a master, of sciences and arts unknown to Balliol and Heidelberg.

It was pretty certain, at any rate, that he was a thought-reader, a telepathist, of no mean order; that he was clairvoyant; that he was a most potent hypnotist; that he could do things—or profoundly impress one with his power to do things—that seemed miraculous, be the secret and solution what it might— conjuring, juggling, sleight-of-hand, legerdemain, or hypnotism.

Anyhow, the ignorant firmly believed that he had the power of raising the dead, or if not of raising the dead, at any rate of restoring life to the very recently deceased. There were attested tales of how he had been called in to heal, cure, or even resuscitate peasants, workers in field and jungle, who had been stricken with illness, met with serious accidents, or been bitten by poisonous snakes. Tales of how he had brought children back to life and restored them to their distraught mothers; of how men, swept away and drowned when fording rivers, had been made to breathe again, and had gone on their way rejoicing; all sorts of amazing and apparently well-authenticated tales of his miraculous supernatural powers.

Well, be that as it might, he had certainly made the District Superintendent of Police look silly that day; pricked the bubble of his conceit and vanity very suddenly; done what, in its small way, really did give the impression that he had very remarkable powers indeed.

It was not as though he had seen the Pathan's face.

Of course it might have been a shot in the dark; he might have been drawing a long bow at a venture.

But no, it wasn't that. The Swami had known him on sight.

By the way, could it be possible that the Swami had known that he was coming? Could one of the Brethren have sent off a wire from Bhawalgarh station to Kotgur telling the Swami that the District Superintendent of Police, disguised as a Pathan, had just taken a ticket to Kotgur? It could be done in code. It could be sent to the Kotgur ticket-collector, say, and he could immediately have sent information to the Swami, whom he knew to be camped half-way between Kotgur and the old abandoned fortress said to be used by the dacoits.

Yes, that was quite possible. Quite possible that the station-master or booking-office babu was one of the Brethren, and that the Swami, having been advised, was simply sitting waiting for a Pathan to come along.

Well, supernatural power or "grape-vine" underground message, the Swami had known him, mocked him, laughed at him, shown him that he knew what Steele was doing there near Kotgur.

Well, he laughs best who laughs last; and, on the whole, perhaps, when all was said and done, it was the D.S.P. who had scored and who was one up on the Swami, for certainly the Swami did not know what a lot he, Steele, knew about him. He wouldn't know that the miserable Lalchand Vasu had unintentionally and unconsciously given the whole show away, implicated the Swami, and revealed him as being the leader of the Brethren in Bhawalgarh, an arch-plotter, a prominent member of the gang who had brought the "failed murderer" from Kashigunge to redeem his character in Bhawalgarh.

No, perhaps on the whole, the poor stupid blundering Policeman was just one jump ahead of the so-clever, so-learned, so-accomplished Swami. Possibly, once again, the plodding, slow-witted, ridiculous tortoise might out-distance the hare, the clever, tricky, turning, twisting, doubling hare, and reach the winning-post first. . . .

If he could only find out whether the date was fixed and what that date was! The tortoise would beat the hare to it then, all-right. The lumbering creature would fix a date of his own, an earlier one, a date for the arrest of the whole gang of them, or at any rate of the ring-leaders. Get them on some charge or other, though at present he had nothing more to go on than the blundering meanderings of a terrified half-wit—and a talk with an English girl.

Or could that lad Lalchand Vasu have been playing a part? Acting? They were all born actors, the whole lot of them.

If so, it was a marvellously fine piece of work.

It was possible, for they were clever devils, undeniably clever; brilliant. If the agitators had character to equal their cunning, guts as good as their brains, it would be a bad look-out for the future of the Indian peasant.

Of course the whole thing, including the anonymous bomb-letters and the over-loaded pistol bunged up with high-velocity smokeless powder, might have been eye-wash and play-acting; a comedy staged by the grim joker Ranjit Singh, with Lalchand Vasu as the star actor; and, for safety's sake, no powder put in the priming-pan of the pistol at all.

But what would be the object of the joke?

Something more than endowing the local authorities with a fine sense of insecurity, suspense, anxiety and worry.

Probably, if this were the right solution, and Lalchand Vasu had been acting the whole time, it was still a red-herring, but one of a different kind.

But if it had been acting, why should Lalchand Vasu have talked about the placing of time-bombs, and told him the names of the places that were to be blown up? Told him practically everything except the date?

Could it be that they had announced the programme, broadcast it among their sympathizers, told them precisely what would happen and when it would happen, and, moreover, told them that the English had been warned; that they had informed the English of what they were going to do, just as plainly and clearly as they had informed their friends and sympathizers— and they were going to carry out their promise?

It might be that. They would have said—to the students, for example, of the Government College, of the American Mission College, of the definitely seditious and disloyal Lala Gangadar College,

"We are going to blow up every important Government building in Bhawalgarh next month, and we've informed every British official of the fact. All fair, square, and above-board. Now watch us do it.

"We've not only written to them, giving them the fullest information—except the date, which is not yet fixed—but we have sent an emissary to tell the Superintendent of Police himself. And he cannot arrest one of us, for he has nothing against us.

"And there they all are, just quaking in their shoes, sitting beneath the sword of Damocles, suspended above their heads by a hair; or sitting waiting for the bomb of Damocles to be placed beneath them, with a hair . . . trigger."

Lord! How one's thoughts did run on.

Steele yawned long and loudly, stretched himself, and rose to his feet. Time he went to bed.

For a minute he stood staring out into the compound.

Hullo! What was that moving? Almost looked as though somebody passed across the drive into the darkness of the gold-mohur tree. As though running away out of the house. Fancy, probably.

The date . . .

That was the vital point, unless the whole thing were a malicious malignant scare-monger's jest, and a gang of young students were having him on a string—Lalchand Vasu their leader. Damned good actor if he were!

The mischievous young apes! . . . Quite likely Lalchand Vasu was back in his College by now—and the whole lot were roaring with laughter at the glorious leg-pull he had brought off, the really lovely trick he had played on the fat-headed District Superintendent of Police.

It would not have been so funny, though, if the fat-headed District Superintendent of Police had taken a different line, and run him in for attempted murder. Then, of course, they'd all have come forward in a body and proved that the whole thing was a practical joke, a put-up job to make a fool of the District Superintendent of Police. And what a laughing-stock he'd have been!

Nevertheless, the boot would have been on the other foot, the laugh on the other face, if he had taken his riding-switch and given Lalchand half a dozen on the seat of his pantaloons, as he called them. But, of course, they had counted—quite rightly—on there being no danger of that. Or, if he *had* been so foully tyrannical, murderously brutal, criminally wicked, as to take the law into his own hands to the extent of paying (for an apparent murderous attempt upon his life) with half a dozen flicks of a switch, what an action for savage assault and battery would have ensued!

But, no—somehow, Mr. Lalchand Vasu, failed B.A., had rung true.

If the whole thing were a students' practical joke, then Steele had learned something from them; he had learned that he wasn't the man he thought he was; that he was a gullible fool who wasn't fit to be a commissioned policeman at all—scarcely fit to be a uniformed beat-pacing constable—if he could be taken in as easily as that.

Yes, Lalchand Vasu was genuine, or Anthony Steele was a fool and a failure.

Gad, if it were a practical joke! . . . Well, if so, he handed it to them. They had taken him down a peg.

And suppose it were all that it seemed to be; that Lalchand Vasu was the tool of a terrorist organization; that the D.S.P. was right in his surmise that the clumsy attempt at the murder of the Collector (or himself) was partly red-herring and partly anxiety-inducing strategy? Suppose that the anonymous bomb-placers had arranged it as a manifesto to all whom it might concern, that they were a power in the land, a power so prepared, so immune, and so potent, that they could afford to announce beforehand precisely what they were going to do—and then do it?

Grim jest or deadly earnest? And if the latter, had they fixed the date, and when would it be?

The date . . .

If they were going to wait until the date of the Governor's arrival to open the new hospital, there was plenty of time for the police to catch Ranjit Singh, for whom there was already a warrant out; round up the dacoits; implicate the Swami; raid the *To-day and To-morrow* offices, search the whole premises and see if there were really a *cache* of arms, explosives or other contraband there; put the fear of God, or rather of the Government, into the Gopaldas brothers; and get something definite to go upon in the matter of guilty connivance on the part of Babu Purshotamdass, Moulvie Abdul Haq, Bhojraj Shahani and Sant Arjun Rama.

For, quite apart from anything that Lalchand Vasu

had said, there could be no doubt about it that that lot met at the Gopaldas house; and most certainly they did not meet to talk Comparative Religion.

There, of course, he had checked-up on Lalchand Vasu's story.

Or had he merely put names into Lalchand Vasu's mouth; and had the young devil, consummate actor that he was, gravely accepted them, admitted them, repeated them—and fooled him to the top of his bent?

What a morass it was.

Anyway, whether jest or earnest, he must act as though it were the latter and, at the earliest possible moment, find out about the date. Why, if the whole thing were not a practical joke the date might be to-morrow, to-day, to-night, *now*.

No, if Lalchand Vasu had not been puffing his leg, the date wasn't fixed; and wouldn't be, until "Number Seven" arrived and fixed it. And if it were a practical joke, of course there was no date at all.

Number Seven. Who could he be? And where was he coming from?

Number Seven. And the date.

Round and round like a squirrel in a cage. The date of the Governor's visit? The Governor would be spending the night at the Commissioner's House of course— which, incidentally, had been mentioned as one of the places to be blown up.

Why, of course, the date of the Governor's visit wasn't fixed. Was that the reason why the conspirators hadn't fixed their date?

And suppose it were an earlier one? What likely dates were there? Were there any anniversaries; anything commemorating some noble deed in the Mutiny?

Of course there had been lots of conspiracy talk in 1907, the fiftieth anniversary of the Mutiny. Some people had been a bit anxious and uncomfortable on May the Fourth that year.

Now what was there about 1857? He'd made quite a study of the Indian Mutiny, as every policeman should; and he remembered something about the date. Yes, of course, 1857 was the centenary of the great Battle of

Plassey. June 23rd, 1757. That was it. Good memory for facts and dates. June 23rd, 1757. Battle of Plassey.

Yes. What about June the twenty-third? If there were a really big comprehensive bomb-plot, and the date were not to coincide with that of the Governor's visit, what about June 23rd?

Had the leaders fixed that date and kept it a secret among themselves, so that nobody knew except this Number Seven, Ranjit Singh, and the Swami?

How could he find out? He'd write again to Tweedale-Roscoe and tell him suddenly to spring "*June 23rd*" on Lalchand Vasu—if he had got him there in Srinagar—and see whether he re-acted at all.

But most probably the lad didn't know the date, and was genuinely under the impression that they hadn't fixed one.

The date—if any . . .

An idea! Betty Gopaldas.

Would it be possible to learn about the date through her? Just possible. Naturally they wouldn't tell her; but could she find out? And if by any chance she could, or came to know accidentally, she wouldn't tell him.

Or would she, if he put it to her that it was her duty, as an English girl, to do anything in her power to avert an appalling catastrophe that threatened her compatriots; her duty to do anything she could, to thwart a blow aimed to overthrow the British Raj?

Of course she would.

Poor child, as though her position weren't sufficiently anomalous, invidious, difficult, at the best of times and under the most favourable conditions, without having that added to it—being given the choice between loyalty to her husband and loyalty to her country.

Yes, Betty Gopaldas would have had enough to contend with if her husband were staunchly loyal, and a true friend of the British. But if he were a conspirator, plotting the deaths of her fellow-countrymen and taking up arms against the British Crown . . . And such arms. Time-bombs!

What line would she take if she discovered that her husband was a plotter, a conspirator, a terrorist, a potential and intending murderer? Would she denounce him, or would she feel that he had first claim upon her—and upon her loyalty, devotion, service?

Anyhow, the problem was, how could he himself make best use of her? By keeping her in ignorance and learning what he could by questioning her, and putting two and two together in the light of whatever information he could get from her; or by taking her into his confidence, telling her the whole truth, informing her that her husband was a false and treacherous enemy of the English, a seditionist, a terrorist and a cowardly murderer engaged in a plot for the killing of her friends in Bhawalgarh?

Her friends? Afraid one could scarcely call them all that. No, she hadn't received any particularly warm friendship from most of the Europeans in Bhawalgarh. Still, she'd count the Commissioner and Mrs. Cornwallis as friends. And Herdie—and himself.

Himself? That was an idea. What about taking the personal line?

What would her reaction be if he put it like that? If he told her that her husband was a leading member of a gang who were plotting to murder him, and would she help him to—well, save his life?

It was the personal aspect, the personal element, that appealed to women. Just as they put intuition and instinct before reason so they put persons before principles. Not perhaps necessarily principles in the sense of ethics, morality, "high principles," but in the sense of theories, arguments, politics, that sort of thing.

Should he make love to her? Rather a low trick, but if ever there was a case of the end justifying the means . . . And it wouldn't do her any harm. Might do her a world of good to have an interest in life. It wasn't as though she had a loving husband like Jenny Herdie had. She couldn't possibly be in love with Ramrao. Probably infatuated, swept off her feet, when she was a silly, romantic, and inexperienced ex-flapper, ex-school-girl, and the noble Ramrao was something novel, strange and attractive, something from the glamorous East, an Indian Rajah. They were all Rajahs when in England. But *now*. . . .

As soon as she got out to India, and found what life with an Indian was, for an Englishwoman, there must have been a revulsion, violent and prompt.

No, of course she couldn't be in love with Ramrao. So there'd be no difficulty from that point of view, and no harm done.

What a wonderful help she'd be if she would really work with him whole-heartedly; work for him. That was probably too much to hope; but you never knew. Very much depended on her frame of mind, her state of feeling with regard to the Gopaldas *ménage* in general, and to Ramrao in particular.

Difficult, but very interesting. Piquant. Probably nothing very much would come of it, but it was certainly worth the time and trouble. At best, it might make all the difference; and, at worst, good fun and no harm done. Of course the whole thing would have been much easier if she'd been a different type of girl.

The date . . . ?

Yes, at the moment Betty Gopaldas was his second string, and Lalchand Vasu his first string. They were his best hope of discovering it, unless of course, once again, there was no date, the whole thing was a myth, a practical joke, and Lalchand Vasu an impudent young rascal who'd pulled his leg very cleverly indeed.

Was he?

Well, he'd soon know. He'd get a letter in a week or two from Tweedale-Roscoe saying that Lalchand Vasu had arrived, or else enquiring what on earth Steele was talking about, as no such person had arrived in Srinagar with a note from the District Superintendent of Police of Bhawalgarh. Then he'd know.

Yawning and stretching himself once again, he closed and bolted the lattice doors of the verandah, turned out the lamp, went into his sitting-room, locked the door, turned out the lamp there, went out to the back verandah, locking the door of the sitting-room behind him, bolted the back verandah doors, and, taking the lamp from a table at the foot of the stairs, went up to his bedroom.

Arrived there, he put the lamp down on the chest of drawers, turned up the wick of the small wall-lamp, and proceeded to undress.

Having done so, and put on the pyjamas which hung over the back of a chair in front of his bare dressing-table, he went to get his air-gun from where it stood in the corner of the room by his bed, which was some three or four feet from the side wall. It was his nightly custom to have a little of what he called sport-without-danger combined with the perusal of light literature, by way of distracting his mind from the cares of the day, and disposing it for sleep.

Arrived at the other side of the mosquito-curtained bed, he suddenly noticed something that caused him to stand perfectly still, staring hard at the bed—now between himself and the two lamps, its interior lighted by them. Someone was lying asleep on it.

An observer might have noticed that no particular expression appeared upon Steele's face, or rather that its habitual calm, quiet, somewhat uninterested expression did not change. He merely stood perfectly still and stared—as well he might.

Whoever it was, lay on his (or, of course, her) right side, back toward him, head on pillow, shoulders hunched, sheet—there being no other bed-clothes— drawn well up.

And who the devil might *this* be?

Not infrequently he had arrived home to find an unexpected visitor ensconced in his sitting-room, with the whisky and soda and cheroots at his elbow; a colleague, friend, semi-official or official messenger, or what-not; but he couldn't remember that ever in his life he had come home to find that an unbidden guest had arrived and gone to bed in his house without leaving any message. Certainly none had ever settled himself thus comfortably in Anthony Steele's own bed. Quite all-right, of course, within limits, if that had been the only bedroom in the house. But there were two more, one on either side of this one, complete with beds and mosquito-curtains, not to mention couches downstairs, shake-downs and canvas camp-beds that could be produced and put up at a minute's notice.

Well, well! Cool, to say the least of it. Now, who could it be?

Not Mike O'Halloran the D.S.P. at Jhalni, as he'd had a letter from him that morning. Whoever it was, was mighty tired and sleepy, for Steele had made a fair amount of noise, pulling out a drawer and throwing wide the slatted doors opening on to the verandah, and so on; not to mention whatever row he had made bolting-up below.

And yes, he had come upstairs fairly noisily, heavy boots on bare boards, and he had yawned with more than a maiden's sigh once or twice. Perhaps the fellow was shamming sleep, for some reason best known to himself?

The fellow? Suppose it were a lady fair? Hardly likely. Not his line of country at all, that sort of thing. There had never been a lass in the house since he'd had it, as far as he knew.

Jenny Herdie! It couldn't be . . . ? No, she'd never do that. Fool enough for almost anything, but she'd never come over to his bungalow and hop into his bed like that, and then fall asleep as though she were in her own, surely? . . . On the other hand, if she had done such a thing and had been there long, she might have fallen asleep.

Of course she wouldn't have done such a thing— apart from the fact that he'd never given her the slightest encouragement. Surely it had been fairly obvious, only last night, that he was trying to dodge her invitation to dinner.

And what should he do if it were she?

But of course it wasn't.

Then who was it?

The quickest way to settle that question would be to find out. But perhaps, on the whole, he'd keep quite still, just a little longer.

Yes, or perhaps a good deal longer. It must be a

man. If the gentleman had been waiting for him, he could wait a little more. Puzzle him a bit. Hitherto he had had Steele, his quarry, his prey—if that were the idea—in sight, himself completely invisible, owing to the light from the lamps falling on the white mosquito-netting and rendering it just as opaque as a wall of white marble.

Now the position was reversed. Steele had got him between himself and the light, and if the fellow wanted to see what his intended victim was up to, he'd have to turn over, or at any rate turn his head. Very awkward and uncomfortable situation for the poor chap, as soon as he began to wonder what the devil Anthony Steele was doing there behind him. Before very long it would take absolutely superhuman self-control to prevent him from looking round to see what was happening. He'd get frightfully worried .as the minutes ticked by, and absolutely nothing happened.

Steele kept perfectly still. There was no sound in the room. The situation grew more and more unbearably tense.

The intruder would simply have to budge sooner or later, if only to satisfy his curiosity, and find out how on earth the man who had just been clattering about the room had suddenly vanished.

A little trial of patience.

If this were a trap, it was going to close on the individual who set it.

On the other hand, if it were a trap—and it certainly looked like something of the sort—it was a queer one. What exactly would the idea be? If this were another tool of the terrorists who'd been sent to do the thing properly this time, told to conceal himself in the bungalow and await his chance, surely he was over-doing, or perhaps under-doing, the concealment. One had heard of dacoits, thieves, murderers, hiding themselves under beds, but it was quite a new technique to get into them.

But of course one had to keep up to date and move with the times. This might be the latest thing, the new method.

And as a matter of fact the fellow had, as it happened, been completely concealed behind that mosquito-netting, the lamps being where they were. Well then, why hadn't he taken a pot-shot before this? He couldn't have missed at that range—not with his target almost touching him, as Steele had been, two or three times while he was undressing.

Or hadn't they given this one a pistol; not even a blunderbuss? And was it the old Shivaji-Afzul Khan trick again? Get close up and then slash or stab?

Was the would-be murderer to lie doggo in the bed, until his victim untucked and raised the mosquito-net, and then was he to strike?

Not a bad idea either, inasmuch as the light would have been turned out, and there would be nothing but the glimmer of the little wall-lamp.

It was quite possible, indeed quite likely, that Steele would have noticed nothing unusual until he had pulled up the mosquito-curtain; and then, with both hands encumbered and raised, he would have been an easy prey. . . . Probably that was it. A daring, risky, but really quite sound scheme. And, in point of fact, but for his happening to go round to the other side of the bed, and thence glancing through the net, it would all have worked out neatly and quite successfully.

Yes, the more one thought about it, the cleverer it looked. An ideal trick for getting your man close in front of you, with his hands raised and his body exposed to a stab. Quite a different thing from attacking a man whose hands were free and who, unhampered and unencumbered, had time to defend himself.

But why not have used a pistol downstairs? Why not have had a shot at him from the outer darkness, as he sat in the lighted verandah opposite the open door? It could hardly have been a question of escape; because, although a pistol makes a loud noise, there would have been plenty of time for the murderer to get safely away. It was doubtless well known to the terrorists that the District Superintendent of Police never had his garden patrolled, his house guarded;

never had a police-orderly sitting at his front door except as a messenger during the day-time; that his servants were allowed to clear off to their houses at the bottom of the compound as soon as their work was finished after dinner; that he kept no *chowkidar*[38] to spend the night loudly coughing and clearing his throat when he was not snoring.

No, it would not be a question of difficulty of escape after firing a pistol shot, any more than it had been in the case of Lalchand Vasu—if that were a genuine attempt.

Queer.

Anthony Steele leant back against the wall behind him, assumed as comfortable and restful a position as he could, folded his arms, and settled down for the trial of patience. If he knew anything at all about such matters, the man—or woman—on the bed would, before long, be suffering a strain unbearable. It must have been bad enough, lying there while his victim was in sight and his actions could be watched. Quite bad enough, inasmuch as at any moment he might, for all the watcher knew, have moved the lamp to the other side of the room, caught sight of him and reached for a weapon.

It must have been bad enough lying there, waiting for the moment when the mosquito-curtain was pulled out from under the mattress and raised; the moment when the feasibility of the scheme was to be put to the test. A pretty good trial of coolness and nerve.

But what must it be now, when the positions were reversed; when the watcher was watched; and the erstwhile victim might, at any moment, become the attacker, the assailant be himself assailed, the killer be killed?

Yes, unless the individual on the bed had nerves of steel, he must be having a pretty bad time of it. The question,

"What's he doing? What *is* he doing?" must be rising from a whisper to a scream in his mind. "What is he doing? Why doesn't he *do* something?"

---

[38] *Watchman.*

He must be on a perfect rack of suspense and apprehension. He would know, of course, that there was no door or window by which Steele could have gone away from the room without his seeing him go.

There he had lain, gripping the handle of his knife, ready to strike, the moment the mosquito-curtain was lifted and Steele stood before him, almost touching him, his hands raised as high as his face, his sight for a second obscured by the raised curtain, his body offered, absolutely unprotected and defenceless, to the blow.

Who would the assassin be? Certainly not one of the terrorist gang. They did not risk their own precious lives. Not one of them would ever do that, unless it were Ranjit Singh who had been a soldier and was tough. Even he, however, would probably take the view that in the terrorists' army he was a General, and a General's place is not in the front line.

Nor would it be another hungry, half-baked, windy-minded student of the Lalchand Vasu type. They could get them—plenty of them—to lob a bomb at a Blood-stained Hireling Tyrant of Satanic Government, to hold a pistol up against his back and pull the trigger, or even to take a shot at him at short range, but they would not find one who'd do a thing like this. This wanted real nerve.

Nor would it be a hired *thug*, one of Bagu the Dacoit's band. They'd do a job all-right, at union rates, but they'd do it their own way. Old-fashioned con-servative workmen who followed their profession as their fathers had taught them, and used the time-honoured technique of their trade. You'd never get a professional to do anything as unorthodox as this. Never. You couldn't offer him enough money to do it. For quite a reasonable fee and expenses, he'd go to your house in the middle of the night, dressed in nothing whatsoever but a suit of oil, and with even his head shaved and oiled so that you couldn't grab him by the hair, and he'd stick a knife in you as you slept, take away anything attractive and portable in the way of money and small valuables, and depart into the jungle whence he came, or take the high road in dirty *puggri*, shirt and loin-cloth as an itinerant mendicant, pedlar, or pilgrim, like a million other what-nots.

But you'd never get him to pose himself like that in a bed under a mosquito-curtain and a sheet. He'd sooner go into a police cell than into such a trap as this.

It was going to be very interesting indeed to discover what manner of man this was, since one could safely rule out actual conspirator, student dupe and tool, professional robber, *thug* and hireling murderer.

Well, whoever he was, he'd got patience, coolness and a fine control of his nerves. Yes, he'd got courage and was a stout lad.

It must have wanted a bit of doing—to make his way into the bungalow of the District Superintendent of Police, get into his bed, tuck the mosquito-net in, all neat and tidy, pull the sheet right up over him until all but his eyes were hidden and then just . . . wait.

The waiting must have been Hell.

And how the fellow's heart must have beaten when he heard him begin to move about, lock up, come upstairs, come into the room.

Of course he had calculated, quite correctly, on the fact that Steele would be carrying a lamp which would dazzle his eyes as he came into the room; and that he would put the lamp down in the obvious and practically only place, on the chest of drawers there, where its light would be reflected from the white mosquito-curtain without penetrating it.

Very well thought out. And yet wasn't it a bit too well thought out, too elaborate for an Indian of this type?

Certainly it would be, if the man were a mere jungle dacoit or bazaar *budmash*. There was a brain behind this scheme.

And wasn't it the brain, probably, of someone pretty well acquainted with European habits and domestic interiors; someone who knew that mosquito-curtains were pulled down and tucked in all round the mattress at dusk when the mosquitoes began to fly into the house from the garden? Someone who knew that there was almost always a tiny hand-lamp burning in the bedroom or adjacent bathroom, and that a bigger, brighter lamp was either carried upstairs by the person who came to bed, or that otherwise there was a bracket wall-lamp that he lighted when he came into the room?

Was it possible that one of his servants was an accomplice?

No, he thought he could rule that out, but one never knew. And when one was engaged in the work of detection, it was folly to rule out anything that was humanly possible.

All very puzzling. Quite a new technique.

Presumably they would not have worked this way if he had been sleeping on the ground floor.

His mind went back to the last time that he had had an adventure of this sort, when sleeping in a one-storey bungalow. That had been a remarkable feat of—whatever it was. Worthy of the Swami himself. To this day he did not know, and he never would know, whether it had been a case of hypnotism, drugging of his drink, or poisoning of the atmosphere. He had taken ten days' leave and gone North to visit a friend of his school-days, now a Forest Officer, who had offered him some shooting. The Forest Officer, a bachelor like himself, had given him an end room, of necessity on the ground floor, as, like the majority of Indian bungalows, it had no upper storey.

After dinner they had sat in front of a pleasant log-fire, the night being sufficiently cool to make it acceptable, smoking, yarning, and recalling events of their school-days. At about midnight they had had a final whisky and soda and gone to bed, his host coming along to Steele's room for a last look round, to see that he had everything he wanted; lamp alight in the bathroom and bedroom; a covered jug of home-made lemonade on a table beside the bed; cigarettes; matches . . .

Yes, everything all-right.

Having undressed, he had taken a book from his cabin-trunk and lain down on the bed, thankful to be in a place where mosquito-curtains were unnecessary. It had, for years, been his custom to read a few pages of a book and then to lay it down and compose himself to sleep, having discovered that when he failed to do this, he lay awake thinking of his work, cogitating over clues and cases, sometimes far into the small hours of the morning.

On this occasion he had, to his surprise, very suddenly found himself extremely drowsy; so much so that although he was within a few lines of the end of the chapter, he could not keep his eyes open to finish it. His hands had drooped, relaxed, and the book had fallen on to his face.

But even this had not properly awakened him, and had only aroused him sufficiently for him to notice that the window opposite to his bed, a window that opened inwards in two halves, had been pushed open, and that a man, standing without, was staring fixedly at him, with bright, penetrating, unwavering eyes.

He could only see the head, and realized that it was not only bare, an unusual thing in India, of course, but shaven and glistening with oil.

And yet, strangely enough, it perturbed him not at all that an extremely villainous-looking native should have opened his bedroom-window and be staring him out of countenance. On the contrary, he had felt agreeably soothed, calmed, rested, and delightfully sleepy. He felt no surprise; much less disapproval, resentment or annoyance. He felt grateful to the man. He was a kind, helpful, beneficent person who was sending him off to sleep. Very nice fellow. Sort of good fairy, though he looked a most uncommon bad one. But one mustn't judge by appearances. Standing out there in the night, keeping watch and ward, he was a guardian angel, if he did look more like a devil—more like the Devil himself, in fact.

Never mind. Handsome is as handsome does; and this fellow was doing him a good turn, sending him off to sleep peacefully, just when he'd been feeling very wakeful, and thinking he was in for one of his white nights.

Very nice. . . . Good man. . . .

And he had closed his eyes and drowsed off into a dreamless sleep.

But he had been awakened again by a sound in the room, or perhaps by a consciousness of movement. He had opened his eyes and found that the obliging fellow was now in the room, was actually standing beside his bed, still looking him straight in the eyes as hard as he could stare.

Well now, that was very, very attentive of him, making a thorough good job of it, not just putting him to sleep like *ayahs* do the babies—clearing off without waiting to see whether they really were properly asleep.

Why! There were two more, as well. And they were carrying his cabin-trunk out of the room, walking one behind the other with the trunk between them; the man in front, with his hands behind him, holding one handle of the trunk, and the other man in the rear with his hands in front of him, holding the other handle.

They must be the station-coolies his boy had brought; and they were carrying his trunk out to put it on an *ekka*[39] or a *byle-ghari*[40] to take it to the railway-station, five miles away.

Yes, the mail train went through there at four o'clock in the morning. Mail trains always do go through these places at four o'clock in the morning. But he hadn't realized that it was to-morrow morning, or rather this morning, that he was going. But there it was. Obviously it must be, or the coolies wouldn't be taking his trunk. That was quite obvious, wasn't it?

And of course that was why this good fellow had stayed—had come into the room—to see that they didn't wake him up; or to send him off to sleep again if they did wake him. Well, now that was very nice.

In the second or two that he had kept his eyes open, these thoughts had dimly and dully struggled through his mind; he had then closed his eyes again and sunk into a deep slumber. . . .

---

[39] *Pony-cart.*
[40] *Bullock-cart.*

And in the morning when his boy brought him his *chota hazri*[41] lo and behold, his trunk had vanished. And he had never seen it or its contents again.

Rather humiliating for a Police Officer, and definitely annoying; but infinitely more interesting and puzzling. How on earth had it been done?

Had the man, without speech or movement, hypnotized him from the window, twelve or fifteen feet away? It certainly didn't seem likely; because the drowsiness had come upon him with the utmost suddenness, and before he'd looked in the direction of the window, or seen the man at all. And when, opening his eyes, he had seen him, he had already been so drowsy, sleep-sodden, and bemused, that he had not re-acted as normally he would have done. He had not only taken the man for granted, but had accepted him quite simply, as one does in a dream. Surely the fellow could not have hypnotized him before Steele saw him; could not, unseen, have cast a spell upon him as he lay there reading a book, without catching his eye and holding it as the mesmerists and hypnotists invariably do?

Dismissing the idea of hypnotism, what about drugged drink? The whisky and soda that he had had between dinner and bed-time had come from the same bottle and syphon as that which his host had drunk, and the latter had not suffered the slightest untoward consequence. They had both had the same small quantity of whisky; and, far from being drowsy, the Forest Officer had attended to some correspondence before going to bed, and had not only written two or three letters, but also his diary for the day.

No, it was not the whisky and soda. In that case, the obvious thing, of course, was to suspect the jug of lemonade, of which he had drunk a tumblerful. But, in the interests of detection, the Forest Officer had volunteered to drink the rest of it, and had done so without experiencing the slightest inconvenience or ill-effects.

There remained only the theory of a drug in the air, the poisoning of the atmosphere of the room by

---

[41] *"Little Presence"* (*morning tea*).

dhatura dust, a trick of which he had heard, but in which he did not believe.

According to his informant, a native police-agent, these *thugs* dried and powdered *dhatura*, placed a quantity of it in the end of a hollow bamboo or other tube, went to the window or door of the room in which the intended victim was sleeping, and blew it towards him as one blows a pea through a pea-shooter. The sleeper, inhaling the dust, was drugged by it, and slept as though he had taken opium, morphia, or other powerful soporific.

Was this what had happened to him that night? It was possible but, he thought, highly improbable; and indeed he simply did not believe it. But the fact remained. Something, somehow, had drugged him so suddenly, so completely, that although he had seen what was going on in the room, he had not understood it, and had never, for one second, thought of thieves.

Very lucky for him that he had not, for if he had realized that his trunk was being carried out of the room by a couple of dacoits, while a third one stood by, he would have sprung up, and would equally surely have got a knife through his throat or his heart, as he did so. . . .

And now the rôles were reversed. The intruder and his knife were on the bed, and it was the intended victim who was standing by, and watching.

And how much longer was he going to stand and watch? How much longer would the murderer be able to bear it?

Yes, he really must hand it to him, for nerve and self-control. It must be incredibly difficult to lie there and keep perfectly still, knowing that something had gone wrong; knowing that the game was probably up; knowing that he was caught in his own trap. It must be a ghastly strain, waiting for what would befall, and wondering what it would be—a shot, a stab, a stunning blow.

How much longer would the man stand it; and what would he do when he did do something? Spring up and make a jump for it—on the other side of the bed? Twist round and go for Steele—on this side? Whip out a pistol, and shoot? Or a knife; and spring up and stab?

Well, whatever it was, he wouldn't bring it off, for, at the slightest movement, except of the head, Steele would act first. He'd tear down the mosquito-curtain as the man moved, close with him, and envelop him in it. And incidentally, if he fought, he'd give him a poke he'd remember.

Hullo, what was that? Did the head move slightly?

Or had the lamp flickered?

Or was it pure imagination?

Could it be a woman? . . . Jenny Herdie? . . . No, it must be a man.

How much longer?

An iron nerve . . . On the other hand, it would require as much courage to make a move as it did to lie still, for the fellow was at a tremendous disadvantage. In fact, he hadn't a chance at all.

How much longer was this to go on? He couldn't stay here all night, waiting for the *thug* to do something.

At length, moving for the first time since he had taken up his position on that side of the bed, Steele stepped swiftly forward, his bare feet making no sound. Bringing his face close to the taut mosquito-curtain, he peered into the interior. A very faint odour was perceptible; elusive, reminiscent, an odour vaguely suggestive of garlic, of coco-nut oil, of Indian clothing. Yes, and the little that he could see of the hair looked very black.

The confounded, infernal, maddening impudence! To get into his bed! Attempted murder was one thing. It might or might not come off; and in either case the Law provided the penalty; and a District Superintendent of Police in these merry times must count it among the little rubs of his profession; the little risks he expected to run; all in the day's work.

But to get into his bed! Really it was unpardonable. He had never struck an Indian yet, except in self-defence, but he'd be sorely tempted to teach this fellow a lesson he'd remember. He felt really angry. He also felt that this had gone on long enough; that the situation had been unduly prolonged.

"Hey, you! Turn over on your back," he said suddenly, in Hindustani. "Towards me. Come on. . . . If you try to get off that bed, I'll kill you."

The figure on the bed made no movement, no sound, no sign that it had heard.

A sudden thought struck Steele.

Was it possible that he had been standing there all that time staring at a dummy!

A dummy in his bed—and he'd stood there for God knew how long, staring at it.

Well! If this was another practical joke, they'd brought it off all-right. A very good joke. But perhaps a bit beyond a joke. And he'd give a month's pay to have a quiet word with the joker.

Clenching his right fist, ready to strike, Steele thrust his hand in under the edge of the mattress, seized the calico border of the mosquito-curtain and pulled it out.

No movement from the figure on the bed.

One moment, though. It might be a dummy; and the dummy might be a booby-trap; and a booby-trap of the most unpleasant kind—a fatal trap, in fact. If the whole thing weren't humbug and moon-shine from beginning to end, and if Bhawalgarh in general and he in particular really were up against the cream of the Brethren of India political-murder gang, headed by the Swami and Ranjit Singh themselves, not to mention Number Seven, they were dealing with some of the cleverest and best-equipped terrorists in India, and probably in the world.

This might be one of the placed bombs that his young friend had been talking about last night. When he went to disturb the dummy on the bed, he might pull a lanyard, touch a spring, make a contact, that would explode a bomb that would blow him to pieces.

(That was the expression they'd used in the letter sent to Herdie, wasn't it? There was going to be an explosion that would "blow him to dust." It had seemed quite to upset poor old Herdie.)

It was probable that the terrorists were now in possession of that sort of bomb—the kind of thing you just put in a drawer, a trunk, or a box of some sort, and the victim, by opening it, does the rest.

Quite likely.

But on the other hand he had gathered from Lalchand Vasu that there was to be a simultaneous explosion of bombs all over Bhawalgarh; time-bombs that were all to go off together.

God, what havoc they'd make!

But there was no telling how much Lalchand knew, supposing him to be genuine at all—and how much he'd told of what he knew.

Or was this just a demonstration on the part of the gang that they were quite competent to do what they intended; a little object-lesson? If they could place a dummy, with or without a bomb, not only in the District Superintendent's own bungalow but in his very bed, presumably they could place them in the Commissioner's House, the Collector's bungalow, the *kutcherry*, Post and Telegraph Offices, Railway-station, Banks, Fort, anywhere they chose.

Had he been a fool always to refuse, somewhat ostentatiously perhaps, to have any personal bodyguard, any protection for his bungalow; always to refuse to have orderly, *pattiwallah*, *chowkidar*, or even a servant in his house after they had cleared away his dinner and finished for the evening?

Slowly he raised the mosquito-curtain.

No, this wasn't a dummy. It was a man.

"Hey, you!" he growled again. "Turn over, will you. Come on, this way."

No reply. Not a move. No sign that the man had heard. No sign of life.

No sign of life?

No. And surely no-one could keep quite as still as this man had done for the last—how long?

Still keeping his right fist clenched, poised, and ready, Steele drew down the sheet, exposing an Indian dressed in cotton coat and trousers.

"Hey! Come over, will you," said Steele again, and suddenly clutched the man's shoulder and left arm, pulled him over toward him, and found himself face to face with Lalchand Vasu.

Yes, he'd expected it; known it really, before he turned him over.

How had they killed him?

By terror—from the look of him.

Yes. Lalchand Vasu certainly looked as though he had died of fright.

And, so far as Steele could discover, there was no sign of any wound or external injury whatsoever.

Well, well! Very interesting. Very interesting indeed. Also instructive, informative. This told him a good deal; told him where, to some extent, he was; gave him a little firmer foothold in the middle of the morass.

In the first place, Lalchand Vasu had been genuine. Poor old Lalchand Vasu, failed B.A. and failed murderer, had not been a joker. He might have been a joke—to the terrorists—but he was genuine. He had come to kill the Collector Sahib and bungled the job badly; had waited outside the wrong bungalow, shot at the wrong man, and had killed neither himself nor anybody else.

Almost certainly it had been intended that he should do one or the other; make a demonstration; and, according to the result of it, either bolt to the station and escape; or lie a corpse, or at any rate a gory mess, with his face blown off.

Yes, his first theory had been right, he felt pretty sure. Lalchand Vasu had been a red-herring, but where the plot had miscarried had been in the failure of the pistol to explode, and in Lalchand's failure either to run away or perish.

Obviously the poor wretch had then been caught in the act of disobeying the conspirators, and escaping in the wrong direction. When questioned as to what he was doing and why he was doing it, he must have admitted that he had fallen into the hands of the District Superintendent of Police and must have shown the gang that, intentionally or unintentionally, he had given him a good deal of information. They'd find

Steele's note to Tweedale-Roscoe.

The gang would see that the red-herring had turned into a whale; and think that the authorities, instead of smelling a rat, must now smell an elephant.

Undoubtedly there had been a general meeting of the terrorist-gang and they had decided that the first thing to do was to eliminate Lalchand Vasu, not only as a hopelessly failed murderer but as an unprofitable servant who meant well and did ill; knew too much and did too little. Not so much a case of more useful dead than alive, as quite useful dead and quite useless living. His corpse, returned to the clever District Superintendent of Police, would show the latter that he must be an even bigger fool than they thought him, if he imagined for one moment that he could detach the meanest of their servants, the humblest of their employees, and spirit him away to safe-keeping, as future King's Evidence and present source of further information.

That was it; and it really was a bold and clever stroke. They had killed the poor lad in some horrible way, and Ranjit Singh, with or without help, or possibly Bagu the Dacoit and one or more of his merry men, had simply carted the corpse along after dark, dumped it in a quiet spot in the big garden, and carried it into the house by the back entrance, either while Steele was sitting in the front verandah, or when he was out of the place altogether.

Yes! He had seen someone in the garden—apparently running away—just before he came up to bed.

Probably dacoit work, the delivery of the body; and an amazingly clever piece of work, too. But then, they were very clever at that sort of thing. There was the case of the Railway Traffic Superintendent whose house was cleared one night. They had simply emptied the place, including the room he was sleeping in, so that when he woke up in the morning there were himself and his bed and nothing else. It was a wonder they had left him that much.

Yes, no doubt the gang had killed Lalchand Vasu. Probably in their secret meeting-place in, or under, or behind, the *To-day and To-morrow* offices. And the professional thieves had done the dumping for them.

One of the amazing phenomena of India, these criminal tribes, of which every man, woman, and child was a born, bred, professional criminal, openly and admittedly so, living by crime and by nothing else; a caste, a hereditary guild.

Yes, that was what had happened; and now he could rule out any practical-joke theory, and could get down to the job of piecing together the various clues, and finding out how far Lalchand Vasu's information had been correct; find out something that would be legal evidence and give him an excuse to act, warrant his arresting the lot of them.

He could pretty safely go on the assumption that Lalchand had believed all he had said; and, on the whole, the probability was that it was accurate; that the men who met at the Gopaldas house, as Betty had told him, were the Bhawalgarh branch of the Brethren of India; were an active terrorist gang; and that, as Lalchand Vasu had told him, Ranjit Singh was here in Bhawalgarh; that the Swami was one of the leaders; and that there was a big, ambitious, comprehensive plot for a massacre in Bhawalgarh, a tremendous up-heaval, with murder, rapine, riot, and destruction, the date of which was not fixed but would probably be that of the Governor's visit or, if earlier, that of some significant anniversary.

It was also probably true that decision on the subject would not be made until the arrival of Number Seven, who would act, and issue instructions, according to circumstances.

But not one scrap of tangible producible evidence had he got, as to the existence of a plot, much less as to its date.

The date was the all-important thing.

If only he could know it as soon as it was fixed; know as soon as the conspirators themselves. Would it be possible to get an agent into their meetings? He'd have had just a faint hope, or at any rate would have toyed with the thought, of doing something in that line himself, in his Pathan disguise, but for his somewhat humiliating encounter with the Swami that morning.

It was probably out of the question, anyhow. Extremely unlikely that anyone would ever set foot in their secret meeting-place except Number Seven, the Swami, Ranjit Singh, Ramrao Gopaldas and his brothers, Babu Purshotamdass, Bhojraj Shahani, and the Moulvie Abdul Haq.

It was more than probable that anybody who came to them in the guise of a messenger from Midnabad would get extremely short shrift. There'd be some password, signature, or token, some piece of knowledge, the lack of which would be his undoing.

And that brought him back to his second string, his other hope—now that Lalchand Vasu was out of it—Betty Gopaldas.

He'd certainly make the utmost use of the second string to his bow.

Meanwhile, what to do about this poor dupe and broken tool?

Probably secrecy would still be his best line; and he'd only be playing the conspirators' game for them if he gave to their extremely disturbing and sinister deed the publicity which they would like it to have. It would not do anything at all towards soothing apprehensive minds, if it became known that a member of the terrorists' organization, an agent whom the District Superintendent of Police had nobbled, had himself been promptly murdered and tucked up in the District Superintendent's own bed, to be their very eloquent, if dumb, messenger.

No, he'd have Lalchand taken quite secretly to the police mortuary, and get the Civil Surgeon to do an autopsy and report to him privately.

And now, what about a spot of sleep. . . .

Carrying the lamp in one hand and his air-gun in the other, Anthony Steele went into the next room and lay down upon the unprepared bed, refraining, as was his habit, from lowering the mosquito-net until he had had his read and sport-without-danger for the composing of his over-active mind: by no means his troubled, agitated, or anxious mind; for neither by habit nor by nature was he disposed to allow his mind to be troubled, agitated, or anxious.

Opening his book, a light and pleasing work of travel by a whimsical dilettante, he deliberately switched off the current of his former thought, put all professional cares and cogitations from his mind, and achieved detachment.

While reading and visualizing the travel-author's well-described Malayan scene, he listened attentively.

Complete and perfect silence reigned.

Prolonged silence.

There it was. Very faint, but quite unmistakable. The almost inaudible sound of a slight scurry, the faintest possible suggestion of a soft and tiny thud. And then a distinct tinkle of glass in the bathroom.

Moving with extreme slowness, Anthony Steele laid the book down on the bed beside him, and took up the air-gun, a powerful toy from whose rifled .22-bore barrel, the pellet was discharged with remarkable accuracy and sufficient force to drive it through both sides of a tobacco-tin.

Another faint flurrying scurry and a faint squeak. A rush across the taut ceiling-cloth above his head. Tiny sounds from the other bedroom. A moment later, a large rat appeared in the doorway leading from the bedroom in which lay the corpse of Lalchand Vasu.

The animal sat up, looked around, and Steele pulled the trigger.

Got him!

A feeble kick, and the rat lay still. One pest, and potential disseminator of bubonic or pneumonic plague, the less. Beastly vermin, how he loathed them. Snakes were preferable.

What an enormous great beast. Perhaps that was the identical brute that came and gnawed his hair the other night, and then woke him up by biting his ear. Call him Number Seven.

When was the real Number Seven coming? And would he come by train or by road? On foot; in a bullock-cart; or in a luxurious motor-car?

Steele reloaded the air-gun, laid it on the bed beside him, and took up his book again. He must not start thinking about Number Seven now. He had shut up shop for the day.

A faint scratching sound.

Glancing in the direction whence the noise came, he saw another rat sitting on top of the opened door, either washing its face or nibbling at something it held in its fore-paws.

Keeping the book still, in his left hand, he very slowly took the air-gun in the other, rested the barrel on his knee, sighted, and pulled the trigger.

The rat fell from the door with a soft thud, kicked, and lay still. And perhaps that was the one that gnawed half the hair out of his shaving-brush. If so, he wouldn't do it again, the fat brute.

Call him Babu Purshotamdass.

Again he reloaded and resumed reading.

Something fell with a light clatter in the bathroom. What would that be? Tooth-brush?

Perhaps if one baited the rat-traps with shaving-brushes, tooth-brushes, hair-brushes, shaving-soap, tooth-paste and such things, the rats would go into them instead of avoiding them, as they did when baited with cheese. Did the rat mind, through generations of bitter experience, associate the smell of cheese with rat-traps, and rat-traps with the smell of cheese? He certainly got more rats this way, with his air-gun, than the *hamal* did with the traps.

To think that the foul vermin were responsible for the deaths of millions of people, through plague. For every man killed by a snake, a thousand were killed by rat-fleas.

Hullo, there was another sitting up and eyeing the dead bodies of his friends and relations, without consternation or alarm.

Just as Steele was about to shoot, the rat dropped on all fours and ran across the room. He took a snap shot, and, either by good luck and a fluke or by good shooting, to his great satisfaction got it through the hind-quarters. As it lay kicking, he shot it again.

Call him Ranjit Singh—whom he would catch on the run too, he hoped, before long.

As he reloaded the gun a fourth rat dropped through a hole in the ceiling-cloth in the corner of the room, landed on its paws, sat up, appeared to wink at him, and dashed off through the doorway.

"Call him the Swami," smiled Steele.

A few minutes later he arranged the mosquito-curtain, turned out the lamp and went to sleep.

III

Saturday morning!

Saturday morning had come at last. She would love Saturday morning for the rest of her life. Every Saturday morning, when she woke, she would remember this day.

One may lose anything and everything that one values: one's home, friends, country, one's faith, hope, trust, and the little personal things one loves and values; but memories remain. Nothing, while she lived, could take away the memory of this Saturday morning; and in an hour's time it would be a quarter to seven and she could start.

Betty Gopaldas looked round the hateful room, with its dirty, torn and sagging ceiling-cloth, its dark-blue washed walls, with the virulent pink borders framing the doorways and the barred unglazed windows; its stained, frayed, and ragged floor-covering of plaited palm-leaf; its lack of furniture, curtains, hangings and bric-à-brac; and its total absence of comfort.

How terribly hot it was, although the sun could never shine into the room. How dark, airless, unwholesome and horrible. But, by contrast, how glorious must be the morning outside; almost cool; with dew on the grass.

Lovely until the sun rose to smite and to slay, blasting the beauty of the day. But against the beauty that was in her mind and soul, the sun would be impotent. Nothing—neither the sun nor the "Maharani" Subhadra; neither heat nor weariness; neither physical pain nor mental anguish—could spoil the inner beauty with which this day should endow and fortify her.

A depressed and cringing female, dressed in a plain dirty-white cotton *sari*, entered, bringing a somewhat bent and rusty tray on which were an enamel tea-pot; very large jug, containing a very little milk; a brass bowl in which was a small quantity of sugar and a smaller quantity of dust, dirt, spare-parts of ants, and ther foreign bodies; and two cups which, with their respective saucers, were representatives of three different tea-sets. Frequently Betty had wished they ould have managed four. If only the two saucers had not been alike. . . . One day she would break one of the saucers, and then nothing would agree with anything; and a more desirable, because complete, heterogeneousness would be achieved. With two alike it was merely slovenly. The other in its complete incompletion she could regard as chic, novel, a new fashion of her own. One day, when feeling particularly courageous, wild, wicked, wanton and devilish, she would break the large pink saucer on which was inscribed in Gothic letters of gold *God Help You Now*. Altogether too *à propos* and apposite.

In the next bed, her husband, Ramrao Gopaldas, sat up, stretched, yawned and cleared his throat generously, comprehensively, loudly, thoroughly; yea, with abandon.

"Good morning, Ramrao. Tea?"

"Yes, dear. It is this morning that you are going riding with Mr. Steele, isn't it?"

"Yes."

"Going to make a fixture of it?"

"How do you mean?"

"A weekly event. A ride every Saturday morning."

"No. Not that I know of. Mr. Steele didn't suggest it."

"Would you like to have a regular morning for riding with him?"

"Yes," replied Betty promptly. "I should. . . . Much better fun than riding alone."

"Why not suggest it, then? I've no doubt Steele would like it."

"Oh, I shouldn't care to do that. Mr. Steele is a pretty busy man, I expect."

"Oh, but he goes for a ride almost every morning."

"Does he? I shouldn't care to ask him, anyhow."

"But why not? He'd jolly well like it."

"Well, he can say so, then. I'm not going to."

"It would be awfully jolly for you. Look here, if he suggests another ride within the next fortnight, you go. And then if, after that one, he asks when you'll have another ride with him, you fix it up—within the fortnight."

"Right. I will," agreed Betty, passing a cup of tea to her husband.

"Only don't fix anything up with him for any day after a fortnight hence."

"Why not?"

"Won't be here."

"What! Mr. Steele won't? . . . Well, in that case he wouldn't ask me to ride with him."

"No, I mean you won't."

"I?"

"Yes, you, my dear. We are all going down to Dhargaum for a change."

"*What?* To Dhargaum? All of us?"

"Well, I shall be going to and fro, I expect. Motiram or Jaganath will be with you, no doubt; and Tulsiram, because he will be enjoying vacation."

Betty's heart sank.

"But this is the first I've heard of it."

"I didn't hear of it until last night."

"Your mother, I suppose."

"Yes."

"How long shall we be there?"

"Oh, who knows? Perhaps till the Rains. Yes, I expect till the Rains."

"Ramrao, I don't want to go to Dhargaum with your mother."

"No, my dear. Nor do I. But we are going."

She knew that it was useless to argue. Worse than useless to say anything at all. If the lady Subhadra had said that the family was going to Dhargaum for the rest of the hot weather, the family would go—and stay there till the monsoon broke. Only those members of the family whose business kept them in Bhawalgarh would remain.

"That is that, then, I suppose," she said with resignation in her voice.

Oh, well, she might have known that it was foolish to give way to happiness. . . . To give way to happiness! What an expression. What a thought. It was to misery, fear, despair that she must not give way. It was at happiness that she must clutch.

But anyway, this was Saturday morning, and she was to ride with him. And perhaps at the end of the ride they'd rest the horses and get off and sit down and talk. And perhaps he'd not talk about Comparative Religion this time. Perhaps he'd talk about his work; about himself. She would try to make him talk about himself.

Slipping out of bed, she went into the bathroom, not noticing this morning, in her happiness, the greasiness of the floor, the stained, discoloured ugliness of the blue-washed walls, the ugly discomfort of the little zinc wash-tub; the gloom; the dank smell.

Having tubbed and dressed in her white riding-habit and topi, she made her way along dark passages and down carpetless wooden stairs to the courtyard at the back of the house, a dusty, untidy place enclosed by high walls.

Before she had unbolted and opened the back verandah lattice-door, she was aware that neither horse nor syce was awaiting her. A dirty ancient, with a stiff grass hand-brush, was raising clouds of dust, to the end that it might settle back in the place whence he had disturbed it.

"Go and call the syce. Tell him to bring my horse at once," said Betty in Hindustani.

Without reply the old man shuffled off, to return five minutes later and announce that the syce was coming.

"Is the horse ready?" asked the girl.

"No," replied the old man, and resumed his futile brush-work.

With growing uneasiness that was fast turning to anger, she waited until the syce, an ill-favoured ruffian, wearing the remains of a pair of baggy trousers and a fez cap, slouched round the corner of the house.

"I ordered you to have my horse here at a quarter to

seven," said Betty.

"Horse gone lame, Mem-sahib," he said.

"I don't believe it. It wasn't lame yesterday."

"It's lame to-day," replied the man half insolently.

Fool that she had been not to think of this. Forgetful fool. She might have known it. Give way to happiness indeed! What an idiot she had been to tell Ramrao last night that she was riding with Steele to-day. Promptly he had told Subhadra—and the horse was lame.

Or had he himself given orders to the syce that the horse was to be unfit for work in the morning? If so, what underhanded deceitfulness, for he had pretended to be quite glad that she was going to ride with Anthony Steele.

Unshed tears of anger and disappointment scalded her eyes.

She might have known it!

Before she could speak she heard a footfall behind her and, turning, saw her husband, arrayed in pyjamas and patent-leather shoes, coming from the darkness of the bare and empty window-barred room that opened on to the verandah.

"Not gone yet?"

"No, the horse isn't here. The syce says it is lame."

"What?" asked Ramrao, turning to the syce who stood at the bottom of the steps that led from the verandah to the compound. "Lame?"

"Yes, lame," grinned the man.

"Who says so? Did the 'Maharani' say so?"

Again the man grinned.

And, suddenly snatching his wife's riding-whip from her hand, Ramrao sprang down the steps, slashed the man across the face with all his strength, kicked him violently and, as he turned to flee, struck him again and again across the neck and bare back.

"*Lame*, you swine! *Lame!* You lying black-faced son of a sow! *Lame?*"

And punctuating his high discourse with heavy blows, he pursued the man, shouting,

"Bring that horse, and if he *is* lame—I'll lame *you*—

for life."

This was a Ramrao whom Betty had never seen before. As he turned back into the verandah, his face, distorted by rage, looked devilish.

A new Ramrao indeed. Never for one moment had she imagined that he could have given such an exhibition of temper and violence.

Could it be true, as true as regrettable, that she experienced an unwonted feeling of respect for him?

But why this sudden change? Why this entirely novel defiance of the 'Maharani's' orders; this bold and unfilial self-assertion? Or was the whole thing a piece of acting, a realistic impersonation of a man justly incensed to righteous wrath. The syce must have found it a fine piece of realism, anyway.

Could it be that after what he had said about her riding with Steele, he must make a show of doing his best on her behalf, knowing perfectly well, the whole time, that, inasmuch as the 'Maharani' had said the horse must be lame, it was going to be lame?

How distrustful of him she was becoming. But how could it be otherwise? How could anyone be anything but distrustful of a person who was utterly unreliable, who could never be pinned down; who apparently never meant what he said or said what he meant; whose promises were worthless; and of whom the kindest thing that you could think was that he liked to say whatever he thought would please you, quite regardless of whether it were true or not?

Anyhow, that grinning beast of a syce had deserved all he had got, for he was a leering, impudent liar and rogue.

And here he came, leading Star, who obviously was no more lame than she was herself.

"Cured him, have you?" snarled Ramrao.

The man bowed low, touching his forehead.

"He has got better in the night, Master," he whimpered.

"Yes, I thought he would have. And he's going to stay better, do you hear? If you play any more tricks, it won't be the horse that'll be lame."

So she had wronged her husband. He hadn't been siding with the 'Maharani' against her, after all. And that had been genuine anger, a wrath as real as the blows had been.

But why? She had been fooled and foiled a dozen times like this before; and he had never said a word, except mildly to chide her when she had hinted that the horse was lame to order—the 'Maharani's' order.

Was it the beginning of better things? And was he taking to heart her expostulation against his weakness, cowardice, childishness, where his mother was concerned; his lack of loyalty and his meanness toward herself; his hitherto invariable habit of putting his mother first, always fulfilling her wishes and desires where they clashed with those of his wife?

"Thank you, Ramrao," she said. "It was about time that man was taught a lesson and made to understand that it is my horse. Star is not going to be lame any more, is he?"

"No. I won't have it. Why didn't you tell me?"

Oh, Ramrao, Ramrao! "Why didn't she tell him!" Had she not told him a dozen times that the horse was said to be lame, and that she did not for one moment believe that it was lame, and would he please discharge the syce and get one whom she could trust?

Well, better say nothing, particularly at the moment when he had done the right thing.

"You tell me if it happens again, my dear," continued her husband, "and I'll give the rascal a thrashing and fine him a week's pay."

"Understand?" he shouted in Hindustani, turning to the syce. "Next time that horse is lame I'll flog the hide off your back and cut your pay as well. . . . A week's pay every time. Do you hear me?"

The man abased himself.

"Master, what shall I do if the 'Maharani' . . ."

"*Chuprao, tum!*[42] . . . You will do as I tell you. Any time the Mem-sahib orders the horse, you have it ready to the minute. Well fed and well groomed. And you polish that saddle better."

---

[42] *Shut up, you!*

Really, thought Betty, it might almost be an English-man speaking. What had happened and how long would it last?

Why, he'd be helping her to mount next, giving her a hand for a leg-up. He'd probably do it now if he knew how.

She mounted from the step without help.

"Thank you, Ramrao. I'm so glad you interfered."

"Of course, dear, of course . . . You should have sent for me at once. Enjoy yourself. Good-bye."

It was going to be a Saturday morning to remember after all.

§2

How splendid he looked. How absolutely . . . right. What a pleasure to one's eyes, to meet straight forthright-looking grey eyes after so many unreadable brown ones. How cool, calm, strong, assured, he looked—and was. What a tower of strength and reliability. Curious that she should always have been so fond of Browning, and that her particular favourite should be *The Last Ride*.

> *Then we began to ride. My soul*
> *Smoothed itself out, a long-cramped scroll*
> *Freshening and fluttering in the wind.*
> *Past hopes already lay behind.*
> *What need to strive with a life awry?*

But of course this was not going to be the last ride. It was the first real one; the first that they'd arranged together; but it was not going to be the last; particularly as Ramrao, far from objecting to her riding with Anthony Steele, had actually suggested that she should try to make a weekly fixture of it.

That she could not and would not do—but what a joy if he suggested it.

Anyway, he'd be sure to suggest another one; and perhaps, each time, they would arrange for another.

What if we still ride on, we two,
With life for ever old yet new,
Changed not in kind but in degree,
The instant made eternity—
And Heaven just prove that I and he
Ride, ride together, for ever ride?

What was he saying? She felt so idiotically happy, her heart was singing so loudly, and she was listening with such joy to the sound of his voice, that she had actually missed the meaning of the words.

Religious discussions?

No, she simply was not going to discuss religious discussions.

"I really don't know," she said. "I haven't the least idea as to what they talk about."

"But they all came last night?"

"Several of them did, I know. What an interest you take in them."

"I do. Sant Arjun is a remarkable man, and it will be extremely interesting to see whether he makes any headway with so mixed a lot as those; a Mussulman; an enlightened free-thinker like your husband; an Arya-Samaj; a Brahmo-Samaj; a Hindu; and Sant Arjun himself, by birth a Brahmin. . . . Wonder if he's ever tried to make a Sikh convert?"

Oh, why would he talk about the wretched creatures? Was a study of Comparative Religion his hobby, combined with the sort of psychology and ethnology that would have a bearing on the subject, and be of special interest to an intellectual Police Officer? Or was it that he thought that she herself was particularly interested in the matter, as she was so immersed in Indians and India, so to speak?

Well, she'd tell him, before long, that she had more than enough of India at home. What she wanted to talk about was England, and about himself and his work.

"You know a Sikh when you see one, I suppose?" he asked.

"Oh, yes. Quite unmistakable. Not only the turban and dress, and not entirely the fact that the beard, moustache, and hair are never cut. I think I should know a Sikh by his face, apart from that. Fine sensitive faces as a rule."

"Yes, as a rule," he agreed. "Not always. There are exceptions of course. I have seen some very heavy, bloated specimens, ugly and pock-marked; but, as a race, they are splendid. I have the greatest admiration for them. They have a fine religion and they live up to it. Or rather, it is part of their lives. . . . Have you ever seen a Sikh come to the house—to one of the meetings, I mean?"

"Oh, Mr. Steele, don't let us talk about that sort of thing. I believe you think that I am keenly interested in Indian life and thought. So I am, up to a point, but . . ."

"Yes, I know. I understand. You want a change, eh? Got all the India you want in the bungalow. Quite so. What shall we talk about?"

"I'm very interested in detection, police-work, crime, and how you catch criminals, dacoits, terrorists . . ."

You are, by God, are you! thought Anthony Steele. We are going to talk about how we catch terrorists, are we?

"Well, one thing at a time, Mrs. Gopaldas."

"D'you know, I wish you wouldn't call me that. I want to forget all about India altogether, for an hour, and imagine I am riding with you in England. If you wouldn't mind calling me Elizabeth, or perhaps Betty . . ."

"I wouldn't mind a bit," replied Steele gravely. "It would give me no pain whatever. And if you wouldn't mind calling me Anthony . . ."

"I wouldn't mind a bit," smiled Betty. "It would give me no pain whatever."

"Good. Well, as I was saying, one thing at a time, Betty. Let's tidy up as we go along. I've got a tidy mind, you know."

And a lovely tidy person, thought Betty, and I'm sure your bungalow is tidy and your office and your dressing-table. How I'd love to see inside your bungalow and put some flowers in it.

"What was I saying when you so rudely inter-rupted? Oh, yes. . . . Has Sant Arjun contrived to rope in a Sikh?"

"Well, I don't know about roping-in. There's one comes."

"By Jove, how interesting! He *is* a go-getter, the good Sant Arjun, isn't he? Is the Sikh a little tiny wizened old chap? If so, I think I know him."

"Oh, no. On the contrary, he's enormous for an Indian. Huge, big, strong-looking man."

"Pock-marked?"

"Yes. Like so many Indians. It must have been dreadful before vaccination was made compulsory."

A huge, big, powerful Sikh, pock-marked. Ranjit Singh for a tenner!

"Oh, well, Sant Arjun won't convert that chap. Still, it's wonderfully interesting. What a medley of an audience he harangues. I should love to be present and listen to them. Wouldn't you?"

"No," replied Betty. "Not much, I'm afraid. It would probably be over my head. Phrases like 'metaphysical transcendentalism' don't thrill me much. I'd sooner listen to the idlest gossip about Home, at the Gymkha-na."

"And you wanted to talk about police-methods, eh, and how we catch dacoits and—terrorists?"

"Yes."

"I was hoping to surround a dacoit den to-night; catch 'em alive-o, and run them in. They've been raiding villages and looting, over in Almera State; and doing a bit of highway robbery, too, here within twenty miles of Bhawalgarh. They beat up a poor old *bunnia* and pinched his hard-earned savings of a life-time over at Sulri last week. Must have made a fine haul, too, for he's a scoundrelly old money-grubbing usurer. Burned all his books, as well. I rather fancy the villagers joined in there, after the dacoits cleared off, as there wasn't a man of them who wasn't up to his eyes in debt to him; twenty per cent, per mensem interest, and his fields mortgaged for security. Boys will be boys, we know, and all *sowcars*[43] ought to be beaten up—but it's the police who get into trouble when it happens."

Now, what would she make of all that? Tell him that it was not anti-dacoit methods that interested the Gopaldas family, but immediate anti-terrorist action?

"And are you going to raid them to-night? How I should love to go."

"What, and stop a pot-leg fired from a blunderbuss, or a hammered copper-wire slug from a *jezail*? No. Raid's off. I was on my way to spy out the land and have a look at the general lay-out of the country, with the view to surrounding their hiding-place and rushing them at dawn to-morrow, when I ran into the Swami and he knew me at once, although I thought I was pretty well disguised. . . . Didn't your husband tell you about it?"

"No. How would he know?"

"True. How would he know, of course.

"Until the Swami told him," he added.

"Does he know the Swami, then?"

"Doesn't he? Doesn't he come to the house with the others?"

"What's he like? How does he dress?"

"Well, I have only seen him dressed in grey ash and a rag, but perhaps he has less or more of a lounge-suit for calling."

"Less or more?"

"Well, grey ash and a rag is very lounge, isn't it? Perhaps he wears a less 'lounge' suit than that when he calls—and that would be more of a suit, wouldn't it?"

"What's he like?"

"Oh, very intelligent-looking chap. Thin; ascetic; fine forehead; aquiline nose. Really a very fine face. In point of fact, much more like an Arab sheikh than a *faquir*."

"I don't think I've seen him," said Betty. "I may have done, but not among the people my husband has introduced to me."

"I wonder," thought Steele.

---

[43] *Usurers.*

"And you've never heard your husband refer to anybody as 'The Swami'?"

"I don't think so. I don't remember his doing so. But here we are—talking about them again."

"Yes, and we were going to talk about the wicked police, weren't we?"

"Yes. I should think it's the most thrilling life in India, isn't it? More so than a soldier's because a Police Officer is always on active service, isn't he?"

"Fairly active. Though a good deal of his action takes place at his office table, you know."

"Well, yes. The same with a soldier, especially if he happens to be Adjutant.

"As my brother is," she added.

"Oh? In India?"

"No, unfortunately. Hong Kong. . . . Yes, I should think a Police Officer's life in India is the most interesting there is, because you have a very considerable spice of risk and danger. And then, what you do at your office table must be extremely interesting work—following up clues, sifting evidence . . . deduction. . . . You've had some narrow escapes, haven't you—Anthony?"

"Yes. A nail worked up in my boot and I got quite a nasty go of blood-poisoning."

"Any others?"

"I cut my face shaving and got a microbe in that way, too. Narrowly escaped lock-jaw. Got so bad I could only open my mouth for four drinks instead of five. And could only use short words."

"Like 'Bo' to a goose, I suppose. . . . Any others?"

"Fell off my horse once."

"Did it stop and cause you to fall forwards; or go on and cause you to fall backwards?"

"I fell sideways, as a matter of fact."

"What for—fun?"

"Saddle not properly girthed. Syce got the fun. I only got the fall."

"Any others?"

"Only the night before last. Didn't your husband tell you?"

"Night before last? But you were at the Meeting."

"I was; but I went home from it. I suppose it was really a joke, wasn't it?"

"What?"

"Didn't Ramrao tell you?"

"No. What was it?"

"Oh, only a joke."

"But you said it was a narrow escape."

"It was."

"You narrowly escaped death, do you mean?"

"Yes. I might have died of laughing."

"At what?"

"Poor old Lalchand."

"Lalchand? Lalchand whom? Do I know him?"

"You know Lalchand, surely, Betty? Why, Lalchand Vasu."

"Never heard of him."

"Sure?"

"Quite sure."

"Perhaps by some other name he smelt as lovely."

"Why did you nearly die of laughing at him?"

"I didn't. I said I might have done. I should have done, if I had."

"You'll confuse me in a moment, Anthony. Now then, what did Lalchand do to you whereby you were in danger of death—by laughing or otherwise? What do you mean?"

"Well, Lalchand fired his funny old pistol at me."

"Fired a pistol at you?"

"Yes."

"But what happened?"

"What they call a 'sinister and threatening click'. . ."

"Don't joke. Do tell me. Was it an attempt on your life?"

"Well, Lalchand drew his keen-edged pistol from its sheath, put it up to his right eye—the north end inward, the south end pointing at me—and pulled the trigger. And there was a distinct click. I heard it."

"Anything else?"

"Only a few sparks."

"It didn't go off?"

"No. Lalchand went off. To my bungalow."

"But was it a proper pistol?"

"Most proper. Most respectable-looking pistol I ever saw. You know—Victorian. Solid. Solid mahogany. The wooden end, anyhow."

"Was it loaded?"

"Over-loaded. I was never so frightened in my life as when I saw the charge."

"It would have killed you, then, if it had gone off?"

"More likely to have killed poor Lalchand. Didn't Ramrao tell you?"

"No. Why should he? How should he know? Have you told him?"

"No."

"How could he know, then?"

"I don't know whether perhaps he was in the know. In the joke, I mean."

"But was it a joke? Do be serious. I believe there *was* an attempt made on your life, the night before last."

"*Why* do you believe that?"

"Because you've just told me so."

"Oh, I see. . . . You didn't really know anything about it, then?"

"No, of course I didn't. Do tell me."

"That's all there is to it. Just a joke. But I say, it was no joke for poor old Lalchand, was it? . . . Afterwards."

"I don't know what you are talking about. I don't know Lalchand. I don't know the joke."

"Well, ask Ramrao. He'll tell you. Ask him—and tell me what he says, will you?"

"Yes."

Yes, certainly she'd ask, and most certainly she'd tell him—because that would mean seeing him again. Was he going to suggest another ride—so that she could tell him? And would it be only for that reason that he would suggest it? Was the subject of the fate of Lalchand and the fact that for Lalchand the joke was no joke, so very interesting? And had he really had a narrow escape on Thursday night after the meeting?

"Anthony. . . ."

"Yes, Betty?"

"When I ask 'Honour bright?' when you tell me any-thing, will you tell me the absolute truth—or not tell me at all if you don't wish to?"

"Certainly."

"And when I say 'Joking apart,' will you be seri-ous?"

"Of course I will."

"Did you have a narrow escape the other night after the Meeting?"

"Not really. I don't think there was much danger to me."

"Any danger at all?"

"Practically none."

"Good. But you have had some narrow squeaks, haven't you?"

"Oh, only in the way of business."

"It's pretty safe here in Bhawalgarh, I suppose?"

"Oh, quite. No danger here whatever. Don't need any police in Bhawalgarh at all, really. No crime. Not to speak of. No political trouble. No—terrorists."

If that were going back to Ramrao and Co. it might do a little good in the direction of "false security and fools' paradise." On the other hand it would not square with the obvious fact that Steele tried to help Lalchand Vasu to escape them. They must have read his note, that Lalchand was carrying to Tweedale-Roscoe. That in itself would show that Lalchand had given the show away sufficiently to make the police think him worth holding for further usefulness, and perhaps for King's Evidence.

Or had Lalchand destroyed the note in time? Had he stoutly denied having told Steele anything at all? Had he confessed to nothing except failure and an attempt to escape them?

Perhaps. But if so, why had they killed him and dumped him in Steele's bed? Of course, that might possibly be just a little jest of Ranjit Singh's, to puzzle and worry the authorities; and with the added incen-tive that if Lalchand Vasu had turned traitor, his murder and the disposal of his corpse would show the District Superintendent of Police that he wasn't as clever as he thought he was—and certainly not as clever as the terrorist organization that he was up against.

All very puzzling.

"No, no crime in Bhawalgarh, Betty. Nice peaceful spot this. Lazy police earn their pensions by sitting down and getting fat. No crime or rumours of crime. That's why I want to nab these dacoits, butting in here and spoiling our blameless record."

"Perhaps they'll go away," she said.

"What, now the Swami's warned them, you mean; told them that I was snooping round their home-town in fancy-dress, and looking something like a Pathan?"

"The Swami told them? What has he to do with dacoits?"

"Well, he knows them by sight, doesn't he?"

"How? Why? . . . I mean, how should he?"

"He shouldn't. Very wrong of him. But he does. He knows them by sight. Told me that he'd seen them pass by where he was squatting in the jungle. . . . Does Ramrao know Kotgur?"

"I don't know. I have never heard him mention the place. Why?"

"That's the nearest station on the railway to the place where the dacoits settled down when they came over the border from Almera State. It's a few miles through dense jungle, and up into some broken rocky hills. There's an old fort there that used to be a sort of robber-stronghold in the good old days of the Pindaris and what-nots."

"And that's the place you were going to surround when you raided them?"

"Yes. But they seem to have got *khabar*.[44] They'd gone—or the Swami said they had. And in any case, he'd warn them, wouldn't he?"

"Would he?"

"Well, wouldn't he?"

"Anthony, you are talking in parables, or else we

---

[44] *Information.*

are at cross-purposes. How on earth should I know what the Swami would do? I never heard of him till now."

"Sure?"

"Practically certain. I see very few people, you know —though quite as many as I want to—and Ramrao doesn't talk to me about his friends and his doings. I have never heard of the people you've been talking about this morning."

"Except Ranjit Singh, of course, Betty. You know him."

"Ranjit Singh? No. I have never heard his name, though I seem to remember it as that of a Sikh king, Maharaja, I mean. Wasn't he the Lion of the Punjab? I used to read all I could about India—before I came here."

"There's the temple," said Steele. "Let's sit down in the shade and have a chat, shall we?"

"Yes, let's."

Steele dismounted and held the horses while Betty swung herself down. He then ran the stirrup-irons up the leathers, unfastened the girths, bumped the saddles up and down a few times, re-fastened the girths loosely, unfastened the bits, took the reins over the horses' heads, and led them to where Betty had seated herself on a fallen pillar in the shade of the front of the old temple. He dropped the reins, and the horses stood as though tethered.

"Why did you bump the saddles like that?" she asked.

"To restore circulation in the horses' backs—like I rub my legs and insteps when I pull off tight riding-boots."

"I see. Good horse-mastership, eh?"

"Well, a horse likes to slacken his belt as much as I do."

Seating himself beside the girl, Steele put his hand on hers as it rested between them on the stone.

"Betty," he said, "let's go all serious and sober-like, shall we?"

Turning her head and flushing as usual, she looked

him in the eyes.

He held her gaze with his, smiling.

Yes, a candid face this. Nice truthful, steady, honest eyes. And most obviously she was interested in him, liked him. A man could . . . However, he was a policeman. A policeman first, anyhow.

"I want a real heart-to-heart talk with you, Betty my dear. . . . Eh?"

"I'd love to, Anthony."

"No jokes—and 'honour bright.'"

"Yes. If I say I'm not joking I shall not be joking. And if I say 'honour bright' I shall be telling you the absolute plain simple truth. If I can't do that, I shall not tell you at all."

"Good enough, Betty. . . . Do you like me?"

"Yes, I do. Very much. I have always liked you. . . . Do you like me?"

"Yes. I do. I have always liked you, too. Let's be friends. Special friends, I mean, Betty. Help each other."

"How could I help you?"

"Would you, if you could?"

"I'd love to. There's nothing I'd like better. How could I help you?"

"Oh, lots of ways. You said just now that you thought police-work must be about the most interesting occupation there is. You could help me with my police-work."

"Could I, really? How?"

"By telling me things. Things that I couldn't find out for myself, but that you could; and perhaps only you."

"How? What sort of things?"

"Well, for example, now, I may want to know the whereabouts of a certain individual at a certain time, might be very interested to know whether he were in Bhawalgarh or not; and if he were in Bhawalgarh, where he lived, where he spent his time; or where he spent some particular period of time."

"What, a criminal, do you mean?"

"Well, he might, or might not, be a criminal. He might be a perfectly innocent person himself, but he might consciously or unconsciously be in some way connected with criminals. Or he might be a person who was in no way criminal in the ordinary police-court sense of the word, but he might be a political offender. He might be a fire-brand; an agitator. His motives might be above reproach; but his actions might be undesirable and the public result of his actions deplorable."

"But how could I, of all people . . . ?" began the girl.

"Why, for example, a person of that sort might come to your husband's house. Your husband might, quite unintentionally, be entertaining a dangerous criminal. It might be that, unknown to your husband, the man was a professional agitator; even, possibly, a terrorist, who had come from some other part of India, and was hiding in Bhawalgarh in disguise, and under an assumed name. And his method of hiding might be to make friends, locally, with respectable citizens, visiting their houses and leading an obviously blameless life while the police were looking for him elsewhere. Then, if suspicion did fall on him here, he'd have plenty of good friends, of known respectability and unimpeachable character, to vouch for him."

"I see," said Betty. "But wouldn't it be better to get my husband to help you? Surely he'd be much more useful."

"Well, it's difficult, Betty. You see, you are English; and perhaps you and I could understand each other better than Ramrao and I could do. You'd see my point of view. That's what it is, really—that's the important thing—the point of view. You take the English point of view and he, being an Indian, would naturally take the Indian point of view."

"But he'd be on the side of law and order."

"Oh, in an ordinary criminal matter, a matter of highway robbery, arson, assault, burglary, murder, that sort of thing, of course. Oh, yes, naturally he'd be on the side of law and order. . . . But suppose it weren't a criminal matter at all, but something purely political. Suppose some active politician with, shall we say, rather extreme views, had gone beyond the very,

very wide limits allowed by the Law. That would be
different, wouldn't it? Your husband might in his heart
be inclined to agree with the politician. Might sympathize with him. All a matter of the point of view. Our
point of view, the Government's, the English point of
view generally, mine—and yours—would be that the
man was a potential danger to the peace, a fomenter of
disturbance, a very possible cause of rioting, looting,
bloodshed; and, as such, not to be encouraged. In fact,
definitely to be discouraged. You see, the two points of
view might be so widely divergent that from the one
he'd be regarded as a patriot, from the other as a rebel;
from the one point of view, a public benefactor; from
the other, a public danger."

"And how, with the best will in the world, could I
help you in a case like that?"

"Well, for example, by telling me if a man whose
name (or *alias*) I could give you, and whose appearance
I could describe, were in the habit of coming to the
house—or, indeed, if he came there on one occasion; or
you caught sight of him in, or about, the house; or
heard his name mentioned; or knew that he were a
friend, acquaintance, or—colleague—of your husband."

"Without my husband knowing that I told you?"

"Yes."

"I couldn't do that. I couldn't tell you things that he
wouldn't like me to tell you."

"No, I suppose not. I hardly meant that, though. . . .
I didn't think you'd do anything that would make you
feel—disloyal. I thought perhaps you could help me
without that."

"I should so love to help you, Anthony. But you
wouldn't have me spy on my husband, would you? I
couldn't watch him and report to you what he said or
did. . . . Why, I might get him into trouble."

"Do you think he does anything, then, that might
get him into trouble—if it were known?"

"No, I don't. Of course not. What I meant was, I
might tell you something that would give you that
impression—quite wrongly. I might tell you something
that he had said, and you might put a wrong

construction on it. Or I might tell you of some visitor who might prove to be a dangerous politician, though my husband did not know it."

"That wouldn't get him into trouble, Betty. It might save him from trouble, mightn't it? Don't you see? We might be able to open his eyes to the real character of such a visitor. Might be able to inform him that his new acquaintance wasn't worthy of his friendship."

"Y-e-e-s-s. . . . I see. Well, if it couldn't possibly do my husband any harm; get him into any sort of trouble —in fact, save him from getting into trouble through being imposed upon by a dangerous man who was really in hiding—that would be different."

"Yes, it would. Very different. Suppose you left it to me, Betty. I mean, trusted to me not to ask you to tell me anything that would get your innocent husband into trouble; cause him to be accused of anything he had not done; bring him under unjust suspicion. Would you help me then?"

"I'd just love to be of use, and I'd do anything to help you, so long as I wasn't being disloyal to my husband. But of course I might have known you wouldn't ask that. I am sorry I said what I did—about not spying on him. Of course you wouldn't ask me to spy on him."

"My dear, I wouldn't dream of asking you to get any innocent man into trouble, least of all your own husband. . . . Thanks so much for promising to help."

And the hand that lay over the girl's closed upon it and gave it a warm pressure.

Betty Gopaldas smiled up into his face and placed her other hand upon the one that held hers.

"Anthony, you do make me feel happy. I feel happy for the first time since I came to Bhawalgarh. I have been so unutterably *lonely*—and you make me feel I have a friend."

Steele took both hands in his and drew her round toward him. What a sweet face it was.

Damned shame really . . .

Still, the lives of the good men and true, working down there in Bhawalgarh; the *Pax Britannica*; the British Raj itself, perhaps, were at stake.

"That's what I want, Betty. I want you to feel you have a friend in me. And I want you to be my friend. I want you to help me."

That undoubtedly was the best line to take. She'd do things for him, personally, that she wouldn't dream of doing for any such abstraction as the *Pax Britannica* and the British Raj. Undoubtedly the best line; and he'd pursue it carefully, gradually, slowly. Work up to the point he wanted to reach. He mustn't rush his fences. Go slow and see how she re-acted. But time was everything. He must hasten—slowly. *Festina lente.*

"You can help me enormously Betty," he said.

"I will help you; and I'll trust you not to ask me to do anything that I feel I cannot do, or ought not to do. . . . But you won't do that, I know. . . . Can I really help you—on those terms?"

"Help me, Betty? You can save my life."

"Oh, we weren't going to have any joking. Not just now, I mean."

"Well, that's no joke. It's very nasty—being in a position where you have to have your life saved."

"Anthony"!

"Yes, really. Literally and truly. Joking apart. You could give me help that not only might, but almost certainly would, save my life.

"And some more valuable lives than mine," he added.

"Anthony! Is your life really in danger?"

"Oh, well, any Police Officer's life is in danger now-adays. Mine no more than anybody else's; but it is definitely threatened just now."

"Here, in Bhawalgarh?"

"Yes."

"Those dacoits?"

"Oh, they're nothing. A little rough-and-tumble with them is neither here nor there. All in the day's work and quite good fun. What's known as 'clean fun.' Dacoits are funny without being vulgar."

"What is it, then? Something . . . political?"

"Yes. There's a plot being hatched by a terrorist organization."

"To kill you?"

"To murder every gazetted official in Bhawalgarh."

"*Anthony!*"

The girl's eyes widened in horror; her lips parted in fear.

"To murder *you*? . . . And the Commissioner and Collector?"

"Yes, and everybody else of the other Services, too."

"But you will prevent it? You will be able to stop it?"

"Hope so. In fact I'm going to. If you help. The chief thing I want to know is the date. Of course I want to know all I can possibly learn—who's in it; where they meet; where they store their weapons and explosives; and so forth. But the most important thing is the date. If I knew that, I could act first. Try to arrest everybody whom I suspect, on some charge or other. Arrest all I can, anyhow. At present it's all suspicion. I know nothing with any certainty. I can prove nothing. And some of the people whom I suspect are not the sort who could be arrested on suspicion. You can run-in a bazaar *budmash* for loitering with intent, as he's pretty certain to be doing that at any time. But I couldn't arrest a man like Sant Arjun Rama, for example, for loitering—in Commissioner's House where he is, at present, an honoured guest—could I?"

"But Sant Arjun isn't a conspirator, he is a . . ."

"Or Bhojraj Shahani; the little pleader chap with the pointed beard and big gold-rimmed spectacles, tussore silk suit, collar and tie, little brown pill-box cap."

"But surely he's not . . ."

"Or Babu Purshotamdass; the huge, great fat man, frock-coat, bare calves, pink socks, patent-leather shoes, short hair, who goes bare-headed."

"Yes, I know him, but do you mean to say . . ."

"Or the Moulvie Abdul Haq; tall chap, European dress, with *tarboosh*—fez cap."

"But they all come to . . ."

"And the Sikh who may not be Ranjit at all. . . . The great powerful-looking chap, beard parted in the middle and brushed up sideways and tucked under a blue turban, pock-marked face."

"But, Anthony! . . ."

"I couldn't arrest *them* for loitering with intent, or on some trumpery excuse of that sort, could I? They're prominent citizens, men of mark and standing, and they're . . ."

"But Anthony . . . wait a moment. They're the men who come to the house. They . . ."

"Yes, my dear, they come to the house, don't they?"

"But—they're not *conspirators*?"

"That's what I want to know. I want to find out all I can about them. As I say, they are not bazaar *budmashes* whom a beat-constable can pick up and gather-in."

The girl withdrew her hands from Steele's.

"Anthony," she whispered, "do you mean to say that those men are conspirators, terrorists, murderers—and that they meet at our house?"

Holding her eyes with his, Steele slowly nodded his head.

"But . . ."

The girl rose to her feet in horror.

"Does my husband know? . . . Know what they are? . . . Know what they're doing?"

What should he say?

This was his chance; his moment. The lives of men, those men his friends, depended perhaps on what he said, what he did, now.

Had he read her aright?

Was he equal to his task; fit for his job; worthy of his responsibility; deserving of promotion; was he a man of skill and ability commensurate with the ambition that urged him to aim at the highest rank and position in his great service?

A false step now, and untold evil might result, immeasurable injury ensue, not only to life and limb, but to the country of his adoption, to the Indian people he loved, to the Government that he served, and to England. The flame of a great explosion here might light such an Indian jungle fire as should never be put out until the country was scorched, withered and blasted from end to end.

He held out his hand and the girl placed hers in it.

"Sit down, Betty," he said. "Tell me this. Suppose
. . . Just suppose—and I am only asking you to
imagine something, and then to try to give me a clear,
firm and certain answer . . . suppose Ramrao *did* know
that these men were members of a dangerous political
organization; a terrorist group; in fact, a gang of
determined and desperate murderers who were plotting, contriving and intending to kill me . . ."

He felt the grip of the girl's hand tighten upon his
own—unconsciously, doubtless.

"And what is much more important, to murder the
Commissioner, the Collector, Judge Sherdley, the Civil
Surgeon, Colonel Campbell, Professor Torrens, Major
Hector Grant at the Fort, Major Murdoch at the Gaol,
and in fact every European military and civilian officer
in Bhawalgarh. . . . Suppose he *did* know it."

"But, Anthony! He'd . . . he'd tell . . . He'd denounce
them."

"Suppose he knew . . . and didn't—tell?"

"He couldn't do such a thing. He'd . . . he'd . . . Tell
me, *does* he know?"

"Suppose he not only knew but *was one of them.*
Suppose he was a terrorist, a potential murderer, and
doing everything he could to bring about this massacre, this slaughter."

The girl sprang up again.

"You are only asking me to imagine it, of course. I
don't know why, but . . . Well, I'll try to imagine it."

"Thank you, Betty. I'm only asking you to try to
imagine it, because you've promised to help me. And
you are going to help me. Very well, imagine that
Ramrao is a terrorist and intends to be a murderer;
that he hopes and intends to kill me; and has, in point
of fact, already made the attempt. . . . Now then, Betty,
what would you do if it were true?"

And Steele, rising to his feet, towering over her,
exerted all his will-power, all the force of his personality, to dominate, to compel.

The girl's eyes fell. Her mouth twitched.

Damn it! Was she going to cry? God knew the job was difficult enough without that.

Placing his hands upon her shoulders,

"Answer me, Betty," he said, "answer me. Help me. What would you do if it were true? If you knew it were true?"

The girl tried to speak.

Putting his hand beneath her chin, he raised her head.

"Look at me, Betty. What would you do? Would you help me—or him—or neither of us?"

The girl swallowed, moistened her lips, and answered, "I'd help *you*."

"Of course you would, my dear," he whispered. "Of course you would. You'd help me—and England. Sit down."

And as they sat down again, he put his arm about her shoulders.

What was the expression on her face as she turned it to him? A little difficult to read.

Gratitude?

For what? For his friendship; his confidence; his putting his arm about her shoulders?

Was it love?

Anyhow, there was warmth in her eyes, a glow in her face—if an unusual firmness, almost hardness, about her mouth.

"*Is* it true?" she whispered.

"I don't know."

"I think you do know."

"Honour bright, Betty. You remember?"

She nodded and her eyes smiled.

"I don't know whether it is true or not. I want to find out—and I want you to help me. Will you?"

"Of course I will. I'll do absolutely anything that you tell me to do. If there is even a possibility that it's true. But I cannot believe it. I can't. I *can't* think that of Ramrao."

"No; well; look, Betty. If you will help me in the way I ask you, you will be clearing him of suspicion. If you can help me to find out that he knows nothing about it—doesn't know anything at all about who these men really are and what they are really up to—you will be helping him as well as me, won't you?"

A long silence.

"But suppose . . ." began the girl.

"Suppose it were true, you mean," he said. "Suppose he were one of them—a leader among them? Well—oughtn't he to be found out? Before it is too late? Oughtn't these murders to be prevented? Wouldn't you help to prevent them?"

"Of course the murders ought to be prevented," replied the girl, indignantly, flushing angrily as she spoke. "Any murder ought to be prevented. Of course I'd help you. Naturally, I'd do anything to prevent the murder of my worst enemy—let alone my . . . best friend."

"And suppose you found out, beyond any shadow of doubt, that your husband was implicated, what then?

"Well? Tell me, Betty," insisted Steele, as the girl hesitated. "What would you do?"

"I don't know. I feel that it would be all wrong of me to tell about him . . . denounce him. I should feel such a sneak, as schoolboys say. So treacherous. It would be a dreadful thing for a wife to do."

"Any wife to any husband," mused Steele aloud. "And of course the Law does not compel a wife to give evidence against her husband.

"But could you, and would you, sit quietly by while it went on? Sit and wait for the massacre?" he asked.

"No, I wouldn't. That would be ten times worse. I should go mad."

"Looks like a choice of evils then, doesn't it? Either you do anything you can to prevent murder—wholesale slaughter in fact—by finding out all you can, and telling all you know; or else you do nothing at all, and become accessory before the fact."

"Perhaps it isn't true. Perhaps he knows nothing about it."

"Exactly. Quite so. Perhaps. And in that case he should be cleared of suspicion, as I said, shouldn't he?"

"Yes, certainly he should."

"If he is under suspicion," she added. "Is he?"

"He is."

"Who suspects him?"

"I, for one."

"Can you tell me why you do, Tony? You know that I'd never dream of whispering a syllable of anything that you told me, don't you?"

"Yes, my dear, I do. I'll tell you. There are certain men whose arrival here in Bhawalgarh, at different times, was notified to me. They came from different parts of India, and are suspected of belonging to different branches of an extremely active political organization of terrorists calling themselves the Brethren of India. 'Enemies of India' would be a much more appropriate name for them. It is a seditious subversive society of political malcontents, and its avowed aim and object is the overthrow of the British Government. Their *raison d'être* is to wage war on His Majesty the King Emperor; their methods are the murder of the King's officials and the instigation of rioting, fire-raising, the spreading of consternation and alarm among His Majesty's subjects and the fomenting of disorder; their weapons are the bomb and the pistol; their tools, men generally better than themselves, men who have what they lack, courage and genuine, if misplaced, desire for political martyrdom. Well, some prominent members of this Society have, as I said, come to Bhawalgarh. Now, what first drew my attention to Ramrao and his brothers, Motiram, Jaganath and Tulsiram, was the discovery of the interesting fact that those different men, coming from different parts of India—each with the same sinister record—all, without exception, met at your husband's house.

"Isn't it a little curious and interesting that there is a Hindu agitator from Calcutta who has been in prison for openly preaching sedition and incitement to riot; that there is a Mussulman from the 'Hindustani fanatics' of Asmas, whose particular job in life is to bring about a working understanding between Mahommedan and Hindu terrorists; that there is a Brahmin politician from the Deccan, who wields the most subtle, dangerous, and virulent pen in India, and who was amazingly lucky to escape when a young *protégé* of his, undoubtedly trained by him for the purpose, was hanged for the cowardly murder of the Collector of Madrutta; that there is a very powerful preacher of revolution, who is wanted for the writing, printing, and dissemination of the most foully lying pamphlets that ever were circulated by cunning knaves among ignorant fools; that there is a master of propaganda who has been specially and intensively trained in America and Moscow by the enemies of England; and that there is also a man whose speciality is the undermining of the loyalty of sepoys and police, who, incidentally, is wanted for plain murder as well as for high treason; and who, to give him his due, is a bold fellow, a man of his hands, a fighter as well as a cunning devil, and probably the most courageous of the lot. . . . Isn't it a little curious and interesting that they should all meet in Bhawalgarh—and meet in Ramrao's house?"

"Those men meet at my husband's house?" asked Betty.

"They do, my dear."

"You are sure of that?"

"I know it! . . . Can you offer any explanation at exculpates Ramrao—and his brothers?"

"Ramrao may not know who or what they are; and he may be their innocent tool himself. I mean, they may meet at the house under the guise of a sort of philosophical society discussing—comparative religion."

The girl paused and looked Steele in the eyes.

"Anthony, did *I* say anything that made you suspect Ramrao, when we were talking about religious discussions, the night before last?"

"No, no, Betty," Steele assured her. "You told me nothing that I didn't know. Of course I knew that they met there. Didn't I describe them to you?"

"Yes. But mightn't it be as I say, that Ramrao doesn't really know what sort of men they are? He thinks they come to talk to Sant Arjun Rama and each other about . . ."

"Well, he hears what they talk about, doesn't he?"

"Isn't it possible that he goes out of the room and leaves them to talk together?"

"Is it likely?"

"Or mightn't they use a sort of code language that he doesn't understand? I mean, just to give each other information or warning—that sort of thing?"

"Is it likely?"

"Well, mightn't some of them whisper to each other when Sant Arjun or somebody else is addressing them?"

"Is it likely, Betty? Anyhow, there it is. They do meet at the house, and that *does* bring Ramrao under suspicion, doesn't it?"

"Yes."

"Well, let's try to clear him of suspicion; and if, in doing so, we find that it is quite impossible—well—we shall know where we are, shan't we?

"And you will know what to do, won't you?" he added.

"I shall. For I shall do exactly as you tell me."

Steele breathed a sigh of relief.

So that was that. Thank Heaven. A very fine morning's work. This looked like real progress, and as though he'd got the girl where he wanted her. And no harm done.

"Betty," he said, again covering her hand with his, "you are going to do something for England."

Flushing, the girl looked him in the eyes again, her unspoken thought,

"I'm going to do something for you. Don't you know I'd do anything for you, anything on earth?"

"I'm going to do what you ask me," she said, aloud.

"Good. Now there are two things I want you to find out if you possibly can, will you?"

"I will. Only show me how I can, and I will do my utmost."

"Well, the first thing is the date. From information received, I have every reason to believe that on a certain date, which may or may not be fixed, there is going to be a simultaneous attack upon Government Offices and Government officials in Bhawalgarh. Also upon the Banks, the Railway-station, the Post and Telegraph Offices and the Gaol. All to be blown up simultaneously. Not only will there be hideous loss of life, and destruction of property by that act, but the explosion will be the signal for rioting, arson and murder; probably indiscriminate slaughter and looting of wealthy shop-keepers, money-lenders, and people of that sort; and the rioting will quite quickly lead on to the inevitable Hindu-Mussulman clash, defilement of mosques and temples, street fighting, and more slaughter.

"Now, the most important thing in the world for me just now is the date."

"You don't suppose they'd tell me that?"

"I don't. No. Of course not. But with your usual woman's wit and unusual intelligence, you might be able to put two and two together. . . . Now, think hard. Could you remember anything that has been said or done that might possibly give a clue?"

The girl sat silent, frowning in thought.

"The only thing I can think of, myself," continued Steele, "is some anniversary date, like June 23rd. That's the anniversary of the Battle of Plassey. It is just possible that, having no particular reason to choose one day more than another, they would choose a great day like that. It is the sort of thing that has been done before, both in Indian and European history. Have you heard any reference to dates, or can you think of any date of any sort or kind in the near future that they might choose for any reason?"

A silence fell between them, while he watched her narrowly.

The girl's hand turned over inside Steele's and took his.

Suddenly she spoke.

"The Governor's visit!"

"Good. Clever girl. Yes, I'd thought of that, too."

"Is the date fixed?" asked Betty.

'Was the date fixed?' Should he tell her it was; tell

her it was a strict secret; that, so far, only the police knew? Should he name a date which would undoubtedly be a later one than that on which the Governor would come? If it went home to Ramrao Gopaldas, might that affect their plans at all? Postpone their own date? Should he mislead her?

How suspicious and distrustful this work made one. But could a police officer, especially in India, be too suspicious, too distrustful? He might. It was just possible he might overdo it, miss chances, forfeit help that he would otherwise have got. He must trust somebody, sometime.

Yes, one of the qualifications of a good police officer was knowing whom to trust and how far to trust them. This girl was sterling. He would back his judgment— and trust her absolutely.

"No, in point of fact it isn't fixed," he said, "and, for that very reason, the date of the plot may not be fixed. If I could know for certain that no definite day had been decided upon, I should say that the announcement of the date of the Governor's visit would fix it."

"And you'd be sure that you were safe until the Governor came. I mean you'd feel sure that the conspirators would do nothing until then."

"Yes."

"Is it likely they would wait until the Governor came?" she asked.

"Well; yes and no. There's no particular reason why they should attempt to get him in Bhawalgarh if they were going to get him at all. It would be just as easy, or difficult, to shoot him or bomb him in his own Government House at the capital. On the other hand, it would be a sort of crowning triumph for the devils if they could include the Governor himself in the holocaust here."

"What grounds have you for believing that there is such a plot, apart from the fact that these suspects . . . ?"

"They are more than suspects, Betty. They are known agitators, seditionists, terrorists. Some of them are known criminals, in fact. Yes, apart from the fact that these men are here in Bhawalgarh and are known to hold meetings, I caught one of them, or rather one of their employees, dupes, tools—and got it out of him."

"And couldn't you make him tell you the date?"

"No, he didn't know it. Of that I am convinced. And that again is one reason why it may be the date of the Governor's visit."

"I suppose you couldn't turn him into a police-agent and use him to . . ."

"No, he's dead. They killed him."

"Is he the one who tried to kill you?"

"Yes."

"Oh, what *can* we do? You cannot arrest them all?"

"I can't. I've nothing against any of them, except the Sikh, if he is the man calling himself Ranjit Singh. He's for it, the moment we can lay hands on him. Meanwhile . . ."

Suddenly the girl turned to him again.

"I have just thought of something. I've just thought of something . . . that may be helpful. Ramrao told me this morning that he is sending me away."

"*What?* When?" asked Steele eagerly. "Sending you away? By Jove! When, Betty? *When?*"

"In a fortnight's time."

The girl scanned his face. Was there the slightest expression of regret? No. But then, so far as she knew, his face never showed what he felt, never showed any feeling at all. Was there any sign of regret in his voice?

No. And she mustn't be selfish, self-centred. He had something much more important to think about than a trifle like that.

"Tell me exactly what he said."

"I'll try to remember exactly. Now wait a minute, and I'll try to get it exact, word for word. He said,

"'You are going riding with Mr. Steele to-day, aren't you?' and then asked me if we were going to make a fixture of it; was it to be a weekly event, a ride every Saturday morning. I told him that nothing of the sort had been suggested. And then he asked me if I wouldn't like to ride with you regularly."

"And what did you say to that?"

"I told him that I should, for it was very much nicer to have company than to ride alone."

"Yes?"

"And then he asked why I didn't suggest it."

"He did, eh?"

"I told him that I shouldn't do that, for doubtless you had something else to do."

"Yes?"

"And then he said it would be very nice for me to have someone to ride with, and told me, at any rate, to fix up another ride. Any time within the next fortnight."

"Yes?"

"And I said that if you asked me to ride with you again, I should do so. And then Ramrao said—and I remember his exact words—

"'Only don't fix anything up with him for any day after a fortnight hence.'"

"That's plain. And you asked him why not, of course?"

"Yes, and he said,

"'You won't be here.' . . .

"We are all going down to Dhargaum with his mother; and he went on to say that he might be going to and fro, but that either Motiram or Jaganath would probably remain in Dhargaum; and if they did not, Tulsiram would, as the College would be closed."

Steele's face showed nothing of the joy, the triumph, the intense interest, enthusiasm, relief, that he felt. Here was news indeed. Here was something much more solid, useful, probable. After all, June 23rd had been the merest shot in the dark, and the date of the Governor's visit a speculative idea, a possibility.

"You didn't happen to remark that it was a bit sudden, did you, Betty?"

"No. Well, I did in a way. I remember saying,

"'This is the first I've heard of it.'"

"Yes, and what did he say to that?"

"He said, 'I didn't hear it myself until last night.'"

"And then?"

"I said that I supposed it was his mother's idea, and he agreed that it was."

"And then?"

"I asked how long we should be there, and he said,

"'Probably until the Rains.'"

"Any more?"

"No, except that I told him I didn't want to go to Dhargaum with his mother; and he said neither did he, but that we were going nevertheless. And that was that."

"Was that all?"

"Yes. Not another word. Do you think it has any bearing?"

Steele studied the girl's face. Open, honest, eager, transparently ingenuous.

"I do, my dear. I do think there is something in it. And I think you've helped me enormously."

"Oh, I *am* glad."

Again the girl took the man's hand in hers.

"If I could only be a real help to you."

"I believe you have helped me enormously. And you are going to help me a lot more. . . . 'In a fortnight.' You are absolutely certain of that?"

"Absolutely. He said it at least twice—that if you invited me to ride with you again, I was to accept 'any time within the next fortnight.' "

"Then it looks as though I've got a fortnight's respite . . . a fortnight's safety . . . a fortnight to work in."

"Have you really?"

"Yes. It's not as though it were a hardy annual, this visit to—where was it, Dhargaum? The family doesn't go there every year, does it?"

"No. I've never heard of their going. They didn't last year, I know."

"Why Dhargaum, I wonder. And as we said, it's a bit sudden."

Silence.

The girl realized that she was stroking the hand that she held, protectively, anxiously, quite unconsciously.

It was all-right. He hadn't noticed it.

"Betty, when you get back, will you do something for me?"

"I'll do anything I can."

"Could you pretend to be a little—what shall we say? A little mutinous—about the Dhargaum business? Say, in fact, that you are not going; that you refuse."

"I will. But it won't make the slightest difference, of course."

"No, but it might make him give some reason for his wanting you to go."

"He'd only say that it is the 'Maharani's' wish, as though that were good and sufficient reason for anything."

"And suppose you say that it is not your wish. In fact, it's your wish and intention to stay here in Bhawalgarh. That wouldn't make any difference to your going, of course, but might it not compel him to give some further and better reason than Subhadra's whim?"

"I doubt it. I really think that he considers that to be quite sufficient reason for anybody."

"Yes, but suppose you said that you didn't consider it so."

"It wouldn't make any difference, and I don't think he'd pretend to offer any other reason."

"No, but it might perhaps disclose the *fact* of urgency, if not the reason for any urgency, mightn't it? An attitude of refusal and real obstinacy on your part might provoke him to say something. I mean, something that would show how absolutely imperative it is that the family should get out of Bhawalgarh in a fortnight's time. Do you see what I mean?"

"Yes. And I'll try."

That would mean trouble, bad trouble with old Subhadra. If she really stuck out and gave the impression that nothing on earth would induce her to go, she'd probably "fall ill" again—one of those mysterious illnesses that were apt to follow upon defiance of the terrible old woman. Not that that would deter her from doing as Anthony asked her.

It would mean trouble and she would suffer, but it would be a delight to suffer for him, if it would help him at all.

Of course they'd tell her anything in the world but the real reason for going to Dhargaum. But as Anthony said, it would show how imperative it was that they should go; and that would tell him something. It would not be proof, but it would be an indication that for some reason—whether personal safety or the averting of suspicion—the Gopaldas family must be out of Bhawalgarh at the time of the explosion. They would all go to Dhargaum; and doubtless Ramrao and any of his brothers who came thence to Bhawalgarh, would do so secretly.

Yes, she would absolutely refuse to go. She would defy the 'Maharani,' and make them use actual physical force. And if they did so—Anthony would know.

But even that would prove nothing, of course; though it would go far to confirm suspicion.

Couldn't she do something that would give proof, one way or the other? As Anthony had said, if Ramrao were innocent, he had nothing to fear. On the contrary, she might be able to show that he was quite innocent; and that if this dreadful plot existed, he knew nothing about it.

Would it be possible for her to be present at their next meeting, or to overhear what was said?

Wild ideas of disguising herself and getting into their midst in the rôle of an emissary of another branch of their Society flashed through her mind, only to be dismissed as absurd. Equally absurd was any idea of listening at a key-hole, hiding in the room in which they met, or successfully spying upon them in any other way.

"Well, Betty?"

"I was just thinking. Couldn't I do anything more helpful than refusing to go to Dhargaum and thus finding out to what lengths they would go, to take me away with them?"

"I was just thinking the same thing, but I don't, at present, see what you could do."

"I wonder what would happen if I tried to join them, offered to work with them and for them?"

"Well, the first thing that would happen would be that they would not rest until they'd found out how you knew anything at all. They'd probably begin by being tremendously amused. They'd ask each other how long you'd been insane; and if they found out that you really knew anything at all, they'd probably decide that you knew too much."

"And then . . . ?"

"Then I've no doubt they'd take steps to see that you didn't find out any more."

"Sticky end, d'you mean?"

"I should certainly be anxious about your health, Betty. I should say that old Subhadra is just about six-teenth century; a lady who'd thoroughly understand, admire, and approve the Borgias and their methods."

"Yes, I've been taken ill once or twice already, after a row with my mother-in-law. Pure coincidence, per-haps."

"Pure cause-and-effect more likely.

"No," continued Steele. "I'm afraid we can do noth-ing along those lines. You see, it is not as though you could be the slightest good to them, Betty. If you were in a position to say to them,

"'I know all about it. I'm with you heart and soul, and I can be of enormous help to you,' it would be a different matter. They might give you a chance to show how helpful you could be. They might suspend judgment or, rather, defer sentence—and put you on probation. But they know perfectly well that you couldn't be of the slightest use to them. With all the will in the world, you couldn't help them. There was that shocking case where they got at a wretched girl student, and perverted and debauched her mind so horribly that she actually fired three shots at the Governor, at a public meeting. It doesn't bear thinking of. A thoroughly nice, innocent school-girl and college-student until they got hold of her, and now a degraded wretch serving a life-sentence as a convict in the Andaman Islands. Aren't they heroes, the brave fellows that put the pistol in the child's hand?

"Well," he continued, "they know quite well that

they couldn't use you in that sort of way. And there is no other. No, I'm afraid you'd pronounce something uncommonly like your own death-warrant if you told them you knew their names, records, and intentions; and that you knew all about their plot for a wholesale bombing of Bhawalgarh."

"Suppose I went to Ramrao and told him that I'd discovered everything, and that I was going to denounce him, and them, to the authorities."

"Well . . . I don't think we should meet again, Betty. I think you'd go either to Dhargaum or to Heaven. Probably to Heaven *via* Dhargaum."

"And it wouldn't do any good? I shouldn't be helping you?"

"No good at all. I should say it would merely hurry on the date. . . . The only thing that might save you would be their knowledge of the fact that you have no evidence at all; that, in point of fact, you know nothing at all, you merely suspect what, in point of fact, is the exact truth."

"And of course you know nothing yourself, really?"

"In a way, nothing. I know their names, and that they meet at your husband's house; and I suspect that they meet at another place and that they are hatching a most comprehensive and wholesale murder plot. I haven't the slightest proof or any producible evidence, and my one possible witness has been murdered— which murder is proof positive to my mind, but is no evidence at all in a Court of Law. With the exception of Ranjit Singh, for whom we are looking, not one of them is a 'wanted' man.

"Suppose I arrested the men I believe to be the ring-leaders. No committing Magistrate would send one of them for trial on the evidence that I have got. If I could get them committed for trial, no Sessions Judge would convict. And suppose a Sessions Judge, being morally certain of their guilt, did so, there is still the High Court, and the High Court would rightly dismiss the case. There simply *is* no case because, as I say, I have got no proof.

"I have only got certainty," he added bitterly. "Certainty that we are all condemned to death, thanks to the cumbrous British Law and 'Justice' that protect them."

Silence.

"Anthony, I've got another idea. You think that Ramrao may have meant me to tell you that I should only be here another fortnight."

"Yes, I do. What I am wondering is whether he said a fortnight because it is a week—or a month. I took it at its face value when you told me; but I've been thinking. In the first place, why should he be keen on your riding with me, and suggest that you try to make a fixture of it? . . . Because he wants you to tell me something. He wants you to be a channel of information, or rather misinformation, between him and me. What would it matter to him if you made an appointment you couldn't keep? Why should he be so particular as to your not making an appointment for any date beyond a fortnight hence? Pure pretence— and obviously because he wants you to tell me that you will be gone, after a fortnight. And why should he want you to tell me that you and his family will only be here another fortnight? Simply because it will be some other period than a fortnight.

"The false security again," he mused. "At first, you see, I fell headlong into the trap; chuckled to myself, and said, 'Ah, I've got a fortnight to work in.' Now I realize that you were intended to tell me that I had a fortnight to work in. Therefore I have not. You feel sure, yourself, that he meant you to tell me?"

"Yes, I do. Thinking back, I feel sure that I was intended to tell you that I should only be here another fortnight; and that's what gave me the idea."

"What is it?"

"Why, if he can use me to send you misinformation, couldn't you do the same thing?"

"Just what I was thinking, Betty. In the first place, when you get back, and he asks if I invited you to ride again, you say,

"'Yes. We are going for another ride on Tuesday.' When he asks if I made any suggestion of more rides

542

after that, you say that I told you that I always ride once a week in the early morning before inspection-parade, and I asked if we should have a ride on those days, at any rate.

"When he asks whether you told me it could only be for a fortnight, you reply that you did mention it. When he asks what I said to that, say it didn't appear to interest me in the slightest degree. I just said,

"'Righto, we'll have some more when you come back, then.'

"Are you a good fibber, Betty?"

"Haven't had much practice, but I'll manage that all-right."

"Good. Now, it will interest me very much to know what other questions he asks you. Especially if he enquires whether I happened to mention the date of the Governor's visit, and secondly, if he asks you whether I told you of anything that happened to me on Thursday night or last night."

"I'll remember every word he says. What am I to reply?"

"That the date of the Governor's visit is fixed for to-day month; that he'll arrive on the Saturday, stay over Sunday, and go on Monday. Remember that?"

"Yes, a month to-day. Saturday, stay Sunday, and go on the Monday."

"Good. And about Thursday night and Friday night I made no mention whatever. You see, it would be quite natural that I should have advance information about the Governor's visit, and that I should tell you, as a matter of interesting gossip. But it isn't likely that, in casual conversation, I should talk to you about so serious a police-affair as the attempted murder of myself, and the actual murder of the man who had bungled the attempt."

"It will be pretty significant if he does ask me if anything was said about an attempt on your life, won't it?"

"Yes, most significant and interesting. But of course he wouldn't put it like that. It will be quite sufficiently noteworthy if he seems to be hinting—fishing for information, trying to find out about it, won't it?"

"Yes. Or if he shows the slightest interest in what we talked about. He has never displayed any interest in my doings outside the house before, much less in the subjects of my conversation with friends.

"Not that I have any friends," she added. "I should have said acquaintances."

"Well, you've a friend now, anyway, Betty."

This marched indeed. How amazingly he had changed her in the course of an hour. Changed her from "I couldn't possibly spy upon my husband" to "I'll tell you exactly what he says."

But he mustn't take credit to himself. Subconsciously no doubt, however much her conscious mind might deny it, she detested and despised the man, loathed his family, and abhorred the life she had to lead with them.

No, there was little credit to himself, for of course he was amazingly lucky in the fact that she obviously— well—liked him; and was more than ready to be liked by him.

"There's one thing," said Betty. "Granted that the fortnight was pure misinformation, I don't think there's the slightest doubt that we are going to Dhargaum. If, from that, you argue that it is either for reason of the family's personal safety when there is rioting, looting, and bloodshed; or else for reason of establishing an alibi at the time of the massacre—then nothing terrible will happen while they are here in Bhawalgarh."

"Yes. Their departure will be like that of rats from the sinking ship. Their going will be a signal. . . . We'll make fairly frequent appointments to ride together, and so long as you are here, the probabilities are that the date isn't fixed. Any time you don't turn up I shall be forewarned."

"Yes. . . . I wonder if I could communicate with you."

"We'll think about that. . . . Of course, the date *may* be fixed, and they may rush off to Dhargaum the day before, or the same night, but I don't think so. That would look a bit suspicious. You see, Ramrao will know that you've told me that the family is going to Dhar-gaum, a thing they haven't done before; and he'll know it would look definitely odd if it happened that they cleared out just in time to escape both danger and implication. Escape danger of the explosion as well as of the looting and rioting, and escape suspicion of being implicated in the rising.

"No, I should say that the date is not fixed, and if it is, that he will leave Bhawalgarh well before the day—a week at least, probably.

"Now about communicating with me if there is any news, any warning. I suppose you've no trustworthy person by whom you could send a message?"

"Absolutely none. I haven't a soul in whom I could place the faintest reliance. If I wrote a note to you and gave it to one of the servants, it would be taken straight to Ramrao, or more likely to Subhadra."

"And you've no conveyance of your own—no *tum-tum*,[45] victoria, or car?"

"Nothing whatever. The only time I can get out alone is when I ride, and more often than not the horse has a diplomatic illness."

"Yes, I remember you told me on Thursday night. He 'evolves lameness out of his inner consciousness,' doesn't he?" smiled Steele.

Oh, how delightful. He'd remembered what she'd said. That was nice.

"Yes, and by the way, that reminds me. I don't know whether it is of importance. The horse was declared lame this morning and Ramrao followed me downstairs—a thing he's never done before—to see me off; or rather to see that I got off. I am quite sure he expected to find the horse was lame. He did, and he very soon cured it."

"Oh? How?"

"Beat the syce unmercifully. And the horse was miraculously healed, cured, *un*lamed. And Ramrao was really in a frightful rage. I'd never seen him like that before. I didn't dream he had it in him to assert himself like that."

---

[45] *Trap; dog-cart.*

"In fact, he was determined that you should get your ride, a thing that has never interested him hitherto, eh? In short, he was determined that you should ride with me. Why? So that you could give me certain misinformation; and also that he might find out whether you'd received any genuine information, such as the date of the Governor's visit; and whether I had anything to say, any speculations to make, as to the interesting events of Thursday and Friday night at my bungalow. That's it. Good again, Betty."

"But if I could get you something really definite, tangible; because when all is said and done, this is still all suspicion, isn't it?"

"Yes, based on pretty solid ground, though. And with quite solid results and conclusions, thanks to you, my dear. Whether I am right or whether I am absolutely wrong, I'm convinced that there will be no explosion before the family goes to Dhargaum. Also that, for some reason or other, Ramrao intends you to ride with me and to hoodwink me unintentionally. And there is some good reason behind that, of course."

"And you cannot think of anything else that I can do at present, except to mislead Ramrao?"

"No, I'd give anything for confirmation on the subject of the date; and I'd give a very great deal to know some more about a man whom they call 'Number Seven'; who he is; where he is; when he's coming here; how he's coming; and exactly why he's coming. Of course, the last is fairly obvious. He's coming to put the final touches on the plot *bandobast* and to do any gingering-up that might be necessary. But whether he's coming for the purpose of bringing any special explosives, infernal machines, time-bombs, I don't know, of course. They may be here already; or the component parts may be here, and he may be the expert who puts them together. I suppose you've never heard any reference to 'Number Seven'?"

"No, I haven't."

"Naturally. I don't suppose you will. By the way, does Ramrao talk in his sleep?"

"Well, as a matter of fact, he does. He's what one

might call a noisy sleeper. He frequently wakes me up. I hear him tossing and turning and grinding his teeth. He shouts fairly frequently, too."

"Goes in for nightmares, eh?"

"Yes. I can't say I have ever heard him say anything coherent in his sleep."

"No, that's a very faint hope. I generally shut the book when I come to the page where the villain gives himself away by babbling things in his sleep. Detective thrillers interest me very much, nevertheless. They are so damned funny. *Really* funny, to a police-man. No, I don't suppose he'll sit up one night and suddenly begin a dream conversation with the words, 'My dear Mr. So-and-So, otherwise Number Seven.' We won't count on it, Betty."

"No. I wonder what would happen if, suddenly *à propos* of nothing at all, I said,

"'Ramrao, who is Number Seven?'"

"Yes, an interesting matter of speculation—but I shouldn't carry it beyond speculation. Consequences might be unpleasant, drastic; and he certainly wouldn't tell you.

"By the way," he continued, "can you sit at a window or at an aperture in the verandah lattice-work that overlooks the front entrance to the house? Quite naturally and without incurring suspicion?"

"Yes, I could. Very often when it is stiflingly hot in the bedroom I go out into the verandah that looks on to the street—it is all shut in with pretty close lattice-work, apertures hardly big enough to poke your finger through—and open the lattice 'window.' Why?"

"Well, I was thinking that any time you happen to see Purshotamdass or Bhojraj or Sant Arjun Rama or Abdul Haq or any other of the philosophers come in, it might mean that there was going to be a meeting that night, and if you watched, you might notice a man whom you'd never seen before. If so, and you could describe him to me, it might lead to something. He might, or might not, be the mysterious Number Seven who, I believe, is the most important of them all, and the mainspring of the works of this particular plot."

"Yes, I'll keep the sharpest look-out that it is possible for me to do without arousing suspicion. But they don't come in at the front of the house. There is a way into the courtyard at the back of the compound."

"Oh? That's interesting. Then they must come through another house that backs on to yours?"

"Yes. I have never attempted to go out that way, of course, nor down that horrible smelly little lane beside the house, but it is from my bedroom, which also has a small verandah at the back, that I have seen these people come across the courtyard. I shouldn't have thought anything about them except for the fact that I was surprised to know there was a way in at the back, like that."

"But it was at night?"

"Yes, there is quite a bright lamp over the door in the back verandah—at the top of the steps. When any-one comes and the door is opened, he naturally looks up. That's how I noticed Purshotamdass and Bhojraj and the Mohammedan. . . . I have been so bored, sitting upstairs hour after hour with nothing to do and nothing to read, that I've sat at the verandah lattice 'window,' both at the back and the front, and it has been quite an event to see people arrive, somewhat mysteriously, at the back of the house."

"Who admits them?"

"I don't know. I can't see from above. But I do distinctly see the visitor as he raises his head and comes up the steps from the compound to the ground-floor verandah level."

"H'm. . . . So a police agent, shadowing the front of the house, naturally wouldn't have anything to report about visitors. Now I wonder through which house—or rabbit warren—they get into your compound. . . . We must watch for the gentlemen in the street behind yours. That's Borah Bazaar, isn't it? Yes. . . . Thanks, Betty. That's useful again. I had no idea there was any way in at the back."

"That in itself is suspicious too, isn't it. . . . ? I didn't think of it at the time, or if I gave it a thought, I suppose I imagined it was because they were meeting to talk religion, and might get into trouble with their caste-fellows if it were known that they were attending Sant Arjun Rama's—Christian missionary-meetings."

"Quite suspicious, as you say. Or else why should that particular gang meet at night, and sneak in by a back way? Yes—and that accounts for Ranjit Singh."

"How d'you mean?"

"Well, I was surprised when you told me that he came there. I wondered that he had the nerve, though I suppose he has pluck enough for anything. That secret entrance accounts for it."

Suddenly the girl started.

"Anthony," she exclaimed, "I have misled you."

"Intentionally, Betty? Before we—understood each other?"

"No. Just carelessness. I have just remembered. It wasn't there at all that I saw the man you described—the Sikh."

"Eh? Where, then?"

"Why, it was one morning when I was out riding."

"What, passed him on the road, and happened to notice him?"

"No. I was riding along, and saw two men sitting under a tree. One of them was lighting a little fire, and I remember wondering what he was going to cook, and how he was going to cook it—because he certainly wasn't wanting the fire for warmth, although it was about six o'clock in the morning. One of them was a *faquir*—one of the dirty professional beggars—and the other wore a turban and had a sheet round him. I didn't notice his face."

"You noticed a good deal, anyhow, Betty. Good."

"Well, I noticed them because I had never seen anybody at all when riding out this way before."

"Oh, out this way, was it?"

"Yes, and when I rode back, the man who'd been sitting there wrapped in the sheet, got up as I drew near. He came toward me and salaamed, and said, in excellent English,

"'Excuse me, Mem-sahib. I have a message for your husband.' I didn't much like the look of him and got ready to touch Star with my spur.

"'Well?' I said.

"'Will Mem-sahib kindly say that a poor brother is visiting Bhawalgarh?'

"As I said, I didn't like his face at all, so I simply rode on without saying anything whatever."

"Did you tell Ramrao?"

"Yes, I thought I'd better."

"And was he interested?"

"Yes; looking back, I am quite sure he was. Very. Though he pretended not to be. . . . Yes, now I come to think of it, the real reason why I remember the man is because Ramrao asked me to describe him. I remember saying he was a big, powerful-looking man, with a pock-marked face, wearing his beard and hair as a Sikh does."

"I was puzzled at the time by the man knowing who I was," she added.

"Did you notice the *faquir*?"

"Only glanced at him."

"Was he a most repulsive, bloated brute with a hideous thick-lipped, drink-sodden sort of face; a ruffian who looked as though he lived on *bhang*[46]?"

"No, quite the reverse. I remember that much because, although the Sikh's face was nothing like that, it was coarse by comparison with the *faquir's*."

Steele nodded.

"Yes, I thought as much," he said. "That was the Swami; and of course the Swami knows you by sight. He knows everything, according to his own account. He saw you ride by; and, no doubt, told Ranjit Singh who you were and suggested sending a message to Ramrao through you, as the quickest way of letting him know that he was here."

"And he hasn't come to the house? You've never seen him since?" he added.

"No."

"Ah, well, that exonerates my people to some extent. I was a bit perturbed at the idea that he was knocking about the bazaars and calling on Ramrao,

---

[46] Hashish.

and they'd never spotted him. He's the one whom we *can* arrest, though I imagine the plot will go on just the same, if we do.

"Good," he continued. "Well now, about the other man—this 'Number Seven.' Will you keep a look-out, as far as you can, and let me know if those people come to the house again, and particularly if one comes whom you've never seen before. Of course, any number of people whom you don't know, and perhaps haven't seen before, may come in by the front way and be perfectly innocent visitors; but anyone who comes in by the back way and at night, is not only open to the gravest suspicion, but may be the man I want, the man they call 'Number Seven.' I believe him to be of the utmost importance and I have not the faintest idea as to who he is or what he's like."

"I'll do my best," replied the girl. "I'll watch from my bedroom verandah at the back of the house, every night, when Ramrao is not there. I will especially look out for a man whom I haven't seen before. And I will do all I can to find out how urgent it is that the family should go away from Bhawalgarh. . . . How shall I communicate with you, if I have anything to tell you?"

"Well, we'll ride again, as soon as we can, and I shall see you on Thursday night at the Literary binge, I hope. But suppose there were anything urgent? . . . Of course you never go out on foot, Betty? Nobody does."

"No, I have never gone out for a walk; and I don't imagine I should be allowed to do so. I should certainly be followed if I did."

"You could never get out unobserved, I suppose?"

"No. There is always a *chowkidar* or *durwan* or a sort of *pattiwallah*, at the door. At the front entrance, invariably. I've never been in or out without seeing him there. In fact, the door is kept bolted, and it is his job to open it for anyone, and to fasten it after him."

"And the same with the door at the back verandah?"

"Well, I've only been down there when I go riding, and there has always been someone there, too."

"What happens when you post a letter?"

"I have always given my letters to Ramrao, and he either posts them when he goes to his office or sends them with his own, by his clerk or *pattiwallah* to the Post Office."

"It's rather amazing," observed Steele, "but it seems to be a simple fact, that you've absolutely no means of sending a private message to a person living in the same Station. Well, anyhow, we'll have another ride on Tuesday morning, shall we, and then shall I be seeing you again on Thursday evening at the Gymkhana before dinner? And we could ride again to-day week?"

The girl smiled happily. Yes, that would be splendid. Out of this great and ghastly threatened evil would come, at any rate, a little good. No, a great good—the happiness of seeing him more often, and possibly that of being helpful.

"Then I'll tell Ramrao that we are going riding again on Tuesday morning," she said.

"Yes, and it will be interesting to see what line he takes. I rather fancy that he'll agree most readily—and probably send some more misinformation. I'll look out for you again at seven o'clock on the road by the Police Lines, and if you are not there, I'll come to the Gymkhana to tea on Thursday, and ask you for a dance. And I shall see you at Commissioner's House at the Literary Society meeting after dinner."

"But what if I am not there?"

"Then another ride on Saturday morning."

"And if I shouldn't be there then, either?"

"I shall be a bit worried, Betty."

Did he mean on her account or on his own? On his own, of course. Not his own safety; but his work, his duty. But perhaps he was a little worried on her account, too?

"However, I shall know whether the family has gone to Dhargaum or not. I'll have the house and the railway-station watched," he added.

Yes, that would be all-right. Thanks to what the girl had told him, the Gopaldas family would not be able to make a midnight flitting by the back way into the Borah Bazaar, while the police-agent was watching the front of the house in the Sudder Bazaar. And he'd have both the Bhawalgarh and the Chinchgad railway-stations watched by someone who knew the family by sight. And if they hired motor-cars and went by road, they'd be seen leaving the house.

"You really feel absolutely certain in your own mind that they positively are going to Dhargaum?"

"Perfectly certain. You can be sure of their doing that."

It would be very interesting to know when the Gopaldas brothers had decided on this move; how long they had had it in mind. He would have to send a good man down to Dhargaum to make discreet enquiries. It ought to be easy enough for a sharp fellow to find out what house they had taken; when they took it; and, possibly, when they were expected to arrive.

"Anthony," said Betty suddenly, "I'm going to promise you something, and you can really rely on me. . . . I feel so grateful to you for trusting me—and being my friend—that I want to do this for you. If anything happens suddenly; if there is any emergency; if I come to learn anything urgent that I feel you ought to know at once; I promise I will let you know, *somehow*."

"Good," said Steele.

That was the spirit. She'd do it, too. Nothing like young enthusiasm for carrying anything through, especially when allied to quixotry and a little affection, a warm glow of personal feeling. Love, in fact. Damn shame, really, but—the end and the means. The gigantic end and the microscopic means. The fate of an Empire—and the feelings of a girl.

"If I think it is really urgent, then, you shall know. Why, if real necessity arose, I'd run out of the house, straight to the Telegraph Office, and send you a telegram."

"H'm. I don't know about that. Even supposing you got out of the house and reached the Telegraph Office, there would be the question of how much you could say in a telegram *tout au long*. I'm not too sure as to how far the telegraph babu here is to be trusted, either. He may be a Brother himself."

"Then I'll come to your house, Tony."

That was the spirit. He had never done a better day's work in his life. If only there had been some way of getting her into their meetings, their inner councils. But that was hopeless.

Anyhow, he'd get a line on the date, inasmuch as she'd let him know as soon as the family was flitting; and whether a stranger came in by the secret way, a stranger who might be Number Seven.

"Provided you get out of your own house, Betty," he said.

"Yes, but it has just occurred to me that if the servants hate Subhadra half as much as I think they do, and if they only work for Ramrao for their miserable wages as I believe they do . . ."

"I see," exclaimed Steele. "Quite so. A few rupees would do the trick, eh? Yes, it is extremely likely. Love of *pice*[47] and love of intrigue are pretty nearly their strongest passions; their besetting sins."

Betty laughed ruefully.

"What's the joke?" smiled Steele.

"Anthony, I haven't the few rupees."

Steele laughed.

By Jove, that was a bit thick, if quite to be expected. Yes, ordinarily speaking, of course, she'd have no use for petty cash and would have no sort of allowance; and in a joint-family household like this, would have no handling of house-keeping money. Old Subhadra would see to that.

"Oh, well; that's all-right," he smiled. "In any case, you'd be administering public funds. Secret Service money, devoted to the bribery and corruption of enemy agents, eh? Will you administer some for me, Betty?"

"Yes. Though I'm afraid I shan't be able to give vouchers and receipts and so on," she smiled.

"No, the *chowkidar* won't write out an acknowledgment for five rupees for services rendered in deceiving the 'Maharani,' will he? However, I don't think that's a fatal objection. . . . Look here, you take these five-rupee notes and see what you can do in that way."

---

[47] *Small copper coins. Money.*

"I don't like taking the money, but it would be silly to be squeamish about it, because so much might depend on your knowing in time."

"My dear child, the lives of all the Europeans in Bhawalgarh might depend on my knowing in time; not to mention what might follow on the successful demonstration that the terrorists can carry out a thing like this. . . . Have you got a personal *ayah*?"

"No."

"Is there any non-*purdah* woman-servant, who goes in and out of the house and whom you could bribe?"

"I never thought of it till now. I don't know. There's a poor wretched widow who's a sort of half hanger-on, half servant, who does what little there is done in our rooms."

"A poor relation of the Gopaldas family?"

"Something of the sort. By marriage, I should think. Probably the wife of the cousin of the nephew of the aunt of Ramrao's uncle's sister's daughter's son."

"Something close like that, eh? No very strong blood-tie. Do you think she might be useful?"

"Well, Subhadra is extremely cruel to her; treats her really brutally, as though she had some unforgettable personal grudge against her. I've always been kind to the poor thing, because I feel so sorry for her. She is still quite young, but—well, I'd sooner be a dog in the compound than lead her life, and with nothing on earth to look forward to."

"Do you think you could do anything with her?"

"I think it is quite possible. I have only just thought about it, of course."

"Well, you try the effect on her of a glimpse of the corner of a five-rupee note. She'd probably bring a letter to my bungalow. Especially if she got half the reward before she started, and was going to get the other half as soon as you knew of its safe delivery. And more especially as she could probably do it without running much risk of being discovered. A letter would be perfectly safe if she handed it to one of my servants at the bungalow, or to a police orderly."

"Yes. Anyway, you can rest assured that if there is

anything really urgent that I think you ought to know, you shall know it without delay. And if it is really immediate and vitally important, I'll come myself, so as to be sure you get the message."

"I ought to be going back now," she added.

Steele rose to his feet and took the girl's hand in his.

"I can't thank you enough," he said. "I feel twice as hopeful as I did an hour ago. And I am going to rely on you . . ."

"You can."

". . . to let me know *at once* if you learn anything urgent—vital."

"You shall know. I'd do anything for . . . I mean I'd do anything to help."

Should he kiss her?

Damn it, was she going to kiss him?

Of course not. A thoroughly "nice" girl. Absolutely ingenuous. Innocent. Well-behaved. It was only to be hoped she was as much *sans peur* as she was obviously *sans reproche*.

"Come along, then."

And, as they turned to where the horses stood, patient and motionless save for an occasional fly-induced shudder, whisk of the tail or stamp of the hoof, he put his arm about her shoulders and after a kind of brotherly hug, gave her a gentle commendatory pat upon the back.

The girl coloured warmly and gave him a smile that he considered the sweetest and nicest that he had ever received. . . . Good lass! . . .

Having girthed up her horse, arranged bit and bridle, and laid the reins upon its neck, he gave her an expert hand as she mounted lightly. Galloping and cantering back, there was little conversation.

As they parted at the corner of the Police Parade-ground,

"Good-bye Betty," said Anthony Steele. "Take care of yourself. Till Tuesday morning. Here, seven o'clock. Thank you, so much."

"Good-bye, and thank *you* so much," replied the

girl, and turned off in the direction of the Sudder Bazaar feeling, in spite of the insistent clamour of foreboding fear, as though her heart would almost burst with happiness.

§3

Meanwhile, Ramrao Gopaldas, Esquire, M.A. (Oxon), Barrister-at-Law, sought the company of Subhadra, his mother, who, having bathed; having ceremonially anointed her husband's foot with ghee; joined with him and the *parohit* in morning *puja*, prayers and worship; waited humbly upon her husband as he ate and drank; and broken her own fast thereafter with tea and fruit, had seated herself in the favoured corner of her favourite verandah.

"Mother," said Ramrao, after respectful and affectionate greeting, "you forgot to tell that fool Dowlah that the saddle-horse was no longer lame."

"Doubtless you remembered to tell him, my son."

"I did. But between us I am afraid we managed to let Betty know the cause of his lameness. The fool started to ask me what he was to do next time you decreed the horse should be lame!"

"What matter? The girl knows who rules here. . . . Do you think she will tell the Police Sahib, all-right?"

"Undoubtedly. Something will be said about riding again. And she is sure to mention that we are going away a fortnight hence."

"Instead of a week, eh?" chuckled the old woman.

"Yes. There's no telling what that dog Lalchand let out—of the very little he knew. Steele Sahib is a very clever man."

"And Lalchand Vasu a very silly fool," observed the old woman.

"*Was*, Mother."

"Was?"

"Yes. Lalchand Vasu was. We knew he couldn't have told Steele Sahib much when he was alive, but we let him tell him something after he was dead."

"Parables, my son. What message did the dead

tongue utter?"

"The dead body of Lalchand Vasu told Steele Sahib that he was as a child in the hands of the Brethren of India; that the Brethren strike whom they will, strike where they will, strike when they will; told him that servants of the Brethren who fail them are no safer than are the enemies themselves of the Brethren."

"And what was the worst the living Lalchand could have told him?"

"Nothing important, for he knew nothing—except what we have already announced to them all, by letter."

The 'Maharani' chuckled again.

"Steele Sahib had no letter, had he?"

"No. All the other Sahibs were notified by post, but to Steele Sahib we sent a personal message, telling the fool messenger that Steele's bungalow was the Collector's and that Steele would come to it from Commissioner's House at about eleven o'clock. He carried a useless pistol, and fell into Steele's hands as we intended. All went according to plan, up to that point, but then things went wrong. Steele either won him over, bribed him, or frightened the life out of him; and Lalchand failed us, disobeyed us; perhaps betrayed us —as far as he could. Bagu and Ranjit Singh, waiting in the shadows of the compound, followed the poor fool to Chinchgad railway-station and let him take a ticket. It was to Srinagar!"

"Oho! What does that mean?" enquired the Maharani.

"And a letter to Tweedale-Roscoe Sahib, a famous Sahib there, a friend of Steele's. He was to keep Lalchand Vasu safe, of course, until the police wanted him. And meantime, doubtless, Tweedale-Roscoe was to get what more he could out of him. So Bagu and Ranjit Singh did certain things to him. Things calculated to encourage the imparting of information. He imparted—and thereafter he died. And since Steele Sahib wanted him so badly, they returned him to Steele Sahib."

"And you think he only told the Police Sahib just as

much as you told the others in the letters that the Swami wrote."

"What more could he tell him? And what can Steele do?"

"Have you told Number Seven?" enquired the Maharani.

"About Lalchand Vasu? No. Not yet. He'll be at the meeting to-night."

"When does he leave Commissioner's House?"

"That is not fixed, Mother. The longer he is there, the better. Where could he be safer?"

"He is a very very clever man," mused the Maharani Subhadra. "What a brain!"

She broke into a thin cackle of laughter.

"'Number Seven'! To think of him lecturing all the Sahibs! To think of him sitting there in Commissioner's House, hearing all the things most useful to the Brethren. Invaluable information borne to him on a platter. Laid at his feet. And Cornwallis Mem-sahib his obedient servant! The Brahmin convert to Christianity! *He, he, he!* Living in the Commissioner's House at Bhawalgarh. Well, that's one place that will blow up quite certainly when the time comes."

Mother and son laughed in unison.

"Has he decided about the Lāt Sahib?" she asked.

"The Governor. No. He'll decide to-night, in the light of what he has learned from the Commissioner himself. I've no doubt that if there is no special cause for haste, no reason to fix an earlier date, he will wait for the Governor's visit."

"Yes, yes. Tell him I agree," chuckled the Maharani. "Say I said it is always a good thing to get the Governor himself to grace an occasion, if you can."

"Quite so," concurred Ramrao Gopaldas unsmiling. "The Governor's visit lends brilliance to any occasion."

"Brilliance!" sneered the Maharani. "There will be brilliance enough that night, if all goes well. . . ."

"The Governor's presence! An added brilliance, my son," she nodded, still chuckling. "Yes, I think Sant Arjun must wait for the Governor's visit, especially if he can remain at the Commissioner's House until then.

Is it known when the Governor comes?"

"We hear from the Brethren at Jhalni that it is not yet given out, but is quite certain to be soon. They tell us that he will come to Bhawalgarh on his way to the Hills, and he is to reach there on the first day of next month. That would bring him here a week from to-day."

"I suppose the Brethren have a quite reliable man in the Secretariat at Jhalni?"

"Assuredly, and we shall know the date, and the time of his train, as soon as the information is *pukka.*"

"And you told the girl a fortnight?"

"Yes. And it cannot be more than a week, even if Sant Arjun decides to wait for the Governor. Everything is ready except at the Fort, and that will be completed in a couple of days."

"And if it should be postponed, the girl can give Steele Sahib a fresh date for our departure. . . . Your wife cannot serve you as Lalchand Vasu did, of course?" mused Subhadra.

"How could she? She has never heard the word 'plot.' She could tell him absolutely everything she knows without opening her mouth—for she knows precisely nothing. She hasn't even the ghost of a suspicion. How should she have?"

"Steele Sahib is a very clever man."

"Yes, but as they say in their language, you can't get blood out of a stone. You can't get information from a person who has none. All that she can tell him is what we want her to tell him; give him what we want her to give him. On the other hand, she may learn something from him. I'm going to have a careful talk with her when she comes back. He may have mentioned the good Lalchand Vasu to her. He may possibly have jumped at some conclusions (from what Lalchand Vasu said to him and from what Sant Arjun wrote in the famous letters) and may have tried to pump her. I'll find out what they talked about; hear every word that was said, as though I had been there myself."

"You don't think she'd play you false, my son? If she knew anything, that is?"

"Well, anyway, she won't—because she can't. Because she knows nothing and will know nothing."

"I like not this shameless talking with men. This riding. Dancing. Might she not take Steele Sahib for her lover?"

Ramrao laughed.

"My dear Mother, I know exactly how often she has seen Steele Sahib, and exactly what they've said to each other. She has never seen him, alone, until to-day. I will arrange their meetings and I'll send him messages, though neither of them will be aware of the fact.

"Betty's a fool," he added, "and just the right sort of fool—ignorant and innocent."

The Maharani laughed again.

"My son, the most foolish woman alive is cleverer than any man—in certain directions."

"I don't fancy she could fool me, Mother."

"Then you are the fool—to think so," was the uncompromising reply.

§4

Meanwhile the Reverend Byam J. Torrens and his guest and nephew, Sewell E. Lee, having set forth at dawn in the doctor's carriage, drawn by Petra, made their undulating way, slowly but surely, in the direction of Belgad and the disused temple which the Swami Dayanand had named as the rendezvous.

> "*So sudden it rose, so heavy it fell,*
> *They scarce could hear the temple bell,*"

murmured Mr. Sewell E. Lee.

"Eh? What?" enquired the doctor, emerging from a brown study.

"Ever been on the mechanical horse or camel in an ocean liner's gymnasium, Uncle?"

"No, Son. There were neither horses nor camels on the last ship I saw, and I wasn't in the Ark. Why?"

"This *ghari* of yours is better than either the bumping horse or the jumping camel."

"Much better, I'm sure," agreed the doctor. "Would you mind putting your feet up on the seat in front?"

"But that leaves them out in the early morning sun," objected Lee "and I might want 'em again."

"Tut, tut! You don't call this hot," expostulated the doctor.

"No, hot isn't the word I'd use," replied Lee. "Word! I'd use a phrase—if I ever used such phrases. . . . What have we stopped for? Does Petra want to think?"

"Don't stand up, I beseech you," begged the doctor.

Sliding from the *ghari* without touching its floor, Lee discovered that Petra had perforce stopped because the narrow road was entirely blocked by a herd of vast slate-coloured water-buffaloes, whose pale-blue eyes beneath the huge spreading curling horns gave them a most sinister and menacing appearance. An intimidating sight.

All was well, however, as a tiny naked black pot-bellied child of some three summers appeared from behind the herd, ran along its flank and brutally assaulted the colossal leading bull, with a twig.

The bull, admonished and contrite, broke into a lumbering trot, was followed by his friends and relations, the road was cleared, and Petra resumed the extremely uneven tenor of his way.

Passing through the village of Belgad, which consisted entirely of mud, save for the reed thatch of the hovels, Dr. Torrens observed to his companion,

"That's India. There is not an adult in this village who can read a syllable or write a word. The average level of intelligence is just about on a par with that of their buffaloes. They live on the absolute ultimate edge. They own nothing but the right to work in those 'fields,' from sunrise to sunset. The failure or delay of the monsoon means famine, sheer starvation; and, but for the Government, they'd die like flies. An epidemic used to mean death to practically everyone whom it attacked, for they have no stamina; and again, but for the Government, would have no quinine or other medicine, and no sort or kind of medical care, attention, or teaching. They are the most hard-working, the most innocent, the soberest, the simplest, human beings on the face of the earth. I love them. And there are people (and well-meaning people among them) who would hand them over to a Congress—good God—and would take away the one thing that stands between them and even greater poverty, hardship, and danger of death from famine and disease—the British Raj. There are three hundred millions of them, and nothing on earth can be done for them save what the British Government does do; for they are the victims of climate, the climate that is responsible for their lack of food, lack of stamina, and everything else except peace and justice. While the British Government is strong, those two things they have got. And that they may continue, they pray. So do I.

"And who asked me to preach a sermon on a beautiful morning?" he added on a lighter tone.

"Nobody, Uncle. But where's the beautiful morning? Lord, I'm dying of heat-apoplexy."

"I've been doing that for fifty years," smiled Dr. Torrens. "Quite a slow death."

Suddenly, placing his left foot upon the *ghari* step, his right knee upon the seat in front, he prodded the syce in the small of the back with the handle of his umbrella and then tapped him smartly on the left shoulder, whereupon the syce turned off the dusty and rutted road to a cart-track that led away into the sear, drear jungle of apparently dead and dying trees, bushes, and undergrowth.

"Sailing directions," murmured Lee as the doctor subsided into his seat.

"That's another thing I like about this *ghari*, Uncle," he observed. "You don't know whether you are on the road or off it. And you can't say that of every vehicle. And what's more, when you are on it you think you are off it, and when you are off it you're sure you are on. And it's nice to know where you are in life."

"That's the temple," replied the doctor.

Following the direction in which the doctor pointed, Lee beheld a doorless one-roomed stone building, ancient, domed, ornamented with curious carvings.

A couple of sharp blows upon the syce's back brought the carriage to a halt; and, each in his own way, with careful avoidance of the floor, its occupants disembarked.

Peering into the comparatively cool and dark recesses of the temple, Lee saw a practically naked native sitting cross-legged upon the floor. On one side of him was a black-buck's horn, its sharp point tipped with steel, its butt or base bound with iron; on the other, a beggar's bowl.

"Salaam, Swami-ji," the doctor saluted him. "May I introduce my nephew, Mr. Sewell E. Lee of Boston, America, who wishes to have the privilege of meeting you, and is anxious to interview you for his paper, the famous *Boston Herald and Arbitrator*."

"The honour is mine," smiled the Swami, bowing and saluting by bringing his right hand to his forehead. "Will you be seated? What about letting your syce bring cushions from the carriage?"

"Oh, we'll sit down right here, thank you," replied the doctor.

"What shall we talk about?" smiled the Swami, as soon as his visitors had settled themselves with what comfort they might, upon the hard and uneven, if clean, stone floor.

"*Yoga*, please," replied Lee promptly. "And after that, I'd like to have your views on the best form of government for India."

"Quite a programme," smiled the Swami. "It will take us at least an hour to dispose of the whole subject of *yoga* in addition to that of the large and thorny question of the form of government best suited to this unhappy country."

Lee noticed, as the Swami smiled, that his lips were as thin as those of the average European, his eyes peculiarly lustrous, dark and deep, and yet, at the same time, disconcertingly penetrating. A remarkably fine face, with its high and not too narrow forehead, aquiline nose, good chin, and entire absence of any look of sensuality. So often, so monotonously often, had he observed that, from the nostrils up, a face was fine, admirable; from the nostrils down, ugly, heavy, repulsive, with its huge mouth, thick lips, heavy jowls, weak chin and every contradiction of the promise made by the eyes and brow.

"Suppose you question me," suggested the Swami.

"Thank you. I should like to. Could I study *yoga* and become a *yogi*?"

"Undoubtedly."

"What should I have to do?"

"Well, as a tiny preliminary step, abandon every single solitary thing that you possess, and come to me here clad in the minimum allowed by the excellent rules of your admirable police."

"I see. And then?"

"Cut yourself off finally and entirely from your country and your countrymen, your friends, companions, acquaintances, relatives; from your parents and brothers and sisters; from your wife and your children, if you are blessed with any."

"Yes. And then?"

"And then I'll talk with you daily for a few hours, over a period of a few months or years."

"Teaching me *yoga*?"

"No, preparing you for the first lesson in *yoga*."

"Oh. And then?"

"I'll find you a *guru*, a teacher. And you will walk, begging your way, to where he is. Perhaps Benares; perhaps Hurdwar; perhaps Puri. And when you have served him for a few years as his *chela*, and shown signs of worth and grace, he may see fit to give you the first lesson in the preliminary course that leads to the elementary stage through which the candidate passes in the hope of becoming a beginner."

"I see."

"And having survived to that point, how long would it take me to attain proficiency in *yoga*?" asked Lee.

"After those years of preparation for apprenticeship, I should say about—a century."

"Thank you. And should I then be a real *yogi*?"

"No. But, by that time, I think there would be some

hope of your becoming a promising disciple."

"And how long would it take me to become a *yogi*? Such as yourself, I mean, Swami-ji?"

Smiling his puckish, mocking, whimsical smile, the Swami bowed.

"To become so poor a *yogi* as myself? Let me see now. Tempering truth with modesty, I should say some five hundred years."

It was Lee's turn to bow as he smiled somewhat wryly.

"It took you as long as that? "he riposted.

"Oh, far, far longer than that," replied the Swami. "More nearly five thousand years."

Again Lee bowed and changed the subject.

"What I would particularly like to ask you next, Swami-ji, is whether you'd be so good as to give me a small demonstration of the wonderful powers acquired by the study, five thousand years of study, of *yoga*."

The Swami's smile was enigmatic.

"A little demonstration, eh?" he mocked. "But haven't you seen plenty of that sort of thing in hotel compounds, from Bombay to Calcutta, where tourists and trippers most do congregate? The little yellow chicken, the drugged and fangless cobra, the mangy mongoose, the miraculous, if wilted, mango plant?"

"You mistake me, Swami-ji," interrupted Lee, with some dignity. "I have no wish at all to see cheap conjuring tricks, but I have a great desire to know whether any of what one has heard about that aspect of *yoga* is true. There are millions of people throughout the world who'd be deeply interested to know whether these things are true. And it occurs to me that it might interest you to let them know. To tell them, through me, whether it is, or is not, the fact that *yogis*, such as yourself, have learned secrets of Nature that are still hidden from other investigators and scientists; and have acquired powers unknown to them."

The Swami looked at him.

"The Senses are the Gateways of the Soul," he said.

While Lee was yet thinking that this observation was fairly trite and platitudinous,

"Are you fond of music?" enquired the Swami.

"Very," he replied.

"Have you a favourite air?"

"Well," mused Lee. "A favourite? There are so many. I appreciate Liszt's *Liebestraum*."

"Listen," said the Swami.

And like distant elfin pipes of fairy music, a tiny, tiny thread of sound grew and grew until, clear, distinct, and most beautifully rendered, there fell upon his ears the *Liebestraum*.

Fell upon his ears, but their evidence was rejected.

This was plain nonsense.

But it hadn't been the Swami who suggested the air.

He had suggested it himself.

There could be no hidden gramophone. If the Swami had offered to produce the tune, that would have been the solution of the apparent mystery.

Of course it was absurd.

But damn it all, there it was.

There must either be a gramophone and record of remarkable sweetness and purity inside the temple, or there must be a wonderful string band outside in the jungle—which was still more absurd.

No, it was he who had asked for this particular air.

Was his uncle hearing it, too?

Glancing across at Dr. Torrens, he saw that undoubtedly he was hearing it; was listening critically; was, like himself, puzzled, but, unlike himself, acquiescent.

He rose to his feet.

"Excuse me, Swami-ji," he said. "I am sure you will approve."

The Swami smiled; and Lee, walking about the interior of the temple, placed his ear here and there about its walls, looked up into its stone-groined ceiling, blackened with the smoke and soot and dirt of ages, but patently bare and incapable of concealing a gramophone or any musical-box larger than a snuff-box.

Stepping outside into the blinding glare and smiting suffocating heat, he circumambulated the temple, and returned. At no point in his journey about the walls of the building, within or without, had the music sounded nearer or farther away, quieter or louder, more or less distinct.

Wireless?

Again seating himself, Lee eyed the Swami intently, puzzled and speculative.

"Would you like some Indian music for a change?" smiled the Swami.

"No. I'd like the *Star-Spangled Banner*," replied Lee. "And after that the *Marseillaise*, and after that *Land of Hope and Glory*, in that order, at once, and played rather quickly."

That'd stump the bird if there were any hocus-pocus with gramophone records or wireless.

Scarcely had the words left his lips than a brass band crashed into the opening bars of *The Star-Spangled Banner*.

"Like Sousa himself," murmured the doctor.

Having come to its triumphant close, the American National Anthem changed into the strains of the *Marseillaise*, beautifully and wonderfully rendered by a wood-wind orchestra.

The music died away, to revive immediately as Elgar's *Land of Hope and Glory* burst forth from some mighty organ played by a master.

Silence fell within the ancient temple.

"Do you prefer any of our Indian fruits to those of your own richly endowed country?" enquired the Swami.

"Well, it's difficult to say. I certainly enjoy a real ripe Alfonso mango. I had some in Bombay."

"As sweet as this one?" enquired the Swami. "The one you are now tasting?"

And instantly Lee's palate savoured mango; rich, sweet, luscious mango of the best kind, entirely free from the faint suggestion of turpentine which mars the ordinary variety.

He swallowed appreciatively, and swallowed nothing, his mouth being empty.

"*Some* mango," he said, striving to hide his feelings

of wonder and amazement, bordering on alarm.

"Yes, it is a fine fruit," said the Swami. "And I think the best we have in India, though a perfect William pear runs it pretty close. Try this one."

And instantly Lee's mouth was filled and flooded with the rich sweetness of a ripe and luscious pear.

Again he swallowed, and wiped dry lips.

"A good strawberry is very good," observed the Swami, and the flavour of strawberry was as strong in Lee's mouth as ever it had been in all his life.

"Will you have anything else?"

"Peach, please."

"Yes, a ripe Californian cling, fresh from the tree and warm from the sun," smiled the Swami.

And the flavour came, the real miracle seeming to be that no fruit was in his mouth.

"Do you like the smell of incense?" enquired the Swami.

"Can't say I do," replied Lee.

"Then we'll remove it," was the reply, and Lee was aware that the odour of incense, which had undoubtedly assailed his nostrils, was no longer there.

"Attar of roses?"

"So-so."

Yes, that was attar of roses, such as he had smelt in Cairo.

"Your favourite flower?"

"Rose; carnation; camellia."

"Yes, in that order," agreed the Swami.

And it was as though a great fragrant tea-rose was held beneath Lee's nose; then a rich clove-scented carnation; and then a somewhat sickly sweet camellia.

"Of what material is your suit made?" asked the Swami.

"What they call mercerized cotton, I believe."

"Close your eyes and pass your hand down your thigh."

Lee did so. Clearly he was dressed in sand-paper.

"Again."

No, it was satin. Smooth, sheer, and shining. Shining to the touch, he thought. Extraordinary.

"Again."

But it was warm and slippery and wet. Blood? Was his leg bleeding?

"Again."

No, his thigh was a block of ice. Hard and cold as frozen rock.

"Again."

No, it was hairy cloth. It was coarse tweed that he was wearing.

"Again."

Lee started. Hell! His thigh was red-hot iron. It had burnt his hand.

Involuntarily he opened his eyes to look at his seared palm.

The Swami and the doctor were laughing.

"Have you seen the Taj Mahal?" enquired the Swami. "By moonlight?"

"Unfortunately not by moonlight. I must go again for that, at the right time."

"Save yourself a journey," smiled the Swami. "Look there, through the wall."

And staring where the Swami pointed, Lee found that, framed in a window which hitherto he certainly had not noticed, was a very lovely picture. Lovely beyond words, and deserving every encomium that had ever been uttered in its praise. The Taj, by moonlight!

Incredible. Impossible. But there it was. So marvellous.

He was actually *seeing* it. But he must maintain his grip, exercise his critical faculties to the full. He had certainly heard, tasted, smelt, touched, and seen things that were not there; but all of them had been things with which he was familiar.

No, he couldn't say he was familiar with the appearance of the Taj Mahal. He had seen it once, in blazing sunlight. Now he had seen it by moonlight. Nevertheless, he had seen it before, and, by closing his eyes, he could, with a considerable effort of the imagination, have visualized it by moonlight.

Or could he have done? Could he ever, unaided, have conjured up such a picture as this? Perhaps not.

Could the Swami then cause him to see things that not only were not there, to be seen, but that he never *had* seen?

"Have you ever seen a hamadryad, a king cobra?" enquired the Swami.

The question was amazingly *à propos*, for he had never seen one. Could the Swami show him something he had never seen and therefore could not visualize? He had not the least idea as to what the most dreaded snake in India was like.

He had been told, or had read, that it was the only aggressive snake in the country, the only snake that would attack a man unprovoked; that—whereas any other snake would flee with the utmost speed at man's approach, and would never strike save when at bay, when imagining itself to be cornered, when trodden on, touched, alarmed—the king cobra or hamadryad, on the other hand, would chase and attack a man as a terrier would a rat; but he had never seen one.

He had never seen a picture of the snake nor read a description of it. He did not know what colour it was; what was its size; whether it had a hood; whether it closely resembled the ordinary cobra and had the spectacle-markings distinctive of the species.

The Swami pointed to the corner behind him and to his right.

Turning his head, Lee saw, coiled in the corner, a big yellow snake, as thick as his arm and probably some eight feet in length.

As he looked, it partly uncoiled, raised its head, hissed, and produced a loud and curious sound as of the rustling of thousands of dry leaves. Its horrible lidless eyes glared cold hate at him.

He was frozen with horror as the snake, swaying to and fro, raised its head higher, spread its hood yet wider, and drew back to strike.

"Meet my friend *Naja hannah bungarus*, alias King Cobra, alias Hamadryad. Don't be afraid. Let not the red mist of anger or the cold grey fog of terror render you to her virtues blind."

Lee swallowed, and endeavoured to speak calmly

and in his ordinary voice.

"Endowed with virtues, is she?" the journalist managed to ask.

"Yes. An excellent mother. She makes a neat nest of dried leaves, and guards her off-spring—usually thirty-two in number—both in the egg-stage and in their tender childhood with praiseworthy devotion. An admirable parent to her babes."

"Well, she's neglecting them right now," said Lee.

"Go away, *Hannah Bungarus*. The Sahib doesn't like you, Hannah," said the Swami.

The snake dropped back upon itself and, quickly uncoiling, moved writhing swiftly to the entrance. As it passed within a yard of him, Lee noted the amazing and inexplicable movement whereby snakes travel, three-quarters of the body flat upon the ground, the head and remainder raised above it, the undulations entirely lateral, with no upward looping of the body whatsoever. Did it propel itself by means of its scales, or by moving the ends of its ribs which acted like legs enclosed within its skin?

He realized that he now felt more dazed than frightened.

"And so I have seen a king cobra, have I?" he asked.

"Yes and no," replied the Swami. "You have, and you've not. Anyway, you know exactly what one is like, and, as a trained journalist, can doubtless describe in utmost accurate detail the thing you have—or have not—seen.

"As all good journalists can do, of course," he added.

Lee yawned heavily. What was the fellow saying?

"And now you are feeling a little sleepy," came the mocking voice. "My tricks have tired you. A cold douche is what you need."

And as he withdrew his eyes from the doorway through which the great snake had disappeared, and turned in bewilderment to the Swami, he involuntarily ducked as the Swami flung the contents of his beggar's-bowl—ice-cold water—full in his face. The shock made him gasp.

Half angrily he drew his handkerchief from the breast pocket of his coat and went to wipe water from his dry face, dry collar, tie and clothing. There was no water.

Glancing again at the Swami, he saw that he was sitting motionless, the empty beggar's-bowl beside him.

The Swami's face was serious, intent.

"The Senses are the Gateways of the Soul," he said.

"Did you find them open, or force them, Swami-ji?" asked Lee, as angrily he shook himself and rose to his feet.

"What was it—hypnotism?" he demanded. "Illusion?"

The Swami smiled.

"Illusion," he said. "All is illusion. Describe what you have seen—and heard and smelt and touched and tasted—for the benefit of your few million readers, Lee Sahib. Tell them the truth and so tell them the—illusion."

"So truth is illusion and illusion truth?"

"Have you not seen and heard and smelt and tasted and touched?"

"Undoubtedly I have."

"Have you? Undoubtedly?"

"Have I?" asked Lee. "Or haven't I?"

"Well, doubt your doubts—and tell your readers," said the Swami.

"Shall we now re-arrange the Universe, beginning with this portion of it? Arrange for the better government of India?" he continued.

"I shall be more than glad to hear your views, Swami-ji," replied Lee gravely.

"Well, I will tell you. In the words of a more famous man than I, it has been said,

> *"For forms of government let fools contest,*
> *Whate'er is best administered is best."*

"Agreed," replied Lee. "And the meaning of the parable? Without going into the question of the form of Government, what is likely to be the best administered for India?"

"Anything," replied the Swami, "that is administered by Indians. Though the very worst, it will be better than the very best administered by others."

"A hard saying," observed Lee.

"And my last," smiled the Swami, bowing and closing his eyes, with an air of utter finality and dismissal.

"Come along, Son," whispered Dr. Torrens. "This is where we get off."

Nothing loth, Lee rose to his feet, glanced at the apparently unconscious Swami, and walked out from the cool interior into the furnace of the jungle, noticing as he did so, that the track of a large and heavy snake led from the stone floor of the temple away into the deep dust, and disappeared into the undergrowth.

Well, there was the good horse Petra; and there was the syce, sleeping in the shade of the trees. They were all real enough. . . . *To Hell with hypnotism!*

With care and circumspection Lee climbed into the *ghari*, sat down, and put his feet on the opposite seat. As Dr. Torrens was about to follow his example, the voice of the Swami fell upon their ears.

"Torrens Sahib! . . . Torrens Sahib! . . ."

"Half a minute, Son," said the doctor, and turning, went back into the temple.

"Torrens Sahib, I had a thing to say. Like *King John*,

> "I had a thing to say—but I will fit it with some
> better time.
> By heaven, Torrens, I am almost ashamed to
> say what good respect I have of thee.
> Thou hast no cause to thank me, Torrens, yet;
> but thou *shalt* have;
> And creep time ne'er so slow, yet it shall come
> for me to do thee good.
> I had a thing to say—but let it go."

"No—say it, Swami-ji," requested the doctor.

"Will you do a little thing for me, and a great one for

yourself, Torrens Sahib?"

"Why, to be sure, Swami-ji. Apart from the fact that it sounds good. A great thing for myself, eh? What is it?"

"Could you possibly leave Bhawalgarh to-day fort-night?"

"Leave Bhawalgarh?"

"Yes."

"For how long?"

"Oh, only for the night."

"And go where?"

"Anywhere you like. One station up the line—and preach to the 'heathen.' Yes, carry the Lamp of Light into outer darkness, if it is only that of Chinchgad."

"But why should I, Swami-ji?"

"Why shouldn't you?

> "'*Can you whose soul is lighted*
> *With wisdom from on High,*
> *Can you to men benighted*
> *The Lamp of Light deny?*'"

"And why that particular night, Swami-ji?"

"Because I ask you; beg you; implore you. You are not British, you are American, and I want you to be anywhere out of Bhawalgarh, to-day fortnight. And what is more, I want you to take with you any American friends of yours whom you can persuade to go."

"Take my friends?"

"Yes. Take them all down to Bombay for a binge. . . . Or take them up into the hills above Kotgur and build tabernacles, and dwell in them for at least one night."

"But why? Why? What's the joke?"

"No joke at all, Torrens Sahib. It will certainly be no joke if you disregard my warning."

"You mean you are seriously asking me to go out of Bhawalgarh on Saturday, the week after next, and stay away from Bhawalgarh for that night?"

"Yes."

"Why, what is going to happen?"

"It's going to happen that you leave Bhawalgarh, I hope; and take with you your personal friends. Those whom you wish to save."

"Including Indian friends?"

"Er—no. Americans only. Will you go, Torrens Sahib?"

"I don't think so. No, I really don't think I shall go, Swami-ji. Unless you give me some reason for doing so. Can't you give me the reason?"

"No, I can't. I can only beg of you to go. And if you can get no others to accompany you, then go alone— with your nephew. Will you?"

"I'll think about it."

"You won't promise?"

"No."

"Well, will you promise me something else? Will you mention what I have just said—to every European whom you know? That will at least give them a chance, won't it?"

"Well . . . Yes. It will give them a chance to act on it, but . . ."

"But you don't think they will? Never mind. Do your best, Torrens Sahib; and you will have done your duty as I have done mine. I warn you in all seriousness and with all the earnestness and strength that I can, to go away from Bhawalgarh by midnight on Saturday week. A fortnight to-day. And I beg of you to convey this warning to every one of your colleagues and friends. As I say, I have done my duty in the matter, and now I beg of you to do yours."

"But surely you can tell me something more? You can give me some reason—that I can give to them?"

"No. I can't. I am not in a position to give you any definite information. But I am in a position to give you the gravest warning that one person can give another. Go away for the night. And give the warning to your friends—and save yourself a life-time of regret. *Listen*, man! Remain in Bhawalgarh, leave your friends unwarned—and . . ."

"And . . . ?"

But to all appearances the Swami was dead. His

jaw had dropped. His eyes were open but had rolled up so that the irises had disappeared. He had ceased to breathe. Touching him, Dr. Torrens found his body to be quite cold. He shook it angrily.

"Swami-ji," he said aloud, "if I were as clever as you I'd make better use of my cleverness."

And then, feeling uncomfortable, ashamed, as though he had insulted the dead, he left the temple, returned to the *ghari*, and climbed in beside Lee.

"You put all your weight on the floor, then, Uncle," observed the latter. "Nice thing if it had given way under you! "

"I begin to think it will be a nice thing if nothing more than that gives way under me," replied the doctor.

Arrived safely back in Bhawalgarh, Dr. Torrens signalled Sailing Directions by means of his umbrella, and navigated his crank craft to safe anchorage beneath the porch of the D.S.P.'s bungalow.

Steele, it appeared, had just arrived, as his horse was being led away by a police orderly. At the doctor's shout of "*Qui hai!*"—the shout that, in India, is the substitute for the ring or knock of the West—the D.S.P. himself threw open the lattice doors that he had that moment closed behind him.

"Salaam, Doctor Sahib. Morning, Lee. Just in time for a cold drink. Come along in."

"No. I won't get out. I only want just a word. I took my nephew here to see the Swami Dayanand this morning and, after the interview, he gave me a most solemn warning against being in Bhawalgarh to-day fortnight."

"On or during?" asked Steele, his face betraying neither surprise nor interest. "I mean, must you go during the day, or can you spend the whole day here?"

"I am to be gone by midnight," replied the doctor.

"And are you going?" enquired Steele.

"That's what I've come to ask you," smiled the doctor. "Am I going?"

"No, I don't think you are—going. I think you will be gone."

"Now here be mysteries, portents and wonders," said Dr. Torrens. "Where shall I have gone?"

"Heaven," replied Steele. "Heaven, undoubtedly."

"Does that go for me, too?" smiled Lee.

"Ah, that I cannot answer," replied Steele gravely. "But 'Hope springs eternal', of course. Do come in and have a drink, doctor."

"No, no; really. Thanks very much indeed, Steele."

"We've been in and out of the *ghari* once this morning," explained Lee.

"Well, I thought I'd come and tell you, Steele, because the Swami particularly asked me to pass on his warning to my friends—my American colleagues, and every friend I've got in Bhawalgarh—and I thought I couldn't do better than begin with you, especially as you are our official guardian and protector."

"And you couldn't do better than end with me, too, doctor. Another of the Swami's tricks. He's too fond of these leg-pulls. He wants to spread consternation and alarm among His Majesty's lieges. He guessed you'd tell me."

"Just what I thought, my dear Steele. Just what I thought, and it seemed to be my duty to mention it to you."

"Thanks very much indeed, doctor. And if you'll kindly mention it to nobody else, you'll have put a spoke in the Swami's wheel and spoiled what the parrot called 'a damned silly trick, too.' I'll tell you about that parrot some day. Sure you won't come in?"

"No, no, my dear boy. Again many thanks. Good-bye. I'll do as you say, and not mention this to a soul."

"That's right, Padre Sahib. Good-bye."

As the *ghari* turned out of the compound gates on to the white and white-hot road,

"What did that cop mean about your being in Heaven to-day fortnight, Uncle?" asked Lee.

"Why, Son, I take it that he ventured to prophesy that to-day fortnight I shall either be in Bhawalgarh or in Heaven. And personally I think he's a true prophet. I'll say I shall be right there, in one of those two identical places. Steele was pulling my leg, too. If we stay a fortnight we shan't be here at all. We shall all be murdered in our beds."

"Good a place as any," yawned Mr. Sewell E. Lee.

At the same moment Anthony Steele stood gazing at the tiger-skin that lay at his feet.

"A fortnight to-day," said he to himself. "Torrens is warned to be out of Bhawalgarh by midnight a fortnight to-day. And Betty is told that she and the Gopaldas family will be leaving Bhawalgarh a fortnight to-day. And Torrens is to advise every one of his friends to be out of Bhawalgarh a fortnight to-day. And His Excellency arrives a week to-day. Thank you, Swami-ji. A fortnight to-day.

"In other words, a week to-day. Every man-jack of us, including His Excellency—unless I strike first.

"And whom am I to strike?

"And what am I to strike with?

"I wonder if I could arrest the Gopaldas brothers, Purshotamdass, Bhojraj, the Swami, *and* Sant Arjun.

"And what good would it do if I did, with Ranjit Singh free and Number Seven coming?"

Seating himself in his long chair, Steele produced pipe and tobacco-pouch.

"Swami-ji, my lad," said he to himself, "in the Golden Days of old, you'd have been pinched by the *kotwal's* police and tortured until you told all you knew—including the whereabouts of your friend Ranjit Singh.

"So, doubtless, you will be in the bright glad days to come, when the 'Satanic' British Government is overthrown, and Soviet Russia is here, or the Japanese.

"And as it is, I can't even arrest you. I haven't a thing against you.

"No, nor against any of the others, either. And I don't know who Number Seven is, nor when he is coming.

"And I don't really know whether Ranjit Singh is in Bhawalgarh or not.

"And I know, as well as I know my name, that we are all going to be blown to Hell, *this day week*.

"And what can I do?

"I must see Herdie at once. Toddle over unofficially. I'll go to dinner and have a quiet talk with him."

Rising and going to his desk, Steele scribbled a chit to Mrs. Herdie, saying that he would be able, after all, to accept her kind invitation to dinner that evening, if the notice were not too short.

The police orderly who took the note to the Collector's bungalow brought back Mrs. Herdie's reply, a more-than-warm welcome.

§5

Jane Herdie was awaiting Anthony Steele alone in her big drawing-room that evening.

"Ah, there you are, Tony! How are you?"

"Fine, thanks," replied Steele. "All Saturday-nightish. It wasn't tails and white tie, was it? I guessed it wasn't."

In fact, thought Steele to himself, I was perfectly sure it wasn't, and that I am in for a *tête-à-tête.* Very nice and all that, my dear Jenny, but I've got to have one with your husband, too. And I don't go till I get one.

"How do you mean—all Saturday-nightish, Tony?" enquired Mrs. Herdie.

"Well, it has been one of the guiding principles of my well-spent life, religiously to observe Saturday night. 'Now the week is over and Sabbath's drawing nigh' sort of feeling. Even if I know I've got to work all night, I'm glad it is Saturday."

The more he kept her talking, the less she'd have to say. He had had an uneasy feeling, for quite a long while, that Jenny Herdie would say something, one of these days.

Therefore, most said soonest mended, just now, perchance.

Probably quite wrong and very conceited of him to think so, but he had an idea that Jenny Herdie was always manœuvring to corner him for a *tête-à-tête*—to say that something.

"I am so glad you could come, Tony. What happened to the bachelor party?"

"Oh, for one reason or another, they had all cleared out of Bhawalgarh. How is the Collector Sahib?"

"*He*'s all-right. Come and sit down here beside me and tell me what you've been doing since I saw you last. Two whole days."

"No; one whole day."

"But it's forty-eight hours."

"Ah, that may be; but only Friday was whole. I saw you on Thursday and now I'm seeing you on Saturday. Thus one *whole* day. Extraordinary how few women have any head for mathematics."

"Well, never mind about that. What have you been doing since I saw you?"

"Oh, everybody I could. Playing the flute; getting on with my embroidery-work, and all that."

"Embroidery?"

"Yes, I do a lot of embroidering."

"What do you embroider?"

"Stories, mostly."

"And do you really play the flute?"

"Rather. And the piccolo. And the oboe and the yea-bo."

"Do you really? What exactly is the yaboe?"

"Don't you know? So few women have any head for musical instruments."

"Well, what is it like?"

"Do you know what a French trombumpah is like?"

"No, I don't."

"Well, it's like that."

"You must bring it with you some time, Tony."

"Oh, it's much too big to carry."

"Well, then, I must come and see it, and hear you play it."

Had she been leading up to that, or had he himself provided the opening?

"Is it like a euphonium?"

"Well, a cross between that and a calliope and the . . . Ah, here's your husband."

And Steele sprang to his feet as Herdie came into the room.

"Late as usual, Lawrence," observed Mrs. Herdie.

"So busy, my dear. I do apologize."

"Mr. Steele has just been inviting me to come and see his collection of musical instruments."

"Didn't know you were a collector, Steele."

"Well, hardly that perhaps. I . . ."

Paul Jesus Miguel Xavier Manoel Braganza Mascarenhas da Silva, the butler, appeared in the doorway.

"Dinner is served, Mem-sahib," he said, and Steele modestly forbore to continue.

At dinner Lawrence Herdie drank barley-water, Mrs. Herdie nothing at all, and Anthony Steele whisky and soda.

Conversation was light and easy, thanks to Steele's efforts.

When the butler had cleared the table of all but dessert, and had placed finger-bowls and the port and madeira decanters, Mrs. Herdie rose.

"Don't be long, Lawrence," she said, eyeing him straitly.

"No, no, my dear," replied her husband, as Steele held the door open for her. "I want a few words with Steele. We shan't be long."

When the butler had brought the coffee-tray and cheroots, he retired, to return ceremoniously bearing a brazen bowl in which rested a glowing piece of charcoal. This, with tongs, he raised and bore to them, that the Sahibs might light their cheroots from it. To the connoisseur a better method than the use of matches.

When, for the last time, the door was closed, Steele swiftly and succinctly laid before the Collector the whole of his story, from beginning to end, putting him in possession, first, of all the facts that he had discovered, secondly of his conclusions, and thirdly of his suspicions.

Herdie listened in silence and then summed up.

"First; I get anonymous letters, so extremely well put together that I read them through, from beginning to end. One would have thought that they had been written, not only by an Englishman, but by a finished scholar of great literary ability and power. Further, I discover that similar letters have been sent to the Commissioner; the Judge; Wallace, my Assistant Collector; the Principal of the Government College; Major Hector Grant of the Fort; Captain Murdoch of the Gaol; Colonel Angus Campbell of Nicholson's Sikhs, and, in fact, to every gazetted officer to whom I have mentioned the matter.

"Secondly; you learn from Mrs. Gopaldas that certain agitators, seditionists, and notorious political firebrands meet at her husband's house. Also that this person, calling himself Sant Arjun Rama and professing to be a Brahmin convert to Christianity, attends the meetings. Very interesting.

"Thirdly; a student makes an attempt, genuine or otherwise, upon your life, and you extract information from him which confirms what you've already learned about the meeting together of the political malcontents who have come to Bhawalgarh. He also discloses the story of a bomb-plot that bears out the threats contained in the before-mentioned anonymous letters. He also mentions the *To-day and To-morrow* offices as one of the meeting-places of the conspirators.

"Fourthly; you find the dead body of the same student in your bed."

Herdie broke off.

"By the way, what was the result of the Civil Surgeon's autopsy?"

"Oh, yes. Very interesting, that," replied Steele. "Entirely negative. He could find no definite cause of death, and suggests that he probably died of sheer fright. He was a seedy, weedy youth; ill-nourished; and had an enlarged spleen and a weak heart."

"So he might really have died from natural causes?"

"Yes. Vague again, like all the rest of it. But he didn't put himself to bed in my house. And if his end was natural, it certainly wasn't happy."

"Quite so. We've got to go on probabilities—and he was probably murdered," agreed Herdie.

"Fifthly," he continued, "this Swami Dayanand warns Dr. Torrens to clear out of Bhawalgarh on Saturday week—a fortnight hence—and to warn his American friends to do the same thing. And that agrees, in a curious and interesting manner, with what Mrs. Gopaldas told you—that the Gopaldas family are themselves clearing out of Bhawalgarh—a fortnight hence."

"Yes," agreed Steele, "as you say, Sir. So much so, that I thought I'd better tell you the whole story from beginning to end. I didn't want to bother you with it if there was nothing in it; but what Torrens told me this morning decided me. The fortnight and the corpse. Even though that again may be part of a gigantic leg-pull. The whole thing may be a fantastic, practical joke; the death of Lalchand Vasu being so fortuitous and so delightfully *à propos* that they couldn't resist working it into the joke."

"Joke's too good, I'm afraid," said Herdie. "Altogether too good."

"Yes, that's what I felt," agreed Steele. "It somehow isn't quite Indian, is it? The native of this country, generally speaking, has a very poor sense of humour; and he jokes just about as rarely as he laughs or whistles. It was partly the feeling that it was too elaborate a joke to be a joke that decided me to bother you with the story."

"Of course there's this to it," mused Herdie. "It may be all a *banao*,[48] all bunkum and moonshine, but not exactly a joke at all—any more than it is a bomb-plot. They are not doing it as a genuine joke to amuse themselves, but simply out of malice, cussedness, and ill-will—to annoy, to disturb, to upset and worry; to 'cause consternation and alarm' as Army Regulations call that sort of thing. Not a joke in our sense of the word; and not a plot in their sense of the word. They've come here from Calcutta, Bombay, Poona, Madras, Agra, Lahore, Delhi, Chittagong, Midnapore, Peshawar and so forth, for some purpose or other—to confer, hatch schemes, lie low for awhile, meet kind friends from Moscow, Chicago, Cairo and such-like. And being here, with time on their hands, they are improving the shining hour by making a damn nuisance of themselves and keeping us guessing. Don't you think that

---

[48] *Frame-up; concoction.*

may be it?"

"I do think that may be it. Also I think it may not. There may not be a grain of truth or a grain of gunpowder; and there may be half a ton of high explosive. Personally, I think there is sufficient smoke for us to act as though there were some fire. And what I want to know is—how we're to act."

Herdie studied the cigar-ash that he had dropped into his coffee-cup.

"That's what I've been pondering," he said. "We have nothing to go on. We cannot even say there has been a murder. We can't say that the politicians, who meet the Gopaldas brothers, meet to plot. Presumably there is no actual objection to Sant Arjun Rama going from the Commissioner's House to the Gopaldas house, any more than there is any objection to Ramrao going from the Gopaldas house to the Commissioner's House. Sant Arjun Rama may go to the meetings at the Gopaldas house to try to convert them all to Christianity."

Steele smiled as he thought of Betty's theory.

"Exactly."

"And Ramrao might merely have said what he did, to his wife, in a fit of jealousy," continued Herdie. "It might be that he didn't like her riding with you, and didn't like to say so. So he simply told her they were going away. And the Swami may equally simply have been pulling Dr. Torrens's leg."

"Looks rather like collusion though, doesn't it?" observed Steele. "Very curious that both the Swami and Ramrao should have been particularly insistent upon the fortnight."

"Looks like it. But there *may* be nothing in it," replied Herdie. "In fact, it's an infernal devil's-brew of may-be's and looks-like-its. At one moment it is patently absurd and the next it's—patently genuine."

"Exactly how I feel about it," said Steele. "One's mind veers from the folly and stupidity of doing anything at all, to the criminal folly and incredible stupidity of not doing anything at all. And either way, it seems to me we fall into their trap."

"Yes, and there I think you put your finger on the spot," replied Herdie. "And also point to the solution. If, either way, we fall into their trap, let's fall into the little one and make ourselves ridiculous, rather than fall into the big one, the bottomless pit, and make ourselves and Bhawalgarh—victims."

"Yes, I quite agree. I felt sure you'd take that view of it, and decide that we must act as though it were a genuine plot."

"And that brings us round full-circle," smiled Herdie. "Back to the starting-point. How are we to act?

"In the first place," he went on, "there are no grounds for arresting anybody except, of course, Ranjit Singh, if you had the good luck to catch him. And in the second place there are no grounds for a raid on the Gopaldas house. What you might possibly do, is to raid the *To-day and To-morrow* offices, 'on the strength of information received' that the badly wanted Ranjit Singh is in hiding there. Though with such wily men as Purshotamdass, Bhojraj Shahani, Abdul Haq, the Swami, and Ranjit Singh, not to mention Sant Arjun Rama, I doubt whether you'd find anything."

"No; and if one found the gang themselves, the whole lot of them, there's no law against their holding a meeting there or anywhere else. Still, it's worth trying. One might be lucky. Might get hold of something. Or of someone—who'd squeal."

"Well, that's one thing we can do," said Herdie, "and there's another. Although we won't play their spreading-consternation-and-alarm game for them, I'll have a word with all the officials whom this Lalchand Vasu mentioned. See them individually and separately; and say that, while there is no cause for any sort of panic and that kind of thing, there would be no harm in doubling—or quadrupling—precautions against anything in the nature of . . . well, bomb-placing. I'll have a word with Anderson of the Bank of India and Miller of the Provincial Bank; with Murdoch, about the Gaol; and with Hector Grant about the Fort. They'll all probably laugh.

"I'll see the Commissioner to-morrow morning after

church. And I'll mention, for what it is worth, that his wife's *protégé*, though a guest at Commissioner's House, frequents the society of certain notorious agitators and seditionists.

"I'm afraid that'll worry poor old Cornwallis frightfully and get him into trouble with the lady Rowena. And doubtless her Saint will tell her that he has a mission to these bad men and a duty to consort with sinners. . . .

"I suppose you've got some really reliable picked men you could send up to the Gaol and put on special duty when the time comes?"

"Yes, and that brings us to the most important point of all—the time," said Steele. "Does anything suggest itself to you on that point, Sir?" he asked.

"Yes. If the whole thing isn't a damned mare's-nest or a practical joke, I think that that fortnight warning, from two sources, means that the explosion is intended for some time well within a fortnight; and directly I knew that the Governor had consented to open the Hospital I thought of the anonymous letters. And now, what you tell me, brings the Governor's visit to mind again."

"Exactly," agreed Steele. "If there is going to be anything of the sort, any shooting, bomb-chucking, assassination, trouble of any kind, that, I should say, is when it will happen. Is the date of the visit fixed?"

"Had a Confidential to-day," replied Herdie. "He arrives next Friday evening, stays the night, opens the Hospital on Saturday morning, and catches the one-thirty on Saturday night, or rather Sunday morning, to make the connection at Mahommedabad Junction."

"So he'll be at Commissioner's House all Friday night, and on Saturday night until about one a.m."

"Yes."

"Then if there's going to be trouble, it will be on one of those two nights presumably. . . . I suppose there will be an official dinner-party at the Commissioner's House on Friday night."

"Yes, in the ordinary way. In the normal course of events, there would."

"As things are, I should think it'd be quite a sound idea not to assemble the whole of official Bhawalgarh in one building," said Steele.

"Yes; a bomb under the Commissioner's dining-room would save a lot of trouble, wouldn't it? Trouble and expense to hard-working conspirators. About twenty birds to one stone, not to mention the women-folk."

"But of course we could make anything in the nature of the placing of a time-bomb quite impossible."

"But not so impossible for anyone to creep into the garden and chuck a bomb into the room," replied Herdie. "And what about a man disguised as a servant? Every guest will bring his butler with him. A bomb might be thrown, if it couldn't be placed."

"Oh, I don't think there'd be much fear of that," aid Steele. "Forewarned and forearmed. Jackson and I would both be on duty outside; and we'd comb the garden pretty thoroughly, patrol the whole place, and have a picked man watching every door and window.

"As well as one or two on the roof," he added. "And guests could be asked not to bring their servants. That would minimize the chance of an assassin getting into the house."

"Nice state of affairs, isn't it?" observed Herdie. "A Credit to Politicians, so to speak. India had at long last found peace, and settled down into a quiet and con-tented country—until some conceited, windy fool dis-covered that its contentment was 'pathetic'! Did even a politician ever conceive such a notion before? Just fancy a national contentment being *pathetic*. And just fancy it being the high aim and ambition of a 'states-man' deliberately to turn contentment into discontent."

"And even so," observed Steele, "the discontent is only that of the vocal three hundred thousand and not of the silent three hundred million. The people of India are contented enough; and will be, so long as they have their British 'Protector of the Poor' to turn to."

"Yes, if only one could get the truth into the heads of the woolly-witted philanthropists at home, that India's worst enemy is the person who lifts a finger to try to shake the strength and stability of the British Raj, the one bulwark that the aforesaid dumb three hundred millions have, against exploitation, starvation and ruin. . . . And that those who come to England to 'represent' India represent precisely themselves and their little self-seeking clique—and nobody else. . . . Another glass of port? No? Shall we join—my wife?"

As they rose to their feet, Herdie said, "That's all we can do, then. Raid the *To-day and To-morrow* place at the time you think likeliest; warn every British Official concerned in this threat; shadow all suspects; tell the Commissioner that Sant Arjun Rama meets them at Ramrao Gopaldas's house; and, on Friday next, take every possible precaution and act precisely as though we knew there was going to be an attempt on the Governor's life and a general rising and massacre, that night or Saturday night. . . . Surely such places as the Fort, the Gaol, and the Banks can be safeguarded, made bomb-proof, plot-proof, conspirator-proof, since they are forewarned?"

"Surely," agreed Steele. "Granted that any one of us, from the Governor downwards, can be bombed or shot at, just as often as the devils can find a tool to act for them, I really don't see how infernal-machines and time-bombs can be placed in buildings where they are already expected by the occupants."

"No. The more one looks at it, the more one suspects a practical joke. We've both been shot at and so has the Governor; but this wholesale blowing-up of forts, gaols and banks! . . . No, it's a joke."

"Hope so, Sir," replied Steele.

"But it was no joke for Lalchand Vasu," he added, as Herdie opened the door.

In the drawing-room Jane Herdie awaited them, her eyes bright, her colour rather high, her foot and her fan moving somewhat quickly.

Herdie knew the signs. Well, thank Heaven, Steele was there to keep her occupied and happy, for he himself had a long night's work before him. She'd keep Steele there till midnight and then she'd go upstairs. That ought to give him three or four hours of peace, and he'd get through a lot of work in that time.

Quite possibly she wouldn't come down again. She might drink. . . . Herdie's mind shied away like a startled horse from the vision of his wife drinking herself to sleep. The sooner he got to work, the better; and there was nothing to keep him in the drawing-room. Jenny would not mind how soon he went, and Steele would certainly excuse him, knowing how busy he was—especially now. He must write a discreet note to every official in Bhawalgarh. Some he'd ask to come and see him at the *kutcherry*; others could call on him here; one or two he would himself visit. It might be as well if he went up to the Gaol. That would be the danger-spot, if there were real trouble. The releasing of that prize collection of violent criminals—dacoits, murderers, highway-robbers, professional thieves and *thugs*—didn't bear thinking of.

The Fort would be all-right, surely. Of course, women and children—and such men as cared to join them—could be sent into the Fort for safety; but what an appalling false step that would be if the whole thing were a mare's-nest or a practical joke!

That would be playing the agitators' game for them, with a vengeance.

Nothing could be better calculated to "spread consternation and alarm" and to proclaim from the house-tops—and from the Fort walls—the British Government's weakness and fear.

And what of the Native Regiment? Colonel Angus Campbell was a fine soldier and it was a fine battalion—none better—but the same applied to the very ones that mutinied and murdered their officers in 1857. It applied to the regiment that did so in this very place, and after an orgy of bloodshed, rapine, and plunder in the town, settled down to the siege of the Fort; and were joined by hordes of other mutineers, *budmashes*, robbers and criminal riff-raff.

How far were the Sikhs of the regiment tainted, their loyalty shaken, their minds poisoned with infamous lies, their belief in the British undermined by tales of their Faith being in danger. Pity it wasn't a

Ghurka regiment. For the Ghurka stood well-nigh as far outside Indian domestic, political, and religious problems as did the British Tommy himself.

"Will you excuse me, Jenny? I've got a tableful of work I really must get down to. You'll excuse me, won't you, Steele?" he said.

"Very well, Lawrence," smiled Jenny Herdie. "I know you are not really happy outside your office."

"Why, of course, Sir," replied Steele as Herdie glanced at him. "I know how terribly busy you must be just now."

And Herdie, with a kindly smile, left the drawing-room.

"Why is he specially busy just now?" asked Jane Herdie, as the door closed behind her husband.

Steele thought quickly.

"Oh, hasn't he told you yet? H.E. arrives on Friday."

"No, he hasn't said a word."

"Well, he only knew just before dinner. I only knew, myself, after dinner.

"What a shaking-out of morning coats and brushing-up of old top-hats there will be when the news is published," he went on.

"Yes, busy time for Rowena Cornwallis. She'll love it, though."

"Yes, she's a great hostess."

"What a blessing H.E. is a bachelor," observed Jane Herdie. "A Governor in the house must be trouble enough, but a Governess . . . !"

"Oh, the lady Rowena would keep her in her place," smiled Steele. "I'd back the lady Rowena against . . ."

"Do come here, Tony," interrupted his hostess. "I'm not going to shout at you across the room."

And Mrs. Herdie indicated the place beside her on the settee.

A bit of a bore, but if Jenny Herdie wanted to flirt, why shouldn't she? Live and let live. She must find life pretty dull with poor old Herdie. One of the most conscientious men who ever lived, and one of the nicest, but not the right husband for this extremely pretty woman, temperamental and yet stupid. She must find life frightfully dull, being so lacking in interests if not in interest. No mental resources whatever.

What on earth did she do with herself, since she never, by her own confession, read a book, sang a song, set a stitch, wrote a letter, or played a game? Did she play *the* game—by Herdie? Played her own game, more likely.

And now she wanted to play a game with Anthony Steele, judging by the fact that she had just—artlessly and quite unconsciously perhaps—put her hand on his, as it lay on the cushion between them.

"Kiss me, Tony. . . . *Love* me," said Jenny passionately, her hand closing on his with a hot grip.

Good Lord! Sudden—to say the least of it, thought Steele.

"With all the world to see?" he smiled "Suppose your husband walked in, and, with a loud cry of '*Break away*' cautioned me against holding . . . h'm."

Dear, dear! In his confusion and alarm, he had almost said something silly.

Mrs. Herdie's face hardened perceptibly as her eyes glinted beneath frowning brows and her lips were compressed.

"Lawrence will not come out of his study to-night," she said. "Until I go and fetch him."

"He might, you know," smiled Steele. "That's how accidents happen. He might think of something he wanted to say to me, and march straight into the room just at the wrong moment, and cry 'Hold. Enough,' like Macbeth.

"Or perhaps, '*Hold that*,' like a film-director," he amended. "'*Anything you are doing will be used in evidence against you.*'"

"Good job, too."

"No. Bad job. Worse still if St. Paul came."

"*St. Paul?*"

"Paul Jesus Etcetera, your butler. I should blush every time I saw him hereafter. Don't suppose I should see him Hereafter, though, if I did anything so wicked as that."

"He'll not come until I call. . . . Kiss me, Tony."

Smiling imperturbably and gazing into Jane Herdie's eyes,

"*Oh for the hour, the place, and the loved one,*'" he murmured. "Isn't it extraordinary how rarely they coincide!"

"Which of them is missing here, Tony?"

"Ah!"

"Kiss me. You must. You *shall*. . . . You do love me, Tony, don't you?"

"The hour and the place," murmured Steele. "Now's the day and now's the hour, but I'm damned if this is the place, Mrs. . . ."

"Tony, please never call me Mrs. Herdie again—or I shall call you Mr. Steele."

"*Oh!*" reproached Anthony Steele.

"I shall. You are to call me Jenny, and in front of Lawrence too, and everybody else. Kiss me, Tony."

"The place . . . The hour and the place. The hour's all-right, but do you know that we are being watched?"

"Watched! By whom?"

"I couldn't tell you. But everything we Europeans do in India is seen and known—and multiplied by ten—and talked about."

"But, Tony, no-one can see us here."

"How do you know? How do you know who's out in the garden there? This room is brilliantly illuminated and the garden is in darkness. How do you know who's watching us?"

"Tony, you make me quite uncomfortable."

"No more uncomfortable than you make me," thought Tony. "As a matter of fact, I'd rather like to kiss you, but I'd really much sooner slap you. That's what you want, my lass; and it's a great pity Herdie doesn't do it."

"What are you thinking, Tony?"

"I was thinking of you."

"Oh, Tony! *Darling!* . . ."

About time he went home. A long chair, pipe and pyjamas. Then bed, book, air-gun, a little sport-without-danger, and a spot of sleep. He wanted some.

No place like home.

A hand stole up to his chin and turned his face sideways.

"What are you thinking of, Tony?"

"My bungalow," he replied truthfully.

"Oh, Tony! *Darling* Tony."

Then he was thinking of her. Of his bungalow. Of her in his bungalow. Of course he loved her. If only because she loved him so much, he must surely love her.

"Kiss me . . ." she whispered, as Herdie opened the door from his office and walked into the room.

"Sorry to . . ." Herdie stared. ". . . to . . . to . . . talk shop, Steele. Would you give me a minute?"

Steele rose to his feet.

"Certainly, Sir," he replied, turning to go.

"Good night—*Jenny*," he said mischievously.

"Oh, no, no. Don't go," expostulated Herdie. "No, please, Steele. Only a minute."

If Jenny were making love to Anthony Steele, he could doubtless take care of himself—could play St. Anthony. And if he loved Jenny he could . . .

Lawrence Herdie's mind again shied away from the thoughts that strove to approach it.

"Of course you are not going, Tony," cried Mrs. Herdie. "Come back as soon as you can, and have a drink."

"No, really. I must be strong if I can't be silent," protested Steele still more mischievously.

She understood. He must be strong. He must resist overwhelming temptation. He must flee from it, in fact. For this was not the place. He himself had said it—and had spoken of his bungalow in the same breath. That was the place. And until the hour and the place and the loved one were his—he must be strong. But she must not let him go until the hour had been arranged between them.

"Sorry to bother you, Steele," said Herdie, closing the door and seating himself at his desk. "Sit down a minute. I've drafted a carefully worded demi-official to the people concerned, and I shall be seeing all of them to-morrow. But what has just occurred to me is this. Do you think things are so serious that it would be a good plan if I suggested to the Commissioner that the Governor be asked to postpone his visit?"

Steele considered this.

"I do—and it's an idea," he said. "It is certainly an idea.

"Reflects on the efficiency of the police a bit," he smiled, "but it is certainly an idea. If His Excellency postponed his visit, apparently indefinitely, but with the intention of coming to Bhawalgarh on his way back to Jhalni from the Hills, it would give us time, wouldn't it?"

"That's what I thought," said Herdie. "Anything might happen. You might lay hands on Ranjit Singh; Sant Arjun Rama would have gone; you might get something against the others on which we could act; and the situation would probably clarify itself."

"Yes, and if the worst came to the worst," agreed Steele, "and there was a bust-up within the next fortnight, the Governor would be out of it, anyhow."

"Yes; and if the Governor doesn't come—and nothing happens—what are we to argue from that? That the whole thing was a practical joke?"

"Yes, Sir, I think so. That or a mare's-nest. If there really is a big and comprehensive plot, it wouldn't be abandoned just because the Governor changed his plans."

"I agree, Steele. And I'll put it to the Commissioner; tell him all you've told me; suggest that the Governor be put off; and then we'll carry on just as though we had full information that there was going to be—an explosion."

"I suppose the Commissioner will take your view of it, Sir?"

"I think so. I quite think so. I've always found him most ready to listen to the man on the spot—which is the secret of governing India."

"And what about His Excellency?"

"Oh, I think he, in turn, would listen to the Commissioner. Besides, if Cornwallis agrees with us, and

595

decides to put H.E. off, he could give him some other reason. Officially, and at first, anyhow. Tell him the Hospital won't be ready for the opening. Something like that."

"Yes, something of the sort," mused Steele. "I think it's a splendid idea.

"Anyway, it ought to be tried," he added, "for it's a brilliant notion, Sir, postponing the visit. A brain-wave."

"Right. I'll see the Commissioner to-morrow then, and if I don't convince him straight away, I'll get you to weigh in, too. Might be a good idea if I sent for you to come over—if it's necessary."

Herdie rose to his feet.

"Thanks, Steele. Sorry to have worried you with shop again at this time of night."

"Not at all, Sir. I was only too anxious to talk it all over with you. Joke or not, it was getting too big for me to handle by myself."

Herdie went to open the door leading into the drawing-room.

"Do you mind if I go out this way?" said Steele. "I've said good night to Mrs. Herdie."

§6

Meanwhile, that evening, another *diner à trois* was taking place in the bachelor quarters of the Officer Commanding the Fort of Bhawalgarh, a dinner whereat three brother Scots, Highlanders all, discussed trout and salmon fishing; deer-stalking; grouse-shooting; the phenomenon of the Highlanders' power of second sight; personal experiences of curious manifestations of the uncanny, the super-normal and the occult; ghosts; and finally, the ghost of Bhawalgarh Fort.

This last was of particular interest, as the ghost was that of the host's grandfather, Colonel Hector Grant, himself also once Commandant of the Fort and occupant of those same quarters.

"Ghosts," mused Major Murdoch of the Indian Medical Service and Superintendent of the Bhawalgarh

Gaol, as he poured out his glass of port. "An interesting subject and as old as the Bible. Everyone believes in them subconsciously, or rather, in his heart of hearts; and all intelligent people deny their existence, scoff at the mere idea of them."

"Quite so, and quite rightly," smiled Colonel Angus Campbell of Nicholson's Sikhs. "We all know there are no such things. Pure moonshine and nonsense."

"Including the ghost of Bhawalgarh Fort," he added, smiling at his host.

"Quite," agreed Major Hector Grant. "What is your experience—that makes you deny the existence of ghosts so firmly, Murdoch?"

"Mine? Oh, all nonsense, of course. Even if there could be such a thing as the ghost of a human being, how could there be such things as the ghost of a monk's robe, for example?"

"Quite so. What was it?"

"Foolish fancies of an imaginative highly strung child. I used to spend my holidays with an uncle who had an old place at the top of Glen Grannock. It belonged to the infamous Simon Fraser, Lord Lovat, at one time, and was the scene of some dark and dirty doings, both before and after the '45.

"I usually had a little room that I loved because it had an almost octagonal window-turret from which I could see north, south and west. Lovely views of the loch and glen. One time when I went—I must have been about fifteen—I couldn't have the room, for some reason, and was put into another that had not been in use for years. I didn't like it at all, and I couldn't give a reason. I didn't sleep in it well, either, and that was quite a new experience.

"One night I woke up, lying on my left side, and looking along a wall to a window opposite my bed, a high window through which the moon was shining brightly.

"There was a man in the room.

"I was at first astonished and then terrified. He was kneeling, facing the wall with his left side toward me. In the moonlight I could see him sufficiently distinctly to know that he was a monk. He was dressed in a black robe, gathered in at the waist by a knotted cord or rope. This garment had a pointed cowl which hung from his shoulders down his back, leaving his head bare. The top of his head was either bald or shaven, leaving a tonsure of black hair. On his bare feet were sandals. His clasped hands were raised in front of his face, and from his white bony arms the sleeves of the monkish habit fell back, exposing them almost to the elbows. Although I could only see his face *en profile*, I knew that it was emaciated and was contorted by powerful emotion—grief, fear, agony or horror.

"Obviously he was praying with terrific fervour, earnestness, abandon.

"While I looked, he rose to his feet, and I remember seeing a rosary of jet or ebony beads, to which a cross was attached, swing outward from his girdle as he did so.

"Erect, he flung his hands aloft, raised his face to Heaven, and then appeared to embrace someone or something, in the act of doing which he seemed to merge into the wall. It was as though the wall were but a veil through which he thrust his arms in the act and gesture of embracing.

"I think I fainted."

Colonel Angus Campbell withdrew his cheroot from his lips and blew a long cloud of smoke.

"We must, of course, treat this rationally and with proper scepticism, and provide a solution," he smiled. "Obviously it was a nightmare."

"Obviously," agreed Major Hector Grant. "You had been reading Scott during the day, and had dined late and indigestibly with your uncle."

"Quite so. Quite so," agreed Major Murdoch. "A nightmare induced just as you say. And I dreamed that peculiar and particular nightmare again the next night. Or rather, morning. It must have been between four and five o'clock. And a third time, one evening, as I sat with one muddy boot on and one off, weary and worn after a long day's stalking, resting in the middle of the labours of changing for dinner. Precisely the same thing."

"Did you swoon the second time, when you saw it in the grey light of dawn?" asked Colonel Campbell.

"No. It grew fainter as the light grew stronger, much in the same way as a film would do if all the lights in the house were turned on. Faded and disappeared. Or, possibly, I may have shut my eyes in terror before the thing disappeared."

"And the third time when you were sitting in a chair?" asked Major Grant.

"Much the same. There was no light in the room save that of the log-fire. I sat and stared at the thing. As on the two previous occasions, I was filled with a sense of horror, terror. I was almost frightened to death. I was shaken from head to foot. When I could control the rigor and screw up my courage sufficiently, I managed to get a box of matches from my pocket and light two candles that stood on the mantelpiece, these being all the lighting-arrangement the room boasted. When I turned round the figure was no longer there."

"Let us again be rational and properly sceptical, and explain it away," said Colonel Campbell. "You looked at the spot in which your nightmare had located the praying monk. You remembered the scene in detail, and projected it from your inner consciousness so vividly and strongly that you saw it, or rather thought you saw it, with the physical eye."

"That's it," agreed Major Grant. "Association of ideas, dim light, the actual spot, sensitive retentive memory, over-active imagination."

"Exactly," agreed Murdoch. "And this third effort of my imagination was so successful that I was moved to mention the matter to my uncle as we dined alone together that night, under the contemptuous gaze of the eyes of a number of heads of 'royal' stags and of a few ancestors."

"'Oh, seen the Praying Monk, have you? That's interesting. Who told you about him?' said the old chap.

"'Nobody, Sir,' I assured him.

"'Quite off your own bat, eh?' he asked.

"'I never heard a word about him, and I have seen

him three times, Sir,' I said.

"'And you don't like him?'

"'Not a bit.'

"'He's perfectly harmless.'

"'I'm not so sure of that, Sir,' I said.

"'Well, he won't do *you* any harm.'

"'I think he has done me some already. He has taught me fear as I never knew it before. And I don't want to go into that room again, much less sleep there.'

"I think my uncle was somewhat disappointed in me; but although he pooh-poohed the ghost, I never heard that he ever went out of his way to encounter him by sleeping in the room himself."

A brief silence fell.

"Very interesting. I call that very interesting, indeed. First-hand experience of your own, and corroborated by what your uncle said," observed Grant.

"Extremely interesting," agreed Campbell.

"It is; especially when you hear the sequel," continued Murdoch. "I inherited that house, and I own it still. I was thirty years of age when it became my property, a doctor, a fairly widely read and widely travelled man, and particularly interested in the occult, in supernormal phenomena, and in honest and scientific psychic research.

"Shortly after the house had been overhauled and put in repair I went to spend four months of furlough there, from June to September, and the first night of the full moon I slept in the room in which I had seen the apparition fifteen years earlier.

"I went to bed that night wishing, hoping, and intending to see the ghost again.

"I did. That very first night. I kept myself awake as long as possible by drinking coffee from a thermos-flask, smoking, and reading a book.

"The last time I looked at my wrist-watch was at three-fifteen and, some time after that, I fell asleep. I awoke, again lying on my left side, my back to one wall and looking along another to the window in the wall opposite my bed. In the light of the full moon that shone into the room, illuminating the floor and wall between me and the window, I saw the monk again. As far as I could remember he was dressed in exactly the same way, was kneeling in the same position, and behaved in exactly the same manner as before.

"When he rose to his feet, crossed himself and embraced someone whom I could not see, merging, as he did so, into the wall itself, I sat up, threw off the clothes, and stepped out of bed.

"I wasn't horrified, terrified, frightened, this time, but tremendously keyed-up, excited, thrilled. I advanced to the spot where he had been, and where now there was nothing but the blank wall, and tapped with my knuckles at the place where he had disappeared. I had some sort of notion that I might find that there was a door beneath the plaster. The room was distempered, by the way, in a sort of cream-coloured whitewash, and not papered.

"I had visions of discovering a secret passage, a forgotten room, a hiding-place, a chapel, something of that sort. Otherwise, why should this monk, or rather, spirit, astral form, ghost of a monk, appear always at this spot and disappear through this wall?

"What I partly hoped and partly feared to find, was that someone, monk or nun, had been walled up here; for the monk's movement, gesture, as I have said, after praying, was precisely that of the act of embracing. If the man himself had been walled-up here alive, it was hardly likely that his ghost would behave in such a way. But might it not have been a nun; and might not he have loved her? Might not I be upon the point of discovering the relics of an awful tragedy, a terrible love story, one of those barbarous cruelties of which our quite-recent ancestors were capable?

"A walled-up nun!

"Tapping with my knuckles, I learned nothing at all, went back to bed, and slept again.

"Tapping next day with a hammer, I was delighted and quite excited to discover that most undoubtedly I had tapped on wood as well as on stone; and it seemed quite improbable to me that there would be a perpendicular beam just there in the wall itself. And yet the wood that was undoubtedly below the plaster was rather narrow for a door.

"I went over to Inverness and arranged for a firm of building-and-decorating contractors to send a man over to Glen Grannock, as the house was called, to strip the plaster from the wall and find what was underneath it at the spot where the tapping gave forth different sounds and indicated the presence of wood as well as stone.

"This was done, and the workman laid bare a great wooden crucifix, built into the wall itself. Nothing more.

"At the foot of this crucifix the ghost of the monk had knelt, and then, rising, had embraced it as though the wall had not been there.

"No, there are no such things as ghosts, of course. Ask any intelligent person," concluded Murdoch.

"Of course," agreed Colonel Campbell. "My own experience confirms what you say."

"I used to go to Ireland for some hunting whenever I was on leave at the right time. I went once to stay with my late wife's brother who had married a very charming Irish widow, a Fitzgerald of Kildare. I only stayed there once, and I'll tell you why.

"I was dressing one lovely warm sunny Sunday morning in October. Breakfast wasn't until nine-thirty on Sundays, and I had not only taken advantage of the fact, but cut it a bit fine. There was a french window in my bedroom giving on to a big wide verandah, and I had opened it. I was brushing my hair, when a charming little kid ran into the room from the verandah. I was the more surprised in that my host and hostess had no children, and I was under the impression that there were none in the house.

"'Hullo,' said I. 'Where have you sprung from?'

"And the little girl, a regular little fairy she was, laughed, tossed her curls back and ran away again, out on to the verandah.

"That's funny, thought I. I didn't know there was any other door or window opening out there.

"And before going downstairs I stepped out and looked.

"No; it was as I thought. Through my own french window was the only way on to the verandah, one end of which was closed by the bay-window of my room and the other by the railings that ran round the long and the short side of it.

"How had the kid got on to the verandah? And how had she left it?

"I shouldn't have been so surprised had it been a boy, but this dainty, fragile little thing didn't look as though she had been climbing, nor the sort that would be likely to do that kind of thing. And her little white silk frock had been spotlessly clean, which it wouldn't have been if she'd scrambled over that creeper-matted verandah railing.

"I was so puzzled and intrigued that, as soon as I had said good morning to my hostess in the breakfast-room, I mentioned the matter.

"She burst into tears.

"It was rather dreadful.

"Her little girl, aged eight, had climbed on to a chair that had been put out there, reached for a flower, fallen over, and broken her neck.

"Although I knew that my brother-in-law had married a widow, I had never heard that she had had, and lost, a little girl.

"Of course, I didn't say another word to the poor woman, but I asked my brother-in-law if he could show me a portrait of the dead child. It was an extremely good one—of the little girl whom I had seen.

"No, there are no such things as ghosts, of course," added Colonel Campbell. "Any intelligent man can give you an excellent and acceptable explanation of that."

"Of course he can," agreed Major Grant. "And of my own experience, too.

"You know the Mutiny history of this Fort, of course. My grandfather, Colonel Hector Grant, commanded it; and when the Native Regiment in garrison here, mutinied on May 10th, 1857, he did great things with the handful of British gunners he had got, and a few loyal Sepoys who, all honour to them, remained true to their salt, *nimak hallal*, in circumstances under which it took a lot of doing, and at a time when precious few Sepoys had the courage and strength to go against the overpowering current, and do the right thing.

"He was a great character, my grandfather, very eccentric, even before the days when he suffered from a combination of brandy and religious mania. He had received a severe head-wound at Sobraon, a sabre-cut which had obviously affected his brain. He undoubtedly drank tremendous quantities of brandy-*pani*—though there was no record of his ever having been seen drunk or, indeed, the worse for liquor—and he used to preach and exhort with all the fervour and violence of a prophet of old. He looked like one, too.

"There's an oil-painting of him, as a subaltern, at home, done here in Bhawalgarh by a native artist in 1855; and though he was no older then than I am now, he had got a long grey beard and must have looked about seventy. Extraordinary how those beards aged the men of that generation. A be-whiskered subaltern of twenty looked forty, and a field-officer of forty-five looked like Methuselah.

"Well, now, we've all seen portraits painted by native artists, and I have no doubt they've all given us the same impression—that portrait-painting wasn't their strong point. I am no judge of a picture as such, but I do know enough about perspective to see when a picture is absolutely all wrong, and enough of anatomy to know when what purports to be a likeness is quite evidently unlike any human being that ever lived.

"So, the question of colour apart, I have no great admiration for the work of Indian artists, or rather I hadn't until the other night.

"Now I have. For I can testify that that portrait of Colonel Hector Grant, painted here in 1855, was a truly admirable and faithful likeness."

"How do you know that?" asked Colonel Campbell.

"Because I've seen him.

"I met him face to face, in full moonlight, the other

night, just outside a recess in the old disused treasury-house wall, a recess in which there is a door that I have never seen opened. I was never more astonished in my life, and thought for a moment that Brandon or Crawfurd of the Battery had got himself up for a fancy-dress ball as an officer of Native Infantry in John Company days. It was a queer kit, too; shako, neck-curtain, stock, scarlet coatee with tails, white overalls strapped over half-Wellingtons, sash, cross-belt, old-fashioned sword and so on—and then I saw that the long grey beard was obviously not false. And in the same second that all this flashed through my mind I realized that I knew the face.

"I *knew* this man.

"Of course, it was my grandfather himself! There he stood in front of me, in the flesh . . . only he wasn't in the flesh; and the living image of the man in the painted portrait . . . only he wasn't living.

"And I don't mind telling you fellows that I should not have mentioned this, deeply as it intrigued and indeed affected me, but for your own shameful confessions. That was what I had been leading the conversation up to, as I wanted to find out what your attitude was to that sort of thing. I rather wanted to tell somebody, only it had to be somebody sympathetic. And it is an unusual Highlander who's not—sympathetic—to anything connected with second-sight, clairvoyance, and psychic phenomena."

His hearers gazed at Major Grant with deep interest, each of them obviously stirred if not thrilled.

"Well, well! That is amazing," said Colonel Campbell. "It is something to see a ghost at all, a real indubitable authentic ghost, but to see the ghost of one's own ancestor, one's own grandfather, here in India . . . Well, well!"

"By Jove, yes," agreed Major Murdoch. "You know, we three ought to address ourselves to the Psychical Research Society, for we can each of us bear first-hand living testimony to the existence of what are known as ghosts. I had never heard of my praying monk; Campbell had never heard that a child had either lived or died in that house in Ireland; and now you've seen the ghost of your grandfather so plainly and clearly that you can pronounce his painted portrait to be an excellent likeness."

"Yes, and I'll tell you another thing which is pertinent. Something that, when I realized it afterwards, struck me as remarkably interesting. Although the face was the face in the portrait that hangs in the hall at my home, the dress was not the same as that in the picture.

"He had been painted in mess-kit, bare-headed, with epaulettes, and wearing medals.

"The ghost was, as I said, wearing the shako of that day; his coat had no epaulettes; and he was not wearing medals. The ghost had a white belt and shoulder-strap, too; and these are not in the portrait, of course, as he was done in mess-kit."

"That's interesting," observed Murdoch, "and rather cuts the ground from under the feet of the worthy scientists, 'realists,' and sceptics who inform us that every ghost that we think we see is merely the outward and visible materialization—if you can call a ghost material—of a mental conception."

"Quite so," agreed Campbell. "I suppose you had never seen any sort of drawing, sketch, painting, or portrait of your grandfather in the dress in which he appeared to you?"

"Never. I really hadn't the slightest idea as to what kind of head-gear he wore, nor as to how he would dress, for active service. Now I do know, down to the last button, through seeing him as undoubtedly he actually was during the last days of his life, when he was holding this Fort with a handful of men against hundreds—probably thousands.

"And now I'll tell you something else that will interest you. Having seen this ghost and with such amazing distinctness, I naturally thought about the matter a good deal and made all sorts of investigations and enquiries—to try to find out whether it was an old, well-known, and established phenomenon; and if not, whether it had ever appeared to anyone else; also whether anybody now alive had ever seen the ghost of Colonel Hector Grant.

"Well, I have discovered that, to the native personnel at any rate, he's quite well known; that he's a legend among them; that there's a story attached to the ghost—and that there is actually alive at this day a man who has not only seen the ghost, but who knew Colonel Hector Grant himself, when he was Commandant of this Fort and lived in these very rooms."

"Gad, that's interesting," said Colonel Campbell, pouring himself a second glass of port and wafting the decanter in a left-handed circle across the table to Major Murdoch. "And isn't it curious and typical that they know all about this, while no European ever hears a word of it? Probably no European ever has."

"Yes, typical," said Grant. "If only we could know more of what they say, know more of what goes on under our very noses, it would be better for us, for them, and for India.

"Well, in point of fact, there is one other European that knows, another Highlander, too, Donald Mac-Kenzie, one of the best Battery Sergeant-majors that ever lived. Comes from my part of the country, and I have known him practically all my life. When I started making discreet enquiries among the European personnel, I naturally began with him. He didn't seem a bit surprised, and admitted at once that he had seen the ghost. He's a thoughtful educated chap, and took the view that what he had seen wasn't really there, as he put it; and that had there been anybody with him at the time, that person would not have seen it.

"Curiously enough, although he has actually seen the ghost, it is his opinion—or was, until I spoke to him—that there are no such things as ghosts at all, save in the way, and to the extent, that there are such things as dreams. You 'see' a dream, but it is not real. Same with ghosts. To him, the ghost was a waking dream—a day-dream, one might say; a vision."

"Hallucination, in fact," observed Colonel Campbell.

"A figment of the imagination," murmured Murdoch.

"Yes. But now that I have told him that I had seen the same ghost—and in the same place, by the way—and that we have agreed precisely as to the details of its dress, he is reconsidering his opinion on the matter. What he would like now, would be that he and I and a third person should endeavour to see the ghost together. The third person, paraphrasing what Donald said, would preferably be a fat-headed, unimaginative, ignorant fellow, who would never see anything that wasn't there, and damn little that was.

"We are going to try, anyway."

"Let us three try too, shall we, Grant?" suggested Murdoch.

"Yes, and we might have Donald MacKenzie with us, since he has seen it. But wait a minute. This is what I was going to tell you. There is alive at this moment an aged party of the name of Pandurang Hari who, as I say, actually knew Colonel Hector Grant. Not only knew him, but knows his ghost, and knows the story connected therewith.

"Pandurang Hari was not—unfortunately for the sake of making a neatly rounded tale—actually a loyal Sepoy who fought under Colonel Hector Grant in the defence of the Fort. He must have been fourteen or fifteen years of age when the Mutiny broke out in May, '57. Not old enough to be a soldier, but quite old enough to get around and see everything, to understand what he saw, and to remember it—which he does, to this day.

"He was the son of an employed pensioner in the Fort; and he was undoubtedly inside the Fort for at any rate part of the time that it was besieged.

"Pandurang Hari's son, following in father's footsteps, as is inevitable in India, was a Sepoy and is now himself an employed pensioner working here as rifle-range-*pattiwallah*, barrack-*chowkidar*, target-mender, and cleaner and oiler in the armoury. He's Atmaram Pandurang and sort of unofficial batman and factotum to Sergeant-Major Donald MacKenzie.

"Knowing that this Atmaram Pandurang had been in and about the Fort from childhood, and that his father, Pandurang Hari, had also been in and about the Fort from childhood, like *his* father before him, it occurred to Donald MacKenzie that anything that these two did not know about the Bhawalgarh Fort would not be worth knowing.

"Directly he tackled him, Atmaram Pandurang said,

"'Oh, yes, everybody knows that the *bhut* of the old Colonel Grant Sahib walks in the Fort whenever bad trouble is coming.'

"Had he seen him himself?

"'Oh, yes, several times,' he said at once. And so had his father, Pandurang Hari. Father had known the Colonel Sahib himself, cleaned his sword and revolver, pipe-clayed his straps, polished his boots, and carried his gun when he went out for *shikar*.

"Sergeant Donald MacKenzie promptly bade Atmaram Pandurang bring old Pandurang Hari along for a *bukh*. This he did; and MacKenzie, having had a long talk with him and found him amazingly interesting, brought him along to me. As MacKenzie rightly said, I was sure to be interested in somebody who had been here in the Fort in Mutiny days, and who remembered my grandfather most distinctly.

"Well, this is what I learned from Pandurang Hari. That, as my grandfather died, he cursed the mutineers, in Hindustani, with the utmost violence and ferocity. He called them what they undoubtedly were; and he prophesied a fitting end for every treacherous, disloyal, murderous son-of-a-pig among them. He said that not only would the Sirkar blow the ring-leaders from guns and shoot those who obeyed them; but he himself would haunt them as the most terrible of *bhuts*, both here and Hereafter. Apparently he cursed them to such purpose that they slunk off and left him to die in peace, in that very room through there.

"He must have been a tough old bird, for according to Pandurang Hari, he had got about a dozen bayonet wounds in the last hand-to-hand scrap, as he and his gunners were driven back from the walls to the foot of those steps, which they held for quite a while with bayonet and musket-butt.

"Then, soon after the Mutiny was suppressed and this Fort re-taken, a rumour arose that the ghost of Colonel Grant Sahib had been seen—and according to Pandurang Hari, in the same spot where I and Donald MacKenzie saw it, too.

"Apparently the story was quite unknown to the Commandant and the officers and European personnel of the half-battery here, but it was common talk among the Sepoys. Just after the first appearance of the ghost, the big fire of 1858 occurred, and several lives were lost, including those of Major Jackson and three European soldiers belonging to the Arsenal, when the burning building in which they were salvaging collapsed.

"Pandurang Hari swears that he saw the ghost himself on that occasion, as did at least two sentries and a *chowkidar*.

"As is always the case with the uneducated native, it is extremely difficult to get dates more than approximately, though the chronological sequence is generally correct. Anyhow, it was some time after this that the ghost was seen again, and old Pandurang Hari connects this reappearance with the fact that a floor in the Barracks gave way, owing to the ravages of white ants, and three gunners were killed, or rather, a gunner and two drivers, one breaking his neck, one being buried and suffocated, and the other dying of loss of blood owing to falling on an earthenware *chattie*, a jagged piece of which severed his jugular vein.

"Later, it appears, there was a very bad outbreak of cholera and the garrison of the Fort suffered severely. In one barrack-room, according to Pandurang Hari, all the men whose beds were along one wall died, while none of those whose beds were along the opposite wall took the disease at all."

"Quite likely," said Major Murdoch. "I know personally of a case where men in alternate beds, with the utmost regularity, fell victims during a cholera epidemic. Inexplicable, and probably pure chance and coincidence—and possibly not."

"Well, just before the epidemic, the Colonel's ghost

was seen again; and by this time, so Pandurang Hari tells me, they had begun to connect the appearance with approaching misfortune. Doubtless the tale is embroidered, and any misfortune that occurred was always connected-up with the last appearance of the ghost.

"Anyway, it seems that it was seen before that nasty business in the 'Seventies, when an officer here was not only accused, but convicted, of cheating at cards after Mess one guest-night. I forget the name of the officer and it is better forgotten, but the story is quite authentic. He went across to his quarters and blew out his brains. I remember my father talking about it at dinner one night, with old General Rose, a crony of his.

"Apparently the ghost turned up again and again, and each time a disaster was foretold and invariably came to pass.

"Perhaps. Perhaps not.

"But this struck me as interesting. Old Pandurang Hari says he appeared (and it was one of the occasions on which he himself saw him) one dreadful hot night in July. Then everybody—except the Europeans, of course —knew that something was going to happen. But nothing did. Nevertheless it was remembered, later, that the night on which he appeared was that before the Battle of Maiwand. At that battle, as you know, the British guns were captured and every single artillery-man killed. And it is an interesting fact that the half-battery stationed here in Bhawalgarh Fort had been sent up to Afghanistan and had joined the very brigade that Ayub Khan defeated.

"According to the evidence, for what it is worth, this was the only time that the Colonel's ghost appeared without some disaster or other occurring in the Fort itself.

"The last time that Pandurang Hari, or, so far as I can gather, anybody else, saw the ghost, was when a Sepoy ran amok, went *ghazi* and shot the Commandant, bayoneted a couple of officers, and then jumped off the wall and broke his neck.

"Curiously enough, all these appearances have

been at, or about, full moon, and in the hottest of the hot weather."

"And now you've seen him," observed Colonel Campbell, fingering the stem of his wine-glass. "It is full moon to-morrow night, I think; and it is certainly the hottest of the hot weather."

"And quite independently and authentically, Sergeant-Major Donald MacKenzie has seen him," said Major Murdoch.

"Yes, and so now I'm wondering what is going to happen in Bhawalgarh Fort," smiled Grant.

"Yes, by Jove! I hadn't thought of that aspect of it," said Campbell. "By Gad, it will be interesting if something does happen."

"Yes. Be almost worth the disaster, to see the story carried on—and carried out," agreed Grant.

"It would be a redeeming feature of it, wouldn't it?" said Murdoch.

"Yes; I shouldn't at all mind a mild misfortune," agreed Grant again. "Not that it would prove anything, naturally."

"No; prove nothing at all, of course. But still, I think it is up to you to have a recognizable disaster of some sort, Grant," smiled Campbell. "We don't want any murders, suicides, fires, cholera epidemics, defeats, or anything like that, of course, but . . ."

"No. But isn't the whole thing—interesting?"

"One of the most interesting things I have ever come across," said Murdoch. "Goes one better than my praying monk. For that, although it actually occurred and was real enough, was quite—pointless—so to speak. No-one knew the story connected with it, who the monk was, or anything about him; but this is doubly interesting with that story attached.

"Trebly, as a matter of fact, since the ghost is that of his own grandfather. And it will be mighty interesting to see whether anything recognizable as a disaster, calamity or misfortune follows," said Colonel Campbell.

"*Very* interesting," agreed Major Grant, a trifle wryly.

IV

Police-Sepoy Hashmat Dad Khan, specially chosen by the District Superintendent of Police by reason of his proven ability, keenness, and courage, and more especially for his intelligence, which was of an order far higher than that of the average Mahommedan police-man or soldier, leaned idly against the wall of the house at the corner nearest to the offices of the anglo-vernacular newspaper *To-day and To-morrow*, which he had been sent to watch, chewed a stick of sugar-cane, and looked as stupid as he could. With some difficulty he had shed all his wonted smartness, spruceness, and neatness with his uniform, and assumed the air, manner, and mien of a bazaar loafer and *budmash*, along with the appropriate clothing.

With an ill-wound dirty *puggri* on one side of his head, its end hanging down his back signifying a certain swashbuckling truculence, long filthy shirt worn outside dirty baggy trousers, and heavy thick-soled heel-less slippers of which the toes curled over toward his instep, he chewed and spat, chewed and spat, and with dull observant eye appeared to note nothing but the diminishing proportions of his juicy morning meal.

A sacred Brahminy bull meandered along the bazaar, nosed at the chewed fragments, and was loudly cursed as a loafing lump of worthless Hindu idolatry.

A plump young woman passed, clad in a tiny brief bodice and adequate loin-cloth that left bare her magnificent arms and legs and exposed the powerful muscles of her back as well as most of her abdomen. In the eyes of all who beheld her, she was nevertheless dressed with correct and becoming modesty, according to her caste, creed and station.

The loafer bestowed upon her a leer, a gesture, and a brief remark which elicited a reply that made him laugh. That was a good one! And, in acknowledgment, he spat, into the basket which she carried, a contribution from the waste products of his mastication.

A Hindu Police-Sepoy sauntered past twirling a truncheon; spick-and-span from his high-built, tightly bound red *puggri* to the equally tightly wound blue putties upon his thin legs, putties that, oddly to the unaccustomed eye, joined bare knees to the bare feet upon which, fastened by a single toe-strap, were stout sandals. His dark-blue cloth uniform was speckless, his buttons and belt refulgent.

"What a remarkably dirty scarecrow!" murmured the loafer, to be answered by a scowl, a flash of white teeth, and a significant motion of the truncheon.

"What a *particularly* dirty pig," he remarked as the Sepoy swaggered on.

Good. The fool had not recognized his friend and comrade Sepoy Hashmat Dad Khan.

A piteous object rounded the corner, a leprous creature that dragged itself along the ground, using its hands as feet, its arms as legs. Dust-covered, clad—almost un-clad—in torn rags, slobbering, dribbling and drooling, it emitted monotonously a hoarse cry, an appeal for alms.

Ceasing its slow and miserable progress at the feet of Police-Sepoy Hashmat Dad Khan, it peered up at him through long matted locks, and begged.

Again the loafer contributed of his superfluity. The prostrate beggar cursed him mechanically, and, without troubling to shake the chewed fibre of the sugar-cane from his head, dragged his body painfully on, his hands grasping a pair of carved and much-worn wooden objects which, shaped something like dumb-bells, kept his knuckles from contact with the ground.

In course of time he reached the steps that led up to the entrance of the offices of the *To-day and To-morrow* newspaper, and collapsed on their shady side, with his head upon the bottom step.

Here he lay and moaned pitifully to passers-by until, later, kind charitable hands raised him from the ground and bore him within.

Here, the door having been closed, he rose to his

feet, laughed, shook himself, and, removing the huge foul wig from his head, became the Swami Dayanand.

After conversation with the sub-editor and a compositor of the *To-day and To-morrow* newspaper, the Swami made his way to a back room in which there was little but a copying-press, chairs and a file-cupboard. Near this last the Swami seated himself and was soon joined by the acting-editor of the paper, one Jeshwant Ghokale, and Ramrao Gopaldas, with whom he talked, while obviously listening carefully for an expected sound.

Meanwhile a coolie, bent almost double beneath a great load of faggots, kindling-wood, branches and sticks, passed the loafer, presenting nothing more to his uninterested gaze than a pair of long sturdy legs and a mound of fire-wood. A thin protruding twig brushed the loafer across the face. Promptly he raised his foot, with swiftness and some force, in such a manner that it propelled the human beast of burden forward, sending him staggering along and causing him to break into a jog-trot. Apparently he accepted the kick as a Manifestation of the Inevitable, for, without stopping or straightening his body, he went on his way uncomplaining.

Almost before the gaze of the amused loafer had been withdrawn from him, in search of objects of greater interest, the burden-buried coolie turned up a lane or passage so narrow that his extremely bulky, if not very heavy, burden almost brushed the walls on either side.

Definitely he would have been a nuisance and an obstacle to the progress of passers-by, but fortunately there were none, for the alley into which he had turned was a *cul-de-sac* ending in the great high wall of the Fort itself.

At a door in the blank wall on the left-hand side of the lane, the coolie stopped and kicked. The door was opened, and, bending even lower, he forced his crackling load of faggots and brushwood through the doorway. Following the man who had admitted him, he staggered to the back door of the house, cast his burden sideways to the ground, straightened up, and revealed himself a big, powerfully-built, burly man with a bearded, pock-marked face—an obvious Sikh.

Entering the house and proceeding by dark and devious passages, crooked and unlighted stairs, he made his way to an attic, the right-hand wall of which did not quite meet the edge of the raftered roof. By means of a short rough ladder such as is used by builders' *maistris*, he climbed to the top of the wall, squeezed his body horizontally through the aperture between the wall and the roof, and dropped on the other side. The man who had admitted him removed the ladder, carried it downstairs, out into the courtyard, and deposited it in an ancient and dilapidated shed, already cumbered with much rubbish.

The Sikh, walking carefully along a rafter-beam, raised a trap-door, lowered his body and, ere his arms were extended to full length, touched with his feet the floor of a room. Standing on the side of a string-and-frame bedstead, he closed the trap-door and made his way down by rickety stairs and secret passages to the ground floor of the house.

Here he entered a room furnished with a *dhurrie*, an aged, circular blackwood table, huge and heavy, some cane-bottomed chairs of various shapes, sizes, and stages of decrepitude, and an almirah or clothes-cupboard.

Seating himself in a long leg-rest chair, he took his ease.

After a while, nothing having happened, he unlocked and opened the almirah, and slid the whole of the back of it to one side. This exposed another expanse of wood-work, to a knot-hole in which he placed his ear.

Reassured by what he heard, he tapped thrice, once, twice, and thrice—whereupon there was a sound of the turning of a key in a lock. A door was opened, another wooden partition was pushed aside, and the Swami Dayanand appeared.

"Hail to thee, blithe spirit," said he, taking the hand of Ranjit Singh, who drew him through into the room in which he had been waiting.

"Any luck?" he asked, seating himself.

"Yes and no," replied Ranjit Singh. "Jemadar Gujar Singh is making headway with his men, and can absolutely count on Havildars Fateh Singh and Pratap Singh, two or three Naiks and a couple of dozen or so of their various relatives. And there are also my own brothers and cousins. These all definitely and undoubtedly will make a move in the right direction on the night. They will shoot all the officers—and then who is to lead? Jemadar Gujar Singh. Unfortunately, that wooden-headed fool Subedar-Major Nikka Singh is absolutely hopeless. The owl is rabidly pro-British."

"Well, since he throws in his lot with theirs, he shall share their—lot," observed the Swami.

"Yes, he shall certainly get his, when they get theirs. But it's a pity; a great pity. If we could have got the Subedar-Major, we should have got the Regiment, or at any rate, all we wanted. It's bad luck, for the man's a power—and he's more English than the English. Thinks more of his Kitchener Sahib and Roberts Sahib and the rest of his Sahibs than of Nanak Chand[49] himself, Govind,[50] and all the Gurus. Thinks more of King's Regulations than of the Granth.[51] Buckingham Palace, where the King of England shook hands with him, is more to him than the Golden Temple of Amritsar."

"His grandfather was one of the Sect of the Nikalseinis, wasn't he?" enquired the Swami.

"Yes, fought under Jan Nikalsein[52] at Delhi in 1857, after fighting against him in the Sikh Wars."

"Well, it's no good trying to do anything with that type of renegade swine."

"No, they've got him, body and soul, and he values his five decorations above his five K's—*Kesh, Kanga, Kuch, Kura* and *Kirpan*."[53]

---

[49] *The first Sikh Guru and founder of the Sikh religion, circa 1469.*

[50] *The great Tenth Guru, 1675-1708.*

[51] *Sikh Bible.*

[52] *General John Nicholson.*

[53] *Uncut hair, comb, shorts, iron bangle and dagger (all of which every true Sikh must have).*

"Give him five more—with your automatic—when the time comes," said the Swami.

"And then some," growled Ranjit Singh, who had sojourned in America.

"Is Jemadar Gujar Singh a man of light and leading? Clever?" asked the Swami.

"Clever enough—and a really useful man; but of course he hasn't got the Subedar-Major's influence."

"I suppose you've promised them—everything?"

"Yes, including another Lion of the Punjab who shall one day be the Lion of Hindustan, too. Free land; no taxes; monopoly of money-lending; free irrigation; the army of India to be entirely Sikh; Amritsar to be the Capital of India; pay and pensions to be trebled for all ranks. . . . Oh, all sorts of remarkable things."

"And I suppose the war-cry on the day is to be *Khalsa ji ki fateh?*"[54] smiled the Swami.

"Naturally," replied Ranjit Singh.

"And without allowing the wish to be more than great-grandfather to the thought, what do you think really is, on the whole, the spirit of the Sikh sepoys of the Regiment?"

"Well, the spirit of any Indian regiment is, to some extent, indeed to a great extent, that of the Subedar-Major; but there is a lot of discontent, and Jemadar Gujar Singh has got a pretty good following. He'll have a far bigger one from the moment of firing the first shot —and killing the Colonel. They'll follow him all-right. There has been a lot of unrest ever since the suppression of the Gadr Sikh revolt; the Amritsar massacre; and the time the Government mismanaged the trouble when the hundred and thirty Akhalis[55] were shot or burnt alive by the Mahant[56] of the Udassis[57] at the Nankhana Shrine. Why, over five thousand Akhalis, most of them old soldiers who had fought for the Sirkar, were thrown into prison. Then, of course, Gandhi has been extremely helpful to us with his

---

[54] *Victory to the Khalsa.* (*God's chosen—the Sikhs.*)
[55] *Fanatical Sikhs (from religious war-cry Akhal! Akhal! The One! The One!).*
[56] *High priest.*
[57] *Sikh sect.*

wonderful incitement to sedition. His 'no violence' idea has caught on splendidly all over the Sutlej country, and *jatkas*[58] of Sikhs marched right across the Punjab in military formation. . . . And of course the regiment was getting letters from home every day, telling them about it all."

"'No violence'!" smiled the Swami. "Gandhi's an amusing old gentleman with his Gandhi caps, his fasts, and his salvation by spinning-wheels. No violence! I asked him what he was going to do when the English left India and the Pathans and Afghans swooped down to take their place.

"'I shall use soul-force,' he said. Can you beat it? Gandhi and his 'soul-force' versus the Ghazi and his knife! . . . But he has been mighty useful—to us.

"Yes, he has been very useful . . ." he continued. "And it must have done a lot of good for us among the Sikhs when the Congress held its camp-meeting in Amritsar with more pomp and circumstance than the Viceroy himself holding a Viceregal Durbar Camp."

"Yes," agreed Ranjit Singh. "It was really very funny, for when they proclaimed the Republic of India and pulled down the Union Jack from the flag-staff and ran up the National Independence Flag, it was the Police themselves who had to fight to protect the camp, from a *jatka* of pro-British Sikhs, old soldiers gathered and led by an *ex* Native Officer! They'd have burnt the Congress camp and their flag too, and made the fat Congress spouters run for their lives—but the Police protected them nobly and threw a lot of the pro-British assailants into prison. They are funny, these British. Here were the purest revolutionaries openly preaching sedition, rebellion, war and revolution; trampling the British flag underfoot and replacing it with their own— while the 'forces of law and order' were desperately fighting to protect them from loyalists, and to ensure their 'sacred right to freedom of speech.'"

"Under the Union Jack," smiled the Swami. "Only it was over it, for the flag was under the feet of as many of the worthy Congress-wallahs as could trample on it."

---

[58] *Large parties.*

"Yes, all that sort of thing has had an excellent influence on the Regiment, but one cannot honestly say it is really *quite* ripe yet."

"Not up to the 1857 fine and mellow maturity," smiled the Swami.

"No; what with Subedar-Major Nikka Singh and his relations and followers, and the wretched doubters who whine their shameful slogan,

> "*Angrez hun jande,*
> *Pinshun kithu ande?*"[59]

"Anyhow, there's plenty of discontent and a strong element of unrest with Jemadar Gujar Singh as its nucleus; and, mind you, in '57 that's all there was in a good many of the regiments," he continued. "More than half the mutineers followed their ring-leaders instead of their officers because they thought the former would win, and the day of the British was over. And it's the same now. Just like an avalanche. One stone can start a million-ton avalanche that will grow into a complete landslide.

"Yes, and Jemadar Gujar Singh is the stone," he added.

And as the two worthies talked, a pair of shapeless bundles of humanity passed the loafer yawning at the street corner.

"Allah! The cow and the calf!" he grinned. For the bigger of the two *burka*-covered women was truly enormous, the other small and slight.

The *burka*, like the good deed, may cover a multitude of sins. It is an outer garment of calico worn by the *purdah* woman, not only over her clothing but over herself, covering her as completely as a pillow-slip covers a pillow. From the crown of her head to the slippers on her feet she is completely concealed, there being no opening or aperture in the extinguisher-like garment, save a muslin-covered slit through which she may peer.

---

[59] *Now the English* go
Whence will pensions come?

The loafer forbore to make ribald comment that might offend their ears, for these were *purdah-nashin*, ladies whose moral and social respectability and consequence were attested by their public privacy, their complete withdrawal from all that life and activity in the midst of which they walked.

Like nuns apart, they made their respected and unimpeded way along the busy crowded street, unobtrusively turning aside into the house that stood between the offices of *To-day and To-morrow* and the one into the courtyard of which the firewood-laden coolie had made his way a little earlier.

In this house the veiled ones removed their heavy *burkas*, revealing in the one case, the corpulent form of Babu Purshotamdass, and, in the other, the slight figure of Bhojraj Shahani.

These gentlemen then entered the *To-day and To-morrow* offices by the roundabout route of stairs that led to the roof common to the two houses, and stairs that led down again to the printing-room next door. Although in the same house that contained the conspirators' meeting-room, they could not go to it direct, as all access to it from the front of the house had been bricked-up, permanently closed and concealed. After brief conference with Mr. Jeshwant Ghokale, acting-editor of *To-day and To-morrow*, and Ramrao Gopaldas and his brothers, they proceeded to the conference chamber in which the Swami Dayanand and Ranjit Singh awaited them.

Leading the way to the back of the printing-house, Jeshwant Ghokale unlocked the filing-cupboard, again removed piles of newspaper-files, letter-filing boxes, books, leaflets, and other impedimenta, drew out the three shelves, slid the back of the cupboard to one side, and knocked thrice, once, twice, thrice, on the back of the almirah which stood in the conspirators' room in the next house.

Unlocking the almirah in that room, Ranjit Singh slid the back of it to one side and admitted the Babu Purshotamdass, Bhojraj Shahani, and Ramrao Gopaldas.

Jeshwant Ghokale, the editor—being but a figure-head and man of straw, retained for the purpose of going to prison whenever the paper was prosecuted for preaching sedition, and its editor sentenced—was not of sufficient importance, eminence, and worth to have a seat in the council.

Bowing respectfully and humbly, he slid the back of the filing-cupboard into place, returned the shelves, files, filing-boxes, books and other impedimenta to their places and restored the filing-cupboard to apparent innocence. He then locked the door of the cupboard and went about his editorial business.

Ranjit Singh, who lived in the conspirators' house—from which he only went out in the rôle of a load-carrying coolie, a human beast of burden—did the same, on his side of the wall, sliding the back of the almirah into place, replacing the clothing on hooks, and locking the heavy teak-wood doors.

"Is Sant Arjun Rama coming?" asked the Swami of Ramrao Gopaldas.

"Yes, but he'll be a little late," sniggered the latter, "as he has gone to church with Cornwallis Mem-sahib! I saw him last night, and he told me that he has no doubt that, at our next meeting, he'll be able to say for certain what day the Governor arrives. The Commissioner has had a Confidential, saying that it will be Friday, and this is probably *pukka*, but possibly false pretence. Our friends at Jhalni will know for certain to-morrow, or Tuesday at latest. That he goes to the Hills is fixed and certain; that he breaks the journey here at Bhawalgarh is almost certain. But we are not to let that make any difference. Friday night it is to be, or, rather, three o'clock Saturday morning, whether the Governor is here or not. If he is here, so much the better. If he is not, his train is going to be de-railed in the jungle between Kotgur and Mohammedabad Junction; and, should anything go wrong and he is not shot or otherwise killed, he is to be bombed when changing trains at Mohammedabad. That is being arranged, and has nothing to do with us. But Sant Arjun Rama will tell us himself when he comes."

"When do we bring the 'eggs' from the Ratnapur and Kotgur temples?" asked Babu Purshotamdass. "Because I . . ."

The speaker was interrupted by the sound of tapping, as though someone knocked on the floor beneath their feet.

"There's Mister Luxman," he said.

Quickly the heavy table was pushed to one side and the *dhurrie* turned back, exposing a trap-door in the floor.

Ranjit Singh raised the trap-door by means of a ring attached for the purpose, and the one who had knocked from below climbed out from the cellar into the room, to be warmly greeted by the rest of the Brethren.

This man, known to his fellow-conspirators as Luxman, was a remarkable character, an unusual Indian in that he combined great capacity for physical labour, great manual ingenuity and dexterity, a very wide knowledge and experience of mechanical and electrical engineering, with a studious inclination, marked literary ability, and a considerable poetic gift.

He was also a fine practical chemist.

In the eyes of these, his friends, he was two men. In one manifestation he was a manual labourer, a skilled mechanic, a trained engineer with extensive and peculiar knowledge of electricity and chemistry; in the other, a scholar, a student of economics and sociology, a writer, an orator, a poet and a patriot.

That a man endowed with these latter qualities, powers, and abilities should soil his hands with manual work was, in their opinion, indeed amazing. But nevertheless, it was to them a thing for which to thank whatever gods there be.

Luxman Dhonde was indeed one of the most dangerous of the agitators working in India for the overthrow of the British Government.

The younger brother of Narayandas Dhonde, hanged for the peculiarly treacherous and cold-blooded murder of the Collector of Ahmedpur while the guest of Dhonde and his friends, he had cherished the bitterest hatred against the British from the days when, as a schoolboy, he had sat at the feet of such men as Bal Gangadar Tilak; and had, almost as a child, conceived the idea and intention of devoting his life to "avenging" his brother's death and waging war against the Government.

With the intention of learning all he could about bomb-making, he had enrolled himself, on leaving school, as a student at the Government Engineering College at Kalkee, and had specialized in chemistry and electrical engineering. Thus equipped, he had gone to America and worked in an explosives-factory.

From America he had gone to Europe in the pursuit of further knowledge and skill, the whole time combining subversive political activity with the study of lethal and destructive mechanical-engineering and chemistry.

In India he was an eloquent and violent preacher of armed rebellion; and on several occasions had been directly and personally responsible for the fomentation of riots and uprisings in which there had been serious loss of life and damage to property.

Thrice he had been arrested and tried for his part in seditious plots, and had served three sentences of imprisonment, the last of which had been for two years.

The events of the year 1914 had given him the opportunity of a life-time. He had immediately set to work to foment active rebellion, had put himself at the disposal of German agents in India, had worked heart and soul, night and day, at the various plots for the embarrassment of the Government, and for the prevention of the transferring of troops from India to the various fronts. He it was who had conceived the plot, and done a great deal of the work, which almost brought a second Indian Mutiny in 1917, an event of which the British public knows nothing—and of its principal manifestation, the murderous mutiny of the Fifth Infantry, stationed at Singapore, but little. But for the presence and prompt action of British and Japanese men-of-war and the F.M.S. Volunteer Corps, this explosion would have started a conflagration which might have spread across India and blazed up at every regimental depôt throughout the country. The old army was sound to the core; the new army of recruits was tainted by the poison of the enemy and by subsidized seditionists.

When in Berlin, Dhonde had made himself known to the right people, he had impressed them with his personality, and, on the outbreak of war, he was entrusted by them with the handling of enormous sums of money, all of which he had honestly devoted to the purposes for which they were intended.

An extremely successful master bomb-maker, he was a less competent but still reliable and courageous user of bombs, albeit he preferred the placing of the time-bomb to the throwing of the hand-grenade.

He had been the leader in four of five bomb outrages, and though hitherto unsuccessful in the killing of any very prominent official, the affairs had served to give him experience and aplomb, at the slight cost of the killing and maiming of a few dozen harmless and innocent Indian bystanders. Twice in Calcutta he had shot at the Inspector-General of Police and once had thrown a bomb at him, but had only succeeded in wounding him—and killing an aged road-sweeper, a little girl and a goat. But even though he had not hitherto succeeded in the murder of an important official, his work, he considered, had naturally shaken the nerves of his intended victims as well as those of the community, and had been generally damaging to public *morale*.

Throughout the war he had contrived to escape arrest. So powerful and competent was the organization of the Brethren of India, of whom he was one of the leaders, that he was able to go from place to place, certain of assistance, protection, and a safe haven of refuge. Never was he betrayed or discovered, and it was not until after he had perpetrated some outrage that the police, too late, came to learn that he had been in the town, village, or district in which they kept watch and ward.

This man it was who—having decided that Bhawalgarh was, owing to its record (dating from Mutiny days) of disloyalty, sedition, and turbulence the most suitable place—had hatched and propounded the plot for making it the scene of an explosion that should, as he said, shake India to its foundations and the British Government to its downfall.

Stepping from the ladder into the room, he displayed a wiry, well-knit, athletic-looking frame; a strong, harsh, determined countenance lit up by compelling fanatical eyes which showed curiously pale in his dark face, the irises being a light greenish-blue; and an air and presence of authority and power.

"Where's Sant Arjun Rama?" he asked, looking round. "He should be here. I have news for him. News! . . . News! . . . News!"

"Tell us, Luxman," said Ranjit Singh.

"What is it, thou sharp-headed worm that dieth not? Is it done?" asked the Swami. "Has the worm bored through?"

"It has, Swami-ji, it has," chuckled Luxman Dhonde, rubbing powerful, long-fingered, grimy hands together. "I'm through. I'm through at last; and the plan will go to time."

"Through into the Fort?" asked Babu Purshotamdass. "Man, it is wonderful."

"Through into the Fort," said Luxman Dhonde proudly. "At any moment I like. My hand has been into Bhawalgarh Fort and I go in myself whenever I wish, and after but another hour's work. . . . Yes, we are ready now. . . . Where's Sant Arjun?"

"He'll be here soon," replied Ramrao Gopaldas. "He's doing *puja* in the Christian Temple."

Luxman smiled grimly.

"What?" he asked.

"He's at the English church with the *Burra Memsahib*,"[60] giggled Motiram Gopaldas.

Ranjit Singh, a Sikh to whom alcohol and tobacco were by religion anathema, eyed the latter with disfavour, for he smelt of both; and, though anything but

---

[60] *The great lady.*

drunk, was not as serious and sober as a conspirator of the Brethren of India type should be. Still, the creature had his uses, and it takes all sorts to make a world, particularly an under-world.

"Let's have a look at your work, while we are waiting for him, Luxman," suggested the Swami.

"Yes, show them, Luxman," said Ranjit Singh. "I'd like to put my hand into that Fort now, too. My grand-father set foot, as well as hand, in there, shed his blood and died there, striking a blow against the *fer-inghis*."

"All-right," said Luxman Dhonde, nothing loth to display his almost-completed work. "Swami-ji, Bhojraj Shahani and Babu Purshotamdass will be enough at one time."

"I'll come too," said Ranjit Singh. "I did a lot of the work and I should like to see the finish. See through the hole, too. You, Ramrao, keep an ear for Sant Arjun's knock. We shan't be ten minutes. Here's the key of the almirah."

Pushing the table aside, turning back the *dhurrie*, and raising the trap-door, Luxman Dhonde descended the ladder and led the way down into the cellar.

This extended under, and for the length of, the small courtyard at the back of the house, being terminated by the wall of the Fort itself.

Probably it had originally been intended and used for the storing of merchandise, and as a hiding-place for valuable or forbidden property, goods, the knowl-edge of the possession of which would be likely to rouse the cupidity of the *kotwal* or other rapacious and oppressive official in pre-British days, those good old times, "those golden days of Mother India, when no cow ever died, no epidemic ever raged, no monsoon ever failed"—and the tax-farmer took everything upon which he could lay his hands.

It was an examination and exploration of this cellar as a possible place for a workshop, and for the storing of explosives, weapons, and bombs, that had given Luxman Dhonde his brilliant idea when endeavouring to think out a means of entering and blowing up the

Fort.

Observing that the majestic fortress, though a magnificent Colossus of War, had feet of clay, inasmuch as, although it was built of stone, its surrounding walls consisted of bricks of sun-dried mud, and its defences, thirty feet high and ten feet thick, were thus only mud-walls, he had realized how extremely easy it would be to tunnel through them.

Here, in this underground cellar, he was only ten feet from the interior of the Fort. Between him and his goal was only a paltry ten feet of dried mud—child's-play to an engineer with unlimited time and money, and adequate labour at his disposal.

Realizing his wonderful opportunity, he had smiled grimly, rubbed his hands gleefully, and told his friend and colleague, Ramrao Gopaldas, to procure forthwith from the Bhawalgarh Gymkhana Library, a copy of that admirable and exhaustive work, well known in India, *The Bhawalgarh Campaign*, written in 1848 by General Sir Havelock Wigram Laurence, which contains a most detailed account of Bhawalgarh Fort and, what was of much more interest to Luxman Dhonde, a ground plan of its walls and buildings.

A careful study of this ground plan, and of the illustrations to the chapters dealing with Bhawalgarh Fort, showed Dhonde that a tunnel from the cellar would come out under or in the enormously strong building, known in the earliest records as The Prison; later as the *Toshi-khana* or treasure-house; and, at the time of the conquest of Bhawalgarh, as the *Top-khana* or arsenal.

What was most probable was that the little ten-foot tunnel would lead into vaults below this building.

As the tunnel had neared completion, Dhonde had worked alone, with the utmost care against unnecessary noise, and in the small hours of the morning, being in ignorance as to what might be on the inner side of the wall. He had no intention of breaking through into a prison cell, into any kind of room which had an occupant, or into a vault outside the door of which a sentry was posted.

And now his work was done. He had penetrated the wall successfully and secretly.

The four men climbed down the ladder and crossed the cellar, beneath which was a board-and-earth-covered pit filled with bombs, weapons, and ammunition; and, as Luxman Dhonde switched on the electric torch, saw the gaping hole at the far end.

"Is it now big enough for me to go in? I stuck before," whispered Babu Purshotamdass.

"Yes," grinned Dhonde. "You can try, anyway, and we can drag you out by the feet if you stick again."

"There's no fear of the tunnel collapsing on me, or behind me?" asked Babu Purshotamdass.

"None whatever," whispered Dhonde. "It's like crawling through a sewer or an iron pipe. You'll be as safe as if you were crawling down the barrel of the *Malik i Maidan*, the Big Gun of Bijapur.

"I'll go in first and listen again," he added. "Don't make a sound."

And into the tunnel Dhonde crawled, on hands and knees, to return a few minutes later.

He was trembling with excitement.

"I have let a ray of light into the darkness," he whispered. "Indeed I have shed a light. I have this day lighted such a torch as . . ."

"Don't spout," growled Ranjit Singh. "Did you look in?"

"Yes. As it was pitch-dark and utterly silent, I became impatient. . . . I went mad with triumph. . . . I shone the light inside. . . . It is a cellar like this! . . . It's a vault, an underground store, with a small door at the side."

"Empty?" asked Ranjit Singh.

"No. It's a store-chamber of some kind, and opposite our hole are stacks of great old boxes, strong, iron-bound, clamped, locked."

"*Treasure?*" whispered Babu Purshotamdass. "Money? Rupees? Gold-mohurs?"

"How do I know?" shrugged Dhonde. "Certainly the building above these vaults was once called the Treasury, but these boxes may contain nothing but paper records. They may be empty. Or they may be filled with coined gold."

"Hardly that," said Bhojraj Shahani. "Money would be at the *kutcherry* in the Treasury."

"Of course it would—current coin of the realm," said the Swami. "But suppose this is no longer current. Suppose this is treasure that has lain there from the days of Akbar. Treasure unknown to the British Government. This Fort was captured by Laurence after a siege. The defenders would have hidden their treasure before surrendering. They might have buried it in this vault, and bricked-up the entrance. On the other side of the door that he has seen. Isn't it likely that our friend has stumbled on the forgotten vaults of the Fort Treasury of those days?"

"It is posseeble! It is posseeble!" agreed Babu Purshotamdass. "Treasure there must have been; and it would have been kept in the vaults of the Treasure-*khana*. That might not have been discovered by rapacious conquerors."

"Well, we'll soon find out what it is, anyhow," said Ranjit Singh. "Let's break in now and open a box."

"No, not yet," objected Luxman Dhonde. "It is possible the place is in use—to the extent of being visited once in a while, though I don't believe so. I shouldn't think the vault has been opened for a century."

"Well, let's break in now, then," urged Ranjit Singh.

"No, man. Wait," repeated Dhonde. "I've been impatient enough as it is. Taking a risk and showing a light in the tunnel. Not only that, but shining it into the vault.

"Anyone going in there from the Fort would carry a lamp and would never see the hole, but if we make it big enough for us to get through, it might be noticed. It might be reported to the Officer Sahib. And then, what?" he asked.

"They'd discover this cellar, find the trap-door and enter our council-chamber."

"Well, and what if they did?" asked Ranjit Singh. "There's always somebody down here; you, or I, or another. There'd be plenty of noise. We should hear them coming, if we happened to be in session in the Council-chamber. There'd be ample warning."

"Don't talk nonsense," snarled Dhonde. "Suppose we did have time to clear everything away and get out? If they found nothing else, there's the tunnel, isn't there? We don't want them to know that there's a tunnel leading from near the *To-day and To-morrow* cellars straight into the Fort, do we?"

"When are you going to break through, then, Luxman?" asked the Swami.

"Thursday night," was the reply. "Twenty-four hours before I blow the place up. We must take that much risk of discovery. I shall break through on Thursday night and investigate that little door. The door wouldn't still be there if the entrance had been built-up and closed permanently. I should think it leads into another vault. If it doesn't, it'll be at the bottom of a flight of steps leading up to the ground level. It must be one or the other, and there won't be a sentry there. Why should there be? It won't take me long to deal with the door, and I shall know what is on the other side of it very quickly. There must be a way from the vault into the Fort itself, naturally. I shall reconnoitre on Thursday night, and make my plans and arrangements according to what I discover. And wherever there is, or is not, an explosion on Friday night, there will be a mighty one in Bhawalgarh Fort! "

Babu Purshotamdass was moved to embrace the speaker.

"Well, I'll go and have a peep, Luxman," said the Swami; and taking the electric torch he crawled into the tunnel.

Ten minutes later he returned and, though displaying no outward and visible signs of excitement, spoke with warm enthusiasm.

"Wonderful, Luxman! You are a great man, and I shall live to see your statue in the market-place of Bhawalgarh. Wonderful! A very little quiet work and you can walk straight into the Fort. I believe that is an underground treasure-chamber. Think of it, my brothers. If Luxman Dhonde not only plants a time-bomb, a high-explosive infernal-machine in the very heart of Bhawalgarh Fort, but also discovers a vast hoard of gold-mohurs of Mogul days, at one stroke he impoverishes the enemy and enriches the Brethren!"

"The enemy bleed to death and new life is poured into the veins of the Mother," said Babu Purshotamdass. "Stream of gold. Man, it is meeraculous."

"But I don't think I will crawl in," he added.

"I shall. Give me the torch," said Bhojraj Shahani.

"Yes, yes, you go. You are small," urged Babu Purshotamdass.

"My heart is big," replied Bhojraj Shahani, and entered the tunnel.

A few minutes later he emerged, trembling with excitement, babbling, and almost incoherent.

"It is the Day! The Day! . . . We win! We win! . . . Oh, Luxman, you are truest son of the Mother. Your name shall be inscribed in letters of gold on the walls of our parliament at Delhi. . . . It is Victory! It is Victory! . . . You will blow them sky-high."

"Well, don't make so much noise about it," growled Ranjit Singh.

"No, no," giggled Bhojraj Shahani hysterically. "Luxman Dhonde shall make the noise, the noise that shall resound throughout the world—resound with his fame and downfall of tyrants."

"Come on back," said Ranjit Singh. "Sant Arjun should be here by now."

And the conspirators returned to the Council-chamber to find that Sant Arjun Rama and Abdul Haq awaited them with the Gopaldas brothers and the proprietor of the *To-day and To-morrow* newspaper, one Lala Ratansi Mangal.

The loafer at the street corner had noted that a bazaar *ghari* in which were seated two topi-wearing *Klistans*,[61] as he called them, had driven quickly down the street and stopped at the entrance of the *To-day and To-morrow* offices.

The occupants of the *ghari* had entered the building and the *ghari* had driven rapidly on. Its number, the

---

[61] *Christians.*

loafer noted, had been concealed by the usual bundle of hay tied on behind, the pitiful handful that is the exiguous meal of the ever-hungry Indian bazaar-tat.

As the two *Klistans* had been obviously men of substance and position, one of them bearing a large official-looking envelope, Hashmat Dad Khan had not considered the incident to be of interest or importance. Evidently gentlemen having business with the paper, probably the insertion of advertisements. . . .

Quickly the good news of the completion of the tunnel was told to Sant Arjun Rama and Abdul Haq by a chorus of eager voices, ere Sant Arjun Rama took the chair at what his presence there constituted the head of the round table. They expressed their delight and approval, and Sant Arjun Rama bestowed congratulations and praise upon Luxman Dhonde, promising that skilful engineer that he would commend him in the highest quarters.

He then came to the business of the day.

"Now, gentlemen," said he, "this is our last meeting but one, before a Day that shall go down to History, a Day as great as any that have yet dawned in the annals of the great story of Mother India, our Bharat Mata.

"Before we begin, I trust that nobody has with him any sort or kind of incriminatory paper, letter, pamphlet, memorandum, list of names, note or other document. *To-day and To-morrow* is going to be raided. It may be raided while we are in session here to-day. Almost certainly the secret of the filing-cupboard, next door, will not be discovered. Should it be, and this room be invaded by the armed myrmidons of the law, nothing must be found upon which they can take action. We have a perfect right to meet here if we wish to do so; and in any case the warrant for the search of the premises next door does not apply to this house. So, provided no incriminatory documents are discovered here, there is no possible excuse for the arrest of any one of us, save that of our admired and honoured friend, the great patriot Ranjit Singh."

"And I shall not be here," grinned the great patriot,

nodding in the direction of the trap-door beneath the *dhurrie* which was spread under the table around which they sat.

"Well; no papers, no pamphlets, no letters?" continued Sant Arjun Rama. "No. And nothing must be written now. Right, then; this is final and definite. Official, so to speak.

"The Governor comes here to Bhawalgarh on Friday, sleeps here Friday night, and departs (or thinks he does) on Saturday: and the explosion—the manifold explosion—takes place on Friday night at three o'clock. At that late hour all have retired to rest. At that early hour none has yet arisen.

"At three, then, on the first stroke of the chime in the clock-tower of the market-place—we act.

"First, the Fort.

"Let us all thank and praise whatever gods we severally honour, worship, and obey, that our noble, self-sacrificing, indefatigable brother, Mr. Luxman Dhonde, has made it possible that the greatest explosion of them all will take place at the most important point of all. At the Fort of Bhawalgarh. There the explosion itself will be greatest, and also the moral effect upon the Government will be greatest. The explosion that blows in the gates of the Gaol may be more practically useful at the moment, as upwards of five hundred dangerous criminals will be released—but the explosion at the Fort will most appeal to the imagination of India; to the imagination of the world; and will strike the greatest terror to the hearts of the Satanic Government.

"Secondly, the Gaol.

"At the same time that the Fort is blown up, the gates of Bhawalgarh Gaol will be blown in. That invaluable work is, as we know, in the hands of our sturdy and faithful Ranjit Singh. He, with certain chosen stalwarts who can use guns, will come along the road on Friday night just before three o'clock, as though they were peasants going to Saturday market or elsewhere, with a bullock-cart.

"Behind them will follow Bagu the Dacoit and his

band, with another bullock-cart. In the bullock-carts will be guns for these two parties and a great number of *tulwars*[62] sickles, knives, and *lathis*.[63] With Ranjit Singh goes a man especially trained by Mr. Luxman Dhonde in the placing and exploding of the bombs, one for the outer gate and one for the inner. These it may not be necessary to use to force an entrance, inasmuch as the payment of two hundred and fifty rupees and the promise of two thousand five hundred rupees more, to each of three of the Gaol personnel may have provided quieter keys. In such case, the bombs will be used—after the liberation of the prisoners—for the demolition of the Gaol.

"On the stroke of three o'clock, at the moment of the explosion at the Fort and the Gaol gates, two chosen men throw hand-grenades into the bedroom of the Governor of the Gaol, and, should he survive to run out, they will shoot him as he does so.

"The prisoners released from the Gaol will be armed with the swords and *lathis*; and those among them who, being dacoits, understand the use of guns, will be provided with them.

"These released prisoners will be in need of all things, poor fellows; and the bazaars, shops, houses, the Treasury and the Banks of Bhawalgarh will be at their disposal. Also, each man will be provided with a box of matches and something that burns nicely. Yes, we have thought of everything.

"Thirdly, the Post and Telegraph Office and the Railway-station.

"Simultaneously with the explosion at the Fort and the Gaol, the Post and Telegraph Office will be blown up. We have an excellent man there, as you know, in Mr. Mohan Roy, the telegraph-babu, himself one of the Brethren. All he has to do is to place a certain little box, neatly tied up as a brown-paper parcel, in a drawer in his desk, and leave the office a little before three o'clock. One imagines that, on this occasion at any rate, Mr. Mohan Roy will be a clock-watcher. At

---

[62] *Swords.*
[63] *Thick iron-bound bamboo staves.*

three precisely, a time-bomb will blow the Post and Telegraph Office and all its instruments to pieces, and both telephone and telegraph will have ceased to function.

"Similarly, at the Railway-station, Mr. Mulchand Prasad will be watching the station clock with great interest, as the hands draw toward three. He too will have placed a parcel precisely where it will do most good.

"The Railway-station will be wrecked; telegraph posts will fall, snapping the wires; the signal-box will be blown to pieces and, in the space of a second, Bhawalgarh will be entirely cut off from the outside world as to telegraph, telephone and rail.

"And I here give you a piece of news which will interest and delight you. Arrangements have been made that precisely the same thing will happen, at the same moment, at Mohammedabad Junction on the one side of Bhawalgarh, and at Jhalni on the other. The railway will not be available for troop trains, or any other, in time for there to be the slightest interference with the—er—rejoicings at Bhawalgarh.

"Fourthly, as to the Banks.

"There again, bombs may not be necessary—at least for obtaining entrance—for our invaluable Ranjit Singh has had dealings with their Sikh watchmen.

"Should the bombs be needed, they are provided, and will explode at three o'clock, blowing in the doors, if these have not been opened for us.

"With regard to the Law Courts, their destruction is merely symbolic. Let me withdraw the 'merely.' The blowing up of the Courts of Alleged British Justice will be a sign and a token to all men, and an invaluable one, that their day of misrule is over. A time-bomb explodes inside the High Court at three o'clock on Friday night. It will be left there by the caretaker when he goes home. Similarly with the *kutcherry*. It is right and meet that that should disappear.

"With regard to the Treasury, there may be a slight hitch, but merely as regards time. We cannot say for certain that the Treasury will be blown up simultaneously with the other places. There are difficulties, and it has not been found practicable to bribe the guard satisfactorily. One can never be certain as to what men will be on duty on that particular night, and the Police *havildars* have been found—difficult. Nevertheless, one thing is certain—that the Treasury will be wrecked, looted, and burned. It would be a strange thing if Bagu's band of specialists, the five hundred professionals and enthusiastic amateurs from the Gaol, and the bazaar mob of *budmashes*, helped by the Mussulman butchers, among whom our friend Mr. Abdul Haq has done such good work—it would be strange, I say, if these, armed with guns and incendiary materials, not to mention a few hand-grenades which will be issued to men who have been trained to use them, cannot give a good account of the Bhawalgarh Treasury.

"Then, as to the houses of Officials and other undesirables.

"For the Commissioner's House I have, myself, provided. It will cease to exist at three o'clock on Friday night, and so will the Commissioner. Should His Excellency the Governor keep to his present programme, he too will be sleeping in the Commissioner's House that Friday night—until three o'clock—when an explosion will permanently deprive the State of his invaluable services.

"Of the Judge's house I have little doubt. The *chowkidar*, excellent man, may possibly fail through stupidity, but not from good-will. The spirit is very willing, if the brain be weak. Should he bungle the matter, however, the mob will rectify it. Certain of the released convicts will take a personal pleasure in dealing with the Judge—and his good lady.

"Similarly again with the Collector's bungalow. We have an amusing man there, a worthy character, a Goanese rascal, who, having been a steward on a liner for some years, has an ambition. (I make a study of men's ambitions and use them, where possible, to our ends.) His idea of the Earthly Paradise is to travel to and fro between Tilbury and Bombay, as a Portuguese Gentleman of means and leisure—and to keep Goanese stewards on the run. I gather that he intends to take the high hand with superior servants of the Company, most particularly the Purser, the Assistant-Pursers, the Chief Steward, the Head Waiter and with others of the class who made his life a burden when he was himself a Goanese cabin-steward and waiter.

"He is a good man, faithful to his employer, and he is quite willing, for a hundred rupees down and a *hoondi*[64] for a *lakh*[65] to leave a 'perfectly harmless' brown-paper parcel in the house when he quits it for the night. Just a little gift to the Sahib from an admirer.

"Similarly with the houses of the other European officials."

"What about the American Mission College?" asked Ramrao Gopaldas. "Torrens Sahib is very popular with the students. My brother gives him a good character."

"For which I'm sure he would be very grateful," smiled Sant Arjun Rama. "No, his house will be spared —for two reasons. In the first place we have no desire to antagonize public opinion in America; and, in the second, an American newspaper man, who is also his nephew, is living there. That is a piece of the best luck imaginable. He will send an account of the Bhawalgarh happenings which will be on the front page of every newspaper in America. His presence here is a gift of the gods themselves."

"In any case, I have given Torrens Sahib fair warning," laughed the Swami. "He knows that something terrible is going to happen to all Europeans—a fortnight hence. The newspaper man can tell America how he was specially protected, because of the love we bear his great country."

"You are our *enfant terrible*, Swami-ji," laughed Sant Arjun Rama. "You'll spoil the plot yet."

"It will be all the same a million years hence—or even sooner," was the reply.

"You may notice that I made no mention of bombing the house of the District Superintendent of Police,"

---

[64] *bond.*
[65] *100,000.*

continued Sant Arjun Rama. "I did so intentionally, as I wish to provide for him otherwise. I want him out of the way before Friday. He is getting altogether too busy. He has always been a most active and dangerous enemy of the Brethren of India; he has been the cause of great harm to us; and he annoyed me personally only last Thursday night at the Commissioner's House by endeavouring to bring me into contempt before the company gathered together to listen to me.

"I want him taken alive and brought here on Thursday night.

"I am sure our invaluable Ranjit Singh can be trusted to arrange for Bagu the Dacoit and certain of his followers to get him.

"I think I should like to see Steele Sahib sitting in this very room, bound to this very chair, gagged and watching one of Mr. Luxman Dhonde's time-bombs on this very table, in front of him."

"But, man," expostulated Babu Purshotamdass, "we don't want this room awfully blown to pieces, this house blown all up, and the *To-day and To-morrow* offices wrecked! It will be fearfully fatal and dangerous and destructive."

"Don't be alarmed, Babu-ji," smiled Sant Arjun Rama. "Listen. Steele Sahib will sit watching and waiting for it to explode. I shall not tell him how long he has got to wait. I hear that the Sahibs call him Cold Steele. He will be *very* cold by the time the bomb explodes—for it never will explode."

Ranjit Singh laughed.

"Really! Really!" smiled the Swami in mild expostulation. "Tut! Tut!"

Motiram Gopaldas laughed shrilly. "*He, he, he!*" he giggled hysterically. "While so many of his dear compatriots are dying through explosions, he will die through non-explosion. Many he will hear—but not that one," and he laughed immoderately.

"*Chuprao, tum,*" growled Ranjit Singh. "Shut up! You jackal."

Sant Arjun Rama turned to him.

"Now, as to the sepoys of the Regiment here. Have

you anything new to tell us, Ranjit Singh?"

"No; nothing of great importance," replied Ranjit Singh. "But . . ." and he repeated what he had already told the Swami Dayanand.

"One thing you can absolutely count on," he continued, "is that Jemadar[66] Gujar Singh will see to it that something worthy of the occasion occurs, the moment the explosions are heard. He'll be awaiting them, and so will a good fifty of his followers. He'll have everything arranged for dealing with the officers, who will doubtless run out of their bungalows as the bombs go off all over Bhawalgarh. As they run out they will be shot. The guard on Friday night will be under Jemadar Gujar Singh's cousin, and he will pick the right men.

"With the guard and all the sentries loyal—to us—it will be a simple matter for them to open the armoury and issue rifles and ammunition only to those who are their friends. In all that noise and confusion, with their Officers killed and the Subedar-Major shot before their eyes as a warning and example, there will not be many unarmed men willing to give their lives for nothing. For any who are fools enough to defy them will die; and the half-hearted will follow Jemadar Gujar Singh, taking courage as they see what happens.

"And doubtless the Babu-ji's last pamphlet will have done some good among the waverers, too."

"Yes, yes," beamed the Babu Purshotamdass. "It is good, I think. Obedient to instructions, I have not a copy with me, but I can recite it, in English, from memory."

And rising to his feet the enormous man did so, his usually mild eyes flashing behind his spectacles, his fat face quivering with emotion.

"Wretched misguided Indian Sepoys," he began, addressing the assembled Council of the Brethren as though they were themselves the erring sepoys, "what has happened to you? You are thin and pale and horrible to the sight, through feeding upon chaff and husks and *chupatties* while your masters gorge them-

---

[66] *Subedar*—Native Officer, 3 stars. *Jemadar*—Native Officer, 2 stars. *Havildar*—Sergeant. *Naik*—Corporal.

selves on lovely food. Where is the fierce bright shine of your sweet countenances? Gone, gone; for you live as chained convicts in your huts. Nay, the convicts are better treated, for they are not made to march hundreds of miles, to bear weight of rifles, to walk at night, to stand upright in the darkness as sentinels, and to bow the head before Colonels. And what of your family-members, the nears and dears from whom you have been torn away? How do they pull on? Does the plague stalk fro and to, among them? Yes. And who introduced it into our Bharat Mata? Did not the British—and then blame it on to innocent rat and harmless unnecessary flea? Did it not spread from Bombay, the port at which they imported it? And do your wives send word by returning leave-men that the Sahibs are putting pollution into your wells and calling it purification? What wist they of purification? I trow not. The water in the wells turns pink and your children die. And if your little ones die not fast enough, do not the Sahibs send evil men to your villages to scratch the arms of the bleating babes with sharp and cruel knives? And do not the men pour pollution through the holes thus made, yea, direct into their very bodies? And you bear these things—and call yourselves *men!*

"And is not malaria increasing in your villages through the cunning Sahibs importing malicious mosquitoes whose very gnaw is sharper than all the serpents' teeth? And is not the yield of your fields decreasing so that your family-members cry in vain to you for food, because the Sahibs are exporting all the corn—that they may grow fat and rich while you grow slenderish and impoverish? And why are your faces black and the faces of English soldiers white? Are not both of the same stock? Are you not Aryans also? Then why? Because you are given despicable foods, while English soldiers are fed full and far otherwise and fatter. What pay do you get; and what pay do the British soldiers, whose battles you fought, get? You get *pice* and they get rupees. Have you not sodden the soil of many lands with your blood? And, in reward, are you now set free? No; for still you are drilled in lines and made to walk in ranks. But now shortly comes your deliverance, so *be prepared.* Do as your Jemadar Gujar Singh—mark my words, your Jemadar Gujar Singh—tells you, and . . ."

"And that will be enough, I think, Babu-ji," interrupted Sant Arjun Rama. "Excellent. But sufficient unto the day . . ."

"Very well, then," he continued, addressing the Council. "We can rest assured that, at three o'clock on Friday night, Nicholson's Sikhs will cease to exist as a regiment. Doubtless it will live up to the magnificent tradition of 1857, and having disposed of its Officers and all who would restrain it, will burst forth and take part in the doings of the night."

"And afterwards," remarked Ranjit Singh as the speaker paused, "the Assembly will be blown in the market-place, and the loyal survivors will fall in and march to the Fort. The Jemadars will choose me as Colonel. We will put the Fort back into a state of repair, and be the nucleus of the New Army of Hindustan."

Sant Arjun Rama eyed the speaker coldly.

"Doubtless," he said. "Doubtless. . . . And now, Mr. Abdul Haq, what is the latest news from Almera State?"

"All goes well," replied Abdul Haq, the only Mahommedan present. "The cutting of the telegraph at three o'clock on Friday night will be the signal that the *coup d'état* has been successful. At that moment, rockets will be fired into the sky from the Telegraph Office of Almera City. On sight of these rockets, others will also be fired into the sky from the *sowars'* barracks, whereupon they will mount their horses and ride forth. They are Mussulmans to a man, and their Colonel is the cousin of the Nawab of Almera. He hates the Nawab like poison, and will kill him with his own hand. The Mussulman butchers of the bazaar will lead the townsmen in a great riot in which the moneylenders' houses will be sacked and burned, and there will be great confusion. When all is going well, and the Palace is in the hands of the troops, the cavalry will take the road for Bhawalgarh, arriving here at about six o'clock, or, at any rate, sometime early on Saturday morning."

"And you are quite certain they will prove— amenable?" asked Sant Arjun.

"Absolutely. On the lowest grounds will not the Brethren be their paymasters? Will not the Brethren guarantee and confirm their leader, the new Nawab, on the throne of the cousin whom he has just deceased? Oh, yes, have no fear. . . ."

"I have no fear," Sant Arjun Rama assured him.

"I was going to say, have no fear that the Almera Imperial Service Troops will not be loyal to Mother India, loyal to us, and obey promptly all orders of the Brethren.

"Conveyed to them through me," he added.

"And doubtless the Imperial Service Troops have been promised many things," smiled Sant Arjun Rama, "even as the sepoys of the Indian Army here and else-where."

"Oh, many things; many things," agreed Abdul Haq. "All will become Officers in the New Army in due course, or much quicker. The New Army will eventually be led by a Mussulman Commander-in-Chief, and their pay and allowances will be enormous; their rations remarkable; their quarters attractive; their discipline agreeable."

"And their ruler? The ruler of India?" chirruped the Swami. "Moghul Emperor, doubtless?"

"Doubtless—if we can find one," smiled Abdul Haq. "Failing that, we shall know which of the Mussulman Princes to carry in triumph to Delhi."

"You mean *they* will know," corrected Sant Arjun Rama.

"Of course, of course," agreed Abdul Haq quickly. "The foolish fellows are already debating the question of who will be the most suitable occupant of the new Peacock Throne."

"Anyhow, Almera State and the Imperial Service Troops of Almera rise at three o'clock on Friday night, the signal being the cutting of the telegraph wire?" said Sant Arjun Rama.

"You may count on it with perfect and complete certainty," replied Abdul Haq. "Until that happens, nothing else will happen, and outwardly all will be normal. Peace and order will prevail, every man going about his business as though he knew nothing—until the telegraph fails and the rockets go up."

"That's all-right, then. Good. . . . Now, has anyone any questions to ask, or is there anything anybody would like to suggest?" asked Sant Arjun Rama.

"Where will you yourself be at three o'clock on Friday night?" asked Abdul Haq.

"With the rest of you, at General Head-quarters on the roof of *To-day and To-morrow*. We will all go up there after the explosion in the Fort, all save Ranjit Singh the soldier, the man of action. From that spot we will ride the whirlwind and direct the storm, issuing any new orders that may be rendered necessary by the current of events."

"Good. . . ."

"Then we meet again here on Thursday night, each of us arriving as soon as convenient, or possible, after midnight. And when we quit this room for the last time, we will leave our able and energetic friend Steele behind us. . . . You, my dear Luxman, can no doubt provide us with a bomb of the most convincing description."

"Though dead, it shall be alive," said Luxman Dhonde. "He shall hear it tick. It will tick for a week, though I doubt whether he will hear it for as long as that."

"I doubt it, too," smiled Sant Arjun Rama; "but make it a week, for good measure."

"There shall be an eight-day clock inside it," promised Luxman Dhonde.

"An alarm-clock, indeed!" chuckled Sant Arjun Rama. "Permanent alarm, eh?"

Rising to their feet, the conspirators took leave, one by one, of Sant Arjun Rama with marked respect, the reverence due to his record, his character and his personality.

Leader of the leaders who had gathered in Bhawalgarh, none stood higher than he among the heads of the Brethren of India; among those of the world-wide Secret Society calling itself the Red Flags of Freedom; or of the All-India Society known to itself as the Red Banners of Bharat.

For, in addition to almost lifelong devotion to the Cause, had he not, with his own hand, bombed a Viceroy?

He had bombed a Viceroy.

As the pamphlet, secretly distributed throughout India from the printing-press of the India newspaper *The Edge of the Sword*, had said,

"Almost is this noble and distinguished man a Regicide, for though not quite a Vice-Regicide, he has bombed a Viceroy. Alas, that we may not publish his true name, a name that shall for ever stand in glory with those of Suraj ud Dowlah, Nana Sahib, Tantia Topi, and such heroes."

From the safety of a lofty screened verandah, Sant Arjun Rama had, indeed, lobbed a bomb down into the howdah of the elephant that bore the Viceroy of India as he made his state entry into Delhi. True, the bomb had only blown the mahout's arm off; injured, shocked, and horrified, the Vice-reine, a lady whose life was devoted to improving the lot of Indian women by the provision of Maternity Hospitals and Zenana Medical Missions; and wounded the Viceroy insufficiently to prevent him from carrying on the day's work. The fact that the terrified elephant, deprived of the guidance of his mahout, had stampeded into the crowd, killing, crushing, and maiming innocent men, women and children, detracted nothing from the glory of the great deed.

But, apart from this, which alone would have placed him on a pinnacle high as that occupied by the highest, Sant Arjun Rama was undeniably an extraordinary man, one such as India alone could produce.

On leaving the Hindu College at Madrutta, a College governed and staffed entirely by seditious Indians, in which he had sat at the feet of a *pundit* who recounted the history of India in a way that would have surprised a European, Sant Arjun Rama had studied and practised *Yoga* and the Vedanta Philosophy for a decade.

Such was his progress, so great were his power, his personality and his amazing oratorical gift, that he became famous throughout Hindustan as a *yogi* of almost unparalleled asceticism, knowledge and psychic force.

As with many of his kind, one result of his years of study, extensive and intensive, was to warp and distort his mind through constant contrasting of the great and golden days of Vedantic India—an India that never existed—when the land was yet unpolluted by the tread of alien foot: when men were gods, their knowledge and their powers immeasurable: when the accumulated wisdom of the centuries was the common heritage of all: when to be a Hindu was to be a Vedantist, a conqueror of the flesh, a conqueror of self, a dweller in constant communion with the gods themselves; one who realized, knew, and held within himself, the Infinite Itself; the great and golden days when any man on any road might meet, and have speech with, the Rishis: when God was Nature and Nature was God, and all men could read the Book of Nature; and the beautiful perfect world around them was one vast Harmony.

That was the India by which to judge the India of to-day with its plague epidemics, its famines, its malaria, its tuberculosis; its roaring railways; its bad monsoons, with their sequelae of poverty and suffering; its ugly roads, canals and bridges; its horrible hospitals where terrible things were done to the bodies of poor helpless men and women; its police, with their interference with the grand Vedantic customs of old— *sati*, for example; its materialism; its falling away from the noble standards of the fathers; its growing lack of respect for Brahmins; its deterioration owing to the spread of harmful western education among the masses; its acceptance of terrible doctrines, such as the equality of the rights of man, whereby the bodies of a thousand Untouchables were considered quite equal to the paring of a Brahmin's finger-nail. . . . In short, its utter pollution.

And whence did this pollution come?

From the West.

And when did this pollution begin?

With the coming of the English.

Inevitably, Sant Arjun Rama's real religion became Nationalism. "India for the Indians" was his watch-word. Not so much Indian rupees, Indian products, Indian soil, Indian jobs, posts, and appointments for the Indians—not so much that, as Indian ideals, Indian beliefs, Indian culture for the Indians.

And by Indian he, of course, meant Hindu. Only one degree better than the European *mleccha* himself, was the Mussulman. For what was the Mussulman but another barbarian invader? The European had come by sea, and conquered the country by guile, by lies, by intrigue. The Mussulman had come by land, down through the passes from Central Asia, and conquered the country with fire and sword.

From the New India they should be cast out, root and branch—extirpated, exterminated, massacred as their brethren the Turks massacred the Armenians.

To the people who occupied India for the countless centuries before the invasion of their country by his own Aryan ancestors, Sant Arjun Rama conveniently gave no thought.

What were they, those so-called children of India? Aborigines—Bhils, Gonds, Sonthals, animals in short.
. . .

And what made Sant Arjun Rama peculiarly dangerous among the dangerous men with whom he consorted, the underground workers with whom he plotted against the British Government, was his reversal of the order of their programme.

To the highly educated, experienced, travelled, phil-osophical students of revolution and leaders of revolt, men whose mental equipment was equal to that of any revolutionaries in the world, the proper method for achieving the emancipation of India from British rule was,

First, to raise the politically conscious educated class to fitness for the governing of India.

Secondly, having fanned the fires of Nationalism to white heat, to cause a blaze that should burn up, burn out, burn down, burn away, all that was foreign in the land, and then bring about a mighty revolution that should cast forth, for ever, all that had not existed in the Golden Age of India and was unknown to the Vedas.

But to Sant Arjun Rama, the proper method for the emancipation of India from British rule was precisely the opposite.

First, to fan the fires of Nationalism to white heat and cause a blaze that should burn up all things British and the British with them, and,

Secondly, this being done, to set about the training of the "free" people in the arts of self-government.

Briefly expressed, his colleagues of the Innermost Council would prepare and then emancipate. Sant Arjun Rama would emancipate and then prepare. Not for him the anti-Government pin-pricks, the sporadic pointless murders and easily suppressed outbreaks that should turn the eyes of the world upon India and the eyes of Indians upon themselves, while the goal of fitness for self-government was sought.

For him, a swift and bloody revolution on the French and Russian models, and thereafter, political education, training in self-government and the slow dawning of India's Golden Day.

What Sant Arjun Rama failed to realize, or brushed aside, was the fact that the world has changed somewhat since the date at which he set his mythical Golden Age of India.

What was to happen to the country when the British had been driven out, the Mahommedans put in their place beneath Hindus and given the choice between conversion to Hinduism and death, he did not stop to consider. He concerned himself neither with the problem of exactly how seventy million fighting Mahommedans were to be forced to choose between death and Hinduism; nor with that of how the mild, gentle, peace-loving Golden India should deal with the countless hordes of ferocious bloodthirsty Border Tribesmen who would stream down to her plains on the very day that the British evacuated the Khyber; of how defenceless Mother India would deal with Afghanistan, with Russia, with Japan, with any nation, Eastern or Western, who, observing that she had cast forth her watch-dog and opened wide her door, should say,

"Well, if the British really don't *want* India . . ."

Had anyone asked him about the defence of a country for the protection of whose thousands of miles of coast-line there would not be a single ship of war, he would have indicated the Sepoy army, again ignoring the fact that no Hindu sepoy army ever had, or ever could, protect the country against a European or Asiatic invader, apart from the question of whether it would survive its argument with the Mahommedan sepoy battalions.

The frame of mind of those sane Indians who realize that India has no future whatsoever, save with the help and protection of the British, he could not comprehend.

With their far higher selflessness that realizes and accepts the truth that the Indian must, for a century or centuries, be the protected and guided younger brother, he had neither sympathy nor understanding.

For the admirable Indians who serve India well and faithfully in positions of trust and responsibility under the British Government; men whose hard work is rendered doubly hard by the circumstances of their position, the claims to preferential treatment of not only their kith and kin but of all their caste-fellows, he had nothing but contempt.

With indivisible singleness of purpose, with flame-like energy, with lion-like courage, with immense and most un-Indian concentration, determination, and ruthlessness, he followed his own path, the path of destruction that shall lead to construction.

And destruction, alas, is so much easier than construction.

So to his deeds, to his character, and to his force

and personality, his colleagues paid the meed of honour and respect that was their due. . . .

Ranjit Singh having unlocked the almirah door, listened long and intently for sounds on the other side, and then knocked thrice, once, twice, and thrice, the filing-cupboard on the other side was cleared, its back removed, and the way opened into the rear premises of the *To-day and To-morrow.*

Sant Arjun Rama, Ranjit Singh, and Luxman Dhonde descended into the cellar, that the first-named might inspect the tunnel and look into the vault of the treasure-house of the Fort. . . . The Swami Dayanand, having replaced the *dhurrie* and table, remained to re-admit them to the Council-chamber on their return. The Babu Purshotamdass and Bhojraj Shahani resumed their *burkas* and departed by way of the gate in the lane through which Ranjit Singh had entered; and Ramrao Gopaldas bade his brother Tulsiram send a clerk from the *To-day and To-morrow* offices for the bazaar-*ghari* whose driver was a humble Brother in disguise, and which had brought Sant Arjun Rama and Abdul Haq to the meeting.

"By the way, Ramrao, a word with you," said the Swami, as Ramrao Gopaldas was about to bid him farewell. "I had a thing to say but I will fit it to some better time. I had a thing to say but let it go.'"

"No, don't let it go, Swami-ji," said Ramrao Gopaldas. "What is it?"

"We have a man, a goodly man, a man who soon shall cast a doubt—I mean, a bomb. It is I who have to cast the doubt. He'll cast the bomb into the house of the Governor of the Gaol. I am about to cast the doubt —into your mind.

"This man, who in but six days' time will cast that bomb and several others, doth guard them secretly and well. And where, oh Ramrao Gopaldas?"

"Down in the cellar here, Swami-ji?"

"Nay, nay. As is well known to you, our pet-name for these impulsive things so full of life and to be so tenderly handled is—what?"

"We call them eggs, oh Swami-ji," said Ramrao,

humouring the humorist.

"Eggs, indeed. And what say the wise men? 'Put not all your eggs into one basket.' . . . Now this is but one of our baskets, and another is the crypt of the ancient temple at Ratnapur. And there, sitting on, or near, his eggs, dwells Luxman Dhonde's faithful understudy."

"Yes, we all know that, Swami-ji. And yet other eggs there be in your safe guardianship in the old fort at Kotgur."

"Yes, yes; but we speak of Ratnapur, and of one who dwells there. How long is it since you were at the ancient deserted temple of Ratnapur, my Ramrao?"

"Oh, years."

"Well, it is not years since your wife was there."

Ramrao's eyes narrowed and those of his brother Motiram, large as they were, opened yet more widely.

"She was there yesterday morning," continued the Swami, "and in the company of our friend, Steele Sahib."

"Oh, yes, of course. She went riding with him, not only with my knowledge and consent, but with my blessing, Swami-ji. And something more, too. With a little useful information—useful to us, that is—that in her artlessness she might impart to our friend."

"Well, it was our friend who did the imparting," replied the Swami. "He told her all he knows. And a lot that he doesn't know, but suspects."

"And why not?" smiled Ramrao Gopaldas.

"True. Why not? Always provided the dutiful wife returned and told her husband all about it," smiled the Swami.

"Which she did," replied Ramrao, a little shortly.

"She did? Good. Then she told you that Steele has discovered the plot; has discovered the names of all the plotters; has discovered that we meet at your house and in the *To-day and To-morrow* offices? Told you that he knows what buildings are going to be blown up; what officials assassinated; what our plans are; and, in fact, everything except the date, and the name, identity, and whereabouts of 'Number Seven'?"

"What?" whispered Ramrao, his eyes almost closing

beneath their frowning brows. "He told *her*? All he got from Lalchand Vasu?"

"Yes. And she told you, no doubt. Also that she had undertaken to do her best, her very utmost, to discover the date, as well as the name, identity, and where-abouts of 'Number Seven.'"

"How do you know that?" asked Ramrao hoarsely, while Motiram Gopaldas stared, speechless, with open mouth.

"The guardian of the eggs," replied the Swami. "The door of the temple has been roughly boarded up, to keep out the jungle pig and the biped pig. Hearing the sound of horses' hooves and of voices, the guardian of the eggs, who was squatting beneath his sheet at the hidden entrance to the steps that lead down to the crypt, disappeared as a rat into its hole, down those same steps to the crypt, and proceeded, by way of the secret passage and entrance, into the temple itself.

"Here, with his eye to a crack between the boards that closed the doorway, he beheld Steele and the Gopaldas Mem-sahib dismount from their horses and seat themselves on a fallen pillar, within a yard of him.

"Removing his bright observant eye, he applied his metaphorically bright, observant ear to the same ori-fice, and listened for all he was worth.

"Happily—an English-speaking Engineering Col-lege-trained youth—he understood every word that was said. Understood, too, that she was as clay in his hands; and that he moulded her to his will and as he would. She is his friend; not ours. She is his woman; not yours. My poor dear Ramrao, he kissed her, fondled her. And you know what kisses mean between white folk. She is his obliging little friend."

Ramrao Gopaldas appeared to be stricken dumb; stunned; incredulous.

The Swami beamed upon him.

"Women, dear boy," he smiled. "Women! Inconti-nent creatures. Leaky vessels. And to change the meta-phor, inconstant weather-cocks. Creatures formed for man's delight—and his undoing."

"I can't believe it," stammered Ramrao.

"Well, whether you believe it or not, act as though it were true—for it is," replied the Swami.

"But such duplicity—such . . . such . . . such . . . *treachery!*"

"Such femininity, in fact," smiled the Swami. "How like a woman—to behave just like a woman!"

"But she has deceived me utterly."

"Ah, that is what you can't believe or understand, eh? Not that she should attempt to deceive you, but that she should succeed. Well, well, doubtless the Maharani Subhadra, that great mother-in-India, will know how to deal with an errant daughter-in-law."

"By God and by God she will," swore Ramrao Gopaldas, while Motiram Gopaldas violently nodded his head.

"But mind you, there is no real harm done—to the cause, I mean. Only to you as a husband," the Swami reassured him. "She is no more in a position to do harm to us than the excellent Lalchand Vasu was. Nay, on the whole, the result is good, rather, for she made it clear to him that he had a fortnight within which to perform his wondrous works for the salvation of the British Raj, a fortnight in which to—get busy, in short, if the watcher of the eggs understood all he heard."

"That's what I sent her out with him for," said Ramrao Gopaldas, "to tell him that she would not be able to ride with him again—after a fortnight."

"Well, she made that abundantly clear. And the wily young man sent a message back for you, to the effect that the Governor would not be coming for another month."

"Yes, she reported that all-right," growled Gopaldas.

"To your infinite amusement, doubtless," smiled the Swami. "Well, so far, it looks as though you are one up on Steele. You've fooled him over the date and 'Number Seven'; and he has not fooled you, of course, with his tale about the Governor not coming for another month. And as I say, there is no harm done; but it is only by the mercy and grace of the high gods themselves that it is so, for if you are one up on Steele, Steele would have been ten up on you, save for the watchfulness of the watcher—of the eggs."

"How?" asked Ramrao.

"Simply because the wife of your bosom, my dear boy, the *feringhi* wife whom you imported, is hand in glove with our deadliest and most dangerous enemy. So be wary."

"Forewarned is forearmed," growled Ramrao Gopaldas.

"Yes, and see that it is not four-legged—a four-legged ass. And see that Mr. Four-legged Forearmed Ass is not given horns, if you understand the allusion."

"Of course I understand all allusions," replied Ramrao angrily.

"Well, try to understand all illusions, too. And as I say, be wary. Be not only wary . . . but subtle . . . clever. Don't go home in a rage and begin the Taming of the Shrew with a whip and as you dealt with the syce yesterday morning."

"How . . . ?"

"'How do I know?' It was all retailed to your new rival. But listen. Be a little clever. Use the girl—a little longer. If, and when, she learns something really important concerning the date or 'Number Seven' (I must tell Sant Arjun Rama the joke that his coming is expected!) she is going to communicate the news direct and immediately to Steele. She is going to his house. A good excuse for going, one night, I should say."

"She is, is she?" said Ramrao Gopaldas, a sinister note in his voice, a restraint in his manner that boded ill.

"She is, my young friend. So go you home and smile and smile. . . . Go you home full of loving-kindness and affection, oozing trustfulness and confidence . . . and use the woman. Use her cleverly. Let her learn something that he should really know—and speed her on her way to tell him! We'll think and consider and perpend. We'll consult our Sant Arjun and we'll fill our Steele Sahib full of useful knowledge."

Slowly Ramrao Gopaldas nodded.

"I will," he said. "And one night this week, our lady wife, our sweet Elizabeth, shall join her dear friend

Steele—in quiet contemplation of the ticking bomb. . . .
Go to him, would she? She shall have the chance to go.
And she shall stay with him—if she does go—in
everlasting Hell. She shall join him *here*, too. What say
you?"

The Swami said little, but laughed consumedly.

"Oh, fie, fie, apt pupil of Sant Arjun Rama," quoth
he.

§2

That Sunday evening the leading members of the
Gopaldas family sat in conclave and in camera, the
"Maharani" Subhadra definitely in the chair, though
squatting cross-legged upon the floor in the favourite
corner of what was her own private verandah.

As is the case in innumerable Indian households in
this respect, the mother was the power; the father, the
honoured and venerated figure-head; the sons, the
puppets through whom the mother worked; their
wives, her daughters, and all other relations, her
hectored obedient slaves.

Among the politically-conscious educated classes—
alas, how educated!—the mother is very frequently the
most politically-conscious of them all, the most intran-
sigent, the most stiff-neckedly anti-Government, training her sons as soldiers in the political "army of
freedom," stiffening the back of her husband to fight
the good fight, a wordy fight carried on in debating-
club, public meeting, municipal chamber, University
senate or deliberative Council-Hall and Chamber.

Unfortunately she is, in ninety-nine cases out of a
hundred, ignorant, prejudiced, ill-informed, and of the
narrowest vision and outlook. Nevertheless, a fine
woman; a sturdy character; a noble wife and mother,
according to her lights; and, frequently, a heroine
neither unwept nor unhonoured, though unsung.

The "Maharani" Subhadra Gopaldas was not typical
of the wives and mothers of the politically-minded,
discontented educated class, but representative of the
extremest and most rancorous among them. Her

venomous hatred of the British and of British rule was, as is almost universally the case with such people, a personal matter. It was based upon the fact that her husband had been passed over, when candidate for a Judge-ship—in point of fact, most justly—in favour of a better man. In this she professed to see, and quite probably thought she saw, not only the grossest injustice but the vilest bribery and corruption. Nor had the pain of this running sore of rankling resentment been in anywise eased by the fact that her son Ramrao, "Europe-returned," was not eligible for membership of the Bhawalgarh Club, in spite of the fact of his being M.A. Oxon; Barrister-at-Law, Inner Temple; and the husband of an Englishwoman of irreproachable birth, breeding, and education.

To her, the fact was a studied insult, another injurious injustice, the arrogant and intolerable drawing of a colour-bar. Was not her Ramrao as well educated, well mannered, well accomplished as any of them? She did not stop to consider, and perhaps would have been incapable of understanding, had she stopped to consider, the fact that exiles in a foreign land have not only a yearning, but a right, to provide themselves with some spot, however small, unattractive and alien, in which they may, as far as possible, reproduce the atmosphere, conditions, and customs of their native land. Europeans in India do not exclude Indians from the Clubs because they despise or dislike them. They do so because they want one building, one garden, one little playing-ground wherein they can for a brief space forget India; for a little while be at home; play at being in England as they play; have one place where they can talk freely among themselves without having to remember alien ears, alien misunderstanding and misrepresentation.

Do not Indians rightly, properly, and naturally form clubs "for Indians only," when they are in Europe? Do not the Japanese? Do not all sojourners in a foreign land . . . ?

The English, then, had ill-used and injured her beloved husband, had treated him with the grossest injustice, wrecking and spoiling his life and his career, making of him a disappointed, misanthropic creature obsessed. They had studiously insulted her son Ramrao who was as European as any of them, not to mention her sons Jaganath, Motiram and Tulsiram, who, socially and officially speaking, ranked definitely below the English officials. That the Indian Civil Service was open to these same sons; that they had an equal and, indeed, a rather better, chance of passing its examinations, and themselves becoming members of the Ruling Service, she forgot or ignored; and counted it not to the English for righteousness that, like many another Indian mother, she might well have been the mother of the Collector, the Chief Magistrate, the highest Official of the District in which she lived.

And what of it? When all was said and done, were not the English the conquerors of India, and were not the Indians a subject race? Therefore—Down with the conquerors. Slay them; destroy them; extirpate them . . . and pause not to consider who would take their place, the place of the justest, the fairest, the kindliest rulers who ever administered a defenceless and distracted land, incapable, through its own heterogeneousness, of administering itself.

She gazed in turn at each of her four sons, sitting respectfully at her feet.

The four brothers, unevenly yoked and unsparingly driven by Subhadra, were not a well-matched team, nor the Gopaldas household a happy family. The father, Narayen Gopaldas, a weak man suffering from melancholic mania, owing to insistent brooding on his supposed injustice and wrongs, was a cipher to whom the rest paid lip-service.

Ramrao Gopaldas, the oldest of his sons, with something of his father's weakness, something of his mother's strength, and all the cleverness of both his parents, would have had little dislike of the English but for his mother's constant goadings, her constant whipping-up of a sense of resentment whenever some fancied slight offended his vanity and hurt his feelings. In England he had received much kindness; at Oxford he had been accepted on his merits, treated precisely as though he had been an Englishman, and given complete freedom to compete on equal terms for any honour, position or reward. Like the great "Ranji," his compatriot, he was eligible for the highest cricket honours; the same fact applying to any other sport. He was as welcome as anyone else to speak at any debate, and there was nothing to prevent his becoming Secretary, Treasurer, or even President of the Oxford Union Debating Society. From no club, society, clique, or coterie, whether sporting, social or intellectual, was he excluded by the fact of his being an Indian. That the Indian Civil Service was open to him in all branches and to the highest ranks, he knew, and that he could become a barrister of any of the Inns of Court he had proved. So he had lived in England in peace and comfort, and had returned to India unconscious of cause for discontent or complaint.

Immediately his mother had set to work to disturb this "pathetic contentment," to fill him with a sense of wrong, injustice and oppression; and to make great use of the fact that his wife was undeniably ignored by some Europeans, snubbed by others, and placed by all —as well as by her rash folly—in a category of her own, and apart.

People who look for slights invariably find them, and an imagined slight is as painful, as damaging, and as much resented as a genuine one. Before long, Ramrao Gopaldas was second only to his mother in hatred, resentment and bitterness against the English who would not elect him a member of the Bhawalgarh Club, and who did not receive his wife into the innermost exclusive social circle.

The fact that undeniably he liked and admired most Englishmen, and especially the Commissioner, the Collector, the Judge, Major Murdoch of the Gaol, Major Grant of the Battery, Colonel Campbell of Nicholson's Sikhs, the Civil Surgeon, and Principal Telford of the Government College, he used, curiously enough, as a salve to his conscience, on the rare occasions when that remarkable and somewhat incomprehensible mentor raised a gentle deprecative head.

Did it not prove how disinterested, pure, and noble were his motives? He was at one with the Roman father, at one with all those who had cut out the offending member, scorning the agony caused by the excision; at one with all who took the high road when inclination pointed to the low. Yea, though he loved Cornwallis Sahib, the Commissioner must die. Though he loved Herdie Sahib, the Collector must die. Though he loved, or, at any rate, liked, all the others, with the exception of Steele, they must die. That by perishing in their official capacity they also died in the flesh was true—and pity 'twas 'twas true—but India must be free, and every Ramrao Gopaldas in India must be free —to be not only Chief Judge of the High Court, as at present he was free to become, but also to become— what? Viceroy of India? But there would be no Viceroy. Well, to become free—free to make his own laws for himself and his own class. And for Mahommedans and other non-Hindus too—and serve them right.

No, left to himself, Ramrao Gopaldas, albeit proud, touchy, and sensitive beyond belief, was but a poor hater; and, as such, held no high place in the consideration and esteem of such men as Sant Arjun Rama and the ferocious fanatics of the Centre. Here in Bhawalgarh he had his uses nevertheless, though ranking far below those of such men as Ranjit Singh, Luxman Dhonde, the Swami Dayanand, Babu Purshotamdass and Bhojraj Shahani.

Of different calibre was his brother Jaganath, true son of Subhadra his mother, a fierce, sincere, embittered enemy of the English, whose narrow one-track mind loathed them with unquenchable and tireless hate. Part cause of his difference from his elder brother, Ramrao, was the fact that as a youth he had never left his mother's side and teaching; part cause, that he had never known an Englishman. Pupil of his mother, he had come well-grounded to the finishing-school of Sant Arjun Rama's training, having been recommended to him as secretary, servant, disciple, follower—*chela*, in short—by the Principal of that same

Madrutta Hindu College of which Sant Arjun Rama was himself so distinguished an alumnus.

Rare indeed among Indians of the educated class, Jaganath Gopaldas, intense, burning, perfervidly sincere—as so many of them are—was also tight-lipped and silent, a man who said little and thought the more, observant, thoughtful, taciturn. A genuine introvert, he had that impressiveness, that influence, possessed by all who, competent by knowledge and intelligence to say as much as others, say nothing; for to them is given the respect and regard that is the inevitable tribute of garrulous flatulence to reticence and restraint.

It has been said of the Indian that he has no hobby, whether he be the peasant who labours in his poor fields from dawn till dusk, the coolie, the mill-hand, who toils until he dies, the babu who scribbles diligently throughout the day, or the man of leisure deprived of that great blessing, the need to work. This generalization is too sweeping. It is wholly untrue of the educated class, every single member of which has a hobby that delights him and that occupies his every moment of leisure. His hobby is talking; preferably, far preferably, in public.

The Indian student, once he has emerged from the junior school-boy stage; the Indian member of the clerkly professions, whatever be his age; the Indian lawyer, vakil, advocate, pleader, barrister; the educated Indian, be he who he may, loves, beyond all things, to speak in public, to propose, to second, to declare, to open, to reply, to protest, to inaugurate, to request, to suggest, to rise to a point of order, to appeal, to do any mortal thing that will bring him to his feet and to the attention of his impatient fellows. He will debate eternally "with burning indignation," "without fear of contradiction," with much "yielding to no man in his admiration," his scorn, love, detestation or whatever it may be, and with inordinate and intolerable verbiage.

And here is the true love of Art for Art's sake. For he talks for talk's sake, orates for the sake of oration, and peroration—because ninety-nine times out of a hundred he really does not care one iota for the subject or for the result of his impassioned eloquence. When an English student closes his books and goes to his games as naturally as the river to the sea, the Indian student goes to a meeting, be it philosophical, religious, political, or what not. If there be no meeting ready-made for him to attend, he convenes one, and addresses his fellows upon any subject under the sun, from the wickedness of the British in punishing a cowardly murderer, to the desirability of "moving" the college milkman to use less "and/or" cleaner water to dilute the milk.

Infinitely rather would he do this than play organized games. Here and there a stalwart, driven by an English Principal to the performance of these strange rites, comes really to enjoy them, to play them for their own sake, and to prefer the cricket-ground, the football-field and the tennis-court to the debating-room itself; but such are rare and honourable exceptions. The educated Indian's hobby is talking—in public. Nor must what he says be supposed always to represent what he thinks, inasmuch as what he thinks might not lend itself so usefully to oratory, to the idioms that he understands, and to the phrases with which he is familiar. The speech is the thing, the stringing together of many words. Giving expression to his real views, if any, is not his hobby. Talking is.

That of Jaganath Gopaldas, who had no other, might be described as refraining from talking. And because his silence was due to anything but inarticulate stupidity, he stood higher than his more showy brother in the councils of the Bhawalgarh seditionists. Of him much was expected, and of him good report was made by the great ones, the delegates who from Calcutta, Poona, Amritsar, Delhi and Lahore, had visited that provincial spot. Of him they spoke as being one who would, when bidden, "sacrifice a white goat to Kali"[67]; one who would "take the bride[68] to the bridegroom,"[69] as the terrorist jargon goes.

---

[67] *Murder an English official.*
[68] *Bomb or pistol.*
[69] *Victim.*

Sant Arjun Rama, on the recommendation of the Swami Dayanand (who for long had known and admired the "Maharani" Subhadra) had taken note of the other brothers and put their names upon the list of those upon whom he could depend and call. Jaganath he approved of his own personal knowledge, and had marked him out for advancement.

"It is good, my child," said Subhadra, addressing Ramrao. "It is very good. I am pleased and proud. May the plan prosper. May she live for many long hours, for several long, long days, face to face with her paramour —with a bomb between them. May the plan prosper. We must be cautious, careful and clever. Cunning as they are, and cleverer.

"Now—how to get her to go to Steele Sahib's bungalow on Thursday night so that neither he nor she shall suspect that we have allowed, and intended, her to go. She must go to save his life (Oho! To save his life!) hot-foot and urgent; his Guardian Angel; brave, panting with haste, and palpitating with fear, come to warn him and to save his life at the risk of her own.

"How to tell her, without telling her. Have you a plan?"

"Only to take her into my confidence, Mother. Tell her 'everything.' Tell her that we start for Dhargaum on Friday morning, and that Steele is to be 'punished' on Thursday night. That on Thursday night we intend to do what Lalchand Vasu failed to do. I had thought of telling her that the plot—of which he knows so much! —is still definitely fixed for the famous fortnight hence, but that we want Steele out of the way, as he has somehow come to know too much; as there has been a leakage; as someone has been giving him information."

The lady Subhadra laughed contemptuously.

"Bah! Do you think that sort of thing would deceive her? Do you think that a woman in love, fighting for the life of her lover, is as easily fooled and hoodwinked as that? Why should she believe that you suddenly wish to take her into your confidence? She'd be puzzled as to what your game was, but she'd know it was a game, and would merely make a mental note to tell Steele next time she met him. No, she's got to learn of his danger 'accidentally'—and rush to his house to save him—on Thursday night at the time the good Bagu and his men kidnap Steele."

"Give her an opportunity to listen when Bagu comes here on Wednesday night? And give her no opportunity to get out of the house until late on Thursday night?"

"No. Does the leopardess walk into the trap that she sees the shikari prepare for her? She's no fool. Very far from it. She knows perfectly well that you'd never dream of giving her the slightest opportunity of overhearing conspirators in council."

"Shall I leave a letter, then, for her to find and read? Tulsiram here could write it and post it to me."

"Would she trouble to read it?" sneered Subhadra. "Would she be fool enough to think that a conspirator would write the dangerous truth—in English—and send it to you through the post?"

"Jaganath, my son," she continued, turning to the second brother, "unlike my parrot, you think much and say nothing. Have you a plan?"

"I have, Mother. And I'm sure it is a good one. The plan is good, but the means may fail."

"The means?"

"The means; the implement; the intermediary. I propose to use Motiram. For once in a way he may be useful. His apeing of the *feringhis* may be turned to account."

Motiram glared at his brother, and the youth Tulsiram, student at the American Mission College, sniggered unkindly.

"This is my plan, Mother," continued Jaganath, "based on the fact that Ramrao has surely finished with the evil and treacherous white creature," and he succinctly set it forth, the while Motiram's indignant glare gradually changed to a smirk, to an approving grin, his injured dignity melting into amusement and delight.

Subhadra smiled, nodding her head as the plan

was unfolded; Tulsiram giggled gleefully; Ramrao scowled wry and grim approval, and Motiram roared with uncontrollable laughter.

Motiram Gopaldas represented a different type of the result of the impingement of the West upon the East, of the grafting of English "education" badly conceived, badly imparted, and badly assimilated, upon Oriental culture and a natural indigenous training.

All four brothers were products and types, and Motiram represented probably the least attractive, inasmuch as, in addition to learning to speak the English language and collecting scraps of Western knowledge, he had also learned Western vices.

Far less intelligent, experienced and polished than Ramrao; far less intent, single-minded and determined than Jaganath; he was a waster, a drifter, an idler who, infirm of purpose and devoid of character, aped and secretly admired the English as much as he professed to hate them.

Why he had to hate them he was not quite sure, save because his mother told him to do so; because his elder brother Jaganath would hate him if he did not do so; and because even his younger brother, Tulsiram, would despise him if, wearing complete English dress, and seeking English society, he did not profess to follow where his family led him.

Why, he argued, should they all make such a fuss about his wearing English dress, drinking English brandy and seeking the society of the sort of English people with whom he could scrape acquaintance? Had not Ramrao married an English girl?

Feeling as he did, and feeling so little as he should (as a Gopaldas, a son of the "Maharani" Subhadra), he was the least happy of the four brothers, even more depolarized than they, possessing not even a genuine spontaneousness, and sturdy hatred of his own.

Like the rest of the quartette, he had no religion. Unlike them, he had no work, no active personal politics, and no occupation for mind or body, save only vice.

Supplied by his indulgent mother with far more

than sufficient money for his needs, he spent most of his time in debauchery and in sleeping off the effects of it. Vain as a peacock; mischievous, malicious and imitative as a monkey; idle as a drone; changeable as a weather-vane; weak of will; purposeless, idle, self-indulgent, drunken, dissipated, and very worthless, his chief use to the conspirators was the frequency and number of his contacts, the great variety of his sources of information, his opportunity for hearing the latest Bazaar rumours which in India are amazingly accurate and early.

The bare-headed—and bare-faced—ladies whose society Motiram Gopaldas frequented in the balconied houses of the Bazaar, were human exchanges, tape-machines, post and telegraph offices; and his especial famous friend, but recently chief dancing-girl to the Nawab of Almera, if a mine of faults, was undoubtedly a mine of information.

The news that Motiram brought home from the Bazaar was accepted in the Gopaldas family as is that of a great London newspaper in an English home—and was rarely inaccurate.

And equally useful was Motiram for disseminating information that the conspirators desired should be known. Where a shy retiring terrorist would find some difficulty in making a pronouncement through the medium of the press, he would find none in having it published in the right quarter, in the right manner, and to the right people, by taking advantage of the opportunity provided by the activities of the privileged and gifted Motiram Gopaldas. And Motiram, though not clever, was very cunning.

When, for example, it was desired that a *canard* should be let fly, a false rumour started, Motiram could be relied upon to simulate a sufficient degree of drunkenness to be coherent and convincing, and also to enable him gracefully to retract and apologize later, when the story was found to be untrue.

It was the *shrab* that had been talking nonsense, not the good Motiram Gopaldas. Was it likely he would tell his adored Bibi Zuleika a lie? Would he intentionally mislead Roshanara; tell untruths to Zahara; or give false information, in return for kisses, to Nurmahal, his heart's delight?

Motiram had his uses as secret-service agent; as *liaison*-officer between his betters and the Bazaar; and as intelligence-bureau for the collection and dissemination of rumour. . . .

Curiously enough, the Maharani Subhadra greatly loved and admired this worthless and objectionable young man. She listened with avidity and enjoyment to the stories that he brought home; the strange tales told to his *inamoratas* by far-wandering Afghan horse-coper; by swaggering Pathan Sepoy; amazing merchant from Khiva, Bokhara, Kashgar or Samarcand, who had arrived, after months of journeying, with his rug-laden camels, by way of the Khyber; by cosmopolitan wanderer, home from distant lands, with news and trinkets from Paris, Berlin, Moscow, San Francisco, Chicago, New York and Cairo; by queer and inquisitive strays from Bombay, Calcutta and Peshawar; by students, jewellers, lawyers, rajahs, robbers, silk-merchants, silver-merchants, procurers, money-lenders, jockeys, dacoits. Perhaps Motiram was her eyes and ears; her troubadour, her theatre, novel, cinema; her invaluable contact with the great world from which she was cut off.

And here was a family job for Motiram; one entirely after his own heart.

Yes, her scented, anointed, dissipated prodigal Motiram was not merely and wholly ornamental. He had his uses.

V

On Monday, with the Assistant Superintendent of
Police, a European and a Native Inspector, Steele,
armed with a search-warrant, raided the office of the
To-day and To-morrow newspaper and subjected it,
from cellar to attic and roof, to the most searching
scrutiny. Walls were sounded, floors taken up, every
cubic foot of space accounted for, and nothing whatever discovered beyond—what Steele felt he was probably intended to discover—some seditious pamphlets
in a filing-cupboard in a room at the back of the premises.

These rabid effusions of Babu Purshotamdass con-
travened the Law sufficiently to make them worthy of
confiscation, and grounds for prosecution of the paper,
but could not be regarded in the light of anything but a
most meagre haul.

Smiling benignly, offering every assistance, and
contributing observations that made Steele's blood
boil, the "prison"-Editor, Mr. Jeshwant Ghokale, accompanied him on his search.

In the cellar, which was separated by a stone wall
from that in which Luxman Dhonde worked, Jeshwant
Ghokale suggested that perhaps Steele would like to
dig. Heaven knew what he might find, smiled the
acting-Editor sweetly—cannon, rifles, revolvers, bombs,
infernal-machines—Heaven knew what dreadful
things.

Steele, eyeing the floor of the cellar and feeling quite
certain that its surface had not been disturbed for
many a long year, thanked Jeshwant Ghokale and said
he would not trouble. He would dig, but not there. He
proposed to dig into Mr. Jeshwant Ghokale's past, and
to keep a very interested eye upon his future.

Nevertheless he retired baffled, sore, and angry, for
he knew, as well as he knew his name, that the
terrorists met, or at any rate had been in the habit of

meeting, at the offices of *To-day and To-morrow.*

VI

On Tuesday morning Steele rode again with Betty Gopaldas and learned from her that she feared that this would be their last ride together.

"Not the last, I hope," smiled Steele.

"No, I don't mean that," replied the girl. "I should be very sorry indeed to think it was our last ride, Anthony. What I meant was that I am afraid I shan't be able to come on Saturday morning. My husband has given me clear and definite notice that I must be packed and ready to leave on Saturday and . . ."

"*This week?*" asked Steele.

"Yes, this week."

"They are all going?"

"So I understand. It seems that he may be returning quite soon, but the whole family is definitely going this Saturday."

"Did he tell you to tell me?" asked Steele.

"No. On the contrary he said,

"'Don't mention that to Steele, will you? I don't want anybody to know we are going on Saturday. Neither Steele nor anybody else.'

"I asked him why, and he said,

"'Never mind. I just don't want people to know I am going then. Business reasons. I shall find it difficult enough to slip away as it is. So don't forget. Don't mention it to Steele.'

"I asked him what I was to say if you suggested a ride on Saturday, and he said,

"'Why, say "Right-o, I'll be there."'"

"And did you raise any objection to doing that?" asked Steele.

"No, I thought it would be the better plan just to shrug my shoulders, say nothing, and give the impression that I should do so although I didn't like doing it."

"Saturday, eh? "mused Steele. "That means trouble on Saturday night, I suppose. Unless it's a bluff again, which it probably is. I wonder. Here's the temple. We can get down and talk for a while, can't we?"

"For a little while."

"Well, have you seen any of those men again, since we met?" Steele asked when they were again seated on the fallen pillar.

Luxman Dhonde's understudy, who had seen them coming, removed his eye from the knot-hole and placed his ear against it.

"Yes, I have," replied the girl. "Last night. Ramrao went downstairs from our sitting-room, instead of going to bed, and I went out on to the verandah at the back, and kept watch. I had been waiting there for about half an hour, when, from some doorway that I couldn't see, a man came into the courtyard and crossed to the door in our back verandah. As he came to the steps I heard the *durwan* unbolt the door, and the man looked up. It was Mrs. Cornwallis's guest."

"Sant Arjun Rama," nodded Steele.

"And about a quarter of an hour later, two men came together, and one of them was the big Sikh with the pock-marked face, whom I had seen talking to the *faquir* that morning."

"You are sure?"

"I'm absolutely certain. That lamp above the door is a perfect trap. Every visitor looks up when he starts to climb those steps, and the light falls full on his face. It also prevents him from seeing anything beyond and above it, though I don't think anyone would have seen me peeping over the lattice window-sill two storeys above."

"It was the man who sent the message to your husband that morning—'*A poor brother has come to Bhawalgarh*'?"

"Yes, the same man, beyond any possibility of doubt. I knew him at once."

"And who was his companion?" asked Steele.

"I had never seen him before, but I took very careful note of him and can describe him."

"Good Betty," smiled Steele, patting her hand. "Splendid."

"Thank you, Anthony. . . . He was what I should call a swaggering, upstanding type of man; big and strong and tall; and he walked with a stride. Rather like a big Pathan sepoy in mufti—that type of person—only he was not clean and tidy and smart, as they are off duty. His clothes were dirty and his *puggri* roughly tied."

"Could you say whether he were a Sikh or not?"

"Definitely not. The light fell full on his face, and I could see that he had a moustache and no beard."

"Splendid. You ought to be in the Police, Betty."

"I begin to think so," smiled the girl.

"Now, suppose you had to describe him in one word, what word would you use? For instance, you wouldn't say *babu*, of course; and as he was somewhat ragged and dirty, you wouldn't say *sepoy*; and as he was not dressed like one, you wouldn't say *vakil*. . . . What would you say?"

The girl thought for a minute.

"*Budmash*,"[70] she said.

"Good," smiled Steele. "*Budmash*. . . . Now, suppose you had to say it in English. I don't mean the trans-lation . . . but call him something in English."

"Robber," said Betty.

"In fact, dacoit, eh? My dear, do you know, I believe you've been describing the famous Bagu . . . Bagu the Dacoit. No less.

"Now, how the devil did Ranjit Singh and Bagu the Dacoit get into your compound without my men seeing them? There will be trouble for someone when I get back. . . ."

"Well—we'll meet again at Commissioner's House," said Steele later, when they parted, "and perhaps you'll have something to tell me, if I can get a word with you alone. I can't go to the tea-dance."

"I'll do my utmost, Anthony," promised the girl.

"Until Thursday night, then . . ."

---

[70] *Bad character, ruffian.*

§2

That night Anthony Steele again dined with Lawrence Herdie; talked over the plans and precautions for the safety of His Excellency the Governor of the Province (who by cipher telegram had declined to postpone his visit to Bhawalgarh); told him of his fruitless search for further evidence of the plot, and made various suggestions. When, later, he was left alone with Mrs. Herdie, he treated playfully and discouragingly, as he thought, her complaints of the emptiness of her life, her accusations of her neglectful husband, and her threats of drastic action if he and things in general did not improve. At midnight, ere he tore himself away, she became intense, portentous and dramatic.

"When I can bear it no longer, I shall come to you, Tony," she whispered. "Straight to you. . . ."

Steele laughed, his mind on matters even more dangerous.

VII

On Wednesday night, Major Hector Grant, seated on the verandah outside his quarters in the Fort, watched the recessed entrance to an ancient, rarely opened door, thick, low and spike-studded, through which, or beside which, had appeared the apparition of his grandfather.

Night after night he had sat thus, had watched and waited, for the last week, hoping and half expecting to be favoured with another glimpse of the ghost of the fine soldier who had held the Fort so bravely, so well, and so long, and who had died, there in the room behind him, in the knowledge that he had done his duty.

Major Grant had seen nothing; but, on the other hand, he had had to admit that, during his watch each evening, he had fallen asleep.

To-night he was determined not to do so. It was the last occasion on which the moon would serve his purpose, and he intended to keep awake.

He fell asleep.

Waking, an hour later, he opened his eyes, stared, and then sprang to his feet. A figure, a human form, or the astral form of a human being, had disappeared into the recess leading to the doorway.

The glimpse had been too brief for him to be able to say what manner of man—or ghost—he had seen; but quite definitely, quite certainly, someone, something, had passed into the recess of that doorway—and vanished. Unless he were still there, he must have passed right through the door—for that particular door had never, in Grant's experience, been opened.

Hurrying down the wooden staircase that led from his lofty verandah to the courtyard, he ran, in spite of the heat, across to where the low stone building, ancient, disused, empty, obscured a portion of the outer wall of the Fort.

Yes, as he thought. No-one there, and the door locked, as always.

He'd have it opened to-morrow. Even if the building were empty, he'd investigate. There might be a well, a cellar, a secret passage, a vault. There must be some reason why he should have seen the ghost of his grandfather here, and why, again, this elusive wraith, in the identical spot to-night.

Slowly he returned to his quarters, climbed the stair, seated himself on his chair, and gazed again across the courtyard at the deeply recessed doorway.

No, he was perfectly certain he had not been dreaming. He had woken up and *then* looked; and, just as he had been going to yawn, he had seen something move. He had sat upright and stared, and had seen a figure. Most definitely he had seen it, poor as the light was, and it had vanished into that recessed doorway. But somehow it did not look like the figure he had seen there before. Smaller, and dressed differently.

Yes, he would investigate there to-morrow. Very thoroughly too. No, not to-morrow. He had to go and call on Brigade to-morrow at Jhalni. He'd make a thorough search on Friday. And he'd invite Murdoch and Campbell over, tell them of this second experience, and ask them if they'd like to keep vigil with him that night.

VIII

From the usual Thursday evening meeting of the Bhawalgarh Literary, Dramatic and Philosophical Society, at least one member, who had been present on the previous Thursday, was absent, and her absence was noted by at least three people.

Immediately on entering the big drawing-room, Lawrence Herdie noticed that Betty Gopaldas was not present. He glanced eagerly at the doorway as each car drew up at the vast verandah without, and each new arrival entered the Commissioner's drawing-room.

His wife watched him, a bitter and sardonic smile hovering about her lips.

When Anthony Steele came in and, having greeted his hostess and host, glanced round the room, she waved her handkerchief, caught his eye and pointed to a chair beside her.

Steele bowed, smiled, and refrained from accepting the invitation. He had something else to do than carry on a bored flirtation with Jane Herdie. He wanted to assure himself of the whereabouts and movements of Sant Arjun Rama that night; and he wanted a word with Betty Gopaldas. Quite possibly she might have news for him, or, if not, by answering his questions, might tell him something that would tell him everything.

That Betty would do her utmost, he was certain, but she could not judge the value of her information. She might know something that, to her, scarcely seemed worth knowing, but that to him might be of uttermost importance. Only a week ago, she had, inadvertently, helped him enormously. To-night, most anxious to help, she might tell him something that would enable him to save the situation.

From his point of vantage, leaning against a pillar at the side of the great room, he, like Lawrence Herdie, watched the entrance, and the lines of the sardonic smile about Jane Herdie's mouth grew deeper. So Tony was looking for the girl too, was he? She'd like to whip the minx.

Nine o'clock struck. The Commissioner took the chair. Mrs. Cornwallis disappeared through the curtains behind her seat, and returned leading the beatifically smiling Sant Arjun Rama, still clad in the white apostolic garments and sandals, his anointed head bare and meekly bowed in sweet humility.

Steele eyed him intently. Could that holy man, that pious convert, that modern St. Paul, dwelling in the shadow and protection of his kind patrons and in Commissioner's House itself, be what the fact of his associating with the terrorists indicated?

Could it be true that he was, after all, a genuine convert, a convinced and practising Christian, the content of whose mind was pure theology, and the occupation of whose days was nothing but the pursuit of his religion, the cultivation of his spiritual ego.

Was it possible that the men who were undeniably, and indeed professedly, extremists fooled him and used his presence as a cloak and a blind to give plausibility to the pretence that their meetings were but for religious discussion?

Anyway, the gentleman was worth watching, and he should be watched, followed, shadowed, whenever he left Commissioner's House, as obviously he must do, from time to time.

Steele gazed round the assembly as the Commissioner rose to his feet. Practically all the same people as were here last Thursday. Who would think that every official there knew that, while seated in that beautiful brightly lit drawing-room, they were also seated on the edge of the crater of a volcano that might erupt at any time?

Who would think they knew that at any moment the floor beneath their feet might be rent asunder; that with a shattering, roaring noise and a sheet of flame, the roof be blown from above their heads, the walls collapse upon them, burying them alive in their crashing, smoking ruins?

The Commissioner standing there, cool, calm and quiet as though on an English lawn.

Old Sherdley sitting there with folded arms and placid countenance watching him, and knowing that on any night his wife and himself might be blown from their beds. He had never looked more austerely imperturbable in an arm-chair in his London Club.

Lawrence Herdie, whom, on at least three occasions, they had almost killed. Who would think, to look at him, that it was improbable that he would live out the fortnight?

Dr. Torrens, hands peacefully clasped in his lap, eyes closed, apparently without a care in the world. Who would think that he knew what he knew as to the imminence of hideous danger?

The soldiers, Major Grant, Colonel Campbell. Who would think they had a care in the world; that one of them had had warning from the real and from the unreal world, that his life and, far more important, his charge, was threatened?

Who would imagine that Campbell felt the ground to be crumbling beneath his feet, wondering whether his life was safe among those on whose loyalty and honesty he yet would stake his life?

And Murdoch, was it possible that he realized that, before long, an attempt would be made to turn into a hideous public danger his great charge and responsibility that should be a guarantee of safety to law-abiding people; that it was intended that he should be murdered, and that the five hundred desperadoes in his charge should be set free to wreak their will on defenceless people?

Steele had wondered whether, in the circumstances, the Commissioner would call a meeting of the Literary Society for that evening, and had been delighted to learn that he was doing so, and also a little ashamed of having doubted it. Of course, Cornwallis would carry on; and the last thing he would do would be to show the slightest sign of fear, anxiety, or agitation.

But would that Society ever meet again; or, at any

rate, more than once again . . . ?

Ah, there was Ramrao Gopaldas, coming in at the last moment, and gracefully, if hastily, making his profound apologies to his hostess, while the Commissioner waited for him to do so and to find a seat.

Now, what did that mean? Ramrao Gopaldas alone.

Why not Betty? What was the significance of this? What was behind it? Her last words to him on Tuesday morning had been,

"Until Thursday night, then."

Why hadn't Ramrao brought her, and why had he himself come? For a word with Sant Arjun? He'd watch that.

"Ladies and Gentlemen," began the Commissioner, "I call upon the Honorary Secretary to read the Minutes of the last meeting. . . ."

And the business of the evening began.

§2

After a few words with the Commissioner, the Collector, the Collector's wife, and with Ramrao Gopaldas (debonair, elusive and unsatisfactory), Anthony Steele left Commissioner's House, walking as usual from the gate of the grounds of the Residency to that of his own small bungalow.

God, how hot it was! Incredible though it seemed, it was, according to the thermometer, even hotter than at this time last week. The temperature had actually been increasing steadily since last Thursday though that at the time had seemed to be the limit. A hundred and ten in the shade even then, and a hundred and fifteen now! What a week—with the political temperature rising equally fast!

Well, *tout passe, tout lasse, tout casse*. And both temperatures must drop some time; must end in a thunderstorm or an explosion of some sort.

And as likely as not there wasn't any plot.

He had almost come to that conclusion, watching the amazing Sant Arjun Rama; watching the debonair little Ramrao Gopaldas.

But if so, what of Lalchand Vasu's meanderings? What of the Swami's warning to Dr. Torrens? What of Betty's information as to the meetings of the well-known extremists? And why had Ramrao Gopaldas obviously intended Betty to tell him that the family was leaving Bhawalgarh a fortnight hence; and then changed it to Saturday? And where was Betty to-night?

And how short that same fortnight was getting. Here was a half of it nearly gone; and, if there were a plot, no doubt that "fortnight" meant a week or less. And why on earth couldn't His Excellency have listened to reason and postponed his visit? All very well to be so blooming brave and all that, but what about the unfortunate people who were responsible for his safety? The Police especially. Most especially the Police.

Perhaps it was unfair to accuse H.E. of not listening to reason. No doubt he had listened all-right; had carefully weighed the pros and cons; had agreed that, as the Commissioner had told him, it might all be a mare's-nest; and decided that, in any case, it would be bad policy, from every point of view, to let the terrorists think they had got him rattled, to let them congratulate themselves that the Government had got the wind up.

That would be how His Excellency would argue.

Well, no doubt he was right; but it would have been a mighty relief to Anthony Steele if H.E. had not been so right; if he had just simply cancelled his visit on the excellent grounds that were offered by the Commissioner—that the Hospital would not be ready in time.

There was one thing, anyhow. He couldn't say the Police hadn't warned him. The District Superintendent of Police at Bhawalgarh had gone to the Collector and informed him that he had every reason to believe that a desperate and dangerous plot was being hatched; and that it might be consummated on the occasion of the Governor's visit. The Collector had laid the matter before the Commissioner and had called the District Superintendent of Police in evidence; and the Commissioner had duly communicated the information to His Excellency the Governor of the Province.

And that was that.

But what to do, he simply did not know.

He had kept a watch on the offices of the *To-day and To-morrow*, where the conspirators were said to meet, and where they might have a *cache* of arms and bombs, and had found no evidence of the holding of any such meetings.

He had raided the offices on a warrant, and had searched the premises from top to bottom—and had found practically nothing.

He had combed the town and district of Bhawalgarh in search of the elusive Ranjit Singh, and had failed to find him. Quite probably the man had never been near the place. He was not the only burly pock-marked Sikh in India, or in Bhawalgarh either.

He had raided and searched the ruins of the old Kotgur Fort, and found nothing at all, except a few evidences of recent occupation—wood-ash and so forth.

He had had every suspect in Bhawalgarh shadowed and had only discovered that they were apparently leading blameless lives.

And now, when he had expected to learn something from Betty to-night, she had not attended the meeting. Did the family suspect her? Had they shut her up in that gloomy rabbit-warren? He sincerely hoped, for her own sake as well as his, that she hadn't come to any harm—just when it seemed that she might be useful.

Well, here was his bungalow. And here, in one pocket, was his little flat electric torch, and here, in the other, was his little flat automatic—and if anybody took a pot at him, that fool would damn well "get the works."

He'd rise to remark that Anthony Steele, for once, was fed up.

Let dear old Herdie take the noble line that the Law is our sure shield, its strong long arm our protection. Very nice in theory, but cold comfort to a cold corpse. Any fool who shot Anthony Steele up, henceforth, would get both—a bullet and the Law—in the improbable event of the fool surviving to experience the ministrations of the latter.

Probably Herdie was right, from his own point of

view and in his position as the embodiment of the Law, but Anthony Steele was an arm of the Law; arms have hands; and this particular hand would carry a weapon.

Herdie did not believe in weapons for self-defence, but very wisely took good care to have his bungalow guarded. And there he differed from Anthony Steele, who felt about that as Herdie felt about weapons. Herdie said Steele was a fool, in that respect; and he said Herdie was, in the other; and so they were quits.

Anyhow, Anthony Steele could look after himself in his own bungalow, and would have nobody sitting on his door-step to take care of him. And let anybody who chose to come in, be quite sure he could find his way out again!

Imperturbable Cold Steele was getting warm, was getting toward the end of his long patience.

In fact, Anthony Steele, perplexed, thwarted, baffled, was spoiling for a fight.

He'd have a peg and a pipe and so to bed, for a read, a little sport-without-danger, D.V. and plotters permitting.

But having drunk his peg and smoked his pipe, Steele found that he was not in the mood for bed. He was restless, his nerves on edge. He must be up and doing. Doing what? Anyway, he could not sleep while he felt like this; could not even lie still.

How could a man go to bed and compose himself for a peaceful night's rest when he was listening . . . waiting . . . waiting . . . waiting for a shattering explosion—an explosion that would mean the Gaol gates were blown in; the Fort blown up; his friends murdered; his work undone.

No, it was useless to go to bed while he felt like this.

Equally useless to go up to the Fort. They could look after themselves there, surely.

The same with the Gaol and the Banks.

He had done every possible thing he could think of, in the way of warning, precaution, and prevention. Really everything depended on the loyalty, fidelity and incorruptibility of his police-sepoys—*as the safety of India, from terrorists, anarchists, and revolutionaries, always would depend.*

What could he do, further?

What about strolling round to Commissioner's House again? If that snake Sant Arjun Rama did slip out, he'd follow him himself.

What an extraordinarily stubborn, besotted woman Rowena Cornwallis was, once she had made up her great mind. Wouldn't hear a word against the fellow, even from the Commissioner himself.

Rising from his long chair, Anthony Steele yawned cavernously, stretched prodigiously, and went upstairs to his bedroom.

No corpses in the bed to-night, anyway.

Quickly he changed from dinner-kit into khaki shirt, tunic and slacks, put a fawn tweed cap on his head, pulled it well down over his eyes, transferred his pocket-torch and pistol to his tunic, turned down the lamp, and went downstairs. Here again he lowered the wick of the lamp in his sitting-room, and left the bungalow, closing the lattice doors behind him. He retraced his steps in the direction of Commissioner's House. . . . If he drew blank there, he'd prowl round the Judge's place, and then Herdie's. He'd walk right through the whole damned Civil Lines and the native City too, while he was about it. Walk all night—and give some of his policemen a fright, too.

§3

That Thursday morning Ramrao Gopaldas had suddenly notified his wife that the whole family would, after all, proceed to Dhargaum on Friday, "that is to say, to-morrow," and not on Saturday as he had previously said.

What did this mean? . . .

She must let Anthony know at once.

What could she do?

Bribery failed utterly. The humble widow servant-relative curried favour with the Maharani by taking to her a note that Betty wrote to Steele, and implored, and paid, her to take. The *durwan*, more honestly, said he did not dare let her out—and reported the incident to her husband.

§4

And, on that Thursday night, as Betty was preparing for bed, and agonising as to how she could possibly get word to Steele concerning her husband's apparent change of plans, she heard footsteps on the bare wooden stairs leading up to the suite of three rooms occupied by herself and her husband.

Who was this? Ramrao had mentioned that he would be late, which was his usual euphemism for early the following morning. He had "business" after the Literary Society meeting, the Meeting to which he had firmly refused to allow her to go. To her great anger, consternation, anxiety and fear, he had suddenly said when, after dinner, she had observed that it was time for them to start for Commissioner's House,

"I am not taking you to-night. I do not wish you to go."

And from that he would not budge. To that statement he would add nothing whatever.

What did it mean? What could be behind it?

Something, of course. Long ago she had learned that there was always "something." Something that was not mentioned; some *arrière pensée*; some hidden meaning or motive.

No statement could be taken at its face value and apparent meaning. Always it meant something more than—or less than—or different from, what its words conveyed.

Why had he gone without her? What would have happened had she insisted on accompanying him? Physical restraint as well as deep suspicion as to why she was so set on going? . . . Who was this at the sitting-room door?

Whoever it was, was singing; and, *mirabile dictu*, singing merrily, happily, and with joyous abandon, making a sound rare indeed in that house.

It must be Motiram, and Motiram must be drunk

again.

What could he want?

Frequently Motiram had made her feel a little doubtful; occasionally nervous and uncomfortable. When he was sober she felt suspicious, and when he was drunk she felt apprehensive. Definitely he possessed an "undressing" eye; a face on which a leer sat comfortably; a voice that caressed; a manner that insinuated and insulted.

One of the many things that Betty avoided, with some care, in the Gopaldas house, was the danger of a *tête-à-tête* with this brother-in-law. Jaganath she feared, Tulsiram she disliked, Motiram she detested and despised.

The singer, knocking at the sitting-room door, called,

"Betty! Betty! . . ."

Going to the door between bedroom and sitting-room, she prepared to close it.

"Betty! Betty! Somethi'g to tell you. Somethi'g 'mportant. May I come in?"

What had she better do? Lock the door and ignore him, or hear what he had got to say? It might be something important, as he said.

"Betty! Betty! I've got somethi'g to tell you."

The door into the sitting-room opened.

"Well?" she said, one hand on the handle of the bedroom door and the other on the key.

"You will be sorry if you don' listen to wha' I got to say. Sorry all the res' of y'r henceforth days."

The voice was thick.

"Well, tell me, then."

Motiram burst into the sitting-room, turned, and locked the door behind him.

Immediately Betty closed and locked her own door.

This was a nice thing! A new departure. Was life in this terrible house to go from bad to worse? What would happen if Ramrao came home and found his brother locked in the sitting-room?

Well, he'd find her door locked too, if he burst the other one in. And he and Motiram could settle the matter between them. And what proof would there be, when Ramrao came, that she hadn't only just that minute gone into the bedroom and locked the door—when she had heard Ramrao coming?

No, no. Ramrao wasn't as bad as that. She was exaggerating. If she told him the exact truth, he'd believe it, and deal with Motiram as he deserved.

Or would he?

She flushed with sudden anger as Motiram beat upon the panels of the bedroom door.

"Betty! Don't be a *béwakuf*.[71] I got somethi'g 'mportant to tell you, I tell you."

"Well, tell me, then, and go away."

"I'm not going to shout it un'er the door nor by the hole for key."

What could she do? What she'd like to do would be to throw the door open, march out, and horsewhip the creature. And suppose he proved stronger than she was? Besides, he was drunk. He must be drunk or he wouldn't be hammering on her bedroom door.

"Betty! I tell you it's somethi'g 'mportant. 'S 'bout your boy friend."

What was that? What did the creature mean?

Should she ignore him? Suppose he broke the rotten, rickety door down. A good push and the whole lock, handle, key and everything, would clatter on the floor.

"'S 'bout Steele, Betty. You don' listen, and you won' have any more rides with him. You won' see him 'ny more. Not even to say goo'-bye."

And the rich fruity voice, thick and husky, trolled forth shamelessly,

"*And he didn't even say goo'-bye.*"

This was a trick. Why should he warn her if Anthony were in danger? It would be the last thing he would do.

And suppose it were not a trick? Suppose there were some connection between this and the fact that Ramrao had not allowed her to go to Commissioner's House to-night? Suppose this animal, drunk, had

---

[71] *Fool.*

come to mock at her? Suppose he really knew something; knew that there was to be an attempt upon Anthony's life; and that, this time, it was to be successful?

This fitted in with the family flitting that was to take place on the morrow. Suppose he did know something. Suppose this was why they had confined her to the house since Tuesday morning. Literally a prisoner. Suppose Motiram told her something on which she could yet act—if she crept out of the house in the middle of the night, or climbed out of the verandah and got down, somehow.

This drunken beast might know something; might tell her what he knew, if she gave him a chance.

Anthony's life might depend on her hearing what he wanted to say.

She would risk it. How could it matter what became of her, what happened to her, if Anthony were killed? Wouldn't she give her life for his, give anything, do anything, to save him? Of course she would.

"Wait a minute," she said, pulled on a dressing-gown, unlocked the door, and found herself struggling in Motiram's arms, hugged tightly, strained to him, her face and neck covered with kisses.

With all her strength she fought, got her hands beneath his chin, forced his head back, and, with a tremendous effort, wrenched herself free. Though trembling with rage and indignation, she realized thankfully that she was not frightened, not in the least afraid of this disgusting brute.

"So that's what you had to say, is it?" she said. "Wait till my husband comes home!"

"Yes, le's sit down and wait, Betty," hiccupped Motiram. "Where shall we sit?"

Had he been going to tell her anything at all about Anthony, or was it a filthy trick to get her to open the door?

"What do you think Ramrao's going to do, eh, Betty? Do to ol' Motiram?"

"I don't know. I have never had experience with such people in such circumstances. But I should imagine my husband would throw you down the stairs —break every bone in your body—when I tell him what . . ."

"Ah, but wait till *I* tell him—what. I shall tell him you are a little liar, Betty," smiled Motiram, supporting himself in the doorway.

"Who do you think Ramrao is believing, uh? His own belov' brother, flesh of his flesh and bones of his bones and life-long family member, or white *feringhi*—pup? . . . Yes, pup. . . . Pup? . . . No, bitch—yes, bitch. He'll believe what I say. He'll nob-nobbelieve bitch when I say."

"Oh? And what are you going to say?"

"Ah! You wait. Now I say what you said. 'You wait till Ramrao comes home.' Just you wait. You wait 'long with me, in here. Then you'll know. You'll hear what I'm going to say to Ramrao. S'prise you. Really s'prise you, Betty."

"I don't think so. I don't think anything said or done in this house would surprise me."

"Oh, yes, I'm going to s'prise you, Betty. Really I am. You wait till Ramrao comes home."

"And so you had nothing to tell me after all? You were lying, as usual."

"Tell you? What about?"

"Something about Mr. Steele, wasn't it?"

Motiram laughed and lurched into the room.

"Oah, yess! Something about Steele Sahib. Oah, thass goo' joke, Betty."

"What is?"

"What they are going to do to Steele Sahib."

"Who are?"

"Ah I Perhaps you'd like to know, Betty. I'll tell you if you will be awf'ly nice to poor ol' Motiram."

"And when are they going to do it?"

"Why, to-night, of course. Now; soon."

"Where?"

"In fac'," smiled Motiram, spreading his arms expansively and again lurching forward. "In fac', how, when, where, why, what and—hic—which, eh? You wan't to know a lot, don't you, Betty? You want a lot of information. Then I'll give it to you, if you are an awf'ly good girl. What you give me first, eh?"

And again he staggered yet nearer, his arms extended.

What was this? Was it lies? All lies? Or was it the truth? What could she do? How could she find out. She must not fail Anthony.

She backed farther from the drunken man, her arm outstretched to fend him off.

"How do I know you are telling me the truth?"

"'Tisn't truth. I haven't tol' you anything. Steele's all-ri'. They wouldn't really do it, Betty. Too . . . awfully dreadful. Too . . . horriful . . ."

"Too dreadful? Too horrible?"

"Mush. Mush too . . . *awf'ly* bloody. Yesh, what you call bloody awful, Betty. No, no, they wouldn't do that, would they, Betty? *Bloody* awful!"

"No, of course not, Motiram. Of course not. Come into the sitting-room and let's sit down; and then you can tell me what they—wouldn't do to Mr. Steele."

"Yesh. That's ri', Betty. You be awf'ly nice to me and I'll tell you all they won't do. Be a damn shame, wouldn't it? A nice chappie like Steele. *Pukka Sahib.*"

Seizing the man's wrist, Betty half dragged, half led him into the sitting-room, thrust him into a chair and turned up the wick of the big oil lamp that stood in the centre of the table.

Seating herself as far as possible from the drunkard,

"Now we can have a chat," she said.

"No, no! Thass no goo', Betty. You come an' sit here."

And lurching to his feet, Motiram staggered to the sofa, fell upon it, and patted the space beside him.

"Come along. You come an' be awf'ly nice to poor ol' Motiram."

"I don't trust you, Motiram," she said. "I don't believe you've got anything to tell me at all. Not a word about anything. Neither about Mr. Steele nor anything else."

"Steele? What abou' Steele?"

"You said they weren't going to do anything to him."

"No. *Of course* they're not. Not to-night. I'm not going to give them away. You think I'm drunk, don' you, Betty? You think I can't keep secret. You think I'll tell you what they're going to do to Steele to-night. Wha' they're goin' to do to your boy frien' you go riding with. Well, I'm *not*. See? Nonnuless you make love with ol' Motiram. An' then not. No. You think I'm drunk. Maybe. Nots . . . notser . . . not-serdru'k 's all that. Nolless you gimme lotto lotto kisses, Betty. You kiss me and I'll tell you lotto funny thi'gs."

What could she say? What could she do? How could she get the truth out of this maundering, babbling drunkard? Or was there no truth to be got?

Truth and Motiram Gopaldas! Facts, though. Facts, perhaps. . . . Did he know anything?

Again he made to rise to his feet.

"Stay there! Stay there!" she cried sharply.

What could she do to help Anthony? She must do something—and she'd do anything, if it were really necessary.

"Will you come sit here, then, Betty? Come here."

She would. If anything were to be got from this wretched drunken cur, she'd get it.

Seating herself beside him, she seized his hands. That would give her a chance if it came to a struggle.

"Tell me, Motiram," she begged, and endeavoured to smile and look beseechingly into his eyes. "Tell me something interesting. I'm so dull up here. What is somebody going to do to—anybody?"

"Kill him, Betty. Sush a joke. They're going to kill him to-night and in sush a funny way. Ramrao thought of it. It's his secret, not mine. I . . ."

"Ramrao is going to kill Mr. Steele *to-night*?"

"No, no! Don't talk sush nonsense, Betty."

"No, of course not. It's not Ramrao, is it? Ramrao only thought of it."

"Yesh. He only thought of it. . . . But the dacoits going to do it."

"When?"

"Why, to-night, Betty. Didn' you say to-night? Didn'

you jus' tell me it was to-night? The middle of the night."

"Oh, yes; of course," agreed Betty. "The dacoits. He told me about them. . . . To-night. In the middle of the night. Quite soon, eh?"

"Oh, yesh, qui' soon."

And snatching a hand away, Motiram waved it airily.

"Oh, yesh; qui' soon, I 'sure you."

"Where?" asked Betty. "Where? Is he going to raid them?"

"No! What nonsense you do talk, Betty! I thought you were a sh-shensible girl. He's not going to raid them. He's . . . he's . . ."

And Motiram's bloodshot eyes closed, his head nodded heavily.

"Yes! Yes! He's . . . ?" cried Betty, releasing his other hand and shaking him.

"Eh, wha'?"

"Mr. Steele. The dacoits! The dacoits! They're . . . they're . . . ?"

The heavy-lidded eyes opened.

"I tell you, they . . ."

Again the eyes closed and the head fell sideways on Betty's shoulder.

"Motiram! Wake up! Wake up!"

And with all her strength she shook the inert body beside her.

"The dacoits?"

"Yes. They are going to kill . . ."

"Kill him . . . *Where?*"

Motiram pulled himself together, shook off his drunken lethargy, and eyed Betty with owlish gravity and wisdom.

"Whassmarrer, Betty?"

"What are the dacoits going to do? Where? Where?"

"Why, they are going to get poor ol' Steele and . . . Whass it matter, what dacoits are going to get? I'm going to get kiss. Another kiss."

And Motiram again burst into song,

"And another little kiss wouldn't DO us any harm,"

waving an imaginary bottle and seizing Betty firmly round the waist.

"Kiss me, Betty. You kiss *me* this time."

"Yes, but wait a minute, Motiram. Play fair. You promised to tell me all sorts of interesting things, and you don't tell me anything. Now you tell me all about what the dacoits are going to do; and then . . ."

"And *then*, Betty?" leered Motiram.

"Well, you tell me—and then we'll see."

"Yes, I'll tell you, Betty, and then we'll see. Funny ol' dacoits. Good ol' dacoits. They're going to Steele's bungalow to-night."

"Yes, and then . . . ?"

"And then . . . *he*'ll see. And now . . . *you*'ll see."

And suddenly Motiram flung his other arm about the girl and attacked her with amorous violence and drunken fury.

Again she fought and struggled desperately, as she was crushed, kissed, mauled, enveloped, and all but overwhelmed.

Again, and at length, she struggled free, while Motiram, with a drunken laugh and a smacking of lips, collapsed upon the sofa and closed his eyes.

"Thass goo'!" he mumbled. "Thass very nice, Betty. Goo' girl. You . . . you . . . you . . . you . . . go bed, Betty. 'N' don' you lock that door!"

Horrified, sickened, outraged, the girl stood staring down at the human hog sprawling drunkenly on the sofa, her teeth and fists clenched.

A loud snore. A hiccup. A horrible gurgling sound.

Another snore. And then regular heavy, stertorous breathing.

Hurrying to the bedroom, she flung off the rags of her dressing-gown, slipped on a dark frock, opened her bedroom door, saw that the drunkard lay as she had left him, crept across the sitting-room, unlocked the door, and closed it softly behind her.

Could she creep out of the house? Could she? She could try, anyhow.

Quietly as a mouse she began to steal down the carefully unwatched stairs, along the purposely unguarded corridors, to the open and designedly deserted door that led to the empty front compound and the street.

As she did so, Motiram rose to his feet, sober as a judge, and laughed softly. For a minute he stood listening, a diabolical smile upon his face.

"Now, my good Jaganath," said he to himself, "I wonder if you could better *that* bit of work—clever as you think you are."

§5

Meanwhile, Mr. Lawrence Herdie, C.S.I., I.C.S., Collector and Magistrate of Bhawalgarh, drove himself and his wife home in his long powerful car. Only a minute's drive, a minute's peace, before the storm broke; for, knowing the signs as he did, he saw that this was to be a bad night.

Another bad night . . .

How long, oh Lord, how long?

Sometimes one felt that, if they were all to be blown to dust, so much the better; and the sooner the better. Ashes to ashes and dust to dust, since life itself was dust and ashes in the mouth.

And he had so counted on seeing Betty to-night; on sitting quite still and relaxed for a couple of hours; deep in an arm-chair; his hand across his eyes, as they watched her face.

With that tiny oasis in the desert of his life, he could carry on; the one thing for which he lived, or rather the one pleasure in the life that he lived. For a man could always live for his work.

Ah, well; here was the bungalow. Now for it.

That was the second time, at least, that he had seen a man slip away like a snake, as the light of his head-lamps flashed into the drive. Might be as well to have that police-sepoy changed. He must ask the butler if he had seen anyone colloguing with the night policeman at any time.

The policeman rose to his feet, saluted, and stood at attention.

Explosion

The verandah doors were thrown open by Paul Jesus Miguel Xavier Manoel Braganza Mascarenhas da Silva.

"Good evening, Sah and Mem-sahib."

"Good evening, Paul. Everything all-right?"

"Yes, Sah. All proper."

"Will you have a cup of coffee or anything, my dear?" asked Herdie, turning to his wife.

"I'll have a whisky and soda. Take it upstairs, Miguel."

"Bring some coffee along to my office-room, Miguel. If you will excuse me, my dear, I have a little work I must finish to-night."

"You always have, haven't you? And I must lie awake until you come up, or be awakened when you come, and stay awake the rest of the night."

Well, he would get through as much work as he could, before she came down and began.

Thursday night and no sight of Betty. That would be a fortnight without speaking to her; a fortnight without seeing her, save for a glimpse in church on Sunday.

Thursday night; and the Governor arrived on the morrow. How many of them would be alive on Saturday?

Well, he had done his best, taken the plot seriously, and striven to impress the Commissioner as much as Steele had impressed *him*. What more could he do?

He could but do his utmost, as usual.

What a week it had been since last Thursday. What a hellish week; and at the end of it he had not seen Betty.

The end of it? Yes, he counted his weeks from Thursday to Thursday nowadays—ever since he had fallen in love with her. And he had hoped to have a few words with her at the meeting to-night, while his wife talked, as she was sure to do, with Steele.

How much longer could he carry on? Could he survive another week like this last?

Well, this wasn't work, anyhow.

An hour later Lawrence Herdie crept up to bed.

To his great relief his wife made no sound. He glanced at the whisky decanter. Empty. No wonder she was asleep. Perhaps there had not been much in it, though. On the other hand, the butler would scarcely have dared to bring it up, unless it contained a fair amount.

What could a man do, in a case like this?

Perhaps he could do something when he went on furlough—if he lived to have another furlough. Perhaps a long holiday in Switzerland would be her salvation, the change to different scenes, different interests, a glorious climate wherein one did not feel this constant need for a stimulant. Was it his fault?

Well, it was no good going over all that again; and she was asleep, thank Heaven.

Asleep for the night, obviously. What about another hour's work, then?

With the utmost precaution against making a sound, Lawrence Herdie crept from the room and returned to his office and his work. He'd settle down to it again. Make hay while the sun shone. He was terribly behind, and now that she was so soundly asleep, the night was his. She wouldn't wake much before lunch-time to-morrow.

An hour later, the tired man laid his head on his arms for a few minutes' rest, and endeavoured to switch his thoughts from his wife, his work, the plot, the Governor's visit, and to turn them on to the one path in which they could wander with pleasure, peace and joy—and a minute later fell into the heavy sleep of exhaustion.

Jane Herdie sat up.

Gone back downstairs, had he? Let the selfish creature go. Just what he *would* do when she was waiting, waiting, waiting, for him to go to bed and to sleep—that she might do what she had finally and irrevocably made up her mind to do.

Work was all he thought of. His wretched files and his bed. Was ever a pretty woman thrown away on so unappreciative a block as this? What sort of husband was he to a woman who liked a little reasonable gaiety and pleasure? Did the fool think that all a woman needed to satisfy her was to sit and watch him eat, at tiffin and dinner, and then to moon about the bungalow for the rest of her day?

Well, he was wrong, and he was going to learn that he was wrong, and learn it too late. She had had enough. She was fed up. And he couldn't say that he hadn't had fair warning. She had told him often enough that he was driving her mad. She had told him hundreds of times that she couldn't bear the life he made her lead. She had told him scores of times that she didn't love him, and that she did love Anthony. And now, perhaps, he'd believe it.

And if he heard her going out, and came to her, she'd tell him where she was going and why.

He'd know to-morrow, anyhow.

A little unsteadily she got out of bed and began to dress, and though her hands fumbled somewhat, with fastenings, and occasionally she swayed and lurched, she made no sound.

Finally, taking her shoes in her hand, she crept from the room, descended the stairs into the drawing-room, strove to put a shoe on while standing, failed, sat down heavily on the sofa, and eventually succeeded. Fortunately the shoes required no fastening.

It was a comparatively easy matter to turn the key in one of the slatted doors leading into the verandah, and, as the moon was shining brightly through the lattice-work, she was able to find and unfasten the bolts at the top and bottom of the verandah doors, open these without noise, and, unseen and unheard, descend the steps into the shadows of the drive.

Wasn't there supposed to be a night-watchman here? Well, he wasn't here anyway, and if he had been, presumably he would have evinced no surprise, whatever he may have felt, at seeing the Mem-sahib come out for a midnight stroll. Anyway, he certainly would not consider it incumbent upon him to go into the bungalow, knock at the office-door, disturb the Sahib, and announce the fact that the Mem-sahib had gone out for a walk.

How incredibly hot it was. Hotter just here, even, than in the house. Perhaps it would be cooler out on the road. Thank God it wasn't very far to Anthony's bungalow. What should she do if he had locked up and gone to bed? He never did go to bed until pretty late, he said. When he came in, he always sat in the verandah for an hour or so, before he turned in; and very probably he didn't lock up at all. And it was a fad of his to have no *chowkidar*, no night-watchman, nobody in the bungalow at all, when the servants had finished their work.

Was that because people came and had secret interviews with him—police-agents, spies, informers, and people like that? . . . Women? . . . Was it because he had women to the bungalow? One never knew with these bachelors. Such liars.

How queer and disembodied she felt—almost as though she were dreaming, sleep-walking. Anyhow, she could say she had been sleep-walking, if necessary. Quite a good idea, that. Had that little drop of whisky gone to her head? What a shame if it had. She did not feel any the worse for it, really. Just a little bit giddy, perhaps, but only now and then. A little light-headed and light-footed, but only pleasantly so.

What should she do if Anthony had gone to bed and she couldn't get in? Call his name. He'd wake and hear her? Well, she'd soon know. There was his gate.

To her relief there was a light in the drawing-room, a light upstairs, a light in the verandah, and, yes, the verandah doors were unfastened. Pushing them open, Jane Herdie entered Steele's bungalow.

"Tony!" she called. "Tony!"

No answer.

There were his pipe and glass on the table beside his chair.

Dear Tony. . . .

She went into the bare and, to her mind, uncomfortable, sitting-room. This wanted a woman's touch badly. Well, it should soon have one.

"Tony!" she called again. "Tony!"

Returning to the verandah, she opened doors leading into the dining-room, his office-room, and into a fourth room in which he kept riding and sporting gear. Curious. He would hardly have gone to bed and left the place open and lit up like this. She'd see if he were upstairs; but unless he were sound asleep, surely he'd have heard her calling him?

Going through the sitting-room to the foot of the stairs, she called again, and receiving no reply, went up. There was a light in one of the rooms.

So this was his bedroom. How bare and comfort-less.

She peered through the mosquito-netting of the bed. He must be out.

What was in this next room? Nothing but an un-made bed, an unfurnished dressing-table, and a chest of drawers. And in the other one? . . . The same. He must be out.

Well, he'd have a surprise when he came home.

She would make herself comfortable in the drawing-room—to call it such—and wait for him. Perhaps there would be a drink available, for it was a terribly thirsty night. If not, how was she going to get a servant? That was one drawback to his fad of having the bungalow entirely to himself in the evening and at night. On the other hand, what an advantage to-night; and, anyway, he'd be quite sure to see that the ser-vants always left everything ready for him before they went off for the night.

She returned to the sitting-room. Ah, yes. There was a bottle of whisky, syphon and glass all ready on a tray. Why didn't he make the lazy butler pour the whisky into a decanter? It tasted so much better out of cut glass. Still, the drink's the thing. And she helped herself liberally.

Ah, that was better! And that looked a fairly comfy arm-chair.

Where did he keep his cigarettes?

She posed herself in the arm-chair, facing the door.

What a surprise for Tony. . . . How his face would light up.

A quarter of an hour passed, and Jane Herdie poured herself out another whisky and soda.

Where could Tony be?

She yawned heavily. If he were much longer she'd go to sleep. Not a bad idea, either. A Sleeping Beauty. And Tony would play the part of Prince Charming—wakening her with a kiss.

He was a Prince Charming, too.

Jane Herdie yawned again, relaxed the alluring pose, settled herself more comfortably in the chair, and fell asleep.

A few minutes later, had she been awake, she would have heard a faint crunching of the gravel outside the verandah, a light footstep, as the verandah doors were opened.

Betty Gopaldas looked hastily round the verandah. There were his pipe, glass and chair. The lights were on. He would not have gone to bed. There was no sign of a disturbance, a struggle. God grant that she was not too late.

Her heart beat wildly and then seemed to stand still, to turn over in her breast. He had not heard her come in.

Was she too late?

It would be too incredibly cruel that she should have had the wonderful good fortune to escape from that secret guarded prison of a house, to have been able to run straight here (and she had run the whole way) and then to be too late. But surely if those robbers had broken in here and killed him, there would be some sign? The furniture would be in some disorder. There would be . . . blood.

Should she call? They might be lurking in the house; hiding somewhere; and if she called, they might . . . Or, hearing her, he might come down the stairs, all unsuspecting, and they might . . .

No. Probably he was in the lighted room.

The girl tiptoed across the verandah, looked into the sitting-room—and saw Jane Herdie asleep, a picture of domestic felicity.

Betty recoiled.

Mrs. Herdie asleep in Anthony's sitting-room in the middle of the night!

Waiting for him? . . .

But of course!

Of course, she too had heard of his danger, had come to warn him, had found that he had gone out, and had sat down to wait. Of course that was it. But why hadn't Mr. Herdie come instead? Why—probably he had had to rush off elsewhere. He had suddenly learned something about this plot, and had gone to Commissioner's House or the Fort . . . or . . .

Why, of course, he too might be out looking for him.

Yes, that would be it. Mr. Herdie was looking for Anthony, to warn him; and Mrs. Herdie had come here in case her husband missed him and Anthony came back.

And yet—would she have the courage to stay here if she thought there was danger?

Well—here she was, anyhow.

And so all that terrible experience with the beastly Motiram had been for nothing. Never mind, it had been for Anthony, and she had done her best. She would never have forgiven herself if she had done otherwise.

And what now?

She had better go back home. She could do nothing more. Mrs. Herdie would warn Anthony, and he'd be able to . . .

Jane Herdie opened her eyes, stared . . . and stared . . .

She rose to her feet, apparently unable to believe her eyes.

"*What!*" she said. "O-o-h-h-h! . . . I *see!* . . . *That's* it, is it?"

"Where's Mr. Steele?" cried Betty. "Is he . . . ?"

"Oh, it's 'Where's Mr. Steele?' is it?" sneered Jane Herdie, her voice harsh and bitter, her tone an insult.

"Have you seen him? Have you seen him, Mrs. Herdie?"

"What d'you mean, 'have I seen him'? I've seen you, anyway, you disgusting little . . ."

"Mrs. Herdie, he is in danger. I . . ."

"Yes, so I see. He'll be saved from this particular danger, anyhow, you sickening, shameless . . ."

"Mrs. Herdie, I don't understand. I . . ."

"*I* understand, though. Tell me, is this an appointment or a venture—a try-on?"

It was Betty's turn to stare.

What was this woman saying? And what was she doing here, since apparently she was unaware of his danger.

"I don't know what you mean by a venture or a try-on. I've no appointment with Mr. Steele. I have just heard that they are going to kill him. Here, to-night, '*now, soon.*'"

Mrs. Herdie laughed with less of mirth than of harsh anger.

"Is *that* the best you can think of? . . . Well, I'm glad you admit it is not an appointment, anyway."

"Of course it's not an appointment," said Betty.

Was it possible that Anthony had been murdered, kidnapped, before Mrs. Herdie came?

"How long have you been here?" she asked.

"Look here, I want no impudence from a creature like you," replied Jane Herdie.

"Mr. Steele is not in the bungalow?"

"Mr. Steele is not in the bungalow."

What should she do? Why was this woman waiting here? Could it be possible that, at this moment, Anthony was lying upstairs injured, wounded . . . dead?

"Have you been upstairs?" she asked.

"What on earth . . . ? You brazen, impudent little . . . What do you mean?"

"I mean, is Mr. Steele upstairs?"

"What on earth has that to do with you?"

"He's in danger. I . . ."

"And suppose he is? Are you his protector, or is one to understand that he is your 'protector'?"

"Mrs. Herdie, what are you talking about? There's a plot to murder Mr. Steele."

"So you said before. Would you kindly go back to the Bazaar? You've no business here—and no doubt you'll find plenty there."

Betty turned and went.

Anthony couldn't be in the bungalow or he'd have heard their voices.

What now? Should she wait in the wide empty road, keep a watch in both directions, and warn him? But they might waylay him on the road.

And what was that woman doing in the bungalow?

Surely, if she had been waiting there to warn him, while her husband went to look for him, she would have said so? She never had been civil, but at a time like this, if she knew that he was in danger, and if she herself had come on the same errand, surely she would have said so? Surely she would have laid aside her usual haughty, disapproving manner to the extent of saying,

"It's all-right, Mrs. Gopaldas. My husband has gone to warn him and I've come here in case he misses him."

But evidently it wasn't that at all.

What was it, then?

And now what could she do? Would it be better to wait here?

No, of course, Mrs. Herdie would surely tell him, when he came in, that Betty Gopaldas had just been there, had come with some tale about his being in danger—and he would understand. He would know that she had something to tell him.

An idea. Mr. Herdie was the proper person for her to see. He was the power in Bhawalgarh. If she went to him and told him that she had just heard that there was a plot to kill Anthony that night, he would know what to do. He'd do *something*, and he'd do it at once. He would know, of course, from Anthony, that there was a bomb plot, and that an attempt had already been made on Anthony's life. He'd probably know where to find him.

Yes, she would go and tell Mr. Herdie that they were going to kill Anthony to-night, "*now, soon.*" And he would do something.

She turned and began to run in the direction of the

Collector's bungalow.

§6

Bagu the Dacoit was one of the forthright people of the earth; a man devoid of inhibitions; a craftsman who loved his work; and, albeit grim, ruthless, amoral and wholly conscienceless, was something of a humorist. Something also of a paradox was he, inasmuch as he always told the truth, said what he meant, meant what he said, and was a good, straightforward, honest robber.

It is said that blood and breed will always tell; and Bagu was a gentleman of birth and breeding, son of a broad-acred baron, born in a castle, and brought up on horseback.

It was purely unfortunate that a youthful escapade should have had consequences of a kind considered serious by those who administer the Law of the Government of India, for in the Native State of which his father was an honoured ornament, such pranks are rightly understood and taken at their true value. Within the borders of his own Native State, wherein life and outlook upon life are entirely medieval, a foray is a foray, a killing is a killing, and the first may be natural, correct, and sporting; the second excusable, justifiable, and indeed meritorious. But outside such States views are different; things are humdrum and prosaic; the face of the Law is harsh, its views narrow, its arm long; and one who has grievously and outrageously offended it must either become a *bahir-watia*[72] or go to gaol and perhaps the gallows.

Both of these latter are unsuitable for the brave son of a nobleman of ancient lineage, whereas, in his own code and estimation, there is nothing unsuitable or derogatory about turning highwayman, reiver, free companion, outlaw and—dacoit.

So the high-spirited young gentleman who had fallen a victim to the lure and lust of *zar*,[73] *zan*[74] and

---

[72] *A quitter of the road. One who "takes to the heather." An outlaw.*
[73] *Gold.*

zamin,[75] or at any rate to those of *zar* and *zan*, changed his name, his abode, and his way of life; gathered about him a band of more-than-willing companions, and became the Robin Hood of Derwera.

The comparison is not inapt, for, undeniably, he took from the rich, the *bunnia*, the *sowcar*, the rich usurer, and from the wealthy oppressive landlord, though it is not on record that he gave to the poor.

Undoubtedly the poor frequently benefited nevertheless, inasmuch as they came in for the pickings; cleaned up after him; took whatever he had overlooked, discarded or mislaid; and, when he had departed, assumed cloaks of invisibility or airs of conscious virtue.

When the Police came, the said poor gave them all the information they could possibly think of, while suppressing all that they had got.

Ere long, Bagu became a thorn in the flesh of Authority, but escaped extraction therefrom by reason of the fact that he had a brain and a gift; for he was a born guerrilla leader, a man of infinite resource, as daring, dashing and audacious as he was skilful; and he had the enormous advantages of knowing the country as he knew the palm of his hand, having a perfect Intelligence Service in the peasantry whom he never molested and frequently befriended; and in having possession, knowledge, and understanding of a breed of magnificent camels.

These enabled him to operate at incredible distances from his head-quarters; to carry ample supplies; and to bear away all desirable loot and valuable prisoners. It was his custom to travel fifty miles in a night; rest in desert or jungle by day; travel another fifty miles that night; rest again; travel again; rest again; travel again; and, that night, commit a dacoity, two hundred miles from his base.

Upon occasion, as in Almera State, he would settle in a suitable spot for months; send his camels back that they might be properly fed and tended; operate for a while; and when the place showed indications of

---

[74] *Women.*
[75] *Land.*

becoming too hot for him, would send for his camels and go while the going was good.

Politics he had none, save that by nature and nurture, position and experience, he was an autocrat, a dictator, and a firm believer in personal rule. The British he admired as foemen worthy of his steel, and liked them for their manly, sporting, and war-like qualities. That they would hang him if they caught him, he knew, and this added spice to his delightful life, and lessened his regret when, upon occasion, he took pot-shots at them in the way of business. For the educated politically-minded babu class of Indian, he had the profoundest contempt and dislike; for the active terrorist, a qualified approval and lukewarm liking, as a fellow *bahir-watia* who worked in a different way for a different end, though by means which he could not approve.

In Almera State he had recently met a former acquaintance, one Ranjit Singh, a man after his own heart, bold, fearless, an outlaw with a price upon his head, a man of his hands; one who, but for foolish political pre-occupations, might have joined him as lieutenant of his band. He would have been useful, a trained soldier, practised in the methods of warfare of the English, and knowing their ways and dispositions in attack and defence.

When it had become desirable to leave Almera State, Bagu had, instead of returning home, accepted the invitation of Ranjit Singh to come and sojourn in an excellent spot known to him in the Bhawalgarh jungles, an ancient fort, suitable in every way as a quiet retreat and temporary head-quarters.

Ranjit Singh held out promise of something really good, in return for armed support of a project of his own.

And Ranjit Singh's colleagues of the Brethren of India had approved the arrangement—an offensive alliance between the seditious money-collecting *badhra-log*[76] of Bengal and the dacoits having proved very

---

[76] *Young men of the educated middle classes (who join the dacoits in robbery with violence, on the plea of raising funds for political and patriotic purposes).*

satisfactory and mutually beneficial, in that part of the world.

Warned by his new friends that the Superintendent of Police of Bhawalgarh had his suspicions of the ancient Kotgur fortress in which he was sojourning, Bagu had changed his hiding-place for more distant jungle fastnesses on the other side of Bhawalgarh, and there awaited the dawning of the promised day where-on the sacking and looting of a whole town should be his.

This might well be his last exploit in the way of business. What with banks, *bunnias* and bazaars, not to mention the Government Treasury, he should surely be able to make his fortune and retire.

And now the day had come, the work begun, its pleasant preliminary the kidnapping (not for ransom this time, but for punishment) of the District Superin-tendent of Police himself.

What a jest! What a job! He would attend to it himself, to be sure that it was not bungled. Not only to be sure that it was not bungled, but because it was a feat after his own heart.

"Understand?" he whispered, as he, his lieutenant and two chosen specialists of his band lurked in the dark shadow of trees in Steele's compound, late that Thursday night. "No violence. If any man smites the Sahib or the woman, I will cut his throat from ear to ear and fine him a hundred rupees. They are to be gagged with the *lungis*; legs tied together at ankles and knees with the cords; arms bound to their sides with a turban, and the sacks pulled over their heads. Raja and I carry the Sahib to the *byle-ghari* and tie him down in it. Jasmir and Dewa carry the woman and throw her in. Bahadur will sit on the pole and drive the bullocks. I will sit in the cart and keep the *gora-log*[77] quiet. Jasmir will scout ahead and Dewa and Raja do rear-guard. Any of you got weapons? No. That's all-right, then. Got your silk handkerchief, Jasmir, you *thug*? And you, Dewa, you strangler? Don't choke them

---

[77] *White people.*

altogether, mind. We want them both alive. Now then. Quieter than bats."

Bagu leading the way, the dacoits entered the bungalow. Pointing to the woman asleep in the chair, Bagu put his finger to his lips, made a signal to Jasmir and, silently as a shadow, crept past the sleeping woman and, followed by Raja and Dewa, made his way upstairs.

They had been that way before, on the previous Friday night, two of them bearing a corpse.

Soundlessly they entered the bedroom, looked into the other two and into the bath-rooms, and returned as they had come, to find Jasmir still standing over the sleeping woman, his hands a few inches from her throat.

"The Sahib's not here," whispered Bagu. "We'll take the woman and come back later. . . . *Now*, Jasmir."

A huge paw clamped down upon Jane Herdie's mouth, and she awoke to see grinning evil faces, dark oiled bodies, *hands . . . hands . . . hands . . .* and found she could not scream.

Swiftly her ankles were bound together; her knees. The men jerked her to her feet and bound her arms tightly to her sides.

The horrible hand was removed from her mouth and, as she opened it to scream, it was stuffed full of choking, stifling rag. And as she retched, a cloth was bound about her strained mouth and tied with cruel force at the back of her neck.

As she fainted, a long sack was thrust over her head, pulled down and secured above her knees.

A minute later she was dumped into a bullock-cart that stood waiting in the dark shadows of the banyan trees beside the road.

§7

Meanwhile, Anthony Steele, keeping in the shadows of the trees, circumambulated Commissioner's House.

All appeared to be well, the *chowkidar* awake at his post on the broad front steps, coughing and clearing his throat from time to time, partly to show that he was not asleep, partly to scare off prowlers, *bhuts*[78], thieves, *afrits*[79] and other evil-doers, partly for the sake of making a noise of some kind.

At the back of the house a similar state of security prevailed. The stalwart Sikh orderly strolling up and down, *lathi* across his shoulder, was singing nasally to himself.

If Sant Arjun Rama crept forth, he'd have to wait till one of these two was asleep. Or would they, seeing him, merely salaam and think no more about it? To them, he would be not only a holy man, but the guest of the Commissioner Sahib himself, and doubly above suspicion or question.

Having ascertained that the police sentries, at the points of vantage at which he had posted them, were awake and alert, and having warned them that he would be round again later on, Steele waited and watched a while, on his own account; then took a walk on the road leading from Commissioner's House to the native city, and having met no-one and heard nothing, decided to return and visit the houses of the Judge and the Collector.

All appeared to be well at Mr. Justice Sherdley's bungalow, the *chowkidar* awake and watchful; there also being, according to him, an excellent, active, and trustworthy *chaprassi* sleeping just inside the door of the back verandah.

Going on to the Collector's bungalow, Steele was surprised to see that lamps were alight, and to find that the front verandah doors were standing wide open.

Curious.

And where were the *chowkidar* and the Sepoy who should be here on duty?

This would bear investigation.

---

[78] *Ghosts.*
[79] *Devils.*

§8

Meanwhile, Lawrence Herdie, seated at his desk, dreamed a dream, and wakened from it astounded beyond speech.

Falling asleep while thinking, as usual, of Betty Gopaldas, he dreamed that he and she were together; and he was happy beyond all describing, happy beyond conception, beyond the power and scope of conscious human happiness.

They were in a world of their own, a world apart, a fairyland of extra-human joy and peace and delight. She was gazing at him, speaking to him.

And he awoke to find Betty Gopaldas was gazing at him, speaking to him.

This of course could not be, and yet it *was*.

This was his bungalow, his office—and this was Betty Gopaldas. She was there in the room with him, speaking to him, calling him by name.

How utterly wonderful!

And he had been bemoaning the fact that he had not seen her that night, had not been able to watch her across a room—and here she was with him in his own room.

"*Betty!*" he whispered.

What could this mean?

She must be in trouble, and she had come to him. To him, of all people. What happiness, if he could really do something for her.

Meanwhile, God grant that his wife did not wake and come down. He'd lock the door. No, that would be foolish, and make things worse, if she did.

"What is it, Betty?"

"Oh, Mr. Herdie," she panted. "I've been running . . ."

"Sit down. Sit down and . . ."

"No, no. I have come to you for help. They are going to murder Mr. Steele. My husband's brother told me. The dacoits. . . . To-night, '*now, soon,*' he said. At his bungalow. Mr. Steele isn't there. I went to warn him, and I found . . ."

"Found him? You've warned him?"

"No; he was out. So I ran on here. I saw there was a light in this room. The verandah door was wide open. I thought perhaps you were here, and I came in. . . . Oh, do something quickly, won't you?"

"You are sure? Dacoits? At his bungalow? . . . And you don't know where he is, of course?"

"No, no. I thought possibly you might know where he was, and could save him; stop him from going, unwarned, to the bungalow."

"My dear child, I haven't the faintest idea as to where Steele is."

Anthony Steele walked into the room, saw the girl, and stared in amazement.

"Sorry, Herdie," he said. "I saw your door wide open . . . no *chowkidar* or Sepoy . . . a light here . . . and I barged in."

Subconsciously he glanced at the travelling-clock on Herdie's desk. *It was eighteen minutes past one.*

§9

The bullock-cart, its driver addressing the bullocks unkindly, in the vernacular, its only visible occupant singing nasally, passed along the silent empty bazaars and came to a halt at the mouth of a narrow lane.

Its passenger jumped down and was quickly joined by three other men.

"Bring her along quick, Jasmir and Dewa, while I knock," ordered Bagu. "Drive off, Bahadur," he added, addressing the *byle-ghari-wallah*. "Back to the same place, and wait."

A minute later, the door past which Ranjit Singh had been wont to force his bundle of brushwood, was opened, and the dacoits, bearing their corpse-like burden, passed into the courtyard of the house.

"Only one?" growled Ranjit Singh, as he closed and fastened the door.

"The woman," replied Bagu. "The Sahib wasn't there. Meanwhile—a bird in the hand . . ."

"Not there?" exclaimed Ranjit Singh. "Sure?"

Bagu laughed scornfully.

"Well, you had better come in while I tell Sant Arjun Rama. Come along, anyhow, for it will take the lot of us to get her into the house. If you drop her over the wall upstairs, I can bump her down to their meeting-place. That's where they want her."

Willing hands none too gently bore their burden to the top of the house, and thrust it through the space between the top of the wall and the roof. Ranjit Singh received it, dismissed the dacoits to go and seize Steele, bore it to the trap-door, and dropped it through into the room below.

From here he partly carried, partly dragged it down to the council-chamber, the only entrance to which, from the police-watched offices of the *To-day and To-morrow* newspaper on the other side of that house, was by way of the filing-cupboard and the almirah.

Knocking and being admitted, Ranjit Singh dumped his burden heavily upon the floor.

"They've only brought the one," he said, addressing Sant Arjun Rama as the other conspirators rose to their feet. "The woman. Bagu says Steele Sahib wasn't there. He has gone back to wait for him. Better than hanging about there, with this bundle, till he came."

"Yes, quite so," agreed Sant Arjun Rama. "He'll be back with him in an hour or two, I expect?"

"Meanwhile, this is your affair," he smiled, turning to Ramrao Gopaldas.

"Yes, primarily," agreed the latter, "but it is the affair of all of us equally. This woman, my wife, is a traitress. She was caught there—*there* in Steele's own bungalow—red-handed, in her vile treachery and lechery. Out of sheer devilish wantonness, malice, and wickedness she has spied on our affairs, and told all she could, to our most dangerous enemy. That is a crime for which there can be only one punishment—death—and I am the first to agree to it, although she is (or was) my wife. Also I formally propose the method of punishment. Since she is so fond of Steele, she shall die with Steele. . . . Since she loves him sufficiently to betray her husband to him, she shall share his death.

. . . Let her be bound to this chair, and let Steele be bound to that one on the opposite side of the table. Let Luxman Dhonde place a time-bomb between them, and let them sit, bound and gagged, watching it, and enjoying each other's society until they die of starvation. For no-one will ever find them."

Sant Arjun Rama regarded the speaker with interest. Possibly with a little surprise and increased favour, as who would say,

"Hark at my little dog barking at the big elephants. Isn't he brave?"

From the strained excited countenance of Ramrao Gopaldas, he glanced at the bitter face of Jaganath and noted its look of fierce concentration, repressed rage. In answer to his glance, Jaganath Gopaldas nodded without speaking.

Sant Arjun Rama turned to Motiram Gopaldas who, grinning, licked his lips. Who said Motiram Gopaldas was no good to the Brethren?

To the youngest brother Sant Arjun Rama spoke.

"What do you say, Tulsiram?"

The youth swallowed; and with visible effort scowled savagely.

"Let the white goat be sacrificed to *Kali*," he said. "She is a traitress to her adopted Mother, India."

"So be it," nodded Sant Arjun Rama.

"Offer the lady a chair," he smiled, turning to Ranjit Singh. "Take that sack off and let her join the party."

Ranjit Singh roughly seized the corners of the sack, pulled, and disclosed to the astonished eyes of Sant Arjun Rama, the four Gopaldas brothers, the Swami Dayanand, Babu Purshotamdass, Abdul Haq and Bhojraj Shahani, the face, known to them all, of the Collector's wife.

Mouths fell open, and there was a simultaneous murmur of her name.

"Herdie Mem-sahib!"

"The Collector's Mem-sahib!"

"Mrs. Herdie!"

"By God and by God," exclaimed Ramrao Gopaldas. "What have these bungling jungly coolies done? This is not my wife."

The Swami giggled merrily.

"Oh, fie!" quoth he. "What will our kind Collector say? Not only to us and to Steele, but to the naughty wife!"

"What to do, then? What to do, then?" babbled Babu Purshotamdass.

Abdul Haq smiled wryly at Ramrao Gopaldas, whom he detested even as he detested all Hindus.

"Better try the Collector Sahib's bungalow next, if you want your wife?" he jeered.

Sant Arjun Rama spoke, and all eyes turned to him.

"I am afraid it will have to be a triangular party. 'The eternal triangle' as they themselves call it. We can't very well put her back where the dacoits found her. . . . By the way, I suppose they went to the right house?" he asked, turning to Ranjit Singh.

"Well; Bagu went with them, and did the job himself," was the reply, "and he was in Steele's bungalow last Friday when he took Lalchand Vasu back—after we had done with him. . . . No; Bagu caught her in Steele's bungalow undoubtedly, and thought she was the other woman."

Sant Arjun Rama nodded.

"The manners and morals of our rulers are for our admiration, if not for our imitation," he sneered.

"Well, it cannot be helped," he added. "The lady has only herself to blame. If she had not been alone in Steele's bungalow at one o'clock in the morning, she wouldn't be here; and now she is here she must stop."

"Three of them? How many more come? Quite a congested area," smiled Babu Purshotamdass.

Jane Herdie opened her eyes, gazed round the room and at the circle of cruel faces.

Ranjit Singh lifted her into a chair. . . .

What was this? . . . She tried to scream. . . . Where was she? A different place. Different men. . . . Another nightmare. . . . What had happened to her? But Tony would come and save her. Surely Tony would come.

She fixed eyes of appeal on Sant Arjun Rama, praying, beseeching. Why! It was Rowena's Christian!

Rowena's convert!

These men must have saved her from the others.

Why didn't they set her free, let her lie down, take her home? Above all, take this terrible stuff out of her mouth. She would die of thirst.

"Oh, well, no matter," said Sant Arjun Rama. "The poor lady would have—met with an accident—in any case to-morrow night.

"Now I want a word with Luxman Dhonde. What's the time?"

Ramrao Gopaldas pulled out his watch.

The time was eighteen minutes past one.

§10

Meanwhile, in the cellar beneath the conspirators' meeting-room, Luxman Dhonde tested once again the mechanism of the time-bomb that was to blow up Bhawalgarh Fort.

He would be almost sorry when it went; so delicate and lovely a piece of work; so beautiful a thing; so immensely potent an engine of destruction. He doubted whether a more powerful bomb had ever been exploded, or that one had ever been better placed than this would be, to encompass the maximum of effect.

He ventured to flatter himself that he really had been clever, while not for one moment denying that he had been amazingly lucky.

He had worked out, from the old plans, that his tunnel through the wall would bring him into the ancient *toshi-khana*, and it had done so; but he had never dared to hope that he'd be able to go from the *toshi-khana* to neighbouring vaults and chambers, by way of easily opened doors, and thence through an underground passage into the heart of the Fort itself, and without any necessity for going out into the court-yard of the Fort, where, even in the small hours of the morning, he might have been seen. Only once had he come up into the open, late the previous night, when the Sahib had been sleeping, up on the high verandah; and, for the rest of the time, so far as he could tell, he was in vaults, chambers, and passages unknown to—and certainly unused by—the present occupants of the Fort.

Well, the bomb was ready, the mechanism working perfectly, and he could give it anything from an hour to a day, fix it to explode at any given second that he liked, within twenty-four hours of setting it.

Perhaps the best thing would be to take it along at about two o'clock to-morrow, and give it an hour. It had to go off at three o'clock precisely.

Yes, that would be the best plan. An hour would be most ample time for them all to go out, by way of the lane, and wait round the corner; give plenty of time for everybody to clear out from the *To-day and To-morrow* offices, too. It would be just possible that a brick-bat or two would come hurtling that far from the explosion, and do a little damage. The force of the explosion would go upwards, of course, and so would a good deal of debris. The *To-day and To-morrow* people wouldn't want a few feet of thick beam coming through their roof while they were in the house.

Yes, an hour would be very ample; and there wasn't the slightest risk of anyone in the Fort discovering the bomb between two and three o'clock in the morning. He doubted whether anybody but himself had been into that central underground chamber, vault, store-house, prison, treasury or whatever it was, in fifty years.

Well, that would do for to-night. One more look round, and he'd go up and tell the Brethren that every-thing now was absolutely ready.

Or, now that his work was really finished, and there was absolutely nothing more that he could do, should he have a glance at the contents of one of the old boxes in the *toshi-khana*?

It would be rather pleasing, and delightfully dra-matic to go up into the council-chamber, receive their greetings, wait for silence, strike an attitude, and say,

"My work is done. At three o'clock to-morrow the British will receive a mortal wound, the deadliest blow struck since the Mutiny. Also I have to announce that I have incidentally discovered a *lakh* of gold mohurs. A million and a half rupees for the fighting fund." Something of that sort, if there were any money or treasure there.

Yes, the triumph would be all the sweeter if he could say that, and if there were nothing in the boxes, nothing of interest—merely records, documents, as everyone supposed—he'd not make any reference to them at all, not mention that he had opened one as soon as his all-important task was completed. He'd simply announce that his work was done, the work that would enable the Brethren to overthrow the British Raj.

Taking up a hammer and a chisel from his bench, Luxman Dhonde crawled through the tunnel into the old treasure-house, thrust the cutting edge of the chisel between the lid and the side of one of the chests, and struck hard.

According to the clockwork of his beautiful bomb, *the time was eighteen minutes past one.*

And so, at eighteen minutes past one, that Friday morning, there occurred one of the biggest explosions ever known in the stormy history of India.

For the contents of the strong boxes, stored in the vault of the ancient *toshi-khana* of Bhawalgarh Fort, were cordite and big shells, and Luxman Dhonde had driven his chisel against the detonator of one of the latter.

He caused an explosion indeed, and he was blown to atoms—by British cordite. The tremendously solid stone underground-chamber acted as the breach of a mighty gun, the ten-foot tunnel and the cellar acted as its barrel, and the force of the blast, through this barrel, blew the house of the conspirators to pieces, killing every person therein, and bringing down, in smoking ruins, the houses opposite and on either side.

The conspirators had indeed been responsible for a Great Explosion, and by it they died, to a man. And with them died Jane Herdie.

Bhawalgarh counted its time anew, dating all

things from its terrible red-letter day—that of The Great Explosion.

IX

The Brethren of India—while mourning the cruel loss of their great leader, Sant Arjun Rama; their almost irreplaceable chemist, engineer, and assassin, Luxman Dhonde; the liaison-officer between them and the Mussulmans, Abdul Haq; the great and invaluable Swami Dayanand; the vitriolic Babu Purshotamdass; the astute and most able Bhojraj Shahani; the stout executive, Ranjit Singh; and the four wealthy dedicated sons of the Maharani Gopaldas—the Brethren of India, while mourning these heroes, frankly admitted that, for once, the Satanic Government had been clever. Really clever—for, realizing that the Bhawalgarh Brethren were going to blow up the whole place, the Satanic Government had blown them up first. Knowing that they were mining and undermining, the Satanic Government had countermined.

Those among them possessed of a streak of sardonic humour, smiled, and admitted that at last the Satanic Government had begun to learn something, had begun to realize that, from the Satanic point of view, it was really much better to bomb the bombers than to give them a six months' trial, world-wide publicity, and then let most of them go because the evidence was not of such a quality and quantity as fitted in with the medieval ideas of the British and their creaking, ponderous Juggernaut of Justice.

Yes, they had to hand it to the Satanic Government, and admit that they really had been rather smart.

But at the same time it was awkward. If they really were going to bomb the bombers as a policy, blow up the blowers-up as a practice, life was going to be rather difficult for poor terrorists. It was a cruel shame, too; and what was Justice coming to, nowadays?

Still, the Satanic Government had really been very clever, and the terrorists frankly admitted it.

For nothing on earth would persuade the Brethren

that the Bhawalgarh authorities had not themselves deliberately exploded the bomb in the cellar of the conspirators' meeting-house. The Official Report following the court-martial on Major Grant—accused of dereliction of duty in not knowing the quantity and condition of explosive ammunition stored in the Fort— amused them as a piece of mere childish eye-wash; a farce, during the performance of which every player, including the Commandant himself, must of course, have had his tongue in his cheek.

The Satanic Government could hold a court-martial —with its puerile references to heat-deteriorated ammunition exploding through spontaneous combustion —and publish its proceedings; but it couldn't hoodwink the wise men of the Centre, of the Brethren of India. They knew that the Satanic Government had simply massacred the poor patriots in cold blood.

The "Maharani" Subhadra refused to die of a broken heart at the loss of her sons; keeping herself alive with thoughts of vengeance, and with amazing willpower, while she awaited the return to her house of the errant wife of her oldest son. That one should learn what it was to be a white widow in a Hindu household during such span of life as the "Maharani" should allot to her!

But Betty Gopaldas never returned to the roof of her mother-in-law. On the strong advice of Anthony Steele and the eloquent pleading of Lawrence Herdie, who himself took her to the Commissioner's House and commended her to the care and guidance of Rowena Cornwallis, she took refuge there.

When it was discovered that Jane Herdie, identifiable by certain articles of clothing, had been in the conspirators' house at the moment of the explosion, it was generally assumed that she had been kidnapped from her bed in the Collector's bungalow, and taken there by the terrorists, with some idea of holding her to ransom should their plot fail.

When Betty Gopaldas, innocent of mind and unsus-picious by nature, blurted out that she had found Mrs. Herdie in Steele's bungalow when she had gone to warn him, Lawrence Herdie said nothing, but thought the more; and the conclusion at which he arrived was fairly close to the truth.

For him, Life performed a complete and amazing *volte-face*. Anxiety, pain and misery fell from him like a garment. He was saved. His unfortunate and unhappy wife, by her own act, had run into fatal danger. He was free. And, incredible as it was, Betty Gopaldas was also free. The husband whom she must surely have detest-ed, was dead, his death an amazing example of poetic justice. Lawrence Herdie would see that Betty did not fall into the clutches of the "Maharani" Subhadra, con-cerning whose methods he had no illusions. He would take care that, as quickly as possible, she should leave India and return to her father's house. He himself would wait six months—in decency he could do no less—and at the end of that time he would take furlough, go to England, and ask her to be his wife.

The incredible happiness of the mere thought of it!

Mr. Justice Sherdley behaved in public with the decorum for which he was noted. In private he roared with laughter, patted Elizabeth upon the back, and bade her rejoice; for he felt happy, and considered it incumbent upon her to feel happy too, whether she did or not. He couldn't explain it, but he felt that they had been mercifully delivered, even in the moment when the wings of the Angel of Death were audible in the air about them.

The Hon. Edward Cornwallis felt like one for whom not merely the prison doors, but the doors of the tomb itself, had been rolled aside, permitting him to walk forth into the light, bright purity of God's day.

At the next meeting of the Bhawalgarh Literary, Dramatic and Philosophical Society, he made brief and moving reference to the narrow escape, not so much of Bhawalgarh itself, not so much of themselves and their wives, but of that magnificent institution, so dear to all their hearts, the Bhawalgarh Literary, Dramatic and Philosophical Society.

He called upon the Secretary to read the minutes.

Rowena did so, majestic of mien, calm of face, and steady of voice, but very conscious of the absence of one who had been her latest, her best, her choicest *protégé*.

Of course she still believed in him. Firmly. It was her theory—and her expression—that he had been Done to Death.

"Damn it all," said Colonel Campbell to Major Murdoch. "The old boy's ghost appeared to some purpose this time, didn't it? There's a mighty fine breach in his Fort wall at the very spot where he appears. And I'm afraid they will break poor old Grant. How was he to know there was an old forgotten store of ammunition deteriorating and getting dangerous down there under that disused 'treasure-chamber'? Admittedly there was no record of it. . . . And fancy it going up through 'spontaneous combustion'! Don't believe a word of it! . . . But they must have a scapegoat when there is two-annas' worth of Government property damaged, mustn't they? They'll take it out on him. Damn 'Satanic' I call it."

Quite a little crowd came to the Bhawalgarh Railway-station to say farewell to Betty Gopaldas, something of a heroine since rumour said that she had risked her life, and almost lost it, on the terrible night of the explosion, by escaping from the house in which she was imprisoned, to warn the District Superintendent of Police that the Europeans were all going to be murdered in their beds.

She was to travel as far as Marseilles in the care of Sewell E. Lee, old Dr. Torrens' nephew, as he was returning to America to lecture on the subject of India, and to give his compatriots as true a picture as he could of the work of the British in that distressful subcontinent whose peace and prosperity rested on their strength and on that alone.

Being, as he told himself, mightily interested in the cute little dame, it was as well that he could not read her thoughts when, glancing at him, she felt that she would have given her immortal soul had he but been Anthony Steele.

Oh, if this kindly crowd would only go . . . go . . . go right away . . . that she might say good-bye to Anthony in peace; perhaps hear him say it was not good-bye at all, beg her to let it be but *au revoir*—until he came to England.

The guard whistled.

"Well, good-bye, Betty, my dear. I only wish I had words to thank you," said Cold Steele, holding her hand. "You are going straight to your father?"

"Yes," whispered Betty, blinking bright eyes. "The Rectory, Fonthill Regis, Bucks."

"Good-bye, my dear."

"Good-bye, Anthony. Will you do me a small kindness?"

"I should love to, Betty."

"Send me the Bhawalgarh Gazette every week . . . so long as you are here. . . . Good-bye, Anthony."

NOTE

AUTHOR'S NOTE

A great explosion, similar to the one described in this novel, actually occurred in the old Fort, at Hyderabad, Sind.

Exact extracts from the *Daily Gazette*, of Karachi, giving some account of it, are appended.

The author of this book wishes to state that the Bhawalgarh of the story is not Hyderabad, Sind; and that none of the people mentioned in this book was ever stationed in Hyderabad, Sind; or, so far as he knows, ever lived in, or visited the place.

Verbatim extract from the *Daily Gazette*, Karachi, Sind:

A natural Vesuvius destroyed several villages in Italy and an artificial Vesuvius threatened destruction of the town of Hyderabad. In the Fort, large quantities of ammunition and explosives are stored. On Saturday last, some shells exploded *perhaps* due to the intense heat prevailing there. The explosion brought the roof down, but help arriving in time, the fire was extinguished.

The explosion cracked the walls and injured the roof of the vault in which highly explosive material was kept. If the roof is removed it is feared more cordite may explode in the process of removal, resulting in the blowing up of the Fort and probably of the whole town. If the roof is not removed, it will very likely collapse in a few days, and ignite the explosives, with the same disastrous results. The military authorities have therefore decided to destroy the explosives, either by removing and throwing them into the river—in which case also it is feared it may cause a serious disaster—or getting the whole town of Hyderabad vacated, and then blowing up the magazine by firing into it from Ganja Takar, a hill about two miles away to the south of the Fort. A committee of officers sat yesterday to consider the question.

Later.

Explosion

The latest accounts received of the explosion at Hyderabad show that while the catastrophe was of a sufficiently serious nature, Hyderabad has narrowly escaped very much worse disaster. The main facts are these.

On Saturday the 7th inst. a quantity of the cordite stored in the magazine ignited spontaneously (?) and blew down a magazine in the Fort. A board of officers was held and all the shells, about a hundred tons, and half the powder, fifteen tons, was removed to the polygon building in the Fort, and the remainder of the shells, which were stored in boxes, were saturated with water and the magazine flooded.

It seems probable that only the fact of the explosives being stored where they were, saved Hyderabad from being wrecked. Had the whole of the mass of cordite ignited in the magazine, which is in a low and enclosed situation, the consequences would have been serious indeed. As it is, it is reported that many people have been killed from falling houses, and one Baluch sepoy has since died from his injuries.

The Fort police at once cleared the population out of the quarter in proximity of the Fort. The majority of the inhabitants fled when the explosion took place, and the police and native infantry patrolled the streets the whole night in order to prevent pilfering, and to keep people from the dangerous zone. Next morning the whole of the unexploded ammunition was removed and the inhabitants were advised that they might safely return to those houses which had not suffered so much from the shock as to be unsafe. The damage done appears to have been very considerable; many of the houses have been wrecked and others are unsafe; and, throughout the town, houses rocked and shook as in an earthquake. The doors and windows of hundreds of houses have been smashed, notably in the Collector's Bungalow, the Collector's Kutcherry, the Court House and the Post Office, and many other public buildings. Most of the houses have been badly damaged, and, in many, not a single door or window remains, all of them being broken into matchwood. A portion of the Hyderabad Railway Station has been damaged and the roof of the waiting-rooms has received severe injuries. For a time the traffic of the station was at a standstill, the staff being warned not to remain there.

Strenuous efforts were made by the Military and Civilian officials to prevent further explosions, and to reassure the people who were, not unnaturally, in a state of panic. The European detachment and the native troops were on duty the whole of Sunday night till Monday morning. The

Collector of Hyderabad and all the Military officers of the station were on the scene of the explosion immediately afterwards, and the District Magistrate himself saw the Baluch piquets posted. The Sessions Judge and the Assistant Collector assisted the police in holding inquests on the bodies of the unfortunate victims on Monday.

The alarm among the townspeople has now been fully allayed. Our correspondent further stated that the General Commanding arrived by the Quetta Mail on Monday at noon, and issued a proclamation reassuring the citizens of their safety, and stating that Government would consider the question of the losses suffered by the population owing to the explosion.

Until the result of the official inquiry is known it is impossible to say what measure of blame, if any, is to be attached to the authorities in connection with the cause of the explosion. It would *seem*, on the face of the matter, that not sufficient care had been taken in the first instance in safe-guarding this dangerous material from accident. It is not, however, impossible that some special conditions have been responsible for the catastrophe, and that no effort or foresight could have prevented the occurrence. Be that as it may, once the disaster had occurred, the behaviour of all concerned was admirable, and everything that could be done was done to minimize the amount of injury and obviate further risk.

APPENDIX A

Differences between the

**British
and
American**

editions
of

Beggars' Horses

and

The Dark Woman

Items with a single underline are from the British
edition titled *Beggars' Horses*.

Items with a double underline are from the American
edition titled *The Dark Woman.*

<u>BEGGARS' HORSES</u>

<u>THE DARK WOMAN</u>

Generic differences

Beggars' Horses was divided into a Part I and Part II,
with the "Chapter" numbers restarting with the
"parts". *The Dark Woman* has consecutively
numbered chapters without the word "Chapter."

Beggars' Horses has many hyphenated words, but in
The Dark Woman the words are not hyphenated,
such as
key-stone or keystone
No-one or No one
Sub-conscious or Subconscious
Wren was not consistent himself in the use of
hyphens for the word Subconscious in
that in *Beggars' Horses* he used a hyphen,
but in *Explosion* the hyphen was not used.

Different use of single and double quotes.

British spelling versus American spelling, especially in
"...our" versus "...or" words, such as
labour or labor
and
enquired or inquired

Beggars' Horses uses commas more frequently and *The*

Dark Woman uses semi-colons more frequently.

Past tenses of words are sometimes different, such as
        spoilt or <u>spoiled</u>
        learnt or <u>learned</u>
        leant or <u>leaned</u>

Capitalization differences, such as
        <u>Hell</u> or <u>hell</u>

Word choice differences, such as
        <u>gaol</u> or <u>jail</u>
        the faintest breath <u>of</u> or <u>or</u> suggestion of
           jealousy
        <u>Christ</u> or <u>God</u>
        <u>Leave</u> or <u>Let</u>
        God <u>damn</u> or <u>Damn</u>
        <u>Javanese</u> or <u>Japanese</u>
        disagreeing <u>from</u> or <u>with</u> those who say
        now properly <u>dressed</u> or <u>attended</u> to by the
           surgeon
        He'd <u>have</u> been <u>burnt</u> or <u>burned</u> alive but for
           two Secret Service agents
        pleasant words to that <u>defect</u> or <u>effect</u>
        wedding-notice in every <u>paper</u> or <u>newspaper</u>

Phrases, words, or sentences missing in Beggars' Horses

he frankly admitted that <u>as far as he was concerned</u> he
    didn't want to

growled Captain Hennessy Wogan <u>contemptuously</u>.

The stalking and circumventing, <u>the pitting of the skill
of man against animal cunning,</u> you know,

"if it's <u>originally</u> implanted

I think I'd ask for <u>a</u> very long life

Appendix A

What a dear he <u>always</u> was.

agreed Colonel Harrington-Spens, <u>smiling slightly</u>.

What's a wife to <u>a</u> sailor, except a living expense

who takes his mind off his <u>job</u> <u>doing his job well</u>?

the entire estate should <u>then</u> become his.

rose from his chair <u>in one quick movement</u>.

Perhaps I'm afraid of a <u>solid</u> hiding,

and not <u>try to</u> do something about it.

wrath against Mackleworth <u>in the fight</u> that put

here he was—absolutely <u>and completely</u> happy.

not to mention <u>the barest</u> comforts,

were Mata and Daffy birds of a <u>similar</u> feather?

said Joan<u>, shaking her head</u>.

That <u>very</u> good ivory.

Nobody <u>in this boat</u> ought to accept

Feeling better, now? <u>You ought to, you know.</u> Putting
on

saw you doing it. <u>You didn't know,</u> I say I

looked uncomfortable <u>and stared at his hands</u>.

nor ten years <u>for that matter</u>."

and then use his hands. <u>Like this</u>.

to be tortured <u>just</u> for his Faith?

without leaving the slightest external <u>trace</u> <u>mark</u> of injury!

orang-outang, or<u>, perhaps,</u> a gorilla."

absolutely loyal to her employer <u>at all times</u>.

in the <u>wide</u> world."

Phrases, words, or sentences missing in The Dark Woman

> *<u>The Little Gods laughed to see such sport,</u>*
> *<u>For the Wish ran away with the Boon.</u>"*
> <u>Nursery Rhyme</u>
> <u>(Revised Version)</u>.

<u>To</u>

<u>ISABEL</u>

<u>MY TWENTY-FIRST NOVEL</u>

<u>AND</u>

<u>ALL MY LOVE</u>

> *"<u>What we call Fate is even, heartless, and impartial.</u>*
> *<u>. . . We may fret, fume, and fight; but the thing called</u>*
> *<u>Fate everlastingly sustains an armed neutrality . . . and</u>*
> *<u>in our own hearts we fashion our own gods. . . .</u>*
> *<u>In two senses, we are precisely what we worship.</u>*
> *<u>Ourselves are Fate.</u>"*
> Herman Melville.

squashed flat by the 'Colonel's lady,'" <u>he added</u>.

Appendix A

And incontinently collapsed . . . Bad heart attack.

the absolute utter whole of all his mighty strength.

one of the Seven Sleepers. Dam-me, I'm a dormouse!"

Almighty! There were ants running in and out of her
mouth and nostrils. . . . She was dead!

Available P. C. Wren Titles

from
Riner Publishing Company

The Collected Short Stories

Volume One: ISBN 9780985032609
Volume Two: ISBN 9780985032616
Volume Three: ISBN 9780985032623
Volume Four: ISBN 9780985032630
Volume Five: ISBN 9780985032647

The Collected Novels

Volume One: *The Geste Novels*
    Part A: ISBN 9780985032678
    Part B: ISBN 9780985032685
Volume Two: *The Sinbad Novels*
    Part A: ISBN 9780692639382
    Part B: ISBN 9780692639429
Volume Three: *The Foreign Legion Novels*
    Part A: ISBN 9780999074909
    Part B: ISBN 9780999074916
Volume Four: *The Earlier India Novels*
    Part A: ISBN 9780999074923
    Part B: ISBN 9780999074930
Volume Five: *The Later India Novels*
    Part A: ISBN 9780999074947
    Part B: ISBN 9780999074954
Volume Six: *The English Novels*
    Part A: ISBN 9780999074961
    Part B: ISBN 9780999074978
Volume Seven: *A Mixed Bag of Novels*
    Part A: ISBN 9780999074985
    Part B: ISBN 9780999074992

Further information can be found at
rinerpublishing.wordpress.com